PROJECT CANAVERAL

By: Katherine E. Hether

Book 1 in the series is Project XP38.
Book 2 in the series is Project Wraith.
Book 3 in the series is Project Canaveral.

Printed in the United States of America

Raintree Press, LLC
12180 South 300 East
Suite 1238
Draper, Utah 84020
(386) 256-6527
www.raintreepress.com

A special thanks to Stephen Brown, Will Russell, and Gabby Mobile Productions for the book cover.
A special thanks to Jean Tessier and Jeanie Borden for editing the book.

PROJECT CANAVERAL

By: Katherine E. Hether

This book is dedicated to the defenders of our Constitution and our country, both home and abroad. At the bottom of Cheatham Hill in Kennesaw, Georgia, is a monument that touched my heart years ago. It reads, "Here lies our sons. When duty called, they came. When country called, they gave their lives."
Since September 11, 2001, we face a different battlefield raging throughout the entire world called terrorism. To all the innocent victims, deceased, maimed, and their families, may all the countries in the world stand united to stamp out this evil.

Project Canaveral
Copyright applied for:
Library of Congress Control #2021911444

ISBN #978-0-9993363-4-2

www.katherinehether.com

Contents

Chapter 1

THREE DAYS LATER:
White House North Lawn
Monday, June 29 0900 (9:00 AM EST)

BREAKING NEWS: "This is Robert Morwitz with FNN News. As you can see," he pointed behind him, "I am reporting from the north lawn of the White House. An anonymous source has released two more leaks, this time complete with videos. President Trumore has called for a special counsel to investigate this ongoing problem that has plagued his administration since the day he took office. The first leak had to do with the bizarre shootings at a Light Crimson Concert last Tuesday, June 23, hinting it may have something to do with National Security."

The camera switched to show the original crime scene with officials taping off the arena in Mayport Square Gardens. "We will show you newly released footage of that night we received. Please use viewer discretion due to the graphic content of this video," Morwitz warned. "This is actual footage caught on security cameras inside the arena where twenty people died, six are in critical condition, and 140 were injured. A man and woman dressed in Mayport Security Uniforms entered from the lower-level underneath the stage. They broke into the breakroom, killing two people before rushing up the stairs to the stage, throwing what appear to be smoke bombs. Notice the crazed female began laughing while wildly shooting into the audience as the male heads straight for lead singer, Joe Sherrod."

The camera switched to the second-floor corridor. "Another camera picked up the couple shoving fans aside as they pushed their way down the escalator pulling Sherrod, blinded by the smoke," the camera zoomed in on the escalator. "The source states that two Light Crimson Security Officers, shown circled here, rescued Sherrod by shooting him with a tranquilizer, thus changing his bodyweight. The two then struggled to carry Sherrod to the bottom as fans scattered. The agents then jumped to two large flags overhanging the escalator to avoid the chaos and shimmied down to the bottom level behind the abductors," the camera slowed the speed of the film. "Watch as one of the Crimson Agents shoots the female with yet another tranquilizer.

She instantly drops to the floor, and her accomplice is forced to let go of Sherrod. He then scooped his companion up, escaping in the chaos."

The camera switched to outside the arena. "A camera on the corner of 33rd Street and 7th Avenue caught footage of the well-planned escape. Two snipers positioned on the roof of the Lassiter Hotel kept police at bay while aiding a dark-blue Audi escaping with the couple."

The camera switched to an Aerial of Ponce Inlet, Florida. "Sherrod was rescued a second time in Ponce Inlet, Florida, on Thursday, June 25th. The anonymous source reported Sherrod got away from the safe house and reunited with his capturers. It had something to do with the recent posts on his social media accounts, which have been taken down. Payton Ross, the band's manager, announced the cancellation of all future concerts until further notice. Sherrod and the band members are in a lockdown facility at an unspecified location currently. No group has claimed responsibility yet."

The camera switched back to Morwitz. "The second story we are following derives from the multiple explosions last Friday, June 26th in Miami Beach, Florida," he stated as a picture of President Trumore showed on the left side of the screen. "As a direct result of this new administration's policy on Protecting America First, Homeland Security, and the Coast Guard are shown sealing off the area around Bridgette Océanic Aquarium."

The camera switched to an Aerial of the Aquarium depicting the rubble. "If you remember, a spokesperson from the White House confirmed that beginning at 5:20 PM EST, a series of explosions destroyed a major portion of the Aquarium. Several employees were found dead at the scene. Investigators are working around-the-clock."

The camera zoomed in on Morwitz. "The anonymous source stated the Aquarium closed early Friday to unload several new attractions. This new footage depicts gunshots by the alligator tank. Now watch the actual first blast," the camera froze. "At the same time as the blast, this unmarked semi-truck left the scene," the camera changed views again. "Moments before the last explosion, a ship pulled out of port behind the alligator tank," the camera split the screen showing Sherrod and the Aquarium. "The anonymous source claims that Sherrod's abductions and the Bridgette Océanic Aquarium explosions are connected. However, the source refused to comment further. Stay tuned for more updates as we continue to cover these two incredible stories."

The Exchange Tower
5th Avenue and 23rd Street, Manhattan, New York
Linda Ramsey's Penthouse Condominium
Monday, June 29, 2200 (10:00 PM EST)

"Tom, thanks for taking me out to dinner after the long exhausting day I've had," Linda Ramsey confessed as they waited for the elevator in the lobby of the Exchange Tower.

"We've had a series of continuous long days," Gen. Tom Jenkins admitted as the elevator door opened, and a couple rushed past them.

"That's odd," Ramsey looked back, entering the elevator. "Don and Sharon almost knocked us over and didn't say a word. That's not like them."

"I guess they were in a hurry to catch that cab," Tom assumed pointing to the doorman opening the taxi's door.

"Why would anything surprise me after the unbelievable news this morning?" Ramsey questioned as the door closed.

"Come here," Tom smiled pulling her into his arms, kissing her.

"We need to talk about these leaks," Ramsey affirmed stepping back. "I didn't bring it up in the restaurant because I didn't want anyone to overhear us."

"I've had it up to here with talking about the news leaks," Tom raised his hand over his head. "Congress summoned me to Capitol Hill and grilled me most of the day. Then, I had to meet with a furious president. I need a break!"

"In our jobs, there are no breaks!" Ramsey informed him. "Two years ago, we were able to contain the situation from the reporters. We orchestrated the headlines to read, 'Russian Mafia Drug Deal Turns Bloody,' which was partially correct. Could you imagine the chaos the media would have started if Chameleon were made known? Every militant group in the world would be after it," she admitted as the elevator stopped at the Penthouse on the fifty-fifth floor.

"It's not as easy as it was two years ago," Tom whined stepping out of the elevator. "An arena full of fans saw the gruesome attack and abduction of Joe Sherrod. All day the news stations aired reporters continually interviewing fans. The explosions in Miami that aired were from surveillance cameras from surrounding buildings."

"How did the media get that footage?" Ramsey snapped stopping in the hallway. "All surveillance cameras in the entire area were confiscated by Hiltree's men and deemed classified!" she pointed her finger at him. "You know as well as I do that someone with a very high-security clearance was able to obtain them! To access the Evidence Center, one must produce an ID Badge with clearance and a signature! That should be easy even for you to check!"

"I did have my staff check into it," Tom admitted. "The only people with access were Hiltree and me when we viewed the footage with Manning Pilsner of the FBI, and Chuck Coble of the DOJ. We reported directly to President Trumore. No one else viewed them or had access to them. Someone working in those buildings in Miami could have remotely made a copy before Sydney got back from the hospital."

"That's not true, and you know it!" Ramsey poked him in the chest. "As soon as Sydney was back from the hospital, I had him extract those videos and erase them from the hard drives. He said there was no evidence that anyone accessed them, even remotely. He checked that first since someone remotely set off the bombs. We didn't want to take a chance of them resurfacing like today. That's why we did it, instead of your staff! Perhaps, I should have Sydney check your records. You know as well as I know, that with the technology today someone could have masked entering the room. It sounds like a cover-up from the inside. The entire world knows there is corruption in several of the top agencies."

"Sydney can't do that after what else happened today," Tom countered. "Since someone is leaking classified information, President Trumore ordered NCSD (National Cyber Security Division) to begin massive lockdowns on all government computers. Including changing all passwords, codes, and the timing of major security details."

"The president needs to do some in-house cleaning and pretty quick!" Ramsey declared, pointing at Tom. "After the fiasco of the last administration, President Trumore should not have kept any of those people. And since you're Mr. Head of Homeland Security, you should be leading the investigation! Those videos should have never gotten out! I've already told you we can secure this situation in Cuba without you! You're needed more here!"

"I told the president that it's my job to lead the investigation," Tom insisted. "Instead, he asked Congress to appoint a special counsel to look into it. My hands are tied."

"Your hands aren't tied!" Ramsey declared. "It's the protocol for you to lead the investigation! Did you remind the new president of that?"

"I recited the regulation to him," Tom admitted. "Trumore gave the order and said this discussion was over, period. Then, he left the room."

"Did you call Trumore's councilor, Spencer McAlister?" Ramsey asked.

"Spencer was in the room with us," Tom stated. "When I tried to follow Trumore, she stopped me, and told me the discussion was over and left with him."

"Then, the only thing that saved us was Dr. Sydney blurring the video of Kathe and Jay shimming down the flags," Ramsey concluded. "Sydney also hacked into the media and withheld Kathe's name as Sherrod's deceased girlfriend. I also had him plant the rumor that Sherrod's abduction was due to his recent social media posts and shutdown Sherrod's media sites."

"We discussed that," Tom stated.

"Yes, we did," Ramsey confirmed. "We also approved the only footage allowed to air was from the helicopters at the scene that day. They were far enough back that the only thing it showed was the aftermath of the explosion. Then, this happened!"

"Now, we're arguing over something we can't change," Tom insisted reaching in his briefcase and holding up a bottle of wine. "We need a break from work before we both have heart attacks. We had a nice dinner. Let's finish it off with a little vino and a funny movie. We will wake up in the morning refreshed. Lord knows we can use it. We've hardly slept since we got back from Florida."

"It has been an arduous couple of days trying to get ready to go after the intertwined group we uncovered," Ramsey admitted opening her door.

"What is the status of Estevo Vazquez?" Tom asked.

"Sydney tracked Vazquez to a small port near Havana before we lost him," Ramsey shared entering the living room.

"So, you have no clue where Vazquez is?" Tom questioned turning on the lights.

"Not yet," Ramsey confirmed putting her purse on the credenza.

"Vazquez could be anywhere in the Caribbean," Tom declared. "Why would you send your men to Cuba this early? You know Prado uses various locations. You're wasting precious time and workforce. Why not scout the various islands first?"

"Sydney is in charge of that," Ramsey answered noting Tom fishing for information.

"Then, what about Kathe's family?" Tom continued. "I know Pauli moved them when he moved Joe to a safe house. Are you leaving them there? Because you can't put them in Ponce Inlet again this time."

"You are right about that," Ramsey grinned. "You know Sydney likes to keep things quiet concerning Kathe's family. Especially since Sherrod plastered the pictures of him and Alek all over the Internet," she smiled putting her arms around his neck. "Since we're sharing information, darling, have you finished vetting Rodger Slate to work with Hiltree's team?"

"Look at us," Tom grinned pulling her closer, "we're talking about work again. Now, I'll open the wine, and you find us something funny to watch," he kissed her and walked away.

"I asked you a question, and I want the answer!" Ramsey demanded.

"We'll talk about Rodger tomorrow," Tom sighed walking into the dining room.

"I'd rather talk about Rodger tonight," Ramsey insisted.

"Not tonight," Tom stopped, turned, and grinned.

"Tonight!" Ramsey glared as Tom walked into the kitchen.

"The television," Tom peered around the corner and pointed. "No news."

"Fine!" Ramsey scoffed and sat on the couch. She reached for the remote and turned on the television.

"Ramsey, your phone is off," Sydney whispered, hacking into the sound system. "Can we talk?"

"Tom is in the kitchen," Ramsey reached for her phone. "I turned off my cell while Tom and I were at dinner."

"Alonzo called and warned that Spinello's men are in the area," Sydney relayed. "As I called to warn you, I received two warning signals that your security cameras and elevator are disabled," Sydney opened her security system. "Something is blocking the signals," he continued to type and then pressed enter. "I removed the block," pulling up the primary camera on the roof. "As you can see on your phone, a helicopter is circling the roof about to land," he zoomed in on the camera. "They're getting ready to attack you. We'll deal with this problem, and then I'll free the elevator."

"Of all times for this to happen," Ramsey whined turning off the lights in the room. "Tom doesn't know about the upgrades in my condo, and I wanted to keep it that way."

"That's not feasible now," Sydney confessed. "I don't trust Jenkins either. He can't detect your new earbud. I'll stay online with you and talk you through this without Jenkins knowing. Hiltree, as well as Jay, and Jack have visitors too."

"They're coming after all of us at once," Ramsey acknowledged. "I was afraid of this."

"We are their only threat," Sydney agreed. "Go tell Jenkins. I'll stay with you."

"Copy that," Ramsey replied putting her phone on her belt, and hurrying into the kitchen. "Tom, we've been compromised," she whispered turning off the lights in the kitchen. "Follow me to my panic room."

"What panic room?" Tom asked following her through the dining room and then around the living room furniture.

"Sh, sh," Ramsey shushed him, hurrying toward the master bedroom.

"Ramsey, the intruders have night-vision goggles and semi-automatics," Sydney confirmed uploading the rest of the cameras in her condo. "They are positioning themselves around the large windows. The pilot is going toward your kitchen, two by the west bedroom, one by the east bedroom, and one is going around to the living room. They are securing harnesses to the nearest vents," he reported watching her entering the walk-in closet and securing the door. "Give me a minute while you get ready to engage them. I'm getting a call from Stephen Brown in the Florida Keys."

"Hiltree and my men are under attack," Tom sighed reading a text message.

"We've got to hurry," Ramsey noted touching a leaf design on the slate wall by the door. The leaf opened uncovering a retinal scan. She peered into it, and the wall slid open to an arsenal of weapons.

"I never knew this was here!" Tom whispered reaching for an MT15 with a night vision scope.

"Have you ever known me not to be prepared?" Ramsey quizzed reaching for a Bushmaster AR15 with laser and night vision scope, as well as her night vision goggles.

"Where's your drone?" Tom asked gazing around the room.

"Sydney is upgrading it," Ramsey said reaching for a military LED flashlight. "They are entering from the roof," she pointed to a monitor.

"Oh! You have it on camera?" Tom stammered studying the cameras. "I'll take the ones in the kitchen and the living room. Good luck!" he kissed her.

"Be careful," Ramsey cautioned as Tom left the room. She closed the wall, hearing gunfire spraying her bedroom windows, followed by the sound of boots pounding the glass. Ramsey peered around the doorway of the walk-in closet. She saw one of the assassin's kick through the glass window over her bed. She waited for him to come through the glass to open fire. His body landed on her bed. The second man hit another window at the same time, but the glass did not break. He pushed off, opening fire concentrating on the center of the window as his boots hit that precise spot and broke through. She dropped him with a single shot. He dangled inside the bedroom.

"I'm back online with you," Sydney confirmed. "What did I miss?"

"Two targets in my bedroom are down," Linda explained. "Tom is engaging the one in the kitchen. I can hear the sound of glass breaking in the living room."

"It's the left window by the television," Sydney confirmed enhancing the camera. "The target is squatted down beside the couch."

"I see him," Ramsey studied the camera and then carefully peered out of her bedroom. "I've got this one," she pulled back watching the camera. "Check on Tom before I take this one down."

"Copy that," Sydney agreed glancing at that view. "The cameras in the kitchen and dining room are offline."

"I thought you brought all the cameras back up?" Ramsey questioned.

"I did," Sydney declared. "It's showing that they are offline."

"What?" Ramsey questioned hearing Tom throw down his rifle, returning fire with his Glock. "It sounds like Tom is in trouble."

"I can't help him," Sydney admitted. "The target in the living room is communicating with someone on the roof," Sydney turned up the sound. "They are speaking a dialect of Spanish," he checked. "It's Cuban."

"Interesting," Ramsey whispered watching the target slowly stand up, panning the room with his rifle. He maneuvered his way around the couch toward the dining room. Then he turned toward her bedroom.

"If he sprays the wall with bullets, you'll need to get inside the panic room and hunker down until I send help," Sydney cautioned. "Alonzo's men are on the way. Be careful; he's raising his automatic weapon toward your bedroom."

"Let's see how he likes a strobe light," Ramsey whispered pulling off her night vision goggles and hurling the light in front of the assassin.

"¡Mi ojos!" he screamed, ripping his glasses off and falling to the floor.

"Yes, your eyes," Ramsey whispered leaning around the doorway and shooting him.

"Quick thinking!" Sydney smiled. "The target is down! Kick his gun under the couch."

"Copy that," Ramsey hurried into the room, kicked the gun, and turned off the flashlight. "It sounds like Tom is fighting hand-to-hand in the dining room."

"No!" Tom screamed firing his Glock several times with the sound of the table crashing against the wall, followed by the sound of breaking glass.

"I've got to help Tom," Ramsey whispered.

"No time!" Sydney warned. "The camera on the roof is offline. The last target just entered the guest bedroom. He's raising his rifle toward the wall into the living room! Get down!"

Ramsey put her goggles back on as she hurried behind the love seat. She motioned for Tom to get down as he entered the room.

Tom quickly joined her as they heard the last assassin desperately trying to communicate with his companions inside.

"He's ripping off his headset!" Sydney warned as they heard it hit the slate. "Flip the loveseat over! He's going to spray the room with bullets!"

"Tom, help me!" Ramsey whispered flipping over the loveseat. "He's going to spray the room!"

"How do you know?" Tom demanded as bullets began to destroy everything in the room.

"When the target reloads, run to your bedroom," Sydney ordered.

"Tom, when he reloads, follow me," Ramsey whispered.

"Where?" Tom questioned glancing at her.

"Trust me," Ramsey replied as the big-screen television shattered, spewing glass around the room.

"Okay!" Tom exclaimed covering his head with his hands until the bullets stopped.

"Move now!" Sydney ordered as they heard the clip drop to the slate floor.

They quietly scrambled toward the master bedroom. Seconds later, as they barely cleared her bedroom doorway, he started shooting again.

"You're hurt; stay in here," Ramsey whispered noticing his arm bleeding, and then entered the walk-in closet. "Sydney, where is he?" she asked, opening a secret hallway between the two bedrooms.

"The target is kicking what is left of the bedroom doorframe down," Sydney relayed. "He's entering the living room firing wildly. You can slowly come out of the closet," he stated watching Ramsey follow his cue. "His back is to you checking around the loveseat. Take him down!"

"Copy that," Ramsey stepped around the wall as the target turned sideways.

"Shoot him under the vest!" Sydney ordered watching him fall backward. "That was the last one! You're clear!"

"Thanks," Ramsey sighed hurrying to check his carotid artery. "Tom, we're clear," she called over her shoulder. "All targets are down!"

"Are they?" Tom asked standing in the doorway with his gun pointing directly at her.

"Ramsey, don't trust him!" Sydney screamed. "Look in his eyes; you were the target!"

"Tom, this is the last assassin!" Ramsey declared standing up. "Holster your weapon!" Ramsey raised her gun toward him. "Tom, holster your weapon!" she demanded steadying her finger on the trigger. "I said holster your weapon now!"

"Stop!" Tom shook his head, lowering his gun. "I guess I'm in shock," he sighed looking around the room. "I can't believe this happened!"

"Why don't you sit down while I check the target in the kitchen," Ramsey offered. "You haven't seen combat duty for years. You're injured. We need to get you to the hospital."

"No!" Tom exclaimed hurrying to her. "We've got to get out of here before reinforcements come! I've got to get to my men. Hiltree's text stated there are injuries. He has med-training in the field. I need to get to my men," he checked his handkerchief. "Hiltree can bandage it. Let's go!"

"I agree," Ramsey confirmed.

"Ramsey, I enabled the elevator," Sydney confirmed. "Whatever you do, don't turn your back on Jenkins. The hallway is clear. Alonzo's men have secured the building."

"Let's go," Ramsey opened the door wide. "I need to call Wanda and get back to my office."

"Shouldn't we take the stairs?" Tom insisted rubbing his arm. "If there are reinforcements, they will come from the ground this time," he said opening the door to the stairwell. "Besides, the elevator isn't working."

"Why would you suspect the elevator isn't working?" Ramsey grinned pushing the button. "We were the last ones to use it," she said as the door opened.

"I just thought," Tom stammered, "since it was a well-planned attack, they would disable it."

Over the Allegheny Mountains en route to Newark-Liberty International Airport, Monday, June 29, 2250 (10:50 PM EST)

"Cessna Mustang Citation AARS2881, this is Keith Gordon," Keith introduced.

"This is Capt. Jordan Mills," he answered.

"Jordan, I have you on radar coming over the Allegheny Mountain Range," Keith stated. "I noticed three small unidentified aircraft took off from Burnsville on the same flight path as you. They can't climb to your altitude, and I'm showing turbulence ahead, which will force them down. I want you to stay mindful. We're dealing with enemies that seem to come out of nowhere in multitudes."

"Keith, I see them on the radar," Capt. Yorg Vuslick joined the conversation.

"Ah, Capt. Vuslick, what caught my attention is that small airport," Keith said checking the computer screen. "It's used mostly for crop-dusting. It's a little late for that kind of work."

"You've got the point," Yorg concurred. "We will keep an eye out. Thanks for watching our backs over and out," he said and cleared the line.

"We're just getting into the turbulence," Jordan acknowledged hitting unsettled air. He reached for the fasten seatbelt sign and then the intercom to call the cabin. "Kathe, we're coming into some turbulence. Keith warned it might get pretty rough up here."

"Thanks, Jordan," Kathe answered. "I'll keep everyone seated. Most of the passengers are sound asleep. Let's hope a little turbulence is all we have to worry about tonight."

"I hope so, too," Yorg agreed watching the radar. "It looks like the planes are changing course to land near Williamsville Airport. After what happened on the ground in New York, Keith is cautious with us."

"I'll leave you two to fly the plane," Kathe said. "I've got to get Bob a pillow. He can't get comfortable."

"He's not the only one uncomfortable," Jordan stated as the jet tousled around. "I have to admit. I'll be happy when we touch down at Liberty. Who would have thought that my training in the military would come in so handy?"

"I never knew you were in the military," Yorg shared.

"I was a pilot during peacetime," Jordan said. "I flew some in the Congress around to meetings overseas. After I got out, I went to work for Alby."

"Maybe, your background is the reason Ramsey chose you to fly with us," Yorg replied. "She knew in the face of danger you wouldn't flinch. Ramsey still wants to keep Kathe and me out of sight as much as possible. Even though Ramsey never mentioned our names the day of our fate, if certain people found out we're alive, it would be detrimental to all of us."

"Gen. Jenkins was one of those certain people at the time," Jordan reminded. "I'm glad he's on our side now."

"Don't be too sure about that," Yorg cautioned. "The jury is still out on that question?"

"Regardless," Jordan sighed, "I am glad that Ben, Patti, and I got to be some of the few people that know the truth. I knew Kathe had a dangerous job, but somehow it didn't register until I saw her with the team in action. These last few weeks have opened my eyes. I have a new respect for all of you."

"It looks like our worries are over," Yorg pointed to the screen. "There go the three unidentified aircraft. Just like I thought, they didn't make it to Williamsville Airport. Most likely, they landed at another crop-dusters private airstrip."

"Thank God," Jordan sighed. "Ever since Keith called, I've been wondering how we can defend ourselves up here. The Citation is top of the line for luxury and speed, not weaponry."

"Yet," Yorg hinted. "One reason Sydney wants the Citation in Newark is to add a few more surprises to this jet."

"I didn't know that!" Jordan exclaimed. "Is he going to train me on how to use it?"

"Some of it we will operate," Yorg explained, "I understand Sydney will also activate some things from his HUB. I know he's working on programming the computers onboard to fly this plane remotely."

"Capt. Vuslick," Keith interrupted again.

"What can we do for you this time?" Yorg asked.

"Alonzo called and said his sources spotted several of Spinello's men near Williamsville," Keith reported. "I also noted that two Leer Jets have taken off from that same small airstrip minutes after the three from Burnsville landed. Also, be advised that another Leer has taken off from a private airstrip 50 miles south of West Augusta. It could be a trap to bring you down. Dr. Sydney is looking for possible places to land."

"Understood," Yorg answered. "We will be watching." He cleared the line and called Kathe. "We may have company soon."

"Sydney sent a text to me as soon as Alonzo got wind of what was happening," Kathe shared. "Alonzo and Pauli have changed course to join us. Their ETA is one hour. Let's pray that the turbulence is all we have to worry about," she said glancing around the cabin. "Ylia is the only one awake. Alek is laying across her lap asleep."

"She's very good with him," Yorg replied. "However, it's better for all of us to have a Plan B ready to implement in case of trouble. I'll talk to you soon," he cleared the line.

"Wanda," Sydney called. "I need you to run a little interference while Keith activates the program I installed on his computer."

"Okay, give me a second," Wanda cringed. "I hope the tower doesn't figure out what we're doing," she hurried into Keith's office. "Sydney said to activate the program that he hid on your computer while I distract the tower. Who's in charge of the Citation in the tower?"

"Give me a minute," Keith pulled up the schedule. "Arnold Brundage has the Citation's flight plan."

"I'll give Brundage a call," Wanda rushed back to her desk.

"Sydney," Keith called. "The program is activated, and I enabled LogMeIn to access my computer."

"Thanks," Sydney said moving his mouse around the desktop. "The Citation may have some unwanted company, and we need to land it secretly. I'm cloning the Citation's track on the radar to show that it's staying on course. I'll activate Chameleon when I'm ready to take it off the radar."

"I understand," Keith agreed watching the mouse accessing the tower's radar.

"Okay, that will do it," Sydney smiled. "Deactivate the program and hide it again."

"Copy that," Keith complied, and then walked to his doorway and signaled Wanda.

"Arnold was clueless," Wanda grinned hanging up the phone. "I did find out that L'Simonette was in there earlier this evening asking questions about the Citation's flight plan."

"I'll report that to Ramsey," Keith sighed. "Sydney needs to hack into L'Simonette's phone records and see who he is calling. It looks like the Citation could be in trouble, and L'Simonette could be part of it."

"Arnold said he documented L'Simonette probing for information concerning the flight plan," Wanda advised walking back to Keith's office. "Even Arnold questioned L'Simonette motives."

"I'll make sure L'Simonette doesn't erase it from Arnold's log," Keith said pulling it up. "It's still here," he looked at her. "I'll take a screenshot of the page in case he tries."

"Good idea," Wanda agreed. "I can't wait for CC to arrest that rat. For what L'Simonette has cost this airline, I hope they throw away the keys."

"Cessna Mustang Citation AARS2881, this is Dr. Sydney," he alerted. "It seems that we are going to have to land your aircraft."

"Copy that, Sydney," Yorg answered. "Have you found a place?"

"You're approaching Deerfeld," Sydney stated. "It's an old coal-mining town with a population of 108. I'm showing quite a few abandoned structures in that area. These three Leers are on a course straight for you. Keith thinks that L'Simonette gave someone your flight plan. I'll check his phone records when I get a chance."

"That doesn't help us now," Yorg sighed. "They can easily match our altitude and speed."

"Correct," Sydney agreed checking the Internet. "Since we don't know what kind of firepower they have, it would be better to engage them on the ground. I'm showing an abandoned hangar a mile from the airport. I think it still could be stable enough to house the jet. It's the only thing I can find, and it's worth a try. Records dating back quite a few years show that a local crop-duster used State Road 209 as an airstrip. I'm showing it is 3,300 feet long and straight. The Citation can easily use this road to land and take off again. You'll have to use caution; I'm showing they haven't kept up the rural roads. You'll have to land like a CAT III. I'm downloading the exact coordinates to JAKE now. Once you're down, continue until the road splits, take the right fork on Tennessee Valley Road for a half-mile. There is an abandoned farm with a crop-dusting hangar. Hopefully, it's sturdy enough to hide the Citation inside. I've asked Kathe to put JAKE on the console, and I'll activate Chameleon from here. Once I take the Citation off the grid, JAKE will change course for Deerfeld."

"Copy that," Yorg concurred as Kathe entered the cockpit.

"I heard you needed JAKE," Kathe smiled grabbing hold of Yorg's seat as the plane bounced around. "Put JAKE on the console between you two," she requested handing JAKE to Yorg.

"Sydney, we're ready when you are," Yorg reported.

"Copy that," Sydney took over JAKE as it lit up, communicating with the dual computers onboard. "Excellent! You're off the grid! JAKE is changing your course and will assist you in a safe landing."

"Copy that," Yorg replied. "We've picked up the extended runway for Deerfeld."

"It's late," Sydney noted changing computer screens, and checking Google Earth. "There are only two houses on SR 209. A daytime Aerial of the street shows most of the homes are extremely old and abandoned. Hopefully, the residents living in the two houses will be in bed and won't hear you land. Hide the Citation in the old hangar. Knowing Spinello, this may only buy you some time. Alonzo warned Spinello's very well connected all along with this mountain range. I'll keep you informed when the three Leers leave the area, and then we'll reroute you to Liberty," he said as Stephen called him again.

"Copy that," Yorg agreed. "We've already picked up the glide slope for Deerfeld Airport. We're twenty miles out. JAKE shows we are seven miles to touchdown on SR 209. I'll contact you when we're down," he said, clearing the line. "Kat, you need to get back in your seat. You heard, we're landing on an unlit, unstable surface," he said slowing the speed to begin its final descent.

"At least, this isn't the first time we landed on an unstable road together," Kathe chuckled. "I hope it's smoother than the one in Russia."

"That was a CAT III landing with the latest report from the man plowing the runway," Yorg winked. "This will be a walk in the park compared to that."

"In that case, I'll sit down," Kathe smiled leaving the cockpit.

"This night keeps getting better," Jordan sighed as Kathe closed the cockpit door. "Maybe, I should remind Patti where we keep the Wills."

"I don't think we're to that point yet," Yorg laughed. "I've landed on poorly kept roads many times in Russia. Watch and learn, brother-in-law," he said as Sydney illuminated the precise landing route on their screens.

"Is that what I think it is?" Jordan marveled.

"That man's a genius!" Yorg smiled as they approached SR 209.

"Nose light on," Jordan reported watching the screen. "Sydney just gave us an assured safe landing," he said reaching for a lever. "Landing gear is down and locked. We are 250 degrees and 100 knots."

"Copy that," Yorg stated. "Nose light and landing gear down and locked."

"There's the road!" Jordan exclaimed as the pavement illuminated underneath them.

"I see it," Yorg confirmed lowering the nose and then the right gear. "Hold on!" Yorg warned, hitting a bump as the jet began to swerve. "I've got this," he re-steadied the plane and then lowered the left gear. The plane bumped around for a second as Yorg re-centered it again. "We're down," he threw the engines in reverse, gently pumping the hydraulics as it continued to slow.

"We made it!" Jordan sighed with relief as the plane slowed to taxiing on the road, still hitting a few bumps. "I hope the noise of landing didn't wake up anyone."

"If we woke anyone up, we'd see inside lights turning on," Yorg concluded turning to the right at the fork on Tennessee Valley Rd. "We should find the hanger on the right side of the road," he said, turning on the spotlight. "There it is," Yorg said turning and stopping in front of an old hangar. "Sydney was right about not maintaining the road or the hangar," he concurred observing the surroundings.

"Let's face it," Jordan said gazing at it. "It doesn't look safe enough to put this bird inside. If you open the hangar doors, what is left of the structure may crumble."

"Well," Yorg said unbuckling his seatbelt. "You stay here while I check it out," he opened the cockpit door. "Close the main door behind me, in case something goes wrong."

"If you say so," Jordan agreed. "If you think it's safe enough, I'll pull inside."

"You worry too much," Yorg chuckled. "I'll have Kathe check the surroundings with JAKE."

"Dad, that was an awesome landing!" Pete exclaimed running to Yorg.

"Where are we?" Bob sleepily questioned looking out the window. "This isn't Newark."

"Are we in a cornfield?" Jeannie asked looking out the window.

"Everything's okay," Yorg assured them patting Bob on the shoulder.

"Yorg, are we in trouble?" Ylia asked. "Should Jeannie and I wake the children and be ready to leave?"

"No, Sydney is extra cautious since there were problems in New York," Yorg explained. "We made an emergency landing until he checks it out. I'm sure we'll be on our way soon."

"Pete, I'll have to teach you how to do this sometime," Yorg grinned. "I've landed on roads like this when I was your age with my uncle. Pilots are always looking for a place to land in an emergency."

"I can't wait to do this!" Pete exclaimed. "That was exciting! You re-centered the jet twice with ease!"

"That's not as easy as it looks," Yorg smiled glancing at the younger children asleep. "You have your runway touch-and-goes down pat. It just takes some practice to land on dirt or bumpy roads. It would be best if you went back to your seat," he said as Kathe joined them. "We're going to move the jet inside that structure in a few minutes. I need everyone to stay put. I must check out a hangar before we can pull inside. He handed JAKE back to her.

"The hangar looks pretty rickety?" Kathe questioned.

"Sydney said it should work," Yorg whispered as Kathe followed him. He reached into the closet for his backpack. "I do need you to check for any unfriendlies in the area."

"I'm going with you," Kathe insisted closing the closet door. "I heard Spinello has eyes everywhere."

"Sydney picked this abandoned hangar," Yorg replied turning on his earbud. "I have to check it out. Jordan's ready to remind Patti where he put the Wills. Jeannie's worried we are in a cornfield. I've got my earbud. After you check, I'll keep in constant touch with you."

"Okay," Kathe agreed following Yorg down the steps, holding JAKE toward the hangar. "JAKE, are any human life-forms inside the building?"

JAKE lit up, scanning the building, and showing Kathe several small life-forms. "Kathe, no human life-forms inside the building."

"I'll keep an eye on you inside in case there's some unforeseen danger," Kathe said releasing the mosquito-drone from JAKE. "JAKE, warn me if any human life-forms approach the building."

"Kathe, continuing to monitor the surroundings," JAKE replied as the screen remained lit.

"It's all yours," Kathe approved watching Yorg approach the hangar with his gun drawn. "I'm taking the drone inside," she moved it ahead. "Be careful, the hangar is missing quite a few walls, and the roof is missing in several areas."

"I need to check how sound the remaining structure is," Yorg shared. "We've got to hide this bird before daylight."

"Other than possibly a few rats, it's pretty safe to go inside," Kathe approved.

"Would you please join Jordan?" Yorg asked. "He's a nervous wreck."

"I bet," Kathe chuckled hurrying up the steps and into the cockpit. "Yorg wants me to show you what we're up against," she laid JAKE on the console as they watched Yorg open the hangar door and slowly walk inside.

"Kat," Yorg informed her moving his flashlight around. "There is a large portion of the roof missing on the back-left side. The back-left hangar door, along with part of the supporting wall, and the roof, is gone. The back-right door is partially hanging," he relayed checking outside. "The runway used to exit the hangar and go back to the street looks as rough as the road. Only by the Grace of God, the front hangar doors and supporting walls are still mostly intact," he surveyed as he ran the flashlight across both. "It's sketchy but doable."

"Are you sure the remaining roof is stable?" Jordan asked. "The only plane parked here was a single-engine, propeller plane. The jet's engine will shake the structure."

"We have no other place to hide," Yorg warned. "Bring it inside very slowly and stop. I'll open the doors and direct you inside."

"Dear Lord, be with us," Jordan sighed making the Sign of the Cross.

"Jordan, it's now or never," Kathe smiled. "Follow Yorg's instructions."

"You're looking good," Yorg guided the jet slowly inside. "Stop, and cut the engines," Yorg crossed both arms in front of his face. "Good job, it's still standing. I'll close the doors while you and Kathe join me."

"It's not the Taj Mahal," Jordan noted, opening the door, and walking down the steps with Kathe.

"To that mother cat sneaking back to her kittens, it is," Kathe laughed moving the mosquito inside the structure behind some debris. "I'm sure the noise of the engines scared her off."

"It's not perfect," Yorg said joining them. "But it should hide the Citation from the three Leers. Hopefully, they'll fly over without seeing us, and keep going."

"Will the Citation make it through the back exit?" Jordan asked gazing out the back.

"I have to clear some of the debris, but it should," Yorg approved as they walked outside. "It's not going to be a smooth takeoff, but we'll make it," he said following the taxiway to the road.

"I've done touch-and-goes in a small Cessna on a dirt road before," Jordan stated, "but it was smooth."

"This is nothing," Kathe chuckled. "In Russia, we had to takeoff in a field with people shooting at us after we stole the plane."

"You did what?" Jordan demanded.

"Kat don't scare him," Yorg chuckled walking back inside. "He'll text Patti next the phone number to remind her of the Life Insurance Company."

"Very funny," Jordan smirked entering the hangar. "Patti can't take the stress."

"Patti's not the only one," Kathe laughed swatting Jordan.

JAKE interrupted, "Kathe, sensing two human forms 300 yards away and closing."

"Shouldn't we get back inside the Citation?" Jordan asked. "Maybe, we should takeoff and take our chances in the air?"

"No, we are still safer on the ground," Yorg confided handing Jordan his ankle gun. "We don't know the fire-power the jets carry. Follow the procedure and lockdown the plane. Tell Bob and Pete what is happening. If one of us tells you to takeoff, do it. Pete will co-pilot for me. Sydney will direct you to Newark."

"Go through the checklist with Pete," Kathe cautioned following Jordan inside, reaching for her backpack in the closet. "Be ready to takeoff. Alonzo and Pauli are en route. We've got this," she promised leaving the plane.

"I've got the people on infrared," Sydney stated emailing some instructions to Stephen. "They have stopped and are standing together in the center of the cornfield. You two head toward them quickly, so they can't get near the. Yorg, use the mother-drone, and, if necessary, use that mosquito. Kathe, work the camera on the iPad."

"Copy that," Kathe agreed hitting the icon to bring her mosquito back.

"Use the cornfield and rocky terrain to your benefit for cover," Sydney instructed watching them hurry toward the targets. "Jordan, I'm closing and locking the Citation's door for you," Sydney stated pressing enter on his computer. "You and Pete go through the checklist while we check out our visitors. I'm disconnecting you for now."

"Kathe, I added another special safety feature to the Citation," Sydney confessed. "You don't have to worry about anyone breaking into the Citation while you're outside."

"How's that?" Kathe asked as they moved over two rows of corn almost parallel to the people.

"Let's say that anyone who tries will be sorry," Sydney chuckled.

"What's that supposed to mean?" Kathe asked.

"How can I put this," Sydney chuckled, "it's electrifying."

"How did you add that feature?" Yorg asked as he and Kathe stopped behind a rock at the edge of the field. He opened his backpack and pulled the mother-drone out, while Kathe took out the iPad.

"It's a form of Chameleon," Sydney admitted keeping an eye on the cornfield. "I modified it to the electrical system on the main computer onboard. This modification is only for the two of you to know. I haven't told Ramsey yet. Currently, she's safely in the building, showering before joining me. It was apparent the staging of the attack was to kill her. After she neutralized the last target, Jenkins came out of the bedroom, pointing his Glock directly at her. I saw in his eyes that he wondered if he could get away with killing her and warned her."

"Have you talked to Hiltree about it?" Kathe asked as Yorg lifted the drone.

"I sent Hiltree the video for his opinion," Sydney confirmed. "He wasn't shocked. He confirmed what I saw. Also, CC confirmed Hiltree's suspicions about Jenkins' secret comings and goings in the penitentiary meeting with Macaby. There's no record of any of Jenkins visits. Everyone else is documented entering and leaving, including the warden and guards. Hiltree sent CC the footage tonight, instructing her to add more proof to her investigation. We must possess ironclad evidence to nail Jenkins. We have too much to lose, and Jenkins has all of it to gain," Sydney explained enhancing the infrared feed from the satellite. "We're getting some action in the cornfield again."

"I see another smaller life-form is approaching them," Kathe confirmed.

"I see that," Sydney concurred as Yorg hovered the drone over their heads. Sydney switched from infrared to the live feed.

"Maybe they're coon hunting," Kathe suggested watching from the iPad. "The moon is bright enough and we are in the Appalachians."

"You have a point," Sydney stated zooming in closer. "Let's see who is joining them."

"The heavy-set-middle-aged man must have left his house in a hurry," Kathe observed. "He's wearing his striped pajama top stuffed in his overalls and holding a Remington Rife. His companion is also wearing pajamas. He's a little younger with an old shotgun."

"Maybe, they decided to go late," Sydney noted watching a small boy running up to them.

"Oh, my!" Kathe gasped watching the elder man raise his rifle straight at the child. "The child froze in his tracks! I retract my last statement. This doesn't look like coon hunting."

"Amos, what are you doing?" the younger man demanded.

"Let me filter out the wind rustling the cornstalks," Sydney cautioned typing on his computer and pushing enter. "We need a perfect recording."

"What are you doing here, boy?" Amos forcefully whispered as the boy stood in front of him.

"Pa," the boy began. "I heard a loud noise in the front yard, and I got up to look out my window. It saw a fancy airplane turn at the fork before our house. Then, I heard the phone ring and saw Uncle Rufus pick you up. I followed you here on my bike."

"Angel, you dumb, stupid kid!" Amos scoffed. "Of all the step-kids in the world, I end up with one dumber than a stump! Not to mention, I can barely understand your English! If I didn't need your ma, I would have shot you a long time ago! I didn't buy or ask for you! They called you a free bonus. I didn't need a free bonus! I needed a woman to raise my boys!"

"I'm sorry, Pa," Angel looked down at the ground. "I just wanted to see the fancy plane. I never saw anything like it!"

"This is none of your business!" Amos got closer to him. "I told you never to call me Pa unless it's in front of your ma! You'll never be one of Amos Tucker's boys! Get your Cuban-self, back to the house! And don't tell anybody what you saw! You got that boy!" Amos pushed Angel with his rifle. Angel hung his head as he walked away. "Run home, you ninny!" Amos aggressively whispered as Angel hurried off crying.

"Amos," Rufus calmly whispered, "you shouldn't have done that. The little fellers got feelings. You're stuck with him. I'm your brother, and I warned you not to deal with those strange people. Pa always said to only place our trust in mountain folks."

"Shut up, Rufus, or I'll shoot you, too!" Amos snapped. "We need to get to that hangar and report to our contact."

"Did you record that?" Kathe shivered.

"Yes," Sydney answered. "It looks like more than Spinello's men have visited this mountain. Let's take these two targets out now so they can't report. Don't kill them. Let Spinello deal with them."

"With pleasure," Kathe smiled as Yorg looked at the bottom of his iPad and touched the orange X. A small door opened on the mother-drone, releasing a tiny mosquito-drone.

Kathe split the screen on her iPad. One side showed the camera, and the other side controlled the mosquito. She flew the mosquito-drone down to the two men, still arguing about the boy. She went behind Amos first and tapped the orange X on the bottom of her iPad. The mosquito landed on his neck and injected him, and then Rufus.

"Both targets are down," Kathe grinned at Yorg.

"I'm bringing the mosquito back while we secure the two clowns," Yorg stated.

"Hold on," Sydney replied, "Alonzo is calling. I'll add him to our conversation," he said merging the calls. "Alonzo, I have Kathe and Yorg on the line."

"Good," Alonzo began, "my source called and told me that Spinello's men have changed course to Deerfeld Airport. My source will keep us informed when they land and how many men we're facing."

"Can your source stop them for us?" Sydney inquired.

"Yes, and no," Alonzo chuckled, "the source is well equipped. But it's not the kind of relationship you think. It's complicated. Pauli and I are landing at a private airstrip in about ten minutes. By the grace of God, we'll land before Spinello's men."

"Copy that," Sydney smiled shaking his head. "We will leave your association with your source out of this."

"I'm not a priest, old friend," Alonzo chuckled reading instructions on his phone. "Kathe and Yorg stay off the roads. My source warned that these people are very clannish. Go through the woods straight across from the hanger. You'll have to be careful. The terrain is difficult leading to a small river. Cross the river and keep heading straight southwest. My source says to look out for bears. If you get into a cornfield, you need to head more south and stay in the woods heading toward Hamilton Creek Road. You'll come to a clearing and find a large, horse stable, barn, hangar, and a house. We'll meet you at the house in twenty minutes. We must take Spinello's men down before they get near your family. Your children have seen enough violence."

"Copy that," Kathe agreed as they put on their night-vision goggles. "We'll meet you there."

"I'll download the address and instructions to JAKE," Sydney offered as Alonzo sent Sydney the information.

"Thanks, Alonzo," Kathe appreciated. "First, we have to secure these two clowns, and we'll be on our way."

"Kathe," Sydney said reading another text message. "I need to go offline for a while and talk with Stephen. Ramsey is in transit," he said before answering Stephen's call. "Yes, Stephen, I'll send you the information you need. I'll need to take over the camera for a few minutes. I must install some special software that I finished. I'll have to explain what it does on an as needed basis."

A few minutes later, Kathe and Yorg finished securing the two brothers by zipping-tying their hands to some smaller trees. "I wonder what they'll think when they wake up like this," Kathe smiled, using JAKE to melt their cell phones.

"Like they woke up in a nightmare," Yorg chuckled. "The big, bad men with deer hunting rifles never saw what happened to them," he said checking the time. "Let's go," Yorg urged, adjusting his goggles. "We've got less than fifteen minutes to get to the house. We passed a large ranch-style house on the left when we landed," Yorg explained as they crossed Tennessee Valley Rd. "We now know that Rufus owns that house. It's evident that Spinello's men already alerted them to watch out for us."

"That confirms what Angel said to Amos," Kathe agreed as they carefully crossed the road. Kathe stopped, "Sh...sh... she listened. "I hear someone crying," reaching for JAKE. "JAKE is there a life-form near us?" she asked as the screen lit up.

"Kathe, there is a small life-form through the trees, ten-feet to your left," JAKE stated pulling up the directions.

"It has to be Angel, and it's dangerous out here," Kathe cautioned.

"You're always a loving mother," Yorg smiled following her. "No man should ever treat a child, like Amos just did."

"There he is," Kathe peered around a tree. "He's sitting under a tree next to his bike. Wait here for a minute," Kathe stepped out. "Angel," Kathe calmly called putting her hands up slowly approaching him. Yorg stepped out behind her. "We're not going to hurt you," Kathe said as Angel jumped up. "Please, don't run. We saw and heard the way Amos treated you."

"No child deserves that kind of treatment," Yorg declared. "We have children on the plane you saw tonight. We are trying to protect them from Amos."

"We tied Amos and Rufus to some trees," Kathe admitted. "They are alive. The evil man that sold your mother to Amos is after us. I promise that when this is over, we will help you and your mother get back to your family in Cuba," she said as Angel ran to her, throwing his arms around her.

"Really?" Angel asked, looking up at her.

"I promise," Kathe smiled. "And I always keep my promises."

"Angel," Yorg explained bending on one knee. "It's dangerous out here. Your house is across the street. We'll watch you get inside, but you must promise not to tell anyone, including your mother, that you saw us."

"I promise," Angel hugged Yorg and got on his bike. "You'll help us get back to Cuba?" he asked, looking over his shoulder.

"Todo el camino de vuelta a Cuba," Kathe promised. (All the way back to Cuba.)

"Gracias," Angel smiled and crossed the road. (Thank you).

Chapter 2

Deerfeld, Virginia
Tuesday, June 30, 0050 (12:50 AM EST)

Kathe and Yorg watched Angel get off his bike, walk up the front porch steps, and open the door. They waved to Angel as he went inside and then crossed the road behind the barn.

"We've lost too much time with Amos and Rufus," Kathe admitted checking the terrain through the woods to the ranch. "Look at this ravine we have to cross. GPS shows a drop-off of twenty-five feet straight down into a five to eight feet deep river with a swift current. Alonzo's friend warned it is difficult. That might be an understatement."

"The cliff isn't straight down either," Yorg pointed out. "It's very jagged. That will take a lot of time to climb down. Not to mention this forest is bear-infested. Are you thinking what I'm thinking?"

"Absolutely," Kathe grinned. "The moon is bright enough that we don't have to turn on the lights. No one should see us."

"Amos doesn't take care of his property," Yorg looked around. "The rickety old barn does have an old, Chevy truck inside. Hopefully, it still runs. Let's look," he led the way inside the barn. "No keys, no problem," he smiled checking under the hood. "It looks good. I can hotwire it under the dash."

"There's a half-eaten banana on the dashboard in front of the steering wheel," Kathe noted. "Looks like he drove it a few hours ago."

"That's good enough for me," Yorg grinned rolling the window down, and putting it in neutral. "Help me push it back out the barn and down the road before I start it."

"I'll push from the front while you push and steer it from the side," Kathe agreed walking around it.

Deerfeld, Virginia
Tuesday, June 30, 0100 (1:00 AM EST)
Saundra Smith's Ranch

"Alonzo DiMeglio, it's been a long time!" she greeted as Alonzo walked down the steps of the Leer Jet.

"Bernadette Rocca!" Alonzo chuckled giving her a big hug. He stepped back and looked her over. "You haven't aged a bit! You're as beautiful as the last time I saw you! I've sure missed you!"

"Alonzo!" Bernadette blushed, "you look great yourself." She hugged him again as Pauli joined them. "Pauli Pachino!" Bernadette jumped in his arms, and he swung her around. "It's been such a long time!" she smiled looking him in the eyes. "I didn't get to see you nor say goodbye before I left."

"I hope Alonzo told you goodbye for me," Pauli smiled putting her down. "I had to run a little interference for you to leave that day. You know how it is?"

"I owe you big time!" Bernadette exclaimed hugging him again. "I heard you had your hands full that day." She stepped back. "A day hasn't gone by that I don't thank God for our family bond. You always have our backs," Bernadette reached up kissing him on the cheek, and then glanced at Alonzo. "Where are my manners? You must be hungry and tired. Come inside while we wait for your friends. I made tea and some snacks," she said walking to the house.

"I see your horses are already gone," Alonzo noted the empty stables.

"I told the few people I interact with in town that I sold them two weeks ago," Bernadette sighed. "I've sent them ahead as usual. It's funny," she admitted walking into the house, "there's no such place as a paradise for people like us. Here, I go by the name of Saundra Smith. I must control myself with most of the Hillbilly men. They seem to own their wives and treat them with little to no respect. They act as if I'm deaf when I'd pass them in the stores as they make snide remarks."

"Bernadette?" Pauli laughed reaching for some cheese and crackers. "That's more than control. I've worked with you; you deserve an Oscar for that performance!"

"Thanks, Pauli," Bernadette accepted tipping her teacup to him. "I didn't want to blow my cover. As you well know, in our profession payback is sweet. I always knew it was a matter of time before I'd have to leave. With each crude remark they would make; I would smile at them. I plan to show them the real me before I leave."

"And you are so good at that!" Pauli agreed tipping his cup to her.

"We all have specialties," Bernadette grinned shrugging her shoulders.

"Bernadette let's get serious for a minute," Alonzo changed the subject. "What's going on up here? It's not Spinello's usual business location."

"No, it isn't," Bernadette agreed. "I volunteer at the pitiful airport to see who's coming and going. About three months ago, some men came to the mountain and met with several of the church's men. The so-called minister set the meeting up. It wasn't Spinello, but I could tell he sent them. A Cuban was with them. Amos Tucker, one of the head clansmen, had already dealt with the man through the minister. From listening to their conversation, Amos bought his new Cuban wife and her son about a year ago. They only referred to him as Montez. I checked all my sources and couldn't find anything on him. He made a lot of financial promises to the townspeople for some high favors. After that night, I started noticing the fear element in most of the women in town. Ladies who always opened their arms to me no longer did. I didn't want to get involved or be recognized, so I began my departure. I planned on slipping away next week until you called. I figured you'd need my help."

"We are out-numbered," Alonzo admitted. "I didn't want to blow your cover, so I didn't ask."

"If it wasn't for Mr. LaBasco, you, and Pauli," Bernadette confided, "I wouldn't be here. I'll stand beside our family any day," she said as an alarm sounded on her phone. "Someone is walking through the cemetery at this time of night," Bernadette warned hurrying to the dining room, and opening the hutch. She pulled out the keyboard and then turned-on multiple security cameras. "It's kind of late to visit a grave, don't you think?" she questioned watching the minister hurrying to the back door of the church. "Well, I see the good reverend is going to the church at this hour."

"Kathe, there are cameras all around this property," JAKE warned as Yorg parked in the woods.

"JAKE, call Alonzo," Kathe requested getting out of the truck.

"Kathe," Alonzo answered walking away from Bernadette and Pauli.

"We see the stables, and JAKE warned of multiple cameras," Kathe informed him.

"Just a minute," Alonzo said walking back to Bernadette and Pauli. "My friends are close and noticed the cameras facing them. They don't want a recording of them in this area."

"I don't know how they detected my cameras," Bernadette glanced back at him. "I've never had anyone detect them."

"They are very high-tech, like you," Alonzo admitted. "I've used some amazing gadgets with them lately."

"Okay, the cameras are off," Bernadette reported. "Tell them to come to the back door of the house and come in," Bernadette responded turning off the house alarm with her cell phone. She continued to listen to the men in the church.

"Kathe, Yorg," Alonzo greeted a few minutes later in the kitchen. "We're in the dining room watching some of the men from town meet with the minister at the church," he relayed leading the way. Pauli greeted them as Bernadette turned up the volume to the microphone in the church.

"This better be something at this late hour!" Rev. Woods exclaimed as two men armed with rifles entered from the back door of the church.

"I think those people Montez is looking for landed here tonight," Bubba stated leaning his rifle against the first pew. "If it's them, we have to call that number."

"What are you talking about?" Rev. Woods demanded.

"Amos called me tonight and said Rufus saw a plane land on the road in front of his house," Bubba declared.

Rev. Woods reached for his phone and checked the screen, "I missed a call from Amos!" he snapped bringing up his voicemail. "He didn't leave a message. What else did he say?"

"Rufus said it took the right fork in the road," Bubba explained. "They were going to check it out and call me back. He wanted me to call you and then get Billy to meet them. He never called back. His old lady said he hasn't returned," he reported as Rev. Woods's phone rang.

"It's Montez," Rev. Woods cautioned answering the phone. "No, Amos and Rufus are still checking. We're calling all the men to help. When you land, why don't you wait at the airport until I get the information. I realize you brought your people to get them. However, it's dark out here, and we've got no shortage of black bears. Your men don't know the area. My people know about this mountain. We'll find them . . . okay. I'll call you as soon as we know." He turned to Bubba, "That was Montez. He wants to know their location. Did you try to call Amos again?"

"Yeah, it just goes to voicemail," Bubba stated as Rev. Woods tried.

"That's odd; his voicemail is full," Rev. Woods noted.

"I tried to call Rufus and got the same thing," Bubba reported as the young man behind him started nervously pacing the aisle.

"I don't like this!" Billy snapped. "I never trusted these people! They'll get us all killed for their favors!"

"Billy," Rev. Woods sighed placing his arm around Billy's shoulder. "We talked about this at several meetings before they came. Our town has become a ghost town after the coal mine closed! All we must do is give them some information and take in a few strays from time-to-time. They'll give us quite a bit of money in return."

"That's not true!" Billy exclaimed moving away and glared at the reverend. "They're smuggling criminals into our country and want us to harbor them!"

"What harm can it do?" Rev. Woods defended. "They promised these people wouldn't hurt us, and they wouldn't be here long."

"You're a man of The Cloth!" Billy declared. "You're supposed to teach us to live as the Good Book says!"

"I am a man of God," Rev. Woods defended. "I'm taking care of my flock as the Good Book says. Your grandpa is sick!" he snapped pointing at him. "The doctors in that fancy hospital in West Augusta turned him away twice already. If you're scared to be a part of this, then go home! We won't give you any of the money! The choice is yours!"

"I went from making good money in the coal mine to nothing," Billy sighed glancing at the floor. "You know I lost everything and had to move in with grandpa. I can't even take care of him. I have no choice."

"That's my best friend!" Bubba exclaimed throwing his arm around Billy's shoulder and squeezing him. "It's not the first time we've done this together!"

"Don't remind me," Billy shivered walking away from Bubba.

"Both of you start calling all the neighbors and asked them to help find the intruders," Rev. Woods ordered.

"Hot dog!" Bubba laughed picking up his phone. "We're gonna hunt people again!"

"Watch your mouth!" Rev. Woods snapped. "The other men think we're just trying to hold the people they are looking for," he said reaching for his phone. "We don't want them to know the truth!"

"Spinello's men haven't landed yet," Bernadette reported turning around. "Well, so much for the good reverend and his flock. I knew Rev. Woods was a fake the first time, which was the last time I went to his church. That's when I installed my cameras. I always knew Bubba wasn't all there. Bubba's father owns the only funeral home in town, Clifton Mortuary. People from all over the country come here for hunting season. Now, I know why some hunters die in accidental shootings, and Sheriff Potter looks away. Evidentially, Bubba kills them, and his father makes $10,000.00 shipping the body's home to the poor loved ones. They probably split the money."

"That's the going rate for funeral homes transporting bodies across state lines today," Alonzo agreed as several alarms sounded on Bernadette's warning system.

"Enough of being blind!" Ramsey snapped listening to them. "Sydney, get us into Bernadette's camera system! We need to see this!"

"She's got an excellent firewall," Sydney noted pulling up a program. "But it's not as good as my new program," Sydney smiled continuing to type commands on his computer. "Give me one more second . . . and now," he grinned, pressing enter.

"Wonderful!" Ramsey exclaimed watching the cameras open one-by-one on the screen. "How many cameras does she have?"

"She's running twelve individual cameras," Sydney stated as the last one opened.

"Okay, team," Ramsey interrupted, "as you just heard, we're inside Bernadette's security camera network."

"Sydney, I need an Aerial map," Kathe requested.

"It's on its way," Sydney smiled downloading one to JAKE. "I'm highlighting Bernadette's cameras in the area."

"Bernadette, bring up the church again," Alonzo requested turning to the monitor. "Sydney, can you run a facial scan on the Rev. Woods? He looks so familiar."

"He sure does," Pauli agreed walking closer to the monitor. "Can you make him a little younger, perhaps?"

"Who is Sydney?" Bernadette questioned glancing at Alonzo.

"Sydney, make him younger with black hair?" Alonzo requested.

"Sure, give me a minute," Sydney answered cloning the picture of Rev. Woods. "Does this help?" he asked changing his appearance before their eyes.

"Could that be Geraldo Carbone?" Alonzo declared. "

"But it can't be?" Pauli denied. "We went to his funeral. It was an open casket."

"It's apparent now that Bencivenni put a mask on a different corpse," Alonzo realized.

"Who accessed my network?" Bernadette demanded as Alonzo cleared his throat. "Alonzo, who is Sydney?"

"Sydney is my IT Man," Kathe answered. "Sydney is how I knew where your cameras were on the grounds. He and our boss, Linda Ramsey, are connected to all of us via earbuds. Sydney hacked into your system to help us. The only thing I can tell you is that we have very high-security clearances."

"If Bernadette is going to help us, she needs to know everything," Alonzo declared. "I don't keep secrets from family."

"I agree," Ramsey confirmed. "Just give Bernadette the basics to start."

"A little over two years ago, two U.S. Officials approached Mr. LaBasco and me to steal a top-secret weapon system from Russia. They stated it was for the U.S. National Security. When Charles escorted them out at the close of the meeting, the Senator touted having a Middle Eastern buyer to the general. That horrified Mr. LaBasco due to the number of terrorists coming out of that part of the world. Mr. LaBasco called them and told them to come back after he thought about it. I researched Senator Frank and General Thompson and confirmed my findings with my source at the State Department. They were guilty of setting up people to take the fall while they kept their hands clean. Mr. LaBasco declined the offer. Mario Jr. was furious and argued with his father. We tried to make Mario Jr. understand that the weapon would be used against other nations in the wrong hands. Mario Jr. refused to listen and went behind his father's back and made the deal."

"I heard rumors that Mario Jr. deemed his father weak and wanted to take over the business," Bernadette confessed.

"Yes," Alonzo sighed, "Mr. LaBasco sent me to join with Kathe's team and stop Mario Jr. Unfortunately, Frank and Thompson also offered the deal to Antonio Falcini Sr. We also discovered that Pietro Bencivenni joined with Spinello in a hostile take-over of the Falcini Business. Spinello is in business with a Brazilian named Carlos Prado in Miami. Prado has a massive worldwide network of connections. Now, they want the weapon for different reasons. We must stop them!"

"I heard the rumors about the Bencivenni take-over," Bernadette admitted. "It seems the younger generation doesn't believe in family loyalty," she confided glancing at the screen with the church. "Rev. Woods does look familiar. I tried to match him with some of the associates of clients Luca and I knew. I came up with nothing."

"Alonzo," Sydney announced speaking through the computer microphone. "I'm showing his name is Gerardo Carbone," Sydney reported pulling up his rap sheet. "It says he is deceased."

"For someone who died in his late thirties, he sure did age; and not well at all," Alonzo stated.

"Tomme Boy Dano had that contract," Pauli remembered. "That's the third person Dano killed that has shown back up with Spinello's men recently."

"We need to locate Tomme Boy," Alonzo declared. "This proves he double-crossed the people who contracted his services and collected from both sides."

"It sure does," Pauli agreed. "That's crossing the line, even in our business."

"Who else did Spinello bring back?" Bernadette questioned. "I need-to-know who we're going up against."

"Vinnie Issac and Tito Morado that we know of," Alonzo confided.

"Those two animals!" Bernadette exclaimed. "When Luca and I heard they were dead, we went to confirm it. We knew something was wrong when we found closed caskets with around-the-clock guards posted inside and outside the funeral home. We talked with Spinello. He said someone badly riddled their bodies with bullets. That's why the closed caskets. We never believed Spinello. But we had no idea it was something like this."

"The year before they died, Mr. LaBasco got wind that Spinello was back in the Alps," Pauli remembered. "Our men on the ground said he visited a small village of 230 people, fifty miles west of Corippo.

That triggered a red flag since Spinello's family agreement was to stay in the United States. Mr. LaBasco sent us straight to the village to see what Spinello was doing. By the time we got there, the town was empty. The villagers had been slaughtered; blood was everywhere. We found a fresh mass grave by a bulldozer on the site. Just as we were leaving, we heard some children crying. We found them in a basement under the rubble of what once was a house. It took us a while to dig them out. They said their parents hid them when it started. In all my years, I never want to witness something like that again."

"I checked and found out the bulldozer was rented by Geraldo Carbone," Alonzo confirmed. "I never thought Spinello would sink so low as to do something like that. When Spinello tried to kill us in Ponce Inlet, I made him a promise that I will keep!"

"I can't believe Tomme Boy is involved with Spinello like this," Pauli admitted. "At one time, he was the most sought-after hitman."

"Luca and I always suspected Dano worked both sides," Bernadette admitted. "He always lived more lavishly than his contracts paid. We worked for some of the same people. We would hang out together in between jobs. Alonzo and I were working in Brazil at the time Luca was murdered. No one could have gotten the edge on my Luca. I knew it had to be someone Luca knew and trusted. Tomme Boy was supposedly out of the country that day, too. But I could never find out where, nor could I prove he killed Luca."

"Excuse me," Sydney interrupted as an alarm sounded on Bernadette's system. "The gas station suddenly has someone inside the store," Sydney noted checking another screen.

"That's Walter Greene," Bernadette recognized. "He owns that station."

"It looks like they are checking to see if Kathe and Yorg are heading toward the airport," Ramsey surmised. "We're also getting action at the country store, as well as the feed store."

"It's the store owners," Bernadette noted. "Ramsey is right. They will call Bubba if they see something. They may be carrying weapons, but it's for protection from the bears. They are too religious to pull the trigger on a person. They are clannish," Bernadette chuckled, "but too religious to get their hands too dirty."

"That's interesting," Ramsey sat back in her chair, "but they are not above spying and reporting?"

Bernadette smiled and threw her hands up, "I know these people. It doesn't make any sense, but that's the way they are."

"Carbone's main job was to relocate people for Spinello," Alonzo remembered. "This town sounds like a haven for him to work."

"It does," Ramsey affirmed. "Bernadette, what is on this mountain that would interest Spinello enough to bring Carbone here?"

"Nothing," Bernadette explained. "The only thing this town has going is hunting season a couple of times a year."

"I searched the Internet for a reason they chose this location," Sydney answered putting it up on the screen. "It has a very karstic topography. Mainly composed of sinkholes, underground streams, and caverns. It's tucked away in the mountains and very secluded."

"So, now they have everything they need to finish their project," Ramsey assumed. "In Miami, we discovered that Bencivenni is known for making dead people reappear somewhere else. Spinello is known for smuggling, and Prado transports goods and services worldwide. Alonzo said Carbone was known for relocating people for Spinello. My best guess is that this is a perfect town to hold people before relocating them worldwide."

"Yes, it would be," Bernadette concluded. "That's why these Hillbillies are afraid of them."

"Deerfeld fits the description," Ramsey agreed.

"Pauli and I found out that Carbone stayed in the Alps for two years," Alonzo continued. "He had a high, solid, wooden border wall built around the village. He brought in armed guards to keep anyone out. Several people tried to find out what they were doing and vanished. One of our people witnessed a van picking up eight men and four women in the middle of the night at an obscure site. The van went straight to the village. It stayed there for less than a half-hour and left empty."

"You just gave me a terrible visual for them to use Chameleon to smuggle terrorists in and out of our country easier," Ramsey gasped as another alarm sounded on Bernadette's system.

"Spinello's men landed at the airport," Bernadette announced. "What is our next step? With what Alonzo said Carbone did to those villagers in the Alps, these poor Hillbillies don't deserve that fate."

"Now, we know why they're trying to shut all of us down tonight," Kathe surmised.

"Yes, we do!" Ramsey snapped, tapping her pencil, and then breaking it in half. "They know we're the only ones that can stop their worldwide domination plot."

"It appears that Rev. Woods is getting very agitated," Sydney noted. "Let's listen," he said turning up the sound.

"What do you mean, none of the men are coming?" Rev. Woods screamed.

"They all said they want nothing to do with these people," Bubba declared. "They changed their minds and don't want blood money."

"That does it!" Billy exclaimed. "I don't either! I'm going home!"

"Oh, no, you're not!" Rev. Woods proclaimed. "If you don't help us, I'll have Sheriff Potter arrest you for the murder of those hunters!"

"You know I didn't kill them!" Billy exclaimed as Bubba turned his rifle on him.

"You were with me," Bubba declared. "That makes you an accomplice."

"I wasn't even with you when you did it!" Billy refuted. "You made me help you move the bodies!"

"Just like Bubba says," Rev. Woods smiled. "You are an accomplice. You could have slammed the door in Bubba's face," he declared as his phone rang. "We'll be right there to pick you up," he looked at them. "Montez is at the airport. He wants us to pick them up."

"Ramsey," Alonzo cautioned, "it's important we find out who employed Tomme Boy. These people he supposedly killed ended up with Prado smuggling them out of the country. Now, they're showing up in various locations around the states. That means this was in the planning stages for years. We need to know some answers, and good, ole Tomme Boy has them."

"You're right," Yorg agreed. "This could tie them together with the search for Chameleon and Gen. Yetsun in Cuba."

"Absolutely," Ramsey confirmed. "In your business, the term double-cross isn't tolerated. For Tomme Boy to fake the death of his marks, someone helped him. Dano could tie Bencivenni, Spinello, and Prado to the real boss we believe is in Cuba. I'll assign Tomme Boy and Montez to CC. She can find out about them while we are busy."

"Alonzo," Bernadette looked him in the eyes. "I want Tomme Boy!" She threw him a set of keys. "These are to the black Jeep outside."

"Deal!" Alonzo laughed catching the keys. "I'm sorry, Ramsey. Luca only trusted three people, Bernadette, me, and Tomme Boy."

"Kathe," Sydney interrupted, "give Bernadette an earbud so she can communicate with us. We'll operate her cameras and keep everyone informed."

"Copy that," Kathe affirmed handing an earbud to Bernadette as they left the house.

"Ramsey, the trucks will split up at the gas station," Bernadette surmised after putting her earbud in place. "That is where SR 209 and SR 211 meet. Both roads end up on Tennessee Valley Road, where the Citation is hiding. They'll try to cut you off."

"I agree," Alonzo confirmed. "Bernadette is a lot like Kathe. She knows her adversaries."

"Bernadette and I will take care of those coming this way on SR 211," Pauli stated. "Then, we'll rejoin you."

"Copy that," Sydney agreed.

"Pauli!" Alonzo exclaimed. "Fill Bernadette in on why Carbone is important to the family."

"Consider it done," Pauli agreed as Bernadette drove off.

Alonzo threw Yorg the keys and got in the backseat of the Jeep. "What is the fastest way to SR 209?" Yorg asked putting on his night vision goggles.

"Drive between the stable and the barn," Alonzo instructed. "Bernadette always has multiple routes in and out of her places. They'll be narrow with lots of turns through the woods to hide them. She is good at what she does."

"I saw a narrow clearing behind the stable when we arrived," Kathe remembered. "It has to be an exit," Kathe said as Yorg slowly circled behind the stable. "Turn right now!"

"It's narrow, but you're right," Yorg declared immediately turning right and then left.

"That will bring you out in front of the church," Sydney relayed checking the satellite.

"There's the opening to the road," Kathe reported. "We have the church insight. We're heading toward the airport."

"Yorg, stop at the gas station," Sydney advised. "Rev. Woods picked up Montez and his men. They are leaving the airport. I counted twenty men squeezed into three trucks. The airport is ten miles from the station. That's where they will split off."

"Copy that," Yorg answered. "We're passing the country store right now. What do we do with the owner inside?"

"Leave him for now," Sydney instructed. "Bernadette says he's just a snitch. Head for the gas station and persuade that owner to go home."

"I can be very persuasive," Kathe smiled. "I assure you that Walter won't want to be a snitch anymore."

"Play nice," Ramsey chuckled. "These men aren't used to a woman giving them orders."

"Ramsey," Kathe grinned, "I never play nice. You taught me well."

"That, I did," Ramsey smiled.

"We see the station," Yorg reported pulling into the woods behind some trees. "We'll go in on foot."

"Be careful," Sydney cautioned hacking into the Allegheny fuel records. "You're not in the range of the camera yet. I found the schematics of the gas station. I've highlighted the cameras and sending it to JAKE now," he said, pushing send.

"I've got it," Kathe confirmed showing Yorg and Alonzo. "Is there a security system with a monitor inside the store?"

"You've got to be kidding," Sydney chuckled. "I'm showing the only signals coming from any of these buildings are the ones Bernadette placed. I mirrored the three cameras to your phones."

"Kathe, get the owner out of there!" Ramsey ordered. "Montez will be there any minute!"

"I'm already out of the Jeep and at the back door," Kathe whispered trying the doorknob. "The door isn't even locked."

"Why does that not surprise me?" Ramsey shook her head, burying her head in her hands. "Just save Mr. Snitch!"

Kathe drew her Ruger LC9, cautiously entering the back door into the store. She checked JAKE to see where Walter was.

"Ramsey," Kathe whispered. "Walter is sitting at the counter next to the cash register."

"Continue," Ramsey requested. "The outside is clear."

Kathe carefully went left, behind the last set of shelving units across from the back door, and then made it to the end near the bathroom. She ran to the next shelf, as Walter turned toward her direction for a moment. When he turned back, Kathe hurried to the last row, closest to his counter. She glanced outside and saw it was clear. "Walter Greene," Kathe stepped out into the open with her gun pointed at him.

"Oh, my!" Walter gasped slowly turning toward her.

"Rev. Woods isn't who you think he is," Kathe explained. "He's a criminal with a very different agenda for your townspeople than he promised. He's on his way to your station. According to Saundra Smith, you're a not willing participant in Rev. Wood's scheme, or I'd drop you right now. You need to go home to your wife and lock your doors. There's nothing but danger for you here. The choice is entirely yours. What will it be?"

"Rev. Woods is trying to help us mountain folk," Walter stammered as he slowly held his hands up. "The government closed our coal mine. We have little to no income. He's trying to help us."

"His real name is Gerardo Carbone," Kathe declared. "He works for a crime syndicate, which I've already alerted the FBI of his location. He's almost here with three truckloads of hired killers. By the way, Rev. Woods is a good buddy of Bubba. We know Bubba is the one killing the hunters and that Sheriff Potter looks away. Tell me, are they splitting the $10,000.00 funeral home fee from shipping the bodies back to their loved ones with you? You know that would make you an accomplice," she advised as he stared at her. "Walter, I'm trying to save you and your people from the havoc they are about to reign down on your town. President Trumore is reopening the coal mines again. Your people will have income, and more people will move back to the town. Since you're hesitant to believe me, let me show you who I am. Hold up your cell phone."

He hesitated, not moving a muscle.

"I'll give you to the count of three to hold it up, or I'll change my mind about letting you live," Kathe declared. "I know Montez is with Rev. Woods."

"Oh," Walter gasped in disbelief.

"Yes," Kathe admitted. "I know all about Montez. What will it be?"

He slowly held up his cell phone.

Kathe reached for hers, "JAKE, melt the battery."

JAKE lit up, and instantly Walter dropped his burning, hot cell phone.

"Kathe, it is done," JAKE answered as Walter's eyes widened.

"What is that?" Walter asked shaking his burning hand.

"That could have easily been you," Kathe stated. "I don't need bullets to kill you. Now that you know who you're dealing with, if I were you, I'd run home!" Kathe exclaimed as three trucks pulled into the station. "They're here! What is your decision?"

He slowly turned looking over his shoulder at Rev. Woods and Montez getting out of the first truck.

"Leave!" Kathe ordered. "Rev. Woods is sending Bubba and his men down SR 211. He's coming inside here next," she said stepping behind the shelf.

"Yes, ma 'am!" he exclaimed running past her out the back door.

"Showtime, Kathe!" Ramsey warned as Kathe kicked Walter's cell phone under the counter. "Get out of there!"

"Kathe, you can't go out the back," Sydney cautioned changing the angle to the camera outside. "One of the trucks is there," he said pulling up the building's schematics.

"I've got the back door," Alonzo declared running through the woods.

"No one is getting out yet," Sydney relayed.

"Copy that," Alonzo answered. "I've got them in my sight."

"Kat, I'm watching the front," Yorg reported. "Most of the men are still in the truck."

"Kathe," Sydney noted enhancing the camera inside by the corner. "I'm showing a door on the back-right of the station. It has to lead inside the garage."

"Copy that," Kathe sighed moving to the end of the first set of shelves, quickly running to the back of the store. "I found the door," she replied opening the door. "You're right. I'm in a garage."

"I'm showing a tall workbench on the right wall by the door," Sydney relayed maneuvering that camera, and enhancing the picture. "There are some boxes underneath it on the far-right. See if you can hide behind them."

"Copy that," Kathe agreed getting on her knees and moving the boxes. "There is a box that doesn't have one behind it. I can hide there," she shimmied behind it.

"Good job, I can't see you," Sydney reported. "Put JAKE on infrared mode. That way, you can watch the cameras, and the light from the screen won't show."

"Copy that," Kathe agreed.

"Rev. Woods is walking into the station," Ramsey observed. "Everyone, hold your positions. Montez is staying by the truck with his men."

"Walter, are you in here?" Rev. Woods called, drawing his weapon, cautiously walking into the dark store. He turned on the lights and looked around the counter.

"Well, it's nice to see the good reverend carries a Glock," Ramsey cautioned. "So much for carrying only the Good Book. He's carefully checking around each shelf now. He's opening the back door and walking outside."

"Billy, have you seen Walter?" Rev. Woods asked.

"No," Billy answered. "The door was closed when we got here. There's no sign of anybody out here."

"Meet me around the front," Rev. Woods ordered closing the door, checking around the right side of the shelves.

"Kathe, he's coming in the garage," Ramsey warned as Woods opened the door. Kathe held her breath as he entered and put JAKE on silent. "Walter are you in here?" he asked waiting for a moment. Woods walked around the oil pit and looked down inside it. He walked toward the door again, noting the large boxes under the workbench.

"Be careful Kathe, he's checking the boxes," Ramsey warned. Kathe held her breath as Rev. Woods pushed several of the boxes against the wall. Kathe held her body against the largest one in front of her to steady it. Rev. Woods pushed it back with his foot.

"It worked," Ramsey sighed. "Woods is going back into the store. He's walking back toward the front of the store. He's looking behind the pay counter again. Something caught his eye. He's picking up an old rifle and leaving. He's walking over to Montez. Let's listen," she said as Sydney turned up the volume on the outside camera.

"Something's wrong!" Rev. Woods exclaimed holding up the rifle. "Walter's rifle was inside behind the counter. He never goes anywhere without it. Billy, take your men and comb the woods behind the station. Montez, translate instructions to your men. Have them look for an older, thin man, wearing faded, green Bib over-all's and a fishing cap. Leave some of your men to look around out here, and bring some inside with us," he said as Montez translated the instructions.

"Yorg and Alonzo, I'm downloading my infrared camera feed to your phones," Sydney said pushing send. "You need to see where they are. Kathe, he's already checked where you are. Just stay put until the guys can get inside to help you. You've got four men coming inside with six more outside in the back."

"Copy that," Kathe reported. "I'm watching the cameras inside of the building."

"Copy that," Sydney affirmed. "We've got your back."

Alonzo watched Billy drive around to the back of the station and park. He watched as the five men jumped out of the back end of the pickup truck and went in different directions into the woods. One was approaching Alonzo to the left of the station as he moved behind a large bush. Alonzo quietly walked up behind him as the man passed him, putting his arm around the man's throat, choking him. The man struggled for a minute, and then his body slowly went limp. Alonzo twisted his neck, dropping him quietly to the ground, leaving him behind the bush. Then Alonzo checked the screen for his next target. One by one, Alonzo followed them through the woods, taking them out. He came upon Billy last. Billy looked frightened, looking through the scope, moving from side-to-side. Alonzo edged around a large tree trunk as Billy passed by him. Then Alonzo snuck up slowly behind Billy, throwing his arm around Billy's neck. "Billy, I know you don't want to be a part of this," Alonzo whispered as Billy dropped his rifle, trying to struggle free. "Saundra Smith says you're worth saving. Do you want to live or end up like the other five? They're all dead."

Billy stopped struggling, shaking his head, yes.

"I'm going to let you go," Alonzo warned. "If you yell or change your mind, I will kill you! Do you understand?"

Billy shook his head, yes, again.

"Saundra and I believed you when you admitted you didn't help Bubba kill those hunters," Alonzo admitted turning him loose.

"I didn't," Billy swore, slowly turning to face Alonzo.

"Get in your truck, go home, and take your grandfather to the hospital in West Augusta," Alonzo ordered pointing toward it.

"I can't," Billy gasped. "If I do, Rev. Woods and Bubba will tell Sheriff Potter to arrest me for murdering hunters, or they'll just kill me."

"Dead men, tell no tales," Alonzo promised. "My boss will pay for your grandfather's treatment. You were right to question Woods as a reverend. His name is Geraldo Carbone. He plans to kill the townspeople and take over the town. I've already seen his work in the Swiss Alps. We're going to save your town from him."

"I always knew there was something wrong with the reverend," Billy admitted. "Thank you," he cried shaking Alonzo's hand. He picked up his rifle and ran to his truck. Alonzo watched Billy speed around the front of the station, not stopping.

"The back is clear," Alonzo confirmed checking his phone.

"The front is clear," Yorg said as his last target fell to the ground.

"Ramsey and I will help you get inside," Sydney stated pressing enter. "I switched your phones to the live camera feed inside the building."

"Copy that," Alonzo affirmed. "I'm coming in the back door."

"I'm coming in from the right side of the garage," Yorg whispered turning the doorknob.

"Copy that," Sydney confirmed as he and Ramsey watched. "I see both of you."

"Aguilae, vea si la puerta de garaje colgante esta abierta," (Aguilae, see if the hanging garage door is open.) Montez ordered as Aguilae hurried over to the door.

"No, señor," (No, sir.) Aguilae answered.

"Entra desde la estación y revisa dentro del garaje por Walter." (Enter from inside the station and check inside the garage for Walter.) Montez ordered.

"Sí, señor," (Yes, sir.) Aguilae answered hurrying inside the station.

"Be careful, Yorg," Ramsey advised. "Montez sent a man named Aguilae to check the garage for Walter."

"I'm inside," Yorg quickly closed the door.

"Yorg, crouch down in the shadows behind the tall, metal locker to your right," Sydney suggested after changing cameras.

"Copy that," Yorg agreed. "I can't reach my phone to check the camera."

"Aguilae is entering the garage," Ramsey reported. "He's turning on the lights. Luckily, it's a dim overhead lamp. He's looking around the room. Now, Aguilae is walking toward the overhead garage door, turning to peer into the pit. Aguilae is nervously reaching in his pocket. He has a flashlight and is checking inside the pit."

"Yorg, stay completely still," Kathe cautioned from under the workbench. "Aguilae is walking around the pit on your side. He's turning toward you. I can't believe he doesn't see you," Kathe quietly moved the box in front of her to the side. "Sydney, do you want me to take the shot?"

"If you have to, do it," Sydney cautioned. "But from that angle, Aguilae will fall sideways. You won't have time to push him in the pit and hide again."

"We've got another problem," Ramsey sighed. "Alonzo, you need to watch out. Woods, Montez, and two men are entering the station."

"Copy that," Alonzo hid. "I see them."

"I think I can squeeze further behind this locker," Yorg whispered slightly moving it as a screwdriver fell off the top onto the cement floor.

"Shoot!" Kathe sighed. "Aguilae is aiming his gun in your direction and not moving."

"He's afraid and might fire randomly," Sydney warned. "Yorg, you're taller than the locker. Take the shot."

"Copy that," Yorg whispered, jumping up, shooting Aguilae in the chest.

"Good job!" Sydney noted. "Aguilae fell backward into the pit."

"What was that?" Rev. Woods demanded.

"Unfortunately, the men in the station heard Aguilae fall," Ramsey cautioned.

"Charles, ve a ver a Aguilae!" (Charles, go check on Aguilae.) Montez whispered.

"Charles is coming inside the garage," Ramsey warned. "Woods opened the door for him. Charles is sweeping the doorway and now entering."

"Aguilae," Charles called walking around the pit with his gun drawn. "¿Aguilae, dondé esta?" (Where are you?)

"What's he doing?" Yorg whispered.

"Charles is making his way around the pit toward you," Ramsey relayed. "He paused for a second, noticing the locker turned sideways. Don't move. He's using his flashlight, looking around the locker."

"I can't believe Charles can't see you," Kathe sighed. "From this angle, I have a perfect view of you."

"Charles didn't see Yorg," Ramsey relayed. "He's turning back toward the pit. He's walking to the edge and shining his flashlight inside."

"¡Aguilae esta muerta!" (Aguilae is dead!) Charles screamed running around the pit toward Kathe.

"Don't let him leave!" Ramsey ordered.

"Got him!" Kathe quickly shoved the box out of her way and fired one shot, hitting him in his left temple. He fell sideways into the front of the pit.

"Montez!" Rev. Woods whispered backing straight back as he kept his eyes on the door. "Did you hear that? Someone is in there. We need more men. Ah!" he tripped and turned around. "Montez!" he gasped at Montez's face down with a knife in his back. He glanced around the room and then bolted out the front door, running straight for his truck, and sped away.

"Alonzo, why did you let him get away?" Ramsey demanded. "You had him!"

"Relax, Ramsey," Alonzo chuckled. "I know exactly where Woods is going. We're on our way," he said as Kathe and Yorg joined him inside the station. "Yorg, let's get back to the church. We've got a rat to catch," he said leading the way to the Jeep.

"How's my family?" Kathe asked putting on her night vision goggles.

"Jordan said all is quiet," Ramsey shared. "We've got the Citation on screen, inside, and out."

"Are Pauli and Bernadette finished yet?" Alonzo asked following Yorg around some thick bushes.

"Almost," Ramsey answered watching Pauli pull his knife out of a target's back and wiping it off on the man's coat. "I have to say, Bernadette is a good shot. She's positioned herself on the Post Office's roof, taking most of them out with a sniper rifle."

"That's my girl!" Alonzo smiled getting into the Jeep. "She uses a laser telescopic lens and never misses."

"I see that," Ramsey confirmed as Bubba ran out of the woods and jumped in his truck. "What?" Ramsey exclaimed watching him speed off toward the gas station. "I don't understand! Bubba just took off in his truck. Bernadette just watched him leave. Why would she let him getaway?"

"She knows where he is going," Alonzo answered. "I know her well. She will kill Bubba face-to-face. She didn't like the snide remarks he always made to her and other women. Let me quote her, 'payback is sweet.'"

"Luckily, I trust you," Ramsey sighed. "Make it quick. We've got to get you back to Newark."

"Of course, you trust me, ole friend," Alonzo chuckled. "You're getting used to the meaning of family," he smiled as Yorg stopped the Jeep deep in the woods.

Deerfeld, Virginia
Tuesday, June 30, 0205 (2:05 AM EST)
Rev. Woods' Church

"We're back at the church," Yorg stated, getting out of the Jeep.

"Good," Ramsey answered. "Sydney just reconnected Pauli and Bernadette to your earbuds."

"Yorg parked the Jeep where Bubba shouldn't see it when he arrives," Alonzo stated walking through the woods toward the middle of the cemetery. "Pauli and I need to talk with the good reverend. We go back several years before his first so-called death. I know he will still have in his possession something that belongs to Mr. LaBasco. You know how it is in our business?"

"No, but I'm learning," Ramsey affirmed as Bernadette's warning system alerted them.

"This is not over!" Sydney interrupted. "We just got another alert from the cameras at the airport. That fourth Leer just landed, and I counted fifteen men getting out," he reported changing the angle of the camera. "It looks like they are taking two of the SUVs parked there. Yes, they are hotwiring them. They're driving off quickly."

"Yorg, Kathe, go to your family!" Ramsey ordered. "They left the airport fast. Rev. Woods made a phone call as he left the gas station," she alerted rewinding the tape. "He looked pretty shocked that we had the upper hand there. He probably figured out the old crop-dusting hangar is where you're hiding. He'll probably meet Spinello's men there."

"We're on our way!" Kathe exclaimed. "Did you warn Jordan?"

"That's my next call," Ramsey cleared the line.

"Kathe, we'll meet you at the Citation as soon as we finish here," Alonzo promised. "I just located Rev. Woods' truck. Since things are deteriorating here, he's probably stopping to grab his possessions to leave. That's the coward we always knew."

"Copy that," Kathe answered as she and Yorg hurried back to the Jeep.

"I'm disconnecting Alonzo and Pauli from you and Yorg for now," Sydney stated pressing enter on his computer. "I'll reinstate them when they join you."

"Copy that," Kathe answered as Yorg sped away.

"I just picked up the two SUVs nearing the gas station," Sydney reported watching his screen. "They're stopping and getting out to check the area. Some are going cautiously inside, and the others are splitting up on the grounds. It should buy you some time."

"We have to take SR 209 straight to the hangar," Yorg realized. "We can't use Bernadette's shortcuts due to the deep ravine. We have to be in the air before the sun comes up over the mountain, so we've got to hurry to get to the hangar before anyone sees us," he said taking off his goggles.

"I'll have Jordan and Bob get ready to leave," Ramsey stated.

"Tell Jordan that I'll help move some of the rubble off the taxiway when we get there," Yorg said. "Pete can help Jordan go through the checklist again while we clear the targets."

"I'll relay the message," Ramsey agreed. "Just hurry and get it done!"

"Copy that," Yorg agreed.

"Alonzo, I'm going to make my way to the back door of the church and enter," Bernadette whispered carefully checking her surroundings. She glanced at her phone as an alert sounded. "Alonzo, I just received an alert that Rev. Woods went under the podium. In the tunnel, he has a safe and several suitcases. He'll surface at the largest tombstone in the middle of the cemetery to make his getaway."

"Thanks," Alonzo whispered. "Pauli just got here. We've found the largest tombstone and are waiting for Carbone to surface. Be careful old friend," he cautioned signaling Pauli to make his way to the right side of the grave.

"As always," Bernadette whispered slipping out of the woods and hurrying to the back door of the church. I'll get in the Baptistery for a Birdseye view, she thought, quickly picking the lock. Slowly turning the doorknob, she promptly opened the door, sweeping it for targets.

She checked the hidden church camera on her phone. She saw Bubba in the church by the Alter as she quietly locked the door from the inside. She hurried down the long, narrow hallway to the steps, calmly walking upstairs. She could now hear Bubba through the thin wall ranting trying to reach Billy. She slowly cracked the door into the Baptistery and reached in her pocket for a small mirror to check the curtains. They are closed, she noted, quietly entering the baptistery, and locking the door behind her. She reached for her Glock and peered through the thick curtains. She noted that only the alter light was lit. Bubba's rifle was leaning against the Alter and his pistol still in the holster on his right side. He was calling around looking for some help, but she could tell no one answered. Bubba turned his back to her as she stepped out of the curtains. She faced him with both hands firmly on the pistol. "Bubba Clifton!" she called as he slowly tried to reach for his pistol. "Don't try it!" she ordered. "Put your hands up and turn around to face me!"

Bubba slowly raised his hands as his fists tightened with anger. "Saundra Smith," he laughed, lowering his hands. "Are you coming against me?"

"Rule number one is to know your opponent," Bernadette informed him.

"Rules for what?" Bubba laughed.

"The Rules of Engagement," Bernadette shot him, grazing his right side.

"You dumb…!" Bubba screamed.

"Don't say it!" Bernadette interrupted as he grabbed his right side. "You're standing on an altar of God."

"You shot me!" Bubba exclaimed looking at the blood on his hand.

"You're going to find out that I don't like to be sneered at and made fun of to my face or back!" Bernadette declared. "Rule number two is never to show your emotions."

"I'm going to enjoy killing you!" Bubba sneered trying to step back to his rifle.

"Really?" Bernadette asked moving her Glock slightly, shooting his rifle in the bullet chamber mechanism. "Not with that! It doesn't work now!"

"Youuuuu!" Bubba screamed as his face turned red.

"Ahhhh," Bernadette said shooting again, nicking his left side. "I don't like to be called names. And my name is not Saundra Smith," she informed him using her native Italian accent.

"Who are you?" Bubba demanded trying to edge to the left.

"Someone who knows you're trying to go to the podium," Bernadette shared shooting him in his right thigh. "There's an escape tunnel under it that leads to the middle of the cemetery. I did my homework."

Bubba fell to the floor, grabbing his leg, screaming in pain, "Who are you?" He shouted glaring over his shoulder at her.

"Tell me, did you show mercy to the innocent hunters you alone murdered?" Bernadette asked shooting him in the right arm as he tried to reach for his pistol.

"Ahhhhhh!" Bubba screamed out.

"I'm sure you know Rev. Woods's real name is Gerardo Carbone," Bernadette declared.

Bubba glared at her.

"I thought so," Bernadette shrugged her shoulders. "How much did Rev. Woods promise to pay you to help him kill the people that landed in the jet tonight?"

"I don't know what you're talking about," Bubba lied.

"How much for the innocent men, women, and children that are on board?" Bernadette demanded, shooting him in the left arm.

Bubba just rolled from side-to-side, screaming out in pain as she walked down to the chapel and faced him.

"Now, you know what the hunting victims felt like when you slowly enjoyed killing them," Bernadette stated. "Yes, I know about that too. I went into the morgue and saw how many shots they took. I wonder how much pain your father will have while working on your body. Is he going to be able to conceal your wounds as he did theirs? What was your cut of the $10,000 for preparing and shipping the bodies? I also know that Sheriff Potter is married to your father's sister. What was his cut?"

Bubba struggled for words, "Who . . . are . . . you?"

"It's people like you who kill for the sport that demeans my profession," Bernadette declared bending next to him and looking directly into his eyes. "When you get to wherever you're going, and I know you're not going to heaven, just say Bernadette Rocca sent you to save God the trouble!" she exclaimed standing up and shooting him between the eyes.

"Bernadette," Ramsey calmly requested as Bernadette holstered her weapon. "Reinforcements arrived at the airport about ten minutes ago. They are still checking around the gas station for survivors. They'll head your way soon and then straight to the hangar. Kathe and Yorg will need your help."

"Copy that," Bernadette replied hurrying out of the church to join Alonzo and Pauli. "We're almost finished here. We just need a few more minutes and then we'll join them."

Ramsey muted the system for a moment and turned to Sydney, "I think she made her point very clear to Bubba. Thank goodness Jenkins wasn't here to see that."

"That would take some explaining," Sydney sighed. "Remember, they're on our side. Let's see if Alonzo and Pauli have the good reverend yet," he said zooming in on the camera facing the cemetery.

"There's Alonzo in the middle of the cemetery," Ramsey noted. "Now, we will see why he let Woods go."

Alonzo watched the large tombstone as the front slowly began to open and a light appeared. Rev. Woods emerged, carefully stepping on the top step. He had a backpack slung over his arm, holding a Glock and a suitcase. Woods cautiously checked around before stepping outside. He had a grin on his face as he closed the secret door.

"I always knew you were a rat," Alonzo chuckled, stepping out from behind the tall headstone across from the reverend with his gun drawn. "I think the moon is bright enough for you to see me."

"Alonzo DiMeglio!" Carbone sighed raising his Glock.

"I don't think so!" Pauli exclaimed pressing his pistol to Carbone's temple. "I'll take that," Pauli said taking the Glock and then flinging Carbone on the ground at Alonzo's feet. "You won't be needing this where we're sending you."

"Pauli, I can't believe my eyes," Alonzo chucked. "Look who is back from the grave; no pun intended."

"I never thought that I would see you again," Carbone tried to stand up.

Pauli whisked his feet out from under Carbone, "You don't need to stand!"

"I can't believe you're here!" Carbone scoffed sitting on the ground, taking deep breaths.

"I can't believe how good God is either," Alonzo laughed shrugging his shoulders. "What a coincidence? And what a small world it is? It is odd after you helped massacre the villagers in the Alps that you would come back from the dead as a minister. But since you did, I have a confession to make," Alonzo pointed at him. "I didn't go to your funeral. Now, that's off my chest!" he grinned. "You know," Alonzo continued, "speaking of confessions, I think you have a confession to make yourself. You took some important papers from Mr. LaBasco and killed his nephew, Milo, to get them."

"I don't know what you're talking about," Carbone scoffed as Pauli reached down, grabbing his right hand, breaking his index finger.

"Ahhh!" Carbone screamed, grabbing his hand. "That wasn't necessary!" he glared at Pauli.

"I just wanted to jar your memory," Pauli laughed. "Did it help?"

Carbone just looked away, holding his hand against his chest.

"You know Pauli, Carbone's traveling extremely light for leaving town," Alonzo noted.

"Yes, he is," Pauli agreed. "Wasn't he the one that was always dressed to the T when we ran into him?"

"He was," Alonzo confirmed. "Mr. LaBasco always wondered what tailor Carbone used in Marseille. Since he's now a reverend, I wonder what he's taking with him?" Alonzo questioned pointing at Carbone again. "By the way, I'm sorry we foiled your new business deal with all your new partners," Alonzo said as Carbone glared at him. "I see I struck a nerve! Yes, we do know all about them," he admitted glancing at Pauli. "Pauli, aren't you curious to see what he's taking with him on such short notice?"

"I am," Pauli chuckled, grabbing his backpack and ripping it down Carbone's arm with the broken finger. "Here you go," Pauli handed it to Alonzo as tears filled Carbone's eyes.

"Let's see what's in here," Alonzo said rummaging through the bag. "Passport, money, and a new identity," he looked at Carbone. "What? Are you not going to be another minister this time? After all, you did return from the dead. I think it's only fitting for you to save lost souls, don't you?" Alonzo grinned waiting a minute. "Since he's not answering, Pauli, let's see what is in the suitcase?"

Pauli opened the suitcase and pillaged through the clothes. He dumped them out and ripped open the bottom. "Well now, look what we've got here," Pauli said showing Alonzo. "A secret compartment with all kinds of envelopes and money," he handed the envelopes to Alonzo.

Alonzo opened the first one. "This is about Philippi Spinello; interesting reading for the Feds," Alonzo looked at Carbone. "I'll be sure to give this to one I know personally," Alonzo smiled looking sideways at him. "You weren't thinking of double-crossing Spinello, were you?" Carbone began to squirm as Alonzo looked through several more. "Well, Pauli, just what we thought," he said holding up some documents. "How did you get these?" Alonzo asked shoving them in Carbone's face.

Carbone didn't answer.

Alonzo signaled Pauli. "For the record, I did ask nicely," Alonzo held his hands up and grinned.

"Let me ask him again," Pauli offered knocking Carbone flat, stomping on his chest, reaching down, and breaking his other index finger.

Carbone screamed out in pain, "Stop it! I'll tell you!" he cried and took several deep breaths. "Tomme Boy Dano gave them to me," he said as Bernadette listened from behind another tombstone.

"Did Dano say where he got them?" Alonzo asked looking through another envelope. He looked down, "I'm waiting," Alonzo signaled Pauli again.

"Stop!" Carbone screamed, "I'll tell you! If you spare my life."

"Carbone," Alonzo held his hands up, "you know I never make deals." He returned to reading through another contract. He glanced down at Carbone, "I'm still waiting."

"Dano admitted he followed Milo LaBasco when he left the fortress that afternoon and killed him," Carbone admitted.

"Anything else you'd like to get off your chest?" Alonzo asked handing Bernadette two of the contracts. She slowly read through them as Alonzo continued. "We lost two men that week," Alonzo admitted as Bernadette crumpled up the documents in her hands. "By the way, I did notice the contracts I just handed to a friend standing behind you are copies. Tell me; you weren't going to double-cross Dano, were you?" Alonzo smiled as Bernadette walked alongside him.

"Saundra!" Carbone sighed. "Thank God, you're here! These men think I'm someone from their past. Please, tell them who I am."

"What?" Bernadette asked shaking the documents at him. "A man of the Cloth lying with these in his possession?"

"I don't know how those got in my suitcase," Carbone denied.

"Geraldo Carbone, look who's not the only one using their real names," Bernadette laughed. "I'm surprised you didn't recognize me. I haven't changed as much as you have. I guess being responsible for killing innocent people takes a toll on one's age. We briefly passed each other at Falcini's house on several occasions when Luca met with Antonio. I'm Luca Donatelli's widow, Bernadette Rocca. Not only have you aged, but also, you've had your fingerprints changed. That's why I couldn't find out your identity. Now, I find out that you possessed copies of the contract for Luca's execution all along!" she shouted reaching for her weapon.

"A beautiful woman like you doesn't want to go to jail for murder," Carbone begged. "That was a lifetime ago."

"Not to me!" Bernadette shot him between the eyes. "Alonzo," she lowered her weapon starring at Carbone. "I always wondered why Spinello asked for you to witness the hit that day," tears filled her eyes. "That has always haunted me."

"Spinello asked Mr. LaBasco if I could witness Luca shooting Chubby Waldron for trying to take over the family business," Alonzo confided. "That's why I acted surprised when I met you at the hotel in Vienna. As soon as I landed back at Corté de Azuré, Mr. LaBasco and

Pauli were waiting for me at the airport. They told me about Luca's death. We flew straight to your side. On the way, I asked myself the same question. Why us? Pauli found out a year later at a Christmas party when Giano was drunk that Chubby wasn't a blood relative. There was no need for an outsider to witness a family member's execution. Mr. LaBasco felt the best way for you to heal was to relocate you to the mountains to enjoy your horses."

"We can't fix the past," Pauli consoled putting his arm around her. "Now, we know Bencivenni helped arrange Luca's death for him to plot the actual takeover. In time, Luca would have figured it out and stopped him. Luca stood for honor and loyalty for his entire life."

"Yes, that was my Luca," Bernadette agreed. "He hated disloyalty more than anything. We need to help your friends get safely away. Ramsey said Spinello's reinforcements landed and are at the gas station. They'll be heading here soon for Carbone and then the hangar. I'll help you get your friends off safe, and then I've got to pay an old friend a long overdue visit before I visit Spinello."

"I'll have my nephew, Mikey, send a special flower arrangement to Carbone's funeral from the both of us," Alonzo said hurrying to her truck.

"Tell Mikey to have a matching arrangement made for Spinello," Bernadette added. "He'll be next!"

"You can have Dano," Alonzo proclaimed. "Spinello is mine! I made him a promise that I will keep," he said getting into her truck.

"Alonzo, you need to hurry and get away from there," Sydney warned watching the cameras. "The reinforcements are leaving the gas station. They took Montez's body with them and split up. One SUV is heading down SR 211 toward Bernadette's ranch, and the other one is heading toward the church."

"They took the body to hide the fact that Montez is an illegal alien," Alonzo realized. "Bernadette, we need to get off this road!"

"No problem," Bernadette laughed. "I know a short cut," she turned left through the woods. "You better tighten your seatbelts and hang on!"

In the HUB, Sydney glanced at Ramsey, "It's interesting that Spinello hasn't showed his face. With this much at stake, you'd think Spinello would come after Yorg himself, instead of sending amateurs."

"You have a point," Ramsey affirmed. "It's almost like someone else is calling the shots."

"Let's get this bird up in the air with our people home safely, and then we'll figure that out," Sydney agreed. "They just finished clearing the taxiway."

"Okay," Ramsey agreed reaching for her phone. "I need to ask Pauli a favor."

Deerfeld, Virginia
Back at the Old Hangar
Tuesday, June 30, 0330 (3:30 AM EST)

"I can't believe how quickly we cleared the taxiway," Jordan said walking back to the Citation. "There was debris everywhere."

"I know we had Devine help," Bob added glancing at Kathe. "Some of that mess was pretty heavy, even for the four of us."

"Great job," Sydney declared, checking the satellite, and lowering the steps to the Citation. "One of the SUVs passed Bernadette's ranch a minute ago. Make sure the Citation is ready to leave as soon as we tell you."

"We'll be ready," Jordan stated hugging Kathe. "Be safe, Sis."

"Always," Kathe grinned. "Sydney tinkered with my Ruger. It now has a laser and a mosquito-drone."

"Jordan, have Pete help you with the checklist and be ready to leave," Yorg told him. "Follow Sydney and Ramsey's instructions. You may have to leave without us. We will follow you in Alonzo's jet and meet you at Liberty."

"I understand," Jordan answered hurrying up the steps.

"Bob, it's important to keep the blinds pulled down and don't let anybody open them," Yorg cautioned. "You may hear gunfire near it. Keep everyone as calm as possible."

"You can count on me," Bob assured him hurrying up the steps.

"Jordan, pull up the steps and close the door," Sydney requested. "Team, the jet is hot again," Sydney advised rearming the electrical program. "Do not touch the outside until I say so."

"Copy that," Yorg answered as he and Kathe hurried outside the hangar.

Sydney enhanced the satellite image of the area around the hangar. "Okay, team, we have two SUVs converging on us from different roads. One of them has stopped at the church. They are spreading out to check for Rev. Woods," he changed the angle of the satellite. "The second one has pulled into the woods by the junction of Hamilton Creek Road and Tennessee Valley Road," he announced zooming in on that area. "Seven men are getting out, and they are splitting up. Three are crossing the road on the east side. They are heading deeper into the cornfield toward the back of the hangar. Two of the four are splitting up. Two are heading toward the farmhouse through the woods on the west," he watched for a minute. "It seems that the other two are heading into the woods on the south side of the hangar. They are probably going to come in from the front door."

"Copy that; I'll take the two by the farmhouse," Yorg answered reaching for Kathe's hand. "Father, arm us with Thy strength to protect our family from this evil," he kissed Kathe. "I love you. Be careful."

"I love you," Kathe smiled making the Sign of the Cross. "I'll take the other two from the front," Kathe said checking for the best position.

"May God protect you," Sydney added watching Yorg make his way through the debris from the taxiway on the east backside of the hanger. "Kathe, I'll tell you as soon as the targets come out of the woods," Sydney declared checking on the ones in the back cornfield. "It looks like the three in the back are waiting for you to exit the hangar that way," he changed to the farmhouse. "Yorg, one is in the wooded area by the front of the barn. He will probably try to get into the hangar from the opening in the sidewall," he changed the angle. "The second target is making his way to the back of the farmhouse. He will more than likely try to come in from the back of the hangar."

"Copy that," Yorg said crouching down in the rubble.

"Oddly, no one is making a move," Ramsey noted watching the satellite image.

"They may be waiting for the others to arrive," Sydney assumed changing the satellite's angle. "They found Carbone and Bubba. The others are about five minutes away. They are probably waiting to rush you all at once."

"Sydney," Alonzo interrupted, "we are almost to the hangar. We are coming in from the west. Bernadette knew a different way through the woods. At one point, we were airborne across the narrowest part of the ravine."

"What a rush!" Pauli chuckled. "This woman can drive!"

"Copy that," Sydney affirmed glancing at Ramsey. "Glad you made it across. We need your help," he said checking outside the hangar.

"I have to say," Alonzo laughed, "when Bernadette says tighten your seatbelts and hang on, she means it! We're coming in just past Rufus's house on SR 209," he relayed as Bernadette turned into the thick forest and stopped. "We heard where their people are; where do you want us?"

"Stay put for a minute," Sydney stated. "An SUV has pulled into the woods by the stream at the junction of SR 209 and Tennessee Valley Road," he checked Alonzo's position. "Two men have gotten out and are on foot making their way through the woods. They are positioned across from the front of the hangar. The other SUV is passing Rufus' house. They'll probably come in from the back of the cornfield. Heads-up, there is a bear entering from the back-right of the cornfield, so be careful."

"The ones in the back are gathering cornstalks," Ramsey cautioned. "They look like they're planning either to flush you out into the open or set fire to the hangar."

"I'm going to get close enough to the farmhouse and climb a tree," Bernadette declared slinging her rifle around her back. "I can see better from up there."

"Pauli and I will work on the ones from the back of the cornfield," Alonzo relayed hurrying through the cornfield.

"The way you're heading, you'll run into where their SUV is parked," Sydney cautioned. "It looks like Ramsey is right. Three of them are walking closer to the hangar," he zeroed in on them. "They have cornstalks and lighters in their hands."

"Let's try not to let them light the cornstalks," Ramsey advised. "The stalks are dry, and so is the hangar."

Yorg watched through his scope. "I see one at the backside of the farmhouse holding his lighter near the cornstalks." He squeezed the trigger, "One down, and he isn't lighting anything." He turned toward the second target.

"Pauli and I have the targets from the second SUV in sight," Alonzo admitted signaling Pauli. "Give us a few minutes to clear them."

"I'm in position now," Bernadette whispered.

"Copy that; fire when ready," Sydney answered bringing up the camera under the Citation. "Kathe, the two on the east-side have made their way to the front of the hangar. I can see one of them bobbing his head in and out of the doorway."

"I see him," Kathe watched as the target dropped to the floor and rolled inside. She raised her Ruger, shooting him as the other one flung a metal bar into the doorway. He entered carrying a piece of the metal roofing as a shield, trying to make it to a pile of debris for cover. "The second target is inside," Kathe shot him in the right hip as he turned the metal, trying to hurry under the Citation. He struggled to make it to the back-left wheel as she lowered her weapon. "No shot, the second target is under the Citation."

"Copy that," Sydney replied watching the camera. "Pray that he touches the metal. Kathe, he's raising his gun toward you."

"I've got him," Kathe whispered watching the target. "He's leaning around the metal wheel."

"Come on, touch it!" Sydney begged watching him lose his footing, grabbing onto the wheel. "Yes! He's gone," Sydney grinned watching the man floundering around until Sydney turned off the electricity, and then he fell to the floor.

"I see your latest addition to the software works," Ramsey smiled. "Kathe, check him," Ramsey ordered watching Kathe hurry over to the victim, kicking the gun out of his hand.

Kathe bent down and checked his carotids, "He's terminated."

"I've got the one trying to get in front of the farmhouse," Bernadette declared squeezing the trigger. She pivoted around, "Alonzo, fall to the ground," she warned shooting multiple times at a bear stalking him.

"Thanks, Bernadette," Alonzo sighed getting up and staring at the bear. "I didn't hear it."

"I see another target," Pauli alerted. "Give me a minute," he cautioned pulling his knife out of his boot and throwing it. "I got him."

"Yorg, a target from the back is getting close to the hangar," Sydney warned.

Yorg turned looking through his scope. "I've got him in my sites." He squeezed the trigger. "Thanks, Syd, he was about to light the cornstalks."

"Kathe, there is a third target entering from the east sidewall!" Ramsey warned.

"Copy that," Kathe whispered hurrying behind a crumpled part of the roof on the left side of the Citation. She heard the mother cat hiss at the target as he tried to hide between the debris. Kathe got a glimpse of him as he hurried in between the two piles coming toward the back of the jet. "I remember this guy from my house in Ponce," Kathe whispered watching him scurrying to the last pile of roofing near the front door. "Tell Bob to make sure the children can't see out the windows."

"I don't like the sound of that!" Ramsey exclaimed. "What are you doing?"

"Evening a score!" Kathe whispered making her way to the edge of the rubble closest to the door. She waited for the target to get to the end of his pile. She watched as he held his pistol out, peering around the stack to see his friend under the plane. She tagged him with her laser on his right hand and shot him in the wrist. He panicked and turned toward her as she hit his right femur. He cursed, falling to the ground rolling back-and-forth as she walked over to him. "Remember me?" Kathe asked raising her Ruger to his forehead. "I remember you from Ponce Inlet and the video from the Police Station on Anguilla Island. You murdered several friends of mine and helped Benedicto Teodoro escape," she stated standing over him. "I learned one lesson then! Never leave any loose ends!" she declared shooting him. "These three won't terrorize anyone again," Kathe reported melting his cell phone and gun with JAKE.

"Yorg has cleared two more targets from the back," Sydney stated. "Bernadette reported the last two across the street are down. Alonzo and Pauli have cleared their targets. I don't see any more. You're free to leave as soon as you're ready."

"Copy that," Kathe sighed as Yorg joined her.

"Oh, no, Rufus!" Bernadette exclaimed taking several shots. "I just killed a bear that tore Amos apart and was heading for poor Rufus.

Amos deserved it, but Rufus isn't that bad. He once stood up for me in town against Bubba. He had to go to the hospital with facial and head injuries. I'll rescue him before I take Alonzo and Pauli back to their Leer. Then, I'll get ready to leave town. Ramsey, please call me when you find Dano."

"Copy that," Ramsey agreed. "I already have CC working on it. As soon as she locates him, you'll be the first to know."

"Thanks for helping save my family," Kathe stated. "Happy hunting!"

"Don't thank me," Bernadette laughed. "We're all family now. Our paths will cross again."

"You can depend on that," Alonzo added waiting for Bernadette to climb down the tree. "Kathe, we'll see you at Liberty."

"Copy that," Kathe said as Jordan lowered the steps to the Citation.

"Pete, you can take the copilot seat for me after I help Jordan takeoff," Yorg said peering into the cockpit. "It's time you fly into a large airport. You're ready for this."

"Thanks, Dad," Pete grinned handing him the headset. "I can't wait!"

Tuesday, June 30, 1400 (2:00 PM EST), Alby Airlines Security Headquarters, Liberty International Airport, Newark, New Jersey

Yorg held the door for Kathe as they entered the Security Department.

"Kathe, Yorg!" Wanda jumped up from her desk and hugged them. "Thank God, you got out of Deerfeld in one piece!" she exclaimed as she stepped back. "Whenever you two are under attack, I don't know if I should come to work or go to my church? My prayers never ceased all night for you."

"Now, Wanda," Kathe laughed. "If you don't come to work, who's going to keep the Ole Girl in line?"

"You've got the point," Wanda sighed walking back to her desk. "It is a talent. I am the only one who can control her mood-swings and fury, not to mention keep her from killing Gen. Jenkins."

"Now, that is an accomplishment," Yorg laughed. "She and Jenkins are like beer and ice cream, with Ramsey being the beer and Jenkins being the melting ice cream."

"You hit the nail on the head with that one," Wanda laughed. "His latest brag is that he singlehandedly cleared the targets from Ramsey's condo."

"That sounds just like Jenkins," Kathe concurred. "He does all the bragging, and Ramsey does all the work. I must hand it to her. She is good at figuring out the next sneaky scheme slithering out of his mind."

"Thank God, Sydney and Ramsey are covering their backs, as well as ours concerning Jenkins," Yorg affirmed. "He's nothing but trouble for us," he said glancing at Ramsey's office. "Is Ramsey in her office?"

"Yes, she's been impatiently waiting for you," Wanda cautioned. "She expected you here at 0800 (8:00 AM EST) when she got here."

"We landed at La Guardia at 0600 (6:00 AM EST)," Kathe defended. "We do require a little sleep and nourishment, don't you think?"

"I reminded her of that," Wanda stated. "She said, and I quote, 'If I can make it to work on time, they should too.'"

"Thanks for the warning," Yorg grinned leading the way to Ramsey's office.

"Well, look who finally showed up to work?" Ramsey snarled glancing up at them.

"This isn't the same Ramsey who congratulated us on a job well done a few hours ago," Kathe contested. "Would you like to tell us what's wrong?"

"Kat's right," Yorg stated. "You were up all night with us. Why the sudden change?"

"Do you want to know the truth?" Ramsey asked glaring at them.

"It would be nice," Kathe smiled folding her arms.

"I'd rather be at work!" Ramsey admitted. "Instead of sleeping with one eye open and my pistol under my pillow."

"Sydney told us that someone staged the intrusion to kill you," Kathe relayed.

"Yes, I'm waiting for Pauli to check on something for me," Ramsey confided. "If my suspicions are correct, we have a mystery person to find."

"Speaking of mystery people, have you found anything on the man I recognized in the hangar?" Kathe asked.

"I had CC and Sam check out his identity from the video at the jailbreak on Anguilla Island," Ramsey said looking through her notes. "His name was Roberto Bono. For some reason, he is the one that took his black mask off inside the van."

"Bono was one of the three men that killed Officer Daniel Wilbur at point-blank range when they were breaking Teodoro out of jail," Kathe reported. "He would have witnessed Teodoro brutally beat Officer Renee Parker to death."

"Well, that's one of your loose ends we don't have to worry about," Ramsey said as they sat down on the couch. "CC and Sam need to dig a little deeper into something we suspect happened in Anguilla. They will be joining us this evening for the briefing."

"CC had her eyes opened two years ago to what was happening in the Bureau," Kathe shared. "Especially, when she discovered what the last administration was hiding from the public."

"The last administration brought such division and corruption to this country," Yorg declared. "The tactics they used are no different than the corrupt leaders of my country. With all the checks and balances, your government has in place, it's a wonder they got away with multiple forms of treason."

"That rang out loud and clear to CC," Ramsey agreed sitting back in her chair. "CC's good at skirting where she gets her facts and still gets her father-boss, Terrance, to act on them. And don't underestimate President Trumore. He and AG Kolouski won't let the bad actors get away with it."

"CC's following in your footsteps as I did," Kathe smiled.

"We've all had to learn who we can trust in this business," Ramsey admitted.

Tuesday, June 30, 1600 (4:00 PM EST)
Dr. Sydney's parent's home
4500 Reynolds Dr. in White Plains, New York

"Christy, look at the entrance to his house!" Heather exclaimed as they pulled into the black, wrought Iron Gate. "You can't see the house from the driveway," she said straining to see around the front seat. "It has a rolling, thick, grassy hills with rounded beds of beautiful flowers around some of the trees!"

"Look at the benches scattered around the hills," Christy noted. "It's breathtaking for sure," Christy answered as they slowly approached the house. "Oh, my, gosh! Look at that house! It's made of cobblestone!"

"It looks ancient and mystic with the ivy growing up the walls," Heather noted.

"I can't wait to roll down the grassy hills," Pete grinned admiring them.

"I've never done that," Joey replied. "Is it scary?"

"No, it's fun," Pete declared. "I'll teach you and Alek how to do it. You're going to love it!"

"This is nice," Ylia smiled looking out her window.

"I know that I will have fun with the boys in the forest," Bob added. "I wonder what kind of animals live in there?"

"My father and I used to hunt deer in that forest," Sydney shared. "We even got a wild turkey for Thanksgiving every year."

"I guess we can't apply for a hunting license," Pete sighed. "We have to be ghosts again so no one can find us."

"That would be true if I didn't own the forest around the house," Sydney grinned. "You don't need a permit, and I have several rifles locked up in my office that you can use. I'm sure Bob can help you."

"I'm hoping they won't be here that long," Kathe said picking up Alek and kissing him.

"Your mother and I stayed here while I trained her," Yorg recalled. "There is a running stream in the backyard with fish," he said as the limo came to a stop.

"The stream is now filled with exotic Koi Fish," Sydney explained getting out of the limo. "I had to put a screen across the top of the stream. The resident raccoons ate the Koi as fast as I could buy them. Let's go inside."

"This is awesome!" Jeannie exclaimed glancing around the living room. "It has a real stone fireplace!"

"That's the one thing I had in Ponce Inlet that I barely used," Kathe said walking over and flipping the gas switch. "It was only cold enough to use it once when I was there on an R & R."

"I loved living on the ocean in Ponce, but I missed the seasons in Colorado with our fireplace," Jeannie confessed. "It makes the Holiday Season so cozy and warm with the gusty winds and snow outside."

"Yes," Kathe agreed turning it off, "but in July, it's too hot. Now, you will enjoy the 4th of July fireworks. The City of White Plains goes all out for a holiday. I sat out on the front porch and watched them with Sydney and Yorg. It was the best I've seen in years."

"Yorg told me about watching the fireworks with Kathe," Ylia remembered. "That's the first time I noticed he was coming out of his shell."

"Thinking back," Yorg agreed. "I knew I was falling in love again."

"That was obvious to me," Sydney confessed. "Let me show you around the rest of the house," he offered leading the way to the staircase.

"What's upstairs?" Joey asked.

"Let's go see," Sydney smiled. "My father built this wooden staircase with hand-carved railings to overlook the living room. The balcony has a large window with a view of the city below. And this is the boy's bedroom," he said opening the door at the end of the hallway on the right.

"I bet this was your bedroom growing up," Pete said scoping out the room. "I bet you have a secret room somewhere in the closet," he opened the walk-in closet peering inside.

"You know me well," Sydney chuckled walking ahead of them. He reached on the right side of the back wall and opened a hidden doorway. "This goes to the girl's bedroom next door."

"Syd, you never cease to amaze me," Yorg said, following them into the next room. "When did you begin thinking like this?"

"At a very early age," Sydney confided. "Having a father with one of the highest security clearances in the FBI opened my mind to ideas other people only dreamt. Dad was a workaholic in the office, as well as at home."

"Seems to run in the family," Kathe grinned. "I can picture you and your father working on these projects on the weekends."

"We did," Sydney smiled. "I spent my time watching my father on his computer, designing hidden rooms, and going to the science museum with my mother. I loved to study the body exhibits. My mother would help me understand how the muscles and skeletal systems worked. She would quiz me after dinner each Saturday. Then, as I started middle school, I would go to the university with her to sit in the lecture hall and observe surgeries. I would listen to Mom intently explaining the procedures. I was mesmerized!"

"Not your average childhood," Jeannie chuckled. "I can see how you designed Kathe's Ponce Inlet house with secret passages."

"My father taught me that the element of surprise is the biggest gamechanger in dangerous situations," Sydney admitted.

"You mention that you hunted deer when you were young," Bob changed the subject. "When you went deer hunting, did you help your father butcher it?"

"Dad took me hunting," Sydney smiled. "My mother taught me how to field-dress the animal and get it ready for the freezer."

"I'm surprised you have a girl's bedroom," Heather questioned gazing at the incredible pictures around the room. "These drawings are of the same girl from childhood to adulthood. I thought you were an only child."

"I am an only child," Sydney explained. "These drawings are of my younger cousin, Paris Olivia Sydney. My father's brother and his wife were both Counter-Intelligence Agents. In that line of work, her birth was rather a surprise to them. Paris lived with us as soon as my aunt was able to return to work. Let's go downstairs. There is more to see," he said turning to leave.

"Wait a minute," Christy begged. "Why is Paris wearing the same locket in all the pictures?"

"I'll show you," Sydney said picking up a picture on the dresser. "When Paris was five years old, the First Lady gave her a gold locket. In this picture, she is putting it on Paris. The White House is on the front, and her family is on the inside. Paris never takes it off."

"Why did the First Lady give Paris a locket?" Heather asked.

"To honor her parents for service to our country," Sydney remarked. "Let's go downstairs. Jeannie needs to see the kitchen."

"Where is Paris now?" Heather asked.

"After college, Paris moved to Wiltz, Luxembourg, and owns an art studio," Sydney shared. "Her paintings and sculptures are all over Europe. Jeannie's waited long enough. Let's go."

"Look at this kitchen!" Jeannie exclaimed as they entered. "It has a sub-zero refrigerator with lots of cabinets! Bob, pinch me! I think I died and went to heaven!"

"Thanks, Sydney, I'm never going to hear the end of this," Bob sighed.

"Where are the appliances?" Jeannie asked.

"The appliances are in the pantry," Sydney explained. "They all work. I come here for R & R when my job gets to me. Jeannie, you'll have plenty of time to explore when we leave."

"How often do you come here?" Bob asked. "You're always in Newark."

"I come here every time I get a chance," Sydney admitted. "I clear my head and work on some of my father's ideas. He left a library filled with them. I learned to think outside of the box, reading his manuscripts. Come, I'll show you the library."

"The bookshelf takes up three entire walls from floor to ceiling!" Bob gasped. "Are these all his manuscripts?"

"Yes, most of them," Sydney acknowledged. "He also collected old books about the White House and government buildings. He loved sitting by the fireplace and reading about the tunnels under the area for new ideas."

"I remember reading some of his manuscripts in the evening after training," Yorg stated. "Your father was a genius and way ahead of his time."

"He was," Sydney sighed.

"When we stayed here," Kathe shared, "this is where Yorg and I read articles his father wrote on surveillance and spook-stuff. It was here that I learned to think situations all the way through, and more importantly, how to react."

"This was Paris' first attempt at sculpturing," Sydney gleamed walking over to a bust of his father in the middle of the bookshelf. "Dad added this feature," he said, touching it as the bookshelf slid back into the wall, exposing a doorway.

"A hidden room!" Bob sighed entering behind Sydney. "The craftsmanship on that desk is amazing. One of my hobbies is studying furniture from different centuries. I don't recognize this."

"Dad studied the desk of several past presidents and designed this U-shaped one," Sydney shared running his fingers across the top. "I designed the one in my Newark HUB after it. I also included a wall that opens to hidden surveillance camera screens like these," he showed pressing a button under his desk. "There are twenty cameras around the outside of the property, as well as cameras in every room. To access the security cameras, open this drawer under the middle of the screens for the keyboard."

"The pictures are clear for older equipment," Bob gasped gazing at each one.

"I upgraded the cameras to 4K," Sydney admitted. "I like a perfect view day or night," he said reaching for the iPad next to the keyboard.

"This runs the drone that flies around the property if something doesn't quite look right. Yorg can teach you and Pete how to fly it."

"I've been waiting for one of these!" Pete exclaimed reaching for it. "A drone is at the top of my Christmas list."

"It's you," Yorg laughed patting Pete on the back. "You can probably teach me how to do some things with it by the time we get back."

"Dr. Sydney, I see you have a new patriotic painting signed by a Paris L'Ville here in your office," Heather noticed reading the name. "I thought Paris' last name was Sydney?"

"Paris took on my mother's maiden name, L'Ville, for her professional name," Sydney confessed. "Paris said it was because my mother raised her as a daughter."

"If you're so close to her," Jeannie interrupted, "how come Kathe and Yorg never mentioned her?"

"We know of Paris," Kathe answered. "However, we haven't met her on purpose. As you can see, her paintings and sculptures are renowned worldwide. If the wrong people saw her with us, it could be detrimental to her."

"I think it's time for your children to go out in the backyard and check out the Koi Fish in the pond?" Sydney suggested reaching for the iPad.

"Should I go with them?" Ylia asked.

"No, you need to be aware of some of the safety features in this house," Sydney admitted.

"Let's go," Pete said taking Alek by the hand and leading the children outside.

"Dr. Sydney, thank you for letting us stay here," Bob appreciated after Sydney went over more security items in the house. "Just look at the children," he pointed to an outside camera. "They are already having a great time."

"The little, wooden bridge goes over to a private play area," Sydney pointed to another screen. "It's great for picnics and to play with water toys to cool off from the summer heat. I have toys in the closet on the patio."

"It's also perfect for Martial Art training," Kathe stated. "I hit that ground hard many times, learning to fight. And I nailed Yorg right in the middle–two times."

"Yes, you did," Yorg declared. "It was then I knew you were ready to go to work."

"I can see how this library inspired you to become the woman you are today," Bob admired glancing out the window at the children. "I never understood what made you change from a housewife to a security agent. Even after the accident, I thought you would come home to us."

"Don't feel alone," Jeannie admitted. "I, too, had a hard time understanding until I saw Kathe in action."

"Bob," Kathe stood beside him, "like Sydney, Ramsey, Yorg, and my team, I opened my eyes one day and realized that terror comes in many forms. I turned a blind eye for so many years until one day; I couldn't. Then, I looked at the world from a different perspective. It hit me that if I kept turning my head, evil wouldn't go away. It would take over the people and the world I love. That's why we do what we must do to defend our liberties."

"I had a grasp of that idea when I saw you in action in Ponce," Bob admitted. "Then, when I thought we lost you again, it didn't make any sense. But, seeing you again in action and where you trained, I understand the risk all of you take to keep us safe."

"Speaking of keeping people safe," Yorg added. "Bob, make sure Pete and Heather practice sparing, and their katas. Also, they can help Joey with his practice."

"They need to stay sharp," Sydney replied. "I bought some pads and gear for that reason," he turned to Bob and Jeannie. "The security on the property is like I have in my HUB. Kathe and Yorg will also be able to check on you with their cell phones, as well as Ramsey and me. No one can get on this property from any direction without us knowing. You and the children can go outside safely, day or night. The military police also patrol the neighborhood. Most people that live here are high- ranking military personnel who work at the Pentagon, or in Congress."

"This was a haven for his parents due to his father's high-ranking office," Kathe answered. "And since Sydney has a flair for spy-tech, he has added more escape routes on a need-to-know basis."

"I was wondering when Sydney was going to get around to that," Bob laughed. "This wouldn't be Sydney's house without it."

"I do have a few surprises here," Sydney admitted checking his text message. "Kathe and Yorg stay and have dinner with your family. That will help Ylia, and Jeannie get your family settled before you join us to leave. Ylia, spend the night to help Alek feel comfortable with Jeannie. Then, go to my HUB in Newark and finish what you were working on with the Genero file. I've got a few more details to work on with Stephen."

Tuesday, June 30, 2330 (11:30 PM EST), Alby Airlines Security Headquarters, Liberty International Airport, Newark, New Jersey

"Wanda," Kathe greeted entering the Security Office with Yorg, "you're working overtime tonight."

"I'm helping the Ole Girl get ready to leave," Wanda admitted. "If I don't oversee the last-minute details, she'll forget something. After yesterday, her mind is in thirty different places at once."

"And rightfully so," Kathe answered stopping at Wanda's desk. "Ramsey is not used to being confronted with assault rifles."

"No, she's not," Wanda smirked. "She's used to the two of you being on that end of that equation. I've never known her to shoot anyone."

"Ramsey does go down to the range and practice," Yorg joined in the conversation. "I've practiced next to her. She's as good as we are."

"I knew Ramsey went there to practice," Wanda confirmed. "But this time was different. She had real targets."

"We don't know everything about Ramsey's past before she worked here," Kathe admitted. "I always wondered how she came up with the idea for JAKE Technology."

"I never thought of it that way," Wanda agreed. "And I thought I knew everything about her."

"Something in Ramsey's past had to spark the idea," Yorg concluded.

"Well, between Ramsey and CC, I've got to say that both women have surprised me," Wanda stated answering her phone. "Yes, ma'am, we'll be right down," she said clearing the line. "Everyone is waiting for us in the HUB. Let's go," she said reaching for her iPad. "We're taking the shortcut in Sydney's office."

"I was beginning to wonder if you were joining us," Ramsey yawned glancing up at them from the U-shaped conference desk.

"Thanks for the heartfelt approval to stay with the children until they get used to the new surroundings," Kathe grinned. "Hi, everyone. Sorry, we're late," Kathe greeted sitting next to Yorg. "Alek lost his Teddy. We went crazy searching the entire house. I finally used the drone and scoured the grounds. I found it by the Koi Pond under a tree. After that, Alek was so upset; I had to sing him to sleep."

"Teddy is Alek's security blanket," Yorg explained. "Without Teddy, there would be no world to come home to after we saved it."

"I've called Jeannie a couple of times when she was about to rip her hair out looking for that stinking bear," Ramsey chuckled. "She said Alek doesn't go to sleep without it."

"Since Teddy stands between National Security and our team," Sydney chimed in, "I'll have Ylia install a GPS and download it to our phones before she returns to Newark. We surely can't go after terrorists if there's no world to come home to when we get back."

"Now that we've solved that crisis," Ramsey sighed. "Sydney, show us what you and Stephen are doing to ready us for Cuba."

"If you will turn your attention to the wall across from the desk," Sydney said opening the wall to a big-screen television. "From the data, Kathe copied from the main computer at the Bridgette Océanic Aquarium. We know their strategies. It confirmed that Gen. Yetsun is in Cuba. Metarha rerouted people from the Middle East to train with some Cuban Soldiers to send back into the United States. Eduardo joined forces with Yetsun and operates there. I found one of Eduardo's satellites, ESPGOTU1000, but there is probably another one over Japan because South Korea, China, and Russia have unexplained missiles destroyed from that region."

"That information was worth almost being killed for," Kathe commented.

"Now, we understand Eduardo's tactics better to keep everyone safer," Ramsey added. "We're grateful that you and Hiltree dared to stay there long enough to get it."

"Ramsey's right," Sydney explained. "I've enhanced the drones and added more safety equipment to take with you," he confirmed splitting the screen to show a semi-truck near the beach and a map of the Keys. "I sent Stephen and his crew ahead to the Florida Keys to locate the targets. On the screen is Stephen's HUB," he stated zeroing-in on the semi. "Inside is a complete 8-K mobile, movie studio with Realtime filming capability. That way, as the drone films, we can view the live footage. Stephen set up camp over the Seven Mile Bridge on the Gulf of Mexico side before Big Pine Key Island. We will be joining Stephen and his men in the morning. He also has valuable spy-ware for us to use as part of his camera crew for your cover. Stephen is finishing a new documentary on Hummingbirds. He already has footage from around the globe, except the Keys and Cuba. The documentary ends by focusing on the extremely rare Bee Hummingbird. These birds only reside in the mountains of Cuba. Stephen has already pulled the necessary permits to film and use drones over the Keys. He is still waiting on approval from Cuba. He said they are scrutinizing his company since he was filming in Miami when Bridgette Océanic Aquarium exploded. They've already asked to view his footage of Althea Beach."

"Does Stephen have such a thing?" Ramsey questioned. "He cannot use our footage taken over the Aquarium!"

"Stephen is a man of preparedness," Sydney confirmed. "The City of Miami hired Stephen's company to film a commercial of Althea Beach to bring back tourism. While we were working, his video editor, Skip, filmed everything legit and put it together. They will release it next week."

"I told Stephen when I met him two years ago at Centennial Park in Holly Hill, Florida, that he thought out of the box like you do," Kathe smiled as Pauli got a text and left the room. "I can't wait to see what you two cook-up next for us."

"We did 'cook-up something' as you put it," Sydney grinned. "We completed a two-year-long project. We'll unveil it when we get to the Keys; any questions?"

"Not with that," Alonzo began. "We have a major old problem to discuss before we enter Cuba," he glanced at Ramsey. "What are we going to do with Jenkins?"

Ramsey took a deep breath, "That has preyed on my mind all day. After yesterday, I think Jenkins staged the attacks to score points with Spinello."

"It looks that way," Alonzo agreed. "I've known Spinello for years. He never lets an outsider in his inner circle. I thought he had better sense than to trust Jenkins."

"Wait a minute," Kathe grinned. "Jenkins is Head of Homeland Security. Spinello knows Jenkins can open lots of doors for him."

"Like smuggling the illegal Cubans into our country with their weapons?" Jay surmised.

"That is very plausible," Ramsey agreed. "I believe Pauli left the room to get me proof of the suspicion I had yesterday."

"If that is correct," Jack questioned. "What about Hiltree?"

"Hiltree told me in Miami that he stopped trusting Jenkins during Barrick's questionable Foreign Policy Deals," Kathe interjected. "That is before he knew anything about our operation. He caught Jenkins looking the other way, instead of following security protocols."

"Hiltree sent me the footage of the attack at Ramsey's condo after he reviewed it," CC shared. "I talked with Hiltree after Sam, and I viewed it with my father. Dad agreed they were lucky yesterday. Hiltree needs to guard every step he and his men take like we are."

"Yesterday proved it's not if, but when Jenkins strikes again," Ramsey admitted. "However, if we don't stop these people, every country around the world is in trouble."

"Hiltree is a patriot and will stand with us to the end," CC confirmed. "Hiltree confided that he first suspected Jenkins was lonely right before and after his wife died. He thought Jenkins had a mistress and didn't want anyone to know. After working with us, Hiltree seems to believe Jenkins was visiting Macaby regularly after they secured her in prison. Hiltree noticed a pattern between Jenkins receiving phone calls around the same time each week. He would leave immediately and didn't return until the next day. Sometimes he returned after the weekend. He always came back happy. When pressed about his whereabouts, he changed the subject."

"That behavior is Jenkins' MO from past, personal knowledge!" Ramsey snapped.

"Hiltree and Jenkins' offices were next to each other in the Pentagon," Sam added. "Hiltree surprised Jenkins several times and caught him laughing with someone. Jenkins always abruptly ended the call. Once Jenkins was on speakerphone, and Hiltree heard Jenkins laughingly refer to the female as Brina, as Sabrina Macaby."

"Jenkins knows too much about us, including Sydney's skills," Alonzo cautioned. "He's got the authority to arrest us all and throw away the keys."

"Jenkins is shrewd enough to try to frame us," Ramsey agreed. "But he'll wait until we eliminate his competition."

"I'll see what I can do to help keep Jenkins away from us," CC suggested. "Since my father oversees finding the terrorists Metarha placed around the states, Jenkins should be present with Dad when he makes the arrests. That will keep him away for a while."

"Good, that will give us some time to work freely," Ramsey stated. "And give you and Sam time to find something legally against him."

"That's not going to be easy," CC admitted. "Jenkins is good at covering his tracks. Sam and I couldn't hack into the prison records. Sydney had to help us get into them. Everyone who encountered Macaby had to sign in and out, including the staff. Officers in the security department also had to watch from the camera located above the cell door and document it. Judge Vickers, who presided over the case, wrote that stipulation in her sentencing. The only documentation noted Jenkins being there was the day Macaby arrived. Warden Thornhill documented that Jenkins and Hiltree escorted her there. The warden also noted that Jenkins only called him from time-to-time to check on her."

"Who is second in command at the penitentiary?" Alonzo asked. "Thornhill has to have a day off or leave sometimes."

"Officer Janice Patterson," CC answered. "Her notes were added to Thornhill's reports once or twice a week when he was off. There was no mention of Jenkins visiting Macaby. Thornhill arrested the three officers on the take from the Falcini's' that perpetrated the switch with Macaby and Lauren Sinéad. There is a federal warrant out for Macaby's arrest. All other employees thoroughly checked out."

"There must be another mole inside," Ramsey declared. "Jenkins didn't know about the switch with Macaby and Sinéad. We had to prove it to him by showing him the video from the drone camera we placed in Macaby's cell."

"You scared him!" Kathe exclaimed pointing at Ramsey. "I bet you had Jenkins worried if there were any other drones placed around the prison."

"Did you check the records in personnel to see who hired Patterson for that key position?" Yorg asked.

"I didn't think of that," CC stated making notes.

"But you said all the employees now check out," Yorg replied. "What information did you use to base your assumption?"

"Thornhill said he cleaned house," CC affirmed.

"I checked out Warden Thornhill," Ramsey confirmed. "His reputation is impeccable. I didn't have time to check out the rest of the staff, so I assigned it to CC and Sam."

"CC, Sam, did you get copies of the court transcripts of Gen. Thompson's trial?" Alonzo asked. "He was court-marshaled extremely fast. Jenkins put Macaby at the same prison a few days apart."

"Jenkins could have something to do with the Thompson's speedily trial," Ramsey realized. "His office was across the hall from Gen. Thompson. They were close friends."

"Jenkins arrested Gen. Thompson," Jay interjected. "We watched it on the news."

"Then, they weren't that good of friends," Jack laughed. "I bet Jenkins was a little ticked that Thompson didn't let him in on the action."

"If that weren't true, I'd laugh with you," Ramsey admitted. "But it is."

"Jack has a point," Sam agreed. "The trial happened in record time for any court-marshal, much less a general charged with treason. We'll order the transcript today."

"CC, check for sealed files on Patterson," Ramsey requested. "Jenkins would hide evidence of being involved in her placement. The three officers that Thornhill arrested couldn't have pulled this off without someone at the top."

"Yes, ma'am," CC sighed.

"I also think that they should make sure Thompson is still in prison," Kathe stated. "They switched Macaby under Thornhill's nose. Thompson could already be gone."

"I hope that's not the case," CC sighed. "I'll check on Thompson's status."

"Pauli and I will also do some checking," Alonzo shared. "It is cause for alarm for Spinello to let Jenkins near his inner-circle."

"That would answer the question Jay and I have," Jack wondered. "How did Spinello find all of us so fast? We were in different areas in the city. Kathe and Yorg were on a secure flight that only Ramsey, Sydney, and Keith knew about."

"Spinello knew strategically where and what time we would be at each location," Jay added as Pauli returned and whispered to Alonzo. "This smells like an inside job. If it weren't for Alonzo and Pauli warning us, we would all be dead."

"It does reek like an inside job, doesn't it?" Sydney confirmed opening an app on his phone. "Somehow, Spinello knew every detail," he walked around the conference table, waving his phone over each person. "No bugs can transmit within this HUB. Every time I receive a phone call from each of you, my phone scans for threats. Jay has a good point," he said stopping at Ramsey. "Your phone is compromised," Sydney confirmed reaching for Ramsey's phone. "Let's see inside," he pried opened the phone and scanned it. "It's a homemade transmitter with a small, thin wire about the size of one strand of hair. It's activated and deactivated by one other phone."

“Other than the people in this room, only Jenkins knows not to activate the bug around Sydney or me,” Kathe realized.

“Correct,” Sydney answered. “Jenkins knows that we have JAKE Technology; not all of what it can do. He’s fishing for what they know about Chameleon, and what kind of fire power they must stop him from taking it. He knows that with Chameleon and JAKE, he can take over their plot,” Sydney confirmed typing commands on his phone, frying the bug.

“That worm!” Ramsey snapped. “Jenkins planted it the night before our attack! I charged my phone on the nightstand by my side of the bed. I noticed the next morning it was in a different place. That didn’t sit right with me. While Jenkins was in the shower, I went through his pockets and found a small, black bag. Inside it was an expensive female frat-looking ring. I almost tried it on when I heard him turn off the water. I put it back and hurried to the kitchen. I asked him at breakfast about my phone. He said he got up in the middle of the night and accidentally knocked it off the nightstand,” she said glancing at Kathe and Yorg. “That’s why the leak didn’t specify everything that happened in Deerfeld. When we left my condo after the attack, I took a cab to headquarters. I began wondering how they could find all of us at the same time. I shut my phone off for a while. I turned it back on to call Sydney when I got stuck in traffic.”

“But that doesn’t explain how Spinello’s men zeroed in on us so quickly in Virginia,” Yorg stated.

“Before I met Jenkins for dinner that night, I got an update on your location from Keith,” Ramsey admitted. “Then I turned my phone off again to meet Tom for dinner.”

“I’ll have Amy bring you a new phone,” Sydney replied calling his secretary. “That bug is too complicated for Jenkins. Where is Rodger Slate?”

“It’s odd you asked that,” Ramsey remembered. “When I noticed Jenkins’ fishing for information at my condo last night, I asked him that same question. He changed the subject.”

“Then we need to find out where Rodger is quickly,” Alonzo declared. “I remember what he did at Kathe’s house. Rodger has skills almost as good as Sydney.”

“You’re right about that,” Ramsey agreed as Amy knocked on the door and entered.

“Excuse me,” Amy apologized handing Sydney a phone.

“Amy, I heard you wanted some real action and were joining our team,” Jack teased. “Ramsey, I’ll volunteer to be her partner!”

"Not on your life," Amy grinned. "I have all the action I need assisting Sydney with his inventions."

"So, I take it, you like the more geek-type?" Jack winked.

"Serious-type is what I call it," Amy winked and left the room.

"You're wasting your time," Jay laughed. "She's never going to date a field operative."

"Let's stay focused on work," Ramsey frowned.

"Ramsey, I'm downloading your secure data, and then you can have your phone," Sydney stated. "I also sealed it where Jenkins can't open it again. Where were we?"

"We were discussing how someone manipulated the security cameras at my condo like those at Kathe's house in Ponce Inlet," Ramsey continued.

"Hiltree called me a couple of days ago and asked me if Rodger was working with my father," CC reported. "He hasn't seen Rodger since Jenkins took him to DC to vet him."

"That's not a good sign," Ramsey said. "CC, Sam, check on Rodger's family."

"They should be safe," CC stated. "I made sure that Jenkins doesn't know where my father placed them."

"Just check on them and report back to me," Ramsey ordered.

"Yes, ma'am," CC made a note.

"Pauli has information that has a direct bearing on what we are discussing," Alonzo admitted. "Pauli, go ahead."

Pauli looked around the room, "Ramsey asked me to have my clean-up crew check the targets and the ammo specifically at her condo. None of the five men at her condo were Spinello's men. They had no identification on them. They carried Cuban rifles and ammunition."

"I ran a scan on the last target's voice as he tried to communicate with his companions inside," Sydney stated. "He was speaking a Cuban dialect of Spanish. Please, continue, Pauli."

"Just like Ramsey suspected, there was no corpse found in the kitchen or dining room, where only Jenkins fought," Pauli declared. "The helicopter was gone, and since the cameras were offline in those two areas, we have no idea what time it left. The only casings found in those areas were from Ramsey's MT15 and Jenkins' Glock. As for your neighbors across the hall, someone called them and told them they had a gas leak. They were told that only that floor contained the leak. Don't panic the other tenants, just pack a bag and leave immediately. They would contact them when it was safe to return. My men checked with the management office personnel. No one called them or was aware of any gas leak. They would have evacuated the entire building, not one floor."

"That's what I suspected when Jenkins came out of the bedroom with his Glock pointed at me," Ramsey confided. "Jenkins was safe all along. The cut on his arm probably happened when he shot my mother's vase that he always hated. God rest her soul; leave it to my mother to reach from the grave and bite him back. She always did get the best of Tom."

"We need to find out who piloted that helicopter," Kathe declared.

"Yes, we do," Sydney concurred. "Someone hacked into the cameras and the elevator. It appears Jenkins forced Rodger to do it since I'm having trouble finding the IP Address."

"Are you alright with this, Boss?" Wanda asked studying Ramsey's face. "You don't look so good."

"Yes, Wanda," Ramsey sighed. "I believe what saved me was Jenkins saw a side of me that he didn't know existed."

"God can have what's left of Jenkins when you're done, right, Boss?" Wanda grinned.

"If there's anything left of him," Ramsey beamed glancing at Pauli. "You may continue Pauli with your report."

"As a result of what my men found at Ramsey's condo," Pauli explained, "I checked with the other two clean-up crews. And the targets at Jay's apartment and Hiltree's ambush were also Cuban."

"CC, Sam, we need to know exactly how these men got into our country with their weapons," Sydney advised. "If Jenkins smuggled them into the country, there should be a flight plan registered from the U.S. to Cuba and back."

"The area in New York where Ramsey lives is near Wall Street," Sam declared. "All aircraft in that area are strictly controlled. Tracking down the pilot of the helicopter should be easy."

"The attack on Hiltree and his men prove Jenkins tried to eliminate them along with us," Kathe surmised. "Especially, since CC noted Hiltree began questioning Jenkins' motives."

"Jenkins knows he cannot manipulate Hiltree to his side," CC shared.

"Hiltree needs to be in on these meetings with us," Alonzo stated. "Pauli and I are entering Cuba with him. We will bring him up to speed."

"What about the targets sent after us?" Yorg asked. "Kathe recognized some of them as Spinello's goons."

"Yes, a few of them were Spinello's men," Pauli answered. "But most of them were Cubans. Somehow Montez easily flip-flops across the border. That's why the people in the fourth plane tried to take Montez's body with them. Since none of those men survived, my men slipped into the morgue to check Montez's body. He had no identifying papers like the others."

"We only found out Montez's name from the good reverend," Ramsey stated. "CC, Sam, add Montez to your growing list. He was leading the attack in Virginia."

"Which brings us back to Jenkins," Alonzo declared. "We know Jenkins deems Kathe with JAKE as a direct threat to his plan. He also knows Yorg has a vendetta against Yetsun. That's why the attack on Kathe and her family. Jenkins found out about the details of how Yorg was sent to work at Alby Airlines. If Yorg would be so grief-stricken by their deaths, he could dangle Yetsun at Yorg to get to Chameleon."

"Now that Jenkins has seen me in action, he knows he can't control me or match my skills," Kathe added.

"When Yetsun murdered Mikél, I was young and naïve," Yorg declared. "I'm not the same person."

"Yorg, we've all learned our lessons the hard way," Sydney comforted. "Jenkins doesn't know everything Kathe and JAKE can do, nor that you have an implant. Before we left Newark to go to Miami, Jenkins said something that bothered me. He said if someone kidnapped me, they controlled the world with Chameleon."

"You just gave me chills!" Ramsey gasped. "I had the same feeling. Always watch that man's eyes, and you can tell what he's thinking. When Jenkins realized that Sydney could morph Chameleon to do other things, his eyes widened with dollar signs in them."

"Then, why didn't Jenkins' target Sydney instead of you?" Jack wondered. "You said it yourself; he knows Sydney skills."

"That's a good point," Ramsey discussed. "I think Jenkins planned to make my death look like a terrorists attack. In coordinating all the teams together, it made it appear more credible. That's why they attacked all of us, including Hiltree, before the Citation. With us out of the way, he would have eliminated some of the main people who stand in his way. He was setting a trap for Sydney. By kidnapping Yorg, Jenkins knew Sydney would rescue him. Then Jenkins had everyone he needed to use Chameleon. Worse yet, he had Sydney to morph it into what he wanted."

"And Jenkins would arrest the rest of us for his crime," CC finished. "He would have gotten away with Chameleon scot-free."

"For this reason, I do not want Jenkins to know about Stephen's HUB, period!" Sydney exclaimed. "Or what kind of drones we are using. That's our only ace in the hole."

"What about Hiltree's men?" Jay asked. "Can they be trusted?"

"Ramsey had us check Smalley and his men's backgrounds," CC shared. "They are all patriots that are concerned with the changes in our country. The two men injured in yesterday's battle are committed and coming with Hiltree to Cuba."

"With that said," Sydney concluded closing the wall with the remote. "Ramsey and I will be off the Cuban Coast on a Coast Guard cutter with Master Chief Petty Officer Ian Smalley and his men. Are there any other questions?"

"I just thought about something," Jack laughed. "We're in a no-win situation. We're darned if we stop the criminals and darned when we do."

"I think you summed it up nicely," Wanda giggled throwing her hands in the air. "And we work for Alby Airlines and shouldn't be involved in any of this mess."

"No, we shouldn't be involved," Ramsey agreed. "However, since Alby got drug into this mess, we must see it through. Somehow, we'll be victorious!"

"At least, we have some of the most brilliant minds sitting at this table working on the solution," Kathe pointed out.

"Speaking of brilliant minds," Ramsey delegated, "Wanda, assign Captain Mills to use the Mustang Citation and take CC and Sam to locate Tomme Boy Dano."

"CC, Sam, when you locate Dano, do not apprehend," Ramsey ordered. "I owe Bernadette a favor; she'll handle him."

"I've already reassured Bernadette, that your word is your bond, and you would call her," Alonzo interrupted. "Dano will know some of the answers to this puzzle. Bernadette will know the right questions and how to make him sing like a bird."

"While you two track down Dano," Ramsey continued, "I want you to continue your quest concerning Macaby, Jenkins, and the last three subjects we gave you. What you find at the prison should lead you to find out what Jenkins has planned. He always has a back door to slither out of any situation. The rest of us will report to Sydney's Leer and head for the Keys."

Chapter 3

FNN Newsroom, Washington DC, Wednesday, July 1, 0700 (7:00 AM EST)

BREAKING NEWS: "This is Robert Morwitz with FNN News reporting live from the Allegheny Mountains in Virginia," he introduced as Stephen, Will, and Skip watched the morning news in the HUB. "I am in Deerfeld, Virginia, checking on a bizarre story sent from an unknown source to our news station in the wee hours this morning. Deerfeld is a tiny, mountain town with a population of 138. The source said to ask local gas station owner, Walter Greene, what happened to him," he moved the microphone. "Mr. Greene, can you describe what happened last night?"

"I was in my station late in the evening when a woman came in from the back of the store, pointing a gun at me," Walter stated.

"Was it a robbery?" Morwitz asked moving the microphone back to Walter.

"No," Walter insisted, "she said that a newcomer in town, Saundra Smith said that I was a good Christian man and an unwilling participant in Rev. Woods' scheme. The reverend wasn't who he said he was. She was trying to save our townspeople from the havoc Rev. Woods, and the men he picked up from the airport last night were about to reign down on us."

"Did she say what kind of havoc?" Morwitz asked.

"No," Greene answered.

"Did she say the true identity of Rev. Woods?" Morwitz quizzed.

"I can't remember the name, but he worked for a crime syndicate," Mr. Greene remembered.

"Do you remember anything else about your encounter with her?" Morwitz moved the microphone.

"I think she was an alien," Walter confided. "When I hesitated to leave as three trucks pulled up to my pump, she told me to hold up my phone. When I did, a red ray came out of the phone, burning my hand and melting my phone," he said holding it up. "I dropped it and ran out the back door."

Morwitz quickly moved the microphone. "Well, thank you for your comment," he rolled his eyes as the camera swiftly changed, revealing a picture of Sheriff Potter. "There was another unusual thing that happened in Deerfeld last night. According to the local sheriff, something large landed on SR 209 instead of the airport. Sheriff Potter believes a craft hid in this old crop-duster hangar on Tennessee Valley Road." The screen changed to outside of the hangar showing two deputies marking the scene with yellow tape. "They discovered three male bodies inside and several more in the cornfield. Someone cleared the debris off the old taxiway, which showed signs of recently being used. The FBI is en route to assist in the investigation. We will keep you informed as we stay with this third incredible leaked story within the last few days.

Wednesday, July 1, 0800 (8:00 AM EST)
The Florida Keys, Big Pine Key Island

"Well, if it isn't the aliens from the Allegheny Mountains knocking on my door," Stephen chuckled as they entered. "I sure hope Kathe's not going to shoot her red ray and melt my phone, or me for that matter."

"What are you talking about?" Ramsey asked shaking his hand.

"I take it you haven't seen the morning news?" Stephen grinned. "It seems there has been another news leak," he declared filling them in on the newscast.

"Well, at least the leaker didn't cover the other three locations attacked in New York," Ramsey scoffed. "It would be difficult to explain that to the authorities."

"The source seems very selective, don't you think?" Sydney cautioned.

"Yes, not pointing to Jenkins, but always pointing to us," Kathe remarked. "Is that what you mean?"

"Exactly," Sydney agreed. "Stephen, what have you got for us?"

"The data Kathe extracted in Miami was right on the mark," Stephen complimented. "Skip let's bring up the film we took of Cuba two days ago on the TV in the back. We can sit down in there and go over it," he said leading the way to the back of the semi.

"Nice setup," Yorg complimented following Stephen. "I see you can not only film, but edit, and record voice-overs without having to leave the truck," he said peaking in several rooms.

"Yes, I designed it so I can have multiple crews filming on different locations at the same time," Stephen admitted as Skip pulled up the computer. “I can also view what they’re filming in Realtime and make suggestions,” Stephen shared as the team sat around the TV.

“Skip, start at the Aeropuerto Internacional José Martí,” Will suggested handing Stephen the remote. “That is where we located Estevo Vazquez with our drone.”

“That’s a good starting point,” Stephen agreed as Skip brought up a map of both airports highlighted.

“My team will be landing in Havana,” Stephen stated showing the airport. “José Martí is 15 kilometers southwest of Havana in the province of La Habana, in the town of Boyeros. It serves International Flights, Domestic Flights, and Charter Flights,” he changed pictures to show the three terminals. “Sydney gave us the coordinates of Estevo Vazquez as soon as he resurfaced. As Will stated, we located and tracked him here,” he said changing the picture. “Here is Estevo standing by a cab waiting for these two men. We couldn’t identify them.”

“The man on the right is Vinnie Issac,” Alonzo stated. “Tito Morado is the one on the left. Pauli and I figured they would resurface near Estevo.”

“They know we stopped their plan in Deerfeld,” Pauli shared. “They’re relocating Vinnie and Tito to overtake a village in Cuba.”

“The data revealed that Metarha rerouted her people from the Middle East to train with the Cubans?” Ramsey shared.

“Her kind never stops with their objective,” Pauli stated. “Metarha will find another way to try to take down America.”

“What better place than Cuba?” Alonzo agreed. “It’s close and the easiest way other than Mexico back inside the borders. Stephen, what else have you learned?”

“We followed the three men to the Primera Estrella Del Mar Hotel on the beach in Varadero,” Stephen reported. “Inside, they went to the 8th floor. The drone got sluggish around room 809. They stayed for about an hour, and then mysteriously surfaced walking down to the beach with this man,” he said zeroing in on him.

“I don’t recognize him,” Ramsey replied glancing at Sydney.

“No facial recognition,” Sydney said scanning his face. “Stephen, while you continue, I’ll check the Cuban records for him.”

“A small boat was waiting for them onshore,” Stephen continued. “All four men got into the boat. The drone followed them to a Yacht off the coast, where it got sluggish as it approached. We were only able to get close enough to read the name, El Amoré del Sol,” he said zeroing in on the name. "As soon as they got aboard, the Yacht set sail. As we followed it, Will sent a mosquito-drone close to the water, under the blanket-effect, and marked the Yacht with a tag. We followed it to a cove in Matanzas, where we lost both signals. Hopefully, when it leaves port, we can follow the GPS signal again."

"I see for a film company, you're getting good at this spy-stuff," Kathe complimented.

"Sydney got me hooked working on our latest camera for our drone," Stephen grinned.

"I tried to get the drone into the cove several different ways," Will admitted. "Something quickly drained the power. It barely had enough power to reach land. I hid it in a densely wooded area. I'll have to retrieve it when we get to Cuba."

"That's odd that it drained the power so quickly?" Sydney quizzed.

"We've never seen anything like it," Stephen admitted.

"I couldn't believe how quickly the power levels emptied," Skip confirmed. "The source had to be extremely concentrated in that area. I couldn't boost it."

"In New Jersey and Miami, I located the source and was able to boost the battery," Sydney shared. "Someone has enhanced it."

"If Eduardo is as good as we think," Yorg added. "He would upgrade the technology."

"Correct," Ramsey agreed. "The number of illegal trucks going to the hidden warehouse in Jersey proved Spinello used it a long time before we stumbled onto him."

"That's because Nikkoli wasn't as techy as he professed," Sydney declared. "We found that out on the beach in Ponce," he said still trying to hack into Cuba's records. "We need to know all the players on the newly-formed team. I'm still searching who the man with them is, and the owner of that Yacht."

"I'm from the Bahamas," Will admitted. "I have a question about what we're doing. How does stopping Chameleon Technology from getting into the wrong hands, equate to people with new identities living in a small village? And them killing the natives in the village?"

"By getting rid of the natives, they leave no traces," Alonzo answered. "By replacing leaders slowly, no one will realize what is happening until it's too late to stop them."

"What we're uncovering goes beyond the thirst for Chameleon Technology," Sydney assured him. "This is a complex intertwined network of organizations that have joined together to bring a 'One Vision One World' network into fruition. Chameleon Technology will ensure its success. However, to achieve their goal, they need the help of world leaders."

"However, not all world leaders want or will tolerate this kind of union," Alonzo declared. "So, instead of a coup, they are replacing either the leader or their second in command with well-trained look-a-likes."

"This brings chills down my spine," Kathe added. "Several of our presidents talked about a 'One World Vision.' That would explain why several of our trade agreements changed overnight without the approval of Congress."

"Yes, now I remember!" Jay exclaimed. "I read that several of our past presidents, and some world leaders slept in coffins to join a Secret Society for this reason. I thought the concept was far-fetched and blew it off."

"The concept is far-fetched and will never work," Kathe affirmed. "I'll sum it up in one word-greed! Just look at all the top dogs involved that we've uncovered. Once their plan begins to take final shape, the real takers will make their move. It's human nature."

"Don't forget to add Jenkins to that mixture," Ramsey confirmed. "Stephen, you missed the briefing in Newark. We know that Jenkins will use us to eliminate his competition. Then, he will double-cross us."

"Not if we beat him at his own game," Stephen stated. "To do this, we have to have something major on Jenkins."

"CC and Sam are researching that," Ramsey confirmed.

"Stephen, show the team what you have already replaced in the cutter over my desk in our portable HUB," Sydney requested.

"I can't take the credit for this one," Stephen smiled. "After Will observed Jenkins' allusive behavior on the cutter in Miami. Will redesigned one of the electronics in the HUB to zero in on Jenkins. I'll let Will explain how it works."

Will held up a simple, small, round, smoke detector. "I've already replaced the smoke detector on the cutter with one like this," he said turning it around. "What you can't see is this detector has a 4K wide-angle camera on the bottom. I noticed Jenkins walked away from the console every time he received a phone call. Since it sits in the middle of the ceiling, Skip will be able to zoom in on his text messages, caller ID and listen to phone calls, and record them."

"Show them what else you have," Sydney requested continuing to work on his laptop.

"Skip, bring up the video of me entering the Orlando Airport," Stephen requested.

"Here it is," Skip said pushing play and turning up the volume.

The video showed Stephen entering Orlando Airport. It continued to show him walking through the TSA line, talking with security, handing the agent his passport and boarding pass. He then placed his bags on the conveyer belt, walked through the metal detector, retrieved his bags, rode the tram to the next concourse, walked to his gate, and sat down in a chair.

"How did you do that?" Yorg questioned in disbelief. "No one is allowed to take pictures, much less a video going through security."

"Here's how," Stephen smiled pulling his sunglasses out of his shirt pocket and holding them up. "This is also an undetectable 4K video camera with clear sound, as you just heard."

"Can you Realtime that video to your HUB?" Kathe asked reaching for the glasses to inspect them.

"Yes, I can," Stephen chuckled.

"And now, I have another gadget for you," Sydney added looking up from his laptop, and reaching in his backpack. He held up a tiny, square, clear device. "Your glasses are great. However, I may need to talk you through an unforeseen situation," he said reaching for the sunglasses. He placed the device on the inside next to the earpiece and held it up. "This is an undetectable transmitter and receiver. Now, we can talk with you just like with your earbud."

"I worried about not having direct contact with you," Stephen sighed. "That gadget gives me a better peace of mind."

"I knew it would," Sydney agreed. "Before you continue, the man we didn't recognize is Gen. Antan Medina. He works directly under Presidente Castrello. The Yacht, El Amoré del Sol is registered to Espírito Ingeniero, a Brazilian Company," he said hacking into the Brazilian Government Records. "It's an umbrella-company of Alianza Mundial Internacional," he glanced at Ramsey. "Which means, World Alliance International."

"It's following the pattern we've seen with different businesses Catarina Santo Prado owns," Ramsey stated.

"Yes," Sydney agreed. "Catarina is good at masking the country of registration for her businesses. The records I found indicate this company as doing business in Cuba for the last three years. I'm having the computer check the records worldwide. We can continue our discussion."

"Skip, show them the footage we shot yesterday," Stephen requested.

"Okay," Skip replied pulling it up.

"We filmed this with our latest camera," Stephen proudly showcased. "I couldn't wait for Sydney to get here to show it off," he grinned changing the picture to another map. "We figured that Las Tunas and the Sierra Maestra have extremely treacherous jungles. These are perfect places for Eduardo and Gen. Yetsun to hide. Then, we ruled out Las Tunas. The highest point is 302', and our drone found no opposition. We did see three areas that the drone became too sluggish. The first was around the highest peak in the Sierra Maestra. The second was near Mayarí, and lastly near the beach at Santiago de Cuba, close to Guantanamo Bay."

"How high is the tallest peak in Sierra Maestra?" Jay asked.

"It's 6,476'," Stephen answered. "The height is compared to some of the lower mountain ranges in Utah. Thus, the air quality isn't as thin as the higher mountains, so you won't have to worry about hypoxia when we climb."

"That's good to know," Jay replied. "Even at that altitude, we can hold our own with the soldiers and guerillas."

"Isn't Santiago de Cuba where Cuba trains its military?" Kathe asked.

"Some of them," Stephen answered. "There is a larger camp near Bayamo."

"I see what you mean about treacherous jungles," Yorg said viewing the footage of the drone manipulating through the dense jungle. "I've never seen anything like this. The camera shows every direction around the drone perfectly."

"This is our new prize camera drone," Stephen held it up. "It's one of a kind that Sydney and I have been working on for the past two years. It has twelve cameras, each with zoom in and out capabilities. It can take pictures above, north, east, south, and west, as well as underneath at the same time. So, we are now capable of filming 360-degrees with one drone. If we spot something of interest, we can zoom into it as well as listen," he said as his phone rang. "It's Cuba. I've got to take this call," he said handing the drone to Sydney and walking out of the room.

"That drone takes the guesswork out of surveillance," Yorg confirmed.

"Doesn't it?" Sydney agreed taking over the discussion. "It can also travel at 200 miles-an-hour, so it cuts travel time in half. The sleek design makes it virtually non-visual and able to manipulate in tight places. It is also an underwater drone like the one we used in Miami."

"So, you simply combined both drones," Jay surmised.

"Yes, the time it took to switch drones in Miami meant life or death for Kathe and Hiltree," Sydney admitted. "We were lucky at that time."

"The high altitude with rugged terrain and dense vegetation is different than we are used to," Jay noted. "I read online that it is hot with high humidity."

"It will be different," Sydney admitted. "The vegetation contains a variety of critters, some are poisonous."

"That reminds me of the issue I had with an iguana in Miami," Jack mentioned. "What kind of critters should we anticipate?"

"Just one of the snakes, Lesser Racer Caraiba, could chase you," Skip brought up a picture. "Or you could run into a Solenodon," he changed pictures. "It is a venomous shrew-like mammal that produces poisonous saliva that it injects into its prey through its teeth, so watch out for its bite," he warned, fast-forwarding the video to a tree. "Or a Tree Boa squeezing you to death, like this big guy."

"I get the picture," Jack sighed. "Not only do we have to watch out for the two-legged creatures, but the jungle is full of its own. At least, we will be able to breathe without an oxygen mask."

"I hear Cuba has iguanas also," Kathe laughed. "Maybe the one in Miami that had the hots for you has a Cuban cousin."

"Very funny," Jack smirked. "It scared the sin out of me. The worse part was that I couldn't move to see what it was."

"I have to say," Sydney chuckled. "The look on your face as the guy stood above you on the bridge, and you trying not to fidget was priceless."

"Glad to know that I was your entertainment that day," Jack stated. "All I could see was Kathe threatening me to be still as something big and heavy with a long tail stood on my back. How did I know it wasn't an alligator?"

"Don't worry," Jay added. "With this new camera, you can view your performance as it happens on your phone."

"Very funny," Jack scoffed.

"We must be living right," Stephen smiled entering the room. "We've just been cleared to go to Cuba and the use of drones. The Minister of Tourism, Ché Márquez, is excited about this documentary ending with Cuba's specific rare birds. He believes this will bring worldwide tourism. Márquez cleared all my filming sites and said if I need more to let him know. He is also emailing me some sightings of rare birds that are not native to Cuba."

"That's great news," Ramsey declared. "Now we can formulate a plan."

"Skip will monitor the drones from this HUB," Stephen stated. "He'll be able to help us spot something we might miss on one of the cameras and report to us immediately. Will and I are ready to leave as soon as you are."

"I'll call the airport and get you cleared for takeoff within the hour," Ramsey acknowledged. "I've already had your company logo put on my jet, and the registration switched, so everything stays legit."

"Good," Stephen said. "I arranged for several modes of ground transportation for us to use in Cuba also under my company. That way, we keep down suspicions. Will has company ID Badges for each team."

"While you were reminiscing about the Iguana," Ramsey stood up. "I arranged your assignments. Jay and Jack have already changed their appearance to travel as part of Stephen's camera crew," she said turning to Kathe. "Even with Kathe and Yorg changing their hair color to brown, they may have problems. We can assume someone took pictures of Kathe and Hiltree in Miami, either in the underwater control room or getting into the pod. When Gen. Yetsun identified Yorg on the satellite phone, he would have snapped a picture. With the technology we found in Miami, they probably have facial recognition.

It's obvious someone paid the authorities to look the other way. Our targets seem to come and go to Cuba easily. Use caution at the airports and ocean ports. Skip, would you please bring up the Aerial pictures of the map of Cuba again?"

"Is this the one you want?" Skip asked as it appeared on the screen.

"Yes," Ramsey approved. "It will be easier for Kathe and Yorg to use the mini-sub," she said pointing to the map. "You should surface on the coast between Matanzas and Varadero. I want to know why the drone was sluggish in the Hotel. Even with the tag on the Yacht, we have no idea if Vinnie and Tito are still on it. See if you can get close enough to find out. Hopefully, it is a holding place for them until they're ready for them to do their dirty deed. Estevo left alone thirty minutes ago by car and is still on the move. I'll let you know where he goes."

"The first part of this mission is only fact-finding," Sydney declared. "We've got to locate all the players involved before we formulate our final plan."

"I have cameras for Kathe and Yorg to use with a list of birds sighted in that area in case someone stops them," Stephen offered as Will passed them out.

"Hiltree has arranged for Pauli and me to enter Cuba with them," Alonzo reported. "We will be arriving at Guantanamo Naval Base. We will check out Santiago de Cuba before meeting with Stephen at his hotel room in La Playitas tomorrow afternoon," he said checking his watch. "Hiltree is picking us up in thirty minutcs at Fort Zachary Taylor State Park."

"Our ride just arrived outside," Pauli said checking his text messages and replying. "Let's go."

"Here are your ID Badges, as well as Hiltree and his men," Will said handing Pauli a large envelope. "Have a safe trip. We'll see you in Cuba."

Wednesday, July 1, 1100 (11:00 AM EST)
José Martí International Airport, Havana, Cuba

As soon as Stephen and Will landed Gabby Mobile Production's jet at José Martí, a swarm of military vehicles surrounded the plane at the end of the runway.

"Sydney, I didn't expect this greeting," Stephen declared putting on his sunglasses to show the military presence. "Hold on, the tower is contacting us."

"Gabby Flight #226, you are to follow the escort to Runway 9F for clearing customs," he instructed.

"Copy that, José Martí Tower," Stephen answered slowly taxiing behind the lead Hummer.

"Sydney, do you see this firepower?" Stephen asked as a ground crew member gave the signal to halt at the end of the runway.

"It's the new standard procedure in Cuba," Sydney confirmed snapping several pictures. "The government beefed up its security a year ago. I believe it was due to Eduardo's presence. The glasses work perfectly. We can see and hear everything you do."

"That's not as comforting as I thought," Stephen sighed shutting the engines down. "They have guns, and we don't. I knew they would check us as well as the plane, but I didn't expect this greeting since the Minister of Tourism hired us and cleared us. Hold on, the tower wants us to deplane."

"Stephen, I've got your back," Sydney declared. "Jay, deplane first with Stephen. Jack, deplane with Will. Any signs of hostility, you know what to do."

"Copy that," Jay said opening the door. "Stephen, I'm ready when you are. I'll walk in front of you."

"Stephen, another gadget," Sydney grinned. "Any problems, drop to the steps. The rails are bulletproof glass. I'm in their system and will stop all traffic for you to takeoff."

"Anything else I need to know?" Stephen asked following Jay down the steps to the tarmac.

"Make sure you act cool and calm when they greet you," Ramsey added.

"Sr. (Senior) Brown, I am Capitán Montenegro," he introduced as armed guards surrounded them, and a van stopped by the Hummer. "I request your group to retrieve your luggage and then get into the van. We will take you to Customs."

"The luggage compartment is on this side of the plane by the tail," Stephen stated leading the way.

"Have you spotted any unfriendlies yet?" Ramsey asked watching Stephen and the team get into the van.

"Stephen, carefully put your sunglasses in your pocket, so we can see the camera, and switch to the device," Sydney said muting his console. "No, but that doesn't mean there isn't a new player we haven't discovered yet." He glanced at Skip, "Don't worry. I anticipated this. Everything is going smoothly," watching the van speed toward Terminal #3 and stop.

"We've traveled to many countries," Skip gasped watching Montenegro escort the team straight to Chequeo De Emigración at Booth #6. "We've never had this kind of reception."

"They're fine," Ramsey consoled.

"You're passport and credentials, por favor?" Officer Ramos asked as Stephen handed it to him. "Sr. Brown," he smiled, "we've been expecting you. Montenegro contacted me about your arrival since I am an avid, amateur Birder. I took the pictures in this room for tourists to see our wildlife," he bragged pointing around the room. "I am Quito Ramos. It's an honor to assist you and your crew through Customs," he said swiping Stephen's passport. The light turned green as Ramos stamped his passport. "Which region do you think you'll visit first?"

"I'm not sure just yet," Stephen replied. "The sun is shining now, but I heard that the fast-moving Tropical Storm Delilah would brush the coast and head out to the Gulf."

"The last I checked with our meteorologist, Delilah will miss us," Ramos confirmed handing Stephen his passport. "The weather should be nice for your filming. We've had some interesting sightings lately of birds that are not indigenous to this island. I'm sure you'll be as impressed as I am. You are cleared and may stand to the right while we check your crew," he said pointing the way.

Jack was behind Stephen and handed Ramos his passport. "Sr. Davies," he said looking at the stamps on his passport. "I see you just returned from Tasmania," he looked up at Jack.

"Yes, I did," Jack concurred. "Stephen sent me there to work on a project for unusual and exotic birds. Which one is your favorite?"

"It's hard to choose," Ramos sighed. "The Tasmanian Native-hen has bright, red eyes. Or the Eurasian Coot with its bright, red eyes is more vivid against its black feathers and white beak."

"Personally, my favorite is the Masked Lapwing," Jack confessed reaching for his iPhone. "It's black crown and nape are separated from the mantle by a white-collar and underparts. It is interesting the way its yellow bill contours with a bright, yellow wattle that reaches behind the eyes and hangs down beside the chin," he pointed out. "That combined with its long, sharp, yellow spurs gives it an appearance of a Superhero. Especially since it has a loud, penetrating call demanding respect, he's definitely a masked Caped Crusader, don't you think?"

"Yes, I see what you mean," Ramos chuckled handing Jack back his passport. "You have an unusual eye to capture the personalities of birds. I've never heard anyone explain the characteristic of a bird that way. You may wait by Sr. Brown."

"Leave it to Jack to describe a bird like that!" Ramsey exclaimed leaning on the desk and putting her head in her hands. "He's in Cuba; what is he thinking?"

"Stop trying to take the comedian out of Jack," Sydney glanced at her. "It keeps him sane in this line of work."

Jay handed Ramos his passport.

"I see you've just come from Laos and Vietnam," Ramos smiled. "What is your favorite bird in that area of the world?"

Jay pulled out his iPhone and showed his screen. "I'm torn between these two. The Siamese Fireback is a large bird that looks like he's going to do battle. The male has long, grey plumage pulled back like a Chinese warrior with extensive bright, red facial skin, crimson legs and feet, ornamental black, crest feathers, reddish-brown iris, and long, curved blackish tail," he said switching pictures. "The male Silver Pheasant has a bright, red, bare face and legs that radiates against its black and white body. The long, white, tail feathers make it elegant to watch, much like American Peacocks."

"I can see why you are torn," Ramos replied admiring them. "Do you have a website I can view your work?"

"Sure," Jay smiled handing him a business card. "You can see all my photos, and I welcome any comments you might have."

"I will have to check it out," Ramos answered pulling up the website. "I see you have an eye for perfect shots, Sr. Towers. You may stand with the others."

"Thank God, Jay is the straight one of the two," Ramsey admitted. "One more to go, and we've pulled this off."

Will handed Ramos his passport and swiped it. A strange look came over Ramos's face, staring at the picture on the screen, rechecking the passport picture, and then looking up at Will. "Sr. Russell, have you been with Sr. Brown long?"

"We've known each other for over five years," Will answered. "We've worked together for the past two. Why?"

"Have you traveled abroad with Sr. Brown?" Ramos asked.

Stephen watched nervously, "Syd, what's going on?"

"Stephen, calm down," Sydney cautioned. "It appears to be a discrepancy on his screen and the passport. Give me a minute to get into Ramos's computer," he said quickly hacking into it. "Something's wrong with Will's passport. Let me check with Homeland Security's TSA Division. It will take a few minutes," he cautioned feverishly typing.

"Several guards are surrounding Will with machine guns," Stephen warned putting on his sunglasses.

"We see that," Ramsey reported. "Sydney is almost into the records of TSA; just stay calm."

"Armed guards are heading toward us too," Stephen warned.

"Stay calm," Ramsey ordered. "Jay and Jack are right there with you. They've trained to handle this type of situation."

"I was wondering when this would happen," Sydney stated pulling up TSA in San Francisco. "There is a man in San Francisco using the same passport number as Will," he showed Ramsey as Stephen listened.

"It looks like the Head of Security is joining Ramos," Ramsey noted. "Let's listen."

"Sr. Russell, it seems that a hold has been put on your passport," Capitán Juarez stated. "We are going to bring you into custody, as well as your companions until we clear this matter up," he declared, as a guard put handcuffs on Will.

"They're arresting them!" Skip exclaimed. "We'll never get them out of Cuba!"

"Sydney, do something now!" Ramsey exclaimed watching helplessly. "They are arresting all of them."

"I've just completed a retinal scan of the man in San Francisco," he said as his computer brought up a long, rap sheet. "This is illegal, criminal, alien, Gimoaldo Paz Cisneros from Honduras. He's been deported five times and keeps returning to California. He is using the same passport number in San Francisco to board a flight. His picture isn't obvious. An amateur tried to doctor his picture digitally to resemble Will, but it was a terrible job," he said pressing enter. "I just merged Ramos's computer with TSA in San Francisco. They cross-checked it with Homeland and are sending the information to Cuba that they have the real Will Russell."

"Ramos is staring at his computer screen," Stephen noted.

"TSA is arresting Cisneros," Sydney grinned pressing enter again. "They're detaining Cisneros for ICE to pick him up."

"It's no wonder Will had a problem," Ramsey declared reading the rap sheet. "Cisneros has been deported five times from a long list of felonies, including murder in Arizona," she read as Ramos showed Capitán Juarez his computer screen.

"Unbelievable," Skip sighed sitting back in his chair. "That man shouldn't have been deported. He should have been in jail!"

"Remove the handcuffs," Capitán Juarez declared clearing his throat. "Sr. Russell and Sr. Brown, I apologize for any unpleasantness this matter may have caused you," he said as Ramos handed Will his passport. "Sr. Russell, you're free to join Sr. Brown. I hope your stay in Cuba is rewarding."

"According to the Audubon reports and our research, it should be," Will replied joining the others.

"Where are they taking them now?" Skip asked watching Montenegro escort them outside to the van again.

"Stephen and the team have to be with them when they sweep the plane," Ramsey answered. "It is standard protocol for all planes entering a different country."

"I understand," Skip sighed staring at the screen. "This is nerve-racking watching armed guards leading my friends to the taxiway."

"That's because you know the real reason, they're in Cuba," Ramsey explained. "Don't worry. The jet is clean. Hiltree and Alonzo are bringing in the special equipment."

"But they're having Stephen open the Bradley cases," Skip complained.

"Stephen has to show them that the cameras aren't guns or bombs," Ramsey comforted as Stephen opened the case and handed a camera to a guard.

"That is an expensive camera!" Skip declared. "He can't handle it like that!"

"Skip," Ramsey grinned. "Why don't you make us a cup of coffee? The process is going to take a while, and I need you calm."

"It's the guns that worry me," Skip admitted with his eyes glued to the screen.

"We all carry them," Ramsey winked. "How about that cup of coffee?"

Skip came back in the room with the coffee by the time the van carrying the team had pulled into the Hotel Neptuno-Triton in Havana.

"See, everyone is safe," Ramsey pointed to the screen. "They are checking into the first hotel of the journey."

"Thank God," Skip sighed handing them their coffee.

"The airport was the tip of the iceberg," Ramsey added. "It's going to get worse from here on out. You know the people we are going after and why. To ensure your safety, RADM Hiltree sent Comm. Michael Olms to help and protect you. He worked with Stephen and us in Miami. He's very familiar with who we're up against."

"That makes me feel better," Skip sighed. "I prayed for strength in this situation while I made the coffee. After listening to Stephen, these people can't get this kind of technology. I won't let them or you down."

"That's what we needed to hear," Ramsey admitted. "It's our job to have all of your backs. We will disperse multiple teams in different areas at the same time. With the aid of these new hi-tech drones with 360-degree range cameras, we need you and Olms to help us staff them. There are so many angles; you might see something we miss. Stephen's team has one. Hiltree's team has the second one, and CC has the third. If we're helping one team through a situation, your job is to help us monitor the other teams. If there is a problem, you are to alert us. Comm. Olms will take over that situation. That's another reason Hiltree assigned Olms with you."

"That puts my mind at ease," Skip confessed as Sydney picked up the signal from Stephen again.

"Sydney," Stephen stepped out on the balcony, "we are on the 12th floor facing the ocean," he said zooming the camera on his glasses in on the military presence on the beach. "I guess this is how Cuba deals with immigration problems. Do you believe the amount of firepower on the ground?"

"They are all carrying Russian HPE-140," Sydney acknowledged. "That's their version of our M-16."

"It does look similar," Stephen stated. "Our room has a panoramic view of the entire ocean," he showed as he scanned the area. "Jay and Jack are placing a few mosquito-drone cameras in the hallway and elevator, so we don't any have unwelcomed visitors."

"Copy that," Sydney answered. "Alonzo, Pauli, and Hiltree just landed at Guantanamo Naval Base. They will check out Santiago de Cuba before joining you in La Playita tomorrow night. Depending on what your two teams find, we'll know what our next step is."

"Good," Stephen answered. "We're going to unpack some of our equipment and go to a few close locations. I'm sure Ché Márquez will check in with us from time-to-time. I want to validate the reason we are here."

"Copy that," Sydney approved, tapping into the drones in the hallway. "Jay is changing your doorknob for me. It has a unique burglar, alarm system I devised for situations like this one. He will put the 'Do Not Disturb' sign on the doorknob when you leave. Whatever you do, please do not touch it until Jay disarms it. It has several settings, for example, one will stun the person, and the other will do permanent harm six-feet-under. Márquez publicized your visit on the news to promote tourism. That put a bulls-eye on you for vandals wanting to steal your equipment."

"I like your need-to-know gadgets," Stephen chuckled. "I wouldn't want to lose any equipment. It isn't cheap to replace. I need to start gathering footage for the documentary. The faster my camera starts rolling, the faster Skip can start working on it. Talk to you later. See ya."

"That's our cue to head to the cutter," Sydney stated turning to Skip. "Comm. Olms just arrived," Sydney said as an outside alarm sounded. "He's right on time," he pointed to the external camera.

"I'm Comm. Michael Olms," he introduced as Skip held the door open.

"Come inside," Skip shook his hand. "I'm Skip Crowell. Stephen talks very highly of you."

"It was a privilege working with Stephen," Olms admitted. "When RADM Hiltree told me that we were working with a team of civilians that topped the military, I was skeptical. Until I worked with them."

"We'll take that as a compliment," Ramsey smiled shaking his hand. "I'm Linda Ramsey, and this is Dr. David Sydney."

"Ah, the voices in my earbud," Olms shook their hands. "It's a privilege to meet both of you face-to-face. It's been nice working with your team these past few days. Your intelligence operation proved far superior to the government's," he confided reaching in his duffle bag. "Ms. Ramsey, here is an envelope for you, and the keys to the Jeep outside. RADM Hiltree said you are to take it to the cutter."

"I appreciate the compliment," Ramsey smiled opening the envelope. "Our military IDs for us to work on the cutter. Hiltree said you would bring them."

"Speaking of our intelligence," Sydney said reaching in his backpack, "here are new earbuds to connect you to our network."

"Oh, since I'm working with civilians, can you call me Mack?" Comm. Olms requested. "That's what my family and friends call me."

"Okay, Mack, I'll spread the word to the teams," Sydney chuckled.

"I'll show Mack around the HUB and familiarize him with the cameras," Skip assured them. "Just bring everyone home safe."

Wednesday, July 1, 1205 (12:05 PM EST)
Santiago de Cuba

"Sydney, we've just arrived on the border of Guantanamo Bay and Santiago de Cuba," Alonzo reported. "Hiltree has the drone approaching the Cuban Military Base, and it's starting to lose power."

"Copy that," Sydney said pointing the satellite toward them and pulling up the drone. "Give me a minute to locate the source," Sydney stated scanning the area. "It seems to begin just before the target ranges, extending over the barracks."

"Hiltree, I'm boosting your battery," Sydney advised. "You should be able to get under the blanket in half-a-mile and then easily move around. It's afternoon, so the sun is straight up. That alone will mask the drone."

"Copy that," Hiltree answered flying the drone under the blanket. "I got inside. You're right; it's a perfect time to scope out the area. There is not a cloud in the sky. It's a sweltering 98 degrees with 90% humidity."

"Sounds like one time I won't complain about working inside," Sydney laughed. "Hang on. I'll add Skip and Mack to the call."

"I see Mack was impressed working with the team," Hiltree declared. "He only lets his closest friends and his family call him Mack. He comes from a long line of military relatives named Michael Olms. His mother made sure he had a different middle name to use."

"Mothers have that right," Sydney chuckled. "Skip, we are ready for you and Mack to help monitor Hiltree's camera. I'm sending the facial scans of Metarha and Teodoro. It is logical for them to train recruits in Santiago de Cuba."

"Copy that," Skip replied. "We're pulling up those cameras."

"The cameras are loading," Mack replied watching them.

"Copy that," Sydney confirmed. "Ramsey, Hiltree's drone is inside the Cuban Military Base," he confirmed as Ramsey joined him with more coffee. "It seems that not only are some of the officials bought off, but the military as well."

"I can't believe these base shares its facility with Metarha," Ramsey noted. "Hiltree, turn the drone toward the obstacle course. Those aren't Cuban or Middle Eastern soldiers."

"Ramsey, they are the villagers abducted in a raid from a nearby village last night," Pauli stated watching over Alonzo's shoulder. "I overheard some airmen at Guantanamo talking about it after we landed. They took healthy men and young boys ten and older."

"I've got confirmation on Metarha," Mack declared zooming in on the far bottom-right camera. "She's under that canopy to the far-right. The big man with her is Benedicto Teodoro."

"Good eye, Mack," Ramsey complimented.

"On the top-left camera, I see a car speeding past the guard station," Skip noted. "It's heading straight for the obstacle course."

"Copy that," Ramsey checked the monitor. "The car is in a hurry."

"Whoever it is, I hope they see what's going on?" Alonzo sighed. "Unfortunately, the youngest boy couldn't climb across the horizontal ladder. The lad fell to the ground and is face down. With this heat, he's probably dehydrated."

"Metarha and Teodoro are on the way to the boy," Mack cautioned turning up the sound.

"Tell him to get up!" Metarha shouted at the interpreter.

"¡Levánate y cruza esa escalera!" the interpreter screamed as Metarha pushed the boy over with her foot.

"Get up and cross that ladder!" Mack interpreted.

"He's either dehydrated or had a heat stroke," Sydney declared. "The boy is soaking wet with sweat," he noted watching an older man run to the boy.

"¡El necesita agua!" the old man cried falling to the ground to check him.

"He needs water!" Mack relayed.

"That car stopped near them, and the back window rolled down," Skip alerted.

"¡El es mi nieto!" he lifted the boy in his arm and rocked him. "¡Por favor, esta inconsciente! ¡Mi nieto esta inconsciente! ¡Él morirá!"

"He needs water!" Mack stated. "He is my grandson! Please, he's unconscious! He will die!"

"It is Philippi Spinello watching from the backseat," Alonzo identified zooming in.

"Teodoro, get this pitiful, old man out of my sight!" Metarha scoffed.

"My pleasure!" Teodoro laughed kicking him in the head.

"Oh, my God!" Ramsey exclaimed watching the older man fall backward. "Teodoro will kill him!" Ramsey screamed watching Teodoro kicking him in his sides and head.

"Teodoro, stop!" Spinello demanded getting out of the car with his bodyguards. "Shoot Teodoro if he kicks that man again!" Spinello hurried to them.

"This is how I weed out the weak!" Metarha glared at Spinello. "The boy is weak! I'm making a man out of him!"

Spinello bent down by the boy. "An old man and a boy that can't be more than ten-years-old?" he stood up. "Follow me to the canopy. You!" Spinello pointed at the interpreter, "get them some water and take them to the barracks. Have a medic take care of them. They better not die!" he pointed at Metarha and Teodoro.

"Compassion is a side of Spinello that we've never seen," Ramsey declared.

"Interesting?" Sydney questioned. "Skip, Mack, while we are listening to this conversation, I would like you to take pictures of the base and personnel on your cameras. Document them for future facial recognition."

"Copy that," they agreed.

"Metarha, I ordered you to stop killing the villagers!" Spinello warned. "Castrello called our boss. He said the villagers would rebel against him if he doesn't stop the kidnappings and killings! So far, you've killed more people than you've trained!"

"You promised I could bring my people here to train with Cuban Soldiers to send around the country!" Metarha scoffed. "The only people you've given me are nothing more than farmers and little boys! I have to make them fear me to make them strong!"

"That little boy couldn't be more than ten, if that!" Spinello snapped glaring at her. "From what I heard, these people were in sweltering heat from the sun all morning with no rest or water! That little boy and the old man better live!" He started to leave and turned around. "Oh, the guerillas operating in this area wouldn't let your 'so-called' people in the country. They threatened Castrello. That's why Castrello pulled his soldiers. Change your tactics! I'm watching you!" he promised and stormed off.

"No one threatens me!" Metarha clutched the knife on her side, watching Spinello's bodyguard open the car door for him.

"We need Spinello for now," Teodoro cautioned watching them drive off. "He's our key to Chameleon."

"I don't need any man to get what I want!" Metarha glared at him.

"You heard Teodoro," Ramsey stated. "It seems they are plotting to steal Chameleon for themselves."

"Teodoro is a snake," Alonzo stated. "He drifts to the best money. He has no conscience or allegiance."

"Those two are no match for Spinello," Ramsey shared.

"Hiltree, follow Spinello's car and see where he's going," Sydney requested. "Then, we will see you at La Playita."

"Copy that," Hiltree replied. "We are on it."

Wednesday, July 1, 1400 (2:00 PM EST)
Under the Ocean just off the Cuban Coastline

"Sydney, we are seventy-five miles from the Cuban coast and holding steady at fifty-feet under the ocean," Yorg reported.

"Copy that," Sydney approved. "Let me know when you reach the destination."

"Understood," Yorg replied. "How are the other teams?"

"Making progress with their assignments," Sydney stated.

"Good to hear," Yorg agreed. "I'll talk to you soon," he cleared the line.

"I forgot how beautiful marine life under the ocean is," Kathe confessed. "I've never seen such an array of colorful coral reefs in my life. Look at those unusual fish!"

"Well, I'll be," Yorg chuckled, "who said God didn't have a sense of humor. There is a school of yellow, elephant fish."

"I can't believe it!" Kathe chucked. "They have the eyes, mouth, and trunk of an elephant, yet the body and size of a small fish."

"Joey and Alek would want those for our aquarium," Yorg grinned.

"JAKE shows that the bright orange and white-striped fish is a Clown Fish. The bright blue and black one with the neon-yellow tale is a Blue Tang."

"Coming out of that red reef is a Titan Triggerfish," Yorg pointed. "The fish following it is a Goliath Grouper. I heard they are delicious. Pete and I need to take a fishing trip here someday."

"Don't bring Heather," Kathe shared. "Once she saw the sharks circling above them, she would spoil the trip for you boys," Kathe admitted as an alarm on the EICAS panel signaled.

"We've got trouble," Yorg sighed pulling up the side camera. "It's another sub. We need a place to hide now!"

"Where would Cuba get a mini-sub?" Kathe asked looking around. "Look, to the right of me. Is that a manmade reef?"

"Whatever it is," Yorg sighed turning toward it. "It's better than being out in the open. Maybe we can find a place to hide."

"What in the world is this place?" Kathe asked as they entered under a large cement arch. "It's massive. Ahead is a life-sized angel mounted on a box?"

"There's a plaque on the box," Yorg noted maneuvering the sub around it. "It's not a box. It's a tomb for Sybil Anne McIntire, born Sept. 23, 1950, died, January 10, 2018."

"It's an odd place for a cemetery," Kathe admitted reading another plaque. "Mark J. Reed, born January 3, 1929, and died, January 2, 2016."

"Right now, it's a perfect place to hide," Yorg admitted moving toward a sizable lion-statue standing on a large tomb. "This lion should do," he said lowering the sub to the floor.

"How unique," Kathe smiled. "In this tomb rests the Lion family," she read and then glanced at the other sub on the monitor. "Could that be a Russian sub?"

"I'll get a better look after we're out of sight," Yorg sighed turning off the engines. "Now, it shouldn't be able to see us," he affirmed sealing the windows with black shields before checking the cameras. "It's not Russian," he noted zooming in on the sub. "I've never seen anything like it. It's almost as invisible as ours, sleek as a bullet. It looks fast. Look how quickly it turns. It's coming through the arch into the cemetery."

"I was afraid of that," Kathe admitted. "Do you see any markings?"

"No," Yorg affirmed. "One thing is for sure. The people didn't see us. Sydney's warning range is wider than that one."

"Is our sub armed?" Kathe wondered.

"Sydney and his father designed this sub, didn't they?" Yorg opened a panel to his left. "It carries small missiles, and, ah," he grinned as another alarm sounded. "Instead of torpedoes, we have a laser."

"Now, that's our Sydney!" Kathe smiled watching the camera above them.

"A ship above us dropped anchor," Yorg cautioned zooming in on it. "It is a fishing boat. Let me check the weather radar. Delilah is nearing the coastline."

"They are pulling the overhanging poles inside," Kathe stated. "The waves are massive. I guess that it didn't have time to make it to shore."

"That boat is the least of our worries," Yorg warned. "The people in the sub are looking for something. They are stopping at each plaque, and then going to the next one."

"You forgot to say in our direction," Kathe cautioned.

"We can't move," Yorg declared. "If I start the engines, it will generate air bubbles. They'll know exactly where we are. We have to pray it changes course."

"Please, tell me that you can fire the laser with the engines off?" Kathe asked.

"I hope so," Yorg stated as another light activated on the EICAS Panel. "The laser display shows it is on, and the one to the left of it lit up. It has a C on it," he leaned toward it. "It's marked Chameleon underneath that light."

"Activate it," Kathe requested. "We'll know in a minute if it works."

"The sub stopped right above us," Yorg warned holding his finger over the laser control. "I'm ready," Yorg stated staring at the monitor. "I don't recognize the two people aboard," he said snapping a picture of them.

"Chameleon worked!" Kathe exclaimed. "They are leaving! I still can't see any markings on the sub," she reached for the panel. "Let me change the angle of the camera."

"Stop right there!" Yorg requested zooming in on the back. "ESPGOTU420?" he snapped several pictures. "Evidentially, they just found what they wanted. Notice the flashes? They are taking several pictures."

"Yes, they are," Kathe agreed. "At least, the sub is leaving now," she sat back. "Well, we knew Eduardo Santo Prado was here. Now, we know they patrol the entire island and not concentrated in one area. We need to warn everybody to be very careful," she said sending Sydney a text.

"We'll just wait another few minutes to let them get far enough away from us before we continue," Yorg cautioned as Sydney replied to her text.

"Sydney is going to warn the other teams right now," Kathe relayed reading the text. "The idea of burying people under the ocean to make an artificial reef is perfect for the environment. According to JAKE, a company in Florida is testing them before going global."

"An innovated idea," Yorg admitted watching the screen. "Just like I thought that sub has speed. It's already out of our area," he confirmed starting the engines and rising even with the lion's head.

"There is another archway above a tomb that holds several family members, including the names of those that are still alive," Kathe read passing it. "Oh, no! That's what they were taking pictures of! I can't tell what it is for the sharks attacking it."

"I can remedy that," Yorg said pressing a button on the console. "I'm sending out sound waves that repel them."

"It's working," Kathe watched and then turned her head away. "Oh, my God!"

"Someone tied his arm to an angel statue," Yorg marveled circling it. "From the looks of what's left of him, he hasn't been here very long."

"Eduardo has problems with the villagers he shanghaied," Kathe declared. "By taking a picture of this corpse, it shows the other workers what happens to someone that crosses him."

"That's what it looks like," Yorg agreed turning south. "We lost some time with this delay. We need to get moving. Thank goodness this sub also has Stealth-like speed," he said clearing the cemetery and speeding up. "I'm sure glad Sydney updated his father's sub. Without this early warning detection, we could have been toast."

"Me too," Kathe admitted. "Sydney's thinking outside the box has saved us more than once."

"We're already approaching the coast of Matanzas, Cuba," Yorg affirmed. "Delilah shouldn't affect us by the time we get to the cove and locate the Yacht. It's time for you to suit up. Oh, and you're going to love the new convenience of the clear bubble helmets."

"I forgot about those," Kathe smiled. "The team wore the helmets when you rescued us in Miami."

"Yes," Yorg explained. "It hooks airtight into the wetsuit. The air from the tank hooks directly in it. There is a screen just about eye level, which links into Sydney's HUB for visuals. The best part is that you have the freedom to talk as you normally do."

"Excellent!" Kathe exclaimed maneuvering to the back of the sub. She located the button that slid the wall aside to the lockers. Kathe reached for her wetsuit as she looked around for the hatch. "Yorg, do you want me to prepare the hatch yet?" she asked changing into her wetsuit.

"Not yet," Yorg said checking the GPS. "We're almost to the area by the cove; wait until I change."

"That's fine," Kathe agreed securing her utility belt and checking her weapon. "I'm putting the drone in my front pouch. I'm ready except for my air tank and helmet," she reported, admiring the helmet. "You do realize this helmet revolutionizes communications in the field?"

"It sure does," Yorg agreed. "What else does Sydney have for us back there?"

"This sub has everything to sustain us for days," Kathe chuckled glancing at the food in the refrigerator. "I can't believe it even has bunks to sleep," she shared pulling one down on the opposite wall.

"Is there a bunk big enough for two?" Yorg asked as she joined him in the cockpit.

"Only if I'm on top," Kathe gleamed. "Although it might buckle from the weight. It's a small pull-down bunk."

"Sydney is single," Yorg remarked. "Why would he think of accommodating a married couple?"

"We're lucky Sydney designed it with bunks," Kathe defended. "He hardly sleeps. And besides, it's not a hotel; it's a mini-sub."

"James Bond always found a way," Yorg beamed winking at her.

"I know you well," Kathe grinned. "I'm sure you'll figure something out."

"You're safe for now," Yorg smiled stopping near some large rocks. "I think it is safe to park right here. It's deep enough no one can see us leave the sub," he confirmed dropping the anchor. "It has enough cover on shore for us to enter by the park where Will hid the drone. Stephen wants us to retrieve it," he said checking the GPS coordinates that Will gave him.

"There it is," Kathe noted pointing to the beacon. "It's straight out from us and to the left," contacting the HUB. "Syd, we are ready to leave the sub. We located the beacon for Stephen's drone and will pick it up."

"Copy that," Sydney acknowledged. "I need you to wait for a minute. My cousin just sent me a text, which reads 911. She found something and needs to talk."

"Copy that," Kathe answered. "We'll wait."

"Hello, Paris," Sydney greeted. "How's my booming artist?"

"Furious!" Paris exclaimed. "Are we on a secure line?"

"Of course," Sydney stated recording the conversation, and motioning for Ramsey to listen. "What's going on?"

"Dave, I think I found why my parents were murdered!" Paris exclaimed walking around the flat, holding a small camera and micro-CD.

"What did you find?" Sydney asked.

"Your father was right about the hierarchy of the Bureau behind their murders," Paris declared. "The landlord that owns the building my parents last rented in Wiltz is a fan of mine. I've known her for years. I told her I was interested in renting this flat the next time it came available. She said a man she deemed a recluse rented the flat as soon as the police released it. He's lived here ever since. He never associated with any of the other tenants. He would leave sporadically for about a week and return. He always paid his rent in cash. He bugged out last week without notice, left the key, and an envelope with the last month's rent in the door. There was a note saying he wouldn't be back. She gave me a call at my studio after she cleaned it. Yesterday, I finally finished moving into the flat."

"Did you rent the flat using your name?" Sydney asked.

"No, of course, I didn't!" Paris exclaimed. "I studied your father's books."

"Then, are you sure you're okay with this move?" Sydney asked.

"I sure am!" Paris confessed. "And get this, I found several bugs planted around the apartment and one outside my doorway. I remembered in your father's manual how to hack into them and distort the footage. Guess what else? It still has the original furniture. Last night was the first night I slept here. As I got ready for bed, I started having flashbacks. I remember watching my mother hollow out the back of the nightstand to hide something small and thin. It took me a while, but I found a mini-CD in the ridge separating the top from the back. Then, I remembered that mom put me to bed and said that daddy was working. In the middle of the night, I heard a loud noise from the next room. I wandered into the living room and found dad taking the desk apart. There were woodchips all over the floor. He apologized for waking me up. He carried me back to bed and kissed me goodnight. He promised to take me for ice cream the next day after he finished. It took me a few hours, but I found a small camera hidden in a secret compartment. I put the mini-CD inside and turned it on. The only thing that comes up is weird symbols. Uncle David once told me that he and my dad used the same code. So, if anything happened to one of them, the other one would know."

"Dad never mentioned that to me!" Sydney exclaimed. "That's why the Bureau threatened to fire him if he went back to Wiltz!"

"You were away at college when he told me," Paris admitted. "Uncle David once showed me where he hid the key in his study. I'm going to call the airport and head straight to you. I'll see you soon."

"Paris, don't call the airport and stay there!" Sydney cautioned. "I have two agents near you and can be there in less than an hour. Have you secured the flat?"

"Yes, you know me," Paris declared. "No one is getting in here. I changed all the locks and added more. I still have the Walther P38 Uncle David taught me how to shoot. I practice every time I get a chance."

"That's my girl," Sydney stated. "I'm sure you're able to take care of yourself. However, I still want my agents to help you. I'll get them into the building without being seen. Only open the door when I call you. They'll be standing outside your door. I don't want them to knock for fear of waking your neighbors."

"There is a security camera by the street door," Paris warned. "I left it on purpose and rerouted the footage to my phone. That way, I could keep an eye on people coming into the building."

"I've already borrowed a satellite in that area and scanned the building," Sydney confessed. "There are bugs that are hot pointing toward each stairwell. I see you did distort the ones inside the flat and in the hallway by your door. So, we can assume that someone has seen you climbing the stairs. I'll handle the bugs. Be ready to leave."

"I can't believe I missed them," Paris frowned. "But they don't know my identity. I always entered wearing a wide, brim hat and kept my head down. I'll see you soon; love you!"

"I love you, too," Sydney said clearing the line.

"CC and Sam are almost there," Ramsey confirmed.

"After all these years, maybe we can get to the bottom of our family's nightmare," Sydney sighed. "Hopefully, this will finally bring closure to Paris. Let's get back to Kathe and Yorg."

"Kathe, Yorg, we're back online with you," Sydney stated. "Before you leave the sub, in the last locker is a small, dog-like robot. I designed it to carry small equipment on land or underwater. I'm downloading a program on JAKE to move it like you do the mosquito-drone. There is an icon of a dog's face on JAKE's screen. I've programmed the dog to help you locate a safe area for emerging on land. All you have to do is follow it."

"When did you have time to finish working on Chameleon and build a robot?" Ramsey asked glancing at him.

"Dad started working on the robot years ago," Sydney admitted. "I tinkered with it for years on my R & R's."

"Am I glad," Kathe admitted reaching for the dog. "I was worried how to bring the iPads onshore," she said putting them inside and following Yorg to the hatch. "I'll exit the sub first with the robot," Kathe winked and kissed Yorg.

"Be careful," Yorg attached her helmet. "I'll be out in a minute," he said securing the hatch before opening the valve.

"She's out," Yorg reported as the water receded. "I'm leaving now."

"Copy that," Sydney approved. "I'll talk to you topside."

"I'm showing quite a few people in the park," Sydney relayed as they rose to the surface. "Luckily, no one is near the wall where you are surfacing. I'm not detecting any monitors or cameras on either side of the seawall," he said watching them hide the robot and their gear in some reeds. "I have the GPS coordinates of your gear and the robot. When you finish, the robot will take you back to the sub."

"Copy that," Kathe answered taking off her wetsuit. "I brought hats and sunglasses to hide our faces. And a small backpack for the drone and iPads."

"Copy that," Ramsey answered watching them climb over the fence. "Try to make it to the yacht first. I don't want to lose Vinnie and Tito."

"The cove is to the right of you," Sydney affirmed widening the perimeters. "Head for the dense trees and stay in them as much as possible. The fewer people that see you, the better."

"Copy that," Yorg agreed hurrying across a path into the trees.

"You have a clear shot to the cove," Sydney confirmed. "When you pass the next playground, you're free from the crowd to the yacht basin. You should lift the drone from there."

"Copy that," Yorg agreed. "We are almost to the edge of the trees."

"I'm showing the middle of the dock is straight in front of you," Sydney relayed.

"Copy that," Yorg stated peering around a tree. "We have a visual on the yacht basin."

"Let's get this bird in the air and find our targets," Kathe stated unloading the backpack and handing the drone to Yorg.

"Stand back," Yorg requested placing the drone on the ground and activating it with his iPad. "We'll have a clear view once the drone clears the trees."

"There are quite a few yachts here," Kathe declared watching the camera on her iPad. "Yorg, bring the drone down closer to the boats. I need to locate El Amoré del Sol."

"We must be getting close," Yorg acknowledged near several of the last yachts. "Sydney, I can barely keep the drone in the air."

"Something is draining its power quickly," Sydney confirmed scanning the area. "The source is coming from the fourth yacht on the left," he noted freeing the drone. "You're clear. Don't worry about power loss. I boosted the power supply."

"It's the El Amoré del Sol," Kathe declared zooming in on the back. "Yorg, skim the windows starting on the main deck for our targets."

"I'll snap pictures of everyone inside," Sydney relayed. "Gen. Medina and the captain with his crew are the only men on the boat."

"Where's Estevo?" Ramsey asked.

"Estevo is back at the hotel in Varadero," Sydney stated checking his GPS. "He could have Vinnie and Tito with him," he said as an alarm sounded on his computer. "Be careful, you two," Sydney warned widening the perimeter. "I note two people walking past the last playground on the path toward the dock very close to you."

"Kathe, check it out," Yorg requested turning the drone.

"It's Vinnie and Tito," Kathe proclaimed. "They are returning to the yacht. Vinnie has something in his hand."

"It's a map of La Playita," Sydney affirmed zooming in on it. "The small island off the coast circled is La Rosa. It has a population of 98."

"Perfect like Deerfeld," Ramsey groaned. "We've got to warn those people."

"If we do that, we will announce our presence," Kathe warned.

"We have no choice," Ramsey admitted. "We can't let them do the same thing to these poor villagers that they did in the Alps."

"That's for sure," Sydney agreed. "But we don't want to tip our hand just yet. We will have to find another way."

"We've got a few hours to decide what to do," Kathe declared. "The crew is busy getting ready to leave."

"Kathe, Yorg, grab Will's drone and then head to Varadero," Ramsey requested. "Estevo returned to that blocked hotel room. Someone important must be there. We need to know who it is. Sydney hacked into the hotel registry and checked that room. It lists as empty for several days prior, during, and after the last time Estevo was there, as well as now."

"Copy that," Yorg replied hurrying through the trees. "We're heading to the drone now."

"I figured out what to do about the people on the island and keep our anonymity," Sydney grinned bringing up a saved page from the Internet.

"Our military at Guantanamo suspects that Presidente Castrello sends Gen. Medina into villages to force healthy men and older boys into trucks. Their family never sees them again. Spinello confirmed that suspicion when he visited Metarha and Teodoro. We need to find out what they are doing with the villagers. I have a feeling it has something to do with what we're after. Since the yacht is on course to the island, a nice accident could take out three terrorists."

"And we know the perfect two people for the job," Kathe beamed. "It won't bring the people back in the Alps, but it is poetic justice."

"I like the way you're thinking," Ramsey smiled and nodded to Sydney. "This is one loose end we can't afford to overlook."

"And they are excellent when it comes to making it look like an accident," Kathe agreed.

"I'll stay with you until you reach the robot," Sydney explained. "The robot can easily take you back to the sub. Contact me when you get close to Varadero. I have a little surprise to show you how to park the sub."

"Copy that," Yorg said reaching for the drone. "I have Will's drone. See you in Varadero."

Wednesday, July 1, 1600 (4:00 PM EST)
Off the Coast of Varadero near Primera Estrella del Mar Hotel

"Sydney, we are nearing the coast of Varadero," Yorg reported. "We had a rough trip playing hide-and-seek with several of the ESPGOTU mini-subs."

"Copy that," Sydney affirmed pulling up the satellite and zeroing in on the hotel. "I'm showing quite a few swimmers and sunbathers along the coast. There is a small presence of armed guards. You have a better chance to emerge from the south end of the beach. They chose this hotel because thick vegetation surrounds it, which makes it easy to escape," he said checking the depth of the water. "The water is deep near the shore with tall reeds for you to emerge without being seen. I noticed that you've already used Chameleon to hide from the patrols. With Chameleon activated, you can leave and return to the sub. The robot and JAKE can activate the opening port as you approach. The holograms in Ponce Inlet worked the same way. As you noticed, dad originally designed the lockout trunk for two adults and two children. After installing Chameleon, I upgraded the computer for a quick entrance and getaway."

“Syd, you took my concepts to a whole new level,” Yorg confirmed as a warning sounded. “We’ve got company. I activated Chameleon. Give me a minute,” he said maneuvering around the approaching mini-sub. “Multiple subs are patrolling the area.”

“As well as multiple patrol boat topside,” Sydney reported. “I sent you an Aerial picture of them and the hotel.”

“I see what you mean about the patrol boats,” Kathe replied.

“Someone in that hotel wants to stay anonymous,” Ramsey concluded.

“Behind the hotel on the right is another building,” Sydney continued. “That is the service building for the hotel,” he noted zooming in on it. “The main laundry and kitchen are located there. Thick trees around the building hide the building from the guests. On the right side of the trees is a small clearing where guests walk down to the private beach. As you can see, only a few very scantily clad adults use this beach.”

“I see that,” Yorg grinned zooming in on a couple. “They’re preoccupied so that we can sneak past them easily.”

“Good eye,” Kathe grinned swatting Yorg.

Sydney cleared his throat. “Notice on the right side of the private beach, the vegetation goes out into the water, with several large boulders extending into the water. That should hide you from the people on the beach when you emerge. Have the robot hide your gear onshore in the vegetation by the first boulder while you swim to the beach. When out of the guest’s site, have the robot bring you the drone. Then, hurry to the far-side of the service building, where you can launch the drone. That’s where Stephen’s drone picked up Estevo.”

“Sydney, where do the employees’ access that building?” Kathe asked.

“That’s a good question,” Sydney zoomed out. “Give me a minute,” he zoomed in and scanned the area. “Did you see something shiny under the palm tree branches? Let me back up the footage. Yes, the wind blew a palm branch, and I caught a glimpse of a shiny object,” he rescanned the area. “On the far-left side of the main building, nestled between the two buildings is a glass hallway camouflaged by trees, plants, and a net.”

“Much like we found in the Aquarium,” Ramsey admitted. “It’s a good way to smuggle someone in and out of the hotel. The trees and net overhang the roof make it virtually undetectable to spot from the air.”

"That explains how Estevo disappears inside the hotel," Kathe surmised. "Stephen said they were watching with the drone, and suddenly Estevo was walking on the beach with Vinnie and Tito."

"If we're correct, the drone will prove it as soon as it flies near the hallway," Ramsey surmised.

"Correct," Sydney agreed. "I'm also noting that there are guards in the trees and at the end of that beach."

"Copy that," Yorg confirmed slowly turning the sub toward the south. "This is the most concentrated area for the subs. That confirms we are on the right path."

"By keeping Chameleon engaged, it will change shapes to match the terrain," Sydney explained. "The hostile subs won't be able to detect you."

"Copy that," Yorg answered. "It works fantastic. I just maneuvered around two subs and made it to the south-end," Yorg confirmed stopping the sub between the two large boulders Sydney suggested. "Kathe and I will suit up and talk to you topside."

"Copy that," Sydney stated. "I'll help you when you get onshore."

A few minutes later, Kathe exited the sub with the robot and turned around in time to see Yorg emerge from out of a rock. "Yorg," she pointed behind him. "The sub appears to be in the shape of a boulder in the middle of the other two. It was weird watching you emerge from a solid-looking object."

Yorg quickly joined her. "Sydney is Karl Raini on steroids! Let's get topside," he said following the robot.

"The coast is clear," Sydney advised watching them emerge beside the first boulder. "Just try not to let too many people get a look at your faces."

"I have an idea," Kathe gleamed whispering to Yorg as they took off their gear. "JAKE is placing the robot next to our gear in the reeds and turning on the beacon."

"I'm receiving the beacon signal now," Sydney concurred. "You're clear to swim to the beach. There's only one other couple in the water," he reported watching them swim around the last boulder. "You're looking good," Sydney coaxed watching them approach the shore, splashing water at each other.

"It's unusual having married operatives," Ramsey declared watching them stand up in waist-high water as Yorg playfully pulled Kathe under a massive wave with him. "I guess this is the idea she muted from us,"

Ramsey noted as the water receded, and Yorg pulled Kathe into him and then kissed her.

"I realized when Yorg trained Kathe at my house that they had chemistry," Sydney confessed watching Kathe shove Yorg into an incoming wave before running to shore.

"I can't believe Kathe fell for Sherrod," Ramsey admitted watching Yorg jump up and run after her. "Turn the sound up."

"I can't believe you did that!" Yorg shouted running behind Kathe and whisking her in his arms.

"Why?" Kathe laughed and kissed him. "You know that I always get even with you," she kissed him again as Yorg walked past the other people toward the path.

"Kathe, your idea worked!" Ramsey declared. "You made it difficult for people to get a clear look at your faces."

"Now, just walk up the path toward the hotel," Sydney requested. "At the beginning of the clearing on the left side, some of the guests are just setting up volleyball. You'll have to enter the trees on your right and retrieve the drone from the robot. Then, launch it somewhere behind the service building. I'll scan the area for more guards."

"Copy that," Kathe replied retrieving the drone and iPads. "Let's go," she said hurrying toward the building.

"Hold your position," Sydney cautioned checking around them. "I'm showing you've got a guard in the trees 250 yards in front of you. Turn to the right toward the building for about another 200 yards, and you'll be able to launch the drone safely."

"Copy that," Kathe answered leading the way.

"This spot will do," Yorg decided. "We can hide behind this large rock. It has tall, thick plants around the trees behind it if we need to bail for cover."

"Looks perfect to me," Kathe agreed reaching for JAKE. "Are you ready to launch your drone?"

"I'm glad JAKE is waterproof," Yorg grinned setting his drone on a large rock. "You put it in the right spot."

"I'm glad you noticed," Kathe beamed. "It was safe there."

"I'm sure it was," Yorg smiled.

"Okay, you two," Ramsey cleared her throat. "Let's focus on work."

"Oops, busted," Yorg grinned moving Kathe's bangs out of her eyes. "I guess I better keep my eyes peeled for the guards."

"I think that would be a good idea with the fire-power they're carrying," Ramsey declared.

"JAKE, warn me if a human life-form approaches," Kathe requested.

"Kathe, the system is activated," JAKE replied.

"I'm launching the mosquito now," Kathe stated as it rose above the trees. "Where to first?"

"I want a better look at the glass hallway," Sydney requested.

"Why would they use glass instead of solid walls?" Ramsey wondered as Kathe hovered the mosquito over the roof. "It's the same scenario as under the Aquarium in Miami."

"That's because Carlos is the sole designer for his father," Kathe shared zooming the camera inside. "It's a busy place. There are people constantly coming and going."

"I see that," Ramsey noted. "Are there any emergency exits in the middle of the hallway?"

"Sydney, I can't lower the drone any closer, and the battery is beginning to drain," Kathe warned.

"I see that," Sydney answered typing on his computer, and pressing enter. "Try it now. Let's see if I matched the frequency as I boosted the battery."

"It's working again," Kathe reported skimming the entire hallway. "The only way in and out is through the doors of the two connecting buildings. As you can see, there is a constant stream of housekeepers and room service personnel. Wait a minute; what is that?" Kathe questioned zooming in on something entering from the hotel side.

"It's too big for room service cart," Ramsey noted. "It looks like a metal wardrobe box. Get the name of the porter, and then circle above the box."

"The name on his tag is José," Kathe read moving the mosquito.

"That could be an air tank on the back," Yorg noted watching from his iPad. "Sydney, what's inside it?"

"I'm trying to see," Sydney declared. "I can't penetrate it," he said watching the box enter the laundry section.

"Something lead-lined that size would be impossible for one person to push," Ramsey affirmed. "José wasn't breaking a sweat."

"I read that our military is working on a paint that could do it," Sydney confirmed. "But it's only in the developmental stages. Kathe, go over to the other side of the building. I took a picture earlier, and it may have a doorway to the outside."

"Copy that," Kathe complied.

"There's a yacht close to shore," Kathe noticed flying the mosquito over the building.

"I saw that," Sydney agreed. "Yorg, activate your drone and check on it."

"Copy that," Yorg complied.

"I don't see a door," Kathe moved the mosquito closer. "Wait a minute. A hidden door is opening with armed guards coming out."

"Let's see who's inside?" Ramsey requested.

"Copy that," Kathe replied moving the mosquito over them.

"Well, I'll be," Sydney chuckled. "Philippi Spinello has surfaced a second time. The other man has his back to the camera," he said snapping a picture of his back profile.

"Well-groomed, straight, black hair," Ramsey noted. "There's an unusual half-moon-shaped birthmark on the left side of his neck under his ear. He's roughly about 5-foot-9 and 170 lbs."

"He's wearing a wig," Sydney scanned his body. "It's synthetic. That's why it's perfect. Kathe, something solid, is on his face and hands. Move the drone to show his face."

"Do you believe this?" Kathe sighed. "He has a black, mesh-looking veil over his face and hands," she noted zooming in on the mesh veil. "I can't see through it, can you?"

"Negative," Sydney affirmed.

"It has to be Eduardo," Ramsey surmised turning up the volume.

"The veil seems to distort his voice, also," Sydney noticed typing on his computer. "This should fix that," he said pushing enter.

"What are you doing about the slaves rebelling?" the veiled man demanded. "Castrello called me again. The ones that escaped are leading a revolt against his regime. It's spread throughout Cuba. Some of his guards joined the rebellion. He's threatening to throw our operation out of Cuba."

"I assure you that I have solved that problem," Spinello grinned holding up a picture. "The guards recaptured Diego, the leader of the rebellion, after a month of searching for him. He was by the river with one of his daughters. After two days, one of my men wounded Diego trying to escape again. I had them take Diego to that underwater cemetery and let the sharks finish him. Then, I had the guards go back a few hours later to take pictures. His body was half-eaten. They are posting these pictures around the camp and in the villages nearby. That should curtail anyone else thinking about escaping."

“I hope for your sake, it works!” the veiled man snapped. “You assured me that your men could eliminate the targets in the United States and failed miserably.”

“Your soldiers were there as well!” Spinello defended.

“You asked for my soldiers to help you,” the veiled man reminded, “you said you needed them since the Feds are on to you. None of them returned! Not even Montez! He’s been my trusted lieutenant for years! We have too much at stake for them to find us! And with their perseverance, make no mistake; they will come!”

“I’ve double the guards watching this entire island for that reason,” Spinello explained. “When they come, we will find them.”

“You’ve underestimated them from the beginning!” the man bellowed. “The way they are stopping you so easily at all our locations, proves they must have a satellite. My people are searching for it.”

“When they come, we’ll not only eliminate Tierney and DiMeglio, but capture Vuslick to finish the formula with Macaby,” Spinello promised.

“Because of your failure, I’m sending Estevo to help get the island ready for Bencivenni!” the veiled man admitted. “I want you to get rid of Metarha. You brought her here without telling me. My source said that after you left this afternoon, she had Teodoro kill those two villagers because you threatened her.”

“I chose to bring Metarha here because she trained some of the best terrorists in the Middle East,” Spinello declared. “I also thought we could use her to smuggle our people in strategic places. She did that all over the United States for years, right under Homeland Securities noses. We need her to help secretly move Bencivenni’s men around the world.”

“We don’t need her!” the veiled man insisted. “It’s impossible for you to harness her wrath! She’s a sadistic killer! I haven’t had any problem placing our people so far!”

“But the operation is getting too complicated for us to be spread so thin,” Spinello warned. “Bencivenni had to terminate one of the latest replacements last week. Luckily, Bencivenni found a dead ringer for him, and it didn’t take too much surgery.”

“Metarha has one week to prove herself or else!” the veiled man threatened.

“Then, I’ll see you in one week,” Spinello agreed leaving with the guards.

"Ah, ha," Ramsey smiled. "So, it's beginning. There are too many key players with ideas of how this operation should work. Yorg, keep an eye on Spinello."

"The yacht launched a small craft to pick Spinello up," Yorg reported showing them.

"Did you get the name of the yacht?" Ramsey requested.

"I tried while you listened to Spinello talk," Yorg cautioned. "The drone is getting sluggish."

"Try now," Sydney pressed enter and looked at the screen.

"Kathe, a human life-form is approaching," JAKE warned.

"Yorg, Kathe, duck down!" Sydney warned. "You have a guard coming toward you. Yorg, I'll hover the drone for you."

"This way," Yorg said pulling Kathe into tall, thick bushes behind the large rock.

"Something is," Kathe gasped.

"Kathe, quiet!" Sydney warned. "The guard heard you," he zoomed in on JAKE's camera. "It's not poisonous. It's just a Boa. The guard is edging around the rock on the left side."

"Yorg, throw the Boa over the rock!" Ramsey ordered. "He'll think it fell out of a tree."

Yorg grabbed the snake and threw it.

"It worked," Ramsey chuckled. "The Boa dropped by his feet, and he's running away. You're clear to proceed."

"The guard wasn't the only one that was almost long gone," Kathe whispered. "That was one, big snake!"

"Sydney, where's Spinello?" Ramsey asked.

"He just got on board the yacht," Sydney said taking a picture of the stern. "The name is Dragón del Mar with ESPGOTU005. I put a tracer on it."

"That translates into Dragon of the Sea," Ramsey stated. "That could be Eduardo's yacht."

"Kathe, take your drone back to the glass hallway," Sydney requested. "I want to see if the metal box goes back to the room. Yorg, hover your drone over the yacht. It's not leaving yet."

"The same porter pushed the box into the hotel entrance from the hallway," Ramsey noted. "Kathe, see if you can get inside the hotel and head to the eighth floor. It must be Eduardo. Maybe, he'll take the mask off inside the room. I want to see his face."

"Copy that," Kathe said flying the mosquito over the building, hovering it over the entrance.

"A car is under the covered entrance," Ramsey noted. "A porter just finished placing the luggage on the rack and is going inside."

"It's entering with that porter," Kathe said following behind the porter. "It's in the hotel and the elevator. He's getting off on the second-floor instead of the eighth."

"Give me a minute while I activate the button for the eighth floor," Sydney relayed.

"Thanks, it's on the way up," Kathe grinned as the elevator stopped and the door opened. "Something is draining my battery."

"That's because the hallway is heavily blocked," Sydney noted typing quickly, and pressing enter. "Try it now."

"The drone is working again," Kathe reported. "And the battery is recharging," she said as the mosquito got off on the eighth floor. "The metal box is exiting the service elevator," she showed as it passed the drone in the hallway. "We're entering room #809."

"Estevo Vazquez is sitting on the couch," Ramsey identified as Kathe landed the drone on a picture facing the front of the box. "Sydney, get a facial scan of the porter."

"I'm going to have my Capitán take you to join, Gen. Medina on El Amoré del Sol," the veiled man said exiting the box. "I want that island cleared immediately. I don't trust the two that you brought in to do the work. Bencivenni will be ready to have the replacements inhabit it in about a week."

"Pero (But), Vinnie, and Tito did that for Sr. Spinello before," Estevo proclaimed. "That is why I brought them here."

"I trust only you," the veiled man affirmed. "Medina works directly under Castrello. He reported to Castrello that we have problems controlling the villagers. The closer we get to our goal, the more I worry about our partners, especially Spinello. He's beginning to make decisions on his own," he admitted checking a text. "The boat is close. You need to get downstairs. José will take you. Text me when you finish."

"Yes, Sir," Estevo answered standing up.

"Kathe, leave the drone in the room," Sydney requested. "We know where Estevo is going."

"Here comes our rat," Ramsey declared a few minutes later. "José is through the tunnel. The guards are escorting Estevo out to another rubber raft. Yorg, see if that yacht is El Amoré del Sol."

"Copy that," Yorg replied flying his drone to the Yacht. "Sydney, my drone is getting sluggish."

"Got it," Sydney stated watching the drone hover over the stern.

"Yes, it is," Ramsey read. "And it's complete with Gen. Medina, Tito, and Vinnie waiting for him."

"How nice," Yorg commented. "They are having cocktails on the way to a massacre."

"I guess they need it for the courage to kill innocent people," Kathe murmured.

"That kind always does," Ramsey agreed. "Let me check on Alonzo and Pauli. I don't want them late for the party," she said stepping away from the desk.

Wednesday, July 1, 1930 (7:30 PM EST)
Near Tejas, a Small Island Off the Coast
Between Nuevitas and La Playita

"Ramsey, I was about to call you," Alonzo reported. "We're approaching the coordinates of El Amoré del Sol. Pauli located it with our drone and is almost to it. We are ready for Sydney to work his magic."

"Copy that," Ramsey answered. "They are ready for you to take over the drone," Ramsey told Sydney as he brought up the camera.

"Pauli, you're in perfect position," Sydney agreed studying the area. "Pauli, work the camera, and I'll take over the flight," he said connecting to the drone and flying it over the deck. "They are studying the map of Tejas. Let's listen for a minute," he said turning up the audio.

"We go in teams," Estevo announced. "Tito and I will take the south end of the village. Vinnie, and Gen. Medina will take the north end."

"Wait a minute," Tito looked at him. "Vinnie and I work together. No one said anything about splitting us up."

"How can I put this," Estevo hesitated. "Our boss is very suspicious of contracting outsiders. He wants us to execute this plan or nothing," Estevo warned as Gen. Medina pulled out his weapon.

"Are you going to follow orders, or not?" Medina asked raising his gun toward Tito.

"Gentlemen," Vinnie said holding up his hands. "I'm sure your mystery boss needed our help, or he wouldn't have brought us to Cuba. We contracted a job to eradicate Tejas's people and get it ready for habitation, nothing else. Philippi Spinello highly recommended us. He has used our services several times."

"I assure you the only reason you are here is Spinello's recommendation," Estevo declared. "Pero (But) only after our boss checked you out. He contracted you to kill, not torture, and rape the women."

"What?" Tito exclaimed.

"Didn't you think our boss would check you out?" Estevo questioned. "There was a different police report than the one you so-called arranged. We can't afford any bad publicity. Presidente Castrello has already warned us. There are rumors of a coup forming against him."

"That's the first we've ever heard of any of that!" Tito defended. "Where did your mystery boss get that report?"

"It was from an anonymous source," Estevo admitted. "That is why the operation in the Alps will shut down soon and reopen in Cuba?"

"We weren't privileged to any information about the operation," Tito confessed. "After we finished our job, they paid us in cash, and we left."

"Alonzo, I see Estevo took the bait you planted," Sydney congratulated.

"We produced the second police report to deter anybody from hiring them again," Alonzo admitted. "These two are only hired assassins. Spinello gave them free rein and didn't care how they got the job done."

"They are a disgrace to our profession," Pauli confided. "We are businessmen now. It's not liked the old days when we had to 'go to the mattresses.'"

"We've all evolved," Ramsey confirmed. "Notice how Estevo never mentions the boss's name. I'm beginning to believe that no one who works for him knows his name, nor has seen his face."

"That's how their boss keeps his anonymity," Alonzo admitted. "We're anxious to bring Vinnie and Tito to justice for the murders in the Alps. Let's do this."

"I agree," Sydney proclaimed. "Don't let them get too close to the island. It needs to look like pirates at sea," Sydney cautioned flying the drone down the stairs, locating the engine room. "It's a fail-secure locking device, which means it stays locked even when power is lost. Except, when I do this," Sydney smiled typing commands, and pushing enter. "I wonder when Saphirstein invented these locks if he realized someone like me could modify the 15-30 second fire code on the crash bar."

"What did you do?" Pauli asked watching from his iPad.

"It's a trade secret," Sydney grinned as the drone located the three-phase AC power system. Sydney quickly typed commands on this computer and then pressed enter. "That should do it," he grinned as the boat came to a sudden halt. "That jolt is my cue to get the drone out of here."

"You've got company," Pauli warned. "The First Mate and two crew members are on the way down."

"Thanks, I'll keep the drone close to the ceiling by the steps," Sydney replied. "They ran underneath it and went inside. I'm permanently locking the crew inside," he pressed enter. "The drone is up the steps and hovering over Estevo and his friends. Sorry, I just rained on your parade!" Sydney chuckled. "Alonzo, wait about 20 minutes before you pull alongside. I also disabled the communication and radar devices. They're dead in the water-no pun intended. There are no towers out here for their cell phones to connect. They'll welcome you aboard."

"Hiltree is waiting to pick you up," Ramsey added. "He knows what to do."

Twenty minutes later, Mikey pulled his fishing boat alongside El Amoré del Sol. "Ahoy there. We were fishing and noticed your vessel stopped abruptly. It took us a while to bring up our nets to check on you. Are you all, right?"

"Negative," Gen. Medina replied signaling the other three men on deck to go inside. "The Yacht suddenly lost power. The crew went to check and got locked inside the engine room. Our communication system also went down. There is no cell coverage out here."

"Today is your lucky day," Mikey grinned. "I work at a yacht basin in Miami on engines. Permission to come aboard."

"Yes, permission granted," Gen. Medina replied. "Please, come aboard."

"Let me grab my tools," Mikey replied climbing down from the cabin to the main deck, reaching under a seat on the side. "I never go anywhere without my toolbox," he grinned boarding their vessel. "Which way to your engine room?"

"It's down these stairs," Medina pointed. "You may go first. I'll follow you down to the engine room."

"We're saved!" The First Officer and crew screamed, looking through a small window on the door.

"I'll have you out in a second," Mikey smiled giving them thumbs up. "Pretty impressive, it's an electromagnetic fail-secure lock. I'm going to need my meter," he said sitting the toolbox down and opening the lid. "These new locks require a special meter to switch it to open manually."

"What was that noise?" Medina demanded reaching for his pistol. "Something is going on upstairs! Stand up! Who are you?"

"The Calvary," Mikey grinned shooting Medina through the lid of his toolbox with his Glock. "I'm someone that doesn't approve of the reason you're going to Tejas," he stated standing over him. "How much are they paying you to kill your villagers?"

"Do you know who I am?" Medina screamed rolling in pain.

"Of course, I do," Mikey laughed bending next to him. "And I'm the man right now that has power over your life. Tell me who the man in the mesh veil is, and I'll let you live."

"You're a dead man," Medina scoffed.

"No, you are!" Mikey exclaimed standing up shooting Medina. He turned to the crew watching through the window. "Sorry, something fried the electronics. The lock can't be opened," he laughed hurrying up the stairs.

"Mikey, what happened below?" Alonzo asked holding his gun at Estevo, Vinnie, and Tito.

"Medina contracted a bad case of lead poisoning," Mikey admitted. "By the look of their bloody faces, I see you caught them off guard."

"You know I like the element of surprise," Alonzo chuckled taking off a black mask.

"Alonzo DiMeglio!" Tito gasped. "I thought Dano . . ."

"Shut up, Tito!" Vinnie snapped.

"Was going to take me down after Luca Donatelli?" Alonzo questioned. "I guess it's true; you can't believe everything you hear."

"Or, see for that matter," Pauli chuckled. "A few days ago, we ran into your old boss, Geraldo Carbone. Another dead man that turned up in Deerfeld, Virginia. He called himself Rev. Woods. Don't worry, he's not a preacher anymore, and he's not coming back this time. Now, here we are standing in front of the two of you."

"We surely are blessed," Alonzo agreed. "Who would have thought that Bencivenni would do us a favor? Of all the people to bring back to life, so to say, the two people we missed in the Alps."

"You know about that!" Tito gasped.

"Shut up, Tito!" Vinnie exclaimed. "He knows nothing."

"Estevo, it seems that you need to watch the company you keep," Alonzo cautioned. "And I don't mean just these two animals. Who is the man wearing the mesh veil? You know the one you were with at the Primera Estrella del Mar Hotel today."

"I don't know who he is!" Estevo smirked. "No one knows his name."

"For some reason, I don't believe you," Alonzo stated signaling Mikey.

Mikey reached in his toolbox, taking out a needle and a vial. He inserted the needle into the vile, drawing 20 ccs of fluid. "This should help Estevo with his memory," Mikey tapped the air bubble out and then squeezed it until the liquid started to leak.

"What is that?" Estevo begged as Pauli grabbed him from behind.

"Something that you'll never remember," Mikey smiled injecting the needle into the side of his neck. Estevo fell unconscious to the ground.

"Now, for you two," Alonzo promised. "We promised eight little children that we would find who murdered their parents and friends. We're going to take our time and enjoy this," he said pulling brass knuckles out of his pocket. "Pauli, are you ready to dance?"

"I sure am," Pauli smiled reaching in his pocket.

An hour later, Alonzo came out of the bathroom refreshed. "Pauli, I think that was poetic justice."

"Isn't it funny," Pauli chuckled wiping his face with a dishtowel from the kitchen. "They could dish it out to others, but they couldn't take it themselves."

"That kind never does," Mikey admitted. "They are the first ones to beg for mercy and the last ones to give it. This life raft with the name on it is perfect for Estevo to cling to when we drop him off," he tossed it into his boat.

"Hiltree, we're ready for pick up," Alonzo reported.

"Copy that," Hiltree stated. "My ETA is five minutes."

"That gives us enough time to carry Estevo to your boat," Pauli said helping Mikey. "You cross over first and pull him across. We'll drag him downstairs to give him more bumps and bruises."

"You know where to dump Estevo after you interrogate him," Alonzo reminded as the Huey hovered above them. "We'll see you in La Playita," he said as Hiltree lowered the cable.

"I'll be there," Mikey agreed as Pauli hooked Alonzo to the cable.

"Welcome aboard," Hiltree greeted handing Alonzo a helmet.

"Well, I'll be," Alonzo chuckled. "How did you get Yorg's Huey here?"

“I flew it in on a C-130 Hercules,” Hiltree grinned. “Sydney figured we might need it. We can’t use one of our military choppers on this mission. It looks nostalgic but has state of the art technology.”

“I know,” Alonzo adjusted the mic on his helmet. “I watched Sydney land it from a ship like a video game.”

“I wish I could have seen that!” Hiltree exclaimed lowering the cable. “I trust all went well?”

“Yes, all targets acquired,” Alonzo reported. “Mikey is going to interrogate Estevo. Sydney showed him the precise place to dump Estevo overboard in a couple of days. Sydney said the tide would take him to shore. It will look like he washed up from the accident. Mikey took a life raft off the boat for Estevo to cling to on his journey.”

“Hiltree, you missed a good fight,” Pauli chuckled climbing into the Huey.

“I’m sure I’ll have my chance,” Hiltree admitted. “Did you find out who the man wearing the veil is?”

“Negative,” Pauli answered. “If they knew it, they took it to the grave with them.”

“Mikey is far enough away for us to do this,” Hiltree declared checking the radar. “Not a vessel in sight.”

“Which means no witnesses,” Pauli laughed.

“Then, it is time for the barbeque,” Alonzo chuckled.

“Yorg’s new helmet has a telescopic drop-down lens,” Hiltree relayed. “We need to get far away from the drifting ship. By using a laser,” he dropped the lens down, “it won’t leave any traces to show why it exploded. All I have to do is look toward the target and fire.”

“Perfect aim!” Alonzo congratulated. “I can’t believe how accurate a laser weapon is! You shot from this far away, hitting the mark!”

“Not like the old days,” Pauli agreed. “We’d have to gas it down or use dynamite.”

“I didn’t hear that last statement,” Hiltree chuckled. “By the way, none of us were here. My men don’t know about this. I don’t want to get court-marshaled for medaling in Cuban politics.”

“We’re not medaling,” Alonzo chuckled. “We just gave Castrello a black eye. He already told Eduardo he regrets allowing him in the country.”

“Perfect,” Hiltree grinned. “Next stop is La Playita.”

Thursday, July 2, 0400 (4:00 AM GMT + 2) 5 hours ahead of US

Wiltz, Luxembourg

Ramsey handed Sydney a cup of coffee, "What are you doing?"

"I hacked into Luxembourg's satellite and pointed it toward the apartment building," Sydney showed her. "Sam and CC are entering the building. Let me switch to the security camera and help them inside," he said typing commands on his computer. "CC, open the door as soon as you hear the buzzer."

"Thanks, Sydney," CC said hurrying up the stairs behind Sam to the third floor.

"Paris, my agents are outside your door," Sydney declared watching from the hallway camera across from her door.

"Great!" Paris exclaimed opening the door. "I'm ready to leave."

"Paris Sydney, I'm Security Agent, CC Sims for Alby Airlines," she introduced showing her badge.

"I'm Security Agent, Sam Biggs of Alby Airlines," he introduced. "We need to leave now."

"Change of plans!" Sydney exclaimed checking the camera outside. "A car pulled up in front of the apartment building. Two men are getting out. They are entering the building. They have a key to the security door. They are running up the stairwell. You need to move now!"

"Inside quickly," Sam whispered locking the door behind them. "We need to secure this door," he warned glancing around the room.

"They are heading straight to the third floor," Sydney warned splitting the screen to add the street camera.

"Secure that door and find another way out now!" Ramsey ordered.

"I'm not detecting any more unfriendlies outside on the street," Sydney declared.

"Copy that," Sam whispered as CC helped him pull the couch against the door.

"Use this," Sam handed Paris an earbud. "It connects us to Sydney's HUB."

"They are at Paris' door," Sydney reported as Paris connected to the HUB and listened. "They have a key. It didn't work. Now, they're trying to pick the lock."

"Paris, is there another way out?" CC asked.

"I think I remember another way out if it's still there," Paris whispered leading the way to her bedroom.

"Hurry!" Ramsey urged as Sydney switched the satellite back to infrared. "That door isn't going to hold long!"

"Someone with binoculars is watching from the fire escape a building over," Sydney warned showing Ramsey.

"I remember my father showed me an escape route away from the street," Paris whispered. "Sydney, is there anyone near the alleyway in the back of the building?"

"I don't see anyone," Sydney checked. "Infrared isn't detecting anyone or any movement," Sydney stated as CC helped Sam slide the dresser in front of the door.

"I helped my dad put something outside under this windowsill," Paris declared reaching under it. "They're still here!" she exclaimed pulling out two-wire cables with handles.

"Ingenious," Ramsey noted watching the screen.

"I remember Dad had me hold these while he was working outside on a ladder," Paris smiled. "He said it was for an escape," she said as the two men finally broke through the living room barrier. "There are only two of them. I was young, and Dad was going to carry me down on his back."

"No time for stories!" Sydney insisted hacking into the inside cameras. "The men are inside the flat with weapons drawn. Get out of there!"

"Go, I can use my belt," Sam insisted pulling his belt out of the loops. "I'll go last and close the window to mask our escape."

"CC, swing the cable over the metal electrical wire, and slide down," Ramsey ordered. "Then, cover them."

"Copy that," CC confirmed. "As soon as I'm down, it's your turn Paris," CC ordered sliding down to the ground. She reached for her gun and signaled for them to follow.

"Dad always thought of every detail, except me using this escape as an adult," Paris shuttered standing on the ledge, staring down at CC.

"Hurry," Sam whispered. "It's a matter of time before they break the door open. Just hold on tight, and be quiet," giving her a gentle push and following her down.

"Take the alleyway," Sydney advised using the satellite in night vision mode. "There's a fence you'll have to climb that leads to the next alleyway. That will take you to the next street."

"Copy that," Sam acknowledged leading the way.

"Stop!" Sydney cautioned. "I'm showing multiple cars speeding from different routes heading toward the apartment building."

"That sounds like Spinello's men!" Ramsey snapped.

"It does," CC agreed clutching her weapon, crouching behind a dumpster with Paris.

"Syd, wasn't Paris' parents on a long assignment?" Ramsey asked. "It seems they stumbled onto the same thing we did?"

"Spinello and the Falcini's have worked on this for a long time," Sydney assumed. "We'll know when Paris gets to my house. When I was young, I saw my father working on a camera Paris described. I remember Dad said it was one of a kind."

"Sydney, I think one of the cars is about to pass us now?" CC reported. "I see headlights illuminating the dark street."

"Copy that," Sydney stated checking the radar. "It is slowly passing your area. It turned left toward the apartment building."

"We're cut off from our vehicle!" Sam scoffed. "We parked in the other direction! It would be suicide to try to get to it!"

"Copy that," Sydney agreed zooming out. "It looks like they are bringing in more people for the search."

"They're onto us, but how?" Ramsey questioned. "You said Paris didn't use her name when she rented the flat."

"She didn't," Sydney agreed. "Let me recheck Paris' cameras," he said scanning her flat. "Here's why? They heard bits and pieces of Paris' part of our conversation. The camera's mic in the living room failed to distort every other word she said. It did distort her face, so they still don't have a clue who she is."

"That's a blessing," Ramsey confirmed pointing to the screen. "And here comes the police."

"Let's see whose side the police are on," Sydney hacked into the police radio scanners and turned up the audio.

"Great!" Ramsey listened. "Sam, CC, the police have an APB out for a man traveling with two women."

"We might have to split up," Sam suggested. "They'll start canvassing the streets on foot next."

"I have an idea," Paris realized. "Half a mile from here to the north, there is the remains of an old castle. The city condemned it when some kids got into it a few years ago, and one fell to his death. Since then, the townspeople say it's haunted, and no one goes there. Can you find it on the radar?"

"Copy that," Sydney stated locating it. "There is no sign of humans, just probably rats and small animals."

"Can you get us there?" Paris asked. "It's a perfect place to hide and wait them out. Once they quit the search, we can head for the airport."

"They already have people surrounding the Mustang Citation," Sydney stated glancing at its outside cameras. "They're assuming it is yours since they can't find the registration and flight plan. Capt. Mills is hiding in the back. They can't get inside."

"Bernadette!" CC exclaimed throwing her hands in the air. "I forgot about her! If we can get to the castle, Bernadette can pick us up. She's not too far from here. We were on our way to meet with her when Ramsey called. She said she was twenty-five minutes from Wiltz, and she'd wait there in case we needed her."

"I can hack into the outside police surveillance cameras and get you to the castle," Sydney assured them. "Call Bernadette and give me a few minutes."

"Copy that," CC agreed reaching for her phone.

"Hold your position and wait for my signal," Ramsey cautioned. "There is another vehicle coming toward you."

"I can't believe I messed up and caused this," Paris sighed leaning against the wall and sinking to the ground.

"It's not your fault," Ramsey consoled. "We do this every day with several teams. It's beginning to look like your parents uncovered the same smuggling-ring years ago that we recently discovered. These people are ruthless murderers and connected worldwide. Thank God, you called Sydney instead of the police. We'll get you safely to the castle and then to Newark."

"Sam, you can now cross the road without the police knowing and head north," Sydney assured rechecking the perimeters. "Keep to the shadows along the walls of the shops until you reach the woods. I've taken care of all the cameras along the way."

"Copy that," Sam answered helping Paris up. "It's time to leave."

"I'm ready," Paris said as Sam led the way across the street.

"Stay close to me," Sam cautioned following close to the shops toward the end of town.

"Heads-up!" Sydney warned. "A car is speeding toward you from the north!"

"Here!" Sam exclaimed pulling Paris behind an outside vegetable rack. CC dove behind a large garbage can almost knocking it over.

"Oops," CC gasped trying to steady it. "Did they see it?"

"Hold your positions," Sydney stated as Sam and CC drew their weapons. "He stopped the car. The driver put it in reverse. He's not moving yet. The car is out of reverse, and he's driving away. He turned left down the next street. You may continue."

"Move it, people!" Ramsey ordered watching the monitor. "You're almost there," she encouraged as they passed several buildings.

"Duck in that alleyway!" Sydney cautioned as they neared the last building. "That same car is turning around. He's not back to the end of the street yet," he warned watching them turn into the dark alleyway. "Behind those buildings is an easy fence to scale. It backs up to the woods. Keep straight and you'll run into a neighborhood, which is in front of the castle. I'm not showing any animals or humans in front of you."

“Thank God, the moon has enough light for you to see,” Ramsey encouraged watching them hurry through the woods.

“I see the neighborhood across the street,” Sam relayed stopping behind a tree. “Are we clear to cross?”

“Affirmative,” Sydney confirmed. “The houses are very close together. Try not to wake anyone. That neighborhood backs up to the castle.”

“Copy that,” Sam whispered leading the way between houses, crossing several streets. “We’re on the last street before the castle. How do we look?”

“You’re clear,” Sydney advised zeroing in on them.

“What is that in the backyard?” Ramsey pointed to the screen.

“It’s a doghouse with a monstrous dog,” Sydney noted. “Sam, proceed with caution.”

“Copy that,” Sam agreed stopping for a second. “Ladies, we need to walk past the dog quietly. Let’s go.”

“You’re almost to the doghouse,” Ramsey cautioned watching Sam and Paris tiptoe past it. “CC, you’re walking closer to the doghouse than they did.”

“Oh!” CC gasped stepping on a squeaky toy. “This isn’t good!” she whispered raising her foot. It squeaked again.

“Run!” Ramsey ordered. “The dog just bolted out of the doghouse!”

“Run!” CC screamed following Paris to the six-foot wooden fence. “Jump, Paris!”

Paris leaped for the top of the fence next to Sam, trying to get one leg across. “I can’t make it!”

“I’ve got you,” Sam straddled the fence, reaching down, pulling Paris across. “Not bad for a first-timer,” Sam grinned watching CC scale it and drop to the ground.

“That was too close,” CC collapsed rubbing her ankle. “Big Bruiser almost got me.”

“You’re lucky,” Sam checked her ankle. “It’s just a scratch.”

“At least, Big Bruiser can’t make it over the fence,” Paris sighed sitting next to CC.

"No, but Bruiser's trying to get through that loose slat," Sam warned helping them up. "Let's get away from here. The dog's owner turned on the backyard lights."

"There is roughly a hundred-feet of trees, and then the castle wall," Sydney relayed.

"Copy that," Sam affirmed. "We're almost to it."

"I'm showing a helicopter coming in your direction," Sydney warned switching to the police scanner. "The owner called the police. It's heading toward that house."

"Copy that," CC said stopping to catch her breath. "We have the castle in sight."

"Heads-up!" Sydney warned. "The helicopter turned on the spotlight and is searching around the fence."

"I hear it!" Sam reported as they scaled an old stone fence that surrounded the castle and dropped to the ground. "Where to next?"

"By the front door are a few trees with thick underbrush!" Sydney stated. "Hide in the underbrush until I find a way inside."

"Copy that," Sam agreed. "Ladies, cover yourselves with the bushes!"

"I hope there's no snakes or rats in here!" Paris whispered.

"It's better than being shot," CC confirmed as the spotlight shone around them. "Don't move; it's over us."

"Hold your position until that helicopter leaves," Sydney ordered. "Bernadette's ETA is five minutes."

"I hear that dog again!" CC whispered. "And it's getting closer."

"You're right," Sydney confirmed changing the satellite to street view. "The owner and police brought the dog around the fence. The helicopter moved the search to the back of the grounds. The doorway into the castle is ahead of you about fifty feet. The bottom steps are missing, so you'll have to leap to get inside."

"Sam, be ready to use your flashlight on my say," Ramsey added. "I pulled up the article on the boy. He fell to his death in a deep crevice where the first two steps fell through. It is filled with rocks and deadly snakes."

"Just what we needed to hear," Sam sighed.

"The helicopter moved the search to the woods," Sydney relayed. "The police and dog are still walking through the woods. Move now!"

"Copy that," Sam ran, jumped to the third step, and hurried up the rest. "Paris, when Sydney tells you; do what I did. I'll come out and help you."

"That's a pretty far jump," Paris declared.

"There are no other choices," Ramsey confirmed. "You must do this."

"Go now!" Sydney ordered.

"Okay," Paris took a deep breath, ran, and jumped to Sam.

"I've got you," Sam said grabbing her hands, and helping her inside.

"CC now!" Sydney urged. "The helicopter turned to circle the castle."

"Come on," Sam urged as CC jumped to the step, missed Sam's hand, and started to fall backward.

"No!" Sam exclaimed quickly lunging for her arm and pulling her up the steps.

"Find a place to hide!" Sydney warned. "Big Bruiser located where you crossed the fence. He's sniffing your footprints toward the woods."

"CC, don't you have pepper spray?" Ramsey asked. "We need something to deter that dog."

"Yes, I do," CC smiled reaching in her backpack. "I have Counter Assault."

"Perfect," Ramsey agreed. "That's strong enough to keep a Grizzly away."

"It's enough to neutralize that poor dog's sense of smell for quite a while," Sydney added. "Sam, dim your flashlight and check around inside. Let's see our options," he said pulling up the schematics on the castle.

"Copy that," Sam agreed glancing around.

"To your right should lead to a round staircase," Sydney relayed. "I'm showing it goes to the second and third floors. On the second floor to the left is a doorway that leads outside to a private garden. It also has a private stairway to the rooftop. That gives us several options for escape. Have you found it yet?"

"Copy that," Sam answered reaching in his backpack. "It's blocked off with an iron gate and a padlock. Give me a second to pick the lock."

"Paris, do you feel comfortable covering them?" Ramsey asked.

"Yes, ma'am," Paris agreed drawing her weapon.

"This should do the trick," Sam smiled taking off the lock. "I've got the gate open."

"Check the safety of the steps," Ramsey cautioned. "The structure isn't sound."

"Be careful, but you do need to hurry," Sydney requested as Sam tested the first few steps. "Three police cars arrived at the castle. Bruiser knows you're in there. You'll have company soon."

"Follow me one at a time," Sam requested turning the first rounded corner. "They are rickety but holding so far."

"Hold the chatter," Sydney advised. "CC, close the gate and lock it."

"Copy that," CC answered reaching through the gate and locking it.

"A policeman placed a ramp over the broken steps," Sydney relayed. "Here they come with the dog leading the way."

"What in the world!" Ramsey exclaimed watching the dog and people run outside, coughing, and choking. "CC, how much spray did you use?"

"The entire bottle," CC whispered following Paris.

"Well, you just stopped everyone from coming in that way," Ramsey laughed. "The ones that didn't go inside are going around the back. Are you on the second floor yet?"

"Almost," Sam replied rounding the last corner.

"Ramsey, I'm listening to your chatter," Bernadette interrupted. "My ETA is two minutes. First, I'm going to advise the police helicopter to leave. I'm coming in from the south side."

"Are you driving a car?" Ramsey asked.

"Negative," Bernadette chuckled. "After listening to the situation, I borrowed a helicopter."

"There is quite a bit of fire-power also on the ground," Ramsey cautioned. "Do you have weapons?"

"I believe so," Bernadette giggled glancing at the military pilots tied up behind her. "Let's say; I'm well-equipped to take the helicopter and ground crew out. I have a visual. Give me a minute," she said changing frequency. "Wiltz police, this is Luxembourg's Armée de l'Air. I have orders to take over the search. The government wants these people for espionage."

"Armée de l'Air, this is Capitaine de Police Gilles," he introduced. "We have jurisdiction in this situation. You are to stand down at once."

"Brigadier General Lacroix warned us that you would say that," Bernadette smiled, firing a rocket exploding the helicopter. "Next?" she turned blowing up the police cars, and then switched to machine-gun fire at the men below. "What's the matter, boys?" Bernadette laughed as they scrambled in all directions.

"Good job!" Ramsey exclaimed muting the console. "Syd, she's not the ordinary Calvary," before enabling the audio. "Where's the best place to pick them up?"

"The left side of the rooftop at the far-end," Bernadette answered. "I will land there."

"Copy that," Sam confirmed. "We are on our way!"

"I'll be there in a few minutes," Bernadette relayed. "Sydney, have I missed anyone?"

"Let me check with infrared," Sydney checked. "In the front, beside the round tower in the corner, you have one lurking in the shadows."

"I'll take him out and head for the roof," Bernadette complied and then raised the helicopter to the roof. "Sam, push the two pilots out," she requested as he got inside.

"Sorry, guys," Sam apologized shoving them out each door.

"Bernadette, snipers climbed trees at your five o'clock!" Sydney warned.

"CC, Paris, drop down!" Sam ordered.

"Sam, hold on!" Bernadette hollered quickly flipping off the left side, coming around the building's end, toward the trees.

"Ah!" Sam screamed dangling from the door handle, finally steadying his feet on the landing skids.

"Hang on tight!" Bernadette warned maneuvering around their fire. "It's my turn!" she grinned heading their way, returning fire. "One down!" she reported locating the second sniper shimming down the tree. "Got ya!" hovering the chopper. "Sam, will you get back inside!"

"Wow!" Sam exclaimed sitting in the co-pilot seat and putting on his headset. "I haven't done that since Afghanistan."

"Sorry, I didn't have much warning," Bernadette admitted. "One more second, and we would have exploded. They had M-16's," she said landing on the rooftop. "It looks like we weren't the only ones under attack."

"Sam, I'm glad to see you are, okay?" CC declared as she and Paris got inside. "I thought you were a goner."

"Luckily, it wasn't the first time I've done that," Sam recalled glancing around. "What happened here?"

"Well, while I was watching you horsing around outside the helicopter," CC grinned, "Paris spotted movement inside the stairway."

"I signaled CC to get behind an old flowerpot for cover," Paris continued. "CC took out the first one while I worked my way around the remaining part of a wall. The second one pinned CC down while she was reloading. That's when I had a flashback of my father protecting us, and I fired."

"Paris, you save both of our lives," CC admitted.

"Paris, you made the right decision," Ramsey consoled. "Are you okay with it?"

"Yes," Paris answered. "Uncle David and Aunt Deanna would be proud of me."

"I'm proud of you, too," Sydney shared. "We have one more hurdle to overcome at the airport. Capitaine Gilles fled the scene with some men on foot as soon as Bernadette blew up the helicopter. He sieged the

Citation, leaving two men with M-16's guarding it. We can't afford another shoot-out. My primary concern is now they know a young Caucasian female with dark brown hair rented the flat and found something. She's traveling with a Caucasian male and a Black female. And they suspect the Citation has something to do with it. We need to get you in that jet and on the way to Newark ASAP."

"Any thoughts on how you want us to handle this?" Sam asked.

"I'm live streaming the cameras around the Citation to your phones," Sydney stated typing commands. "We need to figure out a way to retake the Citation without drawing too much attention. I allowed them to do us a favor and tow it to the back of the airport near the end of the runway. It's easy to access for taking off. Capt. Mills is waiting for my signal."

"Copy that," Sam agreed checking his phone. "I'm getting the live-feed now."

"Notice the obscurity of the area," Sydney explained. "I can handle the security cameras in that area, but only for a few minutes. After that, they'll know something is wrong and disperse security officers."

"It's just two men," Sam stated. "It shouldn't take more than a few minutes for us to get aboard."

"Sydney, I need to ditch this chopper," Bernadette stated. "I see only two real problems. The engines are cold and clearing takeoff with the tower."

"I can get you cleared for takeoff," Sydney grinned. "Jordan is ready to warm up the engines. He's waiting for you to neutralize the guards."

"Copy that," Bernadette confirmed turning north to come in on the back-left side of the airport. "See that clump of trees?" She pointed to the left. "It should be out of range of the security cameras. We'll land and hike to the back of the airport," she said landing the helicopter.

"Make sure you wipe your prints," Ramsey cautioned watching the blades stop.

Sam got out and opened the back door for the girls and then wiped off the handle. "Which way?"

"Follow me," Bernadette led the way toward the back-right fence and stopped behind some trees.

"Sydney, we have the Citation in sight," Sam reported. "We are ready for you to work your magic with the cameras."

"Hold tight for a minute," Sydney advised. "We have to wait for Wanda and Keith," he said as Ramsey picked up her cell phone.

"Wanda, we are ready for Keith to do the same thing with radar," Ramsey ordered.

"You've got it," Wanda confirmed signaling Keith.

"Give me another minute," Keith warned. "After I did it last time, L'Simonette had the tower put extra security on the Citation," he said blocking the security. "You've got it!" Keith confirmed. "Get them up."

"Copy that," Ramsey grinned.

"Ramsey, it might get a little sticky in here," Keith warned.

"I trust you and Wanda can handle our resident mole," Ramsey confirmed and hung up. "CC, stay put with Paris until the guards are down. Then, get over the fence."

"Copy that," CC agreed.

"Sam, the cameras are off," Sydney reported scanning the area. "You have less than five minutes."

"Copy that," Sam agreed. "The guards are watching a plane takeoff."

"I'll take the one by the cockpit," Bernadette whispered. "On my signal," she hurried to the fence. Bernadette made her way toward the guard by the left-back tire and motioned to Sam. "Now!" Bernadette whispered as the guard lit a cigarette, and another plane taxied past them. As it made the turn, she pulled her knife, grabbing the guard from behind. At the same time, Sam neutralized his target.

"Another plane is approaching the runway," Sam warned as they drug the bodies away from the jet.

"I'm enabling Chameleon," Sydney advised. "Jordan, the cockpit is yours!"

"Yes, Sir!" Jordan jumped into the pilot's seat.

"CC, wait until the plane makes the turn to the runway," Ramsey warned. "The pilot could alert the tower if he sees you."

"Copy that," CC answered.

"Jordan, start the engines," Sydney requested. "CC, they did not see you. It's normal communications with the tower."

"Sydney, I'm lowering the stairway," Jordan declared. "Sam, help me get ready to takeoff."

"Bernadette, show the girls where to cross under the jet," Ramsey requested. "CC, Paris, follow Bernadette's direction, so you don't get sucked inside the engines."

"Copy that," CC agreed leading Paris. Bernadette covered them as they hurried up the stairway.

"Buckle up, ladies," Bernadette requested securing the door. "Sam, the door is sealed. We're ready when you are."

"One more minute," Sydney cautioned pressing enter. "Go now! I've scrambled communications with the tower and radar," he grinned watching Jordan round the corner. "They're blind and scrambling. The runway is all yours."

"Copy that," Jordan answered turning onto the south runway immediately throttling up. "We're up," Jordan heralded rising above the tower.

"Copy that," Sydney said watching the radar. "You're clear as far as I can see. Call me if you need me."

"Copy that," Jordan smiled. "Thanks for the assist."

"Bernadette, do you want us to drop you off?" Ramsey asked.

"Negative," Bernadette insisted as the jet continued to climb. "Spinello and Dano are behind Luca's death. I've already told Alonzo that I'd like to help you bring them down."

"We could use your continued help," Ramsey admitted. "The man that rented Paris' parent's flat after the police released it had to be Dano. The landlord described the man's lifestyle matching the life of a hitman."

"My gut tells me it was Dano, too," Bernadette confided. "That's why I want to see what is on this CD."

"Alonzo already mentioned it to me," Ramsey confirmed. "Welcome to our team. I'll see you in Newark," she cleared the line. "What is the status of our Cuba teams?"

"Stephen and Alonzo's teams have checked into the Playa La Boca," Sydney replied. "I still have to find a spot for Kathe and Yorg to dock for tonight near them. They will meet Stephen's team on the inlet in the morning. Stephen rented a boat. He already checked some of the bird sightings in the area and told Kathe to watch for them."

"How far is the inlet from the hotel?" Ramsey asked.

"A mile and a half," Sydney pulled up the map. "This inlet is perfect for them to meet. Yorg will dock here," he pointed. "Then, they simply walk over to the inlet."

"I hope it's that easy," Ramsey sighed. "That inlet is full of patrol boats and guards."

"All and all, this is going better than we expected so far," Sydney comforted as a news alert flashed on his screen. "Let's see what this is?"

Wednesday, July 1, 2130 (9:30 PM EST)
FNN News
Washington, DC

BREAKING NEWS: "This is Robert Morwitz with FNN News. Cuban officials released these pictures about 2100 (9:00 PM EST)," the screen split showing a patrol boat rescuing a man holding onto a round life raft floating in the Atlantic Ocean. He was identified as Estevo Vasquez, an undercover military officer. Vasquez doesn't recall what happened or why he was found holding onto a life raft from the yacht, El Amoré del Sol. The Cuban government denies any knowledge of the yacht. An anonymous source close to the White House claims this has something to do with the two stories we are following here in the United States. Stay tuned for more information as we receive it," the screen switched to Robert Morwitz. "Now, back to the regularly scheduled programming."

"Jenkins!" Sydney exclaimed. "He is the only one that knows we are here!"

"Yes, he is!" Ramsey snapped. "We've got to figure out a way to expose him to President Trumore without exposing ourselves," Ramsey declared answering her phone. "Tom, we were just discussing you," she said as Sydney connected the call to his console. "We saw the breaking news about Cuba."

"I just got off the phone with President Trumore," Jenkins lied. "He has his Chief of Staff working on it. There is no way that anybody at the White House knows of your operation. The president will call me when he knows something."

"Tom, I hate to tell you," Ramsey scrunched her face. "We had nothing to do with that. We've expected this type of behavior to begin. There are too many bosses with their hands in one pie. It appears someone is eliminating the competition. And by the way, this isn't our operation. The covert operation is yours as well."

"I didn't mean it like that, darling," Jenkins shook his head. "I've had a long day. The president has me working with Agent Terrance Sims locating terrorists in Baja, California. Rodger and I should be joining you soon. I've got another call," he said hanging up.

"What a liar!" Sydney declared pulling up his location. "While you were talking to him, I hacked into his phone and located him. He's traveling across the Caribbean Sea."

"We were afraid of this," Ramsey sighed standing up. "He's using Rodger for something other than Homeland Security. All Rodger wanted when he came to America was a normal life and a family. We promised Rodger that for helping us save Yorg. I'll call CC and have her check on the status of his family. Jenkins wouldn't think twice about holding them prisoner or harming his family," she said yawing. "We need to get some sleep. I'll call CC on the way to my bunk. See you first thing in the morning."

Chapter 4

Thursday, July 2, 0600 (6:00 AM EST),
On the River in La Playita, Cuba

Kneeling beside Kathe asleep on a bunk, Yorg gently moved her bangs out of her face, kissed her, and whispered, "Good morning, Ms. Vuslick."

"Not yet," Kathe yawned, opening her eyes and stretching. "Is it morning already?"

"I'm afraid it is," Yorg kissed her neck. "I've been up for a while. I let you sleep since we've been non-stop. I even made the coffee and found these breakfast bars. We need to hurry."

"Ah, you're such a keeper," Kathe put her arms around his neck and looked into his eyes. "After last night, you let me sleep in, and now coffee with breakfast in bed. What more could a woman ask for?"

"Well, I did have to prove that Bond wasn't the only creative man on the planet," Yorg grinned.

"Oh, you don't ever have to feel inferior to Bond," Kathe smiled playfully touching his nose. "And think, an author's imagination didn't script your performance."

"Maybe, we should do a quick reenactment to make sure I don't forget?" Yorg kissed her as JAKE rang. "Why is work always a phone call away?"

"Because our boss is relentless," Kathe whined. "We will reschedule that bona fide offer, though," she winked answering JAKE.

"Good morning," Sydney greeted pulling up their location. "I trust you had a good night's rest."

"We did," Kathe wrinkled her nose at Yorg.

"Is Yorg up as well?" Sydney asked.

"We are having breakfast," Kathe replied. "You're on speaker."

"I see you docked under the ledge of the mountains where I suggested last night," Sydney noted.

"We did," Yorg confirmed. "I turned Chameleon on like you said, and we slept without any problems."

"Good," Sydney concurred. "That is the perfect location for you to leave the sub and surface. Look at the screen above the right bunks," Sydney enabled it. "As you can see, with the simulated graphics, you have enough space there to exit the sub. Topside, you will enter through a cave where the double-waterfall empties into the ocean. I programmed the robot to locate the opening. That's where you can stash your scuba-gear, as well as change. It is still dark there, so you shouldn't have any company. Stephen and his team rented a boat and are already en route to meet you," he said checking their location. "They are taking it slowly on the river, not trying to draw too much attention. Patrol boats have already stopped and boarded the boat several times. They checked Stephen's credentials and left. It looks like they are about twenty-five minutes out, give or take."

"Copy that," Kathe answered. "We will be there on time."

"The government constantly patrols the river, as well as Spinello's men," Sydney warned. "When you come out of the cave, turn left, and JAKE will lead you to the rendezvous site at the inlet. Stephen sent you a text of the birds you are looking for in case you need a cover."

"Copy that," Kathe replied checking JAKE's messages. "I received them earlier this morning."

"I'll rejoin you when you activate the beacon on the robot," Sydney stated. "I've got to check on CC's team," he cleared the line as Ramsey joined him with breakfast.

Twenty minutes later, Kathe and Yorg used the lights above their helmets to follow the robot. It led them through a bubbling spring into a cave entrance. They emerged, crawling through a small opening that leads into a massive cave with an opportunity to the outside. "This is breathtaking," Kathe said standing up as she panned the walls with her headlight. "Look at the colorful walls and ceiling!"

"It looks like limestone and stalactites with fibrous crystals," Yorg noted walking below the opening to the outside. "The stars in the sky are so numerous. The sky is almost white. And Mother Nature was kind to us." Yorg said pointing to the long tree roots growing into the cave walls. "These roots are hundreds of years old. They should hold our weight to climb out."

"Good," Kathe replied using JAKE to maneuver the robot out of the water. "I can't believe this robot expands to hold clothes, small backpacks, and a camera bag. Here are your clothes."

"We're making good time," Yorg checked his watch stripping off his wetsuit. "I need to find a safe place for the robot and our gear," he walked around some of the stalactites. "Here is a small hidden washout. It might be deep enough for the robot to enter without being detected."

"Let's see," Kathe agreed walking the robot around the stalactites.

“The robot isn’t going to fit,” Yorg noted. “I’ll look for another place.”

“Sydney designed the robot’s legs to lower for crawling into smaller spaces,” Kathe showed him. “How’s that for getting into a tight space?”

“I can’t believe the robot got into it,” Yorg smiled. “Activate the beacon and we’re set.”

“It’s activated,” Kathe said tapping the icon twice.

“Kathe, Yorg, I’m picking up the signal now,” Sydney rejoined them checking the perimeter with infrared. “I’m not detecting any movement topside.”

“We’re ready to go,” Yorg shared. “I’ll go first and cover Kathe,” he grabbed the thickest root, climbed to the top, and waited.

“Yorg, you’re clear to exit the cave,” Sydney watched.

“Kathe, come up,” Yorg coaxed helping her outside. “We’re behind the lower waterfall. Stay close to the wall, so we don’t get our clothes wet, and be careful these rocks are slick.”

“You think?” Kathe slipped grabbing onto the ledge.

“Did you take your ID badges and binoculars out of the camera bag?” Ramsey asked. “You need to look ready for filming birds.”

“Thanks for reminding me,” Yorg sighed. “I’ll get them as soon as we get away from these slippery rocks,” he agreed clearing the fall. He reached to help Kathe.

“It’s almost daylight,” Sydney shared. “I’m beginning to notice more movement along the river. I downloaded the coordinates to JAKE of where to meet Stephen. Earlier, I noticed several campfires sporadically situated around the area. They’re probably camps for the patrol guards or guerillas, so be careful.”

“Copy that,” Yorg stated as Kathe led the way. “We’ll keep our eyes peeled. Anybody could be lurking in this thick vegetation. It’s hard to walk through it.”

“Stop!” Kathe ordered pointing to a thin wire across the narrow path. “It looks like an old-fashioned trip-wire,” Kathe recalled following it with her finger to a net hanging in the tree above them. “We almost went for a ride! And I smell the hint of wood-burning.”

“Unbelievable,” Ramsey stated. “Thank God, you spotted that primitive, archaic contraption. Whoever set that trap returns at night. They can’t be too far away.”

"It does look permanent," Sydney determined. "They probably use it to keep animals or smugglers away while they are sleeping. Kathe, proceed with caution."

"Kat, look under that larger tree to the right," Yorg spotted, "it's a makeshift lean-to. Someone was just there. The campfire is still smoldering."

"There are four patrol guards at the riverbank to your left." Sydney declared enlarging the perimeter.

"Hopefully, they are getting on a boat and leaving," Kathe whispered continuing through the foliage. "We'll stay away from the river long enough for the patrol to get out of sight."

"Stephen's GPS is showing him about ten minutes from the inlet," Sydney advised. "You're pretty close to the rendezvous, also."

"Copy that," Kathe answered. "The trees are changing to mostly scrub oaks, and we smell the river."

"Kat, shush, come this way," Yorg whispered pulling her around a large clump of bushes. "Listen, I hear talking."

"JAKE, are any human life-forms near us?" Kathe asked.

"Kathe, there are no human life-forms near," JAKE answered as they cautiously continued toward the rendezvous spot.

"I'm not picking up anyone on infrared," Sydney confirmed.

"Wait!" Yorg insisted pulling Kathe down behind thick reeds. "Listen, can't you hear them?"

"Yes, I hear voices near us," Kathe checked with JAKE again.

This time JAKE typed on his screen. Kathe, yes, voices to the left.

Kathe typed. JAKE, show me the location.

JAKE typed. Kathe, scan is not showing location.

"Sydney," Kathe whispered, "JAKE agrees about the voice, but unable to locate."

"Hold still," Sydney cautioned. "I'll run a scan," Sydney stated panning the area. "The only humans I'm showing are Stephen and his team. They docked and are onshore. I'm not scanning any other life-forms. Oh, no!" Sydney exclaimed zooming in on a clump of bushes near Kathe and Yorg. "Several men came out of nowhere near you running to the team."

"It's an ambush!" Ramsey declared. "Jay, Jack, several men are heading your way. Stephen, Will, stay calm."

"We have a visual," Jay whispered.

"Stephen, be ready to answer questions," Ramsey cautioned. "Stay cool. Jay, Jack, are ready," she turned to Sydney. "How did we miss that?"

"Ramsey, I see how," Yorg declared moving closer. "They were covered in a thick camouflage blanket about ten-yards away from us. We have a visual of the situation," Yorg confirmed continuing to edge closer to them. "I count nine of them. Stephen is showing his ID badge to the leader. But for some reason, he's giving Stephen a hard time."

"Finally, it is sunrise," Sydney typed pressing enter. "I'm switching the satellite to street-view."

"It doesn't look good!" Ramsey sighed.

"Let me turn up the microphone on Stephen's sunglasses," Sydney shared. "You're right. The leader is arguing that the ID badges are stolen."

"Wait a minute," Kathe noted. "They aren't dressed like the other patrollers. They are drug smugglers."

"Good eye," Sydney affirmed as something flew over the boat, landing in a tree by Kathe and Yorg. "It couldn't be?" Sydney questioned running a scan. "You're not going to believe this, but a Cuban Pygmy Owl just landed in the tree above you."

"Those are on my bird list," Kathe remembered holding JAKE toward the tree. "JAKE, show me an owl."

JAKE's screen lit, displaying the owl. "Kathe, here is the owl."

"That owl might save them!" Ramsey grinned. "They need to act now! Jay, Jack, get ready for anything!"

Jay coughed to signify acknowledgement.

"I have an idea!" Kathe exclaimed. "Yorg, follow my lead and start rolling the film. We're doing a commentary on the owl," Kathe stepped out into the open with her microphone.

"You're on now," Yorg stepped out with the camera on his shoulder and signaled her to begin.

"This is Dr. Karen Reese at the inlet by La Playita, Cuba," Kathe introduced and then Yorg turned the camera toward the owl. "We have spotted a Cuban Pygmy Owl that is endemic to Cuba by this riverbank," Yorg zoomed in on the owl. "It is known for its tiny, plump body with a big head, large, yellow eyes, and two-color morphs, grey-brown and rufous. Its length is close to seven inches tall."

"Yorg, keep the camera rolling," Ramsey warned. "Two of the smugglers are heading your way."

"It weighs about 3.53 . . ." Kathe stopped.

"¡Levanta las manas!" a smuggler shoved her aside.

"Hold up your hands!" Sydney translated.

Yorg kept the camera rolling until the second one shoved a gun in his face. "¡Levanta las manas!"

"Yorg, do what he says," Ramsey cautioned.

"Kathe, tell him this," Sydney spoke. "'Señor, somos parte del equipo de cámeras de Gabby Mobile Production. (Senor, we are part of the camera team for GMP.) Tenemos permiso para filmar en Cuba de Ché Márquez el Ministro de Turismo. (We have permission to film in Cuba from Ché Márquez the Minister of Tourism.) Nos encontramos con Nuestro jefe, Stephen Brown aquí,'" (We are meeting with our boss, SB here.) Kathe showed her ID badge. "Acabamos de encontrar un búho pigmeo. (We found a Pigmy Owl.) Este es mi camarógrafo, Denisov." (This is my cameraman, Denisov.)

"¡No actúes como si no lo vieras su jefe en problemas!" he screamed, nudging her arm with his rifle. "¡Ustedes dos, preparen el bote!"

"Don't act like you didn't see your boss in trouble!" Sydney relayed. (You two prepare the boat.)

"Ah, una hermosa mujer para llevar con nosotros en el barco," the smuggler chuckled. "No nos importan las aves. Queremos tu jehe barco."

"Ah, a beautiful woman to take with us on the boat," Sydney translated. "We don't care about the birds. We want your boss' boat," he laughed reaching for her hair.

"Queremos tu barco," (We want your boat.) Kathe mocked moving away from him.

"¡Hector, los trae aquí!" The leader next to Stephen yelled.

"Hector, bring them here!" Sydney translated.

"Sí Mendoza," Hector waved his hand toward him. "¡Ven con nosotros!" Hector ordered, pushing Kathe along with his rifle.

"Yes, Mendoza," Sydney repeated. "Come with us!"

"This is going to be another one of those eye-opening moments for Stephen and Will," Ramsey noted. "Kathe, once you get over there, use JAKE to get the upper hand on these bozos."

"You'll have to warn Stephen and Will to drop when you're ready," Sydney advised. "Don't worry; they don't speak English."

"Copy that," Kathe whispered winking at Yorg.

"Jay, Jack size up your opportunities," Ramsey advised. "They're not going away without a fight."

"Yorg, the camera has a switch located above the record button," Sydney instructed. "I installed a gun under the extended microphone. The switch opens the gun barrel. The trigger is the record button when the gun is activated. I'm sure you know what to do," he finished watching Mendoza standing in front of Kathe and Yorg.

"Yorg, don't show any emotions concerning Kathe," Ramsey warned. "They won't hesitate to kill you. She's the prize; they'll wish they never saw."

"Ah, ella se ve suave," Mendoza said brushing her cheek with the back of his hand. "La tomaré para mi," he said as Kathe moved away.

"Ah, she looks so soft," Sydney translated. "I'll take her for myself."

"Mendoza, la vi perimero," Hector argued.

"Mendoza, I saw her first," Sydney stated.

"Hector, hermanito ella es mía," Mendoza chuckled pulling Kathe close to him. "Soy el mayor y el jefe."

"Hector, my little brother, she is mine," Sydney continued as they watched. "I'm the oldest and the boss."

"Stephen, Will, this will get messy," Kathe chuckled looking into Mendoza's eyes. "Don't worry. These idiots are clueless as to what I said. When I say, 'ready,' drop to the ground and roll toward the water. Ready! JAKE, laser on now!" Kathe exclaimed cutting Mendoza almost in half with the laser. Kathe pivoted the laser toward a surprised Hector, who fell next to his brother. At the same time, Yorg shot the unsuspecting two standing beside him. Jay and Jack dropped to the ground, rolled away from Stephen and Will, taking out the targets next to them. The two on the boat ran out of the flybridge as Jay and Jack took them out.

"That camera takes weaponry to a whole new level!" Jack chuckled. "Talk about surprising the enemy! I want one of those!"

"Your cameras do the same thing," Sydney assured them. "I couldn't tell you to use them since they were in your backpacks."

"What a toy?" Jack laughed.

"You two, okay?" Kathe asked as Stephen, and Will stood up, dusting the dirt off their clothes.

"Yes," Stephen answered glancing at the bodies. "We didn't figure drug smugglers into our equation since the Minister of Tourism cleared us."

"I did," Sydney admitted. "Jay has a little something for you to carry if you want. Like the cameras, it's hard to detect."

"I'll take it," Stephen admitted. "That was a little too close for my comfort."

"I feel the same way," Will agreed.

"I'll get them for you," Jay said looking around. "As soon as we move these bodies. We don't want them found."

"That's right," Sydney agreed rechecking the radar. "Luckily, the four guards earlier by the riverbank left before the gunfire," he said zooming in on the middle of the small inlet. "Wow! One thing I didn't plan on is a pit not too far from you that has the characteristics of quicksand," he noted running a scan.

"Is there anything else you forgot to mention to us about the terrain?" Kathe demanded. "Yorg and I've been traipsing through this thick foliage only looking for men and varmints. So far, we've found tripwires, lean-tos, camouflage blankets, and drug smugglers!"

"I do owe you an apology," Sydney proclaimed. "I haven't seen anything this archaic in years. And besides, you needed an immediate place to dump nine bodies. What's the problem?" Sydney chuckled. "Sorry, I'll have the computer check for any other unstable areas. Jay, straight out from you in the middle of the inlet, is a circle of sand with no vegetation growing on it. Dump the bodies there, and watch them sink," Sydney explained zeroing in where the smugglers hid. "If you have time, their drugs are probably under the camouflage. It would be fitting for the smuggler to take the drugs with them."

"I like the way you're thinking," Jay answered dragging a body toward the quicksand.

"Kat, we'll get the bodies," Yorg suggested. "You get the drugs."

"One batch that won't make it to the states!" Kathe exclaimed. "It will be my pleasure!"

"Stephen, why don't you and Will get the drone up and look for birds," Sydney suggested. "I'm noting a larger boat that is escorted by two patrol boats coming your way. ETA is about fifteen to twenty minutes," he zoomed in. "It's a government boat. It's probably checking on you."

"You heard Sydney," Ramsey ordered. "People, move those bodies! Kathe, cover up the bloodstains on the ground and in the boat!"

"We'll get the drone up," Stephen answered. "Will, get the drone and iPads," he requested picking up his phone. "Skip, we are in a tight situation. I need you and Mack to help us find and record birds for our alibi. Then, send the pictures back to our cameras. Also, pull up Yorg's camera footage of the Pygmy-Owl and clean it up. Mack will know what to do."

"Copy that," Skip answered. "Luckily, there are reports of several known species near you."

"Stay on earbuds and listen to what camera we need to bring up," Stephen requested. "When you spot a bird, tell Will where to move the drone," Stephen said as Will handed him an iPad. "Once we have some footage, and if they interrogate us, tell each person what they will be showing as I call on them. Understood?" Stephen asked leading the way into the vegetation.

"Understood," Mack replied.

Ramsey muted the console. "They have a lot to do in a short time," she told Sydney. "I hope they can pull this off."

"I have full confidence in them," Sydney consoled.

Twenty minutes later, a government boat escorted by two patrol boats docked on both sides of Stephen's boat.

"Stephen, you've got company onshore," Sydney warned noting Stephen's location in the thicket.

"We're already on our way," Stephen replied. "The 360-degrees cameras already picked them up. Skip and Mack helped us locate several birds as the drone flew over them. With a traditional lens, we would have missed them," he said walking toward the men by his boat.

"Ah, Señor Brown, I'm Ché Márquez, the Minister of Tourism," he introduced. "I hope you don't mind that I came to check on your progress. For your safety, I've had my men keep an eye out for you. These jungles are known for harboring banditos and smugglers."

"I thank you for your concern," Stephen said, shaking Márquez's hand. "This area is buzzing with wildlife. We've found several unusual birds, including one that is supposedly extinct. Jay, bring up the bird you discovered."

"Yes, Sir," Jay answered showing his camera to Márquez.

"It can't be the Ivory-billed Woodpecker!" Márquez exclaimed. "It was said to be extinct for over 73 years in the 1980s by a U.S. Naval Research Scientist."

"I beg to differ," Kathe joined the conversation. "In 2005, U.S. Naval Research Scientist and fellow birder, Dr. Michael Collins, documented the Ivory-billed woodpeckers in a remote nature reserve in Arkansas. The sightings were kept secret for a year, in part to protect the habitat. Then, in January 2017, an article in the open-access journal, Heliyon, published Dr. Collins proving that the Ivory-billed Woodpeckers persist in Louisiana and the Florida swamps today."

"Whom do I have the pleasure?" Márquez asked shaking her hand.

"Dr. Karen Reese," Kathe introduced. "I, too, am an avid birder and a U.S. Naval Research Scientist; the same as my cameraman, Denisov Polinski. Stephen called me to see if we wanted to join his team in Cuba. Today's find is well worth a week's vacation. Incredibly, the woodpeckers migrated this far south."

"The woodpecker alone deems to be a profitable investment for Cuba's tourism," Márquez declared. "I'll report this to Presidente Castrello as soon as I return. You mentioned that you found several rare birds. What else did you find?"

"Karen found a Pygmy Owl," Stephen shared as Denisov showed him the footage.

"It's raw footage," Denisov explained. "I'll edit it for the video."

"Of course," Márquez stated. "Senora Reese, your description of the bird was phenomenal."

"Thank you, Sr. Márquez," Kathe smiled.

"I found a Blue-headed Quail-dove," Jack showed Márquez. "It, too, is endemic of Cuba and considered to be endangered."

"That is a rare find!" Márquez declared. "Presidente Castrello put that bird on the endangered species list last year. Perhaps with finds like these, I should ride along with you for a while."

"I'm afraid we've finished filming by the ocean and rivers for now," Stephen stated checking his watch. "We're meeting another part of my team to go to the mountain ranges of the Sierra Maestra. They're bringing SUVs and equipment to make the treacherous journey."

"Treacherous is right!" Márquez agreed. "There are areas where SUVs won't reach. Perhaps, I should send some of my men with you. The mountains of the Sierra Maestra have many banditos, smugglers, and dangerous animals."

"That won't be necessary," Stephen assured him. "We're used to backpacking our way in and out of all kinds of terrains. And with our use of drones, we're able to spot any unpleasant inhabitants before they get to us. But thank you for the offer."

"Well, in that case," Márquez smiled, "I guess we'll be leaving you. What about your boat?" he asked turning to leave. "There are smugglers in these areas that would love to steal your boat. Should we tow it in for you?"

"That won't be necessary," Stephen answered. "My men always disable the engine, so it's always here when we return."

"In that case, I can have two men stay aboard and protect it from smugglers or banditos ransacking it," Márquez insisted.

"Thank you, again," Stephen replied. "However, I've already got that covered. I assure you that once we leave the boat, no one can board it and live to tell. I'm sure I'll see you when we get back to Havana before we leave."

"Yes, of course," Márquez sighed. "If you're sure you don't need help, I'll look forward to meeting with you before you leave. Adios," he said leaving with his men.

"You handled that well," Ramsey confirmed watching Márquez board his boat. "He was running out of ideas to keep a close eye on you."

"Yes, he was," Stephen sighed. "He wanted to board the boat. It was as if he knew we already had a confrontation."

"Or sent them after us," Yorg stated. "They knew where you were going to dock and were waiting."

"I noticed several of the men on the patrol boats were eying ours closely with binoculars from both sides," Will added. "I was worried they would sneak aboard?"

"Will's right," Stephen agreed. "I did notice while we were talking that Márquez turned slightly and motioned them. What kept them away?"

"Kathe intrigued Márquez with her knowledge of Dr. Collins," Ramsey answered. "After all, Márquez is a birder and a businessman. That, plus Kathe said she and Denisov were U.S. Naval Researchers, detoured any problems for now. Márquez wants tourists to come back to Cuba and their credentials, plus Stephen's company will boost them. Your reinforcements have joined you. Sydney and I need to help CC's team," she cleared the line.

"Will, I have a favor to ask you before I go," Sydney explained and cleared the line.

"Well, I heard we missed all the fun," Hiltree said getting out of the first Hummer.

"Nothing we couldn't handle," Yorg smiled shaking hands. "I heard you got rid of some of our competition."

"Nothing the Huey and we couldn't handle," Hiltree grinned.

"Just remember who owns that Huey," Yorg laughed.

"Just you remember that everything has a price," Hiltree chuckled.

"I see you've been hanging around Alonzo and Pauli," Yorg declared as they joined them. "It's my priceless antique. She's sentimental to me since I restored her."

"You and Dr. Sydney," Hiltree laughed. "He has a unique talent to tweak things with state-of-the-art technology."

Thursday, July 2, 1300 (1:00 PM EST)
On the cutter in the Atlantic Ocean near Cuba

"Our Cuban teams are on the way to the Sierra Maestra," Sydney reported as Ramsey returned to the HUB with lunch. "It seems Márquez plans on checking up on Stephen's team throughout their stay. I asked Will to add a retinal scan to each of the cameras. That way, if Márquez confiscates them, he won't be able to view the footage."

"That would be disastrous," Ramsey confirmed. "What's the status on CC's team?"

"They're an hour out from Liberty," Sydney checked the radar. "I've changed its course to land at my private runway. After Spinello compromised Hiltree at the old Army Base in Staten Island, I had Hiltree install cameras for us to keep an eye on it. I've already seen multiple cars stationed inside some of the hangars. Now, we know why the runway is fully functional. Someone's using it regularly. I've already alerted Bob where the Citation is landing. He was quite shocked. He and the boys passed that area many times and didn't know the runway was there."

"We've only had to use it a couple of times," Ramsey admitted. "But it's worth every dollar we paid to upgrade it. By the way, I'm impressed by how you engaged Chameleon before the Citation took off from Luxembourg."

"The personnel in the tower didn't know what was happening," Sydney chuckled. "They only heard the noise as it flew over them with nothing showing on the radar. My warning signal on our resident mole alerted me after it happened. L'Simonette received a call from Capt. Gilles concerning the events of the Citation. L'Simonette said he didn't know and that he'll get back with him. Then, L'Simonette called someone on a scrambled line. It was a quick call. I couldn't trace it."

"It had to be to Spinello," Ramsey sighed. "That means he'll have Jenkins pay us a visit soon."

"More than likely," Sydney agreed. "Especially since the Citation is now heading for Iceland. L'Simonette can't prove it was in Luxembourg."

"I better warn Wanda and Keith that L'Simonette may show up at their office," Ramsey realized reaching for her phone.

"Boss, you've hit the nail on the head," Wanda grinned. "I just got off the phone with Arnold Brundage in the Control Tower. He said L'Simonette stormed in there, demanding to know who had the Citation on their schedule. Brundage showed him that the Citation was heading for Iceland. L'Simonette declared that it wasn't possible since it took off from Luxembourg. He was furious when he left," she glanced through the bulletproof, glass wall. "Guess who stepped out of the elevator across from our office?"

"You know what to do," Ramsey stated. "Sydney is contacting Keith to shut down his computer and leave his office. I'll watch you on the hidden cameras."

"I hope you enjoy Alby Airlines livestreamed entertainment show today," Wanda giggled.

"Wanda!" L'Simonette snapped walking past her desk straight to Keith's office. "Where is Keith Gordon?"

"Keith is in Dr. Sydney's office getting his lunch out of the refrigerator," Wanda explained as Keith came out of Sydney's office opening a Tupperware container.

"Mr. L'Simonette, this is a surprise," Keith smiled. "What can I do for one of Alby's Vice Presidents this afternoon?"

"For starters, why were you in Dr. Sydney's office?" L'Simonette demanded walking past him into the office.

"I put my lunch in Sydney's refrigerator," Keith answered. "Mine is on the fritz, and Wanda's is too full of her snacks."

"I'm missing some, too!" Wanda snapped. "That's how you know what's in mine!"

"Keith, which office of Sydney's did you stow your lunch?" L'Simonette demanded walking to the bookshelf.

"Excuse me, Sir?" Keith questioned. "This is Dr. Sydney's only office."

"Don't give me that!" L'Simonette shouted. "I know this bookshelf opens to an elevator, which leads to a massive, underground operation. I'm ordering you to open it!"

"I'm sorry, Sir," Keith answered. "I don't know what you are talking about."

L'Simonette pushed past Keith back to the doorway, leading out to the main office, "Wanda, come in here!"

"Yes, Sir," Wanda grinned joining them.

"How do you open this bookshelf to the elevator?" L'Simonette demanded pointing at it.

"Sir, it's only a bookshelf," Wanda stepped back. "It holds books."

"I'll prove it to you!" L'Simonette snapped. "Keith, put your lunch down, and help me move this bookshelf."

"If you say so, Sir," Keith handed Wanda his lunch as L'Simonette started throwing the books on the floor.

"Sir, those are some of Dr. Sydney's antique book collections," Wanda stated. "They're in mint condition."

L'Simonette just glared at her. "Keith, help me pull it away from the wall!"

"Wow!" Wanda exclaimed after they moved it. "Those tiles have gotten dirty! I'm going to talk with housekeeping. They need to start moving furniture when they clean. This is unacceptable!"

"Keith, step on the tiles," L'Simonette ordered.

"If you say so, Sir," Keith complied shrugging his shoulders. "It's a floor, Sir. If it makes you feel better, I'll jump on it," Keith smiled jumping up and down a few times. "See, it's a solid floor."

"I see that!" L'Simonette scoffed. "I don't know how Sydney does it! But I'm going to find out as soon as he gets off vacation!"

"You don't know how Sydney does what, Sir?" Keith asked.

"You know what I'm talking about!" L'Simonette screamed. "I know for a fact that there is an elevator there!"

"Maybe, you dreamt it?" Wanda questioned raising her hands. "I've had dreams that seemed real before."

"It wasn't a dream!" L'Simonette glared at her. "I know some…."

"Excuse me," Wanda looked sideways at him. "You know some-what?"

"Never mind!" L'Simonette growled. "I'll find out how Sydney does this! If it's the last thing, I do!"

"How Sydney does what, Sir?" Wanda cringed. "We live in such a changing world. Dr. Sydney works tirelessly keeping the airline running safely. He deserves a vacation."

"And I guess Keith doesn't know where the Citation is either?" L'Simonette pressed.

"Last I checked, the Citation was near Iceland coming in from London," Keith stated. "Would you like me to recheck the status?"

"No, and it wasn't in London!" L'Simonette shouted storming out of the office.

"That went over well," Keith laughed watching L'Simonette get into the elevator.

"Keith, how did you know that the tiles would be solid?" Wanda asked putting the books back on the shelf. "I held my breath, and my heart skipped a beat, when you started jumping. I was afraid you would fall through."

"Sydney knew Jenkins told L'Simonette about the elevator and the HUB," Keith confessed. "He caught L'Simonette several times, poking around in his office when we were gone. I trust Sydney as Kathe does," he said as Wanda's cell phone rang.

"Job well done to both of you!" Ramsey complimented. "The look on your faces as you questioned L'Simonette's sanity was priceless."

"L'Simonette sure was addled when he left," Keith grinned.

"Addled?" Wanda chuckled. "He was foaming at the mouth!"

"I'm glad you had this discussion with L'Simonette," Ramsey complimented. "Now, we know L'Simonette not only colluded with Spinello for years but added Jenkins to his group. He caught himself before he divulged the name."

"Yes, ma 'am, he did," Wanda grinned. "The only person outside our team that knows the elevator exists is non-other than Gen. Jenkins."

"Thank God, that Sydney has a locking mechanism when he's not in the office," Ramsey shared. "From now on, you two need to be very careful. Either L'Simonette or Jenkins could show up at any time."

"Anything special Wanda and I should do to protect ourselves?" Keith asked. "When Wanda said L'Simonette might have dreamt about the elevator, the look in his eyes said, fire them!"

"Don't worry; L'Simonette is playing it smart," Ramsey shared. "He has no grounds to fire you unless he incriminates himself in cooperation with Jenkins. And, he has no proof of the Citation being in Luxembourg."

Thursday, July 2, 1500 (3:00 PM EST)
Dr. Sydney's Home
4500 Reynolds Dr. in White Plains, New York

"Cessna Mustang Citation AARS2881, this is Dr. Sydney," he contacted. "I'm assisting your landing instead of Keith this afternoon."

"Any reason for the change?" Jordan questioned. "Keith changed our original destination from Newark Liberty to the Army Base on Staten Island. Now, you are changing our destination a third time."

"Staten Island Airbase was compromised when Hiltree and his men were staying there," Sydney warned. "Before they bugged out,

Hiltree put cameras around the base for me. I was alerted about an hour ago of movement at the base. I checked the cameras, and Spinello's men are there, anticipating your arrival. I'm bringing you down at a secret runway. You're going to have to land like a CAT III. I'm already communicating with the computers onboard the Citation. You won't have a visual until the last minute but trust me it's there. My father used it all the time. I'll have you down in a few minutes," he said deploying the landing gear. "You won't have a visual until you clear the trees over the next hill."

"If you say so," Jordan stated as the jet barely skimmed the top of the trees. "Right now, it looks like we are going to crash in the woods."

"You're fine," Sydney said carefully slowing the airspeed. "The runway comes upon you quickly on purpose. Get ready to do your part."

"We've slowed to 130 knots, and we still don't see the runway," Sam cautioned.

"It's there," Sydney promised lowering the jet. "It's very tricky."

"Anything else we should know?" Sam pressed.

"You should get a visual any second," Sydney advised. "Get ready to brake fast. It's a short runway."

"I see it!" Jordan exclaimed as the plane lowered to the pavement. "We have touchdown!" he chuckled throwing the engines into reverse and pumping the brakes. "We're down to 60 knots and slowing."

"At the end of the runway, there is a clearing on the right with a thick, net-like roof," Sydney instructed. "Park under it for cover. Bob is waiting to assist you inside."

"Copy that," Jordan stated turning off the runway and following Bob's instructions under the net.

"Jordan, glad to see you again," Bob exclaimed as they deplaned. "Man, that was the first time I helped park a plane! Sydney is great at giving crash courses. I never knew this runway was here."

"I never knew this runway was here," Paris stated. "And I grew up playing hide-in-seek in these woods with Dave. I'm Paris Sydney, David Sydney's cousin," she shook Bob's hand.

"I'm CC Sims," she introduced. "And this is Bernadette Roca. She's a good friend of Alonzo."

"I'm glad to meet you," Bob said shaking her hand. "Sam, it's good to see you again."

"You two know each other?" CC asked.

"Yes, I met Bob and his family when Ramsey and I helped them move into Kathe's Ponce Inlet home," Sam admitted. "How are the kids?"

"They're happy to be able to be outside in the fresh air again," Bob confessed. "They seem much more relaxed with this safe house. Sydney has a lot of things for them to do. Pete is becoming an expert at flying the drone."

"That's because Pete is a pilot," Sam grinned. "And from what I've heard, he's a natural."

"Yes, he is," Jordan agreed. "I've flown with Pete as my copilot. I gave him the stick, and he flew most of the way from Anguilla to Daytona."

"Let's go inside," Bob suggested. "My wife, Jeannie, has been cooking up a storm for you. Paris, Sydney said that you would be staying with us until this is over. I'll show you the guestroom."

"There is a guestroom now?" Paris questioned following him.

"Yes, Sydney added it near his father's study, since he crashes here on R & R's," Bob shared. "He felt funny staying in his parent's bedroom."

"I can appreciate how Sydney felt," Paris sighed. "The first night staying in my parents' last flat, I started having flashbacks. Which is why I'm here."

"Ramsey explained that to us," Bob confirmed. "You will be safe here with us."

After a late lunch, Jordan and Sam took the kids outside while Jeannie made everyone feel at home.

"If I may, I'd like to excuse myself from the tour," Paris explained. "I grew up in this house. I want to be alone in the study and call Dave."

"Of course," Jeannie smiled.

"I have to stop at the guestroom and grab my backpack," Paris explained. "Then, I'll be in the study if you need me."

"I won't let anyone disturb you while you're talking to Sydney," Jeannie assured her.

Oh, my, Paris thought, entering the study. A momentary feeling of peace just washed over me. I've got goosebumps. She rubbed her arms. I feel so safe when I'm in this room, she thought, walking around, remembering her childhood. I can see Uncle David working in his office, she thought, stopping in the doorway. I can't believe he died sitting at that desk, still trying to find out what happened to my parents. Now, it's Dave and my turn to find the truth. She reached for her phone. "Dave, I like the guestroom you added."

"I knew you would," Sydney explained. "Mom had the plans drawn up for the guestroom for us to come and stay when we had families. I found it in Mom's desk drawer after she passed."

"Aunt Deanna couldn't wait to be a grandmother," Paris recalled. "She always wanted a large family."

"That was Mom, all right," Sydney chuckled. "She always told me not to marry my work like Dad. He left us at the drop of a hat to places he couldn't discuss."

"Yes, he did," Paris agreed. "Remember on one of his birthdays when we were cutting the cake?"

"How could I forget," Sydney laughed. "He walked out of the room, talking on his phone, and didn't return for two weeks. I'm sorry I couldn't be there when you arrived, and like Dad, I can't tell you where I am. Instead of using our phones, I'm turning on the cameras in the study," he pressed enter. "We can see each other on the conference table monitor. I'll watch you as you move around the room. There you are," Sydney smiled. "You're all grown up. Hopefully, when this is over, we can get together."

"I'd love that," Paris agreed sitting in front of the monitor. "It's been way too long since we've been together. We're all each other have in the world now."

"You're the one that moved away," Sydney declared. "I'm still in the same area."

"I needed to search for the truth about my parent's murders," Paris confessed. "It took years, but it finally paid off. The last time I was in this room, I spoke with your father before I left for Europe. Uncle David received one of his mysterious phone calls and hurried into his office. He came out with his crash suitcase and briefcase. Uncle David kissed me goodbye. Then, realizing that I wouldn't be home when he returned, he took the time to tell me about a secret code between him and my parents. He pushed the ladder for the bookshelves over to the left side of his office doorway. I watched him climb to the top bookshelf, reach over the doorway, and opened a secret compartment. Uncle David said that the key to the code was in that compartment. I could hear a helicopter circle over the roof, and he received another call. Uncle David closed the compartment, slid down the ladder, and walked toward the fireplace. He turned to me and asked me to bring him his favorite ink pen on his desk.

When I returned, Uncle David was gone. I always knew it was a diversion for him to slip out of a secret door."

"Mom showed me after Dad passed how he did it," Sydney admitted. "Do you remember where the secret compartment was? Mom never mentioned this to me."

"Yes," Paris declared. "Above Uncle David's office doorway, on the second shelf from the top, by the left side, he did something on the slide pole that opened a secret compartment," she said moving the ladder under the office doorway. "Uncle David moved the books out of the way and touched something on the rung," she said climbing up the ladder, moving the books. "Uncle David said he embedded the family's fingerprint recognition onto the keypad, so no one else can ever open the compartment. We must touch two components at the same time, but I don't remember which ones. He left before I got a chance to see up close."

"Paris, I'm zooming in on the area," Sydney stated. "Did it have to do with putting your fingers under the lip separating the shelf from the door frame?"

"No, I think it had something to do with the ladder and the rolling hook assembly that connects the two," Paris supposed climbing the ladder. "Let me line the ladder up with the assembly closest to the office," she grabbed hold of the bookshelf, sliding the ladder over toward the door. "The ladder still moves as easy as when Uncle David built it."

"Yes, it does," Sydney chuckled zooming in on it. "Let me look closely where the ladder lines up with that metal clip. There's nothing. Move the ladder to the left, just a tad," he requested checking the other metal clips on the doorframe, and then zoomed in to the one by Paris again. "Is the top of that flat clip?"

"Why yes, it is," Paris noted.

"All the other clips have pointed tops," Sydney discovered, checking multiple cameras. "Place your index finger on the top of the metal clip. Now, slide your thumb down on the left side until you feel a groove or something different."

"I've got it!" Paris exclaimed. "It's small but different."

"Good," David complimented. "Now, do the same with your middle finger on the right side and then press both of them at the same time."

"Nothing moved," Paris whined.

"Knowing Dad, it might be a lever," Sydney suggested. "Do the same thing and pull down."

"That's it!" Paris exclaimed. "Dave, it's a lever! The bottom of the shelf raised six inches. You're a genius!" she reached inside. "There's a sealed-envelope," she opened it. "It's a CD with a hole in the middle that fits the mini-CD I found hidden in Dad's desk at the flat."

"Close the secret compartment by raising the lever, and get down from the ladder," Sydney requested. "Then, have CC, Sam, and Bernadette join you in my office. I'm turning on my computer for you. We'll crack the code together."

"Give me a minute," Paris hurried down the hall to the living room. "CC, Sam, Bernadette, please come with me," she requested as they followed Paris into Sydney's office. "Sydney is ready to help us crack the code," she sat at the desk. "Sydney, we're all here."

"Ramsey joined me," Sydney announced reaching for a cup of coffee. "Let's hope this is what we think it is. Paris, see if the mini-CD you found fits inside the one that was in the envelope?"

"It has to!" Paris reached in her backpack and placed her find inside the larger disk. "It fits perfectly!"

"I watched Dad as a young boy design a spy camera that used a small round removable disk," Sydney admitted watching her. "I didn't know at the time that it was for Daniel and Cynthia. Paris, insert the disk into the drive on the side of my computer," he requested. "Let me see if I can open it," Sydney remotely clicked on the CD driver. A message appeared on the screen, which read, 'Mirror to complete access.' Give me a minute. I have to access my father's computer," he moved the mouse to the icon. "This is my father's desktop," he said dragging the CD into the image. "Bingo, we're in!" Sydney exclaimed watching the computer read the disk, bringing up a picture of two men at Charles De Gaulle Airport. A second program automatically opened a facial recognition program. "Perry Newcomb is the man on the left," Sydney identified. "I remember him. He was the Director of the FBI when Dad worked there. He came to our house many times. Aunt Cynthia circled a ring on Newcomb's hand," he zoomed in on it. "I don't recognize the insignia."

"The man on the right is Raymon L'Simonette!" Ramsey identified. "It is before L'Simonette came to work for Alby Airlines. Cynthia circled a ring on his finger as well," Sydney zoomed in on it. "They are identical. Maybe, it's a frat-ring."

Next, the computer pulled up another picture of two men with distorted faces talking to a heavy-set man and another taller Italian. Facial recognition could not recognize the two men with deformed faces. It did identify Pietro Bencivenni, but not Antonio Falcini, Sr."

"That's the men!" Paris gasped. "The heavy-set man was the driver of the getaway car! The other man was in the backseat smoking a cigar!"

"Are you sure?" Ramsey questioned. "It doesn't make any sense that facial recognition didn't recognize Antonio Falcini, Sr. Sydney, recheck it."

"The computer doesn't recognize Antonio," Sydney rechecked. "Why would Bencivenni wait until years later to try to kill Antonio and Mineyo to take over the Family Business? He could have done it there?"

"Ramsey, those are the men!" Paris sighed with tears streaming down her cheeks. "We were crossing the street to get ice cream. Mom froze on the sidewalk whispering a name to my father. The driver started the car when he saw us. Another man ran out of the store shooting in our direction. Dad tried to draw the fire away from us. It worked at first. Then the bullets came at us. Mom pushed me to the ground and covered me. I still have nightmares of her body jerking each time the bullets struck her, covering me. The first thing she whispered was for me to stay still. The last thing she uttered was 'I love you.'"

"Paris, this is too painful for you," CC hugged her. "I'll change places with you. Sam, help Paris sit on the windowsill behind us."

"Of course," Sam complied. "Would you like to lay down or leave the room?"

"No, I want to stay," Paris defended. "It was a shock seeing their faces other than in a nightmare every night."

"I read through all the police records," CC shared. "It never mentioned Antonio Sr.'s name."

"Paris positively identified Antonio Sr.," Ramsey confirmed. "That means Antonio Sr. was in Luxembourg and responsible for the murder of her parents."

"I'm not too sure about that," Sydney stated rechecking. "This program is never wrong. Alonzo said Antonio Sr. never left the safety of his compound after being accused of killing a German businessman," Sydney recalled. "Daniel and Cynthia spoke fluent German."

"Daniel's cover was a German businessman of a dummy company for the government," CC admitted accessing the file on her work laptop.

"Dad didn't know Antonio Sr. was there that day," Sydney confided. "In his notes, I found Dad suspected it but couldn't prove it even after checking Antonio's passport."

"Someone could have falsified Antonio's passport," Ramsey declared. "Then they tried to frame him for their murders. That's why the Bureau made your father stand down. We know that Spinello got to Perry Newcomb after Paris was born and the Luxembourg vacation. Click on the next picture; let's see what else we find."

"That's Bencivenni, and Antonio Sr. with the two men with distorted faces, again," CC stated. "And look who's in the background," she grinned. "It's our old friend, their attorney, Angus Muldanero."

"Notice as you scroll through the file that the newer pictures of Angus Muldanero show him wearing the same ring Cynthia circled," Sam pointed out after viewing several more pictures.

"Spinello admitted to Kathe at her house in Ponce that they killed the real Angus Muldanero because he got cold feet," CC stated. "They replaced him with a look-alike."

"Cynthia and Daniel were the first to discover the meaning of the rings," Sydney realized. "Muldanero is wearing the identical ring as Newcomb and L'Simonette," Sydney confirmed searching the Internet for the ring. "Let's see if it's Bencivenni's frat-ring."

"Jenkins had a female version of that ring in his pocket the last night we were at my condo!" Ramsey declared. "He asked me a few weeks prior what my ring size was."

"Thank God, he didn't put it on your finger," CC stated.

"It's not a frat-ring," Sydney declared pulling up the first couple of pictures they viewed. "Before the Luxembourg trip, Perry Newcomb wasn't wearing the ring. Afterward, he was. It proves that Director Newcomb changed his mind about helping Spinello, or they replaced him."

"To replace someone that fast with a look-a-like shows it was already planned and in the makings," Sam assumed.

"Let me quote Alonzo again," Ramsey shook her head. "By Bencivenni either replacing world leaders or the next in line a few at a time, no one will notice. Please continue."

"It's the same men with distorted faces with Bencivenni in Russia," CC stated.

"I don't recognize the general, but I recognize the place," Ramsey identified. "It's in Baikonur, Russia. That's where the first early-unmanned space rockets launched. Something is handwritten under the general's picture," she leaned forward and read. "Gen. Uilám Yetsun, that's how ESPGOTU1000 got into orbit. That must be Eduardo Santo Prado and Carlos, healing from plastic surgery. Bencivenni introduced them to Yetsun, and Muldanero is in the background to finalize the contract."

"That has to be the original Muldanero," CC noted. "He's not wearing the ring."

"There is one more picture," Sydney stated pulling it up.

"That's Tomme Boy Dano with Bencivenni and Antonio Sr.," Bernadette identified. "They're at a café in Varenna, Italy. It's on Lake Como. I forgot about that city."

"That's the shooter!" Paris screamed rushing to the monitor. "That man ran out of the shop shooting at us!"

"Are you sure?" Ramsey asked. "You were only five, and it took place so fast."

"I told you that I have recurring nightmares since that day," Paris admitted. "I see those faces every time!"

"That means Dano was involved from the beginning!" Bernadette exclaimed. "CC, Sam, we've got to go to Varenna! I'm sure that's where Dano is hiding. Now, I'm sure Dano has the missing pieces to your puzzle. I need to have Alonzo make a phone call for us."

"The pilots need to get some sleep before you leave," Ramsey cautioned.

"We have three pilots on board," Bernadette defended. "One can sleep while the other two fly the plane. I slept the entire trip over the ocean. After seeing and hearing this, I'm ready to leave now."

"I am, too," Sam stated. "Jordan can rest first."

"There is a hidden shed to the right of the airstrip," Sydney stated. "It has a portable fueler inside. Fill up your tank before you leave."

"Copy that," Sam said. "We'll leave as soon as we refuel."

"Have Jeannie fill the little pantry on board with food," Sydney offered. "You have to fly incognito again. I'll give you your new call letters and file your flight plan. That should give you the freedom to move around without fear of L'Simonette knowing your status."

"Copy that," Sam answered. "Let us know when we can depart. We will be in contact with you along the way."

"Copy that," Sydney answered. "Paris, put those disks back in the secret compartment after everyone leaves the room. You are to stay with Bob and Jeannie. Let the professionals handle Dano."

"But I need to go with them and see this through," Paris whined.

"They do this daily," Ramsey advised. "They have one shot at finding Dano and getting him to talk. You're too emotional about the situation and will get in their way. You don't need to witness the vengeance and live with another recurring nightmare. We will finish what your parents started and bring these people to justice. These same people also tried to harm Kathe's children. That's why Sydney and I put them at Sydney's house. You know this house better than anyone and can help Bob and Jeannie keep them safe."

"You're right," Paris sighed. "After seeing what they did to me as a small child, I would hate for them to get their evil hands on these children."

"Paris, you did what you set out to do," Sydney declared. "You helped us identify your parent's murderers."

"Thanks, Dave," Paris said as tears filled her eyes. "I guess this part of the nightmare is finally over."

"Yes, and you proved it like you said you would," Sydney acknowledged. "You're needed to protect the children. We will talk later."

Thursday, July 2, 2000 (8:00 PM EST)
The Florida Keys and Sierra Maestra

"This is the end of the road," Will stated stopping the SUV. "We've worked all around the world. I've never seen such a narrow, curvy road with a steep drop-off like this before," Will admitted pointing ahead. "Even with SUVs, there is no way we can drive up the rocky, narrow trail ahead of us."

"I agree," Stephen confirmed. "Eduardo is shrewd. He chose the area that Fidel Castro hid in for years when he was exiled," Stephen said checking the time. "We have just enough time to set up camp before dark. Let's check with Yorg," he said getting out of the SUV and walking to the other vehicle. "Yorg, this is the end of the so-called road. Let's stay here tonight. We need to head out on foot early in the morning while it is cooler."

"We don't know what's around us," Yorg cautioned. "Let's pull deeper into the woods, and then I'll have Jay and Jack get the drone up to check. Follow me," he said pulling into the woods.

"There is a clearing big enough for two vehicles," Kathe pointed.

"Jay, Jack, get the drone up while I call Sydney," Yorg requested as Will parked next to him.

"It won't take long," Jack shared getting out of the SUV.

"This is more secluded than staying by the road," Yorg shared. "I'll contact Sydney and have him check our surroundings with our drone," he reached for his phone. "Sydney, we're stopping for the night and checking the perimeter around us."

"Let me get back online with you," Sydney confirmed switching the call. "I'm adding Skip and Mack to the conversation. They'll have different angles of the drone's cameras. Hang on a minute. Skip, I need you and Mack to help us look for any unfriendlies near Stephen's campsite for the night."

"Copy that," Skip agreed bringing up their cameras. "Our cameras are fully operational now," he said as the last one loaded.

"The drone just cleared the trees," Sydney relayed. "The 360-camera will give us a better view of what's in the area. I note a waterfall ahead of them. It has a large opening behind it if they need a hiding place. It's high enough to give them the edge against foes. The terrain around the narrow trail is starting to thicken, compounded with large rocks. They'll have their work cut out for them tomorrow."

"I see they're in for a rough climb, especially with the heat and humidity," Skip glanced at each camera. "About a quarter of a mile from the team on the left," Skip zoomed in on the left-top camera. "I see something that could be the corner of a wooden structure high in the trees. "I can't be sure. It's pretty hidden."

"Jack needs to take the drone closer," Mack added. "I've seen guard stations like this before. I'd hate to overlook it, and they're camping in someone's front yard."

"Jack, see if you can find it?" Yorg asked pointing in that direction.

"Copy that," Jack acknowledged bringing the drone down through the trees.

"I don't know who would want to live out here," Stephen declared swatting at a mosquito. "There's nothing out here but bugs, heat, and humidity."

"The poor have to," Kathe stated joining them. "There's so much poverty in Cuba. There's no shortage of electricity at the resorts and government buildings. The houses of the ordinary people at night are either dark or dimly lit with candles."

"Eureka!" Jay reported zooming in on the center camera. "It was hard to see in the dense vegetation. However, it is a treehouse," he targeted the steps. "Someone recently repaired the steps."

"At the end of the driveway, look to the right about 100 yards-back in the woods," Mack reported zooming in on the center-right-bottom camera. "There is a camouflaged canopy. The canopy is covering what could be the bottom of seven metal slats on the front grill of a Jeep."

"Copy that," Jay stated trying to zoom closer.

"Jack, I need you to take the drone under the canopy," Jay requested as Jack complied. "It's an old Jeep that has been involved in gunfire, more than once," Jay said showing multiple bullet holes. "The windshield is riddled with bullets, also," Jay zeroed inside the vehicle. "There are old bloodstains on the front passenger seat. Jack let's see the tag. It's not government, so it will be easier if we must deal with them. Now, go back to the treehouse. I can't wait to see who our new neighbors are."

"Copy that," Jack agreed flying the drone under the top of the roof.

"Stop right there!" Jay requested zeroing in on the inside. "Can you believe this?"

"It's a guerrilla guard station," Mack declared. "I was stationed at Guantanamo Bay for four years. I flew recon over the mountain ranges of Cuba. We heard rumors that the guerillas are protecting something on top of the mountain on a large scale. Our instruments wouldn't work three-fourths of the way up on this side of the mountain, and we had to turn away. We did foil the attempt of several guerrillas kidnapping young females from the villages. They sell the girls to coyotes for drug trafficking."

"I can see why Hiltree chose you to work with Skip," Sydney admired. "You know the hot-spots in the area that compromised your instrumentation within this large theater."

"It was not just the instruments onboard the helicopters," Mack explained. "We lost several drones in the area. The batteries drain instantly, and they fell out of the sky like a rock."

"Copy that," Sydney said making a note. "We've encountered similar devices that block airwaves in multiple locations in the states. However, not on a large scale as this arena."

"It proves we are in the right place," Ramsey noted. "Philippi Spinello used this technique in New Jersey, and Carlos Prado used it in Miami."

"There are enough drugs on that table to kill thousands of people in the states," Yorg declared. "The bags are stacked ten high and cover the entire table," he squinted his eyes. "Can you zero in on the middle row? Those bags look different."

"Sure," Jay complied. "They're marked Fentanyl."

"That's what I was afraid of," Yorg sighed. "Drug dealers lace cocaine and heroin with Fentanyl to keep their clientele hooked. I read 300 people a week are dying from this drug alone."

"By the white powder on their mustaches and tip of their noses," Kathe added watching Jay's iPad. "It looks like they are using their products."

"That mixed with the bottles of tequila on the other table would make them dangerous to handle," Jay pointed out.

"That's putting it mildly," Jack chuckled. "Let's face it. They are hardened criminals that are higher than kites with the strength of gorillas."

"Heads-up!" Mack noted. "We've got movement coming down from the top of the mountain to the right of the trail. Give me a second for them to get into a clearing," he zeroed in. "Two guerrillas are bringing four, young girls for the coyotes," Mack sighed watching them dragging the girls tied together. They're staying off the trail, so our military surveillance cameras can't detect them. Human Trafficking is a big business here."

"Those are extremely young girls," Ramsey sighed as Sydney zeroed in on that camera. "We don't need this kind of trouble. It's the worst timing for us to intervene. It will blow our cover."

"The coyotes use these children to smuggle drugs across the border," Sydney replied. "They are unaccompanied minors that easily enter and stay in the states."

"It was a great feeling when my unit rescued several of these children and returned them home," Mack admitted. "We had to rescue them on the sly. We weren't supposed to be on Cuban soil. If captured, we knew the risk was death or incarceration."

"The same problem we face, stopping these terrorists," Ramsey sighed.

"The guerrillas stopped behind a large rock formation across from the treehouse," Sydney noted. "One of them stayed with the girls. The other one is approaching the treehouse."

"Copy that," Mack noted. "The negotiator checks the guard station against rival groups that try to muscle in on their territory. Let's listen," he turned up the microphone.

"Sosa, Learco," the negotiator called drawing his weapon and firing it in the air.

After a long minute, the door on the porch slowly cracked open.

"Sosa, Learco, es Tajo, mís amigos," he declares reshooting his gun.

"Sosa, Learco, it is Tajo, my friends," Mack translated.

"Ah, Tajo," Sosa slowly appeared. "¿Ah, Tajo, ¿dondé esta Pineda?"

"Ah, Tajo, where is Pineda?" Mack interpreted.

"EL está por allá," Tajo state, pointing toward the trees. "¿Tienes el dinero?"

"He is over there," Mack relayed. "Do you have the money?"

"¿Los recibiste?" Sosa asked.

"Did you get them?" Mack interpreted.

"¡Sí, tenemos algo para ti!" Tajo laughed. "Déjame ver el dinero primero."

"Yes, we have something for you," Mack translated. "Let me see the money first."

Sosa opened the door, "Learco, quieren su dinero primero."

"Learco, they want the money first," Mack echoed.

Learco came out on the porch, "no nos dieron dinero esta vez."

"They didn't give us the money this time," Mack said.

"¿Por qué?" Tajo demanded. "No es así como hacemos negocios."

"Why?" Mack translated. "That's not how we do business."

"Los coyotes quieren ver la mercancía primero que viene esta noche," Learco stated. "Quiero asegurarme de que sean jóvenes; no como la última vez. Los chicas eran demasiado viejas para cruzar la frontera."

"The coyotes want to see the merchandise first," Mack translated. "They are coming tonight. They want to make sure they are young, not like last time. The girls were too old to cross the border."

"Ah, mí amigos," Tajo laughed. "Eso es todo lo que pudimos encontrar en tan poco tiempo. Te gustarán estas chicas. Nos fuimos a un pueblo diferente.

"That's all we could find on such short notice," Mack relayed. "You will like these girls. We got them from a different village."

"¿Qué quieres decir con un breve aviso?" Sosa demanded. "Llegaste tarde y te dije que no iban a funcionar. Tú eres el que insistió podrían cruzar."

"What do you mean by short notice?" Mack echoed. "You were late bringing them, and I told you they wouldn't work. You are the one that insisted they could cross."

"Así que cometí un pequeño error," Tajo chuckled, putting his hands out. "Pineda, traer a las chicas."

"So, I made a small mistake," Mack relayed. "Pineda, bring the girls."

"Aquí estas las chicas," Pineda said dragging them out into the open. He pulled them next to Tajo. "Te gusta?"

"Here are the girls," Mack relayed. "Do you like them?"

"Estas funcionarán," Learco smiled. "Criarlos. Esperaremos a los coyotes y todos nos pagarán esta vez."

"These will work," Mack interpreted. "Bring them up. We will wait for the coyotes, and all get paid this time."

"Sube," Sosa smiled, "tendremos de tequila para celebrar, antes de que lleguen los coyotes."

"Come up," Mack said. "We will have tequila to celebrate before the coyotes arrive."

"The ones inside set up an ambush for Tajo and Pineda," Ramsey warned watching them carry the screaming girls up the ladder. "The coyotes paid in advance for a product they couldn't use. Dealers go to coyotes, not the other way around."

"These poor, innocent children," Kathe sighed as Jack moved the drone to view inside. "They're caught in the middle of this. They can't be more than seven to ten-years-old. We have to stop this!"

"How can we save these children and not tip our hand?" Stephen wondered. "We've had a few bumps, but so far, we've contained our situations. Our cover is working."

"That is true," Ramsey agreed. "We need to think this through."

"However, we can't turn our eyes on this," Stephen insisted. "I couldn't live with myself."

"Stephen, I have the same feelings," Ramsey confided. "After listening to Mack, what we're looking for is definitely on top of that mountain. We need to remain in the shadows. Otherwise, getting to the top will be next to impossible. This mountain is crawling with Eduardo's guards and guerillas; not to forget Márquez keeps breathing down your necks with Cuban soldiers."

"I have an idea, and we don't have to move from this spot," Kathe suggested. "Using the mosquito-drone, I can knock them out. By the time they come to, we'll be long gone with the girls. They won't know what happened, and no one will know we're here."

"You need to hurry and decide," Jay declared zeroing in on the table. "As you can see, Learco is opening a bag of cocaine. Sosa is holding a girl next to the table."

“We’re going to plan B!” Kathe exclaimed listening to the girls scream. “Will, take over the drone. Stephen, take over the iPad for the camera. The rest of us, let’s go!” Kathe exclaimed drawing her weapon and hurrying toward the tree.

“I can’t believe this!” Ramsey snapped. “Use your silencers! Sounds will loudly echo all over the mountain and bring people from all over. We’ll have to do damage control later!”

“Stephen, let me take over the camera for a minute,” Sydney stated as he pressed enter. “I need to see how to get our team safely inside quickly,” he said scanning the cabin. “The steps are very narrow. Only one person at a time can use them. Even with the drones, we’ll have to work quickly, before the coyotes arrive.”

“Kathe, Yorg, and Jay wait near the steps,” Ramsey ordered watching the screen. “Jack, take your rifle and climb the tree in front of the porch on the side facing the road. You can take Learco and possibly Sosa out from there. Let me know when you’re in place.”

“Copy that,” Jack agreed slinging his rifle over his shoulder and hurrying off.

“I don’t have a view of the opening,” Sydney stated. “Yorg, if you gently press up on the trap door, you’ll see where the latch is.”

“Copy that,” Yorg whispered quietly climbing the steps. He gently pressed on the trap door, motioning to Kathe where it was, and hurried back down the ladder.

“Kathe, there’s quite a bit of commotion going on inside the house,” Sydney explained. “They shouldn’t notice JAKE cutting the latch.”

“Copy that,” Kathe answered climbing the ladder. She held JAKE toward the latch, manually turned on the laser, and cut quickly through it. She signaled thumbs up to let Yorg know and then climbed down.

“She did it,” Yorg smiled relaying the message to Sydney.

“Copy that,” Sydney stated. “I’m sending you the feed so you can see what you’re facing,” he said, pushing enter. “As you can see, inside is just an open room. Behind the steps in the right corner, there is a small room. It’s probably the bathroom. Pineda is sitting on a bed to the left of the trap door, against the wall drinking tequila and lighting a cigarette. He has one of the girls next to him. Tajo is sitting on a bed directly in front of the steps, drinking tequila with the youngest two girls on each side of him. Learco is sampling the cocaine on the table to the back-right of the steps. Sosa is holding the oldest girl at the end of the table facing Learco.”

"They will drug that girl first and then abuse her as an example of what's to come to the others!" Ramsey fumed.

"Open borders entice this behavior!" Sydney exclaimed.

"Who would have thought our society would evolve into infanticide and not caring about the lives of the innocent?" Kathe snapped.

"It's up to people like us to make a difference," Stephen insisted.

"Amen to that," Will agreed zeroing in on Jack, shimming up the tree. "Jack is almost in place."

"Copy that," Ramsey acknowledged. "Stephen, I know Jay gave you something to protect yourself. However, there is a gun in the glove compartment in the front seat of your SUV. It's easier to use. I need you to guard the steps and help the girls to safety if we need you."

"Copy that," Stephen agreed hurrying to the vehicle.

"Will, there is also a gun under the driver's seat for you," Ramsey reported. "You can stay with the vehicles and fly the drone from there. Stephen will bring you the girls as we rescue them."

"Copy that," Will agreed following Stephen to the vehicles.

"Jay, if Jack can't get Sosa for some reason, it's your job," Ramsey ordered. "Kathe, your job is to back them up. As they rescue a girl, bring her to Stephen. He can take her to Will by the vehicles for safety."

"Copy that," Kathe agreed following Yorg up the steps.

"We're ready when Jack and Stephen are in place?" Sydney declared.

"Copy that," Jack stated looking through his scope. "I'm green."

"Copy that," Stephen agreed from behind the central tree holding the house up. "I'm green."

"On my count, we go on three," Sydney began. "One, two, three."

Yorg burst through the hatch, shot Pineda, and pivoted his gun toward Tajo, who shoved one of the girls at Yorg, and reached for his gun. Yorg pushed the girl behind a chair next to the steps. While Jay propped his rifle on the floor, pointing at Sosa.

"¡No te muevas! (Don't move!)" Jay yelled as Sosa turned pivoting the girl in front of him.

"No!" Learco screamed throwing the open bag of cocaine at Jay and reaching for the pistol on the table.

"Goodbye," Jack admitted squeezing the trigger, shooting Learco through the front window. Sosa fell to the floor with the girl, pulling her under the table next to him. Sosa reached for his gun and swung his arm around to shoot Yorg in the back.

"No!" Jack declared squeezing the trigger, shooting the gun out of Sosa's hand.

"Great shot!" Ramsey admired as Tajo jumped up, moved the second girl as a shield, and held his pistol pointed at Yorg.

"¡No te muevas!" Yorg reiterated. (Don't move!)

"Jack, do you have a shot at either of them?" Ramsey asked.

"Negative," Jack stated looking through his scope. "I have no visual on Sosa," he moved his rifle. "Tajo is using the girl as a human shield directly in front of him."

"Jay, are you alright?" Ramsey asked watching him on the steps wiping his face with his sleeve.

"Yes, I didn't get the powder in my eyes," Jay answered getting back into position. "Where is Sosa?"

"Mack, do you have a better view of Sosa?" Sydney asked as Mack zeroed in on the bottom-center camera.

"Sosa is crouching down behind a chair under the windowsill in the far-left corner," Mack relayed.

"Kathe, use your mosquito on kill-not stun," Sydney ordered.

"Copy that," Kathe agreed releasing the mosquito from JAKE.

"Heads-up!" Skip warned zooming in on another camera. "Ramsey, we have a truck halfway up the mountain road coming toward them."

Mack looked at Skip's monitor as the truck came around the corner in view, "I see a coyote's tattoo on the driver's neck. They are coming for the girls. Ramsey was right. Drug dealers usually take the drugs and the girls to the coyotes. I've never seen coyotes come up this far."

"Jay, you and Stephen have to stop them," Ramsey ordered. "Jay, give Stephen a rifle. Will, stay with this situation until it's clear. Then, we will move the drone to that situation."

"Copy that," Will confirmed standing between the two SUVs.

"I'll guide Jay and Stephen," Mack stated switching seats with Skip.

"Kathe, we just ran out of time!" Ramsey exclaimed.

"My drone is ready," Kathe stated lifting the drone to the opening.

"We've got to hurry," Sydney warned watching the mosquito pass Yorg, entering the house. "I see Tajo," Kathe said flying the mosquito behind Tajo's neck and landing it. Then, she tapped the red X-icon, injecting him. He instantly slumped over on top of the girl.

"Good job," Sydney stated. "Now for Sosa," Sydney requested watching Sosa slump forward as the girl screamed.

"It's okay," Yorg declared shoving Tajo off one of the girls.

"Gracias, soy Anita," she hugged him.

"Thank you, I'm Anita," Sydney relayed.

Kathe hurried up the steps to the girl behind the chair. "Estás a salvo con nosotros," Kathe told her as she hugged her." (We will take you to safety.)

"Gracias," (Thank you,) she hugged Kathe. "Soy Cambria." (I'm Cambria.)

"Jack, help Jay and Stephen," Sydney ordered. "Will, this situation is clear. I need a visual on the mountain road."

"Copy that," Will agreed as Mack guided Will quickly to pinpoint the location of the truck.

"Kathe, take the girls to the SUVs," Ramsey requested checking the cameras around them. "You're clear to the vehicles."

"Copy that," Kathe agreed.

"Selina, ven con nosotros," (Selina, come with us.) Cambria reached out her arms toward the girl by the windowsill.

"Let's go, Anita," Yorg said walking to the steps.

"¡Espera, mi hermana Mariah esta debajo de la cama!" Cambria pointed to the bed by Pineda. (Wait, my sister Mariah is under the bed.)

"Espera, dejame sacarla de abajo de la cama," (Wait, let me get you out from under the bed.) Kathe hugged Cambria and then knelt, reaching for Mariah around Pineda's body on the floor. "Ven conmigo y estaras a salvo." (I'll get her. Come with me to safety.)

"Ella no puede hablar," Cambria stated. (She can't talk.)

"¿Por qué?" Kathe asked as she looked at Cambria. (Why?)

"Algo le sucedió hace unas pocas semanas y no ha hablado desde," Cambria said as she shrugged her shoulders. (Something happened to her a few weeks ago, and she hasn't talked since.)

"¿Ella puede escuchar?" Kathe asked. (Can she hear?)

"Si y ella entiende lo que decimos," Cambria stated. (Yes, and she understands what we say.)

"Yorg, what's the holdup?" Ramsey demanded. "Get those girls out of there! I need you to help the team."

"Mariah is under the bed and won't come out," Yorg stated. "She's one of the youngest, and she can't talk. Kathe is trying to reach her. She's in shock, kicking, and screaming."

"Who's bigger?" Ramsey demanded throwing her hands in the air. "We've got a truck filled with coyotes on the way with possibly more coming."

“Copy that,” Yorg stated and put Anita down. “Kathe, you heard Ramsey,” he said lifting the head of the bed.

Mariah’s eyes widened, looking up at Yorg.

“Soy estadounidense,” Kathe stated as Mariah began to tremble with fear. “¡Ven conmigo y estaras a salvo!” (I am American. Come with me to safety.) “Mariah, hay más hombres malos se aproximan, ven conmigo. Por favor,” she reached for her. (Mariah, more bad men are coming. Please.)

“Mariah, ven con nosotros,” Cambria cried. “Estas personas nos salvaron.” (Mariah, come with us. These people are trying to save us.)

Mariah reluctantly crawled to Kathe.

“Prometo llevarte a casa,” Kathe said picking her up. (I promise to get you home.)

“Ramsey, we’re coming down now,” Yorg reported.

“Copy that,” Ramsey said watching the new situation. “Hurry to the team.”

“Let’s go,” Yorg said leading the way down the steps.

“Kathe, we might need you against the coyotes,” Ramsey cautioned. “Sydney found a cave under the waterfall near you. See if it’s safe for the girls to hide in if you need to help us. Will, stay by the SUVs and work the drone.”

“Copy that,” Kathe agreed.

“Will, the truck just went around another corner and will reappear in a minute,” Mack reported. “Will, take the drone farther over the cliff for a better view of the entire area.”

“Copy that,” Will agreed moving the drone.

“That’s much better,” Mack stated checking all cameras.

“Mack, I’ll take over the situation now,” Sydney declared. “I want you and Skip to watch for more unfriendlies in the area. There’s no telling who heard Tajo’s gunshots.”

“Copy that,” Mack agreed. “The coyotes will use this as a lesson for anyone else thinking of cheating them.”

“I can’t believe we have to do damage control on two areas,” Ramsey snapped.

“Not necessarily,” Sydney grinned glancing at her. “The coyotes are personally coming to pay these four men a visit. Older girls can’t enter the United States as unaccompanied minors, so they are coming to get revenge on all of them. Sosa and Learco knew the girls were too old and still sold them.”

“Yes, they did,” Ramsey agreed. “But how is that going to help us? We’re left with four bodies to get rid of, not to mention two of them have bullet holes. We can’t set the house on fire due to the powdery, dry condition on the mountain range. And the drugs on the table will explode.”

“But we can put the bodies with the cocaine in the truck and send it over the mountain to burn when it hits bottom,” Sydney smiled. “It will look like a drug deal gone bad.”

“That just might work!” Ramsey grinned. “People, change of plans! Jack, we need that truck to get rid of the bodies and cocaine. Wait until it clears the cliff area before you stop it. We need it intact for the moment.”

“Copy that,” Jack confirmed zeroing his sights in on the road.

“Will, bring the drone closer to the mountain,” Sydney requested. “I want to get a picture of these coyotes.”

“Copy that,” Will complied.

“The truck is getting ready to clear the next curve,” Sydney relayed. “After I document them, we’ll take them down.”

“Copy that,” Jay added. “Stephen and I are in place to take them out.”

“Copy that,” Sydney confirmed. “Since Yorg is there, Stephen, it’s your call if you want to go back to the SUV and wait with Will.”

“Negative,” Stephen declared. “I, like most Americans, got numb hearing this on the news for the last several years. Seeing those frightened little girls and those sick animals pawing at them brought it to reality. I want to stay and help defend them.”

“Copy that,” Sydney stated. “I figured you would say that.”

“Sydney, I’m in place,” Jack reported. “I’m on the tree limb overhanging the road. When the truck comes around again, I’ll be in line with the windshield.”

“Copy that,” Sydney stated. “Perfect spot to stop them.”

“Jack, it’s making the last curve now,” Sydney declared. “Let it pass you first and then disable it.”

“Copy that,” Jack answered holding his finger on the trigger. “It’s on the straightaway to me. As soon as it passes me, I’ll stop them.”

“I don’t want those three coyotes to get away,” Ramsey ordered. “Is that understood?”

“Copy that,” they each confirmed.

“Come to Papa,” Jack whispered peering through his scope.

“Everyone, hold your fire until Jack stops the truck,” Ramsey ordered as the monitor went blank.

“Our cameras are down!” Sydney declared feverishly typing trying to regain the camera. “I repeat. The cameras are down! Will, are you all right? Will?”

“Will, talk to me?” Ramsey begged. “He’s not answering. Something is wrong!”

“Ramsey, I’m on my way to him!” Stephen declared signaling Yorg.

“Ramsey, we’ve got this,” Sydney declared. “You save Will.”

“Kathe, hide the girls, and release your mosquito!” Ramsey ordered. “You’re the closest to him!”

“I’m on my way!” Kathe exclaimed. “We just arrived at the waterfall from the opposite side he’s on,” she signaled the girls to stay put and hurried around to the other side. “I have a visual on Will. I’m releasing the mosquito.”

“I’ve got Kathe’s camera,” Mack declared bringing up her camera on his screen. “Ramsey, I’m sending you the live stream.”

“Now, I see Will!” Ramsey declared. “He is standing between the vehicles looking straight ahead. Kathe, work your way down to him.”

“I’m on my way,” Kathe carefully moved around a boulder behind a tree staying out of sight from his capturers.

“Kathe, I’m taking over your mosquito,” Mack insisted. “Skip will take over the camera to free you up.”

“Thanks,” Kathe released it to them.

“I’ve got the camera!” Skip replied taking it over.

“Mack, raise the mosquito to get a better view of the area,” Ramsey requested. “Stephen, carefully work yourself around to the vehicles. Kathe is almost in position. She’ll need backup.”

“Copy that,” Stephen replied checking his phone. “I’ve already taken out one of them on the way. That’s what held me up. I’m almost to the area.”

“Ramsey, Will thought fast enough to turn off his iPad,” Mack observed. “That way the man crouched down behind him couldn’t see what we were doing with the truck coming up the mountain. He also has his gun at Will’s back. And he is wired with an earbud.”

“So, he’s communicating with someone,” Ramsey assumed. “Skip, can you find the people he’s communicating with?”

“Copy that,” Skip agreed. “Mack, move the drone back down over the vehicles. “Let me check inside and around the vehicles first.”

"Will, I know you're listening," Ramsey comforted watching him slowly nod his head. "We will get you out of this. Stay calm and give us a minute to check our options. Skip, what else do you have for me?"

"There is no one else close to the vehicles or inside them," Skip checked. "Mack, give me a broader view of the surroundings. I need to scan the perimeter of the woods."

"I spot two targets barely inside the woods on each side of the vehicles," Ramsey noted. "They are in a crossfire pattern."

"I see them," Kathe agreed studying the line-of-sight.

"There is also a target in the woods in front of Will behind a tree," Skip zeroed in on him.

"Did Jay give Stephen and Will hidden weapons?" Kathe asked.

"Yes," Ramsey confirmed. "Give me a minute to have the computer check the trajectory and the range of Will's pistol with the target facing him," Ramsey said pressing enter. "The target is barely in range of Will's weapon. There's no margin for error. Will, you must shoot accurately."

"Stephen is coming in on the right side of the vehicles," Skip acknowledged.

"Good," Kathe determined. "I can take out the one crouched down behind Will and the one to his left quickly. Stephen, you need to take out the target on the right of the vehicles. Then, Will needs to take out the target facing him."

"That sounds doable," Ramsey approved. "Mack, fly over the target facing Will."

"The target facing Will is the one giving the orders," Mack turned up the microphone. "Listen to him."

"Copy that," Ramsey listened. "What's he saying?"

"They found the treehouse," Kathe interpreted. "The leader is in constant communication with these three men, since their backup isn't answering him."

"That must be the one Stephen took out on the way here," Ramsey assumed.

"They are each answering questions in order," Kathe continued. "If one doesn't answer, they'll kill Will."

"We can't risk that," Ramsey declared. "Stephen, can you take out Will's target along with the one on the right?"

"I haven't done this since Nam," Stephen admitted.

"Check your phone," Ramsey requested. "I circled each target for you to find them instantly."

"Copy that," Stephen affirmed checking his phone. "I see all four of them, as well as Kathe behind Will a little higher in elevation."

"That's correct," Ramsey confirmed. "That gives Kathe the advantage to pick them off easily. Mack, bring the mosquito above the target facing Will. I should be able to see all targets from that angle."

"Is this what you have in mind?" Mack asked moving the drone.

"That's perfect," Ramsey confirmed evaluating the situation. "Stephen, do you have a clear shot at your target?"

"Copy that," Stephen agreed bracing his weapon against a tree. "I'm locked and loaded."

"Kathe, first you are to take out the target holding the gun directly on Will," Ramsey formulated. "Then, you are to take out the left target."

"Copy that," Kathe agreed. "Will, as soon as you shoot your weapon, drop to the ground. Do you copy?"

"He's shaking his head, and slowly moving his hand down," Ramsey noted. "Will, we are ready. Are you?"

Will tilted his head again.

"Whatever happens, drop to the ground," Ramsey ordered. "Kathe or Stephen will take your target out if you miss."

Will tilted his head again.

"On one, you are to aim your weapons," Ramsey explained. "On two, everyone takes out your targets. On three, Kathe or Stephen will take any remaining targets. Are you ready?"

"Copy that," Kathe and Stephen answered as Will tilted his head.

"My count is beginning," Ramsey warned. "One, two," the shots fired, and "three," Will froze as bullets stuck around him, hitting the windshield of both vehicles and the ground around him.

"Will! Drop!" Kathe ordered moving the angle of her gun around him, striking the last target at the same time Stephen shot.

"Skip, zero in on all targets!" Ramsey requested. "Will, it's safe to stand up now. The situation is cleared."

"Will, are you okay, buddy?" Stephen asked watching him slowly get up.

"Yes," Will sighed. "I'm just mad at myself for missing my target and freezing in my tracks. I've never looked down the barrel of a gun before."

"I don't think I could do it either, if our roles were reversed," Stephen admitted. "It's hard facing an opponent."

"Stephen, your timing was spot-on," Kathe noted. "I wasn't the only one that hit Will's target."

"It was an automatic response," Stephen admitted. "Like I said, working with your team brings back my Nam days."

"Good job!" Sydney acknowledged rejoining them. "We eliminated our targets and loaded the truck with all the evidence. They need to push the truck over the cliff before they join you. I found another drivable site away from this area for them to stop for tonight."

"Copy that," Ramsey stated. "What about these four?"

"It looks like two cartels had a shootout with a double-crossfire," Sydney laughed. "Leave them. Kathe, get the girls ready to travel while you're waiting. There is food in Stephen's SUV for them."

"Copy that," Kathe agreed.

Chapter 5

Friday, July 3
Lake Como in Varenna, Italy 1700 (5:00 PM GMT + 2)
On the cutter off the coast of Cuba 1100 (11:00 AM EST)

"There is nothing like a small, colorful, fairytale village nestled between the base of a steep mountain, melting into a lake," Bernadette sighed gazing out the French doors of the hotel. "I haven't seen Dano in years, but I do know Dano has snitches everywhere he goes," Bernadette remembered putting on a large, brim hat and sunglasses. "I shouldn't be recognized like this. CC, come and see the most romantic city on Lake Como," Bernadette called opening the doors to the private balcony. "I truly forgot how majestic Varenna is."

"I read about Lake Como on the way here," CC shared following Bernadette outside. "It has five cities around an enormous lake."

"Yes, and each city has its own personality," Bernadette recalled taking a deep breath as she gazed at the sailboats. "There's nothing like the gentle, warm breeze off the lake."

"I hear beautiful church bells!" CC exclaimed looking around. "There it is," CC pointed. "I like that the church steeple is the tallest structure in town. It makes it easier for visitors to find."

"I've found in most small towns, the people are very religious," Bernadette shared. "The church is usually in the center of town. After church, at least in this part of the world, they have church picnics every Sunday."

"You've visited so many beautiful places in the world that I never imagined existed," CC confided. "I joined the Bureau to travel and got stuck behind a desk job after my first field job. What made you decide to join this business?"

"Believe it or not, the entire time Luca and I dated, we loved to camp, target practice, and hunt," Bernadette explained. "After we wed, we looked into professions that intrigued us and chose law enforcement. We frequently visited a shooting range in Corté d' Azuré near our apartment. Pauli and Alonzo practiced there from time-to-time. Everyone in town knew who they were but stayed away from them. Then one day, Dano showed up at the range and befriended us. After several weeks of practicing next to us and sometimes giving us pointers, we started going out for a bite to eat and got to know him; or we thought. One day, Dano said he had a business trip to Varenna and invited us to go with him. He said newlyweds deserved a honeymoon to remember, and Varenna was the perfect, romantic getaway. When we hesitated, Dano said it was his treat. He was tired of always traveling alone. After a few days of traveling with Dano, we fell in love with his rich lifestyle. We woke up the third morning to the news of the murder of a prominent British businessman. The military set up roadblocks on all the streets in a massive manhunt. Dano said the news was spoiling our trip. That afternoon, Dano rented a sailboat, and he took us to the next city. We spent several weeks on the boat, visiting each city before we returned home. A few days later, Dano introduced us to Alonzo at the gun range. Dano told Alonzo that we had the skills he needed for his business. Alonzo hired us on the spot, and we went to work for Mr. LaBasco. We thought Dano also did. That's when Dano explained that he was an independent contractor among several families. He promised when we built our reputations; he'd bring us into his fold."

"Didn't you realize that Dano killed that businessman?" CC asked. "It was apparent."

"Not until Alonzo paid Dano in front of us," Bernadette admitted. "Dano used us as his alibi. An eyewitness told the authorities it was a lone assailant. He must have snuck out while we were sleeping. That's when we realized if the authorities had caught Dano, we were just as guilty."

"Then, why did you stay in the business instead of joining the police force?" CC quizzed. "I'm sorry; it just came out! You don't have to answer that question."

"It's okay; it's part of your training," Bernadette chuckled. "I was furious that Dano put us in a dangerous position, but the lifestyle and money intrigued Luca."

"How can you be so sure Dano is in Varenna now?" CC wondered.

"Alonzo and Pauli made a few phone calls," Bernadette smiled. "Never underestimate the worldwide LaBasco family."

"Oh, I don't," CC admitted. "I've worked with Alonzo. One thing he taught me is that the underground has more information than the Bureau's database."

"The LaBasco underground does," Bernadette smiled. "Mr. LaBasco and Alonzo abide by the principle that if you want to stay ahead in this business, you must stay on top of your opposition. Alonzo is the one that formed a network of employees globally. He tightened the organization after Mario Jr. and Giorgio Pulini almost got away with taking over the business."

"That's when I met Alonzo and Pauli," CC shared.

"After Alonzo made some phone calls, he questioned why Spinello's men tried to stop us in Luxembourg, instead of Dano," Bernadette stated. "Dano rented the flat that Paris' parents rented right after the murders. He stayed there all these years until a week ago. It made Dano look weak when he didn't go after who rented the apartment next. Especially after hearing about the bits and pieces of the phone call the woman made," Bernadette shared as Sam joined them. "Ah, Sam, you're back. Were you able to rent a sailboat this late in the day?"

"It wasn't easy," Sam confided. "The owner at the marina denied having any boats left, until I pulled out several Benjamin Franklins, and surprisingly enough he rented me his catamaran."

"Perfect," Bernadette checked the time. "I need to meet with someone while you get the sailboat stocked and ready for the evening."

"When are you going to join us?" Sam asked.

"I shouldn't be too long," Bernadette admitted. "Just start heading toward the bulk of the outside shops and cafés along the lakefront. I'll catch up with you. My connection is waiting. Switch to earbud as soon as you set sail. Oh, and bring all your things, and wipe down the room. There's a possibility we won't be back," Bernadette cautioned reaching for her backpack and leaving the room.

An hour later, Sam and Jordan launched the catamaran. "Patti and I used to go sailing all the time before Jason was born," Jordan recalled maneuvering the boat out of the marina. "Boy, this brings back memories. Patti and I bought a catamaran after I started my first job. It wasn't as high-tech as this one, but it was nice. When I transferred to flying overseas, it wasn't long until she was pregnant, and we had to sell it. It's strange how one child can change everything in your life. I don't know how Kathe and Yorg can be in this line-of-work with four."

"Yes, you do," CC smiled. "You got married, became a pilot, and then had Jason. She had three children when she was forced into this business."

"I know that all too well," Jordan admitted. "I lived through all of the horrible details of her transformation from beginning to end."

"My story is about the same even though we didn't have children," Sam admitted. "After my first tour of duty in Afghanistan, my wife didn't want me to sign up for a second tour. She said she couldn't go through the loneliness and fear of not knowing if I was alive again. I tried it her way for about a year, but civilian life wasn't for this Marine. I couldn't overlook the crime that had taken over America while I was away. She left me the day I reenlisted. I couldn't blame her. She deserved to be with someone that would give her children, a white, picket fence, and come home every night."

"I think most professionals with families that travel fall into that category," Jordan shared. "Patti has a hard time when I'm overseas. She feels like a single mom with a teenager. It's hard today to stay on top of Jason's social life. However, neither of them has a problem with my salary and the lifestyle it affords them."

"Don't worry," CC affirmed. "Jason will probably follow in your footsteps. That's what I did. My mother was a flight attendant, and my father, an FBI Agent. Just like Sam, traveling, and justice is in my blood," she said as Bernadette contacted them.

"Jordan, I'm almost to you," Bernadette stated. "I don't want to draw attention to us by stopping for me to board. I want you to slow the boat down to 10 knots, so I can come aboard and then speed back up. I'm coming from the starboard side. Sam, be ready to assist me."

"Yes, ma'am," Jordan slowed the boat. "I've brought it down to 10 knots. Is this good?"

"It's too slow," Bernadette replied as Sam braced on the back steps, holding onto a rail. "Try 15 knots," she requested getting on the stern of a small speedboat, balancing herself. "That's perfect! Hold that speed! Sam, I'm ready!" she reached for him and jumped.

"I got you!" Sam caught her and pulled her aboard. "Jordan, speed up!" Sam shouted watching the speedboat turn right and then punching the gas.

"We're in the right city," Bernadette declared joining CC on the rear deck. Bernadette pulled out her phone, showing several pictures. "Dano has been seen lately walking with a slight limp and having dinner along this strip. He arrived here a few days ago, on June 28th, according to his passport, but has stayed out of sight until recently."

"That would put Dano's arrival around the time Paris said the flat became available," CC confirmed.

"And the way the landlord described the lifestyle, it's that of a hitman," Sam added. "He only paid rent in cash, which left no trail. He didn't mingle with the other tenants, made him a loner. Occasionally, he would leave for a week or so, and then return."

“Spinello employs several contract killers,” Bernadette assured them. “I wasn’t sure which one it was until Paris recognized Dano in the picture with Antonio Falcini Sr. Then, I knew Dano killed her parents.”

“It’s almost sunset,” CC noticed standing up. “We need to look like we’re having a nice evening, instead of being on surveillance. I’ve set out some drinks and heavy hors d’oeuvres on the front deck,” she said leading the way.

“Can’t say no to food,” Sam chuckled putting several hors d’oeuvres on his plate.

“Jordan, this is where Dano has been seen lately,” Bernadette shared joining him in the flybridge. “Find a place to stop away from other boats, and face the outside cafés,” she received a text. “When you’re ready, come and join us. You need to know the plan.”

“Copy that,” Jordan agreed slowing the boat as he maneuvered it away from the last two catamarans and stopped. “I’ll be right there,” Jordan said securing the anchor and leaving the bridge.

“Here, Jordan,” Sam handed Jordan a wine glass.

“There’s nothing better than a glass of wine at the end of a day,” Jordan smiled swirling his glass, and smelling the aroma. “This is nothing but water?”

“Of course,” Sam chuckled. “We’re on a stakeout, but to the public, we need to look like we’re having a party.”

“Very funny,” Jordan smirked. “After what I’ve been through for the past few months, I’m ready for a R & R on my own catamaran with my family and wine.”

“Gentlemen, we need to get down to business,” Bernadette cautioned as they sat down. “Dano is one of the best in this business. He isn’t the kind of adversary you spot and chase. Dano always has several ways to escape. That’s why he picked Varenna. It has the most crowded shops, and alleyways, with lots of nooks and crannies to hide. We can’t show our hand until we’re ready to take him down. Dano has a photographic memory, if he sees us trying to apprehend him, he will hunt us down.”

“We don’t want a confrontation in the streets with witnesses,” CC warned. “We’re not in the states. The FBI has no jurisdiction here.”

“CC, let me assure you,” Bernadette chuckled receiving another text, “in our business, we don’t leave witnesses. Just a minute; it’s from my source,” Bernadette said reading it. “This answers Alonzo’s question as to why Spinello sent his men to stop us in Luxembourg instead of Dano,” she held her phone for them to see. “Here is Dano a few minutes ago entering the hospital. Notice the bandage on the lateral side of his right thigh just above the knee."

"That wound is still seeping pretty badly," CC pointed out.

"Yes, it is," Bernadette continued reading a text. "Dano went to the emergency room, presenting with a sizable amount of bleeding. My source was able to read his records while the doctor treated him. Dano had a tumor removed a week ago. This is his second visit back to the hospital since the surgery for the same reason."

"I noticed the same men around him in all the pictures," Sam added.

"Bernadette said Dano has snitches everywhere he goes," CC remembered. "Are they snitches or bodyguards?"

"My source confirmed they are Spinello's men," Bernadette assured her.

"Why would Spinello send bodyguards to protect Dano?" Sam asked. "He's just a hitman."

"That's what we have to find out," Bernadette admitted. "With this many bodyguards, it's going to be hard to get him alone. Let's get the drone up and see what our options are," Bernadette said sending a text and quickly receiving another one. "My source will let me know when Dano leaves the hospital," she said receiving another text. "Here is the address of the hospital."

"Where should we release the drone?" CC asked reaching for her backpack.

"Sundown is beginning," Sam stated. "I don't think anyone will notice if I take my iPad to the rear deck and release it. I'll be right back."

"Bernadette, if you'll send those videos to Dr. Sydney, he can add facial recognition to the drone's camera," CC stated. "That will help us keep up with Dano if he gets in a crowd."

"I'll send them right now," Bernadette complied.

"I better report to Sydney and Ramsey," CC said reaching for her phone.

"CC, I just received the videos," Dr. Sydney affirmed opening them. "Whoever took the videos did a great job. I've got perfect facial recognition as well as a retinal," he said continuing to type. "I'm uploading them to your drone's camera right now."

"Thanks, Bernadette took them," CC shared. "Sam is launching the drone, so you can help us figure the best way to take Dano down."

"Copy that," Sydney agreed as an alarm sounded on his console, and he checked the radar. "Jenkins is coming our way. I need to contact

Ramsey while Sam gets the drone up," he cautioned switching calls. "It seems we're getting company; ETA is forty-five minutes. You need to return to the HUB."

"I'm on my way," Ramsey snapped carrying two coffees. "Why is it that every time I go for coffee, something happens?"

"I have to admit that Jenkins picked the perfect time to join us," Sydney declared. "CC's team just located Dano."

"Great!" Ramsey scoffed. "Do you think someone tipped Jenkins off?"

"I'm not a fan of coincidence," Sydney confessed. "This isn't the first time Jenkins surprised us with a visit. I'll alert Skip and Mack. We have technology on board to help us find something on Jenkins. Look at the bright side; he's doing us a favor."

"It's no favor!" Ramsey scoffed. "Now that Jenkins is aware that Chameleon mutates, making it more powerful, he wants the technology even more."

"That is true," Sydney agreed. "But didn't you think I would videotape Jenkins working with us? Jenkins is as guilty as we are."

"Jenkins will deny it," Ramsey declared. "He'll say he was going along with us to catch us in the act."

"Not with the look on Jenkins' face when we showed him proof that Macaby was switched," Sydney grinned. "His facial expressions, along with the questions Jenkins asked, tell a different story. It's not just the evidence we have against him; it's leverage, and how or when we use it."

"I need to contact CC," Ramsey declared. "If Jenkins knows what CC's team is doing, he'll tip Spinello off. They need to hurry."

"Sam barely got the drone up," Sydney pointed to the top of the screen and then pressed enter. "You're on."

"CC, are you all together?" Ramsey asked tapping a pencil on the console.

"Yes ma'am, we are," CC replied watching the drone hovering over the cafés.

"Jenkins is on his way to join us on the cutter," Ramsey cautioned. "We're running out of time. We need the information from Dano. We're not sure if someone tipped Jenkins off about where you are or why he's coming."

"That is alarming," CC sighed. "That shortens our time."

"It does," Ramsey agreed. "However, since Dano plays double-jeopardy with his contracts, I think he already has dirt on Spinello's newest member, Jenkins. Get in and out of there as quickly as you can. Bernadette, do you know who Jenkins is?"

"Alonzo spelled that out perfectly to me," Bernadette admitted.

"It is important to know what dirt Dano has on Jenkins," Ramsey pushed. "Find out all you can about Jenkins."

"I understand," Bernadette declared. "Pauli is calling. I need to take the call," she said switching lines.

"Bernadette, I sent Mikey to help you," Pauli declared. "He landed at Lake Como's Airport a few minutes ago and met with your contact. They warned that the owner at the dock ratted you out. You are to get off the boat and head for the Berkshire Villa on the other side of town. Mikey will meet you there to help you get Dano alone. I've arranged for your connection to take CC and the others to the Citation and guard them."

"With this much at stake, I feel better working with Mikey," Bernadette smiled. "Jordan, we need to ditch this boat immediately! It seems Sam's Mr. Benjamin Franklin, identified him from a photo."

"These people are everywhere!" CC snapped. "Sam, hover the drone over us. I need to make sure no one is following us."

"Copy that," Sam replied as Jordan neared the shore.

"We need a diversion!" Bernadette insisted glancing around. "Jordan, back in close to the third piling on that old, deserted dock. I don't see anyone around the dock," Bernadette noted slinging her backpack over her shoulder. "Stop!" she ordered jumping off on the deck and tying the boat. "CC, jump off and untie the boat when I tell you. It's a double-slip knot; pull the long end."

"Where are you going?" CC asked getting off next to Bernadette.

"You'll see," Bernadette turned and jumped back onto it. "Sam, you need to get off this boat now!" Bernadette warned hurrying past him to the bridge. "Jordan, I'll take over from here. Abandon this ship as fast as you can. Spinello knows about us. They are looking for the catamaran," she relayed placing a small box under the steering wheel.

"Yes, ma'am," Jordan agreed grabbed his backpack and left.

"CC, untie the rope!" Bernadette yelled barely pushing the gear forward, then racing to the back of the boat and jumping off as it pulled away from the dock. "Did anyone see what I did?"

"Not that I can see," CC answered checking the iPad.

"Is the catamaran in view?" Bernadette asked.

"Why, yes," CC answered.

"Keep an eye on it and follow me," Bernadette led the way on the catwalk to the cafés. "The cafés are too open, making it easy for someone to recognize us. Let's go to the park by the museum," she pointed ahead. "That sidewalk follows along the riverbank to a museum and another strip of shops," Bernadette said hurrying through the tree-lined sidewalk, passing a couple kissing behind a tree in the moonlight.

"No one is following us, and the boat is slowly traveling in a straight line," CC reported. "One boat had to veer away from it and blew the horn."

"I hope they don't call the authorities," Bernadette warned. "Everyone, just keep walking casually," Bernadette whispered leading the way over a small, rounded bridge. "It seems the only people out tonight are lovers romancing in the moonlight."

"And what a beautiful moon to be under," CC agreed bending under a low hanging Wisteria limb. "We're still in the clear."

"Wait a minute," Bernadette whispered reaching for her cell phone. "I think we can squeeze through this hole in the thick bushes," she shinned the flashlight through the bushes.

"It looks like lovers hollowed away the inside," CC giggled.

"Ah, to have that young love, again," Bernadette whispered squeezing through it. "It worked. Come on inside with me. Sam, raise the drone and face it toward the catamaran," Bernadette requested watching the iPad over CC's shoulder. "It should be in the middle of the lake alone by now."

"Copy that," Sam stopped turning the drone.

"It is in position," CC showed Bernadette.

"It's in perfect position," Bernadette grinned reaching in her backpack. "I hate to do this to such a magnificent boat," she admitted taking out a small box. "Take one last look at our ride," Bernadette sighed turning the switch.

"You blew up the catamaran!" Jordan exclaimed. "That was a thing of beauty!"

"I couldn't help it," Bernadette admitted. "First, I did it, so Spinello didn't have our fingerprints. Second, I did it because the snitch that betrayed us at the dock took our money and blabbed. I'm sure Spinello's men paid him also. Sam, zoom in so CC can make sure nothing is recognizable about Mr. Snitch's boat."

"You did a great job!" CC complimented checking the wreckage. "No one can recognize it."

"Good, we've got to make it to the Berkshire Villa on the other side of town," Bernadette instructed. "It's not too far from here. Pauli sent Alonzo's nephew, Mikey, to help clear my way to Dano. Pauli also arranged for my connection to take you back to the Citation and guard you while I interrogate Dano," Bernadette explained leading the way through the museum parking lot.

"Pauli sees every detail to the end," CC admitted. "I feel better about you interrogating Dano with Mikey helping. From what I heard, it was Mikey that discovered Spinello's men had Alonzo and the guys pinned down in Miami and evened the score."

"Let's just say Mikey has always been an equalizer," Bernadette smiled.

Friday, July 3
On the cutter off the coast of Cuba, 1400 (2:00 PM EST)

"Dr. Sydney, Gen. Thomas Jenkins just advised us that he is landing his helicopter on the cutter," Chief Petty Officer (CPO) Smalley alerted him from the bridge. "We had no warning, except for a visual. Our radar system is in perfect working order. We are trying to find out how his helicopter escaped it. I've already alerted RADM Hiltree of the situation."

"It sounds like Rodger Slate is with Jenkins," Sydney admitted.

"It's strange you said that," Smalley remarked. "Hiltree said the same thing. I am to let him know if Slate is with him."

"Copy that," Sydney answered. "Please, escort them to the HUB. Do not let them out of your sight. I wouldn't put it past them to try to plant several bugs to spy on us."

"I understand, Sir," Smalley sighed. "Hiltree ordered the same treatment. Are you sure that you want them in the HUB? The general coming in under our radar is too suspicious."

"Forty-five minutes ago, I received a warning about Jenkins heading this way," Sydney confessed. "I didn't alert you because I wanted to see how they approached our ship. By not showing up on the radar, his intentions are clear. I know how he did it, and it won't happen again."

"Aye, if you say so, Sir," Smalley shook his head. "I'm keeping good records on everything he does aboard."

"Ramsey, it's time for you to turn on your charm," Sydney grinned pulling up the cameras on the deck.

"Thanks!" Ramsey scoffed checking the screen. "It's getting harder every time I see that man!"

"You need to play it off like Smalley is," Sydney pointed out. "He's greeting the general with a smile and a salute."

"That's because Smalley hasn't slept with the man for years!" Ramsey snapped. "I've been betrayed in more ways than one."

"And my money is on you being the victor when all is said and done," Sydney grinned. "They are on their way down to us, smile."

"Tom, you finally got to join us," Ramsey greeted them at the doorway with a hug.

"Since uncovering Metarha's smuggling ring of terrorists into our country, it's been non-stop," Tom gave her a quick kiss, reaching for her hands and stepping back. "I've missed my girl. You still owe me a date with wine and a movie."

"We did have to postpone our perfect evening, didn't we?" Ramsey grinned dropping his hands. "We're rude. Rodger, it's nice to meet you finally," she shook his hand. "How does your family like your new position?"

"Gen. Jenkins has kept me so busy; I haven't had time to see them," Rodger stated. "I never got to thank you for saving them."

"It was Sydney that figured out how Metarha was controlling all of you," Ramsey admitted.

"Gen. Jenkins, I'd like to thank Sydney in person," Rodger said walking over to Sydney. "Dr. Sydney, it's an honor to work with the man that saved my family."

"Face to face this time," Sydney shook his hand. "Although I will say, even though it was challenging, we worked as a well-established team. Ramsey and I were wondering when you were going to join us. I heard that Tom has kept you busy."

"Yes, too busy with his agenda," Rodger whispered under his breath as Tom and Ramsey joined them.

"Sydney," Tom shook his hand. "I'm sure you and Ramsey have been busy. We'll pull up a chair, and you can bring us up to date. I'm anxious to hear the progress you've made," Jenkins said as his phone rang. "Excuse me, I need to take this call," he walked toward the door, turning around to face Rodger.

Sydney turned to block Jenkins, "Rodger, what's wrong?"

"Hide this," Rodger whispered handing Sydney a small envelope.

"Rodger, I'm anxious to hear how your vetting went in Washington, DC," Ramsey admitted watching Jenkins get off the phone.

"I'm afraid Rodger and I must postpone that story for another time," Tom quickly rejoined them. "I've been summoned immediately to Washington."

"Unbelievable," Ramsey sighed. "I'm sorry you traveled all this way only to have to leave immediately. Couldn't you handle the problem over the phone?"

"You know it doesn't work that way!" Tom snapped reaching for his phone. "Officer Smalley, have my helicopter ready to leave. I'm on my way to the deck."

"Rodger can stay and help us while you're away," Ramsey declared. "When you get back, we'll be ready to give you a full report on what's happening in the real world."

"Unfortunately, Rodger needs to come with me," Jenkins apologized. "Some young Congresswoman is questioning Rodger's vetting."

"Why would Congress question Rodger's vetting?" Sydney asked. "If you forward me a copy of the forms you filled out, I'll look over it."

"I filled out the forms correctly!" Jenkins insisted. "Rodger isn't the first person I've recommended for vetting."

"There might be some questions you better refuse to let Rodger answer for Congress!" Ramsey demanded.

"I'm well aware of that!" Jenkins turned around. "Rodger, let's go."

"Tom, I'm sure you can handle a new Congresswoman," Ramsey walked toward him. "Don't let her get to you. She's fresh meat to the interest groups. She wants to spread her wings and prove to them she's for sale. After all, she's green around the gills, and you're a seasoned general. Look her straight in the eyes and merely answer her questions with questions. Like asking her what her party thought about it in the past, or what interest group does it affect?"

"Thanks for the pep talk, Dear," Tom grinned. "You're always ready with a quick response. Don't worry. I'll take a page out of your book and not leave her standing."

"That's my man," Ramsey grinned. "I'll walk you and Rodger out."

"Good, I don't know when I'll be back," Jenkins put his arm around her and left the room.

Sydney watched Jenkins and Rodger takeoff on the deck camera as his phone rang. "Skip, I was waiting for your call. Did you get the number?"

"Yes," Skip reported. "The number that called Jenkins began with a New Jersey area code. It was a secure call. By the time Mack hacked into it, Jenkins had told the person, 'It's time to increase the pressure.' He hung up immediately. We ran the number, and it doesn't exist."

"I figured it was a spoofed number," Sydney admitted. "Were you able to run a voice recognition?"

"I tried that," Mack shared. "It didn't match anyone we have on file. I stored it for future use."

"At least, it wasn't a total loss," Sydney declared. "We need to figure out what Jenkins meant by 'turning up the pressure.'"

"You could feel the tension in the air between Jenkins and Rodger," Ramsey admitted returning to the HUB. "What did Rodger slip you?"

"Thanks for running the interference with Jenkins," Sydney appreciated opening the envelope and holding up a small chip. "Rodger slipped me this nanochip," he said inserting it in his drive. "Give it a minute to open it."

"Jenkins didn't take his eyes off Rodger," Ramsey shared. "When you blocked his view while he was on the phone, he was nervous and fidgeting. I'm sure that phone call wasn't from Washington. Something bigger overrode Jenkins' visit, and he didn't like it."

"That was obvious," Sydney agreed. "Rodger whispered to me that Jenkins had him doing his agenda. Maybe, something on this chip will tell us," he said as the file opened.

"Oh, my!" Ramsey gasped. "No wonder Jenkins didn't want to talk about Rodger that night."

"Let me read them," Sydney began.

1. Jenkins threatened to relocate Rodger's family to a hidden location if he doesn't do what he says.

2. Jenkins vetted Rodger to work with Cyber-Security at the Pentagon with Connor Johansson. Jenkins ordered Rodger to embed a set of codes for Jenkins to use that Johansson couldn't trace.

3. Rodger is the one that disabled the cameras and the elevator at your condo.

4. Rodger is the anonymous source reporting what Jenkins tells him too.

5. Rodger put a wormhole into his phone, so that we can communicate through different spoofed numbers he embedded. The calls and text will self-destruct in seven seconds.

6. Jenkins had Rodger add a new encrypted app that is impossible to trace on his phone. Rodger is waiting for the right time to put a virus into it so we can track Jenkins.

7. The coordinates and alarm codes of Jenkins' Island home (Translucent Pearl) 25 miles from the Commonwealth of the Bahamas, and his residence in DC.

8. The codes for Jenkins newly acquired residence in White Plains.

9. Jenkins has a mole at the Naval Station in Miami.

10. Jenkins travels between Cuba and the U.S. without going through customs.

11. Rodger will text us new information as he gets it.

"This information gives us an edge against Jenkins," Sydney admitted.

"It sure does," Ramsey agreed. "We need to check the status of the other teams?"

"Skip and Mack were watching them during our visit," Sydney called. "Skip, what's Stephen's team doing?"

"Kathe and Stephen's team are backpacking up the highest peak of the Sierra Maestra," Skip reported. "They are almost to the village to drop off the little girls. Mack helped them dodge patrols while I snapped some awesome shots of rare birds. Some of which are not indigenous to the region."

"Good, those pictures will sustain our cover," Ramsey noted. "How are they going to get the girls into the village without interaction with the villagers?"

"Tierney said it wouldn't matter if the people see them," Skip relayed. "She said the girls would tell their parents what happened and who saved them."

"Tierney's right," Ramsey sighed. "It's another one of our Catch-22's. What about Hiltree's team?"

"They are checking out the Sierra Maestra," Mack reported. "Stephen's drone was sluggish around the city of Mayarí, implicating something or someone is there. CC's team is on the tarmac waiting for Bernadette to finish interrogating Dano. They will brief you from the air."

"Keep up the good work," Ramsey said clearing the line and turning to Sydney. "We've got our work cut out for us. The people we're after think nothing of collateral damage."

"I'm afraid society has caused this with the so-called 'cancel culture,'" Sydney agreed. "It's the devaluing of precious human life."

Friday, July 3
Varenna, Italy, 1450 (2:50 PM EST)

"Something is coming this way," Jordan warned checking the radar. "What do we do?"

"Let me check," Sam offered tapping his earbud. "Dr. Sydney, we're parked away from the tarmac and have Chameleon enabled. There is something on a direct path toward us. Bernadette is overdue to rendezvous. What should we do?"

"Copy that," Sydney replied checking the GPS on Bernadette's earbud. "Negative, I'm showing Bernadette is on that chopper. Hold while I enable her earbud and talk to her," he said pressing enter. "Bernadette, are you, alright? I see you're heading toward the Citation."

"Yes, I'm okay," Bernadette said. "I'm dropping the thumb drive off to CC."

"Copy that," Sydney answered. "Let me advise Sam of your approach. They need to warm up the engines," he said contacting Sam.

"Bernadette, I talked to Alonzo," Ramsey shared. "He's worried about Bencivenni's replacements. With the upcoming G-Summit, Bencivenni will begin putting his replacements into their new roles."

"I agree," Bernadette explained. "Pauli wants Mikey and me to do recon at Bencivenni's compound for that reason."

"Depending on what you find, we'll decide what action to take against the replacements," Ramey said. "Some of the replacements didn't have a choice in their fate while others volunteered. Either way, it won't be an easy task."

"No, it won't," Bernadette agreed. "Oh, and one thing about the thumb drive, Sydney may have to blip out the screaming before CC listens. She might disapprove of my methods."

"She might be FBI, but she has used a few unconventional methods herself," Ramsey chuckled. "Let me know what you find in the Alps. I'll have CC download the drive to us."

"Bernadette, I have you on the radar," Sydney stated. "As soon as the chopper descends, you can hand CC the thumb drive, and she'll give you a drone. You and Mikey will need it to get inside the compound safely."

"Thanks, that will save us a lot of work," Bernadette agreed.

"I'll get the Citation cleared for takeoff," Ramsey said picking up her phone. "Wanda, I'm ready for Keith to scramble the Citation's IFF Codes again."

"You got it, Boss," Wanda declared hurrying to Keith's office. "It's time."

"Give me a second," Keith cautioned finishing a phone call. "This has been a crazy day for the airline. My phone hasn't stopped ringing," he made a quick notation. "You know, we're going to get another visit from L'Simonette."

"Of course," Wanda grinned. "Isn't it fun to play mind-games with L'Simonette?"

"Last time our plan worked," Keith cautioned. "Pulling it off again might be difficult," he said watching the monitor as he pressed enter. "Ramsey, the Citation is clear for takeoff. I sent the new call letters and a flight plan to the cockpit."

"Copy that," Ramsey smiled turning to Sydney. "We're ready when you are."

"CC has the thumb drive, and Bernadette has the drone," Sydney watched. "Jordan, you're ready to leave."

"Sam, secure the door for takeoff," Jordan announced checking the flight plan.

"Give me a second to run a little interference for you, and you'll be on your way," Sydney typed a few commands and pushed enter. "Jordan, I scrambled communications with the tower and radar. The runway is all yours. By leaving Chameleon engaged again, the people in the tower will not see the jet take off; only hear the noise. There are no records that you were there."

"Too bad we won't see this reported on FNN!" Jordan grinned throttling up and taxiing to the runway. "Sam watch the faces in the tower as we pass it!"

"It gets better each time we do this," Sam chuckled as Jordan pulled the throttle toward him.

"We are up!" Jordan reported. "Sydney, thanks for the assist."

"Copy that," Sydney replied. "As soon as you reach 10,000 feet, have CC download the thumb drive. After we listen to it, I'll know your next destination."

"Copy that," Jordan said turning away from the airport. "Currently, Keith has us on a course to Newark."

Friday, July 3
Mayarí, Cuba 1515 (3:15 PM EST)

"Sydney, the drone is sluggish, and we're losing power over Mayarí," Hiltree reported. "I tried to get to the top of the mountain, and the full battery drained to zip in a matter of seconds. I hit the home key, and it's not responding."

"Give me a minute," Sydney connected to that drone. "Eduardo's changed to a different configuration than he used at Sierra Maestra," Sydney feverishly typed and pressed enter. "It should work now. The new source was double secured. I also boosted the battery power for you. Let me add Skip and Mack to the conversation. This has to be a key location."

"We can use all the help we can get," Hiltree welcomed. "The drone is working fine now."

"The cameras are booting back up," Alonzo smiled. "It will take another minute."

"We need to locate the power source that blocked you from the top," Sydney determined. "Give me a minute," Sydney brought up the city grid of the power company. "It's not coming from the government-run power station. There was a strong power surge from on top of the mountain," Sydney confirmed zeroing in on that area. "That mountain has a long drop off to the ocean."

"I'm almost there," Hiltree relayed as the drone reached the top.

"The only thing here is a large villa surrounded by a solid, stone wall," Alonzo noted zeroing in the center-camera. "The grounds are manicured with exotic flowers."

"There's a barn with two horses to the left of the house," Mack noted.

"It's a little bit of heaven in a dismal country," Ramsey stated as Sydney zoomed in closer.

"There's a helipad in the backyard on the left side," Skip noted.

"I see that," Sydney agreed. "Hiltree fly closer to the front gate. Let's see if there's an address. I can check the city records for the owner."

"That's odd, no address," Ramsey sighed.

"No, but I did locate the signal blocking our drone," Sydney stressed. "It's on the tower above the front door."

"Copy that," Hiltree flew the drone around the tower.

"No house number by the front door," Alonzo stated.

"I see that," Sydney noted. "Skip, Mack, can you spot anything?"

"Negative," they concurred.

"What is the name of the road leading to the house?" Ramsey questioned. "We've got sixteen camera views. One should show it."

"There's no road leading to the front," Alonzo noted as Hiltree flew the drone over the front yard.

"Negative from us," Skip answered as Mack shook his head in agreement.

"I can't believe the only way to that villa is by helicopter," Ramsey stated as Hiltree flew the drone straight over the roof. "A massive blocking devise on a secluded villa with no street address, no roads leading to it, and a steep, long, drop off to the ocean on the other side. I think we've located Eduardo and Catarina's residence."

"It very well could be," Alonzo agreed.

"Hiltree, fly the drone near the left-back corner of the house behind the helipad," Skip requested. "There's an entrance gate and a small path that leads down the side of the mountain."

"It has fresh tire tracks." Sydney checked using JAKE Technology. "I'm showing they're two days old. Follow the path down the mountain."

"Stop right there!" Mack exclaimed. "Go back to the left. Isn't that a cave entrance?"

"It is," Alonzo concurred zooming in the left-middle camera.

"Put the camera on infrared, and stay close to the ceiling," Sydney requested.

"It's not a cave!" Mack admired. "It's a tunnel made of cement with electric lights in the ceiling."

"There's an ATV by the entrance," Alonzo showed. "That would explain the tire tracks."

"Who would have thought," Ramsey sighed as the drone flew out the other side. "It leads to a majestic cove with exotic flowers and trees!"

"That's an understatement!" Skip exclaimed. "It has exotic birds and butterflies from around the world," Skip snapped several pictures. "There are also several varieties of Bee Hummingbirds," he continued taking pictures. "What a find? Wait until Stephen sees these photos!"

"Unless we've stumbled into the Garden of Eden, someone constantly maintains this cove," Ramsey noted. "There isn't a weed in the garden."

"And it's in the middle of nowhere," Alonzo stated. "There's nothing like this in Cuba that we've seen."

"The cove is big enough to turn a small yacht around," Mack noted zooming in the mid-right camera. "And it connects into the ocean."

"Let's see if the cove has a name?" Sydney checked the Web. "According to Cuban maps, this is called Devil's Claw. It states there is nothing but wasteland in this area. It also states that the only way to get to it is by boat. Ramsey thinks this might be Santo Prado's' residence. Let me check their profiles," he rechecked the Web. "No mention of anything relating to Floriculture or Horticulture in their profiles. Eduardo's hobbies are rugby and skydiving. Catarina's hobbies are yoga and horseback riding."

"What about their son, Carlos?" Alonzo asked.

"There's nothing listed for Carlos," Sydney stated. "But the grounds at his house in Florida were similar."

"It was nothing like this," Ramsey clarified. "Hiltree, leave a mosquito-drone in one of the trees, facing the ocean. Then fly the drone back to the villa. I want to look in the windows."

"Copy that," Hiltree placed a mosquito in a tree.

"Let's take the drone straight up," Sydney requested. "I want to take an Aerial picture of the cove. You can go that way to the villa."

"Copy that," Hiltree complied.

"Stop right there!" Sydney ordered zooming in the center-camera facing the mountain. "Hiltree, take the drone through the trees across the stream. I think I see something."

"This keeps getting stranger by the minute!" Ramsey gasped. "It's a glass, A-frame cottage. Hiltree, let's see what's inside."

"Copy that," Hiltree complied.

"Does this remind anyone of the apartment above Madré de Dios Funeralia in Miami?" Alonzo asked. "It's lavishly decorated to impress the guests."

"Absolutely," Ramsey confirmed. "Perhaps diplomats and replacements come here for training before they relocate them. Let's check out the villa."

"Yes, ma'am," Hiltree flew the drone straight up from the helipad toward the sky. "Oh, my gosh! The drone is falling!"

"I've got it!" Sydney boosted the power. "There is another radio-wave blocking device under the helipad," he continued typing. "It's so concentrated; I can't get through it! It must be controlled to allow landing and takeoffs as visitors stay here."

"Someone doesn't want this cove seen from the air," Ramsey declared.

"Or anyone to get in from the air, unless they allow it," Mack added.

"Hiltree, hurry back through the tunnel!" Sydney warned. "The drone probably tripped an alarm system, just like under the Océanic in Miami."

"Oh, my God!" Hiltree exclaimed. "A solid, steel door is sealing the entrance."

"Push it!" Sydney boosted the battery.

"It made it inside, but the other side is closing, also!" Hiltree turned up the speed. "It's not going to make it!"

"There's a red L-icon on the bottom-right of your screen!" Sydney declared. "Turn the drone sideways, aim toward the bottom right of the door, fire, and you'll make it."

"If you say so!" Hiltree followed orders. "The drone is out! Sydney, that was amazing! Why didn't you tell me it has a laser?"

"I learned a lesson at the Océanic," Sydney grinned. "Always be prepared to fight your way out of a situation, even with a drone."

"What do you want to bet that the windows at the villa have closed?" Ramsey watched the screen. "Just like I thought. It triggers more than one alarm. Eduardo knows we're here."

"Not necessarily," Sydney smiled. "When Eduardo checked the cameras, it couldn't pick up the mosquito. No structure is bug proof," Sydney continued to type commands. "I noticed the back of the house has French doors. They're hard to seal. Let's try to enter the mosquito at one of these. I'll monitor the mother-drone."

"Copy that," Hiltree switched to a mosquito-drone, and flew it to the back patio. "I found an opening in the doors. It's heading upstairs. At the end of the hallway must be the master bedroom. The mosquito tried to walk under the door but couldn't get inside the room."

"Let me try?" Sydney asked taking over the drone. "There is a small crack by the bottom door hinge. I think the mosquito can squeeze through this tiny opening if I bring the cursor to touch the wings, and then, press enter, it moves the wings closer to the body frame. Now, it's small enough to fit through the crack. It's all yours again."

"I can't believe you did that," Hiltree chuckled.

"It's all in the wrist," Sydney grinned.

"The wrist and you designed the drone's wings to fold," Hiltree declared.

"Don't take it personally," Alonzo laughed. "Sydney had to help me find a way inside Metarha's house in New Jersey. I must have tried for over an hour. Sydney got the drone inside in less than five minutes."

"Nice master bedroom," Ramsey noted. "Notice how the dresser and nightstands don't have any pictures on them. Find the closet, and maybe we'll find some pictures in there. The door across from the bed should be it."

"Copy that," Hiltree complied.

"Nice spacious bathroom," Ramsey looked at the double vanity with a contoured mirror around it. "Hiltree, turn the drone around. I found the closet. Sydney, when we remodel my condo, that's the kind of closet I want."

"That closet is half the size of your condo," Sydney chuckled. "I like the black, leather bench in the middle, as well as the full-length mirror at the end."

"There's what we are looking for," Ramsey grinned. "Hiltree, go to the dresser in the middle of the woman's side," she requested as Sydney zoomed in on the picture. "There are only pictures of horses with blue ribbons. Try the man's dresser," she watched the drone turn around. "Not one picture on the dresser. Let's try the rest of the villa. We need a picture of Eduardo."

"We won't find anything," Alonzo realized as the drone flew downstairs. "Eduardo has gone to great lengths not to show his new face."

"I'm beginning to get a bad feeling about this," Ramsey confessed. "The house is only decorated with famous artwork."

"Hiltree, leave this mosquito in the master bedroom," Sydney requested. "Hopefully, when Eduardo gets ready for bed, we can see his face."

"Copy that," Hiltree agreed. "Alonzo, and I wondered what happened when Jenkins came aboard the cutter?"

"Someone called Jenkins away as soon as he arrived," Ramsey declared. "Sydney, can you check where Jenkins is currently?"

"Whoever called Jenkins warned him about the app Rodger installed," Sydney assumed. "Jenkins has changed phones. I can't locate him."

"Hiltree, is there any way you can find out the flight plan of Jenkins' helicopter?" Ramsey asked.

"The reason I asked you is that Smalley already checked Jenkins' flight schedule," Hiltree shared. "It's marked classified."

"You know how Jenkins did it, don't you?" Ramsey quizzed.

"Yes, ma'am, unfortunately, I do," Hiltree confessed. "Jenkins forced Rodger to hide his agenda."

"Rodger wants no part of Jenkins or his plan," Sydney declared. "He gave me a nanochip with what Jenkins has done. If I'm right about the app, Jenkins has a replacement for Rodger."

"That can't happen!" Hiltree snapped. "He deserves to live with his family in peace after what they've been through. When was the last time you checked on Rodger's family?"

"Not since CC placed them in her father's charge," Ramsey admitted. "I'll ask her to check on them."

Friday, July 3
Sierra Maestra, Cuba 1545 (3:45 PM EST)

"¡Nuestro pueblo!" (Our village!) Cambria exclaimed, grabbing Mariah's hand, and running ahead with the other girls. "¡Estamos en casa!" (We are home!) Cambria cried as the people in the small village rushed to greet the little girls.

"Mis bebés! (My babies)" María cried as she ran out into the street to greet Cambria and Mariah. "¡Mis bebés! (My babies)" she fell to her knees, throwing her arms around them.

"It's a happy homecoming," Kathe stopped for a minute, watching the girls interact with their families and friends.

"Thanks to a fiery, little mama going into instant protection mode," Yorg grinned taking Kathe by the hand.

"You did notice that we followed Kathe's orders to save the girls instead of Ramsey's?" Jack asked. "And that's not the first time."

"I knew I could count on you," Kathe thanked. "I can't blame Ramsey. A lot is riding on the success of this mission."

"Yes but taking the time to help the innocent is what makes our jobs worth putting our lives on the line for every day," Jay confessed entering the village.

"Do you notice something strange in this village?" Stephen noted. "There are no teenage boys or men under sixty."

"You're right," Yorg confirmed as a helicopter flew over the village, and they witness the people scurrying for safety.

"I take it that a helicopter has stopped here before," Kathe noted leading the way to the middle of the street.

"They probably think that helicopter dropped us off," Stephen assumed.

"They are afraid of us," Jay declared.

"¡No te lleves a nuestros hios!" (Don't take our children!) An older man screamed, walking out into the open, waving his cane.

Cambria and Mariah ran around him straight to Kathe. "¡Espera, abuelo!" (Wait, grandfather!) The other two girls joined them. Cambria and Mariah took Kathe by the hand. "¡Estos son nuestros amigos!" (These are our friends.)

"¡Arriesgaron sus vidas para rescatarmos!" (They risked their lives to rescue us!) Anita cried holding Yorg's hand as one by one the people joined Cambria's grandfather.

"Este hombre me salvo la vida!" (This man saved my life.) Selina stated holding Jay's hand.

"¡Mataron a los hombres que no llevaron, así como a los traficantes de drogas!" Cambria cried. (They killed the men that took us as well as the drug dealers.) "Iban a drogarse y lastimarme primero para que los demás supieran qué hacer con ellos." (They were going to drug and hurt me first so the others would know what they were going to do to them.) "Fue horrible!" she cried as her mother ran to her. (It was horrible!)

"¿Quién eres tú?" Pabló asked. (Who are you?)

"Somos solo parte de una productora de cine," (We are just part of a movie production company.) Kathe began. "Tropezamos accidentalmente con algunos guerilleros que secuestraron a sus hijos." (We accidentally stumbled across the guerillas that kidnapped your children.)

"¿A dónde vas?" Pabló asked. (Where are you going?)

"A la cima de la montaña en busca de aves raras," Kathe answered. (To the top of the mountain looking for rare birds.)

"Debes dar la vuelta," (You must turn around.) Pabló warned. "En la cima de esta montaña, son hombres muy malos. (On top of this mountain are very bad men.) Ellos viniron a nuestra aldea y tomaron a nuestros hombres. (A couple of months ago, they came to our village, and took our men.) Mi hermano menor, Diego, intentó escapar con algunos de los aldeanos. (My son, Diego tried to escape with some of our villagers.) El era el único que lo hizo con vida. (He was the only one that made it out alive.) Unas semanas después, Diego y Mariah fueron al río a buscar agua. (A few weeks later, Diego and Mariah went down to the river to get water for the night.) Los hombres deben haderlos encontrado. (The men must have found them.) Cuando no regresaron, comenzamos a buscarlos. (When Diego and Mariah didn't return, we began to search for them.) Encontramos la muñeca de Mariah a pocos metros del río. (We found Mariah's doll in the woods by the riverbank.) Recogimos la búsqueda a la primera luz y encontramos a Mariah vagando por el rí empapada. (We picked up the search at first light and found Mariah soaking wet wandering by the river.) Tiene miedo al agua y no puede nadar. (She is afraid of water and can't swim.) Ella no ha hablado desde entonces." (She hasn't talked since.) Pablo explained, showing Kathe a picture of Diego murdered. "Ellos vinieron y publicaron estas fotos de el de una semana después." (They came and posted these pictures of Diego the next day.)

"Yorg, look at this picture!" Kathe held it up.

"It's the man that was tied to the angel statue in the underwater cemetery," Yorg identified. "You were right. They used Diego to show what would happen to others that try to escape."

"It was Mariah and Cambria's father," Kathe stated. "Mariah was with Diego when they went missing."

"That's the reason she stopped talking," Yorg declared. "She witnessed the whole thing," he glanced at his watch. "We've got to leave. If they see us here, they'll kill the whole village."

"You're right," Kathe agreed and turned to Pabló. "Tenemos que irnos ahora. (We must leave now.) Gracias por avisarnos. (Thank you for the warning.) Que tendremos cuidado," (We will be careful.) She looked at the girls. "Adios nuesto nuevo amigos," she waved leaving with her team. (Goodbye to our new friends.)

"Look what socialism has done to this country!" Jack scoffed walking away. "One percent of the people are rich, and the rest are starving and pillaged by terrorist groups."

"It is hard to witness," Stephen agreed. "Castrello turns a blind eye to what's happening to his people. How can he sleep at night?"

"It's called the love of money and greed," Kathe declared.

"Castrello destroyed this country," Will added. "My family and I used to come here before he took over. Cuba was the most successful of all the islands. It had the happiest people. Now, they're starving and murdered."

"We need to find out where that helicopter went?" Yorg declared. "Jay, Jack, get the drone up."

"Give us a minute," Jay reached inside his backpack. He handed Jack an iPad and then put the drone on the ground. "The drone won't lift!" He tried again.

"The battery instantly drained," Stephen watched the screen over Jay's shoulder. "You're going to have to recharge it."

"I was afraid of that," Yorg confessed. "Mack said they lost several drones up here. I'll call Sydney."

"I can't seem to get through this electronic barrier," Sydney warned as he continued to try. "We encountered this same problem in Mayarí with Alonzo and Hiltree. It's a different variable from the original formula. It's extremely concentrated and must have multiple sources to cover this large of an arena. I'll get back to you as soon as I figure it out."

"We'll have to do it the old fashion way," Yorg stated.

"Negative, the top of that mountain is covered with Cuban soldiers and guerillas," Ramsey admitted. "It would be suicide to continue without the drone to help you. Move back down the mountain away from the village and set up camp. Use the drone to continue working on your alibi. We just found out that Ché Márquez took off in a helicopter thirty minutes ago. Its flight plan is Sierra Maestra. You're probably going to get company soon."

Friday, July 3
On the cutter off Cuba Coastline 1630 (4:30 PM EST)
Sierra Maestra and Guantanamo Bay 1630 (4:30 PM EST)

"It's been an interesting Friday," Sydney said pressing enter on the computer. "The computer just found the information on the yacht Espírito Ingeniero. It's an umbrella company of Alianza Mundial International owned by Catarina Santo Prado. It was recorded in Luxembourg by an unknown source."

"Catarina is notorious at hiding umbrella companies," Ramsey admitted.

"The same as Spinello," Sydney confirmed. "While the computer works on the formula to break through the radio wave barriers in Cuba, we need to listen to the download with the teams," Sydney said pulling up the recording and contacting CC. "Ramsey and I are ready to listen to what is on the thumb drive. Are you and Sam ready?"

"We are," CC reached for a pen and paper out of her backpack.

"Let me get the other teams on the line," Sydney requested merging the calls. "Ramsey, you may begin."

"People, before we hear the interrogation, we have something to bring up," Ramsey explained Jenkins and Rodger's visit to the cutter.

"I was afraid Jenkins would do this to Rodger," Alonzo confessed.

"The FBI has jurisdiction over the Slate family," Hiltree revealed. "Homeland can't do anything about it."

"Not the way Rodger was acting," Ramsey declared. "Something is wrong."

"That can't be!" CC exclaimed. "Because of Jenkins, I made sure that only the FBI had jurisdiction over them. I'll call my father and find out what happened."

"Rodger is inventive with ways to communicate without anyone knowing," Sydney admitted. "He'll find a way to talk with us."

"I agree," Alonzo declared. "He was creative in Miami."

"Yes, but Jenkins is aware of Rodger's skills now," Sydney cautioned. "Jenkins was with us during all of that."

"That is why Jenkins won't let Rodger out of his sight!" Hiltree scoffed. "Now, what are we going to do?"

"We'll have to wait for CC to find out about the Slates," Ramsey stated.

"Ramsey, we need to hear the interrogation before Márquez arrives," Stephen reminded. "We moved far enough away from the top of the mountain. Jay has the mother-drone up while we make camp to watch for Márquez. Jack put the mosquito inside our tent for you to watch."

"Good," Ramsey approved as Sydney pulled up the cameras.

"This is the conversation between Dano and Bernadette," Sydney said pushing play.

"Bernadette!"

Silence

"Where are my bodyguards?"

"You know me," Bernadette giggled.

"Where am I?"

"Tomme Boy Dano, you have so many questions, and so do I," Bernadette stated. "Let's start with Spinello paying you to kill my Luca?"

"I don't know what you're talking about!" as he screamed.

"Really?" Bernadette asked.

"You're wasting your time!" Screaming

"Am I?" Bernadette chuckled.

Screaming/catching his breath, "You . . . know me better . . . than that!"

"Do I?" Bernadette grinned.

"Don't . . . play . . . mind-games . . . with me!"

"Mind-games, huh?" Bernadette questioned.

Screams/deep breathing "Let me . . . go. I'll . . . have Spinello spare . . . your life."

"You will?" Bernadette laughed.

Scream, "Yes, . . . I . . . swear!" Scream

"What makes you think Spinello's going to spare your life?" Bernadette demanded.

"We're . . . partners."

"Is that so?" Bernadette chuckled.

"Yes, . . . I've got . . . security." Breathing hard

"So, do I," Bernadette admitted.

Yells out, "You've . . . got . . . nothing . . . on me."

"Really, remember these?" Bernadette held up some documents.

Agonizing screams "How . . . did . . . you . . . get those?"

"Alonzo and Pauli." Bernadette declared.

"Your . . . precious . . . Alonzo better . . ."

"Better what?" Bernadette asked. "I asked you nicely."

Screaming "I'll die . . . before I . . ." Agonizing screams "Alonzo . . . forged . . . those . . . to frame . . . me."

"Nice try," Bernadette disagreed. "I was with Alonzo when he got them. The person he got them from was going to blackmail you with them. Lucky for you, I put him out of his misery. Come to think of it, that makes you owe us now."

"I know . . . you're . . . only interested . . . in me . . . because of Luca." Agonizing scream/heavy breathing "Stop . . . Alonzo . . . is helping . . . the Feds." Screams again/sobbing "Join . . . with . . . us . . . This deal . . . will set . . . you for . . . life."

"I'm already set for life," Bernadette stated. "Why did you turn on Luca? He saved your life on more than one occasion. Why?"

Silence/agonizing screams

"Oh, I'm sorry," Bernadette frowned. "Is that the sore that won't heal? Oh no, it's dripping blood pretty badly, now."

"You..."

Bernadette chuckled. "You know better than to call me names."

Yells out/agonizing screams, "Don't . . . do that . . . again!" sobbing "Please, . . . I beg . . . you!"

"Maybe, this isn't painful enough to loosen your tongue," Bernadette wondered. "I'm going to try one more time."

"No, . . . not again!" Screaming/begging "Stop! . . . Spinello . . . wanted me . . . to kill . . . Luca . . . to prove . . . loyalty . . . to him." Screaming/breathing harder.

"Now, you're going to have to prove your loyalty to me if you want to stay alive," Bernadette demanded.

"It's . . . too late. You must . . . have seen . . . the . . . medical report. I'm . . . dying."

"Really?" Bernadette questioned. "That's not what I read. Are you sure Spinello wants to keep you alive? You do know that Spinello controls what care the doctors give you?"

"You're… lying!" breathing heavily.

"Am I?" Bernadette asked. "Think about it. You know all their dirty, little secrets. Why would Spinello want to keep you alive? I know you've been helping Spinello and Bencivenni for over twenty years. I even know all about Daniel and Cynthia Sydney and you renting the flat in Luxembourg. I also know the person your partners joined. I even know they just brought a new partner on board, who brings in high-tech skills. It seems he's taking your place. Now that you've helped each of the main players set things in motion, they're trimming the fat. You are the first of many to weed out."

"No! I . . . am … a partner!"

"No, you're not," Bernadette declared. "You're just a hitman that they paid to do their bidding. People like us are always expendable to people like them. If it weren't for you, they wouldn't have gotten their project off the ground. Have I been wrong about anything yet?"

Sobbing/silence

"I'm offering you a way to get what they promised you, a partnership," Bernadette offered. "Together, we can eliminate them and take over the deal. I know a physician that can heal you. He works with Alonzo. I've seen him work miracles. I want the leverage that I know you have. To show you my good faith, I'll put this down."

Sobbing/silence

"Well?" Bernadette asked.

"Why . . . would you . . . save me?"

"Big money is forgiving," Bernadette lied. "What's done is done? Join us or die. The choice is yours."

"You already . . . know… what Bencivenni … is doing. He controls them . . . with rings."

"How do the rings work?" Bernadette asked.

"He can . . . terminate . . . them at . . . will or . . . if they . . . try . . . to take . . . it off . . . it alerts him . . . and he kills them."

"Why does Eduardo Santo Prado wear a mask?" Bernadette asked.

Sobbing/catching breath, “No one . . . knows . . . Rumor . . . is disfigurement . . . Complications . . . with surgery.”

“What does Eduardo want?” Bernadette drilled.

“Total world . . . domination.” Deep sigh

“Tell me about your new partner?” Bernadette insisted.

“Jenkins . . . has enough . . . information to . . . frame Linda . . . Ramsey and . . . her team.”

“Where is the information?” Bernadette asked.

“Jenkins wouldn’t tell . . . Spinello . . . doesn’t trust him . . . plans to blackmail . . . Jenkins . . .” deep breath “Jenkins has . . . a silent partner . . . at a penitentiary . . . She . . . hired guards . . . and switched . . . two people.”

“What’s her name?” Bernadette asked. “What prison?”

“Jenkins . . . refused . . . to give . . . her name . . . In my . . . coat pocket . . . I have an airplane . . . ticket . . . to find out . . .” deep breath

Steps. “Lambert-St. Louis International Airport. Anything else?” Bernadette asked signaling Mikey to look around for more information.

“Jenkins,” deep breath “wants Alonzo . . . replaced immediately . . . He’s the only . . . reason . . . Ramsey knows . . . what we’re doing.”

“When?” Bernadette demanded.

“I don’t know.” Shallow breathing

“Anything else?” Bernadette quizzed.

“No . . . that’s all . . . I swear. Take me . . . to your doctor . . . I’m getting weaker . . . I can’t feel . . . my leg.”

“Sure, let me get you ready to travel,” Bernadette agreed.

“What . . . kind of . . . needle is . . . that?”

“The only kind I use.” Bernadette insisted. “You know I love my horses.”

“No . . . not that!” horrific screaming/hard time breathing, “My sore!” agonizing screams, “I . . . trusted . . .you!” sobbing “I trusted . . .” agonizing scream.

“Come, come, Tomme Boy, you never trust anybody in our business,” Bernadette reminded. “You’re bleeding to death, just like you killed my Luca. I’m disappointed in you. For someone that never showed mercy to any of your victims, you sure did beg me. I read in your contract with Spinello that he wanted a video to watch it later. Now, it’s my turn to send a video.”

“Bernadette . . . please . . . no!” sobbing harder “I . . . made . . . you!”

“No, you taught me what you were,” Bernadette admitted. “I made myself!”

More screams/gasping for air/silence/gasping for air/then silence

Steps/door opening/ "Let's go. We'll dump Dano on the way."

"I need to give Alonzo and Pauli this information I found in his suitcase," Mikey admitted.

"That's what we needed," CC stated. "We need to go straight to the penitentiary. I've got to question Officer Janis Patterson. It has to be her."

"Negative," Ramsey disagreed. "If you show up there again, it will tip Patterson off. It seems we've underestimated her. She's another piece of this puzzle."

"Dano said the woman slipped two people out," Kathe noted. "We only know of Macaby. Gen. Robert Thompson has to be the other one."

"That's why Thompson was court marshaled and sentenced in record time," Hiltree realized. "I thought at the trial it was odd for Thompson's attorney to wave some of his rights. They knew Thompson already had an escape plan."

"That proves Patterson already worked with Spinello?" Alonzo concluded. "By the time Thompson arrived, motions were set in place for his quick departure. Jenkins wasn't aware of what was going on behind his back at the Pentagon then."

"CC, what is the status of Thompson?" Ramsey asked.

"According to the records, Gen. Thompson is at Merritt Penitentiary," CC reported.

"Where did you get that information?" Ramsey asked.

"The Criminal Justice Department's records show Thompson is in cellblock C-55," CC answered.

"I'm not sure I believe that is Gen. Thompson," Ramsey replied. "We need to check that out. Have you found Patterson's personnel records? We need to know when Jenkins found out about Patterson."

"Yes, I did," CC replied. "But you're not going to like it," pulling up the records. "It is a fairytale! It appeared to be thrown together as she made it up. Some of the government departments Patterson used to reference her past jobs, don't exist."

"Or never did!" Sam added. "I discovered that one of the people Patterson listed as a character reference died before she was born."

"How did you confirm it wasn't someone with the same name?" Ramsey asked.

"I checked the social security number," Sam replied.

"I'll make some phone calls to our people," Alonzo offered. "Pauli and I discovered that Thompson contacted Pietro Bencivenni at the same time his partner, Sen. Bernard Frank, offered Chameleon to Mr. LaBasco."

"That's what Giorgio Pulini set up behind Mario Jr.'s back," Alonzo confirmed. "Jay discovered just before Mario Jr. was killed that Giorgio would leave from time-to-time without telling anyone. We found out after the funeral that Giorgio was on the Falcini payroll for selling Jr.'s information."

"We've learned that most of these people are intertwined," Sydney confirmed opening his browser. "I'm hacking into the security system at the penitentiary," he pressed enter. "I'm in," Sydney continued to type. "I'm finding Patterson's computer. Give me a few minutes. It's a large compound. There's Patterson's office, and she's got her computer turned on. I'm sending in my sniffers. Give me a few minutes to snoop around."

"Okay," Ramsey approved. "Pauli, what Dano warned about Alonzo is very unsettling. Don't let Alonzo out of your sight. They must have a replacement ready to switch."

"I won't," Pauli confirmed.

"Depending on how tight Jenkins and Patterson's relationship is, she might have access to his files," Yorg stated.

"That would make Patterson a danger to us as well," Ramsey admitted.

"If Sydney can't find it in Patterson's computer, we've got to get inside Jenkins' laptop," Hiltree cautioned. "It won't be easy to do since he carries it everywhere, he goes."

"I may have to bring Kathe back to the states," Ramsey confirmed. "Kathe is the only one with JAKE and can work independently of us. CC and Sam have a long list of people to check out. They are spread too thin already."

"I agree," Alonzo affirmed. "We already knew Jenkins would turn on us when we stop this plot. We didn't know about Patterson. She can't be doing this alone. The facility is spread out. We need to search for an accomplice."

"I'll add that to my list of things to check at the prison," CC agreed.

"Stephen, Márquez' helicopter is coming your way," Sydney warned as an alarm sounded on his console.

"The mother-drone picked it up also," Jay confirmed. "It notes his ETA is ten minutes."

"We'll be ready," Stephen stated. "Okay, team, you heard them. Let's get ready for company. Hopefully, this won't take too long."

"We'll pretend to edit our footage," Kathe sat next to Yorg in the tent.

"Skip, Mack, I need you to take some pictures of Kathe and Yorg working in and around their camp," Ramsey requested. "Kathe may need to make a trip for me. Márquez will miss her, and we have to keep up the alibi."

"Understood," Skip agreed. "Mack and I will handle it."

"CC, I just sent you a link to Patterson's screen," Sydney confirmed.

"Can you also leave me a backdoor, so when she's not using it, I can check her files?" CC wondered.

"Of course," Sydney grinned. "Now, you're thinking out of the box. The icon will appear on the bottom-right of your screen. If it's blue, Patterson is on the computer. It will turn purple when she's off."

Friday, July 3
FNN News
New York City 2000, (8:00 PM EST)

Breaking News: "This is Robert Morwitz with FNN News. An anonymous source from inside the White House has reported two more security breaches. The first is that Joe Sherrod, lead singer for the rock group Light Crimson is missing from a lockdown facility. The second is that two guided missiles are missing from the Naval Base near Miami," Morwitz stated as the screen changed to footage from June 23rd at Mayport Gardens in New York.

"If you remember, on June 23rd, an attempt to abduct Sherrod during his concert by this couple, shown highlighted, was stopped by these two security agents, shimming down the flags over the escalator. Somehow a few hours later, while in custody, Sherrod was confirmed missing. He was rescued two days later June 25th in Ponce Inlet, Florida. Two explosions the next day destroyed the Bridgette Océanic Aquarium in Miami. The anonymous source stated these two stories were connected.

"As of yet, we have not been able to confirm any of these stories," Morwitz speculated. "Is this coincidence, or is the rock star involved in espionage? We will keep you advised as these stories unfold."

"You've got to be kidding me!" Ramsey fumed. "There's no way Sherrod could have escaped from the base. Someone is manipulating the truth to frame Sherrod."

"Now, we know what Jenkins meant by 'it's time to increase the pressure,'" Sydney claimed.

"You're absolutely right," Ramsey affirmed. "Skip said the call came from a New Jersey area code. It had to be Spinello telling Jenkins that Dano is missing."

"Probably," Sydney sighed. "Spinello uses spoofed numbers. That's why I can't ping the cell towers to locate him."

"I thought the FCC was clamping down on spoofed numbers," Ramsey stated. "It's about time the phone carriers start protecting their customers from fraud."

"These kinds of people will find another way," Sydney admitted. "I programmed a filter against that within JAKE Technology. That's why our phones and computers are protected," he said as Ramsey's phone rang.

"It's CC," Ramsey put the phone on speaker.

"Jenkins somehow found the Slate family in Tampa where Dad put them," CC reported. "He presented an official document from the Pentagon stating he was to take over the Slate family placement. Charles Lancaster, the Head of Intelligence signed the document."

"When did this happen?" Ramsey asked.

"Yesterday, when we were working with Bernadette," CC admitted. "Dad received a phone call from Agent Lee Pak in charge of them after they left. Dad called Lancaster about the letter, and he denied it. Dad tried to reach me again today when we were listening to Bernadette's recording. After I talked to him, I called Lancaster's office. His secretary told me Lancaster left work yesterday and hasn't returned."

"I can check the authenticity of the document," Sydney admitted. "Did Agent Pak send it to your father?"

"Negative," CC sighed. "Pak demanded to keep it as per regulations, but Jenkins refused. Jenkins claimed he would need it to relocate them."

"That's an out and out lie!" Ramsey slammed her hand on the desk. "Agent Pak knows better than that! It's protocol for Jenkins to leave the document. Now, we have no concrete evidence that Jenkins even took them!"

"Dad documented the event and recorded the phone call before calling Morley at DOJ," CC reported. "Morley said he would look into it. We all know that means he's looking the other way."

"That does it!" Ramsey exclaimed. "I've heard enough to bring Kathe back to help you. Yorg, after Márquez leaves take Kathe to Guantanamo. She needs to meet CC and Sam in Miami. With Sherrod and the Slate family missing, it proves that Jenkins is stepping up his plans to frame us."

"Especially, since Jenkins knows Joe is Kathe's kryptonite," Sydney reminded.

"I agree with Sydney," Yorg declared. "It is evident Jenkins is tying Joe to Kathe in the frame. By Jenkins moving Rodger's family, he's holding them as leverage against us."

"That is so Jenkins!" Ramsey barked. "CC, I'll have Keith reroute the Citation to Miami. You'll meet Kathe there."

"Copy that," CC noticed Patterson turning off her computer. "I need to go. We've got Patterson leaving work for today. I'll log into the camera on her computer to make sure she is leaving the office before Sam, and I check her files. I'll get back to you."

"Okay, let me know what you find," Ramsey requested.

"Patterson isn't leaving!" CC scoffed watching Patterson pull a small laptop out of her backpack.

"She's inserting a thumb drive into a mini-laptop," Sam noted. "It's a good thing Sydney's sniffer's records everything we see. Jenkins knows that Sydney can easily hack into her work computer, so she's keeping this on her personal laptop!"

"She's keeping a different set of notes from Thornhill," CC gasped.

"That and also to protect herself from Jenkins," Sam assumed. "I'm not sold on the idea that Patterson is loyal to Jenkins. You get some rest. I'll help Jordan in the cockpit. After this, I'm not tired."

Chapter 6

Saturday, July 4th
Naval Base near Miami, 1300 (1:00 PM EST)

"I need to see the ID of everyone in the car," Ensign Duggart declared as two officers walked to the back of the car.

"Of course," Sam handed them over.

"Ms. Sims," Ensign Duggart checked her ID, "I wasn't told the FBI was sending agents here today."

In the backseat, Kathe pushed the emergency button on the top of JAKE.

"We've been assigned to an emergency three-fold investigation," CC explained handing Duggart the papers.

"Commander Arroyo and the military police investigated the incident and reported to Homeland Security," Ensign Duggart declared. "Those areas were immediately sealed."

"As you can read, our job is to investigate the conclusions," CC smiled. "Is there a problem?"

"According to orders from Homeland Security, no one is to have access to those areas," Ensign Duggart relayed as another officer walked around the small building and took the point position. "Your access is denied. You need to turn your vehicle around."

Kathe checked the rearview mirror and noted the guard behind her unlatched his holster and was ready to pull his weapon.

"Did you happen to notice who signed my orders?" CC demanded. "We've got a plane to catch this afternoon to DC to meet with The president about these matters."

"Excuse me," Ensign Duggart stepped back into the booth. He scanned the embossed seal on the bottom-left. The scanner on the top turned green, approving the document to be authentic. He returned to the car. "It is official."

"Yes, it is!" CC looked straight at him. "May we enter? We are on a tight schedule."

"Since the areas are sealed," Ensign Duggart stalled. "I need to call Com. Arroyo to clear you," he insisted as the phone in the booth rang. "Excuse me," Duggart stepped inside and answered the phone. "Yes, Sir," he looked at the car. "They just arrived at the front gate . . . Sir, yes, Sir." He walked back to the car as the gate raised. "You may proceed. I'm sorry for any inconvenience," he handed Sam back their ID's. "Chief Petty Officer Nolan Gaines will need to escort you to the areas. I'll have him meet you at Building E."

"Which way to Building E?" Sam asked.

"Go straight until you reach the roundabout," Ensign Duggart relayed. "Then, take the second right. Building E is the third building on the left."

"Thank you," Sam replied and drove away.

"I thought we were goners!" CC gasped. "Who called Duggart?"

"Sydney," Kathe smiled.

"How did Sydney know we needed help?" CC asked.

"I had JAKE warn him," Kathe grinned. "He listened to what was happening and ran a little interference."

"We may need more than interference," Sam declared. "Three crimes were committed, investigated, conclusions filed, and areas sealed in less than twelve hours. To do that, it would have to come from high-ranking officers."

"It has Jenkins' name written all over it!" CC affirmed. "Someone on this base had to be in on it. Be careful. It could be CPO Gaines."

"I'm well aware of that," Kathe admitted. "The conclusions on both matters were nothing more than a coverup. It suggested that one man that, by the way, is not an escape artist got out of a secured government building, and singlehandedly stole another two missiles."

"The quicker we find out what happened and get out of here, the better," CC agreed as they approached the roundabout. "Someone could be watching us. I hope Ensign Duggart doesn't call his commander."

"You don't have to worry about that," Sam grinned. "Since Arroyo investigated the areas and signed off on them, he would not want us to interrogate him. The timing was perfect for Arroyo to have an out if anyone from the government showed up. It's the 4th of July weekend. He is hosting the air show that is just beginning. That noise is multiple jets warming up their engines."

"We still have one problem to worry about," Kathe sighed. "Payton and the band members can't see me."

"Do you think they believed Wanda's cockamamie story?" CC asked as Sam parked the car. "The smoke may have blinded them, but their ears worked perfectly. They're not stupid."

"I know," Kathe sighed as they walked toward the building. "However, the less the members see me, the safer they are."

"Understood," CC agreed. "That must be our guide."

"Ms. Sims?" Gaines questioned as CC showed her credentials. "I'm Chief Petty Officer Gaines. I've been assigned to escort your group around the base. We'll start here. The band members are finishing lunch."

"Thank you," CC entered the building.

"Keep walking in front of me," Kathe requested pushing the emergency alert on JAKE.

"I see you got inside," Sydney grinned. "I programmed your mosquito to hover over you for us to watch."

"What if I have to climb out of something?" Kathe asked following CC.

"It will adjust its height depending on the circumstance," Sydney watched them.

"Sam, and I will interrogate Payton and the band members," CC instructed. "Kathe will interview you and check Sherrod's room."

"Yes, ma'am," Gaines led the way to Sherrod's room.

"Knock, knock," CC smiled as she and Sam entered the room.

"CC, Sam!" Carrie Anne screamed bolting out of her chair. "Finally, it's people I know. Sam, please tell me Ramsey sent you to bring us back to Newark?"

"Ramsey will base her decision on our findings," Sam stated. "She sent us to investigate Joe's 'so-called' escape."

"Is that what they're calling it?" Collen snapped throwing his napkin on the table, sitting back in his chair. "Joe couldn't have escaped! Every window and door inside and outside of this place has a talking security system! We can't go to the loo without the system stating where we are!"

"They also have cameras watching you," Sam pointed to one.

"With this much security, you tell me how Joe escaped?" Collen demanded.

"That's what we're here to find out," CC answered. "Was Joe showing any signs of seclusion, as he did in New York?"

"Not at all," Carrie Anne replied. "Joe never said a word about what happened to him in Ponce Inlet. Brock used a cold laser to speed the healing of the bruises on his face. He told me that he finally felt free from the past to work on the new album."

"Joe was excited with the sales of our last album," Payton confided. "The duet with Carrie Anne, along with the passion in Joe's voice, was what did it. According to the news, Light Crimson is still at the top of the charts, even with us stuck here. Every channel shows fans all over the world holding candle-lit vigils for our return to the public."

"I did see that it's all over the web also," CC mentioned.

"Great!" Payton exclaimed. "We are only able to watch television. We have no other contact with the outside world."

"Joe was thrilled with the fan's response," Troy stated. "That's what pushed him to want to finish the duet for the title song. We worked late last night and had most of the melody completed. Joe was still tweaking the ending when about midnight we called it a night."

"I stayed with Joe and walked him to his room," RJ stated. "The next morning, I went to his room to get him for breakfast, and he didn't answer. I tried to open the door, but it was blocked. The guards helped me bust the door open. Someone pushed a dresser in front of it."

"Did anyone from Homeland Security interrogate you when they investigated the incident?" Sam asked.

"No one from Homeland Security came here," Brock declared. "Com. Arroyo and four military police interviewed us."

"Let's be honest," CC stated. "This isn't the first time Joe escaped from a secure location. RJ, are you sure Joe wasn't acting nervous after the others went to bed, like he was expecting someone?"

"Not a bit," RJ declared. "You heard Payton. They confiscated all our communication devices. After the others went to bed Joe finished the ending. He was pleased. He decided on the name and was going to unveil it at breakfast."

"Interesting," CC received a text. "Did Joe take the lyrics with him?"

"Yes," Collen answered. "But that's not unusual. Joe likes to show his final work to all of us at the same time."

"Has Joe ever mentioned that he wanted to change the name of the band to Joe Sherrod with Light Crimson?" Sam questioned.

"No!" Collen snapped. "Joe's not that way!"

"I didn't mean to offend you," Sam apologized. "Throughout history, several lead singers have done that before they go solo."

"Not Joe!" Travis insisted. "He is committed to Light Crimson."

"I'm sorry," Sam apologized. "I had to ask."

"That's all our questions for now," CC read a text. "Depending on what we find today, Ramsey may move you to a different location."

"Thanks," Carrie Anne sighed. "We would feel safer somewhere else."

"Hopefully, somewhere we are not locked inside," Babs declared. "We're all getting a little stir crazy."

"I'll see what we can do," CC comforted and left.

"Follow me to the hanger where we store the missiles," Gaines said as they got into the car. "It's on the other side of the airport."

"Sydney, what did you find with the security tape?" Kathe asked on speaker as they drove off.

"JAKE was able to tap into the system," Sydney confided. "There are six minutes missing from the timer. I checked with Skip, and he ran it through his equipment. He showed me where someone edited the film and spliced it back together. He said it was done very professionally."

"That's what we suspected," Sam agreed.

"I also had JAKE check outside the windows for tracks," Kathe reported. "Even though the grass was hand-raked, JAKE showed two sets of prints going inside with a third set being drug out. Did you see the images?"

"I sure did," Sydney grinned. "JAKE showed the imprints of the shoes from the dirt underneath the grass."

"Unbelievable," Kathe smiled.

"I see you're using different variables in JAKE Technology as you do in Chameleon Technology," Ramsey concluded.

"Yes," Sydney smiled. "The way Kathe had JAKE scan the area from the bedroom window and then crawled outside walking to the road not only showed the imprints of the perpetrator's footprints but fresh tire tracks on the road. The estimated time of his abduction was 0155 (1:55 AM EST)."

"I'm waiting for your findings at the missile hangar, as to where we send you next, and if we move Light Crimson," Ramsey stated.

"My gut feeling is that we should relocate them," CC shared.

"I agree," Ramsey declared. "I'll work on a plan to relocate them. Did you find anything else?"

"Yes, handwritten song lyrics," Kathe answered. "It must have fallen out of Joe's pocket when they drug him over the nightstand out the window. Its title is 'You're Still Part of My Heart.'"

"Why, for the love of God, can't that man just let you go?" Ramsey bellowed.

"Ramsey," Sam cautioned. "We're pulling up to the hangar. Our tour guide is out of his car."

"Okay," Ramsey agreed and turned up the sound.

Turning off the alarm system and sliding the hangar door open, Gaines led the way inside. "As you can see, we store different types of weapons here. The missing weapons were stored in the middle rows."

"When was the last time the two guided missiles were documented in the hangar?" Kathe asked.

"Yesterday, we did a weekly inventory of our missiles, and they were here," Gaines admitted. "We were preparing to ship them plus several other missiles to the China Sea for the scheduled War Games next week."

"May we see where the missing missiles were stored?" Kathe asked.

"Yes, come with me right here in the middle of this isle," Gaines led the way toward the back of the hangar.

"The sign outside reads 'no cameras allowed,'" Kathe noted. "May I take a few pictures for our investigation?"

"Negative," Gaines confirmed. "Absolutely no pictures."

"Well, it doesn't mean videos," Sydney laughed snapping several still pictures.

"These missiles have the launch weight of 1,500 kilograms," Sam declared.

"That is 3,300 pounds each," Kathe stated walking to the end of the aisle. "So, to move them, you would have to use this reach truck since it can turn around in tight spaces."

"That is correct," Gaines agreed as Sydney took more several pictures.

"Do you always leave the keys in the ignition?" Kathe asked.

"We do not!" Gaines defended. "They have to be checked in and out at Com. Arroyo's office."

"Then, would you like to explain to me why the keys are still in the ignition after Com. Arroyo and the military police investigated in the wee hours this morning?" Kathe inquired.

"What?" Gaines reached for the keys.

"Don't worry," Sydney explained. "I already checked for prints. They wore gloves."

"Where does this smaller hangar door lead?" CC pointed behind the Reach Truck.

"It leads to a taxiway," Gaines admitted.

"Will you please open this door?" Kathe asked. "I'd like to see."

"Yes, ma'am," Gaines disabled the alarm with the code and then opening the hangar door.

Sydney had JAKE video the driveway out of the door as Kathe stepped to one side and walked to the taxiway. "JAKE estimates the last tire tracks were from a vehicle, not an airplane about 0240 (2:40 AM EST) this morning. These tire tracks are a match with the ones behind Building E," he said as he cross-checked the tire prints with the make of the automobile. "We are looking for a Chevy Silverado 350 HD. That can easily carry the weight and not be suspected."

"Can you hack into the security footage last night at the gates to possibly see who's in the truck?" Kathe asked before she turned back to join the others.

"I'm looking," Sydney answered getting into the system. "No, the timeframe we are looking for has been removed."

"I don't know why you walked out to the taxiway," Gaines stated as Kathe returned. "The taxiway has been used all morning to get ready for the festivities."

"I was calculating how much time it would take to steal two missiles and load them," Kathe stated. "The way the missiles containers are built, the perpetrators could take both at the same time. The reach truck is designed to extend the lift to carry multiple pallets."

"It's protocol to move one at a time," Gaines stated. "It's too dangerous."

"I don't believe they were worried about protocol," Kathe declared. "When were you aware the missiles were missing?"

"Breakfast is at 0600 (6:00 AM EST)," Gaines stated. "Joe was reported missing at 0615 (6:15 AM EST) this morning. Com. Arroyo immediately put the base on lockdown. That's when all departments ran security checks. The missiles were reported missing at 0650 (6:50 AM EST.)"

"The report stated that due to the 4th of July festivities, no planes arrived or departed after 0000 (1200 AM EST)," CC checked as Kathe signaled her to leave.

"I believe that is correct, ma'am," Gaines confirmed.

"Well, that's all we need today," CC stated. "Thank you for your time."

"Do you remember your way out?" Gaines asked.

"Yes, we take the roundabout and turn at the second right," Sam stated.

"That's correct," Gaines said, watching them leave.

"Gaines said the keys are located in Arroyo's office and must be checked in and out," Kathe explained. "My gut feeling is that there was no forced entry. We need to check it out."

"Sydney, what building is Com. Arroyo's office located?" Sam asked.

"I finally got the satellite over the area," Sydney admitted. "I'm showing it is in Building M. At the roundabout, take the second exit."

"Copy that," Sam answered. "We're approaching the roundabout now."

"Good," Sydney stated. "I'm showing a camera mounted on Building M is pointing down at the street. I blocked it for you. Stop one building before and let Kathe out. Then drive to the end of the street, turn left, then left again. Park four buildings down to wait for her."

"Kathe, remember to keep an eye out for Gaines," Ramsey instructed. "He had to have realized that you picked up on the alarm systems on the small hangar door. I noted he was nervous about your reasoning ability. He may drive by to see if you went there."

"Copy that," Sam pulled over for Kathe to get out.

"CC, I've arranged for you to take the band members with you," Ramsey reported. "The 'president' ordered Ensign Duggart to have them ready to leave."

"That's pretty bold of Sydney!" CC cautioned.

"That's technology," Ramsey chuckled. "I'll give you the details after Kathe is out of the building."

"Ramsey, there's no signs of a forced entry on the main door," Kathe said using JAKE to turn off the alarm and unlock it. "I'm inside the building."

"I'm showing Arroyo's office is on the second floor," Sydney stated. "Watch for security officers inside."

"I'm using the stairs," Kathe hurried to the second floor. "JAKE, are any human life-forms on the other side of this door?"

"Kathe, I'm not showing any signs of human life-forms," JAKE answered as Kathe slowly opened the door and entered the hallway.

"JAKE, warn me if any human life-forms appear," Kathe ordered.

"Kathe, I'll remind you," JAKE replied.

"Go to the left," Sydney relayed pulling up the directory of the building. "Arroyo's office is at the end of the hallway. I'm blocking the security cameras."

"Copy that," Kathe whispered hurrying down the hallway. "I'm at the doorway. There are no signs of a forced entry."

"I see that," Sydney took a picture.

"I'm going to his secretary's office," Kathe shared. "There are no visible signs of any tampering," Kathe noted panning JAKE's camera for them to view.

"What is in that cabinet behind the secretary's desk?" Ramsey asked.

"Let's see," Kathe reached for the handle.

"Don't touch it!" Sydney cautioned. "I'm showing it's hot. There is an electronic lock on it. Use JAKE to turn off the alarm and open it."

"Done," Kathe said as JAKE opened the lock. "It's filled with keys. There is only one set of keys for each item. The one for the Reach Truck is here."

"Then, someone made a copy of the key," Ramsey assumed as Kathe closed the doors.

"I'm showing Com. Arroyo's office is down the hall to the right," Sydney relayed watching the screen.

"No forced entry here either," Kathe said as Sydney snapped another picture.

"Kathe, sensing a human life-form coming this way," JAKE warned.

"Use JAKE to unlock Arroyo's door," Sydney said as Kathe complied. "Behind his desk on the left is a door that leads to a private elevator or the fire escape. Take the fire escape. I've got the cameras."

"Copy that," Kathe hurried outside and pulled the lever to lower the staircase.

"Kathe, a car is entering the roundabout!" Sydney cautioned. "It's Gaines!"

"I'm half-way down!" Kathe exclaimed. "He'll see me if I go back up. I've got an idea!" she whispered and jumped over the rail behind the bushes around the building. "Did Gaines see me?"

"Maybe not," Sydney whispered. "He was making the turns. We'll know in a minute."

"Are you okay?" Ramsey asked. "That jump was pretty high."

"I'm fine," Kathe whispered. "I had no choice."

"Gaines didn't see you," Sydney said. "He's driving down the street. Hurry to the car and get away from there." They watched Kathe hurry to the next street. "Sam, start the car!"

"I already did," Sam acknowledged. "You're clear on this road. No sign of Gaines."

"Sam, take the first right, and then left," Sydney advised. "That will bring you to the roundabout. Pass the front gate and take the first right. Ensign Duggart has the band members in a black van at a gas station on the right, just before the freeway."

"Won't Duggart tell Com. Arroyo what happened?" CC asked.

"Negative," Sydney smiled. "He's been ordered to report to Jacksonville, Florida's Naval Base ASAP. Sam is to drive the van and drop Duggart off at the bus station on the way to the airport. Remember to wipe the fingerprints clean."

"CC, Kathe, when you're done with the car, wipe it clean also," Ramsey ordered. "I used a bogus company to pay for the rental. There should be no tangible evidence that you were there. Ensign Duggart didn't take a copy of your ID's. You caught him off guard with the presidential seal."

"How did you arrange all of this?" CC asked.

"It's all in the wrist," Sydney laughed. "Jordan has your destination."

Saturday, July 4th
1900 (7:00 PM GMT +2)
Twenty Miles West of Corippo, Switzerland

"Not good!" Bernadette reached for her gun, calling Mikey. "Forget the food! Two of Bencivenni's men pulled up to the store in a dark-blue BMW."

Second in line at the counter, Mikey glances out the front windows of the convenience store. "I forgot something," Mikey muttered to the person behind him, leaving the line. "I see them. They're parking the car," he peered over the top of the shelf at the parking lot. "One of the cashiers must have spotted them drive up," Mikey supposed checking the inside. "He's acting very nervous," Mikey glanced around. "This gas station has two entrances. I'll slip out the other side," Mikey relayed watching two men get out of the car. "The goons are coming inside."

"I'll pick you up," Bernadette slid across the seat and started the engine. "I'm coming around the building now," she slowly drove to the other side, stopping at the closet pump. "I see them inside. You're clear to walk out."

"I'm coming out now," Mikey adjusted his baseball cap, held his head down, slowly opened the door, and walked to the car.

Bernadette slid across the seat as Mikey opened the car door. “Look, who’s at the next pump?”

“Luigi Bianchi,” Mikey identified starting the car and glancing inside the store again. “So far, I don’t think they made me out,” Mikey turned right toward the highway.

“Do you think the cashier recognized you and called them?” Bernadette pulled the visor down to check. “You said the cashier acted nervously.”

“I don’t think so,” Mikey declared. “I kept my head down when I entered the building so that I wouldn’t get picked up on the surveillance cameras. I did notice that as the goons entered, people moved away from them. It’s evident that this is a tight-knit community, controlled by fear.”

“That keeps the people away from Lugino Village,” Bernadette checked her phone. “I’m showing a small restaurant near the highway entrance. We can stop there. I’m sure your Aunt Sophia served dinner an hour ago, and we haven’t eaten all day.”

“How could we?” Mikey asked. “We spotted Bencivenni’s goons at the airport and all along the way. We should have arrived at Corippo hours ago.”

“I was against this fancy, red, sports car with the blackened windows,” Bernadette grinned. “It’s a magnet for trouble. There’s the restaurant,” she pointed on the right. “The gas station was busy. Hopefully, the restaurant isn’t so we can get in and out quickly,” she said as Mikey turned into the parking lot and parked in front of the restaurant.

“I thought the car gives us more of the wealthy tourist appeal,” Mikey disagreed. “I like the car.”

“Still, think so, Dear,” Bernadette chuckled watching two men stop in front of their car to admire it. “The one on the left is Chino Manci,” she reached cautiously for her gun. “I’ve never seen the one on the right. I pray this tint is dark enough that they can’t recognize us. They are drooling over this thing.”

“I guess they decided not to go inside the restaurant,” Mikey watched Chino answer his phone and turn around. “They’re walking back to their car.”

“Chino is off the phone and pointing to this car,” Bernadette watched from the mirror on her visor. “Oh, and now they are unbuttoning their coats and staring at the car again. And yes, they are packing.”

"We might need a little help," Mikey reached for his phone. "Alonzo, we're leaving Locarno toward Corippo. The car's tinted windows are drawing attention. We need some intervention."

"Give me a minute," Alonzo checked his contacts. "I have the perfect person in mind. He's been checking on some unsubstantiated rumors for me about the area we grew up in."

"I've seen Chino with Bencivenni several times," Bernadette held her pistol down. "My gut is warning me they are about to check us out."

"They pulled into the parking space right behind us," Mikey reached for his weapon. "They know we didn't get out of the car."

"They're splitting up to come around on both sides of the car," Bernadette warned. "A confrontation will make it harder for us to complete our mission."

"This car brought us luck," Mikey grinned. "A police car just pulled into the parking lot, and he's passing us slowly. It's a good time to leave."

Bernadette pulled down her visor, checking the mirror, "They're running to their car. They're peeling out!"

"I hear them," Mikey turned onto the road, checking his rearview mirror. "One more red light before the entrance to the highway," he sped through a stale yellow light.

"Our tail ran the light," Bernadette declared listening to the screeching of tires and horns blowing. "They narrowly escaped an accident. We may have to take them out."

"Maybe not," Mikey sped up. "I checked the map on the way over. I chose this car for its speed and maneuverability around the hairpin-curves. That car can't match mine."

"Yes, but if we make a run for it, Chino will call ahead for backup," Bernadette cautioned as Mikey's phone rang.

"Take highway E-43," Pauli requested. "There's a long tunnel about two-three miles ahead. Dominic will be in a light-blue SUV. He's switching cars with you."

"Got it!" Mikey took the entrance ramp. "Thank goodness the traffic is light. I've got to get far enough ahead of them, so we'll have time to pull this off," he passed two cars.

"There's a car coming straight at us!" Bernadette braced for impact. "Roll the car over to the road below us!"

"No!" Mikey punched the gas. "Hold on!" he barely pulled ahead of the lead car. "That was close!"

"Too close!" Bernadette exclaimed, glancing backward. "I don't see them. They're either playing it cool by staying back or called ahead."

"We'll see soon enough," Mikey stated, increasing the speed. "The tunnel is after the next two sharp curves."

"Still no sign of them," Bernadette grinned as they entered the first curve.

"I told you this car would lose them," Mikey took the second curve.

"There's the tunnel," Bernadette relayed. "We might not be out of the woods yet! There are two cars on each side of the tunnel entrance! They will block the entrance!"

"Not with Dominic around!" Mikey sped through the entrance between them.

"Now, they're sealing the entrance," Bernadette turned around.

"There's no oncoming traffic," Mikey stated spotting an SUV stopped on the road in front of them."

"Be careful; it could be a trap," Bernadette warned as Mikey slowed down. "At least, wait until they get out first. I'd like to know who we are up against?"

"Pauli said Dominic would be here," Mikey grinned, watching two men slowly getting out of the SUV. "Never doubt the DiMeglio brothers!" Mikey laughed getting out of the car.

"Mikey, Bernadette!" Dominic lite a cigar. "A little birdie told me you needed a fresh ride."

"Uncle Dominic, Vinnie," Mikey popped the trunk.

"The men that are tailing you are Chino Mancini and Ray Gilleti," Dominic declared. "Rumor has it that they are responsible for several missing visitors to the area. The last man that went missing was a Federal Agent from the states. We've noticed Spinello beefed up security since then. That's why this car almost made you the next two," he said as Mikey glanced at the entrance.

"Don't worry," Dominic chuckled. "The goons just got into a fender-bender. We have all the time we need. We think we found what you're looking for but can't get close enough to check it out. The compound is tighter than Fort Knox. It also has electronic, surveillance cameras. Alonzo assured me that you have a way to get inside. We're here to help you."

"Does Spinello's men know you're here?" Bernadette asked.

"No, not yet" Dominic laughed. "Alonzo and I grew up in this area. We have more family in the area than he's got goons. You better get going. It's almost dusk."

"Thanks for the interference," Bernadette reached for her backpack.

"Hey, what are families for," Dominic threw his hands up. "Bernadette, I'm surprised you got in this magnet."

"Your nephew thought it gave us the 'wealthy, tourist looks,'" Bernadette laughed.

"Mikey always had my sister's flare for glitter and glitz," Dominic chuckled. "Now, get out of here. Oh, and I hope you bought insurance on this car."

"I did," Mikey handed Dominic the keys.

"Good," Dominic chuckled tossing the keys to Vinnie. "Scrap the magnet!"

Saturday, July 4th
2030 (8:30 PM GMT +2)
Corippo Village, Switzerland

"You're checking in late, Mikey," Sophia Conti greeted them.

"Aunt Sophia, did you make my favorite Veal Piccata for dinner?" Mikey hugged her.

"Of course," Sophia stepped back and squeezed his cheeks. "I expected you hours ago."

"You did save us some?" Mikey pleaded. "You are my favorite aunt."

"I even kept your food warm," Sophia smiled. "I know you're in a hurry. But you need to eat. Come into the kitchen. Then I'll show you to your rooms," she led the way.

"Ah, the best Italian cook in the world," Mikey sat at the table. "This makes all that we've been through today worth it," he reached for his plate. "You know Rachel doesn't cook."

"You married her," Sophia chuckled sitting with them. "I told you not to do it."

"But Rachel puts up with Mikey's profession," Bernadette chuckled. "That takes a special woman."

"She is," Sophia agreed. "I see that Rachel made you clean up your language."

"Was I that bad?" Mikey wondered finishing his meal. "Alonzo said the same thing."

"Yes, you were terrible," Sophia confirmed. "How did she get you to quit?"

“Our boys started cussing,” Mikey explained. “Rachel threatened to kill me if I didn’t change.”

“Kids have a way of changing your lifestyle,” Sophia chuckled. “That’s why Vincent and I never had them. Now that you’re finished, leave the plates. I’ll clean them later. You need to get started. Come I’ll show you to your room,” she said leading them up the stairs to the first room on the right.

“Your Bed and Breakfast is so charming,” Bernadette declared.

“Thank you,” Sophia opened the door. “Go ahead inside and look around. I put a cot in the room in case you spend the night. This room has the private balcony you asked for,” she said as a baby cried. “I purposely put you across the hall from the Johnson family with small children. That way, no one can hear you talking. Oh, and the guests in #7 have a teenage daughter, Dakota that sneaks outside during the night to smoke and call her boyfriend. Dakota is very nosy and sneaky. Some of the other guests caught her listening at their door when they opened it. Don’t worry; I plan on keeping an eye on her tonight. She won’t be a problem.”

“Alonzo said your house is one of the last houses built in this rustic mountain village,” Bernadette admired. “You made sure the steps and hallway creaked on purpose.”

“Vincent and I sure did,” Sophia answered. “We retired years ago from your profession and built this Bed and Breakfast. We never stop watching over our shoulders for that one person, still looking for us. What can I say? We were good at what we did. As you’ve already noticed, this place has many ways to escape and different types of alarms. Oh, I seem to be babbling about the good-ole-days. I’ll get out of your way. I’ll keep an eye out for intruders. Let me know if you need anything.”

“Another hug from my favorite aunty,” Mikey hugged her.

“You feed that line to all five of us,” Sophia squeezed his cheeks again.

“Yes, Mikey does,” Bernadette smiled glancing at the look on his face. “But you’re the only aunt that pinches his cheeks.”

“You mean, and lives to talk about it?” Sophia grinned opening the door. “I’m the first person to teach Mikey how to shoot a gun.”

“Yes, you did,” Mikey grinned. “I learned as a small boy to always respect you and Uncle Vincent.”

“You’re the son we never had,” Sophia sighed. “Be careful when you go to your objective. Several people tried to find the compound and never returned. The last one was an undercover CIA Agent that rented the room for a month. He spent one night and left the next morning. I shipped his belongings home with his corpse a week later. Good night."

"Good night," Mikey hugged Sophia again.

"The balcony is perfect for flying the drone," Bernadette stated looking outside. "We can fly it in and out with no problem. I'll get the drone up while you call Sydney."

"Got ya," Mikey handed Bernadette the drone and iPad. "I'll meet you outside after the call."

"Okay, I'll have it up in a minute," Bernadette relayed walking out to the balcony. "I need to know where to go."

"Mikey, Ramsey, and I have Alonzo's team online with us," Sydney declared.

"We heard you had a rough time getting to Sophia's?" Ramsey quizzed.

"Bencivenni and Spinello have taken over the entire mountainside," Bernadette cautioned. "If Alonzo and Pauli hadn't run a little interference, we could have blown our cover."

"I'm connecting everyone's iPads to your cameras," Sydney pressed enter. "Now, we can get started."

"Which way to the village?" Bernadette questioned hovering the drone over the roof.

"Bencivenni's compound is in the Valle Verzasca, between the Leventina and the Valle Maggia," Alonzo instructed watching the screen. "We're looking for a Catholic Church with the clock tower."

"I'm not finding it," Bernadette moved the drone.

"It's half-way down the mountain from your position," Pauli located it.

"Thanks, Pauli," Bernadette moved the drone to the church.

"There should be a road, further down the mountain, with a fast-moving stream that runs parallel to it?" Alonzo quizzed.

"Is this what you're looking for?" Bernadette hovered the drone.

"Yes," Alonzo agreed. "Follow the road to the right until you find a few scattered farmhouses. There should be another Catholic Church in the next village about five-miles-away."

"There are the scattered farmhouses," Mikey zoomed in the camera. "That road sign says 8 km to Leventina. Bernadette, slow the drone down. You'll pass through that small village before you know it."

"I'm not going to get a ticket," Bernadette laughed slowing the drone at the beginning of the village. "Is this better?"

"Very funny," Mikey nudged her arm.

"Leventina is the village with the Catholic Church with a stain-glass window over the front door," Pauli stated. "Dominic said that once we find that we're almost there."

"There it is," Alonzo noted. "From that church, you turn left and follow the main road out of town. It takes you to a dam over the Verzasca River."

"We're coming to a fast-moving river," Mikey noted zooming out.

"That is the Verzasca River," Alonzo agreed. "It has one of the swiftest currents in the world."

"The dam has the only road across it that leads to Lugino Village," Pauli spotted as Mikey zoomed in on it.

"The village is hidden deep in the forest across that dam," Alonzo stated. "They chose that village because they can control who goes in and out. Evidentially, it was a well-kept secret for many years."

"It is heavily guarded," Ramsey noted. "It won't be easy getting across the dam with that number of guards."

"It would be suicide to try to cross the river with that current," Hiltree declared. "I'm a Navy Seal. There is no way anyone could slip across that river."

"Hover the drone for a minute," Sydney requested. "I'm taking pictures and scanning the dam," he pressed enter. "I'm showing a very high-frequency radio wave coming from the inside of that dam. It is more concentrated than any of the dams I've seen. Let me add, Skip and Mack to the conversation and bring them up to speed. We need all the eyes we can get to help you two inside," he admitted making the call.

"We've brought up the cameras and are ready to proceed," Skip acknowledged.

"The village is not only hidden in the forest but has a solid 12-foot-wall that blends into the terrain around it," Alonzo stated.

"Take the fork over the dam to the left," Mack zeroed in on it. "It's a mile and a half down that road to the left. And you're right about it blending into the terrain. I had to zoom in on the area to find it."

"Yes, it is hard to see," Bernadette declared moving the drone closer to it. "The drone is sluggish, and the battery is losing power."

"I've lost the camera feed," Mikey admitted.

"Take the drone higher," Sydney requested typing commands on his computer. "This barrier is similar to the ones we encountered in New Jersey, except it's using a higher frequency," he pushed enter. "Now, you can proceed."

"Much better, Doc," Bernadette confirmed moving the drone over the compound.

"Mikey, your camera should work now," Sydney pressed enter.

"It's loading up," Mikey concurred. "This looks familiar."

"Certainly, it is different from the carnage we witnessed here before," Alonzo admitted.

"I think Mikey means it looks like a smaller version of Kitzbuhel, Austria," Ramsey realized. "Note the colorful row houses with the shops on the bottom floors and outside cafés."

"Yes, I've been there," Mikey stated checking the village out. "It has exotic flowers like we've seen whenever we are on target. Some of which are nonindigenous to this area. Anthuriums and Hibiscus are strictly tropical plants. There must be a greenhouse in the village."

"This too is staged," Alonzo commented. "The villages in this area are more rustic and made of stone."

"It's a pretty active village," Ramsey stated. "People are enjoying the warm summer's evening."

"The couple sitting at the first table outside at the café are dead-ringers for Senator Trace Gentry of South Carolina and his wife, Ellen," Mack proclaimed. "The couple at the table next to them is the replacement for Great Britain's Leader of the Official Opposition and wife."

"The man behind them is a dead-ringer for the primetime commentator for CTN News," Pauli recognized. "I always wanted to wring his lying neck."

"These are copycats of world leaders, their second in command, and news reporters from around the world!" Hiltree exclaimed.

"This is why there is a sudden influx of world leaders turning toward the leftist ways of socialism," Alonzo declared.

"Mikey, can you zoom in on their hands?" Ramsey asked. "Are they all wearing one of those rings?"

"Yes, they are," Mikey confirmed showing them.

"There is a hospital a block from the church's left side with the bell tower," Skip located zooming in on it.

“I see it,” Sydney confirmed. “It is a small hospital-probably twenty beds at the most. Bernadette, I’ll hover the mother-drone over the roof while you release the mosquito. We need to see inside.”

“Copy that,” Bernadette agreed flying the mosquito to the front door. “I guess we’ll have to wait for someone to enter. I don’t see any other way to get inside.”

“Not necessarily,” Sydney chuckled scoping out the door. “Its motion censored. Fly the drone down to the bottom of the right door and find the small electrical box on the door.”

“I found it,” Bernadette replied.

“Now, point the drone directly at the center of the censor,” Sydney requested. “That’s good. Press the green LB on your screen.”

“It opened the door!” Bernadette grinned moving the drone inside the lobby past the front desk.

“You’d think the nurse saw a ghost when the door opened,” Mikey laughed. “She checked the monitor for intruders outside.”

“Luckily, the mosquito is too small for her to see when it passed over her,” Sydney stated. “Let’s see what’s on the first floor.”

“There’s nothing on the first floor, except a tiny emergency room,” Mikey panned the camera.

“Do the same thing to the censor at the elevator,” Sydney requested as Bernadette complied.

“There’s more action on this floor,” Hiltree watched as it passed four nurses working at their station. “Let’s check inside the patients’ rooms.”

“Yes, Sir,” Bernadette flew the mosquito to the floor and walked it inside the first room.

“It can’t be!” Hiltree exclaimed. “The Prime Minister of Israel. He’ll never agree to this plan!”

“An operation like this requires mega-money,” Sydney insisted.

“I agree!” Alonzo exclaimed. “Even with all the Mafia Families involved, this operation exceeds their funding capabilities.”

“We discovered these replacements in the nick of time,” Hiltree declared. “Sydney, document the Prime Minister wearing the ring.”

“It’s already done,” Sydney snapped several pictures. “They’re pretty close to changing the world as we know it.”

“I can’t believe how long this has gone on under our noses!” Hiltree exclaimed.

"That's because they made the changes very slowly," Ramsey answered. "Bernadette, let's quickly check the other rooms."

"Copy that," Bernadette replied while Sydney documented each person.

"They've done their homework," Ramsey noted. "They've replaced quite a few of the free-world leaders or their successors, and news reporters. Even one reporter at FNN, which would never favor a totalitarian dictatorship."

"With this many replacements in one location, it appears they are going to have a massive switch all at once," Mack assumed checking an outside camera. "Outside on the mother-drone, I see Congresswoman Macy of California."

"The Speaker of the House!" Hiltree realized. "The G-Summit is coming up in a few days. World leaders and news reporters from around the world will be at that Summit."

"That's when they plan to switch people!" Ramsey gasped.

"Bernadette let's see if they have an operating room," Sydney requested. "Go back to the nurse's station and go to the left. Since Ricci Falcini was in Florida to sedate Yorg, it proves Bencivenni was planning to open another facility. It will be interesting to see who Bencivenni found to replace Ricci for this one."

"Copy that," Bernadette complied.

"There is only one operating room," Mikey confirmed zooming in on the double doors. "And you're, in luck; it's in use," he showed the illuminated sign above the doors.

"We can't get into those sealed doors," Sydney stated. "Bernadette, is there possibly another door marked Observation Deck?"

"Yes," Bernadette quickly located.

"See if the drone can crawl under that door?" Sydney asked.

"Yes, it's inside," Bernadette confirmed hovering the drone close to the ceiling.

"No spectators tonight," Sydney noted. "Fly the mosquito to the center of the windowsill. Under it should be is a brass button that opens the audio," he watched. "Good, now we can hear them while I get facial recognition of the surgical team," he zoomed in on the speaker. "Bernadette, the speaker has pulled away from the wall. See if the mosquito can get inside that way. I need to see the surgical monitor."

“It might take a minute,” Bernadette agreed maneuvering the drone toward the monitor. “Yes, I got the mosquito inside,” moving it around inside.

“Ladies, this is our last patient for today,” the surgeon informed. “Marsha, are you good with this? Our last patient was a challenge for you to keep sedated.”

“Randy, honestly, I’m tired, but I can do one more,” Marsha answered. “When the last patient woke up in the middle of surgery, he punched me in the face. It took me a minute to come to my senses. I’m thankful you and the nurses subdued him for me to put him back under again. I’ve heard of it happening but never experienced it.”

“You handled it well,” Randy consoled. “And my two sidekicks, Lydia, Barbara, are you good for one more?”

“We’ve worked a twelve-hour day so far,” Lydia glanced at the clock. “This has to be the last. If you’re ready, I’ll document the starting time.”

“Okay, let’s begin,” Randy stated. “Barbara, the scalpel.”

“Sydney, can you see the monitor from this angle?” Bernadette asked. “The space is so tight. I had to find an elusive spot to land it. The only place is eye-level to the anesthesiologist.”

“Not to mention, she is glancing at it constantly,” Sydney understood snapping several pictures. “Not good, the candidate is in trouble. The alarms should have sounded. The heart rate and blood pressure are flatlining. They are losing the patient?”

“Oh, my God!” Marsha noticed. “Lydia, get the Adrenalin!”

“Adrenalin!” Lydia handed a needle to Randy.

“I’m injecting the patient straight into the left ventricle!” Randy informed. “Barbara, any change?”

“No change!” Barbara assured.

“Paddles!” Randy orders as Lydia smeared the gel and handed them to him.

“Clear!” Randy warned rubbing the pads together and then shocking the patient’s chest. “Anything?”

“The rhythm tried to start,” Barbara called.

“Clear!” Randy warned as everyone assisting stepped back again. “Anything?”

“Still no change in the sinus rhythm,” Marsha called out. “Please try one more time! We can’t afford to lose another patient!”

“Clear!” Randy warned hitting him two more times. “Anything?”

"Negative!" Marsha sighed. "We lost him!" she shoved her chair back in anger.

Barbara glanced at the clock. "Time of death is 2307 (11:07 PM GMT + 2)."

"There's no need to document the time of death!" Randy snapped taking his gloves off and throwing them across the body.

"I'm sorry," Barbara cried. "It is protocol."

"You know what to do with the body and his personal belongings!" a guard ordered from the intercom. "I need to report this to Mr. Bencivenni. He's not going to like this!" he turned off the intercom.

"This isn't good!" Lydia cried pulling the sheet over the victim's face.

"Lydia is right!" Marsha snapped. "You heard the guard. Bencivenni isn't going to be happy that we've lost another candidate!" She ripped off her gloves and mask, throwing them on the gurney.

"What can I do?" Randy defended. "I warned Bencivenni that this man wasn't a good candidate! He presented overweight, high blood pressure, and pre-diabetic!"

"Randy," Sydney whispered trying to scan his face. "Look straight at Marsha. I want to see who you are," he pushed enter. "Got it!"

"Because of Bencivenni, this is the fourth person to expire on the table in a month!" Marsha declared with tears streaming down her face. "I interviewed this man before we entered the operating room. He was innocent, plucked from his office on his eighteenth-wedding anniversary in Richfield, Virginia. What a waste of human life."

"Bernadette, move the angle of the drone a little more to the left," Sydney requested. "I need to scan Marsha's face."

"Bencivenni makes the decisions around here, not me!" Randy snapped. "Within the last several months, he's stepped up our surgeries. I warned Bencivenni that the candidates must be physically fit to undergo this type of dramatic undertaking. After losing Tatum, he found this man quick. The only thing Bencivenni cares about is do they fit his criteria of height, body mass, and looks similar."

"My husband is a detective in New Orleans," Marsha shared. "Bencivenni doesn't care about our welfare. I saw it in Bencivenni's eyes after his last candidate died. I thought he reached in his coat for a gun when he handed Randy the new roster of surgeries."

"I did as well," Randy concurred.

"What about you, Barbara?" Lydia asked. "Do you agree with us?"

“I was aware the first morning when each of us woke up wearing identical rings,” Barbara confessed. “I knew Bencivenni wasn’t going to let us live. Bencivenni only needs our skills. As soon as he’s done with us, he’ll activate our rings and get rid of us.”

“Especially since we know what he’s doing! Marsha admitted.

“The more surgeries we do, the longer we stay alive,” Randy comforted. “Meanwhile, we need to be prudent. Every spare minute we have, we need to look for an exit. There has to be another way out other than the main gate.”

“I keep praying that someone will rescue us,” Lydia whispered.

“It’s been so long, our families have given up looking for us,” Marsha shared. “By now, the police have moved our files to the cold case’s file.”

“Finish your work,” Randy requested. “We’ll meet at the usual place and talk more.”

“According to police reports, the surgeon is Randolph D. Keizer,” Sydney read from missing person files. “Keizer, along with his two nurses, Barbara B. Bondi and Lydia S. Cisco, went missing fourteen-months ago. They were last picked up on the parking garage’s surveillance camera at Baltimore’s Lincoln-Mercy Hospital after a late-night emergency surgery. The anesthesiologist is Marsha K. McKinny. She graduated from Lincoln-Mercy and had a job waiting for her in New Orleans. Keizer not only mentored Ricci, but they’ve been roommates since Ricci’s freshman year. McKinny went missing a day later from New Orleans General. Marsha dated Ricci during her last year at college. Barbara and Lydia tutored Ricci after Keizer left. All four graduated at the top of their class.”

“Ricci handpicked them for Bencivenni,” Ramsey surmised.

“Yes, he did,” Sydney agreed. “Let’s see who this victim was supposed to replace? Bernadette, hover the mosquito over the computer. Mikey, zero in on it.”

“I feel like I watched my death!” Pauli sighed.

“Dano said Bencivenni already replaced me,” Alonzo declared. “No one knows my every move, except Pauli. They’d have to replace him to make it work.”

“I know who they used!” Pauli realized. “When I mopped up the Solana mess in Ponce Inlet, I couldn’t find Mazer Solana and Buddy Tatum. Mazer is the closest to me in size and weight. Plus, he was always jealous of me.”

"Keizer said Tatum didn't make it either," Alonzo said. "Who is this man?"

"Robert Rothschild went missing two weeks ago," Sydney read from the file.

"Bernadette, let me take over the mosquito for a minute," Sydney requested typing commands. "I should be able to find a list of each replacement. Surgeries are usually scheduled early in the morning," Sydney advised connecting the mosquito's needle into a drive on the front of the computer. "They did four surgeries today. I'm cloning the files," he pressed enter. "I just saw a file marked rings. I should be able to find how the rings work. Hopefully, I can deactivate the ones on the surgical team. They shouldn't be collateral damage."

"You've got company," Mikey warned as Randy reentered the room and walked to the computer.

"No!" Sydney exclaimed disconnecting the drone and moving it to the ceiling. "I was almost done!"

"He's deleting that man's file," Mikey zoomed in. "It reads Mazer Solana."

"Randy, are you ready?" Marsha asked poking her head in the room. "I sure could use a drink."

"I'm with you," Randy answered pressing enter. "I forgot to shut down the computer.

"Just leave," Sydney coaxed landing the drone on the top-left of the keyboard. "If the mosquito depresses the escape key, it should reboot," he pressed enter as Randy left the room. "I made it! Now, I can finish extracting the files."

"Our next question is what to do with the replacements when we locate them," Ramsey stated. "Some people are innocent."

"Finished!" Sydney exclaimed disconnecting the mosquito. "Bernadette, it's all yours again. Next, check the nurse's station for who they are monitoring in the recovery rooms."

"They blacked out the names," Ramsey noticed watching the camera.

"Yes, they did," Sydney stated as Bernadette flew the drone into the first room. "This man's surgery was probably this morning since they're still keeping him heavily sedated," Sydney noted checking the monitor. "Bernadette, see if the patient is wearing a ring. His hands are under the sheet."

"Copy that," Bernadette agreed walking the drone under it.

"He's not wearing a ring," Mikey reported enhancing the picture.

"They probably don't put the ring on the candidate until they know they are going to live," Sydney declared. "Check around the room for it."

"Copy that," Bernadette complied.

"It's on the sterile draped table next to the bed," Mikey spotted.

"It's the same design as the other rings we've discovered," Ramsey noted.

"Yes, it is," Sydney conferred snapping a picture. "I'm going to take over the operation of the mosquito again. I want to see if I can get a reading on the ring," he walked the mosquito around the top of the ring. "Clever," Sydney admitted probing the Insignia. Then Sydney walked the mosquito inside the back of the ring. "The serial number #594 is around a small hole in the middle," he said injecting the mosquito's needle into it.

"All rings like this have a small hole," Hiltree stated checking his Navy Seal ring. "It's where they attached the stone to the ring."

"Normally," Sydney showed them his computer screen. "Except, this Insignia is a transmitter. The tiny hole on the inside of the ring has a tiny needle filled with cyanide. The circle surrounding the hole is a motion detector."

"So, if they try to take it off, it injects them with cyanide?" Hiltree quizzed.

"That's correct," Sydney confirmed. "Or if they don't perform what Bencivenni dictates, he can terminate them. Or if the target dies by accident, it will alert Bencivenni."

"We can't leave this place or these people standing!" Hiltree demanded. "What they're doing is an act of terrorism."

"I agree that it is terrorism," Ramsey stated. "However, we have to use caution. We now know they forced some participants into this. In the surgical team's case, they haven't undergone surgery to replace a physician caring for a world leader. They have brilliant minds. The FBI can debrief them and send them back to their families."

"One thing that bothers me is who in their right mind would consent to do this?" Sydney questioned. "They have to live through a painful surgery and agree to wear the ring for the rest of their lives."

"Our hands are tied!" Hiltree insisted. "These people cannot go back into society. Unfortunately, they are collateral damage when it comes to the stability of the world."

"We're not God!" Ramsey interrupted.

"Whatever we decide to do, it will have to wait until we have control over the rings," Sydney declared. "I need to find out how to activate and deactivate the rings. Bencivenni must have an app on his phone that controls the rings. It's like the necklaces Metarha used on Rodger's family. First, I need to locate Bencivenni."

"Then, what about the people Bencivenni has already replaced around the world?" Hiltree asked.

"We will make that decision when we obtain control over the rings," Ramsey admitted. "We don't want to start a worldwide panic. Sydney, locate Bencivenni. Alonzo set the takedown of this village in motion with your people. I'll take over the mosquito. Bernadette and Mikey need to join Dominic by the dam."

"Copy that," Bernadette complied using the mosquito to open the elevator and fly inside. "I hit the return button. We're leaving now. It should take a few minutes to join them."

"How are we going to keep Bencivenni from finding out we located this village?" Hiltree questioned. "Spinello's men are all over this mountain. All someone has to do is make a phone call."

"As soon as Bencivenni makes a phone call, I've got him," Sydney declared. "Then, I can use his cell phone to block communications with the outside world for Kathe's team to take Bencivenni down. That way, the rest of the elites won't know what is happening."

"Where is Kathe now?" Hiltree asked. "Once you find Bencivenni, it will take her time to get there."

"And we don't have that kind of time," Ramsey noted. "I saw some replacements packing to leave."

"What are you going to do?" Hiltree asked.

"We can't let them leave," Ramsey decided. "Hiltree's right about these people. Are we in agreement?"

"Unfortunately, you're right," Alonzo agreed. "Sydney, what do you say?"

"I feel the same way," Sydney sighed. "If they replace the people they intend to, it would be detrimental to the world," he checked the console. "Currently, thanks to Rodger reconnecting me to the Jenkins' phone app, Kathe is tracking Jenkins. We've located Jenkins getting ready to land in Missouri. She thinks Bencivenni is taking Joe Sherrod to the Merritt Penitentiary to hide him there."

"I told CC that Jenkins has to have a way in and out of prison without anyone knowing," Hiltree admitted. "I've checked Lambert-International's records, and Jenkins only landed there when we brought Macaby. He hasn't been back."

"CC is with Kathe," Ramsey interrupted. "They are looking into that question for me. Alonzo, are your men in place yet?"

"Pauli reported Dominic and his men are by the dam ready to strike," Alonzo confided. "Bernadette and Mikey arrived a few minutes ago."

"Copy that," Sydney shared. "Bernadette, I need you and Mikey to locate where the high-frequency radio waves are coming from inside the dam. I've noted several cameras outside. I suspect guards are inside monitoring more than the dam."

"Copy that," Bernadette agreed.

"Dominic, wait for Bernadette to take control of the inside cameras before you take down the guards," Sydney cautioned. "Also, disable their transportation. In case someone gets away, they won't be able to warn others."

"We'll do it now," Dominic replied signaling his men. "We are in place, waiting for your signal."

"Bingo!" Sydney sent a text. "I located Bencivenni. He's right where I suspected. He and Jenkins are at the prison. There has to be a private airstrip I missed close by," he said receiving a text. "We can't coordinate the takedown of this village until we control all the communication equipment. Oh, no! I just lost both signals."

"What happened?" Ramsey demanded.

"Someone destroyed the app or phones," Sydney shook his head.

"Then, they found Rodger out!" Ramsey gasped calling Kathe.

Saturday, July 4th
2345 (11:45 PM GMT +2)
Lugino Village, Switzerland

Working their way through the thick forest to the base of the dam, Bernadette and Mikey came across a door. "That is the only door to the inside workings of the dam," Mikey stated.

"The camera above the door has an alarm system," Bernadette pointed out tapping her earbud and whispering, "Sydney, we found the door into the dam. There is an alarm system hooked to a motion-activated, wide-angle camera above the doorway."

"That's not standard equipment for a small country like this," Sydney stated. "Stand down until Ramsey brings the drone over you.

When we're ready, I'll block the camera long enough for you to get inside."

"Copy that," Bernadette answered.

"I have a visual on the scene now," Sydney started typing commands. "I've looped the video footage to show nothing in front of the doorway," he pressed enter. "I also blocked the alarm. You have 15 seconds to get inside. The walls are too thick to use the drone. Once inside, you're on your own. You have eight minutes to make it back to this door to leave. The time is 0020 (12:20 AM GMT +2)."

"Copy that," Bernadette and Mikey, synchronized their watches. "See you at 0028 (12:28 AM GMT +2)." She opened the door. Mikey stepped inside first, sweeping the area as Bernadette entered, and closed the door.

They quietly hurried down the dimly lit corridor to the control room. Mikey signaled Bernadette to open the door. She reached in her backpack, took out a small mirror, and nodded for Mikey to crack the door.

Mikey peered inside, signaling two people, before trading places with Bernadette. She confirmed the two guards were manning the monitors. Mikey motioned her to get ready. She nodded yes. He kicked the door open and took out both guards.

"Oh, no!" Bernadette hurried inside pushing one of the guards off the keyboard. "When he fell over the keyboard, it went into sleep mode!"

"It's 0022," Mikey cautioned.

"I need the password!" Bernadette grabbed her backpack, taking out some loose powder. "Luckily, he just ate a snack," she blew dust across the keyboard. "It's all sevens and nines," she quickly typed different variations of the numbers. "Got it!" Bernadette exclaimed typing commands. "I'm looping video footage of today and mixing it with the last three days. How are we doing?"

"That took time!" Mikey cautioned. "It's 0023."

"One day finished," Bernadette continued.

"It's 0024," Mikey whispered.

"I'm working on the second day," Bernadette reported.

"It's 0025," Mikey whispered listening at the door. "It takes a full minute to clear the building."

"I'm aware!" Bernadette continued feverishly typing. "I'm not as fast as Sydney."

"It's 0026," Mikey cautioned. "I think I hear someone coming. I've got this, keep working," he slipped out of the room.

All I must do is loop them together now, she thought, pressing enter. Bernadette checked the screens and hurried to the door.

"Do you like your coffee black or with cream and sugar?" Mikey grinned holding two Styrofoam cups.

"Cream and sugar," Bernadette reached for one, hurrying down the corridor. "We've got to get outside!"

"We have 25 seconds to open the door," Mikey warned.

"There, it is ahead of us!" Bernadette threw the cup down.

"Skip, Mack, do you see any unfriendlies near the door?" Ramsey asked bringing the mother-drone closer to the dam. "It's almost time for them to open the door. Dominic and his men are pinned down for now."

"Yes, there are two unfriendlies around the door," Mack discovered.

"Hopefully, they'll hear the gunfire and use the metal door for cover," Ramsey stated. "They can't hear me until they open the door."

"I hear gunfire!" Mikey exclaimed stopping at the door.

"We have no choice but to exit!" Bernadette exclaimed. "I'll open the door and use it for cover. Ramsey will tell us where the targets are."

"Do it!" Mikey crouched down as Bernadette slowly cracked the door.

"You've got two shooters," Ramsey warned watching the door slightly open. "They are on the ridge of the hill above you. One is on the right of the door, and the other is to the left."

"We have 11 seconds to close this door!" Mikey checked the time. "We'll have to drop to the ground and roll. I'll take the one on the right."

"Got it!" Bernadette pushed the door halfway open as bullets began to spray it, then stopping as they rolled out with guns drawn.

"Where are the shooters?" Mikey asked panning his weapon from right to left.

"They've got a guardian angel!" Skip shouted. "I spot a woman climbing down a tree! She eliminated the targets!"

"Bernadette, close that door!" Ramsey ordered zeroing in on the doors alarm making sure it rearmed.

"Who is that woman?" Ramsey asked zeroing in on her as she slung her rifle over her shoulder and walked toward them.

"Aunt Sophia!" Mikey ran to her as Bernadette joined them. "How did you find us?"

"When our local sheriff wouldn't help me look for the Federal Agent staying at my place," Sophia explained. "I found his body right around here. On his body was a small camera with pictures of Bencivenni arriving at the airport. He must have followed Bencivenni here. He had pictures of Bencivenni meeting with the guards and going inside this dam. After you left, my sources' confirmed Dominic was in the area. That's when I figured you'd need to know about this entrance and the camera. I hurried here only to find Dominic and his men taking down some guards. He said you went this way."

"Did you bring the camera?" Bernadette asked as Sophia reached in her pocket. "Yes, I knew you would need it for evidence."

"Thanks, this will help us," Bernadette put it in her backpack. It's time we get back to our mission."

"I'll go back and help Dominic," Sophia said. "You two take care. It will only get worse from here. My sources tell me that no one trying to come up here survived."

"We will," Mikey hugged her.

"Bernadette was your mission successful?" Ramsey asked.

"Yes, I looped the cameras inside with footage from the last three days," Bernadette reported.

"Great, that should buy us enough time to get you inside," Ramsey approved.

"Copy that," Sydney returned to the mic. "I'll help you and Mikey get inside the village. While you were inside, Ramsey located two other entrances. I'll bypass the cameras for you. I need you to take out the communication system. I've located two sources I'm sending to your phones."

"I suggest that they start at the ground's building in the back," Mack noted. "It's the most remote location. Easy to get inside, and then we'll help them get to the second communication objective."

"I agree," Sydney confirmed. "Stay within the safety of the forest and head west. We'll get you inside the wall when you're ready."

"We've secured the parking area and around the damn," Dominic reported.
"Thanks, Dominic," Ramsey appreciated keeping the drone over them.

"What is family for?" Dominic chuckled.

"Dominic, a Hummer is approaching," Skip alerted.

"Copy that," Dominic signaled his men and Sophia to be ready.

Friday, July 3
1610 (4:10 PM EST)
St. Luke's Roosevelt Hospital, NY

Breaking News: "This is Robert Morwitz with FNN News, reporting from outside the emergency entrance of St. Luke's Roosevelt Hospital. Ambassador Niew Zambo, of the African Nation of Mutanbo, called an emergency meeting this afternoon for all United Nations Delegates. Shortly after 4:00 pm, Zambo took to the podium. He seemed to be sweating profusely as he pleaded for immediate military intervention. He reported that a different type of terrorist group was trying to seize power over his country before collapsing to the floor. The physician on the scene started CPR, and he was immediately transported here. We will keep you informed on the details as they unfold. Now, back to your regularly scheduled program already in progress."

"Could that be a coincidence?" Ramsey asked.

"I know you don't believe that!" Sydney pulled up the Internet. "I'm checking Zambo to see if he's wearing a ring," he scrolled through the pictures. "It's not showing his hand," he noted as his phone rang. "Ylia, have you found the antidote for the ant-drones yet?"

"I'm close to it," Ylia reported. "But I just received a call from Doctor Pearson at St. Luke's Roosevelt Hospital. I worked with him on Mrs. Genero. President Trumore assigned Dr. Pearson to head a team working on the ambassador who collapsed at the United Nations. Pearson found traces of an unknown chemical in the bloodstream and wants me to look at it."

"We just saw it on the news," Sydney stated. "Ramsey will arrange a helicopter to take you there. Take what you need from the HUB and head to the heliport on top of the building. I'm texting you a picture of a ring. Let me know if he's wearing one exactly like it. If so, you can't take the ring off. It will inject cyanide into him if it hasn't already."

"I understand," Ylia said. "I'll warn Dr. Pearson."

Friday, July 3
1840 (6:40 PM CT)
State Road 67 by Florissant, MO

"Sydney, we are en route to the penitentiary," Kathe reported. "Keith scrambled our IFF Codes to land at STL undetected and had a SUV ready for us. Our ETA is twenty minutes."

"I was about to contact you," Sydney shared. "Sam, I need Kathe to get the drone up as soon as you can."

"Copy that," Sam pulled over for Kathe to get out. "It's perfect timing. There's no traffic at all this time of day. The shift change for the guards was in 1700 (5:00 PM CT)."

"CC, get your iPad ready," Kathe requested placing the drone on the roof and turning on her iPad. "Sydney, which way do we go?"

"I found a blacked-out area just off SR 67 on Junction 407," Sydney explained. "It is one-mile ahead, and then two-miles east at the junction just before the state line."

"The drone is up," Kathe reported getting back in the SUV.

"We're almost to Junction 407," Sam shared.

"Give me a second," Sydney cautioned as an alarm sounded. "Sam, take the junction and pull over. I know I'm right. I just blocked an electronic signal pointed at you. It came from that junction."

"Copy that," Sam took the junction and pulled over.

"The only thing here is a road sign," Kathe confirmed.

"The signal has to be embedded in the sign," Sydney assumed. "I've already scanned everything around it. Hover the drone over the road sign for me."

"I need a closer look," Kathe said getting out of the SUV.

"Me too," CC opened her door.

"Unbelievable!" Kathe exclaimed examining the sign. "There is a mini, wide-angle camera embedded in the sign at the top of the number zero. Whoever put this here is extremely techy. Note the thin, solar panel on the top."

"I see that," Sydney confirmed changing to infrared and then back. "Infrared showed an electrical current cleverly hidden between the pole and the sign. A silver, hair-thin wire, the same color as the sign, connects it to the camera. It is so hidden that I had to pick it up with infrared."

"This road only leads to the penitentiary," CC declared checking the GPS. "It's eight-miles away. Since this facility is for high-tech criminals, it could be monitored by the staff to prevent aided escapes."

"I don't believe so," Sydney declared. "There has to be something further down this road that someone wants to protect."

"I'm sending the drone in that direction," Kathe stated speeding it up.

"Stop!" Ramsey requested zooming in on the top right-left camera. "I think I see something. I can't quite make it out. Kathe, bring the drone down where the trees are separated on the right by the thick foliage."

"It is a camouflage netting," Sydney confirmed as the drone lowered. "I disabled two more cameras located on both sides of the netting. Kathe, take it under the netting. It's covering a makeshift building. Kathe, now I need to see an Aerial of the grounds. The building is an airplane hangar," Sydney discovered highlighting the outline on the screen. "There's a primitive taxiway leading out of the building to a short runway. That could be how Jenkins flies in and out of here unseen."

"As primitive as it is, Jenkins isn't smart enough to do this alone," Ramsey declared. "Hiltree suspects Jenkins has done this for years. Jenkins just met Rodger."

"If memory serves me correct, several inmates were found dead around the time Gen. Thompson and Macaby arrived," Sydney said searching the Web. "Yes, here it is," Sydney confirmed scrolling down the article. "One guard and four inmates were found dead off SR 67 near the town of Pinebrook. The article further states that they were model inmates, slated for upcoming parole in less than a month. They were part of a government-sponsored work detail to earn money for rehabilitating back into society. For the past few weeks, Officer John Ricks oversaw the detail. He left behind blah-blah-blah," he scrolled more.

"What was the result of the investigation?" CC asked as Sydney scrolled further through the article.

"You're not going to believe this," Sydney declared. "The file was deemed classified and sealed by the government. The local authorities tried to file an injunction, stating it was their jurisdiction. The Ninth Circuit Court blocked the request."

"You mean the Ninth Circus Court, don't you?" Ramsey snapped. "How corrupt can they be? It's easy to assess that someone used these inmates to build this hidden airstrip and hangar. Then killed them, dumped the bodies away from the area and sealed the records."

“That’s what it looks like,” CC declared. “Which branch of the government sealed the record?”

“Do you have to ask?” Sydney scoffed.

“Homeland Security?” CC guessed.

“The one and only,” Sydney confirmed.

“This is another reason why I brought Kathe to help you,” Ramsey declared. “What we have is a theory. We need physical evidence to prove Jenkins’ involvement. Kathe, take the drone back to the hangar. Let’s see if there are any windows. I have my suspicion of what’s inside.”

“Negative on the windows,” CC answered. “There is a small doorway.”

“Kathe, use the mosquito to get under the door,” Sydney requested. “CC, take over the mother-drone.”

“Copy that,” Kathe complied releasing the tiny drone.

“At the bottom of the right corner, it looks like a tiny crack,” Sydney found zooming in on it.

“Yes, the mosquito can get inside easily,” Kathe said crawling the mosquito under the door. She flew the drone up to the ceiling.

“That’s what I suspected!” Ramsey snapped. “After the arrest of Gen. Thompson and Macaby, Jenkins became obsessed every spare moment he had checking the Internet. He left his laptop home one day. I got off early and found it. I guessed his password and the screen opened to the website for a private jet, the Embraer Phenom 100. It requires only one pilot and holds six passengers. It has VTOL and can take off or land practically anywhere. It was way out of his price range. Now, I know where Jenkins got the money.”

“Yes, either Bencivenni or Spinello,” Sydney assumed.

“This proves Hiltree was correct about Jenkins constantly visiting Macaby,” CC declared.

“One thing still doesn’t make sense,” Kathe wondered. “Jenkins flew in and out of here alone for years undetected. He was careful not to let anybody know about it or his relationship with Patterson. Jenkins hasn’t let Rodger Slate out of his site since vetting him. Why would he suddenly let Rodger know such a well-kept secret? Or did he leave Rodger inside the hangar, possibly handcuffed to keep him there?”

“Negative,” Sydney noted. “I’m not detecting anyone inside the aircraft or the structure.”

“Wait a minute!” Ramsey realized. “Is Rodger a pilot?”

“No, Rodger is not,” CC stated.

"We overlooked something at my condo," Ramsey explained. "Someone flew the helicopter that landed on the roof and left. That person was in on the entire scheme."

"Is Patterson a pilot?" Kathe asked.

"It wasn't in the fabricated profile I found on her," CC answered.

"We need to find Patterson's real identity," Kathe stated.

"Kathe, I need to see the perimeter of the prison yard," Sydney requested. "Mark the Embraer Phenom 100 with the drone and get back to the prison. We need a closer look."

"Give me a second," Kathe said landing the mosquito on the top of the jet and marking it.

"CC, take the mother-drone to scan the perimeter of the prison," Sydney requested.

"It is on the way," CC complied.

"Perfect," Sydney agreed studying the different camera views.

"What's that?" Ramsey pointed to the front-left camera.

"It's a car next to the middle of the back wall," Sydney zeroed in on the area.

"The monitors in the control room should have picked up that car," Ramsey stated. "Is the camera working in that area?"

"I'm showing it is hot," Sydney confirmed. "With these people, that doesn't necessarily prove it's working," Sydney hacked into the security system. "The camera shows it is live, but it is offline. My computer found less than a few seconds in a time-lapse glitch on the footage. That's why the guards in the control room didn't pick it up. I'm showing no one is in the car. Kathe, let's see the license plate."

"Copy that," Kathe complied flying the mosquito toward the back of the car.

"Missouri license plate #MD J247," Sydney cross-checked it with the DMV. "That tag does not exist."

"Does that surprise you?" CC quizzed. "Isn't everything concerning Patterson a mystery?"

"It's a mystery that we must solve, quickly," Ramsey assured her.

"The first clue we need to figure out is how did that car get through a solid, cement fence with razor blade wire across it?" Sam asked.

"Kathe, follow the tire tracks to the fence," Sydney insisted. "Okay, now over the fence."

"It's obvious the fence opens," Ramsey declared. "Sydney, can you see how?"

"Kathe, outline the section of the fence where the tire tracks begin," Sydney requested scanning the fence. "Now, slowly outline the two panels on either side," he waited. "Now, outline the panels on either side of those. I need to measure each panel. The panels on either side of the one where the tire tracks stop is six-inches thicker than the other panels," he pointed to the screen. "The middle section retracts inside the panel on the left," Sydney circled the motion detector at the bottom of the fence. "It opens and closes electronically, like a garage door. The beam has a separate alarm system attached, which probably goes to Patterson's cell phone when activated."

"Kathe, take the drone back to the car," Ramsey requested. "Someone, drove that car there. Let's see how many people and where the footprints lead."

"Four people got out of the car," Sydney zoomed in on the ground. "Kathe, follow the tracks."

"They're leading into the bushes by the wall!" CC exclaimed.

"Sam, get back on SR 67, and follow the drone toward the prison," Ramsey requested. "Everyone, keep your eyes peeled for a trail or an opening big enough for that car to drive through the woods."

"Yes, ma'am," Sam complied.

"Stop, you just passed it," Sydney grinned. "Back up to the bridge. There is a two-track trail going through the trees on the right."

"Good eye!" Sam said taking the trail. "I couldn't see it from ground level."

"The fence around the prison is a mile ahead of you," Sydney scanned. "Park the SUV out of sight from the trail. Use the cable on your phone to open the gate. I'll take care of the alarm. Check around the bushes to see where the footprints lead."

"Copy that," Sam answered making his way through the trees. "I'm looking for a place to park."

"Kathe, I need you to check Patterson's office," Sydney requested pulling up the blueprints. "I'm showing Patterson's office is on the first floor at the end of the north corridor. "CC, take over the mother-drone and help Sam get inside the compound."

"Copy that," Kathe released the mosquito again. "The mosquito is on the way," she reported moving the drone over the parking lot, through the razor wire covered walkway to the electronic door.

"There's only a skeleton crew around the perimeter," Ramsey noted.

“Interesting,” Sydney rechecked the blueprints. “Whoever parked the car did it in front of solitary confinement.”

“Control utilizes cameras to monitor that area,” CC stated. “Twice a day, guards bring a food tray and put it under the door of the first one.”

“With the holiday, it’s a perfect time for Patterson to move people in and out,” Ramsey suggested. “Especially with Warden Thornhill away.”

“The mosquito is inside the building,” Kathe reported flying the drone over a guard’s head down the corridor. “I’m at Patterson’s office,” Kathe stated walking the mosquito under the door. “I must have just missed her. Her work computer hasn’t time-lapsed out yet.”

“I see that,” Ramsey changed cameras. “Kathe, zero in on the computer screen on her desk.”

“Like this?” Kathe asked.

“Yes,” Ramsey read the screen. “It shows all is well with the compound. Maybe we’ll catch her in the act. Did you see the backpack where Patterson keeps the laptop?”

“No, it’s odd that none of the drawers have locks on them,” Kathe flew the mosquito to check. “Usually, women keep their purses locked in a desk drawer when they’re at work.”

“Patterson must have the laptop with her,” Ramsey noted, “especially, since Rodger enabled his GPS. Sydney which way to solitary confinement?”

“It’s on the first floor by the elevators,” Sydney relayed watching the mosquito find the elevators. “According to the blueprints, the elevator ends at the back of the outside wall. I find that hard to believe. Kathe, open the elevator.”

“Sydney is right!” Kathe gasped electronically opening the door. “It is a standard size elevator. “I’m showing plenty of space behind them to put something.”

“Like the fake wall at the funeral home in Miami behind the elevator?” CC stated. “That means Carlos Prado remodeled the prison and fence. But that would be impossible.”

“Excuse me, Sydney,” Sam interrupted. “There are four sets of footprints leaving the car. They walked to the middle of the wall and stopped by some bushes,” he parted the bushes. “The men stepped across the bushes. Their footprints end at the wall just like we found the tire tracks.”

“The ‘so-called’ deep elevator ends where you’re standing,” Sydney confirmed checking Sam’s GPS coordinates.

“CC, see if you can find out if Carlos Prado ever flew into STL?” Ramsey requested.

“I’m on it,” CC agreed pulling up the file. “Carlos owns a 727. I’m checking private flights as far back as three years,” she pushed enter. “Here we go. Two years ago, a 727 landed at STL from Brazil with a hundred and twenty people on board and building supplies. The company, registered to Espírito Mesa Ingeniero, LLC. rented a private hangar for two weeks, and then left.”

“What was the mandate?” Ramsey asked.

“The remodeling of the only funeral home in Carson City to a Madré de Díos Funeraria,” CC reported. “The story checked out with City Hall. Oddly, the mayor’s family are the only Latinos in the area.”

“That is interesting,” Ramsey assumed. “It makes a good cover for them. With that many men, it would give him enough time to split them up and do quick renovating of the prison and remodel the funeral home. Thanks.”

“Prado is bold to start again so quickly,” CC declared. “I’ll have Dad send some agents over to take a look at the building.”

“I’m interested in what they find,” Ramsey replied. “I bet the building has a hidden room and exit.”

“Kathe, leave the mosquito behind Patterson’s desk and help Sam figure out where the people went,” Sydney requested.

“Copy that,” Kathe said returning the mosquito to Patterson’s office. “It’s in place. I’m on my way to help Sam,” she reported checking Sam’s GPS coordinates.

Friday, July 3
2000 (8:00 PM CT)
United States Penitentiary, Merritt, IL

“Kathe, the footprints lead here and stop,” Sam parted the bushes to show her. “There’s even the heel of one shoe cut off. The wall moves, or we have another wraith on our hands.”

“Or the wall is made to look solid,” Kathe held JAKE toward the wall. “JAKE, scan this wall for a possible opening.”

“Kathe, an outline of an electronic door is on the screen,” JAKE relayed.

"Well, I'll be!" Sydney zeroed in on it. "Ingenious, the grout between the bricks is recessed in the shape of a door. It's undetectable with a naked eye."

"Do you want us to go inside?" Kathe asked. "JAKE can open the door."

"Not just yet," Sydney cautioned. "You two need to hurry back to the SUV. Whoever is inside will leave before the sun goes down. The guards would notice headlights moving through the woods."

"We can't do anything until we see what's going on inside the prison," Ramsey declared. "Bernadette and Mikey located and secured one of the communication centers inside the greenhouse. Once they locate the other one, they'll need to control the rings to rescue the Med team. I'll have to stall them a little longer."

"Maybe, not too much longer," CC cautioned. "We're getting some movement at the wall. Someone cracked the door open. Notice the faint light on the left side."

"Patterson checked the outside for Jenkins and Bencivenni to leave," Sydney noted zooming in on the doorway. "She's closing the door. There must be a way for Patterson to leave solitary confinement from inside the cell."

"You can't leave a cell from the inside without someone on the outside controlling the door," CC declared. "Perhaps, she has an accomplice?"

"Oh, I'm sure Patterson does," Ramsey agreed. "She couldn't pull this off alone. I see Jenkins is getting into the driver's seat. CC, stay with Jenkins and Bencivenni. Sam, keep your distance and follow them. Let's pray they separate. We can't get to Bencivenni if he stays with Jenkins."

"Copy that," CC followed them with the drone. "They are heading toward Junction 407."

"If Bencivenni makes a phone call while the drone is over the car, I should be able to hack his phone," Sydney shared, taking several pictures of the two men together. "Where is Patterson?"

"Patterson is in her office," Kathe reported watching the mosquito's camera she left. "She turned off her main computer and the lights. She's leaving for the night."

"Place another drone on Patterson's vehicle," Ramsey advised watching Patterson leave the building. "We'll catch up to her later."

"Copy that," Kathe secured a drone inside the right rearview mirror.

"The Lord is with us!" Sydney declared. "Jenkins dropped Bencivenni off at the corner of the 407 and SR 67. Strangely, Bencivenni's bodyguards aren't waiting for him. Jenkins is on his way to the hangar to leave."

"Jenkins doesn't want witnesses knowing about his jet," Ramsey assured them. "But Jenkins did give us the perfect opportunity to kidnap Bencivenni. Sam, get ready to engage the subject. Use your silencers. His people can't be too far away. CC, keep the drone high enough for us to watch both areas."

"Yes, ma'am," CC complied.

"We have Bencivenni in sight," Sam declared. "Hold on, ladies!" Sam warned speeding toward Bencivenni, slamming on the brakes, and sliding the SUV sideways.

"He's got a gun!" CC warned as Bencivenni fired at them.

"Get down!" Kathe slid across the backseat, cracking the SUV door open, and slipping out. "I'm going around the rear. I'll disarm him!"

"Use your laser!" Ramsey encouraged. "I want Bencivenni alive!"

"JAKE, laser on," Kathe spoke nicking Bencivenni's hand as he screamed, and grabbed it. "Pietro Bencivenni, stand down!"

"Bencivenni is reaching for his cell phone!" CC warned.

"No, you don't!" Sam shouted running around the front of the SUV, body-slamming Bencivenni to the ground. "You're not so tough without your bodyguards," Sam shouted pulling Bencivenni up by his coat and knocking him out with one punch.

"Way to go, Sam!" Kathe admired.

"We're getting company soon!" CC warned.

"I've got Bencivenni's cell phone," Sam shared.

"With no time to spare," Sydney cautioned. "You have two cars converging toward you from opposite directions. It's Bencivenni's men, and the other is Patterson."

"Shove Bencivenni in the back of the SVU and get out of there!" Ramsey ordered.

"Sam, Bencivenni's too heavy to carry that far," Kathe hopped into the driver's seat. "I'll bring the SUV closer."

"Pop the rear door!" Sam requested dragging Bencivenni to the SUV. "CC, help us get this fat man in the back."

"You've got about five minutes before both cars have a visual on you!" Sydney warned. "Sam, the trees on the first curve towards the hangar are thick enough to hide you. CC, raise the drone higher. I need to view the hangar as well as the two oncoming vehicles."

"Copy that," CC complied.

"Sam, pick me up by the first turn," Kathe pointed, grabbing a small bush, and covering all the tracks.

"You've got it!" Sam turned the SUV around and sped down the junction.

"I have to erase the proof of where Bencivenni fell," Kathe picked up his pistol. "Also, our footprints and tire prints."

"Kathe, get out of there!" Ramsey ordered. "That will have to do! You're out of time!"

"Copy that," Kathe threw the bush in the foliage as she ran toward them. "Sam, I'm on my way."

"I'm waiting for you around the bend!" Sam stopped on the curve. "Get inside!"

"We have another issue," Sydney attested. "Jenkins towed the jet out of the hangar and is warming up the engine. Sam, pull into the trees for cover and wait for Jenkins to leave the area."

"How far into the trees?" Sam slowly maneuvering around the trees. "This is a tight fit."

"You can stop there," Sydney approved. "The tree limbs are thick enough to block you. Jenkins is in a hurry to leave and just engaged the VTOL to take off."

"Jenkins will turn in the opposite direction," Ramsey concluded. "He won't take the chance Bencivenni's men will see him. That's why he dropped Bencivenni off at the junction before his bodyguards arrived."

"You know that man well," Sydney smiled watching Jenkins' lift above the trees and then turning the engines horizontal to takeoff. "The limo pulled over by the road sign. Two men are getting out of the limo checking for footprints. Patterson sped past them as one man tried to flag her down."

"Image that," Ramsey chuckled watching the screen. "Patterson didn't want them to see her."

"Glad you tidied up our mess, Kathe," Sydney grinned. "Four more men just got out of the limo."

"Well, look who we have getting out of the backseat," Ramsey grinned. "It's Arón Sandusky and Nikkoli Giotorra."

"Spread out and look for Mr. Bencivenni!" Nikkoli ordered. "He called me after being dropped off. His GPS signal was in this spot not more than fifteen minutes ago!"

"Then, someone picked Bencivenni up and turned off his phone!" Arón bent down to check the ground. "There should be footprints of him waiting for us. There's nothing! The car with the tinted windows that passed us came from prison! It had to be Spinello's contact. We should go after that car!"

"Did you get the license plate?" Nikkoli demanded.

"Negative," Arón admitted. "Check with the DMV on the way to town for a new, hunter-green, Nissan Altima registered in this area. There can't be that many. We'll check them out."

"That worked out well for us," Ramsey agreed. "That will give us enough time to make the switch."

"It's a good thing we turned off Bencivenni's GPS," CC grinned holding up his phone. "Nikkoli is trying desperately to call Bencivenni. Now, Arón is blowing up his phone."

"Yes, it is," Sydney pressed enter. "I cloned Bencivenni's phone and put it back to factory settings. I further gave Bencivenni's phone a bug to destroy any other device trying to restore his data, including remote storage devices. We now have sole use of Bencivenni's phone."

"The limo is out of sight," CC chuckled.

"Now that's done," Ramsey grinned. "I suddenly feel a two for one special coming on. Put Bencivenni's phone back in the holder and head back to the east wall of the penitentiary. Alonzo and Pauli have a surprise already in motion for Bencivenni."

"Copy that," Sam maneuvered through the trees back to the street.

"What do they have in mind?" CC asked turning around in the seat and placing Bencivenni's phone in the holder.

"There are certain no-no's in the Mafia World that Alonzo needs to rectify," Ramsey admitted. "According to Mr. LaBasco, the other families demand it. Otherwise, others will try the same thing."

"Hold this under Bencivenni's nose for a few breaths," Kathe requested handing a cloth to CC. "This will keep him sleeping like a baby until we want him awake. Then, Bencivenni will wake up and experience what it feels like to be double-crossed."

"Sydney, did Patterson restore the camera facing the east wall before she left?" Sam asked turning off the road onto the trail.

"She did," Sydney confirmed checking the security system. "I reinstated Patterson's loop long enough to get you inside. You'll have less than five minutes to make the switch. That is if I can hold the transmission of an alert to her phone. After that, I'll shut down the entire security system for our other guests to arrive. Control will have to perform a reboot, which will take a while, and then report the incident to Patterson. She won't think anything about a false alarm."

"Copy that," Sam approved. "We're waiting for you to turn off the system and open the gate."

"Done," Sydney pushed enter. "Five minutes and counting."

"We're on our way!" Sam sped to the door.

"JAKE, open the door if there is no life-form by it," Kathe held JAKE toward the door.

"Kathe, the door is opening," JAKE responded as Kathe and Sam swept the doorway.

"JAKE, are any life-forms to the left?" Kathe asked.

"Kathe, sensing two life-forms to the left," JAKE replied.

"The two on the left should be Joe and Rodger," Ramsey declared.

"JAKE, open the door on the left," Kathe requested.

"Kathe, it is opening," JAKE reported as a secret door opened into the cell.

"Kathe!" Joe gasped rushing to her.

"No time to talk!" Kathe insisted walking around Joe. "Rodger, go with Sam and help him bring in your replacement."

"Who's that?" Rodger asked.

"Someone you'll recognize," Sam chuckled leading the way back outside.

"I don't understand what's going on," Joe confronted Kathe. "I woke up two nights ago with Gen. Jenkins and Rodger in my room. The next thing I know, I woke up in an airplane wearing a blindfold. Then, someone took the blindfold off as a man put a ring on my finger. He said if I take it off, it will kill me."

"He is correct," Kathe stated as Sam and Rodger returned with Bencivenni.

"That's the man that put the ring on my finger!" Joe exclaimed.

"Yes, I know," Kathe confirmed. "Lay Bencivenni on the bunk. Sydney, I barely nicked Bencivenni's hand with the laser. It doesn't look like a normal wound."

"That won't matter," Sydney approved. "It looks like an old wound. Your time is almost up. Get out of there."

"Let's go!" Kathe glanced at the time. "Rodger, Joe, come with me."

"Don't leave any traces that you were there," Ramsey cautioned watching Sam lead the way out.

"Yes, ma'am," Kathe replied closing the doors behind them. "Sam, pick me up by the fence," she said, grabbing a limb off the shrubbery.

"We have 30-seconds to pull this off!" Sam warned taking off.

"Sydney, I need to erase the footprints by the building and around our SUV," Kathe declared.

"That's fine," Sydney agreed watching Kathe clear their tracks and run toward them. "The tire tracks coming in the fence won't matter. Seven-seconds to clear the fence," he watched Kathe jump in the SUV, and Sam punched the gas.

"What is that place?" Joe asked helping Kathe to get settled.

"You were in a maximum-security penitentiary," Kathe confirmed handing Rodger an earbud. "Ramsey, Rodger is on earbud now."

"Good job to you all," Ramsey appreciated. "Rodger, that was a true act of bravery. Sydney was able to receive the signal seconds before it was blocked."

"I suspected something was wrong after Jenkins and I left the cutter," Rodger explained. "Jenkins received a phone call and started acting strange. He changed the course from our original destination. He said he needed to stay on track to meet with someone tomorrow. He dropped me off at the naval base in Florida, threatening the safety of my family if I didn't do what he wanted."

"Your family was at a safe house in Tampa," Ramsey explained. "Jenkins pressured Lancaster at the Bureau for their location. Then, Jenkins falsified documents to relocate your family. We're looking for them."

"Jenkins is as evil as Metarha," Rodger admitted. "Honestly, I thought Jenkins was setting me up when he warned me about getting caught. Jenkins didn't return until the wee hours of the morning. We kidnapped Joe as we originally planned and left. Just before we landed, Jenkins said he needed me to wear a blindfold. He said that no one knew the location of one of his partners. I was hesitant to believe him, except he didn't take my phone. We changed to a car. Jenkins picked up another male a short distance away. I could tell we went off road for a short time before stopping and entering a building. I knew then that if I didn't do something, you'd never hear from us again, so I enabled my GPS. A female immediately stormed into the room, grabbed my cell phone, and smashed it. She told Jenkins that I shared my location with someone. Bencivenni went ballistic, screaming the deal was off and wanted to leave immediately! Jenkins pulled his gun to shoot me, but she warned him that she couldn't dump any more bodies in the area. She suggested that it would be better for her to release me in the morning's common area. She has some trusted inmates that would make it look like an accident. She assured Jenkins that my face would be unrecognizable, and she'd tag me as an accidental death for cremation."

"Sounds like Patterson has done that before," Kathe declared while Sydney hacked into the records file marked deceased.

"Two inmates within the last two years died at the hands of another inmate in the common area," Sydney read. "The bodies were picked up by Madré de Díos Funeraria for cremation."

"That doesn't surprise me," Ramsey stated checking the monitor. "Alonzo is putting 'Operation Vengeance" into motion. The mosquito you put on Patterson's car shows her in a secure neighborhood in Maplewood, Missouri. I'm sending Sam the address. We need the information on that laptop, ASAP."

"We're on our way," Sam answered speeding up.

"What do we do with Joe?" Kathe asked.

"Joe will have to stay with you for now," Ramsey answered. "We are pressed for time. We have no choice but to secure Joe with your family. I've already talked with Bob and Jeannie. They'll have a talk with Pete about what he overheard in Ponce Inlet."

"That is mine and Yorg's job!" Kathe disagreed.

"We can't let Jenkins or Spinello get their hands on Joe again," Ramsey insisted. "Sydney's computer just broke the code, blocking our drones in Cuba. Stephen's team is heading up the mountain to look for Eduardo's headquarters. There is a planned launch from the Cape in three days. We've got to stop them from shooting it down. It's carrying supplies for the International Space Station with two astronauts aboard."

"You forgot to mention the G-Summit is in three days, too," Kathe added. "That narrows our timeframe to find out what Jenkins has on us."

"Yes, it does," Ramsey agreed. "That's why you're there, instead of with Yorg in Cuba. Also, Sydney is pretty sure Jenkins took Rodger's family to Metarha. Hiltree's team is on the way to Santiago de Cuba to check it out. I'll let you know what they find."

"People, I located Bencivenni's file concerning the rings," Sydney interrupted. "I need to consult with Ylia before we take the ring off Joe's finger. I'll get right back to you," he switched lines. "Ylia, I emailed you a file found on Bencivenni's phone with the formula of the possible chemical inside the ring. Was the ambassador wearing a ring?"

"Yes, I barely arrived there in time to stop Dr. Pearson from taking the ring off," Dr. Ylia reported. "The ambassador's MRI showed his organs are shredding, just like Mrs. Genero. Dr. Pearson has never seen anything like these two cases. There is nothing we can do," she checked her phone. "I received your email. Give me a minute to figure out a way to extract the chemical," she cleared the line.

"Kathe, while Ylia analyzes the chemical, I'll check the workings of the ring," Sydney reconnected noticing a red flag popping up. "Interesting, another phone mirrors this app. I need to locate that phone and block the mirroring effect."

"How are you going to do that?" Kathe asked.

"By using Chameleon," Sydney chuckled. "Meanwhile, you have the honor of telling Joe the plan."

"Thanks," Kathe whined. "Joe, Sydney, and Dr. Ylia are working on how to take the ring off you safely."

"But you just confirmed that it would kill me!" Joe reminded.

"Bencivenni designed it that way," Kathe confirmed. "However, if Sydney can block the mechanism from activating, or Dr. Ylia can find the antidote, we can take it off. You'll be the first, and then they have several other people to rescue."

"So, what you are saying," Joe questioned. "I'm the guinea pig instead of them?"

"That's a loaded question," Kathe smiled. "You know how capable Sydney is with technology, and Dr. Ylia's expertise is chemical warfare. You couldn't be in better hands."

"Joe, Sydney did something similar for Rodger's wife and two young daughters," CC confirmed. "I was with them. They, too, were just as afraid as you are. They had never even heard of Sydney nor what he could do for them. I was the one that assured them they would be all right. They were relieved the second we took them off."

"Do I have a choice?" Joe asked.

"No," Kathe stated. "Sydney thinks that Bencivenni isn't the only one that can control the rings. We have no choice but to get the ring off your finger."

"Sydney, the ambassador passed away while we were talking," Dr. Ylia reported. "I took the ring, and the computer analyzed the chemical as an altered form of cyanide."

"Good," Sydney continued. "According to the file, the ring has two functions. It either kills instantly or slowly releases into the system, shredding each organ one by one."

"Which is an excruciating death," Ylia commented. "I emailed you the antidote equations."

"I'm receiving them now," Sydney confirmed opening it. "I figured out how to block the activation of the ring. Thanks," switching lines. "Kathe, you may now take the ring off Joe's finger," pressing enter.

"Great," Kathe answered making the Sign of the Cross. "Sydney is ready."

"Wait a minute!" Joe insisted looking into Kathe's eyes. "Whether I live or die, at least it will be at the hands of the only woman I ever loved and the mother of my son," he confessed making the Sign of the Cross.

"I'm so sorry I got you into this mess," Kathe confided. "I'm glad Brock used a cold laser on the bruises and cuts on your face. It's healing nicely."

"I'm going to throw up!" Ramsey scoffed. "Get on with it, Tierney!"

"On the count of three . . . one . . . two . . . three," Kathe quickly pulled the ring off Joe's finger. "Sydney, you did it!"

"How do you know for sure?" Joe cringed.

"It would have killed you instantly, or you'd be screaming out in pain as your organs shredded," Kathe winked at Joe.

"I have a confession," Joe grinned. "As soon as I fell into your eyes, I wasn't afraid."

"I just threw up in my mouth!" Ramsey threw her hands up. "Why does Sherrod keep showing up in our lives?"

"Calm down," Sydney glanced at Ramsey. "That's one major hurdle we toppled. I gave Bernadette and Mikey the approval to interrogate the replacement for the leader of Latvia. It turned out that he is the obnoxious reporter that got his credentials revoked from the White House."

"Do you mean Byron Dunlap?" Ramsey asked.

"The one, and only Mr. Smart-Mouth," Sydney confirmed. "He sold his soul for ten million dollars and the promise to control Latvia."

"That greedy little worm!" Ramsey snapped. "I had Dunlap tagged right all along. It is for this reason that some of these people cannot be released back into society. He isn't a reporter. He is a lobbyist for Jansen and Mills, located in the Middle East."

"I read that," Kathe admitted.

"I need to contact Bernadette's team," Ramsey reached for her phone. "People, it is time to secure the Med team, and then remove the rings. Dominic, your people are to follow Alonzo's orders."

"Consider it done," Dominic replied. "It has to be this way."

"That's it!" Kathe exclaimed. "The simultaneous death of world leaders at the G-Summit would cause that kind of chaos. That is what Jenkins was planning to use to frame us!"

"But we're nowhere near the G-Summit," CC disagreed. "That place is crawling with security worldwide, weeks in advance preparing routes to and from the event."

"We don't have to be there," Sydney admitted. "Patterson has a good IT Man. I barely discovered where he linked the footage Patterson uses to play for the control room. If the G-Summit is in three days, the pictures or videos he faked of us being in Tokyo are a done deal."

"Then, Patterson and Jenkins know all about it and probably have copies," CC gathered.

"Patterson, maybe, but I'm not too sure about Jenkins," Ramsey surmised. "We'll soon find out."

Friday, July 3
2130 (9:30 PM CT)
Maplewood, MO

"Sydney, we're at Patterson's house in the town of Maplewood on the outskirts of St. Louis," Kathe reported as Sam stopped down the street.

"Activate the mosquito and let CC man the mother-drone," Sydney requested. "Ramsey will monitor your team while I help Bernadette and Mikey. I'll break back in to help with Alonzo's list when you're ready."

"Copy that," Kathe answered handing the iPad to CC.

"Good," Ramsey confirmed checking Jenkins' location. "I see Jenkins picked up the Glide Slope at the deserted base in New York."

"Jenkins is not meeting with Congress in the morning like he said," CC stated.

"Another lie!" Ramsey bellowed. "Jenkins would land at Andrews Air Force Base for that. I have a feeling he's meeting someone, possibly Spinello. I'm not sold on the idea that Nikkoli told anybody about

Bencivenni's disappearance. Since Sydney blocked the mirroring effect, there are no signs of a panic mode yet."

"Has Sydney traced the mirroring effect to anyone?" CC asked.

"Not yet," Ramsey shared. "I believe we'll find that Eduardo is the culprit without Bencivenni knowing it. Alonzo said that for self-preservation, Bencivenni would never give anybody access to control his rings."

"And one thing we've noticed about Eduardo is that he is good at skirting the issues," CC agreed.

"CC, give me a look at the neighborhood where Patterson lives," Ramsey requested.

"It's a two-story townhouse with an attached garage," CC showed. "The address is 492 Building B, Overland Blvd. There's a light on downstairs, as well as the upstairs."

"Kathe, find a way to get the mosquito inside the condo," Ramsey requested.

"It's already inside," Kathe stated. "The mosquito found a slight opening near the top of the front door. I'm checking the first floor," she flew it around. "Nothing is unusual in the living room. Let's scope out the kitchen."

"CC, keep an eye on the outside," Ramsey requested watching the mosquito's camera.

"Yes, ma'am," CC complied.

"Kathe, are there any imminent signs of any warnings from her work?" Ramsey asked.

"Negative," Kathe showed the kitchen.

"I see Patterson stopped for Chinese take-out," Ramsey noted. "Try the upstairs."

"Copy that," Kathe maneuvered the mosquito upstairs into the master bedroom. "Patterson is in her office working on the laptop."

"I see that she has the thumb drive in her laptop," Ramsey smiled. "Kathe, insert the needle of the mosquito into the drive next to it. It's so dark in there, she shouldn't be able to see it."

"You're right," Kathe complied.

"Perfect," Ramsey grinned. "I'm copying the data on the thumb drive right under Patterson's nose while she's using it. There's the separate set of books," Ramsey read. "Patterson's adding what happened tonight when Jenkins and Bencivenni were at the penitentiary," she read further. "That's not quite how Joe and Rodger described the events. Patterson is setting

Jenkins up, as we thought. She's making it sound like Jenkins forced her into helping him. Patterson's saving it and emailing it to someone. I can't make out the email address."

"That's because it's encrypted," Kathe noted. "Sydney doesn't have time to break it now."

"Ramsey, I can do it," Rodger offered.

"That would help us timewise," Ramsey answered.

"I'll need to use a phone," Rodger said. "Patterson smashed mine."

"Sure," Ramsey agreed. "Sam, give Rodger one of your extra phones."

"Copy that," Sam agreed reaching into his backpack and handing Rodger an iPhone.

"I keep a backup of my data on me," Rodger admitted opening his wallet to a secret compartment. "Give me a few minutes for my data to upload to this phone."

"You got it," Ramsey agreed watching the monitor. "Patterson is heading back downstairs. Kathe, follow her."

"I can't believe you're spying on this woman from inside a car," Joe mentioned watching over Kathe's shoulder.

"Just for the record," Kathe defended, "this woman was going to kill Rodger in the morning, and then you. You don't think Patterson would let you live to talk about her follies, do you?"

"Point well taken," Joe sighed.

"Patterson's pouring a glass of wine," Ramsey noted. "She's heading back upstairs," Ramsey read a text. "Alonzo said his men are almost in place. He wants us to turn on the camera that Kathe left in the cell. Sydney, Alonzo needs you to live stream it to several of the families but block the ones on the list Alonzo sent you. After that, you're ready to shut down the security system. By the time the system finishes powering down and rebooting, it gives them roughly fifteen minutes. That will give Operation Vengeance enough time to get in and out."

"Alonzo, I blocked the names on the list," Sydney pressed enter. "Let me know when your people are ready."

"I will," Alonzo replied. "I've got my men in place with the families on the list. Mr. LaBasco will tell them what happened when it's time."

"Alonzo, you never said where you got the list?" Ramsey questioned.

"Dano did more than talk to Bernadette," Alonzo laughed. "I told you that Bernadette would make him sing like a bird."

"Did she find anything else?" Ramsey asked.

"She and Mikey have more digging to do," Alonzo chuckled. "Pauli and I need to finalize a few more details for Mr. LaBasco," he hung up.

"Kathe, we need Patterson away from her phone," Ramsey requested. "Start thinking of ways to do it."

"Copy that," Kathe answered splitting the screen to watch both places. "Patterson is getting ready for bed," Kathe moved the drone while she changed.

"Patterson slipped into bed with her wine and a book," Ramsey noted. "She's finally off duty now, thinking she has everything nicely secured."

"Patterson works very hard keeping her dirty little secrets," Kathe stated.

"Kathe, we need a diversion now," Ramsey ordered.

"Patterson did fill her wine glass to the top," Kathe chuckled buzzing the mosquito around Patterson's ear as she reached for the glass.

"That didn't work," Ramsey mentioned.

"Watch this," Kathe laughed landing the mosquito on her forearm, biting her.

"Ouch!" Patterson instinctively swatted at the mosquito, spilling her wine down the front of her gown. "I can't believe this!" she jumped out of bed. "Me, my book, and my new bedspread are covered in red wine!" Patterson screamed hurrying to the bathroom. "My bedspread is ruined!"

"Good reflexes, Kathe," Ramsey grinned.

"Don't look, guys," Kathe smiled flying the mosquito under the door, showing Patterson striping and getting into the shower. "Ramsey, is this what you had in mind?"

"Perfectly," Ramsey grinned. "Have JAKE open the doors at the prison again. I'm shutting off the cameras by her secret entrance and the fence."

"They are open," Kathe said bringing the drone back to the bedroom. "You were right; Patterson can't hear the alarm sounding on her phone."

"What a shame," Ramsey grinned watching five people enter through the door and then into the cell at the prison. "It worked. They are inside. Let's watch this while Patterson's in the shower."

Friday, July 3
2300 (11:00 PM CT)
Merritt Penitentiary, MO

"He's sleeping like a baby," Francesco chuckled standing over Pietro Bencivenni. "Johnny, get this piece of trash ready for confession and penance."

"Yeah, Boss," Johnny answered signaling the other two men. "Tony, bind his hands and ankles with a cloth so it won't leave marks. His death needs to look like a suicide."

"We used to look up to Mr. Bencivenni," Manning sighed tying Bencivenni's hand. "Now, we're glad to be part of his demise."

"The entire family agrees with you after what Bencivenni did," Johnny confirmed. "Let's sit Bencivenni on the floor and lean him against the bed before Mr. Falcini and Miranda enter."

"Bencivenni always was a fat, old man," Tony groaned sitting him down with a thud.

"He's really out of it," Francesco chuckled reaching in his pocket. "This should bring Bencivenni around," Francesco said waving smelling salts under Bencivenni's nose. "He's moving around," Francesco placed a phone call.

"Where am I?" Bencivenni blinked his eyes a couple of times, trying to focus. "Who are you?"

"You know exactly who we are and why we're here," Francesco laughed. "You didn't think we'd forget about you?"

"Pietro Bencivenni!" Antonio Falcini Sr. chuckled entering the room. "Don't tell me you forgot Francesco and the boys already. I hope you don't mind that I brought your longtime lover, Miranda Sejourna with us," he introduced as she entered the cell.

"Antonio!" Bencivenni gasped. "Miranda!"

"In the flesh, and no thanks to you," Antonio stated. "Pietro, my number one, the most trusted man that turned betrayer to the family. Any last confessions you'd like for me to run past Father Leonardo? I promised Father that I'd give you time for your last confession. He even gave me Holy Water to anoint you," he laughed pulling it out of his pocket.

"The only confession I have is that I didn't succeed in killing you!" Bencivenni spit at Antonio.

"Why?" Antonio questioned. "You were nothing more than a thug and con artist, like your parents. I should have left you with them in their gypsy-like carnival. Your masks of famous people gave me the idea of smuggling people in and out of places. That's why I hired you. The ring idea that you perfected was Nikkoli's. Your cunningness is what raised you quickly through the ranks to be my Number One. Without me, you were nothing!"

"Yes, you helped me, but it was both of us that made it successful!" Bencivenni agreed. "It was Adalina that hired me with her money, not yours! For years, I watched Tony and Giano grow up just like you!" Bencivenni spit at him again. "Tony had a mistress and embezzled money to keep his wife from finding out. Giano spent money like water, buying fancy cars, trips, and loose women! Like you, Giano abused every woman he met!"

"What do you think you did to me?" Miranda demanded.

"I had to choose between you and Eduardo's plan," Bencivenni admitted. "It was the only way to slip Macaby out of the country."

"Really?" Miranda snapped. "After twenty years of my loyalty in helping you take care of patients that you mutilated! Do you have any idea of what they went through physically; not to mention mentally? I'm the one that had to tend to them and help them emotionally deal with the changes in their lives! You chose money over me! I was supposed to meet you in Cuba by airplane, not in your coffin scheme! I told you that I couldn't do that because I'm claustrophobic! The last thing Ricci said to me was that you asked a special favor of him! He wouldn't tell me what it was. Luckily, Dr. Sydney woke me up in the coffin and told me it didn't have enough oxygen to get me to Cuba alive! You planned to kill me all along!"

"I didn't need you anymore!" Bencivenni admitted. "You could have turned on me any moment!"

"Well, now look who abuses women?" Antonio chuckled.

"You killed Adalina because you got your mistress pregnant while Adalina was pregnant with Ricco!" Bencivenni shouted. "Now, who's the con artist? I called Spinello and told him what you were doing! That's why Spinello rushed to Adalina's side. She made Spinello promise not to kill you. She said the boys needed at least one parent alive. The final straw was you buying that last flying car company that nearly bankrupted us! It was Spinello that bailed us out!"

"Alonzo showed me proof that you took my boys to Spinello to have him kill them!" Antonio confided. "Alonzo told me that you planned to bring their bodies aboard the yacht after you left Mineyo and me tousling about in the ocean."

"Killing the boys that way was payback for what you did to Adalina!" Bencivenni shouted. "Spinello was so angry after Adalina died that he left the country, and for what? Spinello should have raised the boys, not you!"

"I never knew you felt this way," Antonio sighed. "We did everything together."

"I tried to tell you, but you wouldn't listen!" Bencivenni argued. "You insisted that boys would be boys and to let you worry about them! You told me to focus on our plan!"

"You focused on our plan, all right!" Antonio snapped walking closer to him pointing his finger. "Alonzo told me that you were busy going behind my back for years, setting up deals with Spinello and Eduardo Santo Prado. You lied to me, saying that Prado didn't want to join us! Alonzo showed me proof that you implemented the rings into Prado's plan. I then realized why some of the family leaders suddenly began changing their deals with us. Since I'm the one that paid for the technology of the rings, I thought it would only be fitting for you to die by your invention," he signaled Francesco. "By your design," Francesco handed him the ring, "the rings inject cyanide into your doubles if they don't do what you say. However, your matching ring contains a cyanide pill in case of an emergency."

"I told Antonio your little secret," Miranda laughed. "Don't take it personal. I don't need you anymore."

Francesco opened the top of the ring, taking out a small white pill, and held it up. "Francesco, open his mouth," Antonio ordered.

Francesco motioned for Johnny to help him as he put on rubber gloves. Johnny grabbed Bencivenni from behind as Bencivenni held his jaw shut.

"Open it!" Francesco demanded as Bencivenni clenched his jaw tighter. "Open!" Francesco shouted in his ear. Then, he ripped Bencivenni's neck straight back, pulling his chin down.

"No!" Bencivenni screamed trying to move his head away.

"This will keep it open," Francesco chuckled inserting a dental spreader into his mouth as Tony and Manning assisted. "Let me make it a little wider," he turned the screw.

"Don't cause bleeding," Miranda warned.

"Of course not," Francesco chuckled. "I went to dental school for a while. It won't leave a mark."

"Pietro, I suddenly see the fear in your eyes," Antonio held a picture of Miranda close to his face. "It's the same fear in Miranda's eyes captured in this picture when you put a mask of Macaby on her in Miami to switch them," he dropped the picture. "I don't think I missed anything. However, I do have a confession of my own," he hovered the pill over Bencivenni's mouth. "We are live streaming this to the families that don't have the rings. The family leaders that you replaced will witness a different ending. Mr. LaBasco explained why their leaders changed policies overnight without consulting them. I believe they are dropping dead as we speak. If it weren't for Mr. LaBasco, Alonzo, and Pauli finding out the rest of the families would have the same fate!" he held up several pictures of leaders at Lugino Village. "Recognize these people you created? Don't worry, they are all dead, and the village is burning just like you will be in a minute!" he promised dropping the pill into his mouth and pouring water down his throat.

Bencivenni's eyes widened as he choked a few times before slumping over.

"Johnny, get rid of the evidence and put him back on the bed," Francesco ordered unscrewing the spreader. "Wipe the ring clean and leave the top open on his finger."

"I hope this brings justice to you," Antonio took Miranda by the arm and followed Francesco out to the car. "I'll keep you in the family."

"Alonzo, have you heard from the other families?" Ramsey asked.

"Of course," Alonzo chuckled. "Mine and Pauli's phones are blowing up with calls and text."

"Dominic dropped Bernadette and Mikey off at their jet with the Med team," Sydney confirmed. "They will take them to CC's father for debriefing. Then, they will join you in Cuba."

"Good," Alonzo agreed. "I need to take some of these calls if you will excuse me."

"Sydney, I have more good news!" Rodger interrupted. "I found Patterson's IT man. I'm sending you the link."

"Good work," Sydney answered opening it. "The name on the email address is Connor Johansson."

"I know him!" Ramsey exclaimed pointing to the man. "He's the one that Jenkins gave my funding to for the JAKE Project!"

"Interesting," Sydney read further. "It doesn't say who vetted Johansson to work in the Pentagon. The entire file is very sketchy."

"I can't believe the FBI missed the second spy!" Ramsey snapped.

"Have we missed any more?" Sydney questioned. "His first assignment was to work with Gen. Jenkins' group."

"Maybe Gen. Thompson of the Joint Chiefs vetted Johansson," Ramsey discussed. "Thompson and Senator Bernard Frank colluded with the Russian Gen. Yetsun to get Chameleon. Thompson knew I was working on JAKE Technology and knew it had the potential to enhance Chameleon. Jenkins couldn't grasp the concept of JAKE, so they sent Johansson to help him. Hiltree, have Homeland pick Johansson up ASAP and confiscate his equipment before he warns Patterson. Sydney, do you have the address yet?"

"Give me a minute," Sydney said trying different programs. "It seems to be blocked. Let me try this," he pushed enter. "The address is 42 North State Street, Washington DC," Sydney pulled it up on a satellite. "It's in the George Washington Condominium Complex."

"Copy that," Hiltree agreed reaching for his phone. "It will take me a while to get a warrant."

"Not if you send it to my father," CC proclaimed. "Dad can have someone pick Johansson up immediately. The Bureau suspected someone in that area of leaking classified information but can't pinpoint the location."

"Johansson is also good at covering his tracks," Ramsey stated. "I think it will be poetic justice if Gen. Jenkins signed the warrant," she said pushing enter. "Call your dad. I emailed you the address and warrant."

"I'm on it!" CC smiled hiding Ramsey's email address, sending it to her father. "I'll call Dad to make sure he reads it."

"Copy that," Ramsey smiled. "As soon as they pick up Johansson, I'll make an anonymous phone call."

"Heads-up," Kathe cautioned. "Patterson is finally coming out of the bathroom?"

"How nice," Ramsey smiled watching the camera. "What? She's not going to wash her new bedspread!" Ramsey chuckled as Patterson took her pillow, turned off the light, and left the room. "Patterson's so tired; she forgot her phone. Keep an eye on her. I'll have Skip and Mack edit the video before I send it to Warden Thornhill. Sydney and I have a call coming in from Yorg."

Chapter 7

Sunday, July 5th
0025 (12:25 AM EST)
Sierra Maestra, Cuba

"Yorg, what have you found?" Sydney asked switching cameras to Stephen's drone.

"Thankfully, it's a bright enough moon allowing us to break camp early," Yorg reported. "The drone made it to the top of the mountain. There is a sizable amount of activity in that area."

"With that concentration of soldiers, it looks like you found their stronghold," Sydney assumed checking the various cameras.

"That is what we think," Yorg agreed. "When we took the little girls' home, we noted several helicopters landing and taking off from this area. As soon as you broke through the barrier, we launched the drone immediately and knew we were in the right spot."

"Yes, you are!" Ramsey agreed zooming in. "It's a large, round, grassy knoll surrounded by trees. Those aren't field flowers around the perimeter! Exotic flowers are another sign of Eduardo's presence. Not only does he have an eye for beauty, but he also surrounds himself with it as a calling card."

"It's a perfect place for a retractable dome," Sydney ascertained. "I'm scanning the area. The computer has outlined a retractable dome and a long, underground tunnel woven in-and-out throughout the top. The grass hides the dome's track."

"Jay, leave the mosquito on the tallest tree facing the center of the grassy knoll," Ramsey requested.

"Copy that," Jay answered landing the tiny drone. "How's the view?"

"That gives us a good panoramic view," Ramsey confirmed. "The drone will alert us when the next helicopter approaches."

"While you make your way there, have the drone look for an outside entrance to the tunnel," Sydney suggested. "With the size of the tunnel, there should be more than one entrance."

"The mountain's terrain is thick and filled with dangerous snakes and varmints," Yorg reminded. "It will take us time to walk through it, that is if Márquez leaves us alone. His constant surprise visits slow us down."

"Márquez knows what's up there," Ramsey assured. "It's obvious, the further you climb, the more nervous he will get. That's why he continues to check up on you."

"Stephen asked Skip and Mack to help us keep an eye out for Márquez on our journey," Yorg shared. "Speaking of time, how are we doing Timewise with the other teams?"

"You're on track," Ramsey updated. "Bernadette's team located in the Alps where Bencivenni harbored the new replacements. Dominic destroyed it and made sure that no one got away. Kathe's team apprehended Bencivenni and rescued Joe and Rodger. Let's say, Warden Thornhill will soon get a surprise inmate."

"Bencivenni?" Yorg grinned.

"What's left of Bencivenni after Falcini and Miranda finished with him," Ramsey coughed. "Let us know when the drone finds outside entrances. Alonzo is on the other line," she switched lines.

Sunday, July 5th
0100 (1:00 AM EST)
Santiago de Cuba, Cuba

"Ramsey, Sydney, we have a visual on Rodger's family," Alonzo stated watching the mother-drone's cameras with his iPad. "When Jenkins left Rodger alone at the base, he picked up Rodger's family and brought them straight to Metarha."

"That's what I feared," Ramsey confessed. "Is there anyway Jenkins landed at Guantanamo with them?"

"Negative," Hiltree answered working the mother-drone. "According to the tower's records, Jenkins was with me the last time he landed at Guantanamo."

"That would mean Jenkins lands directly at Santiago de Cuba," Ramsey assumed. "Even with VTOL capabilities, the terrain in that area is too rugged for Jenkins to land anywhere else."

"It also wouldn't work timewise for Jenkins to get back to Rodger and abduct Joe Sherrod," Pauli confirmed.

"I agree," Hiltree admitted.

"I'm bringing up all of your mother-drone's cameras to see the rest of your opposition inside the camp," Sydney relayed as Ramsey sat back in her chair. "Alonzo, release the mosquito and take it inside Metarha's barracks for a closer view of the children."

"I can't believe Jenkins would stoop so low as to put the Slate's back in harm's way with Metarha!" Ramsey snapped watching the mosquito's camera enter the room.

"Greed does a lot to a man," Alonzo admitted zeroing in on the children. "Metarha tied the children's hands to the rails of the bed across from her. She is sound asleep."

"We've seen that before on Anguilla Island," Ramsey admitted. "I don't see Rodger's wife, Jane?"

"They separated the children from their mother," Alonzo reported. "The mother-drone located Jane from the window inside another barrack with Brutus. Jane's sitting on the floor against a wall tied to a meat hook above her head. Brutus has beaten and assaulted her."

"The children are safe and sleeping for now," Sydney suggested evaluating the situation. "First, we need to focus on rescuing Jane. Let me see her."

"Copy that," Alonzo took the mosquito over to the next barrack.

"Oh, my God!" Ramsey gasped starring at Jane. "Where's Brutus, now?"

"Brutus is either passed out or asleep across the room," Alonzo turned the mosquito showing him.

"Hover the mosquito over Jane a minute," Sydney requested scanning her body. "Jane presents with two black eyes and a large cut on her left cheek. She has multiple contusions from head to toe with a dislocated right shoulder."

"Brutus is not to leave that room alive!" Ramsey ordered.

"Don't worry," Alonzo declared. "He won't!"

"The moon is bright enough to light the inside, so night-vision goggles won't be necessary," Sydney explained. "Jane doesn't know you. The less evasive you appear when you enter, the better for Jane right now. She's in shock."

"That's the same look on Jane's face that I saw in the bedroom in Seattle when CC and Terrance rescued them," Ramsey admitted. "I prayed I'd never see that look on her face again. The only difference is that this time, the Head of Homeland Security put them in that situation instead of a terrorist group."

"Don't worry," Alonzo promised. "Brutus will never do this again to anybody."

"The best way for them to get inside the camp is from behind the barracks," Hiltree suggested.

“Hiltree, take over the mosquito for Alonzo, and have Ryan work the mother-drone,” Sydney requested.

“Copy that,” Ryan reached for the iPad.

“Let’s go,” Alonzo walked toward the back of the barracks.

“Alonzo,” Pauli whispered pulling Alonzo behind a tree as a guard crossed them.

“That was close,” Alonzo whispered watching the soldier walk away.

“Hiltree, hover the mosquito over Brutus,” Sydney requested scanning his body. “Brutus is jacked-up on PCP again. Note the white powder under his nose. PCP causes restlessness and jerking in sleep patterns. His rapid eye movement shows he’s hallucinating. We’ve already witnessed several bullets not stopping him in that condition.”

“It’s too dangerous to even go inside without first using the drone to take him out,” Ramsey agreed. “Alonzo, it would be best if you go inside alone. If you startle Jane, she might scream, alerting the guards. Pauli should wait outside; in case something goes wrong.”

“Understood,” Pauli agreed following Alonzo.

“Ryan, raise the mother-drone a little higher for a better Aerial view,” Sydney requested.

“Copy that,” Ryan complied.

“Hold it right there,” Sydney advised checking the cameras. “Two guards have their back away from you talking and smoking. Proceed behind the first barrack.”

“Copy that,” Alonzo whispered sneaking past them.

“Hold there!” Sydney cautioned. “A soldier is on his way to the latrine. Give him a minute to get inside,” he watched the man enter. “You may continue behind the next barrack.”

“Hiltree, use cyanide to take out Brutus before they enter,” Ramsey ordered. “After that, Alonzo, be careful when you enter not to startle Jane. One scream is all it takes to bring the soldiers.”

“Understood,” Alonzo whispered watching Hiltree land the mosquito on the side of Brutus’s neck, injecting him.

“His head slumped into the pillow,” Ramsey noted. “He’s dead. Alonzo, enter now.” Ramsey held her breath watching Pauli slowly open the door for Alonzo to enter the building. “Show her you’re not a threat.”

“Sh,” Alonzo whispered holding his finger to his mouth.

“Oh!” Jane raised her head, widening her eyes.

“Alonzo, Jane’s panicking,” Ramsey warned. “Slowly put your hands up and assure her you won’t hurt her.”

“I’m a friend of your husband, Rodger,” Alonzo whispered slowly approached Jane keeping his hands up. “I’m here to rescue you,” he pointed at Brutus making the slitting motion to his throat. “He’s dead. There are guards outside. I’m going to cut you free.”

Okay, Jane nodded as Alonzo reached for his knife.

“Pauli, Brutus is slightly moving his neck around!” Sydney warned. “We didn’t use enough cyanide for the amount of PCP in his system!”

“Copy that,” Pauli agreed hurrying into the room as he reached into his boot for his knife.

“Who’s that?” Jane asked peering around Alonzo, watching Pauli approach Brutus with a knife.

“He’s a friend,” Alonzo whispered cutting Jane free.

“Ow!” Jane gasped grabbing her right shoulder.

“Alonzo, help Jane lower her shoulder,” Sydney ordered watching Alonzo skillfully maneuver Jane’s shoulder down to her side. He took his shirt off and covered her.

“Ow!” Jane grabbed her mouth and held her breath.

“Brutus isn’t dead!” Ramsey warned. “Pauli, Brutus opened his eyes! Slit his throat!”

“Brutus can’t move his limbs!” Sydney exclaimed. “The combination of cyanide and PCP only paralyzed him! Do it now!”

“That’s right; look at me,” Pauli raised his knife to Brutus’s throat as Brutus’s eyes widened, trying to move his body. “Look into my eyes and see all the innocent victims you murdered! Do you see the innocent 10-year-old boy and his grandfather? Do you see Officer Renee Parker?” he asked as Brutus tried to speak. “Give my regards to Mario LaBasco Jr. for causing all of this!” Pauli exclaimed slitting his throat.

“He’s dead this time,” Ramsey declared checking the cameras outside. “A guard is walking alongside the sidewall of that barracks. It’s so thin. I don’t know how he didn’t hear you?”

“They are probably used to hearing screaming coming out of Brutus’s barracks,” Sydney assumed. “Knowing that Brutus stays there, the guard didn’t want to get involved.”

“You’re probably right,” Ramsey agreed. “Let’s get you out of there.”

“Jane, you need to put the shirt on before we leave,” Alonzo suggested.

“I can’t move my arm,” Jane cringed with pain.

“If we put your right arm through the sleeve first,” Alonzo coaxed. “It won’t hurt as bad. The left sleeve will be easier. We need to rescue your children. They shouldn’t see you like this.”

“Pauli, throw Jane’s torn clothes over Brutus’s body,” Ramsey requested. “We want to send a message to Eduardo.”

“Understood,” Pauli threw her clothes across his body. “Is it okay for us to leave?”

“Pauli, a soldier is leaving the latrine,” Ryan cautioned as Alonzo moved Jane behind him, raising his gun.

“Keep an eye on the soldier,” Ramsey ordered watching the cameras. “We’re not finished.”

“He’s walking straight to his barracks,” Ryan declared. “He’s inside; go now.”

“Finally,” Pauli whispered walking to the door. “Vengeance is served for all the people Brutus beat to death!”

“I’ve got a special plan for Metarha as well,” Ramsey smiled watching them join Hiltree’s men outside in the woods.

“Jane, I’m Alonzo DiMeglio,” he introduced. “We work with Dr. Sydney. We’re going to rescue your children now. Then, we’ll take your family out of there safely.”

“Thank you for saving me from that animal,” Jane hugged Alonzo.

“Ryan, are we clear to get the girls?” Hiltree asked.

“Yes, Sir,” Ryan advised. “A guard just passed behind Metarha’s barracks. You have a clear shot.”

“Alonzo, it would be better for the girls to see their mother with you when you enter,” Ramsey cautioned.

“Understood,” Alonzo whispered to Jane.

“Jane, you need to come with us,” Alonzo explained leading the way.

“Hiltree, on your iPad, is a capital D for Diazepam to use this time,” Sydney stated. “It will knock Metarha out while we take the girls.”

“We do not!” Ramsey ordered. “I repeat! We do not want to kill Metarha. We want to send another message to Eduardo.”

“Understood,” Hiltree complied.

“Alonzo, you’re free to go inside,” Sydney declared watching Metarha’s head sink deeper into the pillow. “Hiltree, have your men guard the perimeter.”

“Jane, Metarha can’t hurt you,” Alonzo assured her. “It will be better if the children see you with us.”

"Are you sure Metarha is out?" Jane questioned wiping her tears. "Brutus wasn't dead."

"That's because Brutus was jacked-up on PCP," Alonzo led the way.

"Oh, my God!" Jane cried rushing to the girls. "Molly, Madeline!"

"Alonzo, Pauli, take the ropes off the girls, and tie Metarha spread eagle to the bed with them," Ramsey grinned. "And find something to gag her, so she can't scream for help in the morning. We want someone to find that witch helpless."

"Copy that," Pauli grinned watching Jane's reunion with her daughters.

"What are we going to do with Jane and the girls?" Hiltree asked. "If I take them on base, Jenkins could find out."

"You're right," Ramsey accessed. "Bring them to the cutter."

"They'll be safer there with you," Hiltree agreed. "As soon as they find Metarha and Brutus, Eduardo will know we're here."

"Eduardo already knows," Ramsey proclaimed. "They've already stepped-up security on top of Sierra Maestra. Eduardo and Spinello still can't reach Bencivenni. With them finding Brutus and Metarha, they'll begin to panic and get sloppy."

"You bet!" Hiltree grinned. "Ryan, get us out of here."

Sunday, July 5th
0215 (2:15 AM CT)
Maplewood, MO

"Rodger, before I reconnect Kathe's team, I wanted to assure you that Hiltree's team rescued your family," Ramsey explained as he walked toward the gas station.

"Thank God!" Rodger sighed stepping around the side of the building. "What happened? Are they alright?"

"Jenkins illegally removed them from the safe house CC's father placed them with a forged document," Ramsey informed him.

"Where did Jenkins take them?" Rodger demanded.

"Straight to Metarha in Cuba," Ramsey answered.

"No!" Rodger hit the brick wall with his fist. "I need to go to them!"

"I spoke with Jane concerning having you join them on the cutter with Sydney and me," Ramsey stated. "Jane was adamant about you staying to fight with us. She witnessed that Jenkins would stop at nothing until he gets what he wants, no matter whom he destroys. As soon as they arrive, Sydney will arrange a secure video call with you. You can make your decision then."

"What did Metarha do to them?" Rodger begged leaning his forehead against the wall.

"Jane made me promise to let her tell you," Ramsey confided. "They'll arrive within the hour. We'll talk then. I need to connect with the team now."

"That's my Jane," Rodger admitted. "After learning about my past, she always wanted me to save the world."

"She said those same words to me," Ramsey comforted signaling Sydney to connect to the team. "Kathe, what is the status of Patterson?"

"She's sleeping like a baby," Kathe reported.

"Perfect timing for me to make a phone call," Ramsey grinned. "I'll get back with you. Sydney, it's time to distort my voice and scramble the call."

"I'm ready," Sydney stated placing the call.

"Merritt Penitentiary Security, this is Officer Tom Yancy speaking," he introduced. "This call is being recorded. How may I direct your call?"

"I thought you should know that you have a dead body in cell number one in solitary confinement," Ramsey stated watching the drone inside the security office.

"Who is this?" Yancy demanded.

"Who I am, is not important," Ramsey chuckled. "Who put the body in the cell is important. It would help if you warned Warden Thornhill that he didn't purge his staff as good as he thought," she hung up.

"Diane, bring up the camera in cell one in solitary confinement!" Yancy ordered. "An anonymous person called and said there is a dead body inside."

"Sydney, work your magic," Ramsey grinned watching inside the security office.

"Done," Sydney pushed enter shutting their system down.

"The camera in cell one is not pulling up," Diane stated trying again. "This can't be! The entire system seems to be shutting down a second time! I'll have to wait for it to finish and then reboot! It will take another fifteen minutes, minimum!"

"We don't have that kind of time!" Yancy exclaimed. "Sound lockdown! Marvin, come with me!" he ordered hurrying out of the room.

"This has to be a prank," Officer Marvin Blais stated as they rounded the corner. "No one has been in that cell in several months."

"Open the door!" Yancy instructed reaching for the light switch.

Marvin reached for his keys and opened the door, "Oh, my God! The caller was right!" He exclaimed rushing inside. "Who is he? He's not one of our inmates!'

"The bigger question is how did he get inside here?" Yancy demanded. "Don't touch him! Is the warden back in town yet?"

"Patterson said Thornhill wouldn't be back until late tomorrow night," Marvin replied. "She left for the evening while you were on break."

"I'll call Patterson," Yancy said reaching for his phone. "Check with Diane to see how the lockdown is going?"

"Okay," Marvin agreed stepping into the hallway.

"Patterson isn't answering her phone!" Yancy exclaimed when Marvin returned. "I'll try again!" he snapped staring at the body. "She's still not answering!"

"You have no choice but to call Warden Thornhill," Marvin instructed. "Make the call!"

"You're right," Yancy placed the call. "Warden Thornhill, I'm sorry to bother you while you're out of town, but . . ."

Sunday, July 5th
0700 (7:00 AM CT)
Maplewood, MO

"Sydney, we just got back from the gas station," Kathe reported as JAKE's alarm sounded. "Sleeping Beauty is finally awake."

"The alarm on the drone alerted me, also," Sydney stated as Ramsey handed him coffee and something to eat. "Patterson's been moving around for a while. I saw where you were and gave you some time. She's rolling out of bed. Stay with her; things will heat up very fast."

"Copy that," Kathe answered maneuvering the mosquito. "She's on her way to the bathroom. I'll give her a little privacy, and then follow her."

"Alonzo warned that Nikkoli and Arón are still in your area," Ramsey cautioned. "Give Joe an earbud. We may have to instruct him."

"I can't believe you said that?" Kathe questioned.

"Are you questioning my judgment?" Ramsey quizzed.

"No, ma'am," Kathe turned to him. "Joe, Ramsey wants you to use an earbud while you're with us."

"I'm getting the hang of stakeouts," Joe grinned putting it in his ear. "Maybe, I'll change professions."

"Joe, I had Kathe give you an earbud in case of an emergency!" Ramsey snapped. "Keep your mouth shut until someone instructs you! In case you forgot, these people play for keeps! Got it?"

"Got it," Joe rolled his eyes.

"Sam, Kathe left a mosquito in Patterson's office," Ramsey instructed. "Sydney downloaded the app to your phone. Please take it to Thornhill's office. We need to know what's going on there as well."

"Copy that," Sam answered opening the app. "It's on its way."

"I see that," Ramsey acknowledged as Sydney split the screen showing all three drones.

"CC, hover the mother-drone for an Aerial view of Patterson's neighborhood," Ramsey requested. "It won't take long for Nikkoli to find her address. We may have to run a little interference. We don't want them to stop her from leading us to Jenkins."

"Copy that," CC agreed.

"Patterson is in the kitchen pouring a cup of coffee," Kathe stated. "She's heading back upstairs now."

"Come on, Patterson, check your phone messages," Ramsey whispered watching Patterson enter her bedroom.

"What?" Patterson glared at the phone's screen. "Yancy, I just noticed I missed several calls from you in the wee hours this morning. I don't know how I missed them. My phone was right by my bed. Is everything okay?"

"Liar," Kathe chuckled hovering the drone above Yancy.

"Officer Yancy!" Warden Thornhill snapped storming into the office.

"I can't talk now," Yancy whispered. "Just get here," he cleared the line.

"You can't hang up on me!" Patterson screamed redialing.

"Warden Thornhill, thanks for coming back so quickly," Yancy stood up.

"I too received an anonymous call in the wee hours this morning telling me to return immediately," Thornhill admitted. "The informant stated something major was going down right under my nose again."

"Yes, Sir, it did," Yancy answered as he silenced his phone. "I tried to reach Patterson several times after I received an anonymous phone call."

"Is that Patterson blowing up your phone?" Thornhill noticed the screen on his phone light up.

"Yes, Sir," Yancy admitted. "I told Patterson to get here immediately."

“Did you give Patterson a reason?” Thornhill asked.

“No, Sir,” Yancy confessed. “With the importance of the situation we discovered last night, I didn’t leave a voicemail.”

“Did either of you tell Patterson what happened?” Thornhill looked at each of them.

“No, Sir,” Simmons responded. “I was trying to find out why our security system shut down twice in a few hours.”

“No, Sir,” Blais responded. “I was securing the lockdown.”

“Good,” Thornhill stated. “There’s no need to tell Patterson about the situation. I have my suspicions for requesting this. Yancy play the recording of the anonymous call you received?”

“Yes, Sir,” Yancy sat down at his computer and pushed play.

“Interesting, it sounds like the same voice,” Thornhill listened. “Would you make me a copy of that?”

“Of course, Sir,” Yancy agreed inserting a thumb drive into the port, pushing copy.

“Now,” Thornhill pulled up a chair, “tell me what happened. Then, we’ll go see the body together.”

“There’s a problem with that,” Yancy admitted. “The FBI showed up an hour ago with papers to take the body.”

“This situation keeps getting better,” Thornhill shook his head. “Tell me what you do know.”

“We discovered a body in solitary confinement cell number one that wasn’t one of our inmates,” Yancy continued to explain the rest of the night.

“I would like you and Officer Blais to check with the police stations and airports about any questionable persons-of-interest in the area within the last few days,” Thornhill requested as Yancy handed him the thumb drive.

“Yes, Sir,” Blais agreed. “Anyone in particular?”

“I’m not sure,” Thornhill admitted standing up. “For the FBI to pull jurisdiction as quick as they did this morning, they know something.”

“I was leery about it as well,” Yancy admitted opening his desk drawer. “Especially since you weren’t back yet. You just missed them. They arrived with a hearse. They came in presenting documents signed by President Trumore, took the body, and left,” he pulled out a file. “Here’s the paperwork with their cards,” handing them to Thornhill.

“This institution is for holding high-profile criminals with extremely high-tech capabilities,” Thornhill stated putting the file under his arm.

"You three are some of the best techies in the business. That's why you're sitting in this control room. We have everything known to man to keep inmates from escaping. You tell me that with all these computers, equipment, alarms, cameras, and your expertise, how a corpse of a non-inmate ended up in one of our Solitary Confinement Cells?"

"I have no clue, Sir," Yancy answered.

"I also haven't been able to find a reason for the system's two shutdowns yet?" Simmons admitted. "There wasn't any loss of power, anywhere in the buildings."

"I checked all the guards posted at each gate, entrances, corridors, and lookout towers," Blais admitted. "Nothing opened, and nothing was unusual. We can't understand how the body got inside."

"It's a mystery that we will not stop looking for the answer until we solve it," Thornhill demanded pointing at them. "I want to know how this, and other weird situations happened under Patterson's watch. Two years ago, four trusted inmates, one month from their release, and a guard were found dead on a single work detail. Around the time, the military placed Gen. Robert Thompson and Sabrina Macaby here for treason a few days apart. Sometime after that, someone orchestrated the switch of Macaby with a look-alike right under our noses!" he held up the thumb drive. "If it wasn't for an informant, that I think is the same one that contacted us tonight, the Ortiz', and a few other bought-off guards would have helped them get away with it."

"Sir, during an attempted jailbreak, a doctor on the scene sent Gen. Thompson to the hospital right before Macaby arrived," Yancy pulled up his file. "He was at Cedar General for two-weeks."

"Yes, Thompson was, wasn't he?" Thornhill questioned. "Again, Patterson was on watch when it happened. During that time, I was in DC working with President Trumore on his new program of pardoning non-harden criminals. During that time, someone tried to execute a significant jailbreak, blowing a hole in the back wall. Patterson oversaw the renovations. On the flight here tonight, I started researching Gen. Thompson. There's no record in Patterson's filed report that Thompson ever left this facility to go to the hospital."

"Patterson filed a report," Yancy insisted. "I proofed it," he scrolled down Thompson's file. "It's not in here!"

"Also missing is a record of Patterson conversing with me or the Pentagon of Thompson's removal during those two weeks?" Thornhill stated. "It's the protocol to get written permission from the Pentagon to remove an inmate for any reason. With such a new, high-profiled criminal, don't you think that's odd?"

"I speak for all of us," Yancey confessed. "We too, have wondered about major activities happening only on Patterson's watch. After the explosion that night on the back wall, an entire crew arrived with building supplies and equipment. It seemed intense, with men working around-the-clock for a week to patch one wall. When we questioned Patterson about it, she said she was in charge and to stay out of the way."

"I want to check on who vetted Patterson to work here," Thornhill declared. "Then we're going to turn that cell inside out."

"Things are heating up," Ramsey grinned watching Thornhill storm out of the office. "Sam, follow Thornhill. He's beginning to put two and two together."

"Thornhill finally realizes that he has a guardian angel watching out for him," Sydney observed. "At least, he's thankful for our help. Thornhill's calling Patterson now. Let's listen," he turned up the sound.

"Officer Patterson, there's no need for you to come into work today," Thornhill stated walking into his office.

"Why, Sir, I'm leaving my house now," Patterson insisted.

"I'm here, and I'll handle everything," Thornhill stated. "Since you always volunteer to work all the holidays, take a few weeks off. We'll see you when you get back, nice, and rested."

"But, Sir," Patterson disagreed. "I'm not sure what happened on my watch. I need to work on this case."

"I'm the warden," Thornhill proclaimed. "I'm ordering you to take time off," the line cleared.

"Did Thornhill just hang up on me, too?" Patterson wondered hurrying into her home office.

"Yes, several things have happened on your watch," Thornhill whispered shaking his head, and opening the file Yancy handed him. "What?" he snapped shuffling through the papers? "There's nothing written on any of these pages!" He held up the two blank business cards. "Who took the body?" he turned his chair around, staring out his window. Who is Patterson, he thought as his mind raced back to the time, he met her? I didn't vet her; he turned his chair around to his desk and pulled up Patterson's application.

"A guardian angel with disappearing ink," Ramsey chuckled.

"Patterson is powering up her laptop," Kathe alerted.

"That's because Johansson bugged Thornhill's office, as well as the main office," Sydney admitted. "Don't worry; I erased her hard-drive and left her a present. She can't do anything."

"What?" Patterson screamed. "My desktop is empty! Someone wiped out my computer!" She reached into her backpack for her thumb drive. At least, I have a backup, she thought, and then screamed. "How could my thumb drive be erased!" she placed a call. "He's not answering!" Patterson screamed trying several more times. "Connor, call me as soon as you can!"

"Well done team, she's panicking," Ramsey grinned as Patterson grabbed her suitcase out of the hall closet as she placed a phone call. "STL Maintenance, this is Lieutenant Janise Patterson. I need you to get my plane ready for flight." Next, she called the tower. "This is Lieutenant Janise Patterson. I need a flight plan for Washington Dulles International Airport, ASAP."

"There's our missing pilot that brought the terrorists to my condo?" Ramsey affirmed watching Patterson pack. "CC, check for a flight plan on June 29th around 2100 (10:00 PM EST).

"I'm already on it," CC agreed pulling up her computer.

"It doesn't look like Patterson plans to come back," Kathe observed. "She opened the filing cabinet, took some files, and slammed it shut. She's bugging out."

"I see that," Ramsey noted. "As we just heard, we have an ace in our pocket whenever we need to use it. We know where she's going. I'll have Keith get the Citation ready to leave. It would be best if you beat Patterson there. We can control the drone watching Thornhill from here."

"Copy that," Sam answered. "When do you want us to leave?"

"After you follow Patterson to the airport," Ramsey requested. "Kathe, once Patterson gets aboard her plane, land the drone inside so we can keep an eye on her."

"Ramsey, I found some interesting information from the Air Traffic Controller's log," CC read. "On June 29th between 2130 and 2230, an unidentified military helicopter was detected in Manhattan airspace. Someone from Homeland Security made a phone call, saying that RAMD Jeremy Hiltree cleared it."

"That has Jenkins' name all over it!" Ramsey exclaimed. "I better warn Hiltree. Jenkins is setting up Hiltree to fall with us just as we thought."

"Someone is trying to hack into the personnel records at the penitentiary," Sydney cautioned as an alarm sounded. "It's Nikkoli Giotorra."

"What's Giotorra looking for?" Ramsey asked.

"He's looking up Thornhill and Patterson," Sydney carefully followed. "He's cross-checking their names with Jenkins. I knew they didn't trust him."

"They know the only place in this area that Bencivenni could have gone was the penitentiary," CC stated. "There's nothing else out there."

"Now, they are checking Patterson's parking permit," Sydney stated. "They're looking to see what kind of car she drives."

"The only car that passed them that day was her hunter-green Nissan Altima," Ramsey remembered. "They aren't stupid. They'll visit Patterson."

"Hopefully, they'll miss her," Kathe smiled. "She's putting her suitcases into the trunk. She's heading back inside. Oh, my God! She's turning on all the gas burners in the kitchen. She's going to blow it! It's summer, and everyone is home! Thank goodness, there are not too many people in the park!"

"Patterson knows we're onto her," Ramsey declared. "She's covering her tracks."

"She's leaving," Kathe noted as the garage door opened. "I'm planting the drone on her car," she said as Patterson drove off. They watched Patterson turn the corner as Kathe jumped out of the car.

"Tierney, where are you going?" Ramsey demanded.

"You know where!" Sam snapped as he and Rodger jumped out and ran into the house after Kathe.

"I've got the kitchen!" Kathe cautioned turning off the gas burners.

"We'll get the windows downstairs!" Sam stated.

"I'll get the ones upstairs!" Kathe ran upstairs.

"I can't breathe!" Rodger choked opening the last one. "It's too concentrated down here!"

"It is," Ramsey watched. "Get out the front door before you pass out! Kathe, get out of that house, too! That's an order!"

"I can't!" Kathe screamed covering her nose. "JAKE detected a countdown device in Patterson's office!"

"Let me see," Sydney ordered. "CC, take the mother-drone inside the office window."

“Copy that,” CC moved the drone after Kathe kicked the screen out. She took a deep breath of fresh air and returned.

“It’s got multiple triggers running at the same time,” Sydney declared as he began typing. “JAKE got the first one,” he kept typing. “Sam, evacuate as many neighbors as you can!”

“I’ll warn the people at the park!” Joe declared getting out of the SUV. “Run to the back of the park!” Joe screamed crossing the street. “There’s a gas leak!”

Sam and Rodger went door-to-door evacuating people!

“Kathe, leave JAKE, and get out of there!” Ramsey ordered.

“No, can do!” Kathe stated. “I have to hold JAKE directly in front of the monitor.”

“Kathe’s right!” Sydney declared turning off the second one. “JAKE’s almost got the last one.”

“I hope it hurries,” Kathe declared. “The timer shows 15 seconds, 14, 13, 12, 11, 10, 9, 8, 7, 6, 5, 4, 3. It stopped!”

“Kathe, have JAKE melt the device,” Sydney directed. “It could reset and blow later.”

“Gladly,” Kathe sighed. “JAKE, melt the device.”

“Kathe, it is done,” JAKE replied.

“We’ve got a worse problem!” Ramsey ranted. “Sam, Rodger, go get Mr. Rock Star before he signs any autographs. Act like you’re his bodyguards.”

“Tell me, Joe isn’t!” Kathe snapped running down the stairs. “The news will tell Jenkins that Joe was here! How stupid could he be?”

“Don’t get me started on that subject!” Ramsey smirked.

“Kathe, I would suggest you get out of there and head for the airport,” Sydney requested. “Jordan has the Citation ready to takeoff as soon as you arrive. Nikkoli and Arón discovered Patterson’s address. They are en route.”

“Copy that,” Kathe said driving the SUV over the curb and into the park toward the crowd.

Sunday, July 5th
1145 (11:45 AM EST)
Dr. Sydney’s House, White Plains, NY

“Aunt Jeannie, can Alek and I play outside?” Joey asked. “Since we weren’t old enough to go with Uncle Bob and look for wild berries, I want to play with my car," he said trying to start it. "Never mind," he slumped pitifully holding it up. "The batteries are dead."

"Well now, that's a pitiful face," Jeannie picked up Joey and sat him on the kitchen counter. "You're in luck. I have batteries in this drawer," she opened the drawer, taking out batteries and a screwdriver. "Uncle Bob explained to you that Paris remembered about the berries. She hasn't been here in years. She didn't know what to expect. Uncle Bob thought it would be best for you to stay with me. Besides, they should be home soon. Uncle Bob said that they almost had enough wild blueberries for two pies. I'm going to make them for dinner," she smiled handing him the remote. "There, the car works fine now," she said hugging him and helping him down. "I have to change the laundry around before I can go out. I guess you can go ahead. I'll be out there in a jiffy."

"Thanks, Aunt Jeannie," Joey smiled taking Alek by the hand. "Come on, Alek. You and Teddy can watch me drive my car. Then, I'll give you a turn."

Jeannie sat her phone on the kitchen counter, watching out the window as the little boys crossed the bridge to the grassy knoll. She waited for a second as Alek sat down with Teddy, watching Joey drive his car around them in circles. Alek was laughing and clapping his hands. They'll be fine for a minute, she thought, hurrying to the laundry room.

"Well, this is enough blueberries," Bob picked up the basket. "Paris, I'm glad you remembered this place."

"How could I forget," Paris admitted. "Aunt Deanna and I used to come here every year to pick berries. I think we also have enough raspberries to make at least one pie."

"I can taste them already," Pete grinned. "Aunt Jeannie is the best cook."

"You better not let Mom hear you say that!" Heather smacked at him.

"I'm just telling the truth," Pete defended ducking away from her. "Mom's a good cook, but Jeannie's got her beat when it comes to baking."

"That's because my mom is only a housewife," Christy admitted. "Your mom has a different set of skills."

"You better not let your mother hear you say that she's only a housewife," Bob chuckled answering his phone. "Sydney, what's up?"

"I see you and the older kids are in the woods behind the house," Sydney checked the cameras around the perimeter of the house.

"Paris showed us where to find wild berries," Bob said. "Jeannie is making fresh pies with dinner."

"Paris and my mother used to do that," Sydney admitted. "I'm calling you as a precaution. Alonzo called and warned his sources spotted quite a few men getting off a chartered flight at Westchester County Airport. The Washington crowd that lives in the area use that airport. Alonzo said to take extra precautions until his men get there. Kathe's team has business in Washington before they drop Joe off to you. Make sure you have that talk with Pete."

"We'll head back to the house," Bob said walking away from the kids. "I don't think I should have that discussion with Pete. That's his parent's job. Pete's very mature for his age. I don't think anybody needs to say anything. Pete knew Kathe was dating Joe before she married Yorg."

"I told Ramsey that," Sydney agreed. "I'll have another talk with her. Leaving Joe there is the only option we have now. The next few days are going to be tough. Just tell Jeannie never mind the talk."

"I'll call Jeannie," Bob stated. "She's with the little boys. I need to tell her to keep them inside," he cleared the line and dialed Jeannie. "Kids, we need to hurry," he motioned to them. "Jeannie isn't answering the phone. Sydney warned that suspicious characters landed at Westchester."

"They may be at the airport, but no one knows about this house," Pete stated picking raspberries. "And it's in a secured military neighborhood. A few more berries, and we'll have enough for two raspberry pies."

"The fact that Sydney called is reason enough to heed his warning," Paris disagreed. "He doesn't play around. We need to head back to the house. We can make another pie later."

"You're right," Pete sighed as Bob's phone rang again.

"Bob, a silent alarm just sounded on the west side of the property, showing four men entering," Sydney warned. "The camera on the east side of the back property shows four more."

"We're over by the landing strip heading toward the house," Bob reported. "We have to cross the grassy knoll. They'll see us."

"I have another way inside the house," Sydney declared zooming in the camera by the runway. "I see four men coming in on your right flank. Go to the fuel tank. The large tree next to it facing the landing strip is hollow. Reach inside the knot on the tree and pull the lever. A door will open. It leads to a tunnel that ends in a safe room under my office. Have Pete immediately get the drone up. The spring's inclement weather must have moved the cameras. We'll have to adjust them later."

"Just a minute," Bob moved the phone away from his face. "Kids, no talking and follow me quickly," he hurried to the tree. He reached inside the knot on the tree trunk, and a door opened. "I found the door," Bob said looking inside. "It's very dark. I can't see anything inside."

"There's a ladder that leads to a tunnel," Sydney explained.

"I forgot about this tunnel leading into the house!" Paris exclaimed taking Bob's phone. "Pete, turn around to climb down first. As soon as your leg passes through the doorway, the motion-censored lights will turn on inside a long tunnel."

"Okay," Pete swung his leg inside, and the lights turned on inside. "Heather goes next, and then Bob. I'll close the door and lock it."

"Good job, Paris!" Sydney noted. "Go to earbuds as soon as you get to the safe room. Ramsey just tried to call Jeannie. She's still not answering the phone."

"I've got this," Paris locked the door. "The escape routes are coming back to me. Here Bob," she handed him the phone.

"Jeannie didn't answer when I called either," Bob admitted following Paris.

"Get that drone up ASAP," Sydney warned checking the cameras. "The men are out of view at the moment," he glanced at the camera facing the back of the house. "The little boys are playing on the grassy knoll. I need to locate Jeannie to get them inside the house," he switched to the inside cameras.

"It's not like Jeannie to let them play alone outside," Ramsey noted as she helped Sydney check.

"I guess Jeannie thought it would be all right since Bob and the older kids are in the woods behind them," Sydney answered. "She is in the laundry room."

"Jeannie's singing so loudly, she can't hear you or the phone!" Ramsey cringed.

"I can access the speaker system," Sydney said pushing enter. "Jeannie! Jeannie! Jeannie! Jeannie!"

"She heard you!" Ramsey exclaimed watching Jeannie stop singing, glancing around the room.

"Jeannie, it's Sydney on the house speaker system!" Sydney exclaimed. "We've had a breach in two areas in the woods behind the house."

"Joey and Alek are playing on the grassy knoll!" Jeannie screamed running into the kitchen, looking out the window. "They're gone!" she cried grabbing her phone off the counter as Sydney called her. "They were just here!" She ran outside, frantically looking around.

"Calm down," Sydney demanded. "They'll hear you. I'm rewinding the tape to see where they went. I'll find them."

"Alek drove the car into the woods!" Ramsey pointed at the bottom camera. "They're following the car to the left of the bridge! They are out of sight. Jeannie, please don't call out to them! Go back to the safe room under Sydney's office. Bob and the older kids just got inside."

"No, it's my fault," Jeannie cried. "I shouldn't have let them outside alone," she crossed the wooden bridge to the woods. "I've got to find them," she insisted stopping to look in all directions.

"Jeannie, stand down!" Ramsey demanded. "I order you to go back inside the house! Pete just got the drone up. As soon as you're inside, Sydney will lock the house down," she stated watching Jeannie hurrying back across the grassy knoll and safely into the house. "Sydney, Jeannie's inside; seal the house!"

"Pete hasn't located the boys yet!" Sydney snapped locking the house. "Ylia was supposed to put a GPS inside Teddy," he searched for the link. "I can't find the link," he called Dr. Ylia. "Ylia, did you put the tracking device in Alek's teddy?"

"Yes, is Teddy lost again?" Ylia asked.

"The boys are lost," Sydney shared as Ylia ran to her computer.

"I forgot to send you the link," Ylia pushed enter. "I just sent it."

"Thanks," Sydney opened the link, sending it to the drone, and JAKE.

"Pete, I just sent a link to the drone for Teddy's GPS," Sydney explained.

"I wondered why the drone just turned by itself," Pete reported.

"It's honing into the device," Sydney stated.

"It's going by the stream on the east side of the yard," Pete stated. "There they are!"

"Yes, I see them," Sydney showed Ramsey. "Alek," Sydney calmly stated trying to get his attention.

"Pete, keep the drone high," Sydney requested. "Ramsey, find the men," he switched to the device. "Alek, it's Dr. Sydney. Can you hear me?"

"Teddy can talk?" Alek smiled holding up his bear.

"Alek, it's Dr. Sydney," he explained. "Can you please give Teddy to Joey for a minute? Please."

"No," Alek giggled. "Teddy is talking to me."

"Are you crazy!" Ramsey snapped. "Alek isn't going to give up a talking bear," she dialed Kathe. "We're not ever going to reason with him!"

"I already sent the link to JAKE," Sydney stated.

"Kathe, we have a serious situation," Ramsey warned. "Sydney sent JAKE a link to Alek's teddy bear's GPS and our drone."

"I'm connecting," Kathe stated sitting behind Joe on the jet. "Why are the boys in the woods alone?"

"Unknown men breached the property, and the boys got away from Jeannie," Ramsey explained. "We need Alek to give Teddy to Joey so Sydney can lead them to safety."

"Alek, it's Mommy," Kathe calmly stated as Joe joined her. "Alek, I see you and Teddy."

"Mommy!" Alek giggled jumping up and down, clapping his hands.

"Alek, give Teddy to Joey for a minute," Kathe begged as Joe watched. "Please, just for a minute."

"Mommy is talking to Teddy and me," Alek laughed. "Mommy, I miss you," he hugged the bear.

"Alek, Mommy misses you, too," Kathe calmly stated. "I miss Joey too. Can I tell Joey?"

"Mommy, where are you?" Alek asked.

"I'm on my way to see you," Kathe stated looking up at Joe, crossing her fingers. "Alek, I need you to give Teddy to Joey for a minute. I want to tell him I'm on my way too. Please."

"All right," Alek whined walking over to Joey, holding up Teddy. "Mommy is talking to Teddy and me. It's your turn."

"Mommy's not here," Joey looked around.

"Joey, it's Mommy talking through Teddy," Kathe raised her voice as Joey looked at Teddy. "Joey, can you hear me?"

"Mommy?" Joey questioned holding Teddy to his ear.

"Yes," Kathe sighed. "Dr. Sydney needs to talk to you. Do what he says. Pete found you in the woods with the drone. I'm watching you through that camera. It's right up above you," she said as Pete lowered the drone for Joey to see.

"Yes, Mommy," Joey answered looking up. "I see the drone."

"Joey, this is Dr. Sydney," he introduced.

"Dr. Sydney," Joey looked around. "We're lost."

"No, you're not lost," Sydney declared. "I need you to hold Alek's hand and be very quiet. Instead of talking, can you shake your head either yes, or no?"

Joey shook his head, yes.

"Joey, there are bad men in the forest looking for you," Sydney explained. "I'm going to get you and Alek back to the house. I need you to start walking toward the stream."

"Come on, Alex," Joey whispered. "We need to go home."

"Good job," Sydney coaxed. "Keep walking. You're almost there," he paused. "Now stop. See the big tree right in front of you?"

Joey shook his head, yes.

"See the big opening in the middle?" Sydney asked. "Go inside the opening. It's a fort I used to play in with Paris. You'll be safe in there," Sydney assured watching the boys walk inside. "Pete, bring the drone down so I can see the boys. Have Bob take over the mother-drone, and then launch a mosquito to go inside with the boys."

"Copy that," Pete complied taking over the mosquito.

"Joey, can you hear the little mosquito flying around your head?" Sydney asked.

Joey shook, yes.

"You've watched Pete practice flying it," Sydney acknowledged. "It has a camera so that I can see you inside the tree. Now, look to the side of the opening. Do you see the curtains on the hooks?"

Joey nodded, yes.

"Pete, be ready to go to infrared," Sydney cautioned.

"Joey, can you pull the curtain across the opening?" Sydney asked. "Can you close the one on the other side," he watched. "Good job!"

"It's dark in here," Joey sighed. "Where is the light?"

"I know it's dark," Sydney agreed. "Do you see the red glow on the mosquito's eyes?"

Joey nodded, yes.

"The mosquito has infrared, so in the dark, we can see you clearly," Sydney explained. "You have to sit down with Alek and stay really quiet. Do you understand?"

Joey shook his head, yes, and then pulled Alek down next to him.

"You're safe there," Sydney promised. "I'll have someone get you soon."

"That was just in the nick of time," Ramsey sighed. "I see four men heading their way," she said as Alek began to cry.

"It's dark!" Alek cried. "Mommy?"

"Alek," Kathe gently called to him. "Mommy sees you. I know it's dark, but you must stay there and be very quiet. I'm watching you," Kathe promised as Alek cried harder.

"I don't see you!" Alek screamed.

"Since it's dark, and it's your naptime, why don't you take a nap?" Kathe asked. "I'll sing your favorite song. Twinkle, twinkle little star, how I wonder who you are. Up above the world so high, Like a diamond in the sky."

"I want Mommy!" Alek cried louder.

"It's not working," Pete gasped watching helplessly.

"Alek's a daddy's boy!" Heather cried. "Dad always sings with Mom."

"Twinkle, Twinkle little star," Joe joined Kathe. "How I wonder what you are? Up above the world so high, Like a diamond in the sky."

"Daddy," Alek smiled clapping his hands.

"It's working," Heather smiled as Alek leaned on Joey's lap.

"Twinkle, twinkle little star," they sang. "How I wonder who you are? Up above the world so high, Like a diamond in the sky. Twinkle, twinkle little star. How I wonder who you are?"

"Alek, Daddy loves you," Joe admitted with tears filling his eyes.

"It worked!" Pete declared. "Alek fell asleep."

"Joey, Mommy's watching over you," Kathe promised wiping her tears. She glanced at the mother-drone's camera. "I see someone outside. Be very quiet, no matter what you hear. The men don't know you're in there."

Joey shook his head, yes, and put his arm around Alek.

"He must have heard Alek crying!" Ramsey gasped. "He's calling someone to help him look."

"Bob, I need Paris and Pete to rescue them," Sydney stated. "Keep the drone at that height and have Heather take control of the mosquito. Paris, go to the fireplace in the library and push in the third brick from the left. A secret door will open on the side of the fireplace that leads outside."

"That's how Uncle David came in and out of the house unnoticed," Paris realized. "I knew it was something to do with that fireplace!" she pushed the brick. "Pete, follow me."

"It's a different tunnel than the one you were just inside," Sydney explained. "Once outside, stay inside the trees for cover. It parallels the stream," he watched them. "You're doing great. You're almost there."

"One man is checking around the fort," Ramsey cautioned. "He's checking around each bush," she changed cameras. "Bob, you have four men approaching the house."

“Don’t worry, Bob,” Sydney explained. “They can’t get inside. The glass is bulletproof, and the doors are solid metal with steel bars across them.”

“They have guns drawn,” Bob noted on one of the cameras. “I’m more worried about the kids.”

“The kids will be fine,” Kathe added watching the cameras. “Pete, Heather, and Paris have trained for this type of situation.”

“Paris, do you remember how we crossed the deep end of the pond?” Sydney asked. “It’s right by the next tree.”

“How could I ever forget,” Paris whispered reaching for the lowest limb and pulling it down. “Follow right behind my steps, Pete. A glass bridge just slid across the pond.”

“The boys are inside our old fort,” Sydney shared watching them cross. “Hurry behind the tree where we carved our initials! A man came out of nowhere! He saw you walk across the stream!”

“I can’t believe we missed him!” Ramsey snapped.

“This was one of the worst springs we’ve had,” Sydney rechecked the cameras. “Some of my cameras need to be readjusted. I’m missing some of the property. The man saw you cross the river and is trying to find where you crossed,” Sydney chuckled watching him take a step on the bridge before Sydney withdrew it. “I hope he can swim. The current is strong there as well as deep.”

“Juno, help!” he fell into the water, screaming all the way downstream.

“That was too close,” Ramsey stated. “Paris, I see you have a silencer on your gun. You may have to use it.”

“Pete, get your Shuriken’s ready,” Kathe requested. “They’re your game-changer.”

“I’m ready,” Pete answered.

“Joey, can you still hear me?” Sydney asked changing cameras.

Joey shook his head, yes.

“Good job,” Sydney stated. “No matter what you hear, I want you to stay there and be quiet. It’s vital to keep Alek quiet, too.”

“Joey, if Alek wakes up, put your hand tightly across his mouth,” Kathe ordered.

Joey shook, okay.

“Good job,” Sydney stated. “Pete and Paris are almost to you. There is one man near the fort, and another one coming up on your left flank.”

“They have guns drawn,” Ramsey warned. “Try not to engage, but you are to protect yourselves,” she watched them shake their heads as they quietly hid behind a large tree. “Good job, he walked right past you. You’re free to go now.” Ramsey watched them maneuver around trees and bushes toward the fort.

“Stop!” Sydney ordered. “Two more men are passing 100 yards away from you. They’re both heading for the stream.”

“Joey,” Sydney cautioned. “Paris and Pete are almost there. Make sure Alek doesn’t scream when they open the curtain. Okay?”

Joey shook, yes.

“Here they come,” Sydney said. “Paris, Pete, go now!”

“There go two of the older kids!” a man shouted shooting at them.

“Ah!” Paris gasped diving behind some bushes.

“Paris,” Pete whispered motioning to her from behind a tree.

“Don’t let him get near the fort!” Ramsey ordered.

“Understood,” Paris whispered steadying her gun.

“Paris, I didn’t see him,” Sydney apologized. “I’m trying to manipulate that camera from here.”

“Pete, aim for his knees,” Kathe ordered watching.

“Paris, you have to take him out,” Ramsey admitted. “He’s seen you.”

“Understood,” Paris agreed.

“He’s calling for help!” Ramsey warned. “Do it now!”

Pete threw two Shuriken’s, striking the man in his kneecaps.

“Terry, Juno, help!” He yelled as Paris shot him in the chest.

“Run to the tree!” Ramsey ordered. “Several others are on the way!”

“Copy that,” Paris whispered hurrying to the tree and crawling inside with Pete right behind her.

“Pete, close the curtain!” Paris insisted.

“One of his companions is close to the tree,” Sydney cautioned. “Paris, you know what to do.”

“Okay,” Paris whispered feeling the inside wall. “I found the lever,” she whispered opening the wall to a ladder. “Pete, go first. I’ll hand you Alek, then Joey.”

“Got it,” Pete whispered turned around, and climbed on the ladder. He reached for Alek.

“Pete,” Alek woke up hugging him. “Where am I?”

“Sh,” Pete steadied himself and climbed down the steps.

“Where’s Joey?” Alek cried.

Pete put his hand over Alek's mouth and whispered in his ear, "He's climbing down in a minute."

"Joey, it's your turn," Paris whispered helping Joey get on the first step.

"Good job," Pete coached. "Hold onto the ladder and take one step at a time," he put Alek down. "Stay here. I have to help Joey," Pete said climbing up the ladder. "I'm right behind you. You're doing a good job."

"I made it!" Joey jumped in Pete's arms as soon as they got down.

"You sure did," Pete smiled.

"Heather, fly the drone down with Paris," Sydney requested. "Paris, lock the door."

"I will," Paris quickly closed the door, locked it, and climbed down.

"The kids just made it," Ramsey stated turning up the sound. "Listen to the men outside."

"Terry," another man joined him. "Jenkins was right about this property being Dr. David Sydney's house. Tierney's kids are here," he held up Joey's car. "I found a new remote-controlled car over there," he pointed.

"I thought I heard a kid crying around this area a little while ago but couldn't find anyone," Terry admitted. "Juno and I heard Reginald scream from this direction. He's not answering my text. And Marco isn't answering either. He was near the stream the last time he checked in with me. Spread out!"

"How long before the kids are in the safe room?" Ramsey asked. "Terry and Juno should find Reginald soon. Marco is the one that fell into the stream."

"The kids are almost to the safe room," Sydney assured her. "This is one of the longest tunnels that Dad built," he said watching them walk down the tunnel.

"There's the doorway," Paris ran ahead and opened it. "Dave and I used to practice getting into this room. Uncle David was adamant about us knowing how to escape enemies that might come after him."

"A couple of the men are above you on the porch," Sydney cautioned watching her climb up a ladder and opening the trap door. "Can you hear them?"

"Negative," Paris answered climbing inside the room. She reached for Alek. Pete helped Joey climb inside and closed the door.

"We're safe in here," Paris acknowledged. "Look," she handed Joey an old, metal car. "This was Dave's dream car. I can't believe some of our old toys are still in here."

"That's where my Bentley went," Sydney laughed. "Paris, you know how to get them into the safe room."

"We're on our way," Paris answered opening a door and leading them inside.

"It's another tunnel?" Pete asked.

"Yes," she opened a door. "Bob, Jeannie, we're back!"

"Boys!" Jeannie ran to them.

"Paris, Pete, I'm so proud of you," Kathe declared watching the reunion. "You never once flinched in the eyes of danger to save the boys."

"I am proud of you, too," Joe sighed. "You're brave like your mother."

"Is that Joe Sherrod?" Pete asked as Ramsey clenched her fist.

"Yes," Kathe sighed.

"I thought it sounded like Joe singing with you, Mom," Heather confessed. "You harmonized perfectly together. Alek quieted down as soon as Joe joined you."

"Where's Dad?" Pete demanded.

"Dads in Cuba," Kathe explained. "Jenkins kidnapped Joe and Rodger's family. You heard the men outside. Jenkins has teamed up with the other side to get his greedy hands-on Chameleon. As soon as I do something in Washington, I must drop Joe off at the safe house with you. There's no other way. I'm sure you'll make Joe feel welcomed. He's in this mess because of me. We'll talk about it after this is over. As soon as I leave Joe with you, I'm rejoining Dad in Cuba. Hopefully, this will be all over soon, and we can be back as a family."

"I understand more than you think, Mom," Pete confided. "I love you."

"I love you, too," Kathe smiled as tears filled her eyes. "You're growing up to be quiet, a strong man."

"Alonzo and Pauli have men almost to the house," Sydney proclaimed. "I just let them through the gate. They'll handle the men outside."

"I'm glad to hear that," Bob said. "They're still looking for a way to get inside the house."

"Don't worry, they can't," Sydney declared. "Pete, take over the mother-drone. I'll let you know when they're gone, and it's safe to move around."

"Copy that," Pete complied.

“Sydney, I forgot about a contract I signed with a new client before this started,” Paris remembered. “I’m supposed to deliver two paintings to Dubai. It’s for the unveiling of a new Presidential Palace.”

“Is there anyone else that can deliver them?” Sydney asked.

“No, it’s a strict, special invitation only,” Paris sighed. “I was asked to personally unveil the paintings in front of the new president in three days.”

“There are no elections in that area that I’m aware of,” Sydney cautioned. “Who contacted you?”

“That’s the strange part,” Paris admitted. “After I signed a notarized form that I wouldn’t reveal to anyone who and what the paintings were about; it disappeared. When I opened the envelope and saw the pictures, it made me feel uncomfortable. A day later, a courier delivered cash for the paintings to my studio.”

“It’s too dangerous for you to leave my house,” Sydney declared. “People are after you, as much as the children. It could be a trap.”

“I understand,” Paris sighed.

“Jordan signaled we’re landing at Dulles,” Kathe shared. “I’ve got to go. I’ll see the children soon,” she cleared the line.

Joe sat next to Kathe and turned off his earbud, “I can’t believe how calmly you watched Alek in such danger. How could you send Pete against men with guns? He’s seventeen-years-old!”

“Joe turned his earbud off,” Sydney turned to Ramsey. “I’m widening JAKE’s perimeter.”

“Not only was Alek in danger,” Kathe looked Joe in the eyes. “All four of my children were in danger, along with my best friends, their daughter, and Sydney’s cousin Paris. As for sending Pete against men with guns, you above all people should be glad Pete trained for situations like this. He helped save your life in Ponce Inlet, or did you forget?”

“I’m sorry,” Joe sighed. “I was out of line.”

“You were!” Kathe snapped. “Now, I’m faced with another problem concerning you. I told you in Ponce Inlet that Pete heard the truth about you and me. I’m so relieved that Pete let me know he understood and will keep the secret. You’re still their favorite rock star. They’ll accept you as another famous friend of ours. Just make sure you keep it that way!”

“I just sang a lullaby to my son for the first time,” Joe shook his head. “You’ll never understand how great that felt for me to watch his face as I sang to him, and he called me Daddy. He calmed down immediately and fell asleep before he heard me tell him that I love him.”

"I understand that you've missed all the first with our son," Kathe stated. "I realize that it hurt you when Heather said Alek's a daddy's boy. Yorg and I will address the situation when this job is over."

"It did hurt me!" Joe admitted. "That's what prompted me to sing with you! Come to think of it. Heather realized that we harmonize great together. It was more than coincidence when we met. You should be on stage beside me. We both know it!"

"Plan B!" Ramsey snapped calling Alonzo. "I see your jet just took off?"

"Yes, we had to wait for the morgue to prepare Bencivenni's body first," Alonzo answered checking the time.

"I need to divert it to Dulles, now!" Ramsey snapped. "They need to bring Sherrod to me," she explained the problem.

"But I have to get Falcini and Miranda back to Florida before the guards make the evening rounds," Alonzo admitted.

"We still have time!" Ramsey stated checking the time. "I'll have them switch to a faster jet! I'll handle everything!"

"I trust you, old friend," Alonzo agreed. "I wish I were there to see the look on Sherrod's face when they put the casket aboard, and the only other passengers are Falcini and a few of his men. I'll make sure Francesco tells Sherrod that it's Bencivenni in the coffin."

"It's only fitting," Ramsey laughed contacting Kathe.

"Kathe, leave Sherrod on the Citation with Jordan," Ramsey stated. "Patterson's back is against a wall. We have no idea what we're up against."

"I'll be happy to leave him," Kathe grinned.

"I also have a little surprise for our, Mr. Prompted," Ramsey confessed. "He's being rerouted and brought to me on the cutter."

Sunday, July 5th
1300 (1:00 PM EST)
Dulles International Airport, WA

"Kathe, I see you're leaving Dulles," Ramsey noted watching that mosquito's camera on the monitor.

"Copy that," Kathe stated. "Patterson parked the plane in hangar #602 and took off in a car. As you can see, she's in a big hurry."

"Sam, stay far enough back not to spook her," Ramsey cautioned.

"Patterson has frantically tried to reach Johansson since she landed," Kathe reported.

"Oh, no!" Sam stopped the car. "She just ran a stale, red light, almost causing an accident."

"Patterson is heading straight toward the Georgetown Apartments," Sydney checked the GPS coordinates.

"CC, what's the status on Johansson?" Kathe asked.

"I just got off the phone with my father," CC reported. "Dad arrived in DC in the wee hours this morning, catching Johansson off guard. They arrested him and searched the house. He's now at a safe house with all his electronics."

"Why a safe house instead of at the Bureau?" Ramsey asked.

"Because the recent leaks were highly-classified and came out of the DC area," CC explained. "Dad doesn't know who he can trust. He also didn't mark the apartment as a crime scene."

"I have to admit, your father is now aware of the corruption in Washington, DC," Ramsey complimented. "I have a feeling when you go back to your office; you won't be working behind a desk anymore."

"You're right about that," CC chuckled. "Dad's amazed at my skills, thanks to you and Sydney."

"Have your father's men gotten into Johansson's files?" Sydney asked.

"Negative," CC answered. "They can't get through his firewall."

"No offense," Sydney stated. "They'll never get through his firewall. Is there any chance you can get Rodger to look at it?"

"That shouldn't be a problem," CC assured him. "I'll call my father."

"As soon as we see what's going on here, Sam will drop you off at a rental car," Sydney explained. "I have a feeling the crucial information we need is in Johansson's computer."

"I do, too," CC agreed.

"Ramsey, Patterson is pulling into the apartment complex," Kathe stated watching her punch in the code. "She knows the code to get inside."

"I'm sure it's not her first time there," Ramsey declared. "She's heading straight for Johansson's apartment."

"Can you believe this?" Kathe questioned as Patterson swung the car into a parking space and slammed on the brakes.

"Why isn't Connor answering his phone?" Patterson exclaimed, slamming her hands against the steering wheel. "His car is here!" she gasped and hurried out of the car.

"Kathe, change to the mosquito and follow Patterson inside," Ramsey requested. "She's putting on gloves."

"It's already up," Kathe stated. "CC has the mother-drone," she handed the iPad to CC.

"I can't believe Patterson's doing this in broad daylight," Sam watched her open the small window beside the door.

"Patterson always manages to find a way inside places," Ramsey noted.

"She's heading straight upstairs," Kathe followed her with the mosquito. "She's entering Johansson's office."

"Did I wake up in an alternate universe?" Patterson screamed hurrying to the desk. "All his electronics are gone!" She rushed to the closet and opened the door. "Oh, my God! The server is gone!" she leaned against the door, taking several deep breaths. "What is Connor doing?" she hurried back to the desk.

They observed Patterson taking papers out of the right, middle drawer, sitting them on the chair.

"The way she's taking the papers out shows it has a fake bottom," Ramsey assumed as Patterson took the letter opener and lifted the bottom.

"That's because she doesn't want anyone to know she was there," Sam declared.

Patterson turned over the bottom, reached for a small envelope, and put it in her pocket. Then, she put the papers back into the drawer and closed it."

"Stay with her," Ramsey ordered as Patterson hurried into the hallway.

"She took the letter opener with her," Kathe said as the mosquito followed Patterson to the next room on the left. "She's going into the master bedroom," the mosquito followed her, hovering close to the ceiling. "This is odd," Kathe watched Patterson climb on his tall bed and stand up. She reached for the decorative top of the bedpost and pulled it sideways.

"I'll be," Ramsey said. "It's a thumb drive."

"Johansson probably stores his information daily on it and hides it there," Sydney proclaimed. "IT techs always has several copies of their daily work, in case of emergencies."

"She's leaving the bedroom with a big smile," Kathe noted. "She's going into the guest bathroom," hovering the mosquito above Patterson.

They watched as Patterson stood on the toilet seat and loosened a tile with the letter opener. She pulled the tile down and placed it on the top of the toilet tank. She opened the envelope.

"What's inside the envelope?" Ramsey asked.

"It's a key," Kathe declared flying the mosquito closer. "She's opening a safe. She's taking out a backpack."

"You've got to be kidding me?" Ramsey snapped as Patterson checked the materials inside. "She's got a passport, driver's license, money, camera with a sizable lens, make-up, and a blonde wig."

"Did you catch the name on the passport?" CC asked.

"Let me check," Sydney rewound the footage. "Anita Sands of Washington DC. Patterson's changing her looks to match the passport and license," he said as she took stage make-up out of the backpack.

"My heavens," Ramsey gasped. "She's a make-up artist. Patterson's changing her looks; right down to blue contacts to go with the blonde wig," Ramsey admired watching her brush her hair toward her face. "She's pretty good," Ramsey commented as Patterson hurried downstairs. "I wouldn't even recognize her."

"A security guard just pulled into the parking lot," CC cautioned. "The officer is checking the license plates of the cars in the complex. He just took a picture of Patterson's plate."

"Let me run her plate," Sydney said as CC moved the mother-drone. "Give me a minute."

"Patterson sees the guard," Kathe stated showing her parting the curtains.

"They've prepared for this day," Ramsey declared watching Patterson reach in the backpack and taking out the camera. She put the camera around her neck. "She's leaving with her keys in her hand."

"The tag is fake," Sydney declared. "Patterson knows she has to get away before he runs the plate."

"She's coming out," Kathe cautioned.

Officer Chad Pierson pulled his gun and hurried toward her. "Put your hands up!" he ordered squaring off at her while contacting the station via his shoulder mic.

"Oh, my God!" Patterson screamed. "What's going on?"

"Keep your hands where I can see them!" Pierson ordered. "I have my body cam showing you leaving a Federal Employee's apartment."

"I'm leaving my boyfriend, Connor Johansson's apartment," Patterson lied holding up her keys. "Connor does work at the Pentagon. I left my backpack with my camera here last night. I stopped by to get them. I work at the Washington Center Mall as a photographer. I'm working the evening shift today."

"She claims to be his girlfriend," Pierson told his sergeant. "Yes, Sir. I need to see some ID and proof of work."

"Of course," Patterson agreed reaching in her backpack, handing him her license and a business card.

"Her name is Alicia Sands," Pierson read while keeping an eye on her. "Her address is 2100 Potomac Blvd., apartment 1603," he held up the card. "She works in Channing Photography in the Washington Center Mall."

"Her story checks out," Sergeant O'Donnell stated running the license. "She's free to go."

"Your story checks out," Pierson stated handing her the articles.

"Thanks for your service, Officer Pierson," Patterson gleamed as she walked to her car.

Leaning his head to his shoulder, "the girlfriend is leaving."

"Kathe, stay with her," Ramsey ordered. "Sam, keep your distance."

"Copy that," Sam answered. "She's pulling into a gas station just before the freeway."

"Kathe, see what she's doing," Ramsey requested.

"Copy that," Kathe answered moving the mosquito behind her.

"Ah," Ramsey grinned. "She wants to know what's on the thumb drive. She's inserting it into a connector that fits inside her phone."

"What?" Patterson snapped. "It's blank! Who does Connor think he is?" she ejected the thumb drive and threw it on the floorboard. Then, she took off the wig and contacts.

"It's a stolen ID," Sydney stated, cross-checking the name with another source. "Alicia Sands did live at that address and worked in the mall. That is a picture of her. The only problem is that after researching it with several searches, Alicia went missing leaving work last Christmas after working late. Someone masked this part of the file. That's why the sergeant let her go."

"Patterson's burying herself deeper as she goes," Ramsey grinned. "Now we know what happened to Alicia Sands. Good viewing for Thornhill when we're ready."

Sunday, July 5th
1515 (3:15 PM EST)
Jenkins' Condo in Washington, DC

"Patterson is one mad lady!" Kathe chuckled retrieving the mosquito as Patterson entered the freeway. "She's questioning Johansson's loyalty."

"She's going into the city," CC said handing the iPad back to Kathe.

"She's going to Jenkins' condo," Ramsey assumed. "It's close to the Pentagon. Patterson's on I-395 East. She'll cross the Potomac River passing Long Bridge Park, and then exit onto East SR 110. Jenkins' condo is in Pentagon City."

"She's doing just that," Sam agreed. "I'm keeping my distance."

"Copy that," Ramsey noted. "There's the exit. Jenkins' condo is not far away on Roosevelt Drive. It's in the gated community of Thomas Jefferson Condominium."

"She just stopped at the gate," Kathe noted. "She's handing her driver's license to the guard."

"Impressive," Ramsey stated. "He saluted her and gave her back the license."

"She's turning on Roosevelt Drive and stopping at the first building," Kathe stated sending mosquito ahead and then handing CC the iPad. "CC, it's all yours."

"Jenkins lives on the top floor, #1017," Ramsey shared as Patterson entered the elevator and pushed the 10th floor button. "And of course, she has a key to his condo!"

"Sorry, Ramsey," Kathe sighed as the mosquito stayed behind Patterson.

"Don't be sorry for me," Ramsey promised. "Be sorry for Patterson and Jenkins."

"I knew that was coming," Sam whispered.

"I heard that!" Ramsey snapped. "I wonder how many times Patterson slept in there after me! What's taking her so long to open the door?"

"She's trying to bypass the alarm system!" Rodger confessed. "Jenkins had me block it."

"Can you let her inside without Jenkins knowing?" Sydney asked.

"If you want me to," Rodger admitted.

"Yes, I do," Sydney approved as Rodger opened his app and pressed enter. "Thanks, it worked. She's going inside."

"She doesn't want Jenkins to know she's been there," Ramsey noted watching her enter the condo.

"Patterson seems to know where to go," Kathe stated. "She went straight to his bedroom and is looking through his desk."

"It's not here!" Patterson slammed the last drawer. She went into the closet, moving his winter coats.

"I didn't know that safe was there!" Ramsey bellowed. "She's trying to bypass it as well!"

"Do you want me to let her open it?" Rodger asked.

"Yes, I sure do!" Ramsey grinned as Rodger allowed Patterson access.

"I saw that Johansson set that up for Patterson," Rodger admitted watching Patterson pillage through the drawers. "Jenkins suspected someone had been in his house but couldn't prove it. I found that she looped the camera."

"Can Jenkins check his camera now?" Sydney asked.

"No, this is my bypass for protection," Rodger confessed. "I knew that Jenkins was going to get rid of me when I discovered he wasn't on your side."

"If Johansson, did it for Patterson," Ramsey speculated, "that means he had access to Jenkins' condo."

"He did," Rodger stated watching Patterson slam the door shut. "I blocked him, too."

"The laptop isn't here, either!" Patterson screamed checking behind clothes. "The only other place is White Plains!"

"Rodger, does Jenkins have a house in White Plains, New York?" Ramsey asked.

"Not that I was aware of," Rodger declared. "After I worked on his condominium, Jenkins took me to a house on an island. From there, we met you on the cutter."

"Patterson is leaving the condo," Kathe noted. "Do you want me to leave the mosquito inside her plane?"

"Yes," Ramsey agreed listening to Patterson contact Dulles for a flight plan to Westchester County Airport. "You're going to White Plains," Ramsey said contacting the Dulles Tower.

"Ramsey, I just contacted an old classmate from college, Stanley Issac," Sydney cleared the line. "Stanley went into real estate in White Plains. Gen. Thomas Jenkins walked into Stanley's office about six months ago, saying he was an old friend of my family. He wanted to buy a house close to ours. So, Stanley sold Jenkins the house at 7200 Eisenhower Drive. Jenkins also had the property recorded in his company's name, Patton Enterprises, LLC. That is how his men showed up at my house. Chameleon found a hidden LLC inside that one, Blue Water Haven, LLC that lists his assets; the Embraer Phenom 100, an island named, Translucent Pearl near the Bahamas, and his DC condominium."

"The Translucent Pearl!" Ramsey steamed. "He must have recently transferred the title of the island to his LLC! Pearl was the name of his deceased wife! That must be where Pearl went when we had our rendezvous! That would have been his getaway after he killed me and got JAKE and Chameleon! Wait a minute. That's a private residential residence. Why would the realtor tell a stranger where you lived?"

"He didn't tell Jenkins the address," Sydney stated. "Every home has a privacy clause no matter who wants to know. Stanley doesn't know what I do for a living. I ran into Stanley the last time I was home on R & R. We had dinner and talked about the good old days in high school and college. All Stanley knows about me is that I became a surgeon like my mother. I have a hectic practice, so I like to come home from time-to-time to get away."

"CC and Rodger, stay in the car while Kathe and Sam move Joe from the Citation to his new ride to me."

"Oh, darn!" CC laughed. "I wanted to see the look on Joe's face."

"For that request, you'd have to stand in line," Ramsey chuckled. "Kathe, you've got to beat Patterson to Jenkins' house," she declared checking with the control tower. "White Plains is only thirty-five minutes away with the Citation. It's cleared and ready to go as soon as you board. It will take Patterson roughly an hour, depending on if there's no tailwind. I also arranged for the tower to slow her takeoff."

"Copy that," Kathe stated. "We're on our way to the airport," she said as Sam passed Patterson on the freeway and entered the airport.

"Good," Ramsey advised receiving a message from control. "Mr. Falcini just landed at Dulles. They are switching planes. Kathe put Joe on the jet with the Falcini's."

"My pleasure," Kathe agreed. "We're going through security as we speak. Just a minute."

"Joe is never going to leave you alone," Sam stated getting on the tram. "I heard it in Joe's voice when he was singing."

"We all heard it," Kathe admitted holding on to the bar over her head. "Why do you think Ramsey went to Plan B?"

“She’s serious about Joe’s safety, as well as your family,” Sam insisted arriving at Alby Airlines on Concourse F. “It’s not your fault Joe keeps getting into trouble. A lot of this Joe brought on himself.”

“Yorg’s in agreement with you,” Kathe understood getting off the tram. “Ramsey, we’re at Alby Airlines. Where do we go?”

“The Citation is waiting for you at Alby’s private hangar,” Ramsey explained. “Captains Roberts and Michaels switched jets and will be ready to leave as soon as Joe and the coffin are on board. The tower will scramble your IFF Codes, as well as theirs. The agent has orders to let you outside the Jetway. You are to take Joe to the jet next to the Citation.”

“Copy that,” Kathe answered arriving at the last gate.

“We’re Security Agents, Kathe Tierney and Sam Biggs,” she introduced as they showed their ID. “Linda Ramsey said we are to exit from your Jetway?”

“Of course,” Agent Noland stated. “Ramsey called, and I have a car ready to drive you to the private hangar.”

“Thanks,” Kathe replied swiping her badge at the door.

“Joe doesn’t know his plans have changed, does he?” Sam asked as they arrived at the hangar.

“Not yet,” Kathe grinned as they boarded the Citation.

“Kathe!” Joe hurried to her. “Where are CC and Rodger? I can’t wait to get to meet your family.”

“They’re not coming,” Kathe looked Joe in the eyes, “and neither are you. Get your things. We’re escorting you to another plane.”

“What do you mean?” Joe demanded. “You said that I was going to the safe house to stay with your family.”

“That was before Ramsey heard what you said after you took off your earbud,” Kathe stated. “Ramsey rerouted the right people to take you to her. I’ve got to get back to work and can’t deal with you right now.”

“I didn’t say that for Ramsey to hear!” Joe exploded as Kathe walked toward the door.

“Well, Ramsey did!” Kathe turned and walked off the plane.

“Why can’t you understand that Ramsey is trying to protect you?” Sam interrupted.

“Protect me?” Joe questioned. “Or keep me from my family!”

“I think you already know the answer to that!” Sam insisted motioning for Joe to board. “You’re holding us up!”

“Captain Roberts,” Kathe smiled hugging him. “It’s been a while. I thought you retired.”

"I tried it for a while," Robert admitted. "But my heart is in the air."

"Welcome back," Kathe smiled. "This is the last passenger you were waiting on," Kathe said as Joe slowly boarded.

"I know," Roberts grinned. "Ramsey informed me. That's why she put Capt. Michaels and me on this flight. Mr. Sherrod and the other special passengers are to stay anonymous."

"Thank you," Kathe smiled.

"You and Ramsey have saved us many times," Capt. Roberts admitted. "Michaels, and I owe you, big time."

"Aren't you going to say goodbye?" Joe asked.

"The last time I said goodbye to you, I made it clear where we stand," Kathe stated as Captain Roberts walked away.

"But you didn't say anything when I asked you, maybe someday?" Joe insisted.

"I didn't say anything because there can never be another maybe someday between us," Kathe declared. "Yorg and I will have to talk about what to do with you when this is over. Please stay with your bodyguards. You pay them to protect you. We might not be around next time to save you," she turned and deplaned.

"You may take any empty seat you like," Captain Roberts said closing and securing the door. "The flight will be light. We're just holding for one more item before we push back."

Joe stood there watching the Citation pushing back. He watched as the jet taxied toward the runway. "I'm not losing you or my son ever again," he whispered.

"I'm Francesco," the man behind him introduced. "You sound like you could use a drink."

"I sure could," Joe answered. "I'm Joe."

"I know who you are, Mr. Sherrod," Francesco declared walking into the galley. "This is an informal flight. You can help yourself. You look like a scotch on the rocks kind of man."

"Is it that obvious?" Joe asked following him. "How do you know who I am?"

"Alonzo told us," Francesco admitted handing Joe a drink. "He rerouted us here to pick you up."

"Are you one of Alonzo's men?" Joe asked following him back to their seats.

"Let's just say we're repaying a favor for a friend," Francesco grinned looking out the left side of the plane.

“Mr. Falcini,” Francesco chuckled handing him and Miranda a drink. “They’re loading the coffin.”

“That’s good news,” Mr. Falcini chuckled taking a sip of his drink.

“Who’s in the casket?” Joe asked.

“Pietro Bencivenni, the man who put the ring on your finger,” Francesco laughed. “You don’t think we could leave him in the penitentiary where you left him, do you?” he laughed and sat down. “Take a seat and enjoy your scotch. We’re leaving soon. We’ve got a long way to travel in a short amount of time with one body to lose!”

“What do you mean, lose?” Joe asked.

“You’re hilarious,” Francesco laughed. “You don’t think we can give Bencivenni a funeral, do you? And he isn’t staying in a box. Let’s say he’s food for thought,” he laughed harder.

“I guess not,” Joe sighed taking a sip of scotch. He looked out the window as the jet pushed back to the taxiway. Why did Kathe put me with these people? He thought as he took another sip. Are they taking me to Ramsey?

Sunday, July 5th
1630 (4:30 PM EST)
7200 Eisenhower Drive, White Plains, NY

“Ramsey, Kathe and I are down the street from Jenkins’ house,” Sam reported. “We’re getting the drone up,” he said while releasing it. “It’s an enormous, three story Southern-style house with a basement.”

“It’s big enough for Jenkins’ ego to live in,” Ramsey chuckled.

“JAKE is picking up several outside cameras,” Kathe cautioned. “I’m shocked. These cameras are old and outdated.”

“I’m sensing that,” Sydney confirmed. “It will be easy for me to loop them. Sam, bring the drone up to give me a view of the entire property. It is one of the hanger homes. President O’Riley owned it. He would come here instead of visiting Camp David whenever he got a chance. My father did some work in that house for him.”

“That’s good to know if we need a way out,” Kathe stated. “Does the realtor know about it?”

“Negative,” Sydney grinned. “Only The president and his secret service knew about it. My father agreed to the project with the understanding that no one other than them could know about it.”

“Your father thought things out to the last details,” Ramsey complimented.

"He kept his work secret," Sydney admitted. "Kathe, release the mosquito. I want to see inside the hangar. I have a feeling the plane that flew Jenkins' men here is inside."

"Copy that," Kathe agreed releasing the mosquito. "It's on its way. I'll land it near the hangar door. Oh, someone landed here recently," she showed the tracks before entering the hangar.

"Just like I thought," Sydney stated checking the registration. "It's registered under the company, Patton Enterprises LLC," he cross-checked it with the FAA.

"Jenkins did his homework," Ramsey declared answering her phone. "Is anyone inside?"

"Negative," Sydney answered. "I already scanned it. Kathe, I've just looped the cameras. Have JAKE bypass the alarm system and get inside. Sam, hover the mother-drone over the house and switch to the mosquito. We need to get in and out before Patterson arrives."

"Our time crunch just got narrower!" Ramsey declared getting off the phone. "That was the tower at Dulles. Someone overrode my request to slow Patterson's takeoff. They apologized for not calling me right away. They had some issues on the runway. They checked her location. She's on the glideslope into Westchester County Airport."

"It's my fault," Sydney admitted checking the drone. "The battery of the drone Kathe left in the plane failed to warn me that it was low," he pushed enter. "I'm trying to boost the battery remotely, but its power is at zero percent. The only way to charge it now is by docking with the mother-drone."

"We've lost our eyes on her!" Ramsey snapped.

"We'll do it the old fashion way," Kathe assured her. "We're inside the house. We'll have to work faster. Sydney, where is the study?"

"I was about five-years-old when I went inside that house with my father," Sydney recalled. "I remember we walked up a lot of steps. Dad had to carry me up the last flight. I believe the study is on the third floor. Dad wanted to prove he could get in and out of the house without the secret service knowing about it. That's why he took me."

"And of course, you did it," Kathe said hurrying up the stairs.

"Of course, they had no clue we escaped until they spotted us outside," Sydney smiled as he brought up the blueprints. "I'm showing that President O'Riley had an elevator installed afterward off the kitchen. But you already know that. I see you located the elevator on the second floor and are inside it."

"Yes, after climbing two flights, we lucked out," Kathe admitted. "Sam found the study. It is on the third floor."

"Jenkins must have bought it furnished," Ramsey noticed reaching for her phone. "The decor is not his usual taste."

"Stanley said the house came furnished," Sydney confirmed.

"There's no laptop on the desk," Kathe said checking the drawers. "It's not in any of the drawers."

"Patterson isn't landing at Westchester!" Ramsey cautioned hanging up the phone. "She passed it and is heading straight for the runway there."

"We need to hurry!" Kathe exclaimed. "JAKE, are there any traces of an electronic device in this room?"

"Kathe, there is not an electronic device in this room," JAKE responded. "Come on, Sam, I'm looking for a safe," she said hurrying into the master bedroom.

"JAKE, are there any traces of an electronic device in this room?" Kathe asked scanning it.

"Kathe, I'm showing a small, electronic device," JAKE responded. "It's displayed on your screen."

"It's behind that painting," Kathe moved the picture aside. "It's a wall safe," she said leaning the painting against the wall.

"JAKE, open the safe," Kathe instructed.

JAKE's screen lit up, "Kathe, the lock released."

Kathe opened the door, "There's a laptop inside," she reached for it.

"Kathe, stop!" JAKE warned. "There is another electronic device inside."

"JAKE's right!" Sydney cautioned. "Do not pick it up! Sam, bring the mosquito inside the safe. I need to take control of it for a moment."

"It's all yours," Sam complied as Sydney connected with it.

They watched as Sydney walked the mosquito under the laptop. "It's a pressure bomb."

"It's a three-two switch," Ramsey noted.

"I've got to see where the power is coming from," Sydney said carefully walking the drone to the back. "There's no plug on the wall or wires coming out," he said walking the mosquito down the wires.

"Oh, my God!" Ramsey exclaimed. "You can't get to the wires!"

"I see that," Sydney concurred crawling the mosquito further down. "There's the connector," he shook his head.

"It has to be controlled by an app on Jenkins' phone," Ramsey assumed.

“Not necessarily,” Sydney said calling Rodger. “Does the FBI have Johansson’s cell phone?”

“Yes, they do,” Rodger answered. “We haven’t been able to get into either of his devices yet.”

“Let me have a look,” Sydney requested changing to FaceTime.

“CC, Terrance, can Sydney have a look at the phone?” Rodger asked.

“Yes, Sydney must have read my mind,” CC smiled. “I was thinking about calling him.”

“We know that Johansson had access to Jenkins’ condo,” Sydney explained. “I believe he mirrored Jenkins’ phone,” scanning the software using a combination of JAKE and Chameleon Technologies. “It only opens with retinal scan, which luckily I can retrieve in his privacy settings,” he said activating the phone.

“You did it, Sydney!” CC exclaimed as her father glared at it in amazement.

“That’s unbelievable!” Terrance gasped.

“I also found what I need,” Sydney confirmed and pushed send. “I sent you a mirror of his retinal scan. See what else is on it. Rodger, I sent it to you as well. Now, you can get into his computer.”

“I need that also,” Terrance declared.

“Of course, I’ll send it to you,” Sydney pushed send.

“Thanks,” Terrance appreciated checking his phone.

“I’m on the computer,” Rodger smiled. “Let’s see what we can find out about Johansson,” he told the agents around him.

“Kathe, I sent JAKE the app to turn off the bomb,” Sydney advised. “Activate it, and I’ll help you get inside the laptop.”

“Copy that,” Kathe said activating the link. “Are you sure it works?”

“You doubt me?” Sydney quizzed. “I’m showing the power module turned green. You may lift the laptop,” he said bringing the mosquito up the wires.

Kathe did the Sign of the Cross and lifted the laptop. “I’ll set it on the nightstand.”

“Good job,” Sydney complimented. “Plug JAKE into the port, and I’ll take over,” he brought the mosquito out of the safe and hovered it over the laptop. “Sam, take over the mosquito,” disconnecting from it and connecting to JAKE. “I’m inside,” Sydney grinned pressing enter. “I’m cloning the files.”

“Patterson just landed and taxied past the hangar to the back of the house,” Ramsey warned.

“I’m reinstating the alarm without the cameras,” Sydney stated. “She can’t see anything inside. The alarm is activated.”

“Patterson thinks she bypassed the cameras,” Ramsey said zeroing in on her phone. “She’s trying to bypass the alarm on the back door. She’s having a hard time. Johansson must have given her the wrong app.”

“It’s close, but not the same app,” Sydney confirmed checking the monitor.

“There’s no honor among thieves,” Ramsey chuckled. “She’s getting frustrated. She’s trying the same thing that doesn’t work over and over. We seemed to have underestimated her. She’s heading toward the last window on the porch. She bypassed the sensor on the window in case of an emergency,” Ramsey discovered watching Patterson opening the window and climbing inside. “Heads-up! Patterson is inside the house with her weapon drawn! You two need to get out of there! She suspects Johansson is inside!”

“We can’t stop,” Kathe advised. “JAKE is cloning the files,” she glanced at Sam. “Keep an eye out for Patterson with the mosquito.”

“Got it,” Sam agreed sending the mosquito down the hallway to the staircase.

“There’s only one escape route,” Sydney cautioned. “It’s in the study.”

“That doesn’t make any sense,” Ramsey disagreed. “Your father is all about minute details. If someone got into the house, the secret service wouldn’t take the chance of using the hallway. There has to be another way.”

“I agree,” Sydney confirmed scanning the thickness of the walls. “I just found it,” he showed her.

“Patterson’s climbing the stairs, very cautiously,” Sam whispered. “She suspects someone is in the house.”

“I see that,” Ramsey stated. “How’s the cloning?”

“I need another five minutes,” Kathe insisted watching the screen.

“You don’t have it!” Ramsey warned. “You’ve got to hurry and get out of there!”

“Four minutes,” Kathe reported.

“Patterson made it to the second floor,” Sam declared. “She noticed the same elevator that we did. She’s waiting for the door to open,” Sam flew the drone above her.

“Sydney, can you slow the elevator?” Ramsey asked.

"Let's see," Sydney declared bringing up the blueprints again. "The electrical panel is in the basement," typing feverishly, pressing enter, typing, pressing enter, typing, and pressing enter. "I've hacked into the unit," he said as it stopped on the third floor. "I'm deactivating the electronics. That should stop her."

"It's done!" Kathe whispered. "It finished early."

"Patterson's panicking," Sam warned. "She's pushing the open button repeatedly. Now, she's pulling the electronic panel off the wall. She's hotwiring the door."

"Kathe, you must erase the computer by resetting it back to factory settings," Sydney ordered. "Sam, I'll take over the mosquito. You two get out of there!"

"Copy that," Sam agreed.

"I erased the hard drive," Kathe relayed unplugging JAKE from the laptop. "Which way out?"

"Go to the tall dresser," Sydney urged. "Simply pull the back-left corner toward you."

"Patterson is in the study searching through the drawers," Ramsey warned.

"There's a larger than normal return register," Kathe stated.

"Push in the middle of the left side, and then pull it toward you," Sydney instructed.

"It worked," Kathe said as Sam entered first.

"It's a tunnel," Sam confirmed.

"She's heading for the master bedroom!" Ramsey reported. "Close the dresser!"

"It's not as easy as it was opening it!" Kathe whispered pulling the handle.

"Patterson is almost there!" Ramsey warned. "Close it!"

Sam reached around Kathe, pulling the dresser back as Patterson entered the room. It closed with a thud.

"She heard the noise!" Ramsey warned. "She's slowly walking toward the dresser, panning her pistol. Keep real still! She's checking around the dresser, ready to fire. She's trying to move the dresser," taking a deep breath. "Thank God, she didn't know the trick to move it. Now, she's carefully checking around the room. She spotted the open safe and is heading to it. You may quietly proceed."

"Connor!" Patterson screamed looking inside the safe. She spotted the nightstand. "The laptop!" She opened the lid and held her phone toward the screen. “It’s not working! Connor Johansson, you’re a dead man!” She took the laptop with her and hurried to the elevator.

“The tunnel leads to a secret elevator behind the study,” Kathe reported. “We’re heading down now.”

“Use caution outside,” Ramsey warned. “Patterson will be leaving from the back window. Sydney is keeping the drone on her.”

“I’m refreshing the battery,” Sydney stated pressing enter. “This one won’t run out.”

“She’s heading straight to the plane,” Ramsey said watching her remotely opening the door with the fob.

They watched as Patterson entered the plane and sat her backpack next to it. She turned on the computer, took the connector out of her bag, and connected to it.

“She’s trying to download the files,” Sydney grinned.

“It’s blank!” Patterson shouted. “Connor erased the files! Perhaps, I can restore them!”

“Somebody is having a terrible day,” Ramsey chuckled.

“Since I’m so close,” Kathe began. “Can I go to visit the children?”

“Yes, but just for a little while,” Ramsey agreed reaching for her phone. “Sydney and I will keep an eye on Patterson. After you leave on your way to the safe house in DC, you can help us go through some of Jenkins’ files. We need to compare it with Johansson’s main computer.”

“Copy that,” Kathe agreed bringing the mother-drone inside the SUV as Sam drove off.

“Ramsey, there is a wealth of information on Johansson’s main computer,” Rodger reported. “For starters, Patterson was the Attaché for Gen. Robert Thompson at the Pentagon. Thompson already deep-vetted Patterson to work at the penitentiary to move people for them. Then he sealed her records.”

“That’s why CC couldn’t find Patterson’s information,” Ramsey stated.

“It gets better,” Rodger continued. “Johansson was given access by the former president to all the files in the top agencies. He had a plethora of names of persons-of-interest to choose from at his disposal.”

“Then, why didn’t Johansson see Jenkins coming?” CC asked.

“He didn’t think Jenkins knew about Chameleon,” Ramsey answered. “Jenkins only found out about it when he was with us before he arrested Thompson. Remember, Jenkins was clueless as to how we handed him, Thompson.”

"After that, Jenkins blackmailed Johansson into hacking into Gen. Thompson and Senator Franks files that were sealed by the former president," Rodger read. "Jenkins placed Macaby at that penitentiary to get access to Thompson, who knew all about Chameleon."

"Jenkins also underestimated how deep Patterson was in on all this," Ramsey surmised.

"We all did," CC confessed.

"According to Johansson's notes, Patterson had him arrange for Warden Thornhill to be on the committee with President Trumore concerning prison reform. That way, Thornhill couldn't come back to the prison while she removed Thompson before Jenkins found out. She arranged for Dr. Pasha Kamenkovich, Yetsun's private physician, to admit Gen. Thompson to Cedar Hospital with a fake illness. Then, Patterson set the charges to blow a hole in the back wall as Prado was landing at the SLT Airport. Johansson coordinated the entire scheme through his contacts. Prado built the escape route out of the prison and arranged for Spinello to fly Gen. Thompson to Cuba to join Yetsun. They replaced him with Jethro Tinsdale, a former intern to Sen. Bernard Franks at the time of his death. He had a gambling debt with the Falcini's. When Franks died, Tinsdale couldn't pay the debt. He agreed to change his looks and live out Thompson's sentence rather than to be beaten to death with baseball bats."

"That would persuade me," CC sighed.

"Tinsdale and Macaby knew enough about Frank's scheme to keep Jenkins' head full of ideas concerning Chameleon," Rodger read. "Patterson wouldn't let Jenkins talk directly to Thompson. Jenkins worked with Gen. Thompson for years. Patterson was afraid that if they talked, Jenkins would immediately know that it wasn't the real Thompson."

"That will be good information for Warden Thornhill," Ramsey stated.

"Exactly," Rodger agreed. "Patterson allowed Jenkins to visit Macaby on a regular schedule. Patterson would sneak Macaby out for dinner with Jenkins in between the guards making their rounds. Sometimes Macaby would spend the night with him."

"That confirms what Hiltree suspected," CC concurred.

"Send me that information," Ramsey requested. "I think it's time to bring Thornhill up to speed. Keep up the good work."

"It's on its way to you," Rodger replied attaching the file and pressing enter.

"CC, have you got anything?" Ramsey asked.

"Dad is going through Johansson's phone while I am going through Patterson's laptop," CC reported. "It confirms what Johansson noted. Patterson was in Afghanistan with Gen. Thompson in the Air Force. She's a sharpshooter and pilot. She saved Thompson from a sniper. That's when Gen. Thompson brought Patterson back to the states to be his Attaché at the Pentagon. She and Thompson were lovers. He took Patterson on expensive vacations all over the world. Of course, his wife and children never found out. It was always on a business trip with the government paying for it."

"It all proves Patterson's loyalty is with Thompson and not Jenkins," Ramsey chuckled. "Send me what you've found so far."

Sunday, July 5th
1840 (6:40 PM CT)
Merritt Penitentiary, MO

"I think it's time to check back with Warden Thornhill," Ramsey told Sydney. "Bring up that drone's camera."

"You do realize that Thornhill will put an APB out on Patterson," Sydney cautioned bringing up the mosquito's camera.

"Of course, I do," Ramsey grinned. "However, I think I can persuade Thornhill to let us handle it. I want to squeeze Patterson and hopefully she'll run to Thompson."

"Let's see what Thornhill is doing on the computer," Sydney said moving the drone behind him. "He's still trying to find out who vetted Patterson."

"Let's give Thornhill some interesting information before we show him his renovations," Ramsey smiled.

"What?" Thornhill exclaimed as Sydney hacked into Thornhill's computer screen. "We already found what you're looking for," Thornhill whispered reading the display. How did you get into my computer? Thornhill typed.

How I got in, is not essential. Sydney typed. The information I will give you is crucial. Are you interested?

Yes, Thornhill replied.

We have proof that Patterson keeps two separate sets of books at work. Sydney typed. On her work computer, she reports the events of her shift that she wants you to know. Patterson keeps the actual events on her laptop in her backpack. She also forwards her encrypted daily files to someone she is working with at the Pentagon. Patterson was the Attaché for Gen. Robert Thompson of the Joint Chief of Staff for the Air Force. She was also his mistress, and he kept her very comfortable.

Interesting, Thornhill typed. Patterson began working with me about five months before Thompson arrived. I can't find who vetted her to work in our high-tech facility.

It was Gen. Thompson that deep-vetted Patterson to work at Merritt Penitentiary. Sydney informed him.

When? Why? Thornhill asked.

Jenkins discovered that the now deceased Senator Frank and Thompson were involved in espionage, resulting in his arrest. Jenkins also arrested Sabrina Macaby for her involvement in the scheme. The former administration appointed Jenkins as Head of Homeland Security for his role in bringing them to justice. Jenkins is trying to get his hands on Thompson's scheme, so he blackmailed Patterson. Thompson's plan is still very active with multiple partners. Patterson arranged for your appointment to work with The president and the 'attempted escape' while you were in DC. I say 'attempted escape' because Thompson did escape that night by Dr. Pasha Kamenkovich. He brought back a man named Jethro Tinsdale, who had a gambling debt with the Falcini's. Patterson coordinated this without Jenkins' knowledge. To get Jenkins to seal Thompson and Macaby's records, Patterson allowed him to get close to Sabrina Macaby. That's when Jenkins deemed them classified and a national security risk.

So, you're telling me that the man in cellblock C-55 is not Gen. Thompson? Thornhill asked.

Correct, Sydney admitted.

Is that the reason for switching Macaby? Thornhill asked.

Yes, Sydney answered.

Who was Patterson sending the sensitive information about Merritt to at the Pentagon? Thornhill typed.

That is classified. Sydney typed.

How do I know this is true? Thornhill asked. I don't know whom I'm talking with, do I?

Because I'm the one who arranged transportation of Lauryn Sinéad out of your infirmary and away from the penitentiary, Sydney confessed. At that time, you were beginning to suspect Patterson's actions. However, you could never prove anything. Go to Solitary Confinement, Cell number one, and I'll show you what Patterson has done in your absence. Sydney requested and ended the conversation.

Thornhill dialed security, "Yancy, meet me at Cell number one in Solitary. Have Diane and Blais watch from the cameras." He requested checking his firewall before leaving his office.

"Thornhill might not want this on camera; block them," Ramsey requested.

I must find out how this person knows what is going on inside my penitentiary, Thornhill thought as he walked to the corridor. The Pentagon designed and regularly upgraded our system. He thought pacing the hallway in front of Cell number one while waiting for Yancy.

"Warden, you look troubled?" Yancy asked joining Thornhill.

"I am," Thornhill admitted. "I had an interesting discussion online with our informant. The person hacked into my computer while I was researching Patterson."

"That's impossible!" Yancy declared. "No one can get through our firewalls?"

"That is what the Pentagon told us," Thornhill declared. "This person evidentially is untraceable. I checked before I left my office, and our firewall works perfectly. I doubted the authenticity of the information about Patterson. I asked for proof, and they told me to come inside this cell, and I would have it."

"You're on," Sydney grinned moving the mosquito over the bunk. "You're the only voice he's heard."

"I seem to be calling myself?" Thornhill questioned showing Yancy his phone's screen. "It even has a picture of me. How can someone hack into my secure phone?"

"I'm as floored as you are, Sir," Yancy declared. "The person went into social media and copied a picture of you. They're not on your phone; it's safe to answer it."

"Hello," Thornhill answered.

"Warden Thornhill," Ramsey stated putting the phone on speaker. "I'm glad you put your phone on speaker for Officer Yancy to listen."

"How do you know that?" Thornhill demanded looking around for a camera.

"How I know is not important," Ramsey stated. "You asked for proof that I'm telling the truth. I am the one that warned you of Macaby's attempted suicide and the corruption in your staff that your security missed. Now, I'm going to show how an unidentified dead man got into your prison. Turn toward the corner of the left-back wall."

"Oh, my God!" Thornhill gasped as a secret door opened.

"Patterson is the one who set the charges to blow up the back wall," Ramsey informed them as they looked inside the doorway. "Patterson hired a company out of Brazil to do this while you were in DC. Her informant arranged your appointment with President Trumore's Task Force for prison reform. That way, you would stay out of town while she helped Thompson escape. A jet landed at STL around the exact time of the 'so-called attempted escape' occurred. Its manifesto stated it had a hundred and twenty men aboard and building supplies. The captain rented a hangar for two weeks. Please, enter the hollowed-out room behind the elevator," she requested watching them. She signaled Sydney to open the back door.

"I can't believe this!" Thornhill exclaimed entering the room as the back wall opened to the outside.

"The cameras never picked this up!" Yancy exasperated.

"If you'll walk straight back to the cement fence, we'll show you how people enter and exit the premises under securities nose."

Yancy called control, "Diane, are you recording this?"

"Recording what, Sir?" Diane asked. "I was about to call you and ask where you were. According to our cameras, no one is at the Solitary Confinement corridor."

"Warden, Diane says the cameras aren't showing us at this location," Yancy reported.

"That's because Patterson put the cameras on an almost untraceable loop," Ramsey confided glancing at Sydney. "Break the loop and show them."

"No way!" Diane gasped as they appeared on the monitor. "How did I miss this?"

"I'll tell you later," Yancy said walking to the fence.

"Patterson allowed the men to replace three of the cement fences panels," Ramsey explained as the middle panel opened, and they walked outside the compound. "These three are a different thickness. An app on Patterson's phone electronically controls the fence. The middle panel slides inside the one on the left."

“How did she pull this off?” Thornhill demanded.

“I think I know,” Yancy realized. “Patterson was meeting with an agent from Homeland Security concerning Gen. Thompson when the blast occurred. She ordered Blais and me to help the guards secure the inmates outside in the common area. Diane was to remain in the control room to monitor the cameras. When we entered the common area, the guards were battling an uprising and needed our help. It was so bad. I had reinforcements from other corridors join us wearing full riot gear. It took over an hour to contain the inmates.”

“I read in your report that several inmates went to the infirmary,” Thornhill surmised. “So, you had to stay away from the area for a while.”

“Yes, Sir,” Yancy recalled. “One inmate had to be transported to the hospital. Blais had to accompany him. It was at least two hours before I got back to the control room and noticed commotion by the back fence.”

“Patterson never contacted you while this was going on?” Thornhill questioned.

“Negative,” Yancy declared. “Diane reported that a construction crew from a local Homeland Office arrived shortly after the blast. They sealed off the area as well as the back fence with thick black tarps. That was an unusual procedure, so I hurried to the fence. Patterson met me behind the prison before I reached the area. She said Homeland needed to take off one of the panels to bring in the equipment to seal the back wall.”

“That’s how Patterson smuggled out Thompson,” Thornhill realized. “She was keeping you at bay.”

“Now that I think of it, Patterson kept me on a wild goose chase to stay away from the area,” Yancy concluded. “Patterson said she was coming to find me and wouldn’t let me in the area. The hospital called, and the inmate died on the operating table. I went straight to Patterson’s office, reminding her that the removal of an inmate had to be witnessed by the two of us. She said Officer Binx of Homeland signed for me since I was on official business. She informed me to stay away from the area because Homeland classified it. She then handed me the file with the paperwork and the agent’s identification cards to document.”

“The file and business cards were blank,” Thornhill declared.

“It couldn’t be,” Yancy stated. “I read through the file and then documented the agents in our records.”

“They used invisible ink,” Ramsey explained. “It lasts for three hours and fades.”

"When you get back to the office, call the Bureau and check it out," Thornhill ordered.

"Yes, Sir," Yancy agreed.

"If you go back inside, we'll close this fence, and I'll show you how she enters back inside the hallway," Ramsey said watching Thornhill take pictures of the open wall with his phone.

Inside as they entered behind the elevator, "If you'll turn this time toward Cell number two," Ramsey requested signaling Sydney to open another secret door leading into that cell. They walked inside as Sydney opened the door to the hallway. "Patterson had them put a sensor on the inside of the wall across from the electronic key panel so she can open it with her phone. She looped the hall cameras and walked out unscathed."

"Yancy, put an APB out on Patterson," Thornhill ordered.

"Now, I'm going to ask you to stand down," Ramsey insisted. "This scandal can't go public. You're already under scrutiny from the DOJ over the death of the guard and four inmates. You're also going to have to answer to the DOJ about another dead inmate."

"How do you know about that?" Thornhill asked.

"I have my ways," Ramsey stated. "With you and your security people fired, Patterson becomes the warden. That way, she's in charge of Merritt, and her secret is safe."

"It does appear Patterson is framing us, Sir," Yancy agreed.

"Patterson and her informant are small pieces of an enormous pie," Ramsey explained. "The dead man in the cell was another piece of the same pie. Patterson had a meeting with your dead man and another man in that cell earlier that afternoon. My people are the agents who removed the body. We will dispose of it. We don't want the more significant pieces to know we eliminated him yet. We intend to make Patterson lead us to the real Gen. Thompson. The man in that cells name was Jethro Tinsdale. At one time, he worked for the late Senator Franks. Thompson will lead us to the ringleader. Don't worry; Patterson and her informant will share the same fate. They'll end up at your penitentiary as permanent guest with no parole."

"I will have to tell the DOJ," Thornhill insisted. "I'll have to show him and request sealing these openings."

"Not necessarily," Ramsey chuckled. "They're electronic. I opened them, and I'm nowhere near you. I can disable them permanently from here. If the DOJ finds this out, it will end all of your careers."

"It's already on video," Yancy declared.

"No, it never was recorded," Ramsey confessed. "I let the two people in your control room see it live and blocked the recording."

"How do I know you're not going to blackmail me?" Thornhill asked.

"Go to C-55 and check for either plastic surgery facial scars around the hairline and eyes," Ramsey insisted. "Tinsdale should also have behind his right ear a half-moon tattoo with two dots. They usually control their replacements with a ring that carries a lethal dose of cyanide. Both items can kill them immediately if they don't follow orders. That will prove I'm telling the truth. Keep watching FNN News. Give us a few days. You'll see Patterson and the others all over the news."

"Why such an elaborate scheme?" Thornhill asked.

"What these people are after would destroy America as well as the world," Ramsey admitted. "When we bring Patterson down, I'll let you watch."

Sunday, July 5th
2100(9:00 PM EST)
Aboard the cutter in the Atlantic Ocean off the coast of Cuba

"Sydney," Rodger called. "I see you have some interesting weather down there."

"Yes, it's only a fast-moving tropical depression brushing the coast," Sydney confirmed. "Smalley says it won't last long. What have you found?"

"I found an email with a large video file attached sent to an encrypted address," Rodger reported. "I'm working with two FBI Agents, and we can't break through the encryption."

"Let me have a look," Sydney requested opening the backdoor to Johansson's laptop. "I've got to go back into the privacy settings," he said typing and pressing enter.

"Johansson used several different languages to mask this address," Rodger shared watching the cursor move around the screen.

"I noticed it earlier when I was inside the program finding the retinal scan," Sydney admitted. "I was in a hurry. However, I did send in a sniffer," he pulled up his program. "The server is offline at the moment."

"It must only turn on when the person is sending or expecting something," Rodger stated. "That way, it's harder to trace."

"Harder, but not impossible," Sydney admitted skimming through his files. "What day was the email sent?"

"It was the last email Johansson sent before Terrance picked him up," Rodger stated. "He was online on the 4th of July about 2130 (9:30 PM EST) when he sent the email."

"The sniffer picked up the last transmission on July 5th at 0220 (2:20 AM EST)," Sydney discovered. "The email address is ESPGOTU01, which is Eduardo Santo Prado," he said breaking the code. "I'm opening the video file," Sydney said pressing enter.

"It's Breaking News, dated July 7th at Osaka, Japan, at 2240 (10:40 PM UTC)" Ramsey gasped. "Sydney put all the teams online with us to watch this video."

"Bernadette and Mikey landed at Guantanamo and are with Alonzo and Hiltree," Sydney reported. "I've got everyone except Stephen and Yorg's team. They are on radio silence."

"Is Terrance with CC to watch this?" Ramsey asked.

"I am," Terrance admitted. "I've been amazed at your work since Dr. Sydney opened Johansson's equipment for us. Your proof of what we've expected for a long time is valuable for us to make the case of the people we suspected."

"Thank you, and good evening, everyone," Ramsey began. "Rodger found the video framing us on Johansson's computer. The email attached reads, 'Carswell will land at the time we discussed. He is bringing the information to the launch site. Here's the video for him to broadcast worldwide during the G-Summit."

"I suspected Charles Carswell's involvement," Hiltree declared. "He and I bucked heads on multiple occasions at the White House."

"What is Carswell's dirty little hands doing with these corrupt people?" Ramsey asked.

"We also need to know how and when Carswell met Eduardo," Kathe declared. "The first week of his appointment as Chief of Staff proved he was anti-American."

"Your real question should be how and when did the man at the top know Eduardo," Terrance stated. "Carswell was Chief of Staff. He reported directly to the president."

"That's been one of our questions," Ramsey admitted. "Play the video," she requested as they watched in utter silence.

"Thank God, you intercepted this video," Skip gasped. "It's practically flawless."

"It's too flawless!" Mack exclaimed. "We've got to tear this apart frame by frame to prove it's a fake."

"CC, you've had time to interrogate Johansson," Alonzo stated. "What have you found out?"

"He's not talking," CC answered. "He demands his right to call his lawyer. He also brags about how he's going to sue us."

"Where's the woman I worked with in Ponce Inlet at the Sheriff's Department?" Sam chuckled. "I watched you get that deputy to sing like a bird. Your technique of persuasion was short and to the point."

"That woman wasn't working with her father-boss at the Bureau," CC frowned. "Thanks, now I'm going to have to do some explaining."

"After the information you've given me, I'm not interested in your methods," Terrance said raising his eyebrows. "On the record, I have to be careful. We're in DC, and the people here aren't friendly to this new administration. My agents are all Patriots, dedicated to protecting this country, the Constitution, and President Trumore. We had certain high-ranking official's dead-to-rights on treason and had to stand down with the last administration. Someone mysteriously lost the proof we gave them. I'm hoping we can get enough hard evidence off the three computers so that I can finally bring those people to justice."

"It's hard to see that America has become a nation of acceptance," Ramsey confided. "People are too busy going about their busy lives to bother themselves with politics."

"We're still missing something," Alonzo cautioned. "Ramsey said from the beginning that Jenkins worked with Johansson trying to steal JAKE Technology at the Pentagon. We're the ones that showed Jenkins that Thompson was after Chameleon Technologies. Then, Thompson deep-vetted Patterson to work at the prison, placing her directly under the warden. If Jenkins worked closely with Johansson, why didn't he know that Johansson was Patterson's, IT man?"

"Because Patterson and Johansson worked in different departments and were never seen together," Ramsey stated. "After Jenkins arrested Thompson, he stopped working with Johansson until Jenkins blackmailed him."

"We also connected the dots for Jenkins to learn that Patterson was keeping secrets from him when we proved Macaby was switched," Kathe declared.

"We did," Sydney agreed. "After we showed Jenkins the video, he left the room and was gone for a while."

"That's right," Ramsey recalled. "He must have called Patterson. When Jenkins came back, he was more aggressive, trying to take charge of us. He threatened to arrest all of us. I had to put him in his place!"

"I don't recall Jenkins slipping away from you any length of time?" Alonzo asked. "He would want to confront them in person. Did he receive any phone calls?"

"Yes," Ramsey recalled. "He had several phone calls where he would leave the room. He said they were from President Trumore."

"While listening to Alonzo, I pulled up June 24th and skimmed Jenkins computer's history," Kathe shared. "When Jenkins took Carrie Anne to the safe house on the Naval Base on June 26th, he documented a meeting with Patterson and Johansson. He threatened to arrest them if they didn't prove their allegiance to him. Johansson mirrored their phones to appease him."

"That's why Jenkins came back in a good mood," Ramsey realized. "He thought he had them where he could control them."

"It's also when Jenkins set his new plan into motion," Sydney declared. "On the video, the layout of my HUB isn't correct. It only shows the back of our heads."

"I note another problem," Terrance declared. "The pictures of the sites in your HUB were of the sites where world leaders are staying in Osaka, Japan. Those sites were just released to the DOJ and Bureau in the wee hours this morning to prevent leaking. President Trumore is en route to Osaka now. We've got to warn him. That video painted the picture that the United States and Israel are behind their planned attack."

"That would turn the world against the U. S. and Israel," Hiltree confirmed.

"We should have all the copies of this video, except for Eduardo's," Kathe stated. "I just found a small video on Jenkins' email and had JAKE open it. It's only pictures of Japan."

"Was it opened?" Ramsey asked.

"Negative," Kathe affirmed. "Jenkins tried to view it from his phone but couldn't open it. He sent a lengthy text back threatening Johansson."

"There's no video on Patterson's laptop," CC confirmed.

"Oddly, Johansson would turn on Patterson," Ramsey reasoned. "Sydney, can you check that?"

"Of course," Sydney agreed hacking into Patterson's files. "It appears Johansson tried to email a large video file, but it did not come through."

"That's why Patterson thinks Johansson has turned against her," Ramsey chuckled. "Especially, since he's not answering his phone."

"What's our next step?" Hiltree asked.

"Oh, I think it's time Johansson sends a text message to Patterson," Ramsey grinned. "She thinks Johansson turned against her. We'll give her affirmation of it. That should force her to run to Gen. Thompson."

"Currently, Patterson's flight plan is to Miami," Sydney checked the drone's GPS. "I believe she will change course to land in Cuba."

"Hiltree, your team needs to get back to Mayarí," Ramsey requested. "I have a feeling Carswell will meet with Eduardo in that little paradise cove you located."

"Copy that," Hiltree agreed.

"Kathe, I'll have Jordan take you to join Stephen and Yorg's team after dropping Sam off to CC and Rodger," Ramsey decided. "The reason for radio silence is because Márquez is concerned about your whereabouts. He seems to have taken a shine to you. He keeps showing up to check if you're back, which is slowing them down."

"Copy that," Kathe agreed.

"Sam, help Terrance and CC make a timeline of events to take to President Trumore," Ramsey requested. "We'll need that soon. That will facilitate AG Kolouski to prosecute them sooner than later."

"Copy that," Sam agreed.

"Skip and Mack, I'll have Sydney send you a copy of the video for you to prove it's a fraud," Ramsey stated.

"Yes, ma'am!" they eagerly agreed.

"We're anxious to get started," Mack declared.

"Okay, you've all got your assignments," Ramsey said and cleared the line.

"Sydney, I'm ready for you to send a text from Johansson's phone," Ramsey sat back in her chair.

"What do you want me to say?" Sydney asked bringing up her number.

"I'm the brains behind our deal," Ramsey began. "I'm cutting the feckless individuals from our group and only working with Eduardo. It has ALWAYS been mine and Eduardo's mission!"

"My pleasure," Sydney grinned checking an alert on the monitor. "I just received word that the other package made it safely, and Mr. Sherrod is landing as we speak."

"That's the perfect finishing touch to my day," Ramsey snarled picking up her phone. "Mr. Smalley, would you take Mr. Sherrod straight to his bunk. I'd like to have a few words with him. I'll meet you there."

"Yes, ma'am," Smalley answered putting on his hat to meet Mr. Sherrod on deck.

"Ramsey don't kill Sherrod," Sydney advised.

"I'm going to put a stop to this once and for all!" Ramsey snarled. "I had Smalley put Joe in the same area as Jane and the children. He wants children; he can entertain hers!"

"I don't like the sound of that," Sydney cautioned.

"Noted!" Ramsey snapped storming out of the room.

Sunday, July 5th
2140 (9:40 PM EST)
Aboard the cutter in the Atlantic Ocean off the coast of Cuba

"Mr. Sherrod, this is your bunk for the remainder of the mission," CPO Smalley ordered. "It's the only private one we have on the ship. Meals are only at certain times of the day. I wrote them down for you and left them on the nightstand. If you miss mess call, you don't eat."

"Thank you," Joe answered. "I don't suppose you can find a guitar I could borrow?"

"I have one in my quarters," Smalley smiled. "I'd be honored to loan it to you if you autograph it for me."

"I'm sure you have a pen for me to use," Joe grinned.

"Yes, would you like me to bring some paper?" Smalley asked.

"That would be perfect," Joe smiled. "I have a song in my head that I've wanted to write."

"I'll bring them to you in the morning after mess call," Smalley offered leaving the room.

"Ramsey, Mr. Sherrod is resting," Smalley reported waiting for her to pass him on the narrow steps to the lower level. "I put Mr. Sherrod down here as you requested. Ms. Slate and the girls are down the hall from him. I'll keep him busy and away from you. I know he's not your favorite person."

"What room did you assign Mr. Glitter Boy?" Ramsey demanded passing him.

"He's in room C-6," Smalley replied. "Perhaps, I should accompany you?"

"That won't be necessary!" Ramsey stormed down the hallway.

"Sherrod's in a world of trouble," Smalley sighed watching Ramsey shove the door open, then slamming it shut.

"Ramsey!" Joe sat up on his bunk.

"I felt sorry for you when Jenkins kidnapped you!" Ramsey snapped.

"The last two years of my life have been a nightmare," Joe sighed standing up. "After my last ordeal, I was finally over Kathe and back to my old self. The band and I began working on a new album. I told Carrie Anne that someday Alek would learn the truth and seek me out. I stayed up late finishing the title song before bed. The next thing I knew, I woke up blindfolded in an airplane. I'm grateful that you sent Kathe and her team to save me," he offered to shake her hand.

"That's not what I heard you tell Kathe after you turned off your earbud this morning!" Ramsey shouted.

"Did you put an implant in me?" Joe demanded. "How do you know what I said to Kathe?"

"I've got eyes and ears everywhere!" Ramsey warned. "There's nowhere you can crawl that I won't know! You brought this on yourself when you wrote those posts about Alek! You put a target on his back and yours! Jenkins discovered that you're Kathe's kryptonite, and by killing you, it would destroy her! I had no choice but to assign them to find you when I needed them elsewhere! For time's sake, I almost put you with Kathe's family! Until I heard the wheels turning in your head to seize the opportunity to gain access to Alek!"

"Another dangerous situation that you put my son in the middle of!" Joe yelled.

"Kathe was calm and handling the situation with the little boys!" Ramsey touted.

"Not until I joined Kathe to sing Alek's favorite lullaby to calm him down before those men got there!" Joe screamed. "They almost killed my son as I watched Kathe's phone screen!"

"Alek wasn't the only one in trouble!" Ramsey snapped. "All of her children were in danger because of you! Her friends, their daughter, and Paris Sydney were also in danger! Kathe kept a cool head, along with Paris and Pete! That is what saved their lives, not the song!"

"You'll never know what it's like to be a famous singer and never get to sing to my own son!" Joe detested. "He called me daddy for the first time! Do you know how many times I've dreamt of that day?"

"I thought you were over Kathe and Alek!" Ramsey quoted.

"I was until I saw Alek in danger!" Joe shouted. "I'm tired of my life being collateral damage for you catching criminals! It is your fault for putting Kathe and me together two years ago in Ponce Inlet. We ended everything and were going on with our lives!"

"I didn't!" Ramsey confessed. "I was ordered to put you together or be fired! I trusted Kathe to be levelheaded! She knew her boundaries!"

"Well, I guess Kathe's boundaries didn't include her emotions?" Joe smirked.

"Even after Kathe let you into her life, you knew what she did for a living and what was at stake!" Ramsey steamed. "You couldn't keep your big mouth shut! That's what caused all this mess! You're still a Glitter Boy! Do you know how many times I've sent my teams to save you?"

"Trust me," Joe confessed. "I wish I was back with my band on tour and never met Kathe."

"That's not what this song is about!" Ramsey reached in her pocket and shoved some papers in his face. "This is the song you were finishing the night you were kidnapped! It's a song about your romance with Kathe! It shows me that you talk out of both sides of your mouth! And I quote, 'you said no one would keep me from my family!' You better never sing this song unless you're in the shower! It puts a Bull's-eye on you and them!"

"There's no way you could know that!" Joe declared.

"I already warned you that I have eyes and ears everywhere!" Ramsey reiterated.

"It's not up to you if I can see my son!" Joe shouted. "Kathe said we'd discuss it after this job! You can't stop that!"

"Do you want to make a bet?" Ramsey quizzed. "Remember who was on the plane with you on the way here and who was in that pine box! They'll never find his body! That's what I'm capable of ensuring! Until this crisis is over, I'm in charge of your life! What you do, and when you do it! Now, there's nowhere on this planet that you can run from me, ever! You're being tracked at all times!" She turned and left, slamming the door behind her.

"I'll take that bet!" Joe hit the wall.

"Ramsey, is everything, all right?" Smalley asked, waiting for her outside the door.

"Everything is perfectly normal!" Ramsey stormed down the hallway.

Chapter 8
Monday, July 6th
0530 (5:30 AM EST)
Sierra Maestra, Cuba

"I feel like I haven't slept in days between our work and the rough seas," Ramsey admitted handing Sydney a cup of coffee. "Even when I get in bed, my mind won't shut down."

"Are you sure it didn't have anything to do with your talk with Joe before you went to bed?" Sydney questioned.

"I got my point across to Mr. Glitter Boy!" Ramsey snapped. "Let's say I made him an offer; he can't refuse. What is the next subject?"

"Did you?" Sydney asked rewinding the footage. "I gave you privacy when you talked to Joe. Here's what he said as you slammed the door," he pushed play.

"I'll take that bet!" Joe hit the wall.

"Once Joe calms down and thinks about what I said, he'll change his tune," Ramsey stated, "because I won't; next subject."

"Tropical Storm Delilah isn't helping Stephen's team either," Sydney reported as an alarm sounded on the console. "It seems that when the weather gives us a break, Márquez shows up," Sydney declared calling Stephen. "Heads-up, Márquez is on his way up the mountain by helicopter. You know what to do."

"Jay just warned me," Stephen admitted. "Has the package arrived?"

"Arrived and intercepted," Sydney confirmed. "It is a little wet but will be delivered momentarily."

"We are ready for the rendezvous," Stephen advised and cleared the line. "Jack, bring up the footage Skip sent us late last night. Will, start the final edits on the last section."

"Yes, Sir," Will agreed sitting down next to Jack.

"I've got the email," Jack stated pulling it up. "I'm glad we sent this to Skip and Mack's computers early last night. They aren't going to be available to help us until they debunk that video."

"It's always good to stay ahead of a situation," Stephen concluded. "That way, when something unexpected arises, you're ready."

"We knew Márquez would be back when he left the last time," Will insisted. "He was firing questions at you as fast as he could. He was trying to trip you up with your previous answers. You handled him perfectly. He was mad when he left."

"He was, wasn't he?" Stephen chuckled.

"Is this where you want to start?" Jack asked.

"Yes, just slow it down," Stephen replied scrutinizing each frame. "It's looking pretty good. I see they changed the layout. Those edits seem to flow smoother."

"I agree," Jack complimented. "I like this revision better."

"I'm not sure about the special effects they used for the title," Will noted. "It shows the sweet, little hummingbirds as violent-warriors."

"You have a good point," Stephen admitted. "I'll have Skip tone it down. Send an email approving the changes, but still considering revising the title," Stephen requested as he received a text. "Jay said the helicopter is landing and the package is very close," he stated texting k to Jay. "I hope Márquez buys Ramsey's idea."

"My money is on Kathe's performance," Jack declared leaving the tent with Stephen and Will.

"I hope you're right," Stephen confessed. "We're in a time crunch to find the cave and he's slowing us down."

"This goes beyond him being nosey," Will stated. "He's suspicious."

"Good morning," Ramsey joined them via earbuds. "My plan will work. Remember to smile and be pleasant."

"Jay, I'm taking over the drone for you to join them," Sydney stated connecting to it. "Márquez needs to see the team together?"

"I hope Márquez buys it and leaves for good this time," Jay commented reaching inside his backpack for his camera.

"He should," Sydney declared. "It's backed up by the film. Ramsey and I previewed it. It looks perfect."

"For all our sakes, I hope so," Jay cautioned joining the others. "The clock is ticking."

"It's too bad you couldn't just shoot Márquez," Stephen chuckled watching him with several arm guards getting out of the chopper.

"Don't think it hasn't crossed my mind," Ramsey confessed. "Márquez is such a thorn in our sides. But all is not lost; you haven't been thrown out of the country yet," Ramsey said watching Márquez hold onto his hat, leaning under the rotor blades, and joining them.

"Sr. Brown, I see you haven't moved from this site," Márquez noted.

"We are working on the final edits to see what we need to finish the documentary," Stephen offered.

"What a good idea," Márquez agreed. "Since you're filming is almost complete, may I preview what you have so far?"

“I never share my work until the final edit is in the can, so to say in our business,” Stephen declared. “I’m afraid you’ll have to wait.”

“You can’t blame me for asking,” Márquez chuckled. “I was also wondering when Dr. Reese was joining you again. Your visa in this country will expire in a few days,” Márquez reminded as his guards turned their weapons toward the trees behind them.

“Senor Márquez, alguien viene!” a guard yelled looking through his scope. (Sr. Márquez, someone is coming!”)

“That is Dr. Reese and Denisov,” Stephen stated. “She texted me that they were close. They’re another reason we haven’t broken camp yet. Dr. Reese said she’s bringing us some footage that would be helpful.”

“Ah, Dr. Reese, you finally returned,” Márquez extended his hand. “I wasn’t told that you reentered the country.”

“I landed at Guantanamo Bay,” Dr. Reese shook his hand. “My boss needed my input on a project we were working on before I left.”

“What kind of project?” Márquez asked.

“I’m not at liberty to discuss my work,” Dr. Reese smiled reaching for her iPad. “Although, why I was there I did copy some photos Denisov, and I took that I thought you’d like to see. I sent a text to Stephen. They are a perfect ending for the documentary,” she said showing a picture.

“Is it an insect?” Márquez asked.

“Yes, in North America and Europe,” Dr. Reese answered. “It’s a Hummingbird Moth. I have several pictures of the Snowberry Hawk Moths and the Hummingbird Clearwing. The Snowberry or Hemaris Diffinis is sometimes called the ‘hummingbird moth’ or ‘flying lobster,’” changing pictures.

“I see you captured a pair mating!” Stephen exclaimed. “These pictures would be an interesting contrast to the documentary.”

“Dr. Reese did a small video about these beauties,” Denisov added pulling it up on his iPad. “We learned that Hummingbirds are warriors. Their beaks are astounding, and they have a penchant for violence. Check this out,” he showed them.

“My footage depicts their striking, majestic colors, mating, and eating habits,” Stephen admitted. “That video brings a different perspective that I only thought was winsomely used in poems and songs. I didn’t think these tiny, cute birds would be violent.”

“Skip nailed the animation on the title page!” Will laughed. “It depicts Hummingbirds as sweet, innocent, little birds, and then switches to a pair violently fighting.”

"That's because I sent Skip the video," Dr. Reese admitted. "I knew Stephen would approve it."

"You read my mind!" Stephen exclaimed. "Sr. Márquez, if you don't mind, Jack needs to send an email to Skip. Tell him I approve the title."

"He may leave," Márquez answered. "I look forward to viewing the documentary."

"Yes, Sir," Jack smacked his hands together. "It's perfect," he laughed walking away.

"After witnessing these birds, I realized that Mother Nature is capable of anything," Dr. Reese admitted.

"Jack, I'll download this footage to your computer," Denisov said catching up with him.

"Perhaps, I should stay and learn how you locate birds and capture such wonderful pictures?" Márquez quizzed.

"What you're asking would violate my trade secrets," Stephen denied. "I'm sure you understand."

"I didn't mean it that way," Márquez apologized.

"Yes, you did," Dr. Reese boldly expressed. "But we'll forgive you anyway. If you'll excuse us, we need to get started," she shook Márquez's hand.

"That's our little-cookie-cutter!" Ramsey exclaimed. "There's nothing like being bold and to the point. Márquez has the power to arrest them and seize their equipment."

"Kathe did put Márquez in his place," Sydney disagreed watching Kathe walk to the tent. "They're leaving, and I think it will be for the last time."

"Yorg, what did you discover while I was gone?" Kathe asked as the team entered the tent.

"We located what we think is one of the entrances," Yorg admitted. "Jack, bring up the footage of the drone Jay left at the clearing."

"It was right where we found the land mines," Jack admitted rewinding the footage. "A helicopter appears to be landing on the clearing. However, watch what happens next," he said slowing down the footage.

"It's just like I thought," Sydney changed cameras and zoomed in on it. "It is an invisible dome. Interestingly, tiny mirrors make up the dome. The mirrors reflect the surroundings, therefore causing a masking effect."

"Sydney, with what we've learned so far about the technology they use," Stephen added, "there were no visible signs of refraction from a glass dome-like in Miami."

“I’m not detecting a high-frequency radio wave jammer, similar to the ones we’ve already found,” Sydney declared scanning the area. “That would cause a blanketing effect.”

“Perhaps, it is only activated while in use,” Ramsey suggested. “That is what we suspected in the cove we found in Mayarí.”

“That is a possibility,” Sydney considered. “It would deter any outside interference.”

“Something turned the dome and the land mines off when I walked over that area,” Jay admitted.

“The forcefield only activates by an approaching helicopter,” Ramsey surmised. “That’s what happens when Eduardo receives an email. Otherwise, his server is off. It’s harder to trace.”

“There has to be another entrance,” Kathe reminded. “Mariah was found wandering by a fast-flowing river. Cambria said Maria was drenched and that Mariah can’t swim. Is there a waterfall in that area?”

“We haven’t found one yet,” Stephen answered. “We’ve had several drones up.”

“If they can mask a heliport, they can mask a waterfall from the air,” Kathe concluded. “You need to follow the river with the drone skimming above the water.”

“Copy that,” Jay answered. “Jack and I will get right on it.”

“While they do that, we’ll break camp and head towards the river,” Yorg stated. “That way, we’ll be close when the drone finds it.”

“Let us know when you find it,” Ramsey agreed clearing the line.

“We’re getting another call from Rodger,” Sydney glanced at Ramsey, answering it.

“Ramsey, the former administration appointed Johansson to be in charge of several security systems,” Rodger reported. “One is the operation of the penal systems.”

“That’s how Patterson was able to control the cameras,” Ramsey assumed.

“Yes, a second was at the FBI,” Rodger stated. “When CC joined us, Sydney blocked the Bureau, and in turn it blocked Johansson. He also has a backup of his data stored in a chip located in his right deltoid.”

“Then, we’re going to have to extract that device,” Sydney admitted. “Dr. Ylia can be there in an hour.”

“I better pick her up at the airport,” CC advised. “Dad doesn’t want anyone to bring attention to this address.”

"Copy that," Sydney understood. "I'll let you know before Ylia lands. Rodger, I need you to run a scan from the beginning to see if you can find who authorized it. This kind of authorization could only come from the top."

"CC, Sam, run a scan on Patterson and Jenkins' computers," Sydney continued. "We need to know when the former administration first encountered Eduardo."

Monday, July 6th
0720 (7:20 AM EST)
Santiago de Cuba, Cuba

"The text you sent to Patterson on Johansson's phone worked," Sydney told Ramsey as another alarm sounded. "Patterson just landed at the airport in Santiago de Cuba. Do you want me to erase Johansson's text off her phone now?"

"Not yet," Ramsey cautioned. "It may come in handy. Bring up the drone's camera and keep the drone close to Patterson. She'll lead us straight to Gen. Thompson, and maybe Eduardo."

"I charged and activated this drone," Sydney smiled pulling up the drone's camera. "That's odd. Patterson isn't leaving the cockpit."

"She's stalling," Ramsey noted. "Patterson seems to be glaring at something out of the window."

"Let me check," Sydney said moving the drone inside the cockpit to see outside the windshield. "From the looks of the limo with the extremely darkened windows driving on the taxiway toward her plane, she has a mystery greeter."

"It's not the Cuban government," Ramsey declared. "There would be armed soldiers surrounding the plane by now."

"Patterson is putting on her headset, restarting the engines, and turning around," Sydney declared. "Let me turn up the sound!"

"This is going to be good," Ramsey grinned.

"Torre de Santiago de Cuba, esta es Cessna CLR8 solicitando una salida inmediata." (Santiago de Cuba Tower, this is Cessna CLR8 requesting an immediate departure.)

"Cessna CLR8, su solicitud ha sido denegada," the Traffic Controller began. (Cessna CLR8, your request has been denied.) "Te trajimos a esta área para estacionar debes desembarcar de inmediato." (We brought you to this area to park you must deplane immediately.) "La persona que le importa que aterrice en nuestro suelo quiere hablar con usted." (The person that allowed you to land on our soil wants to talk to you.)

They watched as Patterson threw off her headset and got out of her seat. She reached behind the pilot's seat, opened the closet, taking out the two laptops. Patterson opened a compartment in the middle of the plane and put them in a hidden area behind a fake wall. Then, she opened the door, and the steps lowered. She watched the limo approach from inside the doorway.

"That doesn't come standard in overhead compartments," Ramsey stated watching her slowly deplane. "The suspense is killing me! If not the government, who gave her permission to land on a Cuban Military Installation?"

"We're going to find out any second," Sydney watched as two people got out of the front seats. "They're opening the back doors."

"It's two of our favorite rats, Spinello and Jenkins," Ramsey grinned watching them emerge. "Oh, Patterson does not look happy. I can't wait to hear this conversation."

"Odd," Sydney noted. "The limo moved away from the plane and stopped. I guess to give them privacy."

"Let's find out," Ramsey requested. "Turn up the sound."

"You look surprised to see us here," Spinello declared holding his hands in the air. "We've tried to reach you, Johansson, and Bencivenni with no luck. Then, you leave your post and show up here. Does Warden Thornhill suspect something?"

"No, Thornhill gave me two weeks off for always working the holidays," Patterson explained. "I couldn't reach Johansson, so I flew to his apartment. His car was in his usual parking spot, but he still wasn't answering my call. I have a key and know the code, so I went inside. The downstairs was untouched. However, when I went to his office, all his electronics were gone. Since Johansson works at the Pentagon, I was afraid he got busted, so I came straight to warn Gen. Thompson."

"Why didn't you call me first?" Spinello shouted. "When we rescued Thompson, I made it clear to you to stay at work, no matter what! I had several other inmates placed there so you could release them."

"You didn't call me either!" Jenkins snapped. "I brought Bencivenni to Merritt to take the two inmates with him for replacements. He picked one for Russia's second in command, and one for Italy."

"That's your fault!" Patterson insisted. "Johansson told me that Rodger Slate turned on the GPS on his phone. The inmates were waiting in cell number two with me to leave with you. Bencivenni went ballistic when I broke the phone and wanted to leave immediately."

"I had to get Bencivenni away," Jenkins admitted. "He called his men the second he got out of the car. I called your cell phone, and you didn't answer, and then I tried to reach you at work. When I put in your extension numbers, it went straight through to Warden Thornhill's office. That's when we put two-and-two together and left the area."

"My phone works perfectly," Patterson defended. "I've been trying to reach you and Spinello. Your phones go straight to voicemail."

"That's odd," Jenkins declared. "I received no calls or messages from you."

"I also tried to reach you as well, after I couldn't reach Bencivenni," Spinello added. "Just like Jenkins said, it went straight to voicemail. I tried for hours trying to reach Nikkoli. He finally answered me and confessed that Bencivenni wasn't at the drop zone. He described the only car that passed them that day was your hunter-green Nissan Altima. He said he tried to stop you, but you sped past them."

"I saw the limo at the drop zone," Patterson admitted. "No one tried to stop me. I thought they picked Bencivenni up and waited for me to pass by them, so we weren't seen together."

"That's strange!" Spinello raised his voice. "Nikkoli and Arón said they tracked you to your condo! It seems that you bugged out and tried to blow up the place. There was a lingering smell of gas that was strongest in the kitchen. Someone was there before them and opened the windows and turned off the gas stove. Then defused a bomb upstairs."

"That's a lie!" Patterson denied. "The remodeling of the prison worked. Warden Thornhill is as dumb as a stump! I tried to call Jenkins to turn around and take the two inmates. I could have still gotten them out. Thornhill's wasn't due back from DC until tomorrow night," she said as a skirmish arose from several men dragging someone out of the limo.

"They got our message loud and clear when they found Metarha," Ramsey grinned.

"That's why they beefed up security on top of the mountain," Sydney admitted. "We had no choice but to save those children," he moved the drone. "Watch Metarha."

"I'll get back to you in a minute," Spinello pointed at Patterson, turning his attention to three of his men having a hard time with wild, vicious Metarha.

"They got their hands full with her," Sydney smiled watching Metarha dropkicked two men, jumping on the third one's back, choking him with the ropes binding her hands.

"She's a highly-skilled killer," Ramsey observed as more men hurried out of the limo and attacked her. "If they didn't have a backup, she would have gotten away in the limo," she chuckled watching them drag her to Spinello and dropping her at his feet.

"Well, well, well, if it isn't the woman that can't follow orders!" Spinello shouted as Metarha glared up at him. "I warned you not to kill that young boy and his grandfather! It didn't take long before Eduardo's informant found their bodies in the jungle! Then, I received another phone call that they found you hogtied to your bed, and Teodoro had his throat slit. Someone threw a woman's torn, bloody shirt across his body," he said as Metarha feverishly tried to talk.

"Should I remove her gag?" a bodyguard asked.

"No!" Spinello snapped. "She doesn't deserve to speak after the brutal beatings of an innocent, defenseless, nine-year-old boy and his grandfather!" he exclaimed pulling out his pistol and shooting her between the eyes. He turned his gun toward Patterson.

"Mr. Spinello, I can prove I'm telling the truth," Patterson pleaded. "It's on my phone! Johansson text me that he and Eduardo are cutting the feckless people involved! That means all of us! That's why I was coming to warn Gen. Thompson! He and Gen. Yetsun need to know this information."

"Show me the text!" Spinello demanded as she reached for her phone and scrolled through her text messages.

"Here it is!" Patterson exclaimed showing him. "I don't know what Johansson and Eduardo have in mind."

"That text message saved you for now!" Spinello confirmed putting his gun away. "Nikkoli and Arón proved to me that I couldn't trust them. I kept them on the phone until my men arrived. Let's say I don't have to worry about their loyalty anymore."

"As I said, after I received the text from Johansson, I bugged out of my condo and came here to prove my loyalty," Patterson lied.

"Come with us," Spinello checked the time walking to the limo. "We've got to clear the runways. A surprise guest is landing to visit Eduardo in a few minutes. Once he takes off, you are to take a helicopter and go to Gen. Thompson and Gen. Yetsun. Jenkins, you are to rejoin

Sydney and Ramsey. We need you to document them in the act of treason with their teams in Japan."

"I've been away from them so long, it won't be easy," Jenkins cautioned. "They'll be suspicious."

"Aren't you Mr. Homeland Security?" Spinello shouted. "If you think about double-crossing us as you did them, you'd better think again! That's not a threat! It's a promise that I will keep! Get in the limo! I'll drop you off at your jet! After the surprise guest takes off, you will too."

Ramsey watched Jenkins glaring at Spinello, walking ahead of him. "That's the same look Jenkins gave me at the condo after the attack," she observed as Jenkins walked around the limo and got inside. "He's got something up his sleeve."

"I'm curious as to who the surprise guest is," Sydney declared hacking into the tower. "The tower is bringing an unidentified craft in now."

"How so?" Ramsey asked.

"The pilot is only communicating digitally with the tower," Sydney declared watching Jenkins get out of the limo by his jet. "It's not identifying its call numbers either."

"It's unmarked as well," Ramsey noted as they got a visual on the craft. "Jenkins is curiously watching it with his phone in his hand."

"Jenkins is videotaping the landing," Sydney declared moving the mosquito over his head. "He didn't shut the door to his plane yet. Jenkins was in too big of a hurry to see who landed. Let's get a closer look," he said flying the mosquito out of Jenkins' jet to the taxiway.

"It's Charles Carswell!" Ramsey gasped watching him deplane and walking to a small helicopter. "What kind of helicopter is that? Can you see the call numbers?"

"Give me a second," Sydney said moving the drone closer. "It's ESPGOTUDR5. It's a single-passenger drone."

"Carswell isn't a pilot," Ramsey declared watching him get inside the cockpit and buckling up the seatbelt. "I know that for sure."

"Carswell doesn't have to be a pilot," Sydney explained. "I thought this was still only in the experimental stages. The computer onboard is programmed to take ordinary people places," he said watching it take off.

"You need to get the mosquito back to Jenkins before he takes off," Ramsey warned.

"It's on its way," Sydney agreed flying the mosquito back inside the jet behind Jenkins. "He documented Carswell landing and taking off in the drone," Sydney said watching Jenkins laugh as he replayed the video. "Look at that grin on his face. He's going to double-cross all of them, as well as us."

"I'll give Hiltree and Alonzo the heads up to watch for Carswell," Ramsey declared reconnecting to them in Mayarí.

Monday, July 6th
0945 (9:45 AM EST)
Sierra Maestra, Cuba

"We're ready," Stephen sighed watching Jack finish pulling up the editing equipment in the main tent. "We'll start where we left off about the title."

"Yes, Sir," Jack answered finding the footage.

"It's time to go to earbuds and contact Sydney," Jay warned docking the mosquito with the mother-drone. "Márquez is fifteen minutes away."

"Sydney, we barely made it back to camp," Stephen reported. "Márquez is on his way to our campsite."

"I was just about to call you," Sydney cautioned. "Things just heated up in Santiago de Cuba. You might be in danger of an ambush. Bernadette and Mikey were with Alonzo. I moved them into a position to protect you. Report what you found before Márquez arrives."

"I was able to skim the mosquito above the water and fly under a very concentrated barrier hiding the waterfall," Jay began. "We found the hidden entrance into the cave. Through a narrow passage between two tall, rock walls that opens into a large, deep cave, midway up to the top of the mountain. The drone's battery began to drain, so I moved it out of the cave."

"The way the mountain curves around to another peak got me thinking about a double-waterfall," Kathe added. "So, I had Jay fly the drone close to the mountain around the curve to the other peak. We found a second waterfall a little higher up. The drone located a small passage leading into a different part of the cave. This entrance was closer to the waterfall so that a person would get wet. There was no path leading down the mountain. It must be the way that Mariah got away from her capturers. Her grandfather said they found her wandering by the river soaking wet early the next morning."

"That got me thinking," Jay continued. "I brought the drone around to the first waterfall and located a well-traveled path. I followed it down to a clearing with a helicopter pad. We witnessed a helicopter land. Ten people got out and headed up the trail to the cave. They looked like engineers coming to work."

"Jay mentioned the drone's battery started to drain inside the cave," Jack added. "This signifies another barrier inside. We're going to have to work the old fashion way."

"Why can't we program the drone to charge off extra camera batteries?" Will asked. "That way, the drone can work underground since the power source will be with us."

"That is possible!" Sydney exclaimed typing the scenario into the computer. "Yes, the Bluetooth capability will work since the power source is within range. We will be able to watch and help you."

"Will and I can use JAKE to program the drone from here," Yorg declared. "It shouldn't take us too long."

"Do it," Sydney requested checking the GPS of Márquez's helicopter. "Márquez will probably pull your visas. Make sure you act surprised. If he tries to confiscate your computers and threatens you, don't worry; give him the password hummingbird12. I programmed that password as a safeguard to delete your hard drives in case this happens. If you must leave Cuba, I'll reroute you back to Guantanamo, and we can finish the job."

"We don't have time for this!" Stephen snapped. "We finally found our objective! Once we get inside that cave, we'll know what they've got planned. We think it's a mini-control room. That shouldn't take us long to destroy."

"We've got enough nitro to blow the facility," Yorg declared. "Will hollowed some of our camera equipment to house the charges, so Márquez can't detect them."

"Good idea," Sydney complimented. "That will save time."

"Someone must have found the coyote's burnt truck, and warned Márquez," Kathe stated.

"I still think Márquez was in on the raid by the river," Jay noted. "Especially since he tried to tag along with us for our safety."

"Márquez did know about that stopping point," Stephen admitted. "I filed it with our itinerary."

"Márquez did try everything he could to board our boat or leave his men to protect it," Jack pointed out.

"I don't think Márquez is a civilian as his profile states," Sydney realized checking Márquez's location. "I'll do more research on him."

"That would explain why Márquez is so suspicious of us," Yorg addressed.

"Smile, you should have a visual of Márquez anytime now," Sydney cautioned. "I'll stay online with you. If there's trouble Bernadette, and Mikey are there now and will take care of it."

"You heard Sydney," Stephen stated listening to the helicopter land in the clearing. "Quiet on the set, lights, camera, action."

"Sierra Maestra, final alibi, take 1," Will stated holding up the clapperboard and then slapping the clap shut.

"Don't get cocky guys," Kathe warned. "If they found the coyotes, they're even more suspicious how we made it through that area unscathed. It's not rocket science to put two-and-two together."

"In that case," Stephen cleared his throat and began adlibbing. "I like Denisov's suggestion that we should hold the Warrior Hummingbirds until the end. That will enhance the title."

"I agree," Kathe took on her role as Dr. Reese, playing along, watching the screen over Jack's shoulder. "We should make a 30-second commercial to intrigue birders across the world to buy the documentary."

"It's a perfect marketing strategy to captivate Márquez's audience," Will agreed. "Márquez will have twice the impact on tourism than he ever dreamt."

"Did I hear someone mention my name?" Márquez asked walking inside the tent with quite a few armed guards.

"Sr. Márquez," Stephen turned around. "Yes, we were discussing some ideas for you to use for marketing strategies. What do we owe the honor of your presence twice in one day?"

"Unfortunately, I'm here on official business this time," Márquez declared as the guards surrounded them. "I'm here to inform you that effective immediately, your visas have been revoked. My men will pack up your equipment. Presidente Castrello wants me to review the footage before we return them. If what is on your computers and cameras are what you say, we will give them back. Then, we are to escort you to your boat and then to your jet. You can send me the final video when you finish it. Then, I will send you the final payment as we agreed."

"Confiscating our equipment was never in our contract," Stephen defended. "My computers and cameras are subject to International Intellectual Property Laws protected throughout the world."

"Presidente Castrello does not participate in world laws," Márquez confessed. "Castrello was apprehensive about letting you enter Cuba.

Especially after you were in Miami when the Bridgette Océano Aquarium blew up, and that you are working with a U.S. Naval Research Scientist."

"Sr. Márquez, I am a Naval Research Scientist," Dr. Reese declared. "I travel worldwide without any problems. I contacted the office of Gen. Antan Medina and received permission to enter your country with the explicit purpose of working with Sr. Brown," she turned over her passport, showing her visa permit. "I'm sure a simple phone call to Gen. Medina will confirm my story."

"That would be difficult to do," Márquez confided scrutinizing her visa. "We found Gen. Medina's body floating off the coast of Tejas yesterday. I'll have Medina's staff check out your story."

"I'm sorry to hear about Medina's death," Reese lied. "He was an avid birder."

"Yes, Medina was," Márquez agreed. "I'm surprised he didn't tell me he approved your working with Sr. Brown. Medina knew Castrello assigned me to the task."

"I guess it's one of those things we'll never have the answer," Reese apologized.

"Sr. Márquez, I sent you ironclad proof that our filming at the Historic Althea Key Beach was purely coincidental," Stephen proclaimed. "We shot a documentary and commercial for them, similar to the one we're doing for you to bring back tourism."

"That's the only reason El Presidente approved your visas," Márquez admitted. "But the situation here has changed with some unusual deaths on the mountain."

"Can we check out a bird that a villager described to Dr. Reese for the ending?" Stephen asked.

"I wasn't aware that Dr. Reese talked to the villagers," Márquez noted.

"Sr. Márquez, you know as well as I do that the locals are the eyes and ears of the area," Reese declared. "If the villager is correct, he described a Hummingbird Topaz."

"The smallest bird in the world!" Márquez marveled. "That would be a record find for Cuba! However, I'm afraid that will have to wait. You and your photographer are to leave with Sr. Brown if all is clear on your equipment."

"I'll have to report this to my commander," Reese stated. "I'm sure you realize the diplomatic problems that could arise by threatening a Naval

Research Scientist. In my many visits to Cuba, I know that Cuba does have to follow International Intellectual Property Laws."

"Sr. Brown," Márquez changed the subject, "I need a password to get inside your equipment. I'm sure you have one for a guest."

"I'm giving you a password with the understanding that I'm turning you into the Board of International Intellectual Property Laws," Stephen promised poking Márquez in the chest with his index finger.

"Sr. Brown," Márquez stepped back as two guards pushed Stephen back.

"That's enough," Jay stood in front of Stephen.

"It would behoove you not to show aggression," Márquez grinned. "This isn't the United States."

"Stand down guys," Sydney cautioned as Jack got in between them also.

"I have Márquez in my sight," Bernadette reported. "Say the word, and he's gone."

"My lawyers will contact you!" Stephen snapped.

"The password, Sr. Brown," Márquez demanded.

"The password for a guest is hummingbird12!" Stephen scoffed. "Again, you're using this at your own risk!"

"Hey, you, be careful with my camera!" Denisov snapped approaching the guard after he threw the camera in a bag.

"Jamel, maneje este delicado equipo con cuidado," Márquez demanded. (Jamel, handle this delicate equipment with care.)

"Sí, podria ser nuestro para mantener," Jamel laughed. (Yes, it might be ours.)

"Team, stand down," Sydney cautioned. "Jamel knows Stephen and Denisov are mad and is trying to provoke a fight. It will look better if they kill you now. That way, Márquez can make a public statement that you are spies and attacked them. Bernadette, keep your eye on them."

"Copy that," Bernadette answered.

"Sydney," Mikey requested. "I'm going to use our mother-drone to check down the mountain for problems."

"Copy that," Sydney approved.

Monday, July 6th
1030 (10:30 AM EST)
Outside of Mayarí, Cuba

"We were right about Márquez pulling Stephen's visas," Sydney told Ramsey.

"We never expected an easy outcome," Ramsey sighed. "Getting into Cuba went like clockwork but getting out will be a challenge."

"We've got the right teams to pull this off," Sydney admitted. "Now, where is Jenkins?"

"Listen, Jenkins is talking to the tower at Santiago de Cuba," Ramsey turned up the sound. "His flight plans state he's heading for Miami. But I don't see that happening now. Carswell's arrival made him nervous. He realized they are keeping secrets from him."

"Ramsey," Alonzo called as Sydney connected to Hiltree's drone. "The mosquito we left in the cove just alerted us of movement from the lake. Eduardo's yacht is entering the cove from the ocean."

"Nice yacht," Ramsey watched the livestream. "Hiltree, have the mosquito check if anyone else is with Eduardo."

"Copy that," Hiltree replied flying the mosquito onto the yacht.

"Eduardo is alone," Alonzo confirmed watching his iPad. "He's getting off the yacht, walking toward the heliport, checking his phone."

"Hiltree, move the mosquito over Eduardo," Ramsey requested. "Let's see what he's doing."

"Eduardo's deactivating the forcefield over the heliport and checking the GPS coordinates of the drone," Sydney noted watching Eduardo's phone screen while typing commands on his computer. "He programmed the single-person drone to land at the heliport. The upper-middle camera shows it's precisely lowering onto the pad," Sydney stated turning up the sound.

"His single-person drone doesn't make a sound, like our drones," Hiltree noted. "That's impressive for something that big."

"They are good for the ecology, including noise reduction," Sydney admitted. "Non-pilot businessmen don't have to worry about traffic. They travel over it to work. The FDA still has them listed in the experimental stages. Eduardo seems to have perfected this one."

"I read where the Postal Service and UPS plan to use something similar to deliver packages," Ramsey declared watching Eduardo slowly lower it.

"That's the biggest mistake any government could approve," Alonzo chuckled. "In our business, it would be an effective tool to eliminate someone and never leave our home."

"Or a terrorists attack from continents away," Sydney admitted. "I already sent President Trumore my report on that very subject."

"How is Carswell connected to Eduardo?" Ramsey wondered watching the door open.

"Carswell hated our Constitution and Israel," Hiltree declared. "He always pushed to eliminate it and take away the Second Amendment. It looks like when that didn't work while he was in office, he found another way."

"Not necessarily," Sydney declared. "While we were talking, I cloned Eduardo's phone. I can control the drone carrying Carswell."

"How did you do that without Eduardo knowing?" Ramsey asked.

"By bundling the security fields of both of our technologies," Sydney proclaimed. "Eduardo does have a strong one, but I noticed a lapse in his defense when he turned off the forcefield. Let's listen to them."

"Charles, I trust you felt safe in my new toy?" Eduardo chuckled shaking his hand.

"Eduardo, this isn't the first time I've trusted you for help," Carswell admitted. "The interference you ran during the failed attempt to save our men in the Middle East was undetectable. It proved to be a financial gain for our backers."

"Not as much as this deal will prove," Eduardo promised.

"Does this mean you've obtained Chameleon?" Carswell questioned.

"Not yet," Eduardo sighed, "but we're close. This deal will work with or without the use of Chameleon. Come inside the cottage and we'll go over the details."

"I warned you that without Chameleon we would not be able to control other world leaders!" Carswell insisted.

"You weren't worried when we pillaged billions from your country and dropped it off to your colleagues in the Middle East," Eduardo reminded. "Remember your buddies who are the enemies of the United States? Did your backers not benefit from it? After that, leaders worldwide admired you and your boss for causing anarchy in America, as you said you would. They voted your boss to lead as the first president of the 'One World, One Vision.'"

"He studied the United States for years," Carswell admitted walking to the cottage. "In college, he concentrated on their laws and how to get around them. Once we used the race card, his adversaries backed off. But I must admit, we had a hard time convincing the Congress that some of the things we did behind their backs was necessary for world peace."

"Come now," Eduardo chuckled. "They were afraid to go against you, thanks to my tutelage and technology. Come inside the cottage. We'll have a drink and go over the video you're going to broadcast at the G-Summit. It will soothe all your fears," he promised opening the front door.

"They carefully never mention Carswell's boss' name," Sydney worried pulling up the Internet. "Since Carswell left office, he hasn't stayed close to anyone he worked within the administration. He hasn't been active in his party. We need to find out who this boss is."

"Did you note a bit of jealousy in Eduardo's voice?" Ramsey asked. "Make sure the mosquito follows them inside. You know what they referred to, don't you?"

"Of course, I do!" Hiltree exclaimed flying the mosquito behind them. "I lost friends that night!"

"The only thing that ever came out of Carswell's mouth that I agree with is that without Chameleon they can't control world leaders," Sydney discussed. "I'll leave it at that for now. Let's listen."

"I believe your drink is scotch on the rocks," Eduardo remembered handing Carswell a glass.

"Your taste in art is exquisite as well as remembering my choice of refreshment," Carswell complimented walking around the room. "Each piece is an original."

"I'm a man that likes to be surrounded by beauty," Eduardo confessed. "Since I've had to live behind a mask, it is the one pleasure I'm able to enjoy."

"Your paradise cove is a reflection of your love for beauty," Carswell agreed. "Some of the exotic flowers are not indigenous to this part of the world."

"You have an eye for detail," Eduardo admired reaching in his pocket and taking out a flash drive. "Let's see if you like what Johansson put together for us."

"Johansson proved to be one of my greatest assets at the Pentagon," Carswell confessed. "If it weren't for him, the administration wouldn't have gotten away with half the things we did behind Congress' backs. The way Johansson sent leaked text messages of phone conversations was undetectable to our 'so-called' experts."

"Do you think the weather will affect our plans?" Carswell asked.

"No," Eduardo chuckled, "it couldn't have come at a better time. If anything, it will back up our alibi. How could a missile from Cuba be fired during a bad storm? The rocket will have to take off tonight due to a window opening in the atmosphere precisely at 2200 (10:00 PM EST)," he grinned pushing play with the remote.

"While they brag and drool over the video," Ramsey interrupted. "I believe it's time for Warden Thornhill to contact FBI Agent Terrance Sims."

"I'll connect you," Sydney said placing the call. "You just gave me an idea. I've got to call Skip and Mack."

Monday, July 6th
1230 (12:30 PM EST)
Federal Bureau of Investigation, Washington DC

Breaking News: "I'm Robert Morwitz, with FNN News reporting live from inside the Federal Building. We are awaiting a press conference from Special Agent Terrance Sims momentarily. The memo that was sent to the press stated that Sims wanted to get ahead of any leaks." The cameraman panned the inside of the room, showing the press corps. "Agent Sims is approaching the podium," Morwitz announced as the camera zeroed in on him.

"Good afternoon," Agent Sims began. "As you read in the memo, I am holding this press conference to stay ahead of any leaks. At 1100 (11:00 AM EST), I received a phone call and then emailed proof from Warden R.D. Thornhill at the Merritt Illinois Penitentiary. After talking at length to Warden Thornhill and reviewing the emails and videos Thornhill sent, I have issued a Federal Warrant for three people. The first is Warden Thornhill's Assistant Warden, Officer Janice Patterson. The second is Gen. Robert Thompson, who was sent to Merritt for a life sentence for treason. Thornhill has proof that Patterson helped Thompson escape with the aid of this man, Conner Johansson. Johansson was an employee at the Pentagon and a holdover from the previous administration. Johansson failed to report to work this morning."

"Agent Sims, how could Gen. Thompson escape a Federal Maximum-Security Facility?" Tom Brioche of CCN News asked.

"I will not take any questions at this time due to the ongoing investigations," Sims answered and left the room, while several reporters shouted out questions. The cameraman zoomed in on Sims walking down the hallway with two agents, ignoring the press.

"Agent Sims stated this press conference was to get ahead of any leaks," Morwitz reiterated. "Sims did state he has proof that Warden R.D.

Thornhill shared with him concerning the three suspects. We will keep you informed as we are given the information," the camera switched to the radar over the Atlantic Ocean.

"The Nation Hurricane Bureaus has downgraded Tropical Storm Delilah," Morwitz showed. "It is dissipating over the Grand Bahama. That is good news for the upcoming scheduled launch this evening at the Cape. I'm Robert Morwitz with FNN News signing off."

Monday, July 6th
1245 (12:45 PM EST)
On the cutter in the Atlantic Ocean near Cuba

"Well, Agent Sims just sent a clear message to Jenkins," Sydney admitted as the newscast ended. "So far, Jenkins thinks he covered his tracks by hiding who deep-vetted Patterson. After Carswell showed up in Cuba, and that press conference, Jenkins will panic."

"Oh, I'm banking on it," Ramsey agreed. "After watching Jenkins' film Carswell landing in Cuba, the wheels in his brain geared up to frame Carswell. That's why he'll double back to Cuba and land at Guantanamo."

"We will see," Sydney stated. "The only problem with that is keeping Jenkins away from Hiltree and Alonzo."

"I'll warn them as soon as Jenkins changes course," Ramsey declared. "What did you discuss with Skip and Mack?"

"A big surprise in Japan," Sydney chuckled sharing his plan.

"A fitting demise of Carswell after what he did to our country," Ramsey laughed as her phone rang.

"Ramsey, Ylia was able to retrieve the implant in Johansson's right deltoid," CC explained. "You won't believe who works with Eduardo?"

"Charles Carswell?" Ramsey answered.

"Yes, how did you know?" CC asked.

"We watched Carswell land alone in Santiago de Cuba and got into a single-person drone," Ramsey declared. "Then, we watched Eduardo control the drone bringing Carswell to his paradise cove."

"Do you know some of the things those two have pulled off while Carswell was in office?" CC questioned.

"We heard them bragging about some of them," Ramsey admitted. "Sydney needs me. I'll call you later. Keep up the good work."

"Bernadette and Mikey are in strategic positions around Stephen's team," Sydney shared checking those cameras. "Hiltree gave them the new motorcycles that I tinkered with and put inside the Huey."

"Bernadette, Mikey, hold your positions until we see what Márquez plans to do," Ramsey requested. "We don't want to spook him."

"Copy that," Bernadette answered looking through her riflescope. "They've just finished putting Stephen's equipment in the helicopter."

"That's strange," Sydney admitted watching Márquez with the mosquito. "Márquez left in the helicopter with the computers and camera equipment. He left guards to escort the team down the mountain by foot."

"Why isn't Márquez flying them out?" Ramsey asked. "He's in a military chopper. There is plenty of room."

"He's planning on ambushing them!" Sydney realized. "Stephen and company, your earbuds are hot. I know you're listening to our conversation. Be ready for anything."

"Do you want me to engage them now," Bernadette asked following them through her scope.

"Negative," Ramsey answered. "That will alert Eduardo that we are near his cave. They won't do anything until Márquez checks the equipment. This will buy the team some time."

"Márquez is not going to be so happy when the hard drives delete in front of his eyes," Sydney cautioned.

"Then, he'll circle back around and demand they open the locked cameras," Ramsey confessed. "With Kathe posing as a Naval Research Scientist, he has to have proof of them being spies. Kathe, have everyone ready."

Kathe coughed signaling they understood, motioning for the others to pick a target.

"Syd, Alonzo is calling," Ramsey picked up her phone. "Stay with Kathe's team while I take this call."

Monday, July 6th
1330 (1:30 PM EST)
Outside of Mayarí, Cuba

"Ramsey, we just got an alert from the mosquito that we left in the bedroom at the villa," Alonzo reported. "Pauli has that drone. Hiltree and I are keeping an eye on Carswell and Eduardo."

"I'm pulling up that camera," Ramsey said. "Pauli, who's in the bedroom?"

"It's an unknown female," Pauli stated following her with the drone. "She walked into the bathroom."

"I see she is wearing a veil, like Eduardo," Ramsey noted pulling up the Internet. "She looks to be about the size of Catarina, Eduardo's wife."

"It has been a while since Catarina surfaced," Pauli admitted.

"Just enough time to have undergone surgery and recover," Ramsey suggested. "That would answer why we haven't seen her. Stay with her. Maybe she'll take the mask off now that she's inside her house. That would tell us who they intend to replace."

"So far, she's keeping it on," Pauli shared. "She's getting suitcases out of the closet."

"She's packing for her and her husband," Ramsey noted. "I'm beginning to have my suspicions of what they're planning."

"The G-Five Summit starts tomorrow," Pauli reminded.

"I don't think they'll show their hands for a couple of days," Ramsey declared. "The schedule for the first day and the morning of the second is usually laying out the itinerary. These two will wait until some of the itineraries are well underway, and votes have been cast to make their move."

"That should give us enough time to get into position," Pauli concluded.

"Good, we have to stay in front of their moves," Ramsey agreed. "Stay with her."

Monday, July 6th
1400 (2:00 PM EST)
Sierra Maestra, Cuba

"Since you left your mosquito inside the helicopter with Márquez, I brought up ours," Bernadette stated.

"There was no other way," Sydney confided. "I have to know who does Márquez's report to. I don't think it is Castrello."

"I don't either," Bernadette confided. "Not with the way Márquez stays on top of this mountain. I have our mosquito watching the team."

"I took our mother-drone up to check the surrounding areas as you requested," Mikey reported. "About two miles down the mountain, I located about twenty guerillas off to the left side. Then, I scouted further down the mountain. I found men around this building in the trees."

“That’s the guerilla’s station the team engaged, saving the four little girls from the coyotes,” Sydney stated. “We were afraid that would give us away.”

“You did the right thing,” Bernadette approved. “Alonzo told us about it.”

“Yes, I have children those ages,” Mikey shared. “We’ll get ahead of this situation. I counted about fifteen guerillas waiting at the station. With the drones, I was able to get around the first wave and am in point position by the station.”

“I notice with Bernadette’s mosquito that they are tightening the team,” Sydney pointed out checking the cameras. “Team, it looks like they are corralling you into the Kill Zone to strike.”

Yorg coughed acknowledging Sydney.

“With the tightening of the team, they may check them for weapons,” Bernadette cautioned.

“That would prove to be the last thing they did,” Sydney answered. “Stephen, Will, if this happens, remember the weapons that Jay gave you.”

Both men shook their heads, yes.

“Okay, be ready and follow Kathe or Yorg’s lead,” Sydney advised. “Bernadette, I note the first wave ahead has fanned out. Is it possible for you to take out a few?”

“My pleasure,” Bernadette reported. “These quiet motorcycles make it easy to sneak up on people quickly,” Bernadette complimented heading toward a lone target.

“One thing I learned from Eduardo in Miami is always to anticipate every scenario,” Sydney admitted calling Stephen’s HUB. “Skip, Mack, Márquez will report what is happening to his superior. I believe he reports directly to Eduardo. We have enough soundbites of Márquez talking. Splice together a tape of Márquez reporting that they have proof on the cameras that the Americans were spies.”

“Copy that,” Skip answered. “We’ll get to it right now.”

“Sydney, a helicopter is approaching the guerilla station,” Mikey warned. “I need to get into a higher position.”

“Be careful, it’s Márquez,” Sydney recognized checking the screen. “Márquez found out quickly that the computers are blank, and the cameras have him locked out. Will installed that feature for me, thank God.”

“Should I lighten the opposition or take them all out?” Mikey asked.

“Hold off for a while,” Sydney requested. “I don’t want to spook Márquez, just yet.”

"Copy that," Mikey agreed. "When the time comes to engage them, I programmed the mother-drone to hover over the area."

"Perfect," Sydney complimented. "I'll be able to help you get them out alive."

"Copy that," Mikey declared.

"Sydney," Bernadette reported. "The guards marched the team through the guerillas. They stayed out of sight and didn't engage. Now, they are following them at a distance. Of course, three are missing along the way so far. I'll keep whittling them down."

"Keep up the good work," Sydney advised. "Márquez landed by the guerilla station to greet them. Mikey is there and ready to engage."

"As soon as I get close enough, I'll get up in the trees," Bernadette declared.

"Good advantage point," Sydney agreed. "The way I've seen these terrorists operate; if we take out Márquez and the leaders, the rest will turn and run. That way, we can take his helicopter and fly straight to the top with no opposition. It all depends on who Márquez is reporting to."

"That would be a game-changer," Bernadette noted. "I'll report my position as soon as I get into place."

"Copy that," Sydney sat back in his chair and glanced at Ramsey. "It looks like we may get a break."

"There is more good news," Ramsey admitted. "Listen to this," rewinding a tape and turning up the sound.

Monday, July 6th
1420 (2:20 PM EST)
FNN Newsroom, Washington DC

Breaking News: "This is Robert Morwitz with FNN News reporting live from our newsroom in DC. We are interrupting the regularly scheduled program to bring you live to Cape Canaveral, Florida. The Private Space Program Timpco is set to deliver a statement," the screen switched showing the space rocket on the launch pad at the Cape in Florida.

"This is Greer Lovell, Operations Director for the Private Space Program Timpco," he introduced. "On July 2nd, Astronaut Samuel Benjamin aboard the space station presented with a slight fever. Physicians for Timpco working with Astronaut Jane Wells, a former medic for the military and aboard the space station, reports that Benjamin's fever has elevated. He is unresponsive to any of the treatments. Wells will accompany Benjamin on the return trip. Astronaut Albert Saul, a Timpco physician, will replace Wells to monitor the astronauts aboard the station."

"As Benjamin's illness worsens, and with Delilah moving swiftly away from the Florida coastline, the manned launch originally scheduled for the 9th will take place at 2200 (10:00 PM EST) this evening. The rocket was originally slated for a routine flight to bring supplies to the station. Now, the rocket will drop off the supplies and bring Benjamin and Wells home. Astronaut LCDR Ross Elliott will replace Benjamin and Astronaut Dr. Albert Saul's will replace Wells."

A picture of Elliott and Saul showed on the screen. Then, the screen split, showing five astronauts on the catwalk walking to board the rocket.

"We will update you as we await the countdown," Morwitz reported as the cameraman switched back to the newsroom. "Astronaut LCDR Ross Elliott returned from the space station last year," a short clip of Elliott getting out of the rocket that landed in the ocean off the coast of Florida a year ago played. "This will be Elliott's third tour of duty. He also trained the crew aboard the space station. So, he is very familiar with each member," the screen switched back to Morwitz. "This is Robert Morwitz reporting from FNN News in DC. We will keep you updated as we get more information."

Monday, July 6th
1440 (2:40 PM EST)
On the cutter in the Atlantic Ocean near Cuba

"That doesn't make sense," Sydney declared. "The astronauts are quarantined for fourteen days before they go into space to prevent common diseases. Physicians monitor them constantly, making sure they are healthy and strong before going into space."

"I think CC found Carswell's boss," Ramsey read a text. "CC discovered that the former president, Omar Barrick, was hospitalized this morning with a mysterious fever and needed to be quarantined," Ramsey sat back in her chair. "Quarantined suddenly seems to be the keyword lately on the news. Curious, now the former president is quarantined with a mysterious fever," she glanced at Sydney. "When the astronauts are quarantined, isn't it recorded?"

"Every minute of it," Sydney smiled hacking into Timpco's computer system. "The disease would have to be dormant for a short time, and then released. I'm scrolling through the footage for the last week," he said and stopped. “I think I saw something,” Sydney rewound the footage and froze the screen. “Recognize this doctor?”

“Dr. Pasha Kamenkovich!” Ramsey exclaimed.

“The camera shows Benjamin in the room sleeping and wearing a headset,” Sydney shared. “Let me slow down the footage using JAKE Technology,” he said slowing the footage and stopping. “Here is a glimpse of Kamenkovich entering Benjamin’s room before the camera goes blank,” Sydney backed it up several days and slowly forwarded it. “There are no other times when physicians are in the room alone,” he fast-forwarded back to catching Kamenkovich. “By using JAKE Technology, I should find the exact frame in the footage,” he stopped it again. “Here is the frame the second it shut down. With using Chameleon Technology, I can not only slow the film down but elongate Kamenkovich entering. Here he is entering and taking something out of his pocket,” he stopped and zoomed in on the pocket.

“It’s a syringe!” Ramsey gasped. “It happens so fast that the cameras couldn’t pick it up. That’s why Timpco’s security didn’t catch Kamenkovich.”

“Exactly,” Sydney agreed checking the system’s history. “Someone hacked into Timpco’s Security System that morning,” he showed Ramsey the time on the recording. “They stopped the cameras long enough for Kamenkovich to enter the corridor. The camera in Benjamin’s room was separate. I got a glimpse of Kamenkovich entering his door before they shut that camera down to administer the shot. Then, they did the same in reverse for Kamenkovich to leave the building.”

“The protocol is to lockdown the building the moment the astronauts enter,” Ramsey stated. “That means someone with a high-security clearance got Kamenkovich in and out. Can you tell who hacked the cameras?”

“I’m checking,” Sydney said typing quickly. “It was ESPGOTU,” he exited the system.

“Then it proves Eduardo wants to take over the space program,” Ramsey suggested. “That’s what we feared when we found the mini-replica of the Cape’s Control Room in Miami. Eduardo has an inside person already planted.”

“Eduardo probably has several people on the inside to pull that off,” Sydney assumed. “He’s beginning to implement his ‘One World, One Vision.’ Taking over the space program would aid in total domination of the world.”

"We can't let Eduardo shoot down that rocket!" Ramsey snapped.

"We won't," Sydney agreed. "But we don't know what disease Kamenkovich implanted into Benjamin. It could be an illness to cause them to bring him home sooner and spread something major to the world. The rocket is scheduled to land back at the Cape instead of Texas. We need to have Ylia ready to help isolate the disease and find the antidote. Benjamin may have infected everyone in space already. That way, when Eduardo is ready, he can waltz into the space station and take it over."

"Oh, my Lord!" Ramsey sighed. "Then, when Benjamin comes back to Florida, he could infect everyone there. That would cause a different kind of chaos happening as Eduardo finalizes the rest of his plan. I'll contact Hiltree. He'll have to recommend Dr. Ylia to work with the physicians at Timpco," her phone rang. "It's CC."

Sydney glanced at the monitor, "Stephen's team is still safely walking down the mountain. Let's hear what CC has found."

"Hello," Ramsey answered as Sydney switched the call to the console.

"Ellie Barrick was moved to quarantine today at 1300 (1:00 PM EST)," CC reported. "The agent's dad sent to the residence filmed the Secret Service following the gurney out of the house and putting Ellie into an ambulance. They followed the ambulance out into the countryside to Sego Lilly Hospital near a small, private airport."

"According to Johansson, Ellie and Omar will accompany Carswell to Dubai," CC reported. "When Eduardo and Catarina leave Cuba, they will blow up the mansion and cove. That will take place at the same time Eduardo launches the missile to blow up the space rocket."

"Then, it looks like Eduardo told Carswell to speed up the plan," Ramsey noted. "Eduardo didn't mention what was said with the Breaking News a few minutes ago?"

"What Breaking News?" CC asked.

"Let me fill you in," Ramsey began.

"Wait," CC put the call on speaker. "Everyone in this room needs to hear what Ramsey and Sydney discovered," she said as Ramsey explained.

"Ramsey, I found more," Rodger spoke after she finished. "Astronaut Benjamin has a fever on the Space Station. Astronaut Wells is caring for him. Timpco plans to send one of their physicians and Astronaut Ross Elliott aboard the rocket to replace them. Dr. Pasha Kamenkovich gave Benjamin a shot. Eduardo exchanged Engineer Scott Lee and Engineer

London Deveron with his replacements. They stopped the cameras to let Kamenkovich in and out."

"We found where they spliced the footage, so security couldn't find it," Sydney shared.

"That goes along with this," Rodger read. "According to Johansson, Barrick still calls the shots in DC with the aid of Carswell and Eduardo. Barrick leads an elite group of politicians that he corrupted with Johansson's help. Johansson leaked the information from inside the White House. I also found a file marked Jenkins. Johansson has videos showing Jenkins lying to President Trumore on security issues. It shows Jenkins leaking to the press private conversations with the president. It even shows proof that Jenkins smuggled the Cubans and their weapons into the states multiple times."

"I have to send this information to AG Kolouski immediately!" Terrance interrupted. "This can't wait!"

"Only if AG Kolouski sifts through the information and doesn't alert Eduardo or Barrick yet!" Ramsey proclaimed. "We're not sure who all the players are in this secret organization. Weren't you listening to what I just said about a possible plague?"

"I was listening," Terrance admitted. "But AG Kolouski needs to be aware of both matters. President Trumore is on his way to the G-Summit. Should we turn Trumore around?"

"No," Ramsey insisted. "If we stop him, it could look like President Trumore was in on it if he doesn't attend."

"I have to warn President Trumore!" Terrance declared. "His Secret Service Agents have to know of this threat. It could get out of hand."

"Yes, you do," Ramsey agreed. "However, you will not tell them how you got this intelligence."

"I've already given you my word," Terrance agreed.

"Ramsey, I found how far Barrick goes back dealing with Eduardo," Rodger stated. "Barrick went by the name of Kenya Baal Akmul in Afghanistan. That is the name the orphanage gave him when he was left on their doorstep. Eduardo and Catarina prey on young teenage boys in orphanages. They watched Barrick in the orphanage for years without his knowledge. The scholarship Barrick received for college was from the Espírito Mesa Ingeniero, LLC. One of the questions was to formulate a thesis on faking one's death in Brazil to receive the scholarship. Barrick researched the most dangerous places in Brazil and chose Sugar Mountain because of the wind sheers."

"That's why we couldn't find Eduardo researching how to fake the plane crash," Sydney admitted checking his monitor. "Barrick did the research for him. I've got to go," he cleared the line.

"Rodger, let me know when you find anything else," Ramsey requested. "Oh, and Terrance, let me know if AG Kolouski will warn the president without you revealing your sources?"

"I will," Terrance promised. "I'll need to show AG Kolouski the intelligence we have for him to warn President Trumore."

"It is what it is," Ramsey sighed. "We can't let anything happen to the president."

Monday, July 6th
1450 (2:50 PM EST)
Sierra Maestra, Cuba

"Ramsey and all teams listen to this," Sydney advised converging the drone's microphone for all the teams to hear. "The mosquito I left in Márquez's helicopter warned me he's receiving a call." Sydney landed the mosquito by the receiver.

"Márquez, our dream is coming to fruition!" the caller exclaimed. "Have you found what the Americans were doing?"

"Voice recognition shows, it is Eduardo," Sydney relayed.

"Not yet," Márquez confirmed. "Their hard drives erased as soon as I put the password in and pushed enter. I can't get into the cameras. I'm having them brought to me to open the cameras now. I am waiting for them at the first checkpoint station."

"If they won't," Eduardo ordered. "Take the female aside first, and let Jamel work her over. He knows how to force women to talk. Make sure she screams loud enough for them to hear her. Tell the rest that you will spare her life if they do what you want. That will scare Sr. Brown into opening his camera. When you get the information, sink their boat. Then, get rid of them and their equipment. The news report will say they were swept out to sea during Tropical Storm Delilah."

"But Presidente, we need to know if they sent the information to Linda Ramsey," Márquez objected.

"Whether they did or didn't, won't make any difference now," Eduardo bragged. "There's no way they can stop us."

"I will get back with you as soon as it's finished," Márquez agreed hanging up the phone. "Jamel, los necesito apúrate aquí. ¿Qué tan lejos estas?"

"Jamel, it is necessary for you to hurry here," Mack interpreted. "How far away are you?"

"General Márquez, estamos a la vuelta de la esquina," Jamel replied. "Estaremos allí."

"Gen. Márquez, we are just around the bend," Mack relayed. "We will be right there."

"Bueno, prisa," Márquez answered.

"Okay, hurry," Mack said.

"Well, that answers the question of who Márquez reports to," Sydney stated pulling up the Internet. "Teams, we're running out of time."

"Jamel refers to Márquez as General," Ramsey noted. "I thought Márquez was a civilian. Why would Castrello appoint Márquez to be Minister of Tourism?"

"I looked Márquez up before we came," Sydney said scrolling through Cuban records. "It says he owned a string of hotels in Cuba. But the way he's acting, this profile is a fake," he hacked into Brazil's military records. "They were faked. Gen. Ché Márquez served in the military with Eduardo Santo Prado in Brazil. His family owns a hotel franchise, Primera Estrella Del Mar Hotel that Carlos Prado designed and built. There are four in Cuba, Camaguey, Habana, Santiago, and Varadero. This gives me an idea," he said typing commands on the computer and pressing enter.

"That's the hotel in Varadero that Kathe and Yorg found Eduardo staying," Ramsey noted. "Now it's beginning to make sense."

"It sure is," Sydney agreed. "Carlos designed the hotel with secret tunnels to move Eduardo around safely."

"Sydney," Hiltree interrupted. "I received word that Jenkins just landed at Guantanamo. He requested the use of a helicopter without any assistance. He said he's checking on an anonymous tip for the president."

"Keep an eye out for Jenkins," Sydney cautioned. "He may show up there. He now knows Eduardo, and Spinello kept Carswell's involvement from him. I don't think Jenkins knows about Barrick yet."

"We will," Hiltree agreed. "However, I don't think Jenkins will come to Eduardo. I think he'll go to the control room on top of the mountain to confront Gen. Thompson and Patterson."

"You have a point," Sydney declared watching the screen. "Stephen's team just arrived where Márquez is located. I've got to help them," he cleared the line.

"Well, well, well, Sr. Brown," Márquez snapped approaching them. "The password you gave me erased the hard drives on both computers before my very eyes. I guess you think you're pretty smart."

"I did warn you that the materials are my intellectual property," Stephen declared. "I simply protected my investment."

"Jamel, es hora de mostrarle al Sr. Brown quién está a cargo." Márquez ordered.

"Jamel, it's time to show Sr. Brown who is in charge," Mack translated.

"Es hora de que respetes al Gen. Márquez," Jamel yelled, hitting Stephen in the back with the butt of his rifle.

"It's time to show Gen. Márquez respect," Mack translated watching Stephen fall to his knees.

"Stephen!" Jay exclaimed reaching for him as the guards pushed him back, raising their rifles at him.

"Well, Sr. Brown, it seems I've underestimated you," Márquez stated. "I guess you won't open the cameras, will you?"

"No," Stephen answered as Jamel struck him again, raising his rifle to do it once more.

"Sugiciente," Márquez shouted as Jamel stepped back. "Es un hombre orgulloso. Moriría en lugar de darnos acceso su equipo."

"Enough, he is a proud man," Mack said. "He'd die rather than give us access to his equipment."

Márquez walked over to Kathe. "I'm sure you might change your mind if Jamel takes Dr. Reese inside the station. There's no telling what he'll do to such a beautiful woman. But I promise it won't be pleasant."

"Stephen don't do it," Sydney ordered. "Kathe can take care of herself. Bernadette and Mikey have your backs."

"I'm going to ask you one more time," Márquez warned. "Give me access to the cameras!"

"Never!" Stephen shouted.

Márquez signaled Jamel.

"He estado esperando esto," Jamel bragged. "Nunca había una Hermosa mujer estadounidense. Voy a disfrutar esto." he held his gun at Kathe.

"I've been waiting for this," Jamel bragged. "I've never had a beautiful American woman before. I'm going to enjoy this."

"Hazlo rápido," Márquez ordered glancing at his watch.

"Make it quick," Mack repeated.

"Sube los escalones," Jamel ordered nudging Kathe with his gun.

"Go up the steps," Mack said watching Kathe slowly walk up the steps with Jamel nudging her with his rifle.

"Yorg, stand down," Sydney ordered as Yorg glared at them.

"I see I've struck a nerve with Denisov," Márquez chuckled. "Did you have a thing for Dr. Reese as well?"

"You need to worry about Jamel," Denisov laughed.

"Oh, Jamel is quite the murderer," Márquez promised watching Dr. Reese open the trap door, stepping inside. Jamel was right behind her, slamming the trap door shut.

"Voy a disfrutar esto," Jamel laughed reaching Dr. Reese.

"I'm going to enjoy this," Mack translated.

"Y yo tambien!" Kathe shouted kicking him between the legs. (And me also!")

"Ahhhh," Jamel screamed falling forward as Kathe clasped her hands together, striking him upwards in the nose. Jamel fell to the floor, dead with blood spewing over his face.

"Sydney, so much for big, bad Jamel," Kathe announced. "I'll play along with the farce for a minute," Kathe screamed dragging Jamel to the trap door. "Márquez needs an eye-opener before we kill him," she screamed louder.

"It's a shame?" Márquez shook his head. "Dr. Reese was a great researcher. When Jamel is finished, there won't be the beautiful woman you knew."

"I have Márquez in my sites," Mikey stated. "Can I take him out?"

"I have the two by Stephen and Will," Bernadette stated.

"Everyone, get ready," Sydney declared. "We need this to go down fast," watching Jay and Jack pivoting slowly towards the guards watching them. "Kathe has a distraction planned. On my mark, Stephen, Will, drop to the ground. At the same time, everyone take out your targets. Kathe, fire at will!"

"Copy that," Kathe slowly opened the trap door.

"I guess Jamel is finished," Márquez bragged. "I told him to be quick."

"Márquez!" Kathe shouted shoving Jamel's body down the steps.

"What?" Márquez screamed watching Jamel's body rolling down the steps.

"Now!" Sydney ordered as Stephen and Will dropped to the ground.

Mikey shot Márquez in his left temple and then began clearing the ones around the tree holding up the station.

At the same time, Bernadette cleared the two targets by Stephen and Will and then helped Jay and Jack.

Yorg grabbed the guard closest to him, breaking his neck and taking his weapon. He shot his way to help Will get Stephen to cover.

Jay and Jack dropped to the ground, grabbing their pistols, clearing some of the guards running away.

Kathe used Jamel's rifle, clearing the pilots scurrying from behind rocks to the helicopter.

"The rest are leaving!" Mikey declared taking out a few more running down the mountain.

"Jay, grab Márquez' phone," Sydney requested. "Everyone, get in the helicopter. Yorg, Bernadette, get that bird ready for taking off."

"With pleasure!" Yorg answered helping Stephen up from behind a rock. "Are you alright? Jamel hit you pretty hard a couple of times."

"I'll make it," Stephen stated getting inside the chopper. "Will, help me find the equipment with the nitro-charges in them. We need to get them ready."

"They're back here," Jay called finding his backpack next to their bags. "You two sit down and buckle up. We're leaving as soon as everyone gets inside."

"Yorg, start thc cnginc!" Sydney cautioned as Yorg complied.

"I trained on one of these," Yorg smiled.

"Bernadette, Mikey, we've got your backs, come on," Jay called shooting a guard behind Bernadette.

"Kathe," Jack helped her inside. "Nice touch throwing Jamel down the stairs. The look on Márquez's face was priceless."

"That was the last thing Márquez saw," Mikey expressed helping Bernadette inside.

"You should have seen the look on Jamel's face when I kicked him," Kathe snickered.

Bernadette hurried to the copilot seat, helping Yorg run through the checklist.

"Get that bird airborne!" Sydney warned. "Some of the guerillas are turning around and doubling back.

"This is a Russian Mil Mi-24," Yorg told the crew as he lifted off. "It's a gunship, attack helicopter that holds eight people. Mikey, Jack, tether yourselves by the doors and cover us."

"I've got the green side," Mikey declared hooking the rope to the ring.

"I've got the red side," Jack shouted as they lifted higher.

"Kathe," Mikey called to her. "Can you bring the drone inside? The control is in my backpack behind your seat," he requested opening the left side door, and firing.

"They are circling the chopper," Sydney warned.

Yorg raised the helicopter above the trees, while Jack and Mikey cleared some of the targets.

"The rest of the guerillas are fleeing," Sydney stated. "Bring the drone inside."

"I've got the drone," Kathe smiled bringing it inside, and then Mikey closed the door.

"Kathe, I sent you a link," Sydney informed her as he typed commands and pushed enter. "Take JAKE and clone Márquez's phone. Then, call the last number and play the link. Skip and Mack finished a program with Márquez voice patterns saying different words. JAKE can use it to clone Márquez's voice to answer different questions. I will listen to the phone call and type what JAKE should say."

"Copy that," Kathe agreed opening the link.

"Here's Márquez's phone," Jay handed it to her.

Kathe placed the call and played the recording. "Presidente, what you suggested worked. The Americans were spies looking for you. Jamel will dispose of the bodies in the ocean. We are in transport to the control room."

"Good," Eduardo congratulated. "Take Macaby to the hotel room in Camaguey, and don't let her out of your sight. I will contact you with the next step from there."

Sydney quickly typed JAKE to respond, "Yes, Presidente. I won't let Macaby out of my sight and await your instructions. Goodbye." JAKE hung up.

"Skip, Mack, your program worked," Sydney grinned. "JAKE mimicked his voice and answered what I told it to say. We just secured Stephen's team a safe trip and landing at the command center.

"Glad it worked!" Skip and Mack cheered.

"Kathe, use the drone to scope out hostile troops in that area before landing," he cleared the line.

Monday, July 6th
1620 (4:20 PM EST)
Outside of Mayarí, Cuba

"I heard that went well," Ramsey complimented as Sydney turned to her.

"Yes, JAKE is evolving like we imagined when we designed it," Sydney agreed. "All I had to do was use the soundbites that Skip and Mack put together with his voice pattern, and type what I wanted to say. Eduardo couldn't tell the difference."

"That's another phenomenal accomplishment for our technology," Ramsey admitted. "Now, we can control our enemies by using their communications against them."

"It was a matter of technology catching up to our expectations," Sydney agreed as the phone rang.

"It's Alonzo," Ramsey answered the call. "Hello."

"Eduardo and Carswell left the cottage," Alonzo reported watching the screen on his iPad.

"I see that," Ramsey brought up that camera. "Hiltree, turn the drone toward the cobblestone bridge; they just walked over. I thought I saw something under the bridge."

"It's a nitro-charge!" Alonzo exclaimed zeroing in on it.

"Are there anymore?" Ramsey asked.

"According to what CC discovered from Johansson, there should be more," Sydney concurred typing commands and pressing enter. "Does this answer your question?"

"He placed them around strategically to destroy the cove," Alonzo saw.

"That's enough to trigger this entire mountain to crumble!" Hiltree exclaimed.

"Hiltree, keep the mosquito over them," Ramsey requested turning up the audio. "Let's hear what they're talking about."

"From now on, my plan will go down quickly," Eduardo smiled. "Pick up the merchandise in DC and take them to the rendezvous. I will meet you there late tomorrow night when I arrive."

"The merchandise will be pleased with the decision," Carswell shook his hand.

"I programmed the drone to take you to your plane at Santiago de Cuba," Eduardo checked his phone. "I doubled the guards around the airport. The tower has cleared you to takeoff as soon as you arrive. We've been alerted to some unfriendlies, possibly in the area. We don't want anyone documenting you in Cuba."

"There was a jet parked off to the side of the runway when we arrived?" Carswell questioned.

"Spinello had to resolve another problem and was late getting out of there," Eduardo acknowledged. "Your anonymity is safe with him."

"Good, then I'll see you tomorrow night," Carswell got into the drone.

"Of course," Eduardo pressed enter watching the drone lift off. "No, you won't," Eduardo chuckled as he flew the drone straight up and out of sight.

"That's a new twist!" Ramsey exclaimed. "Eduardo just lied to Carswell. Someone's not going to Dubai. I told you Eduardo was jealous of Barrick."

"Eduardo told Márquez to go to the control room and to take Macaby to his hotel in Camaguey," Alonzo reminded. "Now, he told Carswell to take the merchandise in DC with him to the rendezvous. It looks as if Eduardo changed his plans to detonate the missile remotely."

"All my sources stated that Carswell hasn't been in DC since he left office," Hiltree declared. "Now, we know there's an underground presence that Homeland wasn't aware existed. Someone has been helping Carswell slip in and out of DC and other places unnoticed."

"We need to identify and locate the mole or moles at Canaveral and in DC," Alonzo advised.

"Yes, we do," Ramsey agreed. "Pauli, have you found anything?"

"Yes," Pauli stated as Ramsey pulled up his camera feed. "The female is on the move. She placed the suitcases by the back door. Now, she is going around inside, placing nitro-charges."

"CC said Johansson noted that they are blowing up the cove and mansion as soon as Carswell leaves," Ramsey shared. "It appears the plans have changed to Eduardo firing the missile remotely."

"Ramsey, are you believing this?" Hiltree quizzed as he flew the mosquito directly to Eduardo. "The helipad is lowering."

"It's coming back up," Ramsey declared watching Eduardo type on his phone. "What does Eduardo have up his sleeve now?"

"It's another single-person drone," Hiltree watched.

"Hiltree, stay with Eduardo," Sydney requested watching him get inside the drone.

"Copy that," Hiltree flew the mosquito inside behind Eduardo's head.

"The command center is in the opposite direction," Ramsey noted watching Eduardo rise straight up and then takeoff vertically.

"Eduardo's landing in the grass by the back door of his residence," Hiltree stated.

"Oddly, Eduardo didn't land on the helipad," Alonzo noted. "He landed in the grass."

"Eduardo is erasing his footprints before he assumes his new identity," Sydney realized. "If he's blowing up the cove and mansion, it only makes sense that he'll blow up the command center too."

"Yes, but how?" Ramsey questioned watching Eduardo get out of the drone. "What's he doing now?"

"Eduardo's opening an outside compartment and taking out a duffle bag," Hiltree noted watching Eduardo open the bag, and taking out several objects.

"Those are nitro-charges, too," Alonzo declared watching Eduardo placing them around the fence. "These don't have a timer attached."

"That allows him to detonate them remotely," Sydney declared.

"A helicopter is coming in from the ocean," Pauli cautioned as it landed on the helipad.

"Well, look who's here?" Ramsey smiled. "I wondered when Carlos Prado would show up," she said as Carlos greeted his father. "This is going to be good!"

"Your mother and I took the virtual tour of our new residence last night," Eduardo patted Carlos on the back. "The Presidential Palace is one of your finest achievements," he said entering the back door.

"I see Mom has been busy preparing for your departure," Carlos noticed entering the living room. "Mother, it's been too long," hugging her.

"Pauli, I'm taking over the mosquito," Sydney declared typing commands.

"However, it is well worth the wait," Catarina admitted. "By changing identities, we will be able to be a family again in the public eye. Our days of hiding are coming to an end today as your father planned all along."

"When you broadcast this video, it will assure our victory," Eduardo declared handing it to Carlos and then pouring drinks. "I'll appoint you as my Chief of Staff, so we will all be together ruling the world."

"I have to admit," Carlos took his glass. "I never doubted this would work with such a genius for a father." They all clang their glasses together. "Before we leave, may I be the first to see my new parents?"

"Negative," Eduardo denied. "We've come too close to have any slip-ups."

"Don't feel bad, son," Catarina confessed. "We've never seen each other. Your father worries about drones watching us from afar."

"I guess I can wait a little longer," Carlos admitted.

"I did leave the implant behind my ear," Eduardo confessed. "Johansson could get greedy and blackmail us. I have a file on him if we need it."

"Do you think we'll ever be able to stop looking over our shoulders?" Catarina asked. "Gen. Yetsun, Gen. Thompson, and Spinello helped you devise the plan."

"Mom, you know Dad better than that," Carlos chuckled. "Dad never leaves any loose ends. Are we leaving before or after the missile launches?"

"We're ready to leave now," Eduardo declared. "I'll oversee the launch after we're gone."

"I believe that will be one of the last times you call me, Catarina," she smiled. "Now, the news will report that I disappeared off the face of the earth as you both did."

"I promised you this would work the morning Carlos and I took off for Rio de Janeiro," Eduardo lovingly cupped the side of her face with his hand.

"I'll get the suitcases," Carlos said finishing his drink and throwing his glass into the fireplace. "Your chariot awaits on the helipad. Pasha is waiting aboard your plane at Santiago de Cuba to take you to DC. Then, I'll takeoff from Havana."

"Skip, Mack, get this downloaded to your footage," Ramsey requested.

"We're adding it now," Skip replied.

"Hiltree, I need to take over your mosquito," Sydney stated. "I want to get a blood sample from Eduardo and Catarina," he said maneuvering the mosquito behind Eduardo's neck.

"I won't miss these!" Eduardo snapped swatting at a mosquito.

"Now for Catarina," Sydney quickly released a second needle into her neck.

“Me either,” Catarina swatted her neck. “There are no mosquitoes in Dubai.”

“There, now we know who’s who when this goes down,” Sydney laughed. “Hiltree, I’m giving you back the mosquito.”

“Thanks,” Hiltree agreed. “With what we witnessed; I need to be in DC to make the arrest. We know who they’re replacing.”

“You can’t arrest them until the real Barricks leave the hospital,” Ramsey cautioned. “If Dr. Kamenkovich doesn’t smuggle them out for Eduardo and Catarina to switch places, it will alert them.”

“But you do understand what Carswell and the Barricks’ fate is?” Hiltree asked.

“Yes, I know what Eduardo meant,” Ramsey answered. “We didn’t put the Barricks or Carswell into that situation. They are just as guilty of this crime as Eduardo and the rest of them. It means our necks along with the takeover of the world if their plan succeeds. Do you have a problem with that order?”

“No, ma’am,” Hiltree agreed. “Not at all!”

“Alonzo, Pauli, after you drop Hiltree off at Guantanamo, use the Huey to join Kathe’s team,” Ramsey requested.

“It’s 1650 (4:50 PM EST),” Sydney checked. “The team is getting ready to land and find the command center. We’ve got to help them stop that missile.”

“Hiltree, take the drones with you,” Sydney recommended. “You’ll need eyes to help you watch and document the event in DC.”

Monday, July 6th
1650 (4:50 PM EST)
Sierra Maestra, Cuba

“Yorg, I see you’re approaching the landing site,” Sydney stated enlarging the mother-drone’s camera on his screen.

“Using Márquez’s helicopter worked like a charm,” Yorg declared. “We passed several military helicopters that simply veered away from us,” he pulled over the clearing to land. “I see several choppers already here.”

“One of them is Janice Patterson’s helicopter,” Sydney recognized looking around. “She’s just entering the entrance to the cave. Stephen, Will, I need you to stay outside of the cave with the mother-drone. We need to control who is entering and exiting.”

"Copy that," Stephen agreed, "I'm showing the area is clear of any unfriendlies at the moment."

"I don't see anyone else," Sydney concurred watching the helicopter land. "Team, exit as soon as you land, and go inside the forest for cover."

"Copy that," Kathe answered looking for the closest way to take cover.

"Jay, take the mosquito with the extra camera batteries into the cave once you're in place," Sydney requested watching them follow Kathe into the woods. "I'll take over the camera on the mother-drone to free up Jack. We've got a little over an hour to get inside and stop that launch."

"Copy that," Jay agreed releasing the mosquito to fly inside the cave entrance. "I'm going to show a quick preview of the inside as far as the mosquito will operate without the extra battery power."

"Good idea," Sydney agreed watching his screen.

"We've got our work cut out for us," Mikey declared watching over Jay's shoulder.

"It looks like a military operation on the inside," Ramsey noted.

"Ramsey," Stephen interrupted. "More soldiers are walking up the trail to the cave."

"With the evening launch, I figured they would step up security," Sydney confided.

"Mikey, what's to say you couldn't borrow a few uniforms and walk in the cave with these soldiers?" Ramsey asked.

"I like your thinking," Mikey chuckled checking the closest soldiers.

"Stephen, I see something moving in the sky in the far distance," Will cautioned. "I'm going to move the drone for a closer look," he advised speeding up the drone in that direction.

"Good eye," Stephen complimented zooming in on them. "Ramsey, we've got another three helicopters approaching. It will take them a few minutes to arrive."

"It looks like the middle one is being escorted by the other two," Ramsey surmised. "Will, let's see who's inside that middle one first."

"Copy that," Will agreed bringing the drone around to the side of the middle chopper just under the roof.

"It looks like engineers in this chopper," Stephen declared. "Four Cuban soldiers are with them," he said as Will brought the drone around to the other two. "These are filled with hardcore guerillas. They are heavily armed."

"It's clear that the engineers aren't there by choice," Ramsey observed. "Hopefully, those two choppers are just the escorts and don't stick around. They already outnumber us."

"I don't believe those two will stay," Sydney concurred. "Eduardo already rigged the cove and his residence to blow. It looks like Eduardo ordered all workers to the cave for the launch. By having them brought there, it would finish erasing his footprints in Cuba when he blows them up, along with his equipment."

"Leaving no witnesses," Ramsey agreed.

"Couldn't Eduardo be traced to Santiago de Cuba?" Jack asked.

"Negative," Sydney explained watching the helicopters approaching. "Spinello mentioned Eduardo has an inside informant that reports directly to him. However, Carswell can be traced landing there to frame him."

"After they land, do you want me to bring the drone back to check for explosives outside the cave?" Will asked.

"Absolutely," Sydney agreed watching the drone speed up. "Our people need to know where they are, in case they have to escape that way."

"I'll help Will mark the explosives and send the information to you," Stephen relayed.

"Thanks, that frees me up," Sydney appreciated.

"Ramsey, I found two ranking officers sitting outside the cave for a smoke break," Mikey said showing Bernadette.

"Those two are about our sizes," Bernadette agreed. "Haven't they heard that smoking is bad for your health?"

"So is lead poisoning," Mikey grinned.

"We'll cover you in case someone steps outside the cave," Yorg stated.

"Thanks," Bernadette answered. "Stephen, is the coast clear for us to grab them?"

"No!" Stephen answered. "Another soldier just joined them."

"I'll take that one," Jack offered.

"Copy that," Ramsey agreed.

"They are sitting on some rocks with their backs to us," Bernadette reported. "Is the coast clear now?"

"Yes, go now," Stephen advised.

"Let's go," Mikey whispered leading the way.

They swung their rifles behind their backs and then quietly climbed up the side of the mountain. Mikey motioned to Bernadette and Jack which one he was going to take.

"The coast is still clear," Stephen declared.

All eyes were on them, sneaking up behind the soldiers, snapping their necks, and pulling them down to the others.

"Jack, help me undress these two while they get ready," Yorg requested stripping one of them. "Kathe, hand this to Bernadette."

"Okay," Kathe hurried to the tree Bernadette was behind.

"Not a bad fit," Kathe noted as Bernadette walked around the tree.

"The pants are made for a man," Bernadette tugged at the hips. "Women are shapelier," she said placing extra weapons in the pockets.

"I sized this guy perfectly," Mikey admitted joining them.

"Jay, bring the mosquito back to the entrance," Yorg requested. "Stephen, is the coast clear for Mikey and Bernadette to enter?"

"They're clear," Stephen declared. "But they must hurry. The three helicopters are almost in range for a visual."

"Kathe, Jack, I need you to stay behind," Ramsey declared. "Your objective is to free the engineers. Those people don't deserve this fate."

"Copy that," Kathe answered. "What do we do with the engineers once they're free?"

"We need to get them to Guantanamo," Ramsey stated. "I'll contact Hiltree. He can arrange for them to land and be placed into protective custody."

"Copy that," Kathe confirmed as Jack lead the way down the mountain toward the landing zone.

"Stephen, are the officers clear to enter the cave?" Sydney asked.

"Clear, this way," Stephen agreed.

"Bernadette, Mikey, you're clear to enter," Sydney relayed. "I'll guide you."

"Copy that," Mikey agreed casually entering the cave holding his weapon to the side of his leg.

"Just inside about twenty feet, the tunnel curves to the left," Sydney informed them. "I count five guards standing around jokingly picking on the smallest one. They're not paying attention."

"I've got the ones on the left," Bernadette whispered checking Jay's screen.

"Yorg, Jay, stand barely inside the cave to wait," Ramsey urged glancing at that screen. "The choppers are almost over the helipad."

"Understood," Yorg replied watching Bernadette and Mikey enter the cave.

"The chopper carrying the engineers is landing below," Ramsey relayed. "Luckily, they didn't see the team."

"Mikey, it's safe to engage when you're ready," Sydney ordered as Mikey nodded okay and then walked upon the soldiers.

"Estás ahí!" Mikey exclaimed. (You are there!) "¿Cómo pudimos acercarte sigilosamente?" (How were we able to sneak up on you?) He asked, raising his pistol and taking out the three of them as Bernadette took out the two on the left.

"Yorg, Jay, you can join us now," Bernadette approved.

"Jay, continue with the mosquito," Sydney requested. "There is a long hallway that curves to the right to the first security checkpoint. Five soldiers are standing around the one sitting at a desk."

"I have an idea," Bernadette whispered to Mikey.

"I like it," Mikey grinned. "That way, the one sitting behind the desk will be visible."

"I see there is a primitive walkie-talkie sitting on the desk," Sydney noted. "That's how they communicate underground. Márquez is supposed to be there by now. They would announce his arrival. Wait until the one sitting at the desk makes the call," he said as Bernadette gave Sydney thumbs up.

"Márquez nos envió para relevarte del deber," (Márquez sent us to relieve you of duty.) Bernadette explained, approaching them.

"Finalmente, el general espera," the guard at the desk said. (Finally, the general is waiting.) the soldier picked up his walkie-talkie. "Gen. Yetsun, Gen. Márquez ha aterrizado." (Gen. Yetsun, Gen. Márquez has landed.) He advised, and listened. "Si, él debe reportarse al centro del comandante." (Yes, he is to report to the command center.)

"No lo creo," (I don't think so.) Bernadette chuckled raising her Glock along with Mikey, taking them out.

"That was quick," Sydney stated. "Bring the military advanced communication device with you. It might come in handy."

"You do mean this old thing?" Mikey chuckled holding up the walkie-talkie.

"Yes, when Márquez doesn't show, they'll call him back," Sydney replied. "I'll have my computer answer for you."

"Copy that," Mikey whispered leading the way to the next checkpoint.

"Sydney," Ramsey glanced at him. "Kathe and Jack are waiting for the engineers to get out of the helicopter. The guards are handcuffing them to a long rope. Some of them look like Americans."

"The two other choppers are leaving," Stephen advised.

"Good," Ramsey acknowledged.

"I recognize one of the Americans," Sydney said glancing at that screen and then pulling up the Internet, checking for missing scientist. "Here he is," he pointed to the screen. "Dr. James Simons went missing four years ago after leaving work at the University of Michigan. He designed half of the new radar equipment for the Department of Defense. He is a pilot and was trying to devise a cloaking device for the Air Force. Dr. Cynthia Jenson has been missing for three years from the University of Baltimore. Dr. Todd Princeman has been missing for six years. He was working late one night designing a new fuel tank for space travel for the Cape. His wife found the car in the driveway and no sign of him."

"The four Asian Americans were scientists on the Boeing Charter Jet from America to Japan three years ago that blew up over the ocean," Kathe recognized watching the soldiers bringing them out of the chopper.

"That's right!" Ramsey remembered. "You researched the passenger's list for possible terrorists boarding with those dignitaries. They were on their way to a conference in Europe."

"Yes, you changed my schedule at the last minute, so I didn't go with them," Kathe stated. "Rescuers never recovered these four bodies among the wreckage."

"Stephen, is the coast clear for Kathe and Jack to engage?" Ramsey asked watching Kathe and Jay steady their rifles. "They will be out in the open for a few minutes."

"Yes," Stephen gave the go-ahead. "Will and I are in a position to help them if they split up."

"Good," Ramsey agreed. "We can't let one of them get away."

"I have them in my sight," Will declared steadying his rifle on a large rock.

"Perfect," Ramsey agreed. "Kathe, when you're ready."

"On the count of three," Kathe declared. "One, two, three," Kathe and Jack took out the two soldiers standing next to the engineers.

"I've got one running down the path," Will said pulling the trigger.

"I've got the one coming toward me," Stephen moved around the tree.

"Good job," Ramsey approved. "Kathe, quiet those screaming women!"

"Sh…Sh…!" Kathe and Jack hurried to them. "You'll bring more soldiers! We're Americans sent to rescue you."

"Hold your hands out, and I'll cut you free," Jack requested reaching for his knife.

"Professor Ohsumi, do you remember me?" Kathe asked cutting him free from the rope.

"Why, yes, I do," Ohsumi admitted shaking her hand. "You worked at the security department at Alby Airlines."

"Yes, it was my job to screen the other passengers onboard your chartered flight for possible terrorist activity," Kathe admitted. "When I heard the fate of the plane, I couldn't believe it. Everybody checked out."

"It wasn't your fault," Ohsumi confessed. "It was one of my colleagues, Ben Matagato. He had a gun and forced the pilots to land the plane. Then, several men boarded and forced the seven of us off. Matagato stood in the doorway, threatening to shoot the copilot if the pilot didn't takeoff. The pilots refused, and Matagato shot the copilot and one of the passengers. We heard the other passengers beg the pilot to takeoff. As soon as the plane was over the ocean again, Matagato exploded it. After witnessing that, we were put on another plane and brought here. A man named Philippi Spinello met us at the airport and brought us here to work in this replica of a space center. They plan to blow up a space rocket at tonight's launch."

"We're here to stop that," Kathe explained.

"I believe you are Dr. James Simons," Jack extended his hand. "My boss read that you are a pilot."

"Yes, but only for single-engine aircraft," Dr. Simons stated.

"Do you think you can fly this helicopter out of here?" Jack asked.

"I think I can," Dr. Simons explained. "I observed the pilots every time we flew, hoping to one day get us out of here."

"We have no other choice," Ramsey declared. "I can't spare anybody. Hiltree sent two fighter jets to escort them, and the tower will talk them down. Kathe, have JAKE set the course for them. Get them up in the air."

"Copy that," Kathe answered. "Our boss approved you to fly everyone to Guantanamo Bay. RADM Jeremy Hiltree advised the tower of your situation and sent two fighter jets to escort you. The tower will talk you down if you need it."

"We can't leave," Simons held up his right hand. "Spinello ordered us to report to the command center. If we don't report to the guards, we will be terminated remotely."

"Sydney, I need you to deactivate some rings on the scientist?" Ramsey asked zooming in on it.

"I've got a minute," Sydney stated. "Jay, guide your team for a minute. I have to help Ramsey."

"Copy that," Jay agreed flying the mosquito.

"Kathe, scan the rings with JAKE," Sydney requested connecting to JAKE.

"Copy that," Kathe agreed holding JAKE over Simons' ring.

"The red flashing light in the center will turn green," Sydney explained. "Then, it's safe to take them off."

"Copy that," Kathe said, quickly disarming each ring. "It's safe to take the rings off now," watching them comply with relief.

"How did you do that with a cell phone?" Ohsumi asked.

"What cell phone?" Kathe grinned. "Dr. Simons, I'll set the course to Guantanamo Bay for you," she led him into the cockpit and placed JAKE on the console. "JAKE, download the coordinates for Guantanamo Bay into this computer."

JAKE lit up, "Kathe, the coordinates are downloaded."

"Dr. Simons, leave as soon as you're ready," Kathe warned. "This mountain is rigged to blow after 2200 (10:00 PM EST)."

"I can't believe what I just saw you do with your cell phone," Dr. Simons insisted.

"What cell phone?" Kathe winked and turned to leave.

"Ms. Tierney," Ohsumi shook her hand by the door. "The next time we meet, I hope it's a happy occasion."

"Mr. Ohsumi let's hope you don't ever have to run into me again," Kathe smiled jumping down as Ohsumi closed the door.

"Clear," Dr. Simons yelled turning on the rotors.

"Thank the Good Lord, we were able to save those innocent people," Kathe sighed moving away from the chopper with Jack.

"Ramsey, they are leaving," Jack reported.

"Good, Hiltree will have them debriefed before they are released into the public after this is over," Ramsey stated glancing at the news.

Monday, July 6th
1700 (5:00 PM EST)
Merritt Island, Florida, Cape Canaveral

Breaking News: "This is Robert Morwitz with FNN News reporting live from inside the pressroom at Cape Canaveral. For the past several hours, the engineers prepared the rocket for 2200 (10:00 PM EST) launch. Stay with us as we cover this incredible rescue mission for Astronaut Benjamin. It is reported that his fever has climbed to 104 degrees."

"Oh, great!" Ramsey snapped. "The countdown is well underway!"

"We work better under pressure," Sydney consoled. "We'll make it."

Monday, July 6th
1715 (5:15 PM EST)
The Main Cave at Sierra Maestra, Cuba

"Sydney, Patterson entered the command center," Yorg whispered. "A guard opened the electric lock and escorted her inside. I tried to guess the code but couldn't. Guards patrol the hallway by the command center every fifteen minutes."

"Kathe, you're needed inside the cave," Sydney stated connecting the two teams' earbuds. "JAKE needs to open an electronic lock for Yorg."

"We're on our way," Kathe agreed hurrying off with Jack.

"It's 1715 (5:15 PM EST)," Yorg cautioned.

"You'll have enough time," Sydney said. "They're climbing up the mountain from the helipads."

"We'll wait by the fourth checkpoint in case someone decides to step out," Yorg shared.

"Copy that," Sydney agreed checking the area. "There is a doorway behind the desk. I'm showing it is a smaller tunnel connecting to the main one. I'm not sure where it begins. This cave has a catacomb of tunnels and dead ends. Put the bodies in one of the dead ends around the corner from you."

"Copy that," Yorg agreed signaling the team.

"It's 1726 (5:26 PM EST)," Yorg checked.

"Relax, they are almost to you," Sydney declared watching them come around the corner.

"Kathe," Yorg smiled sneaking a quick kiss.

"Where's the lock?" Kathe asked.

"This way," Yorg declared.

"JAKE, open the lock," Kathe whispered holding JAKE toward it.

JAKE lit up, "Kathe, the lock is open."

"They're expecting seven engineers and Márquez," Kathe whispered. "Opening the door shouldn't alert them."

"Good, Jay, send in the mosquito," Yorg whispered barely cracking the door open.

"It's set up similar to the one we found in Miami!" Kathe noted watching from JAKE. "It's a large room, holding about fifty people, including guards on each level."

"Macaby is on the third level in the key middle position," Sydney watched. "It's U-shaped around the lower two tiers. That way, they can keep an eye on the engineers below them."

"Can you hack into Macaby's computer?" Ramsey asked.

"Give me a minute," Sydney pulled up his program.

"Patterson is hiding behind a guard on the top landing," Kathe reported. "She has tears in her eyes."

"Gen. Thompson is leaning over Macaby pretty close and whispering in her ear," Ramsey noted. "It's not about work. She's giggling. And Janice Patterson doesn't look so happy. That's a jealousy look as sure as I'm sitting here."

"It sure is," Kathe agreed. "Patterson put her neck on the line to smuggle Thompson out of prison. She's turning and hurrying down the stairs. Heads-up guys, Patterson is coming our way! Ramsey, should we engage her?"

"Negative, let her leave," Ramsey stated. "We still have a mosquito in her helicopter. I want to see where Patterson goes now that she knows Thompson betrayed her. I have a feeling she knows where Thompson will go when he leaves Cuba."

"We'll let her pass us," Kathe agreed hurrying around the corner with her team.

"Ramsey, I'm in Macaby's computer," Sydney confessed.

"Disable Macaby's computer from firing the missile at the rocket," Ramsey ordered.

"Copy that," Sydney agreed typing commands.

"Patterson's leaving out the main entrance," Ramsey watched the mother-drone's camera outside. "Let's see who else is inside the command center."

"The gentleman sitting on the left side of Macaby is the Asian-American Scientist, Ben Matagato," Kathe identified.

"Thanks," Ramsey said taking his picture. "I'll have Mack document Matagato's involvement in this scheme on our video."

"Gen. Yetsun is sitting on the far-right side of the room," Yorg identified. "He looks different. Could he be a double?"

"Give me a minute," Sydney requested pulling up the recording in the Bleau Fountain Hotel in Miami Beach and then recording him speaking. "The voice patterns match. It is Gen. Yetsun."

"Perhaps, Yetsun didn't age well," Ramsey shared.

"The first two tiers have Cuban soldiers guarding the workers," Yorg spotted. "There are only Russian soldiers on the third tier. I recognize some of them that have been with Yetsun since he began this operation."

"Probably, signifying that Yetsun is in charge of the operation," Ramsey assumed. "Isn't he still a fugitive of Russia?"

"Yes, Yetsun has a hefty bounty on his head," Yorg stated as Sydney pulled up the website.

"Dr. Pasha Kamenkovich and his wife, Petra Kamenkovich, also have bounties on their head," Sydney read. "This is interesting. The Russian government executed several military soldiers eight months ago for stealing a new Russian T-14 Armata tank."

"That's the latest next-generation tank," Yorg admitted. "It's nicknamed the Terminator. It is supposed to be indestructible."

"What we need right now is another way to get inside and stop that missile," Ramsey declared. "Any ideas?"

"Carlos solely builds for his father," Kathe brainstormed. "We noticed similarities in his designs in different locations. The one thing they all had in common is an escape room. Jay, turn the drone to the far-left wall," she watched. "If this one is just like the one in Miami, that doorway leads to the escape room. If we enter from there, we have the element of surprise to the third level. With our people standing by the other doors, we should take control of the situation. Here's the door that opens into escape room," Kathe directed using JAKE to open the lock. "Jay, do your thing."

Jay sent the mosquito inside the darkroom as Sydney turned on the infrared.

"There is the doorway that leads into the command center," Kathe pointed out in the middle of the right wall.

"Jay, I saw in the other room that there is a light over the door," Sydney noted. "Hover the mosquito over to the computer on the desk.

Kathe, set JAKE on the computer near the keyboard," hacking into the system and pressing enter. "Yes, if we open the door, the light in the command center will turn on, and an alarm will sound," he typed more commands. "It's safe to open the door now. Wait a minute," he typed faster and pressed enter. "This computer is only set up to work for an evacuation," Sydney pulled up the nano-chip Rodger slipped to him on the cutter. "Yes, Rodger was able to bypass the code giving it access to the main computer," he read typing the code into the computer. "I'm in the main computer!"

"We've got another problem," Kathe sighed. "This room is rigged to explode with hidden explosives," Kathe showed them with JAKE.

"I see that," Sydney sighed reading the chip and checking the cameras in the command center. "Rodger said that Jenkins had him plant hidden charges in the command center also," he scanned the room. "Rodger planted them, and then Jenkins forced him to show him how to create a secret code to explode them."

"Then Jenkins discovered that Eduardo was going to erase any knowledge of him being in Cuba after shooting down the rocket," Ramsey concurred. "Eduardo knows that any of these people could turn on him at any time."

"The escape room is how Márquez was supposed to get Macaby safely out of the cave," Kathe remembered. "Wait a minute! Eduardo said he would remotely fire the missile. This proves Eduardo never planned for Macaby to shoot the missile down from here. It is a diversion to eliminate his competition."

"Would Eduardo plan this costly, elaborate scheme to eliminate his competition?" Ramsey questioned.

"It appears that way," Sydney proclaimed scrolling down the chip. "Rodger didn't tell Jenkins that Eduardo had the codes to the launch pad encrypted. Jenkins never changed the codes."

"That means two missiles are pointing at the Cape!" Ramsey gasped. "We've got to find them! Kathe, Yorg, get inside the command center and shut down that launch! If Macaby tries to launch it from there, it might blow! Sydney, find the other missile and a way to block Eduardo's remote!"

"The countdown at the Cape has stopped," Sydney reported. "The main rocket sounded an alarm. That will give us more time to get inside the command center and find the other missile."

"Ramsey," Alonzo interrupted. "Pauli and I spotted Philippi Spinello in a Russian Mil Mi-24 accompanied by a second one. The one carrying Spinello landed at Eduardo's resident a half-hour after Carlos took off. He stayed in the house for two minutes and came out fuming. Both helicopters are heading for the top of the mountain. We counted twenty-four of his men with him. We're following them. We'll land as soon as they are out of sight."

"Spinello found the explosives and put two-and-two together," Ramsey assured them. "Bernadette, Mikey, you need to help Alonzo and Pauli."

"We're on our way to meet them as soon as they land," Mikey said leaving with Bernadette.

"Stephen, Will, keep an eye out for Spinello," Ramsey requested.

"We heard," Stephen agreed.

"Kathe, I'm sure you heard that you're getting more company," Ramsey reported.

"Ramsey," Stephen interrupted. "We have a visual on Spinello! He didn't fly as high as we expected. His helicopter lifted halfway up the side of the mountain. The men jumped out of the chopper and ran past the first cave entrance. Will, where are they heading?"

"Give me a minute," Will maneuvered the mother-drone ahead of them through the trees.

"It's the third entrance!" Will exclaimed. "It's not behind a waterfall this time."

"I see that," Ramsey congratulated. "We're lucky they didn't use the first entrance. They would know we're inside."

"Pauli and Alonzo just landed in the Huey," Stephen confirmed. "We'll show them where Spinello and his men entered."

"Bernadette, Mikey, there is a third entrance," Sydney alerted. "Check your phone for the location."

"Copy that," Bernadette answered reaching for her phone. "I see it."

"Did I see what I thought was another helicopter!" Will exclaimed quickly moving the drone around the far-right side of the mountain.

"Yes, you did!" Stephen exclaimed. "This ballgame keeps getting better!" he said zooming in on a chopper landing in a smaller clearing, lower down the mountain. "Jenkins arrived and bolted out of the chopper. He's scurrying through the bushes. Will, follow Jenkins."

"It's another waterfall," Will discovered flying the drone carefully behind it. "It's another cave entrance lower than the others directly under the third waterfall."

"It looks like Carlos designed the cave with multiple tunnels to exit," Ramsey surmised.

"Will, don't let Jenkins see the drone," Sydney cautioned. "Move it closer to the ceiling to follow him inside. We need to see where that cave leads."

"Yes, Sydney," Will answered. "I brought another battery in my backpack for this kind of situation."

"Stephen, can you join him?" Sydney asked.

"I'm already on my way," Stephen said. "Will, go ahead; I'll catch up to you."

"Copy that," Will replied slowly following Jenkins.

"Make sure you have your weapons ready," Sydney warned. "We don't know what kind of situation you'll encounter."

"We're packing," Will whispered. "I always wanted to say that."

"Well, cowboy, be careful," Sydney cautioned. "There are no retakes in this movie."

"Don't worry," Stephen clarified. "We've got this. I caught up to Will."

"All teams do not engage unless you must," Ramsey cautioned. "I have a feeling Spinello's men will take control of the command center."

"It looks that way," Bernadette agreed following them. "This tunnel splits. Some men are going to a higher elevation, and some will enter from the bottom tier."

"Which way do you want the mosquito to go?" Pauli asked.

"Go with Bernadette to the higher elevation," Ramsey requested. "Spinello is with that group. Mikey, I want you to stay with the lower group. You'll be our surprise."

"Copy that," Mikey agreed signaling Bernadette.

"Bernadette, you should run directly into a doorway that leads into the main entrance tunnel by the fourth checkpoint station," Sydney advised. "Spinello is heading for the command center."

"Copy that," Bernadette whispered cautiously following them.

"Kathe, move your team out of the escape room," Ramsey ordered. "Spinello is on his way there. It looks like his men are positioning themselves to enter the command center simultaneously from different levels."

"Copy that," Kathe declared hurrying downstairs. "Jack, feel under the bottom of the desk for a button."

"Got it," Jack relayed pressing the button.

"Jay let's see what's inside," Kathe requested opening the door. "Yorg, there's a tank in here with Russian markings."

"It's the missing Russian T-14 Armata!" Yorg exclaimed.

"How could a T-14 end up in a cave in Cuba?" Kathe asked.

"By looking at the tools on the table behind it," Sydney assumed. "I'd say those executed soldiers disassembled it in Russia for Carlos to smuggle it here. Then his men reassembled it inside. That would take about eight months to do."

"JAKE, change the locking mechanism to reenter the room," Kathe held it up.

"Good thinking," Ramsey said watching JAKE light up and comply.

"We're standing by," Kathe replied.

"Bernadette, I see Spinello entered the hallway by the fourth checkpoint," Sydney advised. "The escape room that leads to the command center is around the curve. He's leaving some men to enter at the main door and going to the escape room with the others. He'll enter on the third tier, where the hierarchy controls the launch."

Monday, July 6th
1735 (5:35 PM EST)
Showdown in the Sierra Maestra, Cuba

"Ramsey, we are waiting to enter the hallway after Spinello," Alonzo reported. "Do you want us to engage?"

"Negative," Ramsey denied. "Spinello is positioning his men at several of the entrances for an attack. The fake text message we sent Patterson from Johansson's cell phone worked. Spinello went straight for Eduardo's residence."

"We've noted a growing distrust among the elites all along," Sydney agreed. "All we needed was to speed up the process."

"We nailed Spinello for the double-crosser he is," Alonzo chuckled. "That's been his MO since the first day I met him."

"Spinello's planning to take out his opposition and go after Eduardo," Pauli concluded.

"Spinello's men are by a doorway on the lower level," Mikey added. "One is continually checking his watch. I lost the signal on my phone to Bernadette's mosquito, so I can't see what's happening. But I do know from listening to these thugs, it's going to get ugly real soon."

"I'll reconnect you," Sydney confirmed typing on his computer.

"Thanks," Mikey said watching the inside.

"Spinello is waiting to coordinate the attack," Ramsey stated.

"They plan to take out as many guards as they can and take over the room," Mikey reported.

"That will help us," Ramsey admitted. "Spinello rechecked his watch and smiled. He's giving the signal to enter."

"They are entering with guns blazing from all entrances," Alonzo watched. "He's making a statement to the other partners before he kills them."

"At least, they're not shooting the engineers," Ramsey noted watching workers drop to the floor and get under their desk. "He'll need them to launch the missile."

"It's an unnecessary bloodbath," Sydney sighed watching in disbelief.

"We knew this would happen," Ramsey confided. "Spinello's men are pulling Thompson, Yetsun, and Macaby out from under their desks."

"Yetsun is feisty!" Alonzo watched as one of the men knocked Yetsun to the floor.

"Join the others!" he ordered pointing his gun at Yetsun.

"That was the first real life lesson Yetsun had to learn," Ramsey observed watching him join Thompson and Macaby with hands in the air."

"Alonzo, your team needs to remain by that fourth checkpoint," Ramsey studied the situation. "Spinello may try to exit that way. Do not let him get away."

"Oh, I'll make sure of that," Alonzo agreed watching the door into the command center open. "Pauli, turn up the sound. The cowardly Spinello is about to enter now that it's safe."

"Well, well, well, where do you three people fit in this double-cross?" Spinello asked entering the room.

"What are you talking about?" Gen. Thompson demanded.

"Where's Patterson?" Spinello asked.

"She's at the penitentiary," Thompson stated.

"I saw Patterson in Santiago de Cuba around 1715 (5:15 PM EST)," Spinello declared. "She rented a helicopter to come up here and warn you."

“Warn me about what?” Thompson asked.

“That Eduardo and Johansson have double-crossed us!” Spinello exclaimed.

“That can’t be,” Thompson disagreed. “Eduardo called us and told us that he brought Carswell to the cove. Pasha was taking him and Catarina to the rendezvous.”

“Patterson received a text from Johansson early this morning,” Spinello explained. “Johansson said he was the brains behind this deal and cutting the feckless people. He and Eduardo are taking over. As soon as I read that, I went to Eduardo’s residence! He emptied the safe in the master closet and rigged the place with enough dynamite to blow up half the mountain! Someone picked them up before I got there. I found an empty bottle of wine and three broken goblets in the fireplace. Evidentially, they toasted to their new plan.”

“What?” Gen. Yetsun gasped.

“Where is Márquez?” Thompson demanded. “The first checkpoint reported he landed over a half-hour ago. He never made it here!”

“Matagato, check the tunnel cameras,” Yetsun ordered.

“Can I sit at my computer?” Matagato asked still holding his hands up.

“You may,” Spinello allowed watching Matagato sit down, trying several times to pull up the cameras.

“Someone has turned the cameras off,” Matagato reported glancing at Spinello.

“Tap into Eduardo’s residence cameras,” Thompson ordered. “Let’s see if Spinello is telling the truth. At this point, we don’t know if Spinello is in on this,” he looked at Spinello. “You’re the one that barged in here with a small army murdering our guards. We’re on the same countdown as the Cape. They had to stop the clock due to the main engine problem.”

“Go ahead, I have nothing to hide,” Spinello signaled Matagato.

“The cameras are offline,” Matagato admitted.

“Bring up the footage from earlier today,” Thompson urged.

“I’m trying,” Matagato kept typing commands. “It’s been erased.”

“May I try?” Macaby asked Spinello.

“Sure,” Spinello agreed keeping an eye on her.

“It’s not pulling up!” Macaby exclaimed frantically typing commands. “I do it all the time to check on Eduardo’s residence for him,” she tried another way. “Nothing! The cameras are offline. Someone changed the passwords. I can’t access them remotely.”

"Then, try pulling up the footage at the cottage!" Thompson ordered.

"I know Carswell arrived at Santiago de Cuba to meet with Eduardo!" Spinello declared. "I watched him get into Eduardo's single-person drone. The plan was going as scheduled. My source at the hospital reported that Ellie Barrick was hospitalized on time. My source at the Tower in Santiago texted me a picture of Pasha waiting for Eduardo and Catarina."

"Then, the plan didn't change until after Carswell arrived," Macaby realized splitting the large screen on the first tier and putting the camera feed from inside the cottage next to the countdown. "The cottage is rigged!"

"Check the cameras outside the cottage," Thompson requested.

"The camera is pointing straight at the nitro-charges under the bridge!" Macaby gasped.

"We have been double-crossed!" Yetsun snapped sitting down. "This was my plan! I let Eduardo join with me years ago when I put his satellite into orbit!"

"No one knows what Eduardo even looks like," Macaby sighed. "He could be anyone."

"Eduardo had his face hidden when he and Carlos came to me in Moscow asking for help with their satellite," Yetsun confided. "Eduardo said his face was destroyed by an allergic reaction to the surgical sutures. I never believed him. I tried several times to get a look at him on the camera in his bedroom and bathroom. A thick, black, electronic wall surrounded the shower as soon as he stepped inside. When he came back out, he had the mask on again."

"We haven't seen Catarina in months," Spinello added. "She must have changed her face too!"

"Johansson could have made a second video showing we are guilty, along with Linda Ramsey's team," Thompson surmised.

"Eduardo was always very secretive about Johansson," Spinello admitted. "Whenever I asked him about Johansson, he was very vague. When I talked with Johansson on the phone, he was as well."

"If that's Eduardo's plan, it won't work," Thompson admitted putting his hands down. "Carswell was to come here and pick up the video to take to his boss. Pasha was to sneak them inside the hospital. Even with a super-fast, 'so-called' recovery of a new disease, the CDC will make them stay in quarantine until they are sure the virus isn't dormant, only to regenerate. They can't make it to Japan while the G-Summit is going on since it only lasts five days. Without the video broadcasted before the G-Summit is over, Bencivenni can't activate his rings. We need that to happen to cause worldwide chaos."

"Then, whoever picked up Eduardo and Catarina has the thumb drive to broadcast the video," Spinello surmised. "They'll have the ultimate alibi."

"When was the last time you talked with Johansson or Bencivenni?" Yetsun asked.

"The last time I talked with Bencivenni was when he was waiting for Jenkins to pick him up and take him to the penitentiary," Spinello declared. "I last talked with Johansson the day before to make sure everything at the prison was on schedule."

"Where is Jenkins?" Thompson asked. "His phone goes straight to voicemail."

"He met me here to deal with Metarha and Patterson," Spinello admitted. "Jenkins said there was a warrant for Patterson's arrest. We found Patterson on the runway here just before Carswell landed. I told Jenkins to join Ramsey and Sydney to find out what they've discovered. He had to wait until Carswell took off in the drone before he left."

"Then why isn't he answering now?" Macaby asked hanging up her phone.

"I'm not sure," Spinello insisted.

"Should we scrub the missile launch?" Yetsun asked. "Then, Spinello can grab Eduardo and Catarina out of their fake hospital rooms. Once he kills them, we can resume my original plan."

"We don't need Eduardo," Macaby admitted. "We can pretend to go along with Jenkins as our new leader to keep the authorities off our backs. Yetsun and I can do everything else."

"It would be suicide for me to go to the hospital!" Spinello insisted. "We have no way to prove Eduardo and Catarina are imposters! We'd be shot on sight trying to leave!"

Monday, July 6
1800 (6:00 PM EST)
The Takeover

"Heads-up," Stephen alerted while they kept speculating. "The tunnel Jenkins entered leads behind the command center. He's trying to get into a room to the left of it. He's having a hard time with the code."

"I assume Eduardo changed the code," Sydney stated watching him.

"Jenkins is hardwiring the electric lock to open it," Will announced.

"That's where we are!" Kathe overheard. "Guys, quick, hide!"

"The only place is in the tank," Yorg declared. "Jay, Jack, get that hatch open," he ordered watching them climb the ladders from both sides; and open the hatch. "It's big enough for all of us. Come on."

"Up you go," Yorg whispered helping Kathe reach the first step.

"He got the code!" Stephen warned. "He's opening the door. Will, keep the mosquito with him."

"Close the hatch," Kathe whispered while Yorg pulled her down and led her to the back of the tank. They crawled under it as the door opened, and the hatch closed and locked.

"Jenkins is inside the room," Sydney warned. "He looked at the tank like he heard the hatch close. Everyone stays still. He drew his weapon," he watched as Jenkins walked around it.

"Hold your fire unless it's impossible," Ramsey cautioned.

"Jenkins is satisfied," Sydney took a deep breath. "He's walking to the far-left corner and sliding a small rock about eye level on the wall," Sydney zoomed into it. "It's a TV camera that Jenkins made Rodger install. It was on the nano-chip Rodger slipped to me. Jenkins can see everything happening inside the command center. Now, he's sliding the rock back. He's moving another rock near the door showing the escape room and closing it," Sydney stated. "He's going inside the escape room."

"I know that look in his eyes!" Ramsey scoffed. "It's the same look when he double-crossed me at the Pentagon. He's pulling a small iPad out of his coat," Ramsey noted widening that camera. "He's plugging it into a breaker."

"He's using a direct line into the command center's cameras," Sydney zoomed in to it. "That is on the nano-chip," he read it. "He made sure Rodger showed him how to do it. Now, he's watching and listening to them inside with a big smile," he said turning up the sound in the command center.

"Arguing and bickering aren't helping the situation!" Yetsun shouted. "We've got to find Johansson! He has all the incriminating evidence he needs on all of us."

"It was a setup from the beginning!" Macaby realized. "They manipulated us to help them get what they wanted!"

"Eduardo would still need to keep Jenkins as Head of Homeland for a while to ensure he is accepted as the real Omar Barrick," Thompson declared. "He knows if we live, we will go after him. Jenkins also has enough clout to make the CDC release them early."

"But I don't need Eduardo or any of you," Jenkins chuckled typing on his iPad. "As a matter of fact, I ordered the CDC to keep the Barricks and their Secret Service Detail under quarantine for at least six weeks. Who knows what kind of a deadly disease they contracted? Especially since Pasha infected Astronaut Benjamin before he left."

"Jenkins is the one that arranged the replacements to get inside and let Pasha in a restricted area!" Ramsey snapped.

"Will, move the drone so I can see Jenkins' iPad better," Sydney requested.

"Copy that," Will complied.

"Jenkins is highlighting the charges on the first and second tiers to set off," Sydney warned. "He made sure Rodger installed them so they would be undetectable."

"Ramsey, should we engage Jenkins?" Kathe asked. "He doesn't know we're behind him."

"Stand down for right now," Ramsey cautioned. "I want to see what Jenkins has got up his sleeve. Be sure you've got a way out of there!" she ordered as Jenkins reached in his pocket, taking out a pair of night-vision goggles. "Be ready to go to night-vision. Now, he's climbing on top of a chair, taking a ceiling tile down. It's an AR-15! He's down and shutting off the lights! That sorry excuse for a man turned up the sound in that room to hear the people panicking. Now, he's laughing as he sets off the charges!"

"It's chaos inside!" Sydney reported watching the destruction. "The body count on engineers is high on the first two tiers. Oh, no, Matagato and Spinello are heading for the escape room," he warned as Jenkins opened fire on Matagato, opening the door. Spinello and his men turned around. Two of Spinello's men are trying to take Jenkins down."

"That would save us the trouble!" Ramsey grinned.

"I don't see Thompson, Yetsun, and Macaby on the third tier," Sydney declared checking the drone cameras in the smoky dark room. "Let me check for an escape hatch," he scanned the area.

"Jenkins plans to eliminate his competition and then go after Eduardo," Ramsey declared. "He's no match for them."

"Ramsey, we've got reinforcements inside the tunnel!" Bernadette reported. "I hear them coming from the entrance led by a vehicle!"

"Take evasive action!" Ramsey warned her. "Pauli, I'll take over your drone," she quickly typed commands. "I've got it."

"Thanks," Pauli shoved his iPad in his pocket, and grabbed his Glock. "Alonzo, cover me. This desk is bolted to the wall," he said using his brute strength to pull it away.

"I've got your back!" Alonzo declared keeping the reinforcements from coming around the corner. "Bernadette, be ready if we have to pull back."

"Okay," Bernadette got into position beside the wall.

"I also hear reinforcements in this tunnel," Mikey whispered. "I set a few charges along the way," he pushed an app on his phone. "There's an air shaft above the ceiling. It must end up by the main tunnel. I'll head that way and join Alonzo."

"Go ahead, Mikey," Ramsey agreed. "That's why Jenkins had that look on his face. He sent the reinforcements. That's why he's waiting to enter."

"Here they come!" Bernadette warned joining Alonzo shooting as they stormed around the corner. "Grenade!" she yelled dropping to the floor, crawling behind the desk along with Alonzo.

"Jenkins turned the lights back on, but he's just standing there," Sydney stated. "He's checking his watch."

"Guys, do you hear something by the back wall?" Kathe whispered getting back under the tank with Yorg and reaching for her Ruger.

"Could it be another hidden passageway," Jay whispered. "It sounds like someone's trying to enter," he whispered getting behind the front of the tank with Jack.

"That small room has four entrances?" Ramsey wondered, watching a hidden door open and several guerrillas entering. They headed straight up the stairs to the escape room.

"Miguel, what took you so long?" Jenkins demanded as they approached him.

"These tunnels are very confusing," Miguel stated. "Are you ready to leave now?"

"Not yet," Jenkins answered. "I have to get the files," he said firing wildly at the doorway, killing two men. "Cover me," he led the way inside the command center.

"Sydney don't let Jenkins copy the files," Ramsey ordered.

"I already stopped him," Sydney grinned. "Jenkins' not getting what he thinks. I left him and an old friend for a surprise. Oh, and I found an embedded program and sent it a little surprise as well."

"Jenkins is inserting a thumb drive into Macaby's computer," Ramsey stated moving the drone closer. "He is so predictable. He thinks he's downloading the files on Chameleon."

"I hope Jenkins likes surprises," Sydney smiled.

"What happened to Thompson, Yetsun, and Spinello?" Ramsey asked.

"There have to be secret exits on the top tier," Sydney zoomed in by Yetsun's desk, scanning the wall. "There is a return vent next to Yetsun's desk hanging away from the wall. It has to lead to one of the four catacombs we found behind the escape room."

"That one would have to lead to the tunnel Jenkins used to get inside!" Yorg realized. "Stephen, Will, Yetsun is coming your way! Find a safe place and wait for me. I'm on my way!" Yorg bolted into the tunnel.

"Jack, go with him!" Ramsey ordered. "And seal the door from the tunnel into that room. We don't want Yetsun doubling back to get into that tank."

"Copy that!" Jack replied hurrying behind Yorg.

"Kathe, Jay, stay put a minute," Ramsey cautioned. "We need to see which way Jenkins leaves."

"Copy that," Kathe answered.

"Alonzo, keep an eye out for Thompson," Sydney warned. "He must have taken Macaby with him, exiting from a locker behind his desk. They will come out between the escape room and the command center."

"We would have already seen them," Alonzo stated. "This main tunnel ends past the escape room."

"Negative," Sydney corrected checking the dead end behind the locker. "The small tunnel behind the locker only appears to be a dead end. It is a door that leads to the main tunnel."

"That means there is a door at the dead end leading to the other side of the mountain," Alonzo deducted. "We were so busy; we didn't see or hear them."

"Alonzo, heads-up," Ramsey warned. "Spinello and a few men are exiting through the small tunnel behind locker #21. Stop Spinello, and then find Thompson."

“With pleasure,” Alonzo smiled. “Pauli, stay with Bernadette. Spinello and some of his goons are entering this tunnel by the escape room.”

“Copy that,” Pauli answered firing his weapon.

“Kathe, Jay, Jenkins is finished,” Sydney reported. “He entered the escape room with the guerrillas. He’s exiting from inside a closet behind the main door,” the drone followed them. “It parallels the main tunnel heading away from Alonzo. It must connect to the main tunnel.”

“We’re on our way,” Kathe said as Jay led the way inside the escape room, opening the closet door.

“Spinello is at a dead end,” Ramey noted. “His men are using their cell phone flashlights to check the dirt floor. They’re pushing on the sides of the wall. Alonzo, you should see them in a second.”

Sydney watched as the drone entered the main tunnel when Spinello’s men slowly cracked open the doorway. Alonzo hid around the corner, waiting for them to get inside the main tunnel. As they slowly emerged with guns drawn, checking around the entrance, Alonzo stood still. He watched them signaling Spinello to enter. Spinello slowly stepped into the main tunnel and closed the door. Alonzo quickly opened fire on the four bodyguards, killing them. Spinello tried to get back into the smaller tunnel as Alonzo walked toward him.

“Alonzo DiMeglio!” Spinello froze as Alonzo grabbed him, throwing him on the ground.

“Isn’t God good to me?” Alonzo chuckled making the Sign of the Cross. “The one man I promised to kill in Ponce Inlet walks through a hidden exit into a tunnel right beside me. I even got a bonus. Those four men were in Kathe Tierney’s house when you tried to burn us alive.”

“Alonzo, I know we’ve had our differences,” Spinello begged reaching on the ground for his gun. “But I can make you rich. All I need is for you to help me find Thompson and Macaby. They came out ahead of me.”

“Philippi,” Alonzo chuckled as he straddled him, grabbing him by his shirt, slamming his head against the ground. “You know I never make deals! Money, I’ve got. A safe world to spend it in is on the line because of your greed. What do you say, for once in your life, we put down our weapons and handle this like men? Pauli’s not with me, and now you’re alone. Just uno-y-uno,” he stood up, kicking Spinello’s gun out of his reach and laying his Glock on top of a rock.

"I don't need help to finish you off," Spinello bragged, quickly throwing a handful of sand at Alonzo.

"Is that all you got?" Alonzo moved away, running straight for Spinello, head butting him in the chest. "You've never been anything but a weasel, hiding behind your men. No wonder you left town after Adalina's funeral. How many people did Antonio whack for you when your father asked you to do it? You never had the stomach for it!"

"That's not why?" Spinello denied as Alonzo kicked him in the side. "I found out that Antonio slowly poisoned her. She made me promise to leave him alone. She didn't want the boys to lose both parents!"

"No!" Alonzo argued kicking him several more times. "Adalina knew Antonio would kill you next! The only time I knew you killed a man was when you killed her older two sons with your men there to protect you!"

"Stop!" Spinello yelled rolling away and getting up. He reached for a knife in his boot.

"Did I strike a nerve?" Alonzo asked. "You want to kill me with your bare hands, don't you?" he laughed reaching for his knife, throwing it back and forth in his hands, while watching Spinello's eyes. "What's wrong? You don't have the nerve to kill me!" Alonzo laughed charging Spinello, knocking the knife out of Spinello's hand.

"Don't!" Spinello begged as Alonzo walked toward him. "Please, don't kill me!"

"I see you don't have it in your eyes!" Alonzo charged him again, thrusting his knife into Spinello's thigh.

"Ah!" Spinello screamed falling to the ground, rolling from side-to-side. "We . . . can have . . . it all!"

Alonzo pointed at him, "Remember in Ponce Inlet when you were bragging how all of us were going to die as your men carried Yorg out of Tierney's house and then doused it with gasoline. The words you told her were branded in my mind that day!"

"I . . . don't . . . remember . . . what I . . . said," Spinello gasped still rolling on the ground.

"Let me jog your memory!" Alonzo shouted kicking Spinello in his thigh.

"Ah!" Spinello cried as Alonzo kicked him again.

"You said, 'How does it feel to be helpless?" Alonzo screamed. "Your lover, your children, and your husband's fate are under my control.' Then, you passed me on the way out, stopped and grabbed me by my cheeks, and told me 'To give your regards to Mario Jr. in Hell,'" he kicked Spinello in the head. "I watched you walk out of the house, leaving a few men to make sure we didn't get out, lit your cigar and threw it on the gasoline!" Alonzo stomped his face several times.

"Stop!" Spinello gasped.

"The men you left with us were overcome by Tierney's seventeen-year-old son with a handful of Shurikens!" Alonzo snapped. "He has to live with what he saw and did for the rest of his life!"

"Please," Spinello begged as Alonzo stomped his head again. "Go to Hell and give Mario Jr. mine and his father's regards!" he screamed stomping his throat with his heal. "You cockroach!" Alonzo twisted his heel, breaking Spinello's windpipe.

Spinello gasped for air a few times as his eyes widened. Then his head slumped to the side.

"Pauli, what's the status?" Alonzo asked tapping his earbud as he reached for his Glock.

"Bernadette is pinned between the wall and the vehicle!" Pauli reported. "I'm keeping the guerillas off her," he took several shots.

"I'm on my way," Alonzo reported hurrying back to them.

"Pauli," Mikey whispered crawling further down the air vent. "I've got a perfect shot at the leaders," he said shooting them. "The rest are retreating away from the vehicle."

"Cover me," Pauli said. "Bernadette, I'm coming to get you."

"Wait, Pauli!" Mikey ordered. "One is getting ready to pull the pin on a grenade," he took the shot. "It's clear now."

"Pauli, they have me squished between the vehicle and the wall," Bernadette relayed. "I can't get free."

"Pauli, I'll help you free her," Alonzo joined him.

"The coast is clear," Mikey relayed. "Go," he said shooting toward the next corner to keep the rest of the guerillas at bay.

"I heard one of them say to seal the main entrance," Bernadette warned as Pauli shoved the vehicle enough away to release her.

"Mikey, climb down," Alonzo requested. "I'll cover you now."

"On my way," Mikey kicked the vent out and jumped down.

"Ramsey, we've got to get out of here," Alonzo reported. "Bernadette overheard some of the guerillas setting charges to seal the tunnel from the main entrance."

"Alonzo passed the escape room is another fake door at the dead end," Ramsey declared. "Push it on the right side, and it opens. You can help Kathe's team stop Jenkins and Thompson. It is a continuation of the main tunnel that leads outside on the other side of the mountain. The mosquito needs to charge. It's sluggish in the tunnel already. I'm giving it back to Pauli since he has the battery source. I've got to help Yorg."

"Copy that," Pauli agreed hurrying to the dead end.

Monday, July 6th
1850 (6:50 PM EST)
Finding Yetsun in the Sierra Maestra, Cuba

"Sydney, Will located Yetsun," Stephen whispered zooming in on him. "He's not far from us."

"Stephen, look up," Will pointed to a manmade path against the wall leading up to a guard station above the ground. "You go first. I'll cover you," he said as Stephen hurried up the path to the station.

"Will, come on; he's almost here," Stephen warned watching the mosquito's camera as he reached for his gun. "He's got one more corner to round before he sees you. I'll cover you," he said as Will bent over under the short rail, hurrying toward the station.

"Stop!" Yetsun ordered panning his gun at Will. "Stop! I see you!" he called firing his pistol hitting the top of the rail.

"No!" Will gasped as the bullet ricocheted causing him to drop the iPad over the rail as he dove to the floor. He covered his head as the bullet ricocheted several times before grazing his arm, and then continued bouncing around.

"Oh, no!" Yetsun screamed diving to the ground, covering his head with his hands as it bounced from side-to-side off the walls and ceiling.

"Will, are you okay?" Stephen whispered trying to peer down the path as soon as the bullet stopped.

"Almost," Will admitted turning over on the path, holding his arm. "The bullet grazed my right arm, causing me to drop the iPad," he said reaching for his handkerchief. "Then, it struck the rock beside me and almost hit me again before bouncing over the side."

"You there, in the lookout station, stand up!" Yetsun ordered standing up, pointing his gun. "I know you're in there! Come out where I can see you!"

"Don't shoot," Stephen yelled. "I'm coming out," he slowly stood with his hands up.

"Yorg, Will and Stephen found Yetsun!" Sydney confirmed trying to reconnect to the drone. "I heard a gunshot and lost visual. Do you still have a visual on your phone?"

"Negative," Yorg whispered. "We heard it, and then a man screamed in pain as soon as the gun fired. We heard the bullet ricochet. That's when we lost contact with Stephen and Will."

"The drone is down," Sydney admitted retrying to connect to it. "Yetsun might have shot it," he continued to type.

"Sydney, I'm back," Ramsey stated. "Kathe's team is searching for Thompson and Macaby. They had a pretty good head start through the new tunnel. It will take our team a while to catch them."

"We've got to locate Stephen and Will quickly," Yorg addressed. "We have to go slow around the corners. Yetsun could easily pick us off."

"I understand," Sydney agreed. "Proceed with caution."

"Listen," Jack stopped around the second corner. "It's Stephen."

"As soon as we turn the next corner, it should be a straightaway," Yorg declared. "We're getting closer," Yorg whispered inching his way closer toward the voices. "Wait a minute. Is that a dead end?"

"It can't be," Jack hurried ahead. "There is a large boulder in the middle with paths on both sides. Wait here. I'll check it out," Jack slowly crept around the left side and returned a few minutes later. "I saw Stephen in a guard station above the tunnel. His hands are up, talking to Yetsun. I crawled up the path a little way and saw Will lying down, holding a handkerchief on his right arm. Yetsun has the iPad and is watching the footage."

"Ramsey, did you hear what's happening?" Yorg whispered.

"It's hard without the drone," Ramsey turned up the sound.

"I'm opening the perimeters on Yorg's implant," Sydney stated typing commands. "I reconnected their earbuds."

"Stephen, Will, help is on the way," Ramsey declared. "Try to stall Yetsun until we decide what to do."

"Okay," Stephen whispered as he coughed.

"Ramsey, Yetsun knows about the drone," Yorg whispered. "Listen."

"I'm going to ask you one more time!" Yetsun shouted aiming his gun at Stephen. "Who are you? And how did you get in this tunnel?"

"I told you," Stephen repeated. "I'm a filmmaker from the states. Sr. Márquez at the Department of Tourism hired my company to film a documentary for tourism on rare birds. We followed an extremely rare

Topaz Hummingbird into this cave. We got lost with all the twists and turns."

"I don't believe you!" Yetsun screamed. "You are American spies! How can you film underground?"

"My company only films documentaries," Stephen defended. "I have to be able to film in all kinds of terrains. Will, my engineer, modified the battery system."

"There's no battery system that will work underground!" Yetsun declared holding up the iPad. "How did you film me?"

"We thought we heard something and turned the camera to see if it was a wild animal," Stephen invented. "That's when we decided to climb up here for safety."

"You were looking for me to collect the bounty from Russia, weren't you?" Yetsun demanded smashing the iPad against a rock.

"That iPad you destroyed controlled my expensive camera drone," Stephen sighed. "It is registered to my company by the FAA in the United States. Sr. Márquez cleared me to use it in Cuba. No offense, I don't know who you are."

"Where is your accomplice?" Yetsun demanded. "I'm waiting!" he cocked the pistol. "I saw a man hunched down in the middle of the path and shot at him!"

"I'm right here," Will answered standing up still holding his arm.

"You're not an American," Yetsun surmised. "What are you doing in this tunnel?"

"I'm Mr. Brown's engineer," Will admitted. "We were filming a Topaz Hummingbird and followed it into this cave."

"Are you the engineer that modified the battery system?" Yetsun asked pointing his pistol at Will.

"I am," Will confessed.

"That's impossible!" Yetsun screamed. "If it could be done, my team of engineers would have done it!"

"Yetsun is not buying their stories!" Ramsey snapped. "He's getting very agitated! Get them out of there!"

"Jack, climb up the path and take Will and Stephen to safety while I distracted Yetsun," Yorg ordered.

"But Yetsun is the one that was after you in Ponce Inlet and Miami," Jack hesitated. "He knows the way out of the cave. He'll take you with him to finish Chameleon."

"Jack, we have no choice," Ramsey declared. "Do it!"

"Jack, I'll transfer the mosquito to your phone," Sydney advised typing commands. "Get it up as soon as you can. We need eyes."

"Copy that," Jack agreed connecting to it. "I've got it. I'm rebooting the camera."

"Well, if it isn't Gen. Uilám Yetsun in Cuba of all places to run into you," Yorg chuckled walking around the boulder with the laser tagging Yetsun's heart.

"Captain Yorg Vuslick!" Yetsun turned his pistol toward him. "The man behind the success of Chameleon, right in front of me! I've got you this time!"

"You never had me," Yorg defended as the camera rebooted.

"We've got visual!" Sydney exclaimed.

"Drop your gun!" Yorg ordered. "You never were good with a pistol. I heard the ricocheting of your bullet bouncing off the rocks for quite some time. I see by the dirt on your face that you had to drop to the ground."

"You always were the best at the academy," Yetsun admitted. "That's why I brought you under my command."

"Don't you mean, your control" Yorg chuckled. "You don't have a command anymore. Russia posted a hefty bounty on your head. The word is that the FSB (Federal Security Service of the Russian Federation) and the SVR (Foreign Intelligence Service) are searching worldwide for you. But these two men aren't part of those intelligence agencies. Mr. Brown is only a filmmaker from the states, as he said. When I heard Mr. Brown was filming in Cuba, I checked his credentials. He's telling the truth. On the contrary, I am looking for you and not for the bounty. For murdering, my pregnant wife, Mikél, and crimes against humanity as well as our government."

"You know better than to underestimate me!" Yetsun taunted. "I have my ways of breaking you. O'Brien warned me about Ivan and you slowing the progress of Chameleon. That's when I killed your wife in your new, little apartment. I used to stand on the hill above her grave, listening to you crying and talking to her while drinking Vodka all day long. Tell me, did she answer you back?"

"The last time I went to Mikél's graveside, she did talk to me," Yorg confided. "A calming came over me, and then ways to stop your plan filled my thoughts. Did you forget being alerted by one of your informants that the FSB was planning to question me concerning your involvement in Mikél's death? You knew then that not only was I sober, but I was coming for you."

"I was never afraid of you," Yetsun laughed. "You couldn't get through my security. Like you just said, I have informants everywhere."

"Really?" Yorg smirked. "That's not what Ivan Tulski told me. You were so worried that I would tell the FSB the truth, you arranged for me to work at Alby Airlines in the states on a newly formed Multi-National, Anti-Terrorists Coalition. I found out later that you did it to keep me as an insurance policy if you couldn't find someone else stupid enough to steal a secret, experimental, military jet."

"I'm impressed," Yetsun grinned. "That's why I made sure your sister couldn't leave the country with you. She was my leverage to control you if I needed."

"Kathe and I rescued Ylia from the private hospital you stuck her in, right under your nose," Yorg laughed. "Sorry, Kathe killed your favorite snitch and smuggler, Sean Redmond."

"Not before my men killed your best friend, Ivan Tulski," Yetsun chuckled. "I heard he died in your arms with you weeping."

"Ivan used his last breath to warn me that Mario LaBasco Jr. was helping you steal Project XP38," Yorg proclaimed as Jack tightened the homemade tourniquet on Will's arm. "What possessed you to think you could get away with stealing the latest experimental, military jet carrying Chameleon Technology?"

"Money!" Yetsun bragged. "Mario paid me twice as much as Senator Frank and Gen. Thompson offered. O'Brien and Mario flew it out of Moscow!"

"Your success was short-lived," Yorg laughed. "I watched it blow up along with Mario LaBasco Jr. over the Atlantic Ocean near Brunswick, Georgia, two years ago," he chuckled as Jack motioned for Stephen to join them. "I see you teamed up with Eduardo Santo Prado."

"Eduardo introduced me to Philippi Spinello and Pietro Bencivenni," Yetsun bragged. "Eduardo was the brains behind Spinello kidnapping you in front of your new wife, and Alonzo DiMeglio in Ponce Inlet. He also engineered them to smuggle you into Miami. By the way, I almost didn't recognize you. Your face was so swollen from the drugs they used to keep you sedated."

"That blew up in your face, too!" Yorg chuckled. "Kathe and our team rescued me right under Spinello's nose. I believe Kathe put them to sleep and flew me out in a helicopter. You're still trying to develop Chameleon, while we used a form of it to rescue me. We're way past that stage now."

"You finished developing Chameleon?" Yetsun demanded as Jack led Stephen and Will crawling down the path.

"Let me put it this way," Yorg chuckled. "It has many uses that you never imagined. Like a Chameleon, it takes on different shapes for the good of humanity instead of its destruction. All you ever wanted it for was to take over the world. Your greatest downfall was joining forces with Eduardo and his cronies."

"I have no downfalls!" Yetsun exclaimed.

"Then why are you trying to find Gen. Thompson and Macaby," Yorg chuckled. "Yes, I know about them. By the way, Spinello and Bencivenni are dead. Your plan is falling apart, and your partners are dropping like flies. But that's not what I'm here for, is it?"

"If only you would have done what I ordered, none of this would have happened," Yetsun proclaimed. "We could have had it all, and Mikél would be alive, and a mother."

"No!" Yorg denied. "I would have a bounty on my head, and Mikél's fate would have been the same. The difference between you and me is that I have faith in God. You don't! Everything you do is for yourself! Enough talking and wasting my time; let's finish this man-to-man," Yorg said putting his gun down.

"Yorg, what are you doing?" Ramsey asked. "We don't have time for this. Yorg, do you hear me?"

"Everything is for the good of the people!" Yetsun yelled putting his gun down. "Ordinary people can't make decisions! It's up to leaders to rule over them."

"People are smarter than you give them credit," Yorg disagreed. "Why do they leave Communism and Socialism every time they get a chance?"

"My plan will work!" Yetsun declared charging Yorg.

"No, it won't!" Yorg shouted throwing Yetsun against the wall.

"You are still strong!" Yetsun admitted reaching behind his back and pulling out a stick. He snapped it forward, doubling its size.

"Yes!" Yorg screamed as Yetsun threw him against a wall, shocking him in the back.

"Who would have thought the farmers in Cuba still use old fashion cattle prodders!" Yetsun laughed striking Yorg again as Yorg turned facing Yetsun.

"Is that all you got old man?" Yorg threw Yetsun against the other wall. "Get up and fight like a man!"

"You forget I know your weaknesses!" Yetsun bragged.

"Do you?" Yorg reached in his side pants pocket, quickly throwing three Shurikens, striking Yetsun in his right hand, elbow, and shoulder.

"Shurikens!" Yetsun screamed dropping the prodder as Yorg slowly approached him.

"Tell your cronies in Hell; the rest will be joining you shortly!" Yorg promised.

"Never!" Yetsun yelled reaching for his gun.

"Yes!" Yorg screamed putting Yetsun in a headlock, then turning and pulling Yetsun over his shoulders, snapping his neck. Yetsun crumpled to the ground.

"I understand why you disobeyed me," Ramsey complemented. "Killing Yetsun with your bare hands set you free from your past. You called him out for everything he did to your family and country. Now, do you feel vindicated?"

"In a way, knowing Yetsun will never destroy anyone else," Yorg sighed. "I feel that's what Mikél wanted me to do the last time I visited her graveside."

"Stephen, this tunnel is how they smuggled the villagers inside to work for them," Sydney discovered. "Behind the escape room is a large space. I believe that's where they are kept. Find them and get them out before the mountain blows."

"Copy that," Stephen agreed as Yorg joined them. "You heard our assignment. Let's go."

"Jack, my arm is fine for me to work the drone," Will insisted. "Can you transfer it to my phone? I think this job is growing on me."

"You have my permission," Sydney smiled typing commands. "This job does grow on you."

"It sure did me!" Stephen laughed following Jack. "We will let you know when we find the workers. See ya!"

Monday, July 6th
2030 (8:30 PM EST)
Cape Canaveral, Florida

Breaking News: This is Robert Morwitz of FNN News reporting from Cape Canaveral. We're interrupting your regularly scheduled programs to bring you live coverage of the astronauts getting into the capsule to prepare for the launch to the Space Station to rescue Astronaut Benjamin. As you can see, the astronauts are in the elevator on the way up to the long catwalk with a few engineers. The engineers will help them inside the capsule and into their seats. They will stay there for the remainder of the time to bring up the computers onboard to synchronize with the control room's computers.

As soon as the astronauts are secured, we will zoom in for a close up of them before the engineers leave and secure the door. Then, we will return you to your regularly scheduled programs already in progress until just before the countdown begins. Stay tuned for more coverage from the Cape closer to tonight's scheduled launch at 2200 (10:00 PM EST). This is Robert Morwitz signing off for now."

Monday, July 6th
2040 (8:40 PM EST)
Safe House, DC Area

"CC, Sam, we need to walk around a few minutes," Rodger declared moving his neck from side-to-side. "I'm getting stiff reading the computer screen."

"You're right," Sam sighed noticing Rodger wink. "We've been at this for hours."

"It's fine with me," Terrance permitted following them. "Don't be too long. John will be back with something to eat in a few minutes."

"That's good," Rodger agreed. "We need more time to go over the computers. We won't be long. We need some fresh air to rejuvenate us," he insisted leading the way through the kitchen to the back patio.

"Did you find something you don't want Terrance to know?" Sam asked.

"No, and that's the problem," Rodger began. "I came to an abrupt dead end on the chip. I scanned the chip, and the storage is not full. He has to have another chip."

"But Sydney scanned his body after Ylia removed the implant," CC stated. "He is very thorough."

"I understand," Rodger stated. "Everything we've learned about Johansson from the beginning is that he is methodical in every detail. It doesn't make sense that he would lay the entire plan out perfectly, and then stop before he divulges the final sequence of events."

"Patterson did have access to Johansson's information at the penitentiary," CC realized. "Maybe he didn't want her to know everything."

"I learned that Jenkins only has bits and pieces of the puzzle," Sam shared.

"That assures me that Johansson would have kept it in another place," Rodger insisted.

"But where could it be?" CC wondered.

"Drug dealers sometimes hide drugs in one of their orifices," Sam stated.

"That would have shown on the first scan," Rodger declared.

"Maybe, that final information was only verbal," CC guessed.

"No," Rodger opposed. "Johansson is too OCD for that to happen."

"Let me run this past Ramsey and Sydney," CC declared calling the HUB.

"Johansson is an evil version of Sydney," Ramsey confessed. "Could he mask the signal?"

"Changing the implant's dynamics would mask it," Sydney realized pulling up the setting program on his computer. "Everything leaves a footprint. I'm resetting the perimeters to scan for the slightest emission of an electrical pulse. If it's there, I'll find it."

"I'll get my iPad and rescan Johansson," CC said walking back into the kitchen.

"John just got back with dinner," Terrance held up a plate. "I'll join you in a minute. I have to take this to Johansson."

"That won't be necessary," Sam stated. "I don't think he's going to be hungry when we finish with him."

"What do you mean?" Terrance asked.

"We suspect another implant with the final information on it," CC assumed. "That's why Johansson wasn't that upset when Ylia removed the implant."

"I noticed that, too," Terrance confided. "I documented his arrogant behavior," putting the plate down. "I'm going with you."

"I'll meet you at Johansson's room," CC smiled looking through the kitchen drawers, finding a phone book. "This will work," she held it up. "For something nobody uses anymore, this one is at least two-inches thick. Sam, get the drone. Ramsey and Sydney are ready. I'll grab my backpack and meet you at his room."

"Wayne, you can get something to eat while we talk with the prisoner," Terrance dismissed the guard by the door.

"I'm bringing up your camera," Ramsey said enlarging the screen. "CC, Eduardo began eliminating his competition. We need the final information quickly!"

"Yes, ma'am," CC smiled entering the room. "Mr. Johansson, I think you have something else I'm looking for in that body of yours. Where is it?"

"You've already scanned my body and illegally confiscated my property!" Johansson screamed. "You've denied me of all my rights! I don't have anything to say to you!"

"You have no rights when it comes to National Security!" CC grinned looking at the telephone book. "This is one of the thickest phone books I've seen in years. Are you sure you don't have another implant?"

"You tell me," Johansson laughed sitting on the bed. "You're superior IT man did the scanning."

"I don't have time for this!" CC raised the book with both hands bashing Johansson upside his head.

"You're the one going to jail for kidnapping a Pentagon employee," Johansson laughed. "I'm adding bruising me along with an unauthorized surgery."

"Well, smart man, since you think you know everything!" CC bragged. "Phone books don't leave marks," she hit him across the face. "Where is it?"

"Go to hell!" Johansson screamed.

"Sam, did he just tell me to go to hell?" CC asked.

"That's what I heard," Sam concluded. "I wouldn't do that if I were you. You should have seen what Agent Sims did to the last man that wouldn't tell her what she wanted to know. He used those exact words."

"She's a joke," Johansson grinned.

"Did he call me a joke?" CC asked reaching underneath her jacket, pulling out her Walther P38.

"It sounded like it to me," Terrance shrugged his shoulders.

"What kind of implant is it?" CC demanded tightening the silencer.

"You can't shoot me," Johansson chuckled. "I'm not talking!"

"Last time!" CC warned picking up the pillow beside him. "What kind is it?"

"Go to hell!" Johansson shouted as CC put the pillow between his legs.

"You wouldn't dare?" Johansson yelled.

"Don't look at me," Sam cautioned putting his hands up. "I warned you."

"She wouldn't!" Johansson disagreed.

"Wrong!" CC shouted shooting the pillow.

"I believe Johansson passed out!" Sam admitted watching Johansson fall backward, hitting his head on the wall.

"Terrance, is everything okay in there?" Wayne knocked on the door. "We heard a loud thud!"

"Everything is fine," Terrance covered. "CC dropped a large phone book."

"Some big spy?" Sam chuckled. "Geeks with desk jobs can't handle the real world," he turned to Rodger. "Present company excluded."

"No harm taken," Rodger smiled. "I have to admit. I didn't think CC would do it."

"How do you think we got the information about your family in Washington?" Sam chuckled. "She learned quickly from Ramsey and Tierney how to interrogate a criminal."

"Sam, use the drone to keep Johansson asleep," Sydney requested.

"Copy that," Sam answered injecting Johansson in the back of his neck.

"What did you use?" Terrance asked.

"A little something to knock Johansson out for a few minutes," Ramsey advised. "We need answers now! Eduardo and Catarina recently landed at the private airport outside of DC. Rodger, use gloves, and arrange Johansson's body straight for the scan."

"Yes, ma'am," Rodger complied reaching for gloves in his pocket.

"CC, I'm ready to scan from his head to his feet slowly," Sydney requested connecting to her iPad. "I'm not getting anything yet," he said as the iPad crossed over the area where the first chip was. "I'm showing there is still residue from the first implant site. Take it over the chest and abdomen," he scanned. "Nothing, now take it down his right leg," he requested as the scanner began to highlight an area. "Stop, right there," enhancing the picture. "Rodger was right! I'm showing a slight electrical impulse at the beginning of the gracilis muscle in the fleshy area by the groin."

"Rodger, pull his pants down," CC requested putting on her gloves.

"Sam, hover the drone closer to the area," Sydney requested zooming in the area.

"It's the same markings behind Eduardo's right ear!" Ramsey exclaimed.

"It's not a tattoo!" Sydney exclaimed running a scan. "It's a chip with extra batteries! I didn't pick it up earlier because it emits lighter than usual electrical impulses."

"We need to get that out of Johansson immediately and see what's on it!" Terrance exclaimed. "I need to warn President Trumore before he leaves for the G-Summit."

"Ylia and Hiltree documented Petra Kamenkovich entering the hospital from a tunnel that connects to a house behind the hospital," Sydney reported. "After giving them a shot, Petra took Omar and Ellie Barrick through the tunnel to the house. They drove off in a dark-blue Chevy, Suburban, license plate, ESPGOTU717. Hiltree has a detail watching it. They're heading toward Virginia."

"Then, Petra has the vaccine for the virus," Sydney declared.

"I need the documentation of that," Terrance said. "Can you send me the footage?"

"Of course," Sydney declared scanning the chip. "We don't need Ylia to get this chip. Hold the camera close to the area. I'll use Chameleon to pull out the information and send it to CC's iPad. Kathe is calling us. Give me a minute."

"I'll help Kathe," Ramsey insisted. "You stay with this situation."

Monday, July 6th
2145 (9:45 PM EST)
Cape Canaveral, Florida

Breaking News: "This is Robert Morwitz with FNN News. The launch at the Cape has been put on hold due to one computer signaling an alarm with the main engine. The next window to Cape Canaveral for tonight's launch will be 2255 (10:55 PM EST). As you can see below, engineers are running a check list of the main engine. They are conversing back and forth with the astronauts onboard. If all three computers onboard do not agree, the launch will be moved to next week. We will keep you updated as the night progresses. Now, back to your regularly scheduled programs. This is Robert Morwitz with FNN News."

Monday, July 6th
2145 (9:45 PM EST)
Sierra Maestra, Cuba

"Ramsey, Jenkins located Thompson and Macaby," Kathe confirmed finding them with her mosquito-drone. "They are in an enclosed, mini-command center closer to exit on the other side of the mountain. The two of them were cozy watching the countdown at the Cape. Jenkins watched them through the glass door for a few minutes and burst into the room. We're heading there now."

"I see at gunpoint no less," Ramsey observed bringing up that camera. "Jenkins doesn't want to leave any witnesses. It will be interesting to see if Macaby falls into that category."

"Do you want us to engage?" Alonzo asked. "We're almost there."

"Not yet," Ramsey cautioned. "I need to see if Macaby can launch the missile from that station and what else Jenkins is plotting. Sydney, are you to the point that you can help us get into another computer?"

"Yes," Sydney pressed enter on his computer. "I just finished sending CC the information off Johansson's hidden device, and they are going through it."

"Kathe located another mini-command center," Ramsey explained.

"I'm through the firewall into the computer Macaby is using," Sydney confirmed typing commands. "Yes, Macaby can launch the missile from that terminal."

"Turn up the sound," Ramsey requested. "I'm sure Jenkins will blab his plans before killing them."

"Jenkins put the gun down!" Thompson ordered standing next to Macaby. "We're on the same team! Eduardo and Catarina can't cut us out of the deal. Macaby can launch the missile from here. I have a copy of the video. Macaby can hack into the security equipment at the G-Summit and broadcast it. We can still make this work!"

"We've never been on the same team!" Jenkins exclaimed. "You and Senator Frank originally put this together without me! It wasn't until I stumbled onto Ramsey, and Sydney, tracking Mario LaBasco Jr. trying to steal XP38, that I found out that you orchestrated this entire scheme!"

"It's not a scheme!" Thompson defended. "Eduardo took what we started in Russia, and with Macaby's help, has almost finalized the formula for Chameleon. Eduardo joined forces with all of us to bring his vision to fruition around the globe. We can still use his plan for each of us to oversee a different continent."

"Why would I settle for that when I can have it all," Jenkins laughed. "After all, I am Head of Homeland Security, and you both escaped from a Federal Penitentiary while serving life sentences for treason. My killing you will be justified. Yorg is one the original inventors of Chameleon Technology. I plan to kidnap him, force him to finish the formula, and then kill him. At the same time, I'll have Ramsey, her gang, and Hiltree arrested for conspiracy to commit treason. Then, by controlling Chameleon Technology, I'll take over Eduardo's vision and become the first president of the world."

"Tom, we can have it all just like we planned!" Macaby begged stepping away from Thompson. "I knew you would come and save me."

"I came all right!" Jenkins shouted. "Just in time to catch you cheating on me with Thompson!" he moved the gun toward her. "If you were waiting for me, why did you escape with Thompson instead of staying with me?"

"I didn't!" Macaby denied. "Thompson followed me here! He didn't know about this terminal! Eduardo brought me here one day to program the missile from here. I secretly videoed Eduardo's passwords when he turned on this computer. He took pictures of the Cape and its surroundings. I can still fire the rocket from here," she glanced over at the screen, and then the clock. "It's 2224 (10:24 PM EST). They've restarted the countdown. I must get our missile ready to launch. Please, it will take me a few minutes."

"I don't believe you!" Jenkins glared. "I saw you and Thompson cozy in the other command center as well as in here. How long has this been going on?"

"Baby, you know me better than that," Macaby lied slowly approaching him.

"Stop!" Jenkins ordered keeping an eye on Thompson. "You're trying to distract me!"

"No, I swear!" Macaby cried wiping the tears streaming down her cheeks. "Remember, all the special moments we had in prison and at your condo. You said every time we were together; it was like the first."

"I just threw up in my mouth!" Ramsey snapped watching the screen.

"Want me to off him for you?" Bernadette offered.

"Very tempting," Ramsey groaned. "We need to find out Eduardo's final plan at the G-Summit."

"Tom, I want this as much as you do," Macaby pleaded. "We planned for over two years for this day."

"That's not what I saw!" Jenkins snapped. "Stop, right there!"

"I fell in love with you first," Macaby tearfully confessed. "I confided in you what O'Brien was doing. If I wanted it for myself, I would never have done that. You must believe me. I love you!"

"Then, prove it to me by stopping the rocket!" Jenkins demanded.

"The Cape is at T-12 minutes and counting," Macaby glanced at the monitor. "I barely have enough time to get ready for the launch," sitting down, she began feverishly typing.

"Thompson, I always knew you cheated on your wife," Jenkins chuckled. "It wasn't until my IT man discovered that you paid for Patterson's condo, car, and living expenses that I knew with whom. You both were good at hiding it in the office. From the flirtatious phone records I read, I'm surprised to see you moving in on Macaby. Where's Patterson?"

"At the penitentiary, why?" Thompson stated.

"No, you're wrong!" Jenkins declared. "I was with her and Spinello at Santiago de Cuba's Airport earlier. She was on her way to warn you that Johansson and Eduardo were cutting us out of the deal."

"I don't believe you!" Thompson shouted slowly stepping back toward a desk.

"The countdown is at T-11 minutes and counting," Macaby called out noticing Thompson. "It's time to open the silo doors," she pressed a compartment on the right front of her desk. It opened, and another keyboard popped out. "I'm opening them now," she quickly typed commands.

"We're going to make it," Jenkins grinned glancing at Thompson. "You haven't kept up with the news in the states lately. AG John Kolouski issued a warrant out for Patterson's arrest, as well as yours, and Johansson."

"I'm not worried," Thompson declared. "They know where to meet me and are on their way. AG Kolouski has no jurisdiction where we're going."

"Where's that?" Jenkins demanded.

"Put the gun down and join with us," Thompson bartered. "I'll take you with us and give you an equal share."

"Not on your life!" Jenkins laughed.

"You can't blame me for trying," Thompson shrugged his shoulders. "By the way, Patterson was surprised that you are still living with Linda

Ramsey. Patterson always had to look over her shoulder. Ramsey is one tough woman. I'm surprised that Ramsey didn't follow you and catch you in the act."

"The old saying, 'love is blind' is right," Jenkins chuckled.

"Not as blind as you're going to be," Ramsey whispered.

"Ramsey believes everything I tell her," Jenkins bragged. "Not to mention, she's easy prey for me to get information. I couldn't wait to get rid of her. I had Patterson and Johansson help me plot Ramsey's murder at the condo."

"Patterson told me all about it," Thompson chuckled. "They watched you screw up the whole thing. When you pulled your gun on her, you were smart to put it down. She would have outgunned you!"

"The countdown is almost at T-10 minutes," Macaby alerted typing more commands. "The booster rockets are locked and loaded. Eduardo said to fire the missile at T-10 minutes. Should I engage?"

"Wait!" Thompson ordered. "We're missing something. Turn up the sound."

"This is Bart Jamison of Mission Control," he introduced. "We are coming up to T-9 minutes. Tapley, get ready to put the rocket on hold as soon as it reaches that mark."

"We are at T-9 and holding," Tapley stated halting the countdown.

"Copy that," Jamison answered. "Security, it's all yours."

"This is Commander Jessie O'Riley," he addressed. "All security areas are now in the full review."

"What does that mean?" Macaby asked. "Eduardo didn't say anything about this at our rehearsals," she moved her hand away from the keyboard.

"It means Eduardo set us up to take the blame!" Thompson exclaimed watching the screen. "He should have told you to fire as soon as NASA resumed the countdown. We must take it out before it reaches St. Augustine. If it makes the turn at Jacksonville, it goes into the atmosphere, and we'll lose it."

"If you hadn't turned up the sound, Macaby would have fired too early!" Jenkins exclaimed. "Every television station there would have videoed our missile. NASA would pinpoint the place of origin, and we'd take the blame!"

"I can't believe Eduardo double-crossed us!" Thompson exclaimed. "He is the one that arranged for my double and brought me to Cuba!"

"He strategically chose each of us for what we could bring to his table," Jenkins realized.

"That's why Eduardo let you join us!" Thompson exclaimed. "Everyone involved warned him not to trust you. He needed an easy way to smuggle people and weapons into the states."

"With my position in the government, I'll go in front of a firing squad," Jenkins gasped glancing at the screen. "I never saw this coming."

"You just realize that!" Thompson boasted grabbing his Glock and firing at Jenkins.

"No!" Macaby shouted getting under her desk.

"What the?" Jenkins screamed diving under a desk.

"He was right about your incompetence!" Thompson laughed. "You didn't see me reaching for my gun," he bragged shooting a few bullets sporadically in Jenkins' direction.

"Brina, stay down," Jenkins directed firing at Thompson.

"We knew Eduardo was going to eliminate you along with Ramsey when he was finished with you!" Thompson confessed firing a few more shots.

"Ramsey!" Sydney realized. "Eduardo and Catarina are on their way to DC. He told Carlos that he would shoot it down remotely. He can't at that distance. We have a few minutes to locate the source," he typed feverishly to take over Macaby's computer. "What in the world?" Sydney zoomed her camera to the missile in the silo. "That missile is rigged to explode! Macaby doesn't know about it!"

"Can you scrub the launch?" Ramsey demanded.

"I'm working on it," Sydney declared typing commands.

"The missile!" Macaby screamed getting in her seat. "Stop shooting at each other! I have to be ready!"

"She's going to fire it!" Ramsey declared.

"If I can lock her out of her keyboard, we'll have a chance," Sydney continued typing.

"Someone is locking me out of my keyboard!" Macaby warned feverishly typing commands. "No!" she screamed slamming both fists on it.

"I'm using Chameleon to shut down the electrical system for both the launch and the bomb," Sydney pushed enter. "They are disabled!" he grinned glancing toward Ramsey. "I'm enhancing the footage at the silo for confirmation."

"Thank God," Ramsey sighed answering her phone.

"Ramsey, Estevo Vazquez is on a high-tech submarine about twenty-five miles off the coast of Florida in International Waters," CC read from her iPad. "It will emerge and shoot down the rocket as it resumes the countdown after T-9 minutes."

"Mission Control already halted at T-9 minutes!" Ramsey reported.

"Estevo hasn't emerged yet," Sydney stated checking the satellite. "When he does, I'll pick up his GPS."

"Sydney, I'm sending you the coordinates of the sub," Rodger pushed enter. "Johansson has it spelled out."

"Rodger, see if you can hack into NORAD and put them on red-alert," Ramsey ordered. "You should be able to find what ship is in the area. CC, Sam, keep checking the chip for more information."

"Copy that," they agreed.

"I'm inside NORAD," Rodger declared scrolling down the screen. "The S.S. Carlisle is in the area."

"Then, use Jenkins' name and order them to intercept the sub," Ramsey ordered watching Jenkins moving toward Thompson.

"Look who's reloading his bullets," Jenkins grinned holding his gun on Thompson.

"Tom, please don't!" Thompson begged dropping his gun. "We can still have it all!"

"No deal!" Jenkins laughed shooting Thompson between the eyes, and then turning to Macaby. "You're not on my side! You knew Thompson wouldn't shoot you!"

"No, I didn't!" Macaby cried holding her hand toward him. "Thompson put one of Bencivenni's rings on my finger as soon as he got in here. He said if I didn't help him, he would kill me."

"Sydney, send that clip of Jenkins killing Thompson to Patterson," Ramsey grinned. "That should strike a nerve."

"Oh, my God!" Jenkins glanced at the monitor. "Don't fire the missile! Eduardo rigged the silo to blow!"

"We've got to get out of here," Macaby screamed grabbing his hand and running toward the door. "The exit is this way!"

"Eduardo embedded a second switch to restart the countdown!" Sydney exclaimed watching the screen in the control room. "Kathe, use JAKE to stop it!"

"Copy that," Kathe agreed hurrying around the corner in the tunnel. "Jenkins has a grenade!" Kathe warned jumping back around the corner.

"It's on the ground in front of the door," Pauli warned.

“I’ve got it,” Kathe held JAKE toward the grenade. “JAKE, melt the grenade!”

“Kathe, the grenade is disabled,” JAKE noted using the laser.

“Tierney, whatever you do, have JAKE stop that second countdown!” Ramsey ordered. “The rest of you stop Jenkins and Macaby!”

“They’re not out of the tunnel yet?” Pauli reported as Jay led the way.

“You’ll have to hurry,” Ramsey added. “If Jenkins gets the helicopter up before you get outside, he’ll seal the entrance!”

“JAKE, stop this countdown,” Kathe requested sitting JAKE on the console.

JAKE lit up, hacking into the system. “Kathe, there are several programs attached to the detonator.”

“JAKE, stop all programs,” Kathe ordered watching JAKE pull up multiple programs.

“Kathe, each program is on a separate circuit,” JAKE stated quickly highlighting and eliminating them one at a time.

“Kathe, as soon as you finish, head for the escape room,” Ramsey told her. “Yorg and Stephen’s team will meet you there. They found the villagers underground and rescued them. I have Yorg waiting for you, and then he’ll drive the Terminator out of there.”

“Copy that,” Kathe replied. “We’ve got ninety-seconds to do this.”

“Kathe, a sleeper program has been detected,” JAKE warned.

“There’s not enough time!” Kathe exclaimed. “Sydney, can you help us?”

“Kathe, you have to stop that without my help,” Sydney overheard. “The Cape has restarted the countdown. Estevo just surfaced! I’m hacking into the computer system on the sub,” he feverishly typed commands. “I’m not inside it yet,” he continued typing.

“I’ve got this!” Kathe replied. “Stop that launch!”

“Rodger, once Sydney stops the launch, order the S.S. Carlisle to deploy two missiles to destroy it,” Ramsey ordered.

“I’m ordering the commander now,” Rodger started typing commands.

“The Cape launched the rocket!” Ramsey reported.

“The submarine opened its bulkhead doors,” Sydney typed more commands, pushing enter.

“I’ve got it on the radar!” Rodger reported. “Sydney, let me join your program. You’re running out of time.”

“Okay, the computer runs several programs at once,” Sydney declared as Rodger linked with it. “Rodger, take over the left column. I’ll do the right.”

“Copy that,” Rodger answered highlighting and eliminating each one as fast as he could type.

“We have staging for separation!” Ramsey warned. “They confirmed the separation.”

“I’m almost done!” Rodger reported pressing enter. “Finished!”

“One more,” Sydney declared and pressed enter. “We made it!”

“Then, why aren’t the bulkhead doors retracting?” Ramsey asked watching the screen.

“Rodger, Chameleon detected several different sleeper programs turning on,” Sydney pressed enter, shutting one down.

“This will take too long!” Rodger warned.

“Not if I use Chameleon to shut down the electrical system in the sub,” Sydney continued to type.

“You’re right!” Rodger agreed feverishly typing commands.

“Chameleon is cloning the electrical system!” Sydney exclaimed typing commands. “It’s working! Chameleon shut the entire electrical system down!”

“You did it!” Ramsey declared. “The sub is plummeting toward the bottom of the ocean!” she checked the second screen. “The rocket passed St. Augustine and is heading toward Jacksonville. It made the curve! It’s going into orbit!”

“We did it!” CC exclaimed hugging Rodger and Sam. “Ramsey, Dad is on the phone to President Trumore aboard Air Force One. President Trumore ordered the pilots to turn around back to Andrews Air Force Base. We have forty-eight hours to stop this scheme. He can only delay his arrival. He must attend, or it will appear that he’s in on the scheme. He will warn the Israeli Prime Minister. Trumore wants AG Kolouski to be with Dad when they arrest Eduardo and Catarina at the hospital. Dad told the president that we have DNA samples of them. He wants Dad to share all the information with AG Kolouski.”

“Ramsey, there’s more to this,” Sam interrupted. “Carlos will unveil a new Presidential Palace in Dubai in two days. He’s kicking it off with a Rock Concert with famous bands from around the world. Carlos has the disk to broadcast the video during the G-Summit. Johansson cloned Bencivenni’s app to activate the rings when they’re ready. They plan to kill the dignitaries that wouldn’t go along with the deal in their hotel rooms.

That's when the double will take over for them. Carlos has the workforce to orchestrate his father's vision if anything goes wrong."

"We've got to stop Carlos!" CC exclaimed checking the Internet. "How are we going to do that? It's a special invitation only!"

"CC, our jurisdiction stops on American soil," Terrance cautioned. "I have to play this by the book."

"And we appreciate everything you've done for us," Ramsey declared. "Terrance, you and your men will accompany AG Kolouski to arrest Eduardo, Catarina, and Johansson. Hiltree needs to see this through with our teams overseas. Oh, and CC, your father needs to take the mother-drone with him, and Hiltree will leave him that mosquito."

"Thanks, I appreciate the use of the drones," Terrance admitted. "I've grown accustomed to working with them. From what I've learned from the short time I've worked with you, President Trumore needs to assign you as a Special Task Force against these terrorists."

"Not happening!" Ramsey refused. "We will not share our technologies with anyone or the government!"

"Yes, ma'am," Terrance agreed. "I'll get back to you after I discuss this with AG Kolouski. We're leaving right now to switch places. We'll bring the team with Johansson to Hiltree. They can leave from there."

"Sydney, can you match the invitations perfectly?" CC asked.

"Yes, Paris has an invitation," Sydney shared muting the console except for CC. "She painted a portrait of the new president!"

"Wait!" CC exclaimed. "Paris knows who the new president is?"

"Yes, but as to who it is," Ramsey insisted. "You're the only one that can hear us right now. It's better to keep it a surprise for Kolouski, Hiltree, and your father. They must catch him and his wife in the act. Otherwise, they might have been forced legally to warn them."

"I forgot to tell you that someone hired Paris to paint two paintings for the unveiling," Sydney apologized. "The person that contacted her masked his email address when he sent the pictures. She had to sign a notarized contract not to reveal anything about the two paintings. She said the portrait made her feel uncomfortable."

"We also have access to a second invitation!" Ramsey shouted. "I have the #1 Band on the charts. We'll go over the information on the chip from the air. Jordan is at Guantanamo Bay waiting for the teams. They'll meet you in Dubai."

"We'll get there ahead of them," CC shared. "That will give us time to recon the area. We're close to Paris. Do you want us to take her?"

“No,” Ramsey said. “Bernadette and Mikey will take Paris in a private jet. She needs to stop at her studio in Wiltz and pick up the paintings. You need to locate that Palace and do recon before they get there. We’ve got two chances to get Kathe close enough to Carlos for JAKE to change the chip if we can’t do it remotely!”

“But Johansson orchestrated Kathe meeting Joe, and had L’Simonette keep putting them together,” CC cautioned. “He wrote in his notes that when Kathe got pregnant, it was a bonus for keeping turmoil with her job. Johansson chose playboy, Joe Sherrod because Light Crimson is Carlos’s favorite band.”

“Not as dangerous, as if we don’t stop Carlos from pulling this off,” Ramsey admitted she signaled Sydney to un-mute the console. “Rodger, hack into the venue in Dubai and add a surprise band, arranged by his father as a special gift for the grand finale. We’ll have enough operatives to guard the band members,” Ramsey declared as they heard an explosion.

Monday, July 6
2310 (11:10 PM EST)
Sierra Maestra, Cuba

“What was that?” Sydney checked the cameras. “Kathe!”

“Where was that explosion?” Ramsey questioned checking the monitors.

“Jenkins blew up the entrance,” Sydney pointed to the camera. “Which triggered an earthquake.”

“We’ve lost the drone showing Kathe!” Ramsey exclaimed. “Kathe, can you hear me? Kathe!”

“JAKE stopped transmitting during the quake!” Sydney declared trying to reconnect. “I can’t get through to Kathe.”

“Keep trying!” Ramsey ordered. “I’ll check on the others. Yorg, can you hear me? The mountain is on a fault line. We’ve got to get you out of there.”

“Loud and clear,” Yorg answered. “We felt the quake. I’m surprised this room didn’t collapse around the tank.”

“It’s not finished,” Sydney stated. “Will, check your escape route with the drone before you leave.”

“I’m doing it right now,” Will answered.

“Did Kathe’s team make it out?” Yorg asked.

"Yes," Ramsey rolled her eyes, putting Yorg's earbud on mute. "I can't tell him yet," she glanced at Sydney.

"Jay, can you hear me?" Ramsey asked.

"Ramsey, we barely made it out of the cave when Jenkins fired at the trees sealing the entrance!" Jay alerted. "It felt like a 7.0 earthquake. The ground shook violently for about twenty seconds, knocking us off our feet. Bernadette and Alonzo were near the edge and fell several feet. My Brightex flashlight is lighting up the forest for us to rescue them," he flashed it over the ledge.

"Bernadette is in trouble!" Mikey exclaimed looking over Pauli's shoulder. "She's hanging onto a limb, dangling over another ledge."

"Hold the light over here," Alonzo ordered crawling toward the ledge as the ground began to tremble. "Bernadette, hold on. I'm coming."

"Brace yourselves!" Sydney warned. "The computer is picking up a second aftershock!"

"Alonzo, help!" Bernadette swung around uncontrollably as the ground shook for another few seconds.

"We need to get off the mountain!" Mikey declared moving away from falling rocks.

"Your best option is to climb down," Ramsey studied. "Tie your ropes to some trees. Then, hurry to Alonzo's helicopter at the clearing."

"Pauli, put the drone on hover mode, and I'll work it until you climb down," Sydney ordered.

"Copy that," Pauli complied and then reached in his backpack for a rope.

"Alonzo, have you reached Bernadette?" Sydncy asked moving the drone.

"Not yet!" Alonzo declared. "I can see her below me."

"I see you," Sydney zoomed in. "You're going to have to tie your rope around the closest tree and then lowered yourself to her."

"Bernadette, hang on," Ramsey consoled. "Alonzo is on his way."

"Brace yourselves!" Sydney warned. "Another aftershock is building."

"My hands are slipping!" Bernadette screamed.

"I'm a few feet to your left," Alonzo relayed holding onto the rope. "I'm going to swing closer to you. Be ready to grab my hand!"

"As soon as it stops," Bernadette replied swinging her feet around the limb.

“It’s over!” Alonzo shouted pushing off a rock toward her. “Grab my hand!” he ordered missing her. “I’m coming again!”

“Alonzo!” Bernadette cried letting go of the limb, grabbing his hand as the ground began to shake.

“Hold on!” Alonzo gripped her as she dangled helplessly below him. “Ah!” he strained pulling her up to him.

“Alonzo, hold on!” Pauli shouted over the ledge. “We’ll pull you up!” he said as all three men grabbed the rope.

“You’ve almost got them!” Ramsey coaxed watching the three men pulling with all their might. “You did it!” she cried as Pauli sat on the ground with his feet against a rock, dragging them over the top.

“That was too close!” Bernadette admitted lying on the ground, catching her breath.

“Did Kathe make it out?” Alonzo asked.

“Not yet,” Ramsey sighed.

“We’ve got God on our side!” Sydney exclaimed moving the drone below. “Alonzo’s helicopter is still working. Pauli can fly Bernadette to the other side and get the Huey. It’s the best workhorse we have to begin clearing the entrance to get to Kathe.”

“Keep me informed while I check on the others,” Ramsey requested. “Sydney, that kind of blast wouldn’t happen with a rocket, would it?”

“Negative,” Sydney pulled up the Internet. “Eduardo chose this mountain because it’s on a fault line. That way, he could erase his footprints, sealing any survivors and equipment inside. I’ll help them while you get Yorg’s team out.”

“Yorg, where are you?” Ramsey demanded pulling up Stephen’s drone.

“We are in the escape room helping a few more people inside the tank,” Yorg answered. “Will found minimal damage at the end of our tunnel.”

“That’s what I’m viewing,” Ramsey replied. “It looks like Carlos planned for this moment and made sure his father could make it out alive. That area is reinforced.”

“Ramsey, I’ve come to a portion of the tunnel that the blast sealed,” Will reported. “The drone can’t get through it. I don’t know how far it is to the exit.”

“Let me check,” Ramsey scanned that tunnel. “I’m showing it collapsed about six feet from the exit.”

"Ramsey, this tank is virtually indestructible," Yorg ensured. "I can probably blast our way out of there."

"Yes, but it could trigger further quake activity," Ramsey warned. "Kathe was in a mini-command center on the other side of the mountain when Jenkins fired a rocket sealing the entrance. That's what triggered the earthquake. That's the last we heard from her."

"What about her vitals?" Yorg begged.

"The blast covered the center with all kinds of dirt and debris," Ramsey confided. "The good news is that the room is inside reinforced concrete. It wouldn't collapse."

"What about oxygen in the room?" Yorg asked.

"It probably has a separate air system," Ramsey assumed. "That has been Carlos's MO from everything we've uncovered about him and Eduardo. I need you to get the villagers and your team out. Sydney is working on freeing Kathe."

"This room is safe," Yorg stated. "Stephen and Will can stay with the villagers while Jack and I take this tank and try to locate her."

"Negative, and that's an order!" Ramsey insisted. "The main tunnel continued to the other side of the mountain. That's where Kathe is. Get those people out. She's not far from the exit. Bernadette is bringing the Huey around to help clear the debris. It shouldn't take long," she crossed her fingers.

"I can't lose her!" Yorg screamed. "It's my fault! I should have stayed with her instead of going after Yetsun!"

"We're not going to lose Kathe!" Ramsey snapped. "Time is of the essence! Get moving, Captain! Let me know when you're about to blast out of there! I'll make sure the area is clear!"

"Copy that," Yorg agreed. "Jack, Stephen, get those people inside and sitting down. Will, there's a window next to me where you can work the drone. Let's move out!" he climbed up the ladder.

Monday, July 6th
2340 (11:40 PM EST)
Sierra Maestra, Cuba

"Ramsey, we are at the end of the line," Yorg reported opening the hatch, and looking at the debris in front of them. "Any news on Kathe?"

"Bernadette is almost back with the Huey," Ramsey reported. "The rest of the team placed emergency lights around the area to light up the entrance. You and I need to concentrate on getting your team out now. According to Will's drone's last GPS coordinates, I've calculated that you are in the tunnel's final, straight stretch. Hopefully, it should only take one shot to free you. We want to keep the aftershocks down."

"I understand," Yorg confirmed closing the hatch and locking it. "Are we clear outside?"

"Yes, I'm not seeing anyone in your path," Ramsey advised checking the screen. "Fire at will!"

"Yes, ma'am," Yorg climbed down the latter and turned to Jack.

"We're in for a rough ride," Yorg explained. "Have the people ready to brace themselves."

"I've already explained the situation to them," Jack shared. "We're packed in like sardines, but ready."

"Stephen, Will," Yorg stopped by them. "I don't know what to expect. Our calculations could be off, and we could be buried alive with no way out."

"We were discussing that," Stephen confided. "We're with your decision 100%."

"Thanks for the confidence," Yorg smiled patting him on the shoulder, and then climbing into the driver's seat. "Boss Lady, we're ready," he declared starting the engine, and calibrating the cannon's scope to penetrate the center of a large boulder.

"One minute," Ramsey glanced at Sydney. "Have your team get to a clear area. Yorg's ready."

"Jay, Mikey, Alonzo, get to a safe place," Sydney relayed. "When Yorg blasts his way out of the tunnel, it could cause more aftershocks."

"Copy that," Jay confirmed. "We're on the move," leading them down to the helicopter pads. "We're ready when you are."

"Copy that," Ramsey answered. "Yorg, ready when you are. See you on the other side."

"Everybody in the back, hold on!" Yorg called over his shoulder. "We go on one; three, two, and one!" Yorg fired the cannon.

"Wow!" Ramsey watched from the mother-drone outside. "Careful, it started another tremor when most of the debris flew out!"

"Jay, is everyone alright?" Sydney asked watching the drone's cameras.

"Yes," Jay answered. "It knocked us to the ground!"

"Stay down," Sydney ordered putting everyone online. "Yorg may have to do it again."

“We’re almost out!” Yorg exclaimed. “Ramsey, I’ve got to do it one more time to make it through the tunnel.”

“Fire when ready!” Ramsey agreed watching the blast.

“Here goes nothing!” Yorg yelled as rubble hit the top of the tank. “Hang on!” he screamed flooring the gas. “We’re going to make it or else!” he shouted as the tank jostled over the rubble, pushing the last bit of debris out of the way.

“You’re out!” Ramsey cheered. “You did it!” she watched as trees and rocks toppled on and around them.

“Hold on!” Yorg shouted as the tank rolled over large trees covering the road.

“Is everyone alright?” Ramsey asked as the quake slowly stopped.

“Jack, is everyone alright?” Yorg asked glancing back.

“One person hit the back of his head pretty hard against the side!” Jack answered. “He’s not bleeding. It was a rough ride for all of us!”

“Yorg, I sent you the coordinates to get to the other side faster,” Ramsey said. “We need all the help we can get there.”

“We’re on our way!” Yorg declared programming the GPS. “Let me know the minute you hear from Kathe.”

“I will,” Ramsey agreed.

“One thing is for sure,” Sydney confessed. “They’re on a ticking time-bomb. It’s not if the mountain is going to blow; it’s a matter of when.”

“I know,” Ramsey sighed. “We won’t leave Kathe buried alive! She’ll make it out!”

“Kathe will,” Sydney agreed. “The deepest part of the fault line runs right where Kathe is,” Sydney sighed pointing to the map. “When Yorg fired those two blasts, it caused the area to shake violently. More debris fell in front of the entrance. We don’t know what happened inside the tunnel,” he reached to answer a call.

“Sydney,” Bernadette reported. “Pauli and I are back with both helicopters. I saw you had another tremendous quake.”

“Yes,” Sydney stated opening all the channels. “Jay, Bernadette is approaching. You need to adjust the lights again.”

“We saw her and are waiting for the tremor to stop,” Jay explained.

“Pauli, Bernadette, hover above the landing site,” Sydney advised. “The quake is almost finished.”

“Copy that,” Bernadette agreed. “We’re watching the movement.”

“Pauli, your helicopter is strong enough to pull out small boulders and trees,” Sydney explained. “Wait there for Bernadette to clear the massive ones that fell. Then, you and Bernadette can take turns dragging debris away."

"Copy that," Pauli agreed. "It looks like the ground is steady now."

"I'm showing that also," Sydney confirmed.

"Jay, I'll land and give you a lift up top," Bernadette offered lowering the Huey.

"Thanks, we need to reposition the lights," Jay said. "It shouldn't take long," he said as they got inside.

"Everybody out," Bernadette said hovering above the ledge.

"We're clear!" Jay called.

"Watch your heads," Bernadette cautioned. "I'm going straight up and then lowering the hoist."

"Copy that," Jay declared reaching for it. "I've almost got the chain. Mikey, help me pull it around the boulder."

"I'll help too," Alonzo grabbed hold and tugged. "Is that enough?"

"Just a little further," Mikey pulled the hook around it as Alonzo and Jay put their weight into the stretch.

"Mikey, is it hooked yet?" Alonzo asked stretching as much as he could.

"Got it!" Mikey strained waving over his head. "Bernadette, it's all yours!"

"Clear the area!" Alonzo ordered backing up. "It could fall!"

"Copy that," Bernadette agreed dragging the boulder away from the entrance.

"It doesn't make sense that I still can't reach Kathe," Sydney confessed. "Her mosquito battery shouldn't be empty; it has extra boosters. Even with two helicopters, this is taking too long. Maybe, I can find a spot above her that isn't so deep," he scanned the area.

"We've got company coming our way!" Bernadette spotted waiting for her turn again. "Ramsey, I see what looks like a steady stream of fire heading this way."

"Let me check," Ramsey cautioned quickly moving the drone in that direction. "You're never going to believe it, but it's the villagers. Jorge is leading them with torches, picks, and shovels. They're coming to help us!"

"Every little bit helps!" Alonzo shouted watching the steady stream of torches coming up the mountain.

"I hear something coming through the woods," Mikey warned reaching for his weapon.

"It's Yorg with the tank full of people to help remove the smaller debris," Ramsey said.

"Yorg can't use the tank to get her out," Sydney cautioned. "Even though Kathe's close to the exit, we can't take the chance of another aftershock. Yorg, have the villagers help us as soon as you can get them out of the tank."

"Copy that," Yorg agreed stopping the tank and shutting down the engine. "Jack let's get these people out. We need them to help us dig Kathe out. I'll open the hatch."

"Okay," Jack agreed giving them instructions.

"Stephen, I need you and Will to use your drones and check the missile in the cove," Sydney requested. "Kathe must have shut the timer off, but Eduardo is known for multiple sleepers. I'd hate for one to switch on with everyone on the mountain. I'm sending you the coordinates."

"Copy that," Stephen agreed climbing down. "Will, program the drone to these coordinates, and release it."

"Got them," Will agreed looking over Stephen's shoulder. "The drone is on its way," he leaned against the tank, releasing it.

"At least, the villagers are reunited with their love ones," Ramsey smiled watching the villagers hugging each other.

"¿Dondé esta Kathe?" (Where is Kathe?) Cambria asked running to Yorg and jumping in his arms.

"Kathe esta atrapada dentro del túnel," ((Kathe is trapped in the tunnel.) Yorg admitted hugging her. "Estamos tratando de sacarla." (We're trying to get her out.)

"Le diré al Abuelo," (I'll tell grandpa.) Cambria got down and hurried away. "Abuelo," she cried. "¡Abuelo, Kathe esta atrapado en el túnel!" (Grandpa, Kathe is trapped in the tunnel!)

"Todos vengan conmigo!" (Everyone, come with me.) Jorge insisted carrying Mariah. "Yorg, ¿Que necesitas que hagamos?" (What do you need us to do?)

"Yorg, they can help," Sydney pushed send. "I'm sending you a map on your phone. Have them climb up to where I circled and dig straight down. That is the shallowest part and should be over Kathe's location."

"Copy that," Yorg showed Jorge the map and then opened a side compartment on the tank. "Jack, there are more tools in here and in the back compartment."

"Copy that," Jack answered giving instructions to several men to help him.

"Jorge, iré contigo!" (George, I'll go with you!) Yorg called out following them up the mountain.

"Mariah, siéntate aquí," (Mariah sit here.) Jorge sat her down on a large rock. "Voy a ayaudar a los hombres a rescatar a Kathe." (I'm going to help the men rescue Kathe.) "No llores la encontraremos." (Don't cry. We'll find her.) He wiped her tears and kissed her forehead.

"We've got enough positive energy for this to work!" Ramsey exclaimed.

"Kathe's been in there for an hour," Sydney sighed trying to ping the signal off Yorg's cell phone. "Even by using Yorg's phone, I can't get through."

"Wait a minute?" Ramsey moved the drone around the area. "Where did Mariah go? She was sitting on that rock."

"There she is!" Sydney exclaimed pointing to the screen. "She's walking up the trail toward the ravine."

"She disappeared behind several large boulders," Ramsey moved the drone behind them.

"The path is so narrow her small feet barely fit," Sydney noted. "She's going to fall! Yorg, Mariah is in trouble! She went up the path behind the rock where she was sitting. She's walking around a small ledge that drops off. She could be killed."

"Copy that," Yorg answered. "Jorge, ven conmigo." (George, come with me.) "Mariah esta en problemas!" (Mariah is in danger!)

"Mariah found another hidden waterfall!" Ramsey declared observing her carefully edging her way around the ledge.

"Ramsey, see where the water is going?" Sydney asked as the drone followed the water inside. "Yorg, the waterfall leads to an underground river," Sydney discovered quickly checking the satellite's map. "It's not on the map."

"The ledge is too narrow for us to follow her," Yorg confessed reaching in his backpack, pulling out a rope. "I'm going to have to swing my body around the ravine to the other side. What's on the other side?"

"Look at your phone," Sydney requested sending him the footage.

"I can make it," Yorg said lassoing a large boulder. "Jorge, te enviaré la cuerda." (George, I'll send the rope back to you.)" He said swinging around the corner.

"Thank God, you made it!" Ramsey exclaimed watching him sling the rope back to Jorge. "He made it also!"

"¿Mariah, a dondé vas?" (Mariah, where are you going?) Jorge demanded rushing to her, entering a cave behind the waterfall.

"Podemos llegar a Kathe desde el interior de esta cueva." (We can get to Kathe from inside this cave.) Mariah whispered. "Se abre en un area grande." (It opens into a large area.)

"¿Qué dijiste?" Jorge laughed hugging her. "¡Mi Mariah ha vuelto!" (My Mariah is back!) "¡Puedes hablar de nuevo!" (You can talk again!)

"That was music to our ears!" Sydney exclaimed.

"I knew Mariah would snap out of it!" Ramsey proclaimed.

"¿Me puedes llevar ahí?" (Can you take me there?) Yorg asked picking her up.

"Si, pero de mucho miedo," (Yes, but it's very scary.) Mariah cried throwing her arms around his neck.

"Prometo protegerte," (I promise to protect you.) Yorg hugged her. "¿De que manera?" (Which way?)

"De esta manera." (In this way.) Mariah said leading them inside the cave.

The drone followed Yorg carrying Mariah as they walked through water up to their knees until they reached an upward path.

"Kathe esta arriba," (Kathe is up there.) Mariah pointed. "Arriba bajé a través de esto." (I came down from this.) She pointed inside a round cement tube. "Mi padre me puso dentro de esta diapositiva." (My father put me inside this tube.) "Luego, me empujó después le dispararon." (He said it would take me to safety.) "Dijo que me llevaría a un lugar seguro." (Then, he pushed me after they shot him.) "Lo último que dijo fue que te amo." (The last thing he said was I love you.) She cried harder.

"Los hombres malos se han ido." (The bad men are gone.) Jorge reached for her. "Tu padre quiere que salvemos a Kathe." (Your father would want us to save Kathe.) Jorge hugged her and wiped her tears.

"Lo sé," (I know.) Mariah tried to smile. "Por eso vine aquí," (That's why I came here.) "Él fue muy valiente come tú y Kathe," (He was very brave, like Kathe and Yorg.) She hugged him again.

"Sydney, can you see where we are?" Yorg asked.

"It's a primitive escape route," Sydney said as the drone went up to the top. "There's no way to reach the top from where you are. There must be another way up there. Ramsey, let me take over the drone," Sydney requested flying the drone back out behind the waterfall. "It has to have something to do with the underground river," he said flying the drone down to the river.

“It’s a mini-submarine!” Ramsey exclaimed.

“And there is the doorway inside the tunnel,” Sydney located behind a boulder. “Yorg, you’re going to have to go outside behind the waterfall and climb down to the river. Jorge needs to go back to the villagers and get them off the mountain. The computer is warning me that more tremors will begin soon. We’ve got one shot to get Kathe out, and that’s it.”

“Copy that,” Yorg agreed taking Mariah by the hand. “Ven conmigo.” (Come with me.) He led the way back outside. “Jorge, llévala con los demás y saca la tu gente de la montaña.” (George, take her back to the others and get them off the mountain.)

“Yorg, if they climb down a little way with you,” Sydney noticed. “There’s another trail that leads them back easier.”

“Copy that,” Yorg answered instructing George, tying another rope to a tree. “Mariah, te voy a llevar sobre mi estalda.” (Mariah, I’m going to carry you down on my back.) “Agárrate fuerte y no mires hacia abajo.” (Hold on tight and don’t look down.) He said, swinging her on his back. “Jorge, sigueme.” (George, follow me.) Yorg requested and backed over the ledge.

“You’re looking good,” Ramsey coached as they started down.

“The path is right by you,” Sydney relayed as soon as they were halfway down.

“Jorge, hay el camino a dos demás.” (George, there is the path to the others.) He pointed putting Mariah down.

“Gracias.” (Thank you.) Jorge said taking Mariah’s hand. “Ve con Dios, mi amigo.” (Go with God, my friend.) They waved as Yorg started down again.

“Yorg, hold on!” Sydney warned as a small tremor began. “It shouldn’t last long,” he said watching Yorg holding onto the rope.

“That was close,” Ramsey sighed as soon as it stopped. “You still have a way to go.”

“I’m taking the drone ahead of you to look for an entrance,” Sydney moved the drone as Ramsey watched Yorg hurrying down.

“Thank God, you’re down safely,” Ramsey sighed.

“The doorway is straight ahead of the sub,” Sydney stated. “Carlos built a dock and ramp straight to the door.”

“Pretty fancy for in the middle of nowhere,” Ramsey noted.

“Sydney, it’s got an electronic lock,” Yorg pointed.

“I see that,” Sydney acknowledged enhancing the picture. “Yorg, the number is a combination of 2015.”

"Does it still have electricity?" Yorg sighed trying several variations of the numbers.

"I saw a generator inside the mini-command center that must have kicked on when they lost power," Sydney shared. "It was by Thompson when Jenkins killed him."

"It still works!" Yorg declared shoving the door open with his shoulder. "It's an elevator."

"You can't use it," Ramsey ordered. "There has to be a hidden stairwell."

"Yes, I found the door to it," Yorg hurried up the stairs. "I'm on a balcony that has two ways out. One leads the way I came, and the other one is the slide Mariah used going in a different direction."

"Mariah's father must have worked on this room and knew the secret ways out," Ramsey noted. "That's why they brutally murdered him and displayed pictures of him to the villages."

"The doorway in the middle of the balcony is sealed," Sydney admitted moving the drone around. "I'm sensing Kathe and JAKE are inside. I'm picking up her vitals. She's breathing very slowly."

"Yorg, the code to that door is probably the same as downstairs," Ramsey assumed. "Try that number."

"It is," Yorg said reaching for the doorknob.

"Wait!" Sydney cautioned. "Carlos sometimes uses booby-traps in his designs. Open the door enough for me to get the mosquito inside. We need to see what you're walking into."

"Copy that," Yorg agreed barely cracking the door.

"Kathe!" Ramsey gasped staring at the screen in fear.

"Oh, my God in heaven!" Yorg glared at his phone's screen.

"I need to contact Rodger!" Sydney exclaimed.

"He's on his way to Dubai," Ramsey shared.

"This will take the both of us," Sydney placed the call. "Rodger, as you can see, Kathe is standing behind the main computer desk surrounded closely by laser beams. She is holding JAKE directly at the beam pointing at her face."

"That's the only thing keeping her alive," Rodger sighed as his team joined him.

"How much battery power does JAKE have left?" Sam asked watching over Rodger's shoulder.

"Luckily, JAKE recharges in its holder," Sydney explained checking its power. "It's using a lot of energy blocking the beam. It will run out in less than fifteen minutes."

"Kathe!" Yorg took a deep breath as a tear fell from his eye. "I can see in your eyes that you're listening to us. We were able to get a mosquito inside the door in front of you. I'm right outside it. Sydney and Rodger are working on getting you out of this situation."

"JAKE ran an analysis before the last beam came at me," Kathe whispered with tears streaming down her cheeks. "The source isn't on the computer. There is a secondary system. Before JAKE could locate it, the beam came at me. Instinctively, I used JAKE's laser to block it."

"Did you notice anything unusual before the second system began?" Sydney asked scanning the room.

"There was a set of small tremors that shifted the door entering from the main tunnel, and the beams immediately projected inside," Kathe explained.

"Rodger, I'm picking up a slight electrical impulse coming from the top hinge on the door by the main tunnel," Sydney admitted scanning the door.

"Sydney, one thing we've learned about Eduardo, is that he doesn't use conventional equipment," Yorg emphasized. "That could be the source."

"That hinge is quite a bit thicker than the bottom one," Rodger noted zooming in closer. "It has to be a power source connected by Bluetooth."

"But, to what?" Ramsey asked.

"With this much at stake, it wouldn't be obvious," Sydney admitted.

"Sydney, if you turned off the lights in the room, infrared would pick up the beams," Yorg suggested. "That should make it easier to locate the source."

"Correct," Sydney agreed. "But with the way Carlos and Eduardo wire things, would it cause something worse. Let me run an analytical modal of both scenarios," Sydney typed and pressed enter.

"While you do that, I'm going to try to get into the main-frame of the generator," Rodger began to type. "Just in case we go with this idea."

"It has a 97.8 % chance of not causing a problem," Sydney declared glancing at Ramsey. "It has a 100% chance of causing problems if we don't shut the electricity to it off. It's the only solution we have."

"We're running out of time," Ramsey agreed. "Kathe, what are your thoughts?"

"It's the only chance I have," Kathe agreed. "JAKE's battery is low. My arm muscles are trembling from the exertion of holding JAKE at the same angle for quite a while. Yorg, you have enough time to get out of here. Do it for the children?"

"I'm not leaving without you!" Yorg declared. "Sydney has never let us down! Rodger, can you cut the lights?"

"Affirmative," Rodger held his finger over the enter key on his computer.

"I agree," Ramsey stated. "When you're ready."

"I'm cutting the lights in four, three, two, and one," Rodger pressed enter.

"Infrared is coming on," Sydney relayed moving the mosquito's infrared camera. "The only thing unusual is on the desk above Thompson's body. It looks like a child's large wooden block," Sydney typed more commands and then pressed enter. "I used Chameleon to encapsulate the module. Chameleon is accessing the software and taking it over. I am shutting it down," he pushed enter.

"It didn't work!" Ramsey exclaimed answering her phone.

"Yes, it did!" Sydney exclaimed. "The power cut for a second."

"That triggered another electrical impulse!" Rodger exclaimed.

"Where?" Sydney searched the room. "Infrared is showing the beams are bouncing off the walls back and forth to each receptacle!"

"The source has to be in one of those," Rodger sighed. "But which one?"

"We have another problem," Ramsey interrupted. "Stephen and Will's drone got inside the missile silo in the cove. As they were checking to make sure the countdown stopped, the electricity turned back on! The countdown has resumed! I have no other choice but to evacuate the other teams."

"Yorg, go with them," Kathe sighed. "I can't hold my arm up anymore."

"You have to, Lady!" Yorg ordered. "And that's an order! We've got children depending on us!"

"I keep seeing their faces," Kathe whispered with tears streaming down her cheeks. "Please save yourself. At least, they will have one parent."

"I'm not leaving without you!" Yorg shouted.

"I found the source!" Rodger exclaimed. "I can't pinpoint it exactly, but it's close to the door by Yorg."

“I see what it is!” Sydney declared. “Yorg, above the doorway inside is the only round receptacle. The others are in the shape of a hinge or squares. It has to be the source of the laser.”

“If I open the door, will it set it off?” Yorg asked watching his screen.

“I’m not sure,” Sydney confessed. “It’s far enough away from the frame that it shouldn’t. We have no other choice; open it! Once you’re inside, use the block on the desk to smash it. That should destroy both.”

“Kathe, I’m coming in to get you!” Yorg burst the door opened, grabbed the block off the desk, and smashed the light.

“I heard something snap!” Kathe looked around the room as she put JAKE on her belt and rubbed her arm. “The middle of the floor is sinking!” she screamed as the chairs on both sides slowly began to slide toward the center of the room. “There is a crack starting to open in the center of the floor!”

“Kathe, run to me!” Yorg ordered jumping outside the doorway and reaching for her.

“Kathe, run!” Ramsey ordered watching the crack open wider.

“Oh, no!” Kathe ran toward the door as everything on both sides slid toward the middle.

“You’re almost to me!” Yorg coaxed dropping to the ground and reaching for her.

“Ah!” Kathe screamed dodging objects.

“Grab my hand!” Yorg ordered holding onto the doorframe. “Jump now!”

“I can do this!” Kathe screamed springing off Thompson’s body wedged between the generator and desk.

“I’ve got you!” Yorg grabbed her hand as the floor ultimately gave way, and the room began to shake.

“Get out of there!” Ramsey ordered. “Another quake is starting!”

“Yorg!” Kathe screamed dangling above emptiness.

“Heavenly Father, give me strength!” Yorg exclaimed pulling her up to him. “Kathe!” he grabbed her as the ground began to shake violently.

“Take the slide before it falls apart!” Ramsey ordered. “I repeat, take the slide! Bernadette, meet them at the ledge by the hidden waterfall!”

“With pleasure,” Bernadette smiled as both teams shouted with relief.

“I’ve got you!” Yorg held Kathe between his legs as they slid down the tube together, shielding her head from falling dirt and rocks as the concrete began breaking apart.

“I’ve lost contact with them!” Ramsey snapped.

"I've got them in my sights!" Bernadette screamed hovering over the area, watching them crawl out of the cave.

"Bernadette, lower the hoist!" Jay ordered. "Ramsey, they're almost to us!"

"Thank God!" Ramsey exclaimed sitting back in her chair.

"Yorg's got it!" Jay declared. "Raise the hoist!" he watched as both held onto the chain. "We've got them!" Jay exclaimed with Mikey, Stephen, and Will helping to pull them inside the chopper.

"Everyone is safe!" Ramsey threw her hands in the air.

"Both choppers clear that airspace!" Sydney ordered. "It's a matter of minutes before the entire mountain blows!"

"We're leaving," Pauli declared heading away from the mountain. "Where are we heading?"

"Guantanamo Bay," Sydney advised. "Hiltree arranged for you to takeoff from there."

"What about your father's mini-sub and the drone?" Kathe asked. "Yorg and I left them in La Playita in an underground spring."

"Both are already on the way home," Sydney chuckled. "You didn't think I'd leave my father's toys laying around, did you?"

"Who's behind the wheel?" Yorg asked.

"Chameleon!" Sydney laughed.

Chapter 9

Tuesday, July 7th
1100 (11:00 AM UTC)
Over the Persian Gulf

"Sydney, we're two hours out from Dubai," Rodger called. "I'm sorry it took me a while to read the last chip we got from Johansson. After helping you get Kathe and the teams safely out of Cuba, I had to crash for a while."

"Ramsey and I knew you were exhausted," Sydney admitted. "I couldn't have done it without you. It's unbelievable how Eduardo uses so many different facets in his equations."

"I'm having a hard time hacking into Johansson's firewall on this chip," Rodger admitted.

"I'll join your computer and help you," Sydney said initiating LogMeIn as Rodger sat back and watched. "I see the problem. It has a Russian component inside the Firewall," he typed several commands and pressed enter. "Johansson has one file on this chip. Wait a minute. I saw a blip on the right corner. Johansson has a hidden file! I'll have to use Chameleon to find the encrypted commands. This is what we've been looking for on Jenkins. Johansson has a CYA File for himself!"

"I knew Johansson would have his backside covered," Ramsey grinned reading the screen. "Johansson wrote, 'while Jenkins muscled his way to Spinello right after he put Thompson away, he didn't know anything about Eduardo until Sydney pulled up the obituary.'"

"I remember Jenkins' shouting, 'That's the connection!'" Sydney stated.

"That's because Jenkins knew about the satellite, ESPGOTU1000 that Gen. Yetsun put into orbit," Ramsey continued to read. "Johansson stated that Jenkins was at the briefing with The president about it. He noted that Jenkins didn't tell Sydney and Ramsey about the satellite. That's when Johansson realized that Jenkins planned to double-cross them. One of his last entries stated Jenkins was behind the switch of two replacements with two of the staff at the Cape. Their job was to take control of the computers for the rocket after Eduardo's takeover," she skimmed down. "He has incriminating evidence on how Eduardo adopted Johansson and Omar Barrick and forced them to do his work. He has a CIA ID Badge and credentials claiming he was on special assignment for Carswell."

“Johansson falsified those documents, too!” Hiltree snapped. “I can’t believe that Gen. Thompson put Johansson in the position to sell out our country.”

“Reading through these notations, if caught, Johansson planned to save himself and continue selling our secrets to the highest bidder,” Ramsey declared.

“Rodger, sift through this file and send Skip and Mack some things to add to the video,” Sydney requested. “They have time to send it to Kathe.”

“Sam, go through Jenkins’ file and do the same,” Ramsey ordered.

“CC, finish documenting everything you have on Spinello and Bencivenni,” Ramsey requested. “Check the timeline Skip and Mack are putting together to prove all the individuals involved from beginning to end.”

“Yes, ma’am,” CC answered.

“Ramsey, I have Terrance on the other line,” Sydney alerted.

“Put the call through,” Ramsey requested as Breaking News flashed above the screen.

Monday, July 6th
1900 (7:00 PM EST)
FNN News Breaking News

Breaking News: “This is Robert Morwitz from FNN News reporting on our way to Sego Lilly Airport outside of the DC area. At 1745 (5:45 PM EST), I received an anonymous tip stating that an airplane will explode today over the runway before 1900 (7:00 PM EST). I reported this to the local Desk Sergeant Patrick O’Reilly. He said he had received the same threat for the last three weeks. Each time he sent officers to the scene, it turned out to be nothing. O’Reilly told me that they finally kept the caller on the line long enough to trace the call. It was a teenage boy with special needs. After my editor listened to the recorded call tonight, he still sent me to check it out. The tower is unmanned at this smaller airport due to budget cuts with the air traffic controllers put into effect by the last administration,” he explained as his helicopter lifted off the roof. “Now, back to the regularly scheduled television programming while we investigate this fourth threat to the Sego Lilly Airport. This is Robert Morwitz with FNN News.”

Monday, July 6th
1845 (6:45 PM EST)
Parking lot near Sego Lilly Airport

"Ramsey, I'm with AG John Kolouski and have shown him some of the intelligence we gathered," Terrance reported. "He insisted on coming with us on our stakeout near Sego Lilly Airport. He said our intelligence filled in all the blanks to questions he had concerning Charles Carswell, and the last administration getting away with very suspicious activities."

"I'm sure this has opened his eyes," Ramsey agreed.

"Excuse me, Sir," Agent Wayne Hudson connected his earbud. "I hate to interrupt you, but we've got a jet about to land at the Sego Lilly Airport."

"Terrance, you may put your iPad on speakerphone for the attorney general to listen," Sydney typed commands, pressing enter. "I have distorted our voices to keep our anonymity, and it's untraceable."

"I'll relay the message," Terrance agreed putting the iPad on speaker. "Sir, they have arranged for you to hear what's going on with this takedown. Their voices are distorted, and the conversation is untraceable."

"I understand," AG Kolouski agreed.

"We've been following Petra Kamenkovich since she left that house with the Barricks and Carswell," Wayne reported. "She just pulled off the road alongside the chain link fence near the entrance to Sego Lilly Airport. A single jet is coming in for a landing."

"Let me take over the mosquito," Sydney requested zooming in on it. "It's a Gulfstream G-650 Leer. That is a plush way for the Barricks to travel to their new job. It can travel 7,500 miles before having to refuel."

"That's more than enough fuel to take them nonstop to Dubai," Ramsey declared.

"Why isn't the jet stopping at the terminal to let the passengers deplane?" AG Kolouski asked. "What's it doing?"

"It's taxiing to the other side of the airport to takeoff again," Ramsey assumed.

"And here comes Petra," Terrance noted. "She's approaching the jet as the staircase lowers from the back-right side."

"I need you to document the Barricks and Carswell leaving the SUV and getting inside that airplane," AG Kolouski requested. "With the high-positions they held; I need irrefutable evidence of wrongdoing to bring them to trial for treason."

"They are also doing this without their Secret Service Details," Terrance added.

"Eduardo spared no expense with a covered staircase to keep their identity secret," Ramsey watched the stairs lower.

"Yes, he did," Sydney agreed as Petra parked very close to the steps. She got out and extended the coverage to shield the back door for them to board. "It's a tight squeeze, but the mosquito should be able to get inside," Sydney maneuvered it inside the canopy. "I'll follow them inside the plane and sitting down for takeoff."

"Unbelievable," AG Kolouski watched. "This drone's camera eliminates any reason of doubt against the plaintive. We've got them."

"Look at everything they did to pull this off in broad daylight," Ramsey stated.

"Petra's speeding away before the steps finish retracting," AG Kolouski watched.

"The pilots just ran out of the plane from the front left side!" Wayne exclaimed. "They are running to a car parked nearby. Should we apprehend them?"

"Not yet," Ramsey disagreed. "Put a tail on them and have them wait until the car is out of the area. We don't want them to alert Eduardo," she said watching the jet engines start. "I got a bad feeling," Ramsey gasped watching the Leer accelerate. "Sydney, is there a different set of pilots on board?"

"That's why Petra left so fast!" Sydney realized. "I barely got the mosquito out of the canopy in time," he said flying the drone to the windows of the cockpit. "Negative, no pilots! Wayne, take over the mosquito!"

"Copy that," Wayne agreed handing the mother-drone to the driver.

"Sydney, shut that plane down!" Ramsey ordered.

"I'm trying!" Sydney feverishly typed commands. "The speed is 190 and climbing. It's almost ready for liftoff. It needs eight more miles an hour to climb," he said trying to hack inside the computer system. "The system is jammed! I can't stop it!"

"Oh, my Lord!" AG Kolouski shouted watching the jet explode as it passed the tower.

"Ramsey, I've learned sometimes to hate it when you're right," Terrance sighed.

"The FNN News Helicopter is approaching the airport in the distance," Wayne warned. "He will film the agents following Petra and warn Eduardo! He did say someone tipped them off."

"Sydney hack into the pilot's radio frequency," Ramsey requested.

"You're on," Sydney pressed enter.

"FNN News Helicopter, this is Sego Lilly Airport Security," Ramsey introduced. "You are to stand down and leave this volatile airspace immediately. There are parked planes still exploding."

"This is Seth Conrad with FNN News," he returned. "You have no authority to order the press to leave the area. We were on our way to check out a threat called into the newsroom about this airport. We can see the smoke and flames from this distance. I'll hover far enough away not to get caught in the explosions."

"Let me talk with Robert Morwitz?" Ramsey requested promising him exclusive rights.

"You did it," AG Kolouski noted. "They are turning around."

"Eduardo called Morwitz so he could watch his victory and check if someone was following Petra," Ramsey shared.

"Those people never had a chance for survival," Ylia declared watching the flames rise from the backseat. "They were vaporized immediately."

"What were the call numbers on the tail?" Ramsey asked.

"I got them and ran them before it took off," Terrance declared reading his notes. "The jet is registered to Patton Enterprises, LLC."

"It would be poetic justice if that were true," Ramsey chuckled. "Patton Enterprises, LLC is solely owned by Gen. Thomas Jenkins."

"Gen. Jenkins is Head of Homeland Security!" AG Kolouski snapped. "He has an impeccable record of military service!"

"Sir, that's not what we've uncovered," Terrance disagreed. "Jenkins is in deep with these terrorists."

"When this is over, we need to go over all the proof you have on each person," AG Kolouski declared.

"Yes, Sir," Terrance replied. "With the high-profiled people involved, that's why we needed you to be with us when we make the arrests."

"By this explosion, Jenkins will now find himself under an uncomfortable microscope with the NTSB (National Transportation Safety Board)," Ramsey grinned. "It's about time his lies caught up to him."

“I saved the assets Jenkins’ listed in his well-hidden LLC,” Sydney said pulling it up. “The Gulfstream is not listed. Terrance, I’m sending it to you.”

“Watch it show up in the LLC now,” Ramsey chuckled. “And don’t be surprised if the FAA can’t find the black box, manifest, or flight plan. Eduardo is finalizing the end of his ‘so-called’ partners by either framing or killing them.”

“After what I’ve witnessed in the last few days, that wouldn’t surprise me,” Terrance admitted.

“We’re following Petra with the mother-drone back to the house behind the hospital,” Wayne interrupted.

“Eduardo and Catarina can’t be too far away for Petra to pick them up,” Terrance assumed.

“Look below at the freeway,” Sydney zoomed in on the exit to the hospital. “Eduardo tipped off the Secret Service. It’s record time for Secret Service Agents to show up. They’re beating the local police and emergency crews to the hospital.”

“This particular chaos is meant to establish the new Barrick’s alibis,” Ramsey noted. “They know that agents will have to check on them with chaos so close to them.”

“Ramsey, a plane is landing at the private airstrip by the house behind the hospital,” Wayne cautioned. “She’s pulling up to the plane the same way as before.”

“Let me take over the mosquito again,” Sydney released it with a few strokes of his keys. “Let’s see whose arriving.”

“Wayne, there should be another jet or helicopter in the hangar,” Ramsey wondered. “Check it out with the mother-drone.”

“Sydney, there are no windows in the hangar,” Wayne reported.

“Sometimes under the eaves of these large hangars will be a mesh grid between the walls and the roof for ventilation,” Sydney explained moving the mosquito to the canopy covering the steps. “Try that. I’ve got the mosquito inside the plane that landed.”

“Who are the people wearing the mesh-looking veils?” AG Kolouski asked.

“The replacements for the Barricks,” Terrance answered as they watched the people get inside the SUV and Petra driving inside the garage.

“You flew the mosquito in the car with them?” AG Kolouski watched in amazement.

"Did you notice the doors to the house have electric locks controlled by Petra's phone," Sydney stated hacking into the code. "They're going inside the kitchen."

"I only recognize Petra," AG Kolouski shared watching her open a door leading to the basement.

"The man next to her is Petra's husband, Dr. Pasha Kamenkovich," Terrance said splitting the screen on the iPad to show his file. "He is the private physician of Gen. Uilám Yetsun, and now oversees Eduardo's medical needs."

"I've heard of Yetsun," AG Kolouski admitted watching Pasha open a door into the tunnel. "There is a tunnel!"

"I'll turn up the sound," Sydney offered watching them enter the tunnel.

"Let's see if they are who Paris said she was commissioned to paint in the portrait for Dubai," Ramsey smiled. "They'll have to unveil before entering the hospital room. They won't take the chance of an agent seeing them wearing veils."

"They are at a split in the tunnel," Sydney cautioned as they watched both people take off their veils at the same time.

"It worked perfectly!" Pasha gasped looking at them. "I can't tell the difference!"

"I can't either!" Eduardo exclaimed admiring Ellie's transformation.

"They look identical to Omar and Ellie Barrick!" AG Kolouski gasped. "We just witnessed their murders! Who are these people?"

"Meet Eduardo and Catarina Santo Prado," Ramsey introduced watching them hand Pasha the veils. "They had plastic surgery to become the Barricks. Let's listen to them," she turned up the audio.

"Pasha, give us the shot now," Eduardo instructed. "I tipped off the Secret Service, so we'll have extra protection around the hospital. They will send in someone to check on us any minute."

"I prepared a special dose for you," Pasha agreed reaching in his pocket. "This is an altered form of the virus. It will give you a fever without too many other symptoms. I have the vaccine waiting to give you and Catarina when you're ready to leave for Dubai," he said injecting them.

"We found proof that someone injected Astronaut Benjamin with something at the Cape before he boarded the rocket," Sydney shared. "I used my technology to slow the footage down, showing Dr. Pasha Kamenkovich entering Benjamin's room while he was asleep. He placed a cloth over his nose for a minute to induce a deeper sleep and then injected him. Now, we know for sure it is a man-made virus, and Pasha has the vaccine."

"How did Pasha get into a secure building?" AG Kolouski asked.

"I found in Johansson's notes the proof that Gen. Jenkins forced Rodger Slate to mask Pasha's entrance and exit," Terrance confided. "He also forced Rodger to help him switch two of the engineers with Eduardo's replacements to take control over the facility when he's ready."

"Hiltree also knows about Jenkins' involvement and is helping us stop him," Ramsey added.

"We have Connor Johansson in a van nearby," Terrance confessed. "He was never vetted to work in the Pentagon. We found proof that Gen. Robert Thompson got Johansson the job with a fictitious resume. We have all the documents from each person's computers."

"How did you get their computers?" AG Kolouski asked.

"I simply cloned them before erasing their files," Sydney admitted.

"Why didn't you report this to the president earlier?" AG Kolouski asked.

"With the leaks, we couldn't take the chance of tipping Eduardo's hand before we caught him in the act," Terrance answered. "We learned from the computers of Johansson and Jenkins that they did most of the leaks."

"Sydney, thanks for the tip about the mesh grid," Wayne showed them inside the hangar.

"It's a Global 7000," Sydney recognized. "One of the most luxurious jets in the world. It flies 8,500 miles nonstop from New York to Sydney, Australia."

"Terrance, I'll have CC check to see who owns that house," Ramsey picked up her phone.

"That's good," Terrance replied.

"Wayne, take your drone and hover it over between the house and hospital," Ramsey requested. "With Carlos designing multiple exits, we don't want anyone to get away."

"Copy that," Wayne concurred.

"Once Eduardo's inside the hospital room, he told Carlos that he'd contact him," Ramsey stated. "Once he makes that call, Sydney will clone Eduardo's phone and turn it off. That's your cue to arrest Pasha and Petra."

"We're down the street from the house," Terrance answered. "I gave all the names to AG Kolouski for warrants."

"I just printed out the warrants of everybody involved," AG Kolouski stated lowering the top of his briefcase. "I'm signing them now."

"Ramsey, the virus is highly contagious," Dr. Ylia cautioned. "I brought plastic facial shields, masks, gowns, and gloves for us to wear. Once inside, I'll grab the virus and vaccine. I brought my portable lab to identify the Santo Prado's blood samples. It shouldn't take me long."

"You heard the expert," Ramsey ordered. "Everyone entering that house must wear protective gear. If the virus is what we think it is, it will spread very quickly. Terrance, have your people suit up now."

"Copy that," Terrance agreed getting out of the SUV.

"I'm hacking into the security cameras at the house and shutting them off," Sydney typed commands on his computer.

"The new Barricks are back in their quarantined rooms," Ramsey noted. "Pasha and Petra waited for them to slip into gowns and took their clothes with them. They stopped at the split and hid the veils and their clothes in a secret compartment. Petra sealed it electronically."

"I'll need to have them for evidence," AG Kolouski declared.

"Of course," Ramsey agreed. "Sydney will change the locks once they are back inside the house. He'll open the compartment for you from here.

Now, they are heading back through the tunnel to the house. Terrance, wait for my signal to enter the house."

"Copy that," Terrance stated signaling his men to wait.

"Robert Morwitz is waiting for my signal to start the broadcast," Ramsey shared. "Listen, Eduardo is making the call to Carlos," she turned up the sound.

"Everything went like clockwork!" Eduardo bragged. "We'll watch the fireworks as planned from our hospital beds and then join you," he hung up the phone. "Now to watch what's left of my partners," he chuckled getting into bed.

"Cloning Eduardo's phone was successful," Sydney smiled. "He called Carlos in Dubai. Terrance, I have voice recognition of both for your proof. I found the phone numbers for Pasha and Petra in Eduardo's contacts. I turned them off as well as Eduardo's phone."

"Terrance, you do know what fireworks Eduardo is referring to?" Ramsey asked.

"Yes, ma'am," Terrance answered. "I'm showing AG Kolouski the file we got from Johansson's computer on it. He's looking over it now."

"Eduardo's turning on the television," Ramsey chuckled. "Morwitz is on the air."

Monday, July 6th
1953 (7:53 PM EST)
FNN News Breaking News

Breaking News: "This is Robert Morwitz from FNN News reporting from Sego Lilly Airport outside of the DC area," he said as the cameraman panned across the airport. "At 1745 (5:45 PM EST), I received an anonymous tip that a plane would explode on the runway before 1900 (7:00 PM EST). I immediately called the local sheriff, who said they had received those treats for three weeks. He said they traced the call to a local teenager with special needs. My editor reviewed my call and sent me to check it out. As my crew and I approached the scene, an Air Traffic Controller turned us around from Dulles Airport. They are clearing the airspace until the threat of exploding parked planes is cleared. We just received the green light to fly around the airport.

As you can see, it looks like a war zone," the cameraman zoomed in on the burning planes and tower. "The NTSB is on-site trying to piece together what happened to the plane that exploded when it passed the tower. So far, there is no confirmation how many passengers were onboard," the cameraman zoomed out to the hospital. "Many Secret Service Agents have surrounded Sego Lilly Hospital. It is unclear at this time which high-ranking official is inside or if they plan to move them."

The cameraman switched back to Morwitz. "We will keep you updated as we receive the information. Now, back to the regularly scheduled television program. This is Robert Morwitz with FNN News."

"Just like I planned," Eduardo laughed and turned off the television. "I'm already beginning to feel the effects of the virus. It's not as light as Pasha described. I better get some rest while the takeover begins."

Monday, July 6th
2005 (8:05 PM EST)
The house behind Sego Lilly Hospital

"That's right, close your eyes and rest," Ramsey grinned changing cameras. "Pasha and Petra are inside the house now. They are inside the kitchen, and Petra locked the door. Sydney, change the electric lock code."

"It's done," Sydney smiled pressing enter.

"Terrance, you may enter when you're ready," Ramsey announced.

"We're going inside now," Terrance whispered signaling his men to break the door down.

Two agents nodded approval, and swung the battering ram away from the door, and then swung it toward the door. "Bam!"

Terrance signaled them to hit it again. "Bam!"

"What was that?" Pasha asked hurrying to the kitchen window. "It's the FBI!"

"Pasha, the tunnel!" Petra whispered running to the door, trying to unlock it. "It's not working!" She cried as she heard the noise again, bursting the kitchen door wide open.

"Dr. Pasha and Petra Kamenkovich, FBI!" Terrance entered first holding up his badge. "You're under arrest for crimes against America! You have the right to remain silent. Anything you say can and will be used against you in a court of law. You have the right to an attorney. If you can't afford one, you will be given one."

"We have diplomatic immunity!" Pasha screamed. "You can't touch us!"

"Gag them, and place them in separate vans," Terrance ordered reaching into Pasha's pocket for the vials. "Get him out of here!"

"Yes, Sir," Wingate agreed pushing Pasha toward the door with his rifle.

"Dr. Ylia, I believe this is what you need," Terrance handed the vials to her. "Let's go," he said walking to the door to the tunnel.

"The door is unlocked," Sydney grinned pressing enter.

"We've waited a long time for this," Ramsey declared watching them enter the tunnel. "Terrance, when you get to Catarina's room, Sydney will fly the mosquito inside and knock her out with diazepam. Dr. Ylia will then check her DNA, while Sydney does the same to Eduardo. Sydney cloned Pasha's voice, telling the lead Secret Service Agent that he checked on the Barricks, and their conditions have worsened. They joined the ones guarding the grounds. I had two ambulances delivered to the house, ready for Terrance's men to transport them."

"She looks identical to Ellie Barrick," AG Kolouski admitted looking at Catarina. "She's the same build and skin color. She's even wearing the identical wedding ring that Omar recently gave her at a dinner. My wife and I sat close to them."

"Eduardo is ready for you," Sydney stated moving the mosquito. "You may now enter his room. Terrance, while Ylia checks his DNA, I'm going to land the mosquito on his computer chip to check something before we transport them."

"What are you looking for?" Terrance asked.

"Ylia discovered the same marking behind Catarina's ear," Sydney declared landing the drone. "With them infected with the virus and in a weakened state, Eduardo would have Carlos monitoring their locations. I need to scan the chip for GPS," he checked through the data. "I was right! It has GPS," he said typing commands. "I've now encapsulated it and cloned it to show Eduardo hasn't moved from this location. I'm heading back to Catarina's room to take over hers."

"These two people are without doubt imposters," Ylia confirmed. "These two sets of DNA samples match the man and woman wearing mesh-veils you extracted in Cuba. They do not match the samples of Omar and Ellie Barrick that AG Kolouski provided from their records."

"Both targets are ready for transport," Sydney declared moving the drone.

"Job well done to all of you!" Ramsey congratulated.

"Ramsey, I've arranged for us to take these five people to the brig at Dulles Air Force Base," AG Kolouski shared. "They'll be put in isolation and monitored around-the-clock."

"This isn't over yet," Ramsey stood up and stretched. "We still have five more people to bring into custody."

"I'm aware of that," AG Kolouski admitted. "Since they are on foreign soil, we need a U.S. Marshall to arrest them when you're ready. I'll stay with Terrance to see this through. I want to video Terrance reading the Santo Prado's their rights. Let me know the minute you secure Gen. Jenkins and find the others. I emailed you the warrants."

"Thank you, I did receive them," Ramsey said clearing the line. "I'm leaving as soon as Chief Smalley has a conformation that they're on course for the island," Ramsey placed a call. "Chief Smalley, where is Jenkins?"

"It seems they are making several stops along the way," Smalley reported. "The helicopter is on the deck and ready for takeoff as soon as they're close. I'll get back with you."

"Take a mother-drone with you," Sydney cautioned. "We need to document Jenkins with Sabrina Macaby, an escaped criminal from the penitentiary. That will add nicely to his charges of treason."

Monday, July 6th
2130 (9:30 PM EST)
At the Translucent Pearl

"Ramsey, Jenkins just landed on the island," Chief Smalley alerted as they flew over it. "I'm going to pass over and come in low to land. I saw the perfect place, so that this chopper would be out of sight."

"Good, and it's not very far from the house if we have to go inside," Ramsey agreed sending the mother-drone out the side door. "I've never been to this island, but Jenkins told me it's pretty isolated from the rest of the islands with a gorgeous private beach. I see it took them a while to do some shopping along the way for supplies. They are putting groceries in a wagon to pull to the house."

"Your drone gives us a perfect view even at night with the full moon," Smalley declared as Ramsey hovered the drone above them. "He turned on the lights inside and outside of the house from the plane before he landed. The only thing I see on this island is Jenkins' house, an airplane hangar, and a runway. Now they are pulling the wagon up the ramp to the front door," he looked around the property. "I wouldn't want to live out here. We've had several reports of pirates in this vicinity."

"Knowing Jenkins, he pays the pirates off," Ramsey assumed. "It's time to add AG Kolouski and Warden Thornhill to our cameras," Ramsey connected them. "Work the mother-drone for me while I release the mosquito."

"Yes, ma'am," Smalley concurred. "I see that AG Kolouski and Warden Thornhill have signed in with us. You may speak with them now."

"AG Kolouski and Warden Thornhill," Ramsey greeted. "As you can see, Gen. Jenkins and Sabrina Macaby have just landed and are walking to his house. AG Kolouski, you wanted to witness the takedown of Gen. Jenkins."

"Yes, Ramsey, I do," AG Kolouski acknowledged.

"I've added Warden Thornhill to this call," Ramsey explained. "We're expecting Officer Janise Patterson to join them on the island to incriminate herself involved with this scheme further."

"That's fine," AG Kolouski agreed. "After I had time to review the file on Patterson, I contacted Warden Thornhill. We've already had a rather interesting conversation concerning the renovations at the prison directed by Officer Patterson."

“I’m turning up the audio,” Ramsey declared hovering the mosquito over Jenkins and Macaby. “Let’s listen.”

“Oh, Tom, you’re so romantic,” Macaby kissed Jenkins as he swooped her up in his arms. “You’re carrying me across the threshold of our new home?”

“It’s the only way to start our new lives together,” Jenkins kissed her, stepping inside the living room. “Isn’t it everything I promised you in Merritt Penitentiary?”

“The furniture, and paintings,” Macaby glanced around as he put her down. “I can’t believe you decorated this by yourself.”

“I had to do it,” Jenkins put his arm around her. “I couldn’t let anyone know about this island. I flew everything in from the states. After we sell Chameleon, we can travel anywhere we want and come back to our haven.”

“What a liar?” Ramsey declared. “His wife Pearl redecorated the house a few years before she died.”

“I can’t believe I’m finally free from running from the law,” Macaby kissed Jenkins.

“Yes, you are,” Jenkins grinned. “I told you that I’d rescue you from prison. You did bring a copy of what Eduardo has on Chameleon?”

“Yes, yesterday I embedded a hidden program to email me a copy,” Macaby grinned. “That’s one thing Eduardo didn’t discover.”

“Before we toast to our new lives, I’d like you to download what you have on my laptop,” Jenkins declared. “When I brought the groceries to the house, I left my laptop on the plane. I’ll go and get it while you put the groceries away.”

“After barely escaping thc cavc during the earthquake and Ramsey’s people after us, I’d rather do it tomorrow. It’s late,” Macaby pouted, looking into Jenkins’ eyes. “I’d rather toast our reunion and solidify our love the way we used to at the prison and your condo.”

“Oh, darling,” Jenkins kissed her. “We have the rest of our lives to do everything we want. Selling Chameleon will get us the wealth we’ve only dreamt. We need to make sure we have everything to do that, don’t you think?”

“As soon as Chameleon is sold, Macaby’s a dead woman,” Ramsey observed. “She is Jenkins’ last loose end. He won’t take the chance of her ever turning on him.”

“Of course,” Macaby hesitated fiddling with the medals on his coat.

“I’ll show you to the kitchen,” Jenkins kissed her. “It’s this way,” he pulled the wagon.

"I've never had a kitchen this big!" Macaby gasped walking around. "This is the house of my dreams!"

"I'll be right back," Jenkins put the last bag on the counter. "I'll take this back to the plane and get the laptop," he said folding up the wagon. "I'll be right back."

"Oh, I left my backpack on the plane," Macaby remembered. "Can you bring it also?"

"One laptop and one backpack coming up," Jenkins laughed. "I guess I need to get used to carrying your things with me," he smiled leaving the room.

"I can't believe after everything I've been through," Macaby whispered glancing around the room, "that I'd end up with a fantastic new life." She opened the refrigerator, putting the steaks and vegetables in the drawers. She closed the door and leaned against it. "I'll be married to a famous American General, and together we'll travel first class around the world."

"A penny for your thoughts?" Jenkins asked returning to see her daydreaming.

"I never thought I'd get over Timothy," Macaby confessed putting her arms around Jenkins. "We were together since grade school in a small village in Ireland. But the moment you walked into my life; I realize that we were meant to be together."

"That's how I feel about you," Jenkins kissed her. "I've got my laptop and your backpack," he handed it to her. "After we finish, we'll get cozy."

"Again, Tom, you're so romantic," Macaby sighed following him upstairs.

"Let me show you the master bedroom," Jenkins grinned.

"I can't wait," Macaby smiled hurrying up the steps.

"Just a minute," Jenkins sat his laptop and her backpack down by the doorway. "I have to carry you over this threshold as well," he picked her up again.

"Oh, Tom," Macaby hugged him as they entered.

"What do you think?" Jenkins asked.

"Tom, you remembered I always wanted a king-size bed with the four pillars," Macaby cried as he put her down. "It's everything I ever wanted!" she hurried to the long dresser. "Look at the fancy mirror!" she exclaimed running her fingertips over the latticework with tears in her eyes.

“We’ll have plenty of time to fill those drawers with clothes from London and Paris,” Jenkins smiled watching her opening the empty drawers.

“Ramsey,” Smalley interrupted. “I found a seaplane in a small cove covered with tree branches on the other side of the island,” Smalley cautioned zooming in on the sand. “The footprints lead toward the house.”

“That will be Janise Patterson,” Ramsey grinned. “She’s right on time. Dr. Sydney sent her a nice clip of Jenkins killing her longtime lover, Gen. Thompson. It will be interesting to see how she fits into this love nest. Let’s listen,” she turned up the audio.

“There are no tears allowed in this house,” Jenkins smiled wiping Macaby’s cheeks. “Let’s check your email,” he said sitting down at the desk and turning on his laptop. “It’s all yours,” he traded places. “Now, work your magic, my dear.”

“My pleasure,” Macaby smiled setting her backpack down and pulling up her email. She scrolled down the emails. “Here it is!” she grinned up at him, pressing enter.

“Is this a joke?” Jenkins screamed watching an animated tunnel appear on the screen with a green Chameleon coming out of it. It stood up on its hind legs, faced her, shaking its finger at her. “Bad girl, you’ve just been hacked by the greatest wizard of all! GAME OVER! HA! HA! HA! The fully operational Chameleon Technology has encapsulated your operation!” The Chameleon turned around, shaking its long tail from side-to-side, crawled inside the tunnel, and then the screen went blank.

“That’s what Sydney meant by leaving them a little surprise!” Ramsey chuckled.

“My emails have all been erased!” Macaby screamed trying to restart the computer. “It fried your laptop, too!”

“Rodger said that all hackers have more than one copy of their work!” Jenkins remembered. “I have another computer in my office. Come with me!” He grabbed her by the hand, pulling her down the hallway inside his private office. “Let me turn on this computer,” he sat down bringing it up. “Where is your other copy?”

“I don’t have one,” Macaby confessed. “I couldn’t use a thumb drive. Eduardo would have found out immediately.”

“Didn’t you send it to another email address?” Jenkins quizzed getting up.

"No, I figured out how to elongate the time span long enough to send one email," Macaby cried staring at him. "I only had a split second to do it. There were people around me."

"Rodger added a separate encrypted security protection to this computer!" Jenkins confided. "Pull up your emails. It will be safe!"

"Not necessarily," Macaby sat down. "Just let me think for a minute," she pulled up the eternal clock in the settings. She turned to him, "I've got the answer! My work computer was destroyed. I know Eduardo saved everything to the cloud. I think I can guess his password," she began trying several ideas. "If I can put the clock back an hour before I emailed Chameleon, I can change the name of the file and resend it. That will ensure Chameleon will be intact! The hacker only corrupted the original file name. This shouldn't take too long. I glanced at his phone one day when he was looking it up. He only used a few key phrases."

"Didn't you hear me?" Jenkins shouted. "I had Rodger install a different encrypted security system on this computer! Your file is safe!"

"That wouldn't matter!" Macaby disagreed standing and facing him. "The file was corrupted sometime after I received it! I must change the name and resend it!"

"Do what I said!" Jenkins ordered pushing her down in the chair.

"Macaby would be right, if," Sydney chuckled. "Rodger hadn't given me the key to the encryption. I knew she would try to reclaim it. I thought ahead to backdate it to the time before she received it. Then, I simply had Chameleon's Artificial Intelligence single out the file and encapsulate it. So, no matter how she tried to change the time, rename the file, resend it or whatever. It won't work. It's like Tierney said, 'Don't leave any loose ends!'"

"Please, Tom, don't make me do this!" Macaby cried holding her head in her hands. "I know I'm right!"

"Do it or else!" Jenkins demanded watching her press enter. "It's that Chameleon again!" Jenkins screamed pushing Macaby off the chair. "Move out of the way!" he pushed escape. "This computer won't restart either!" he tried again and again. "I've lost everything I had on Eduardo!" he turned backslapping Macaby across the face. "It's all your fault!"

"No, it's not!" Macaby grabbed her cheek. "I warned you! All I had to do was put the time back before the virus and change the name of the file! Because of you I lost all my hard work!"

"You said you were the best IT person besides Johansson!" Jenkins stood up. "You said Eduardo didn't discover that you emailed it to yourself!" he yelled putting his hands around her throat.

"Tom, you wouldn't listen to me!" Macaby cried.

"You, dumb, stupid convict!" Tom screamed shoving her head against the desk. "You've destroyed everything I wanted!"

"Tom!" Macaby gasped fighting to move away from him.

"Stop," she gasped for air.

"No!" Jenkins screamed squeezing harder.

"Jenkins is going to kill Macaby with his bare hands!" AG Kolouski gasped.

"Not until you're dead!" Jenkins squeezed harder. "Because of your incompetence, I've got to find a way to get back in good graces with Ramsey! She's always smarter than me!" he squeezed harder as Macaby's body fell limp in his hands. "I should have taken you back to prison and kept Rodger!" he threw her on the floor. "This wouldn't have happened!" he kicked her in the head. "Now, Ramsey is my only way to get to Chameleon!"

"Sorry, Ramsey," Smalley sighed, watching Jenkins run to the linen closet in the hallway, grabbing a blanket.

"Don't feel sorry for me," Ramsey sighed as Jenkins wrapped the body in the blanket. "Feel sorry for Macaby. Jenkins used her to get what he wanted. He was never going to keep her. Hover the mother-drone over the house and take over the mosquito. He'll probably kill Patterson next. I can't let him get away this time."

"Ramsey, it looks like someone is behind thc door." AG Kolouski noticed.

"I'm on my way," Ramsey hurried to the house.

"Well, well, well," Patterson stepped around the bedroom door, pointing a gun at Jenkins as she closed it.

"It's Officer Janise Patterson," Warden Thornhill identified.

"Sabrina Macaby is another person you can add to your list of killing today!" Patterson declared. "After blackmailing Johansson and me to get you close to Macaby to learn about Chameleon, you strangled the only person that figured out most of the formula for it! Great job as usual by a bumbling idiot! No one would have suspected anything if you hadn't visited Macaby constantly without signing the roster! I warned you that this would happen! That's what tipped off Ramsey! And she told Thornhill. That's the only way he could have found out!"

"Macaby turned on me!" Jenkins exclaimed. "I had to do something!"

"Liar!" Patterson cocked her gun. "Someone sent me a video of you killing Gen. Robert Thompson, the only man I ever loved! You opened classified documents that Thompson sealed concerning our affair! That's how you blackmailed me! Without Ramsey, you wouldn't have known about any of this! Ramsey was onto Spinello and Bencivenni long before you got involved! And, because of me, you got in with Eduardo!"

"I did you a favor!" Jenkins argued. "I later found him in the mini-command center snuggling up with Macaby!" he chuckled. "You and I can still make this vision work! I know you have a copy of Chameleon and the video to broadcast!"

"Not with a double-crosser like you?" Patterson laughed. "What did that animated Chameleon say?"

"What?" Jenkins demanded.

"Yes, I cracked open the closet door and watched the entire clip!" Patterson laughed. "It said, 'Game over! Ha! Ha! Ha!' and terminated your laptop! I also followed you and watched the virus terminate your main computer! Macaby tried to tell you that she could fix it! But no, you wouldn't listen to her! It reminds me of when you turned on Ramsey at the Pentagon and hired Johansson! You should have stayed with Ramsey!" she screamed shooting Jenkins through the heart as the door swung open. "Linda Ramsey!"

"Yes, drop your gun!" Ramsey ordered holding her Glock at Patterson. "You were a sharp-shooter for the military! I see you shot Jenkins right through his cold heart!" she held up her phone. "We are livestreaming this to AG John Kolouski and Warden Thornhill. It's over! Drop your gun!"

"I don't believe you!" Patterson screamed.

"Officer Patterson," Warden Thornhill spoke. "I've asked AG Kolouski to request that you serve out your sentence at Merritt Penitentiary. Ramsey has offered her assistance in finding all your renovations and correct them before you arrive."

"No!" Patterson screamed turning the gun to her temple, and firing.

"Sorry, you had to witness that, Sirs," Ramsey sighed turning her head.

"I'm not surprised," Thornhill admitted. "I've learned by interviewing some of the community that Patterson bragged about killing the four prisoners that were on a work detail, and the guard. She also forced two of the prisoners to kill other inmates, and some non-inmates that she placed in the general population."

"I'm glad I was able to open your eyes to the corruption Patterson did while you were away," Ramsey agreed dumping out Macaby's backpack and ripping open a false bottom. "This is what I suspected," she held it up. "Antonio Falcini, Sr. never went to Wiltz, Luxembourg as his passport proved. For Bencivenni to prove allegiance to Eduardo, he made a mask for Eduardo to witness Dano's professional hit killing CIA Agents Daniel and Cynthia Sydney. Then, he framed Antonio for their murders."

"The Sydney's were some of the best agents in the field," AG Kolouski admitted. "I saw the evidence that proved they were already onto this scheme and killed for it. Eduardo would have gotten away with it if it weren't for you and your team. I'm joining President Trumore onboard Air Force One to go over your intelligence information without revealing your names or technology. You have my word that I will keep your anonymity. President Trumore will be pleased to know we found out who was doing the leaking, and those who survive will be prosecuted at once."

"Our team has already scrubbed any impertinent footage of our team," Ramsey admitted. "Thank you for keeping our anonymity," she cleared the line. "Smalley, send this new footage to Skip and Mack. They need to add this to the video. I'll meet you at the helicopter."

"Yes, ma'am," Smalley agreed bringing the mosquito back to dock with the mother-drone. "You were right about Jenkins using Macaby. And, that Patterson would come here for Jenkins."

"Sometimes," Ramsey sighed glancing at Jenkins' body. "I hate it when I'm right. I'm on my way."

Tuesday, July 7th
1900 (7:00 PM UTC)
Airport Near Dubai

"CC, I'm lowering the steps for the last team to join us," Hiltree reached for the lever. "Dr. Sydney has activated Chameleon to mask all three jets' identities."

"Thanks," CC replied looking up from her laptop. "I have the presentation ready to show them," she said as the last team entered the C-135 Jet.

"I see you brought my Huey," Yorg shook Hiltree's hand.

"Sydney insisted I bring it," Hiltree stated. "With JAKE and Chameleon installed, nothing Carlos throws at us can stand a chance."

"You're right," Yorg agreed.

"It's too bad the T-14 Russian Tank didn't make it off the mountain in Cuba," Stephen joined them. "Yorg blasted our way out of a cave when an earthquake hit, burying us in dirt and rocks," he looked around. "I see the Huey isn't the only vehicle you brought."

"Sydney gave me a shopping list," Hiltree shared.

"That man is thorough," Stephen agreed. "I see you brought the silent, high-tech motorcycles."

"From what Bernadette and Mikey said about their performance, they'll come in handy," Hiltree admired. "I got a taste of what they're like when I drove them inside."

"They were quiet and stealth," Stephen shared. "I've never seen anything like their maneuverability at high speeds."

"I see that Paris got the paintings," Kathe admired stopping in front of them. "Paris, I see what you meant by the portrait of Omar Barrick bothering you. Did you do what Sydney suggested?"

"Of course," Paris grinned. "Mikey helped me add a few minor changes on the way here. It plans to be an explosive evening, Carlos won't forget."

"Stay close to Bernadette and Mikey," Kathe cautioned placing a lapel pin in the shape of an artist palette on her jacket. "This is a camera and microphone Sydney wanted me to give you in case you're separated. Carlos does not care how many people he kills to reach his agenda."

"Thanks, I heard stories about Carlos on the way across the pond," Paris admitted winking at her. "Just remember, I am a Sydney and grew up in Uncle David's house."

"Yes, you are," Kathe admitted.

"Everyone needs to take a seat," Hiltree requested lowering a screen in front of the Huey. "For you civilians, pull down the jump seats from the sides of the plane. It's a military workhorse and not meant for comfort."

"You've got that right," Carrie Anne complained as Joe and Travis held her seat down for her.

"Speaking of comfort," Kathe wondered, "with the seriousness of this evening, why would Carlos plan a rock concert? The only thing on the itinerary is Europe's top artist, displaying two paintings this evening at the unveiling the new Presidential Palace: but to whom? It doesn't give a guest list. And the guest of honor isn't even present. What are they unveiling?"

"It has nothing to do with entertainment," Alonzo agreed. "This is about a worldwide military coup."

"We think so too!" Stephen exclaimed. "Will and I have discussed this same idea."

"I know," Joe admitted standing up, "that none of you on this plane approve of me based on my past actions. I have endangered not only myself, but also your teams more than once. As a result, I've watched these people firsthand. You can't tell me that Carlos is just a mommy and daddy's little boy. He's a powerful, award-winning engineer. His creativity is much like that of Dr. Sydney in some respects. To me, the point that you're missing is that he's just like me. He's arrogant and a worldwide Playboy. No man is all work and no romance. One thing our band learned from the early days is that we play to our audience. This concert has nothing to do with this evening. Something in his past caused his parents to allow this concert to take place on the biggest night of their new life."

"Joe has a good point," Stephen agreed. "We're in the entertainment business too. It seems like a trap. Were tickets even sold for this event? There are quite a few bands geared to the younger crowd. I've never heard of some of these bands, and after checking them out, I wouldn't listen to their music."

"They both have a good point," Yorg agreed. "Where's the youth coming from, and why?"

"From what we gather, Carlos is in his late thirties," CC realized. "We've never found anything about him other than he is an innovative engineer.

"Not to mention," Babs Thompson added, "he's very handsome."

"I didn't realize that dear," Troy glared at her.

"I'm happily married to you," Babs winked at him. "But I'm not dead."

"I'll have Chameleon check through the computers we cloned," Sydney agreed typing commands. "Let's go continue with what you found from your surveillance."

"I received a text from Terrance saying that Commodore McIntire, with two squadrons aboard the SS Hamilton, is standing by on the Sea of Omar," Ramsey began. "They moved into position if we need them, compliments of AG Kolouski. Cmdre. McIntire covered for us in Miami at the Aquarium concerning the explosions. I waited to tell you after you rested that we have three more villains out of our way," she explained what transpired at the Translucent Pearl.

"Are you doing, okay?" Kathe asked.

"Jenkins got what he deserved," Ramsey admitted. "Patterson saved the taxpayers the trouble of a court-martial. CC, you may now show us what you've learned from the recon of the area."

"Sydney used Chameleon to mask our drones as Sea Gulls," CC began showing an Aerial of the palace. "This place has large drones patrolling it," she showed them. "This is the new Presidential Palace which is located on the peninsula overlooking the Persian Gulf from the front, and the Sea of Oman from the back. We noticed groundskeepers coming out of the hidden doorways within the beautifully landscaped gardens, like the ones Carlos used in Miami."

"So, we're looking at a complete tunnel system under the Palace and grounds," Alonzo assumed.

"That is correct," CC agreed. "The exotic flowers from around the world told us that Eduardo planned to be the president all along, instead of Omar Barrick. He just needed the face of someone well-known around the political world. Some hidden doorways are in the colorfully lit water fountains surrounding the grounds, giving it a luminous presence at night. The swimming pool behind the house has multiple waterfalls laced with exotic flowers, and a full bar in the middle," she switched showing the long driveway. "It is a half-mile from the street to the rounded driveway leading to the palace. Guardhouses are located at the four corners of the property. We saw one guard in each one with four on the rooftop."

"It looks like a replica of the White House," Jay noted.

"That's the first thing we noticed," CC agreed.

"That goes along with Eduardo's jealously that Omar was well-liked while in office," Ramsey assumed. "It was Eduardo writing Omar's speeches that got him elected."

"That's true," CC agreed. "Another signature of Carlos' parents coming here is the stable on the back-right, near the guard tower where the horses are kept," she noted showing the drone flying inside.

"The black stallion is Champion Tyrus," Bernadette recognized. "The white filly is Sugar Treat. They are both Show Horses that I've watched win amazing Blue Ribbons over the years. The way those horses perform together in dances is almost like they're human. The owner's name was Catherine Van Ness."

"Catarina is Spanish for Catherine," Alonzo shared. "We discovered before you joined us that Van Ness is her maiden-name."

"So, knowing your love for horses," Jack grinned, "I gather that when we level this place, you're taking the horses home with us?"

"Exactly!" Bernadette grinned.

"Getting back to the tour and the mission," CC cleared her throat. "In front of the rounded driveway on the lawn is where the rock concert will be held. We discovered that Carlos designed a stage to rise and lower for different events."

"Using the mother-drone, we saw the stage raising from the ground," Hiltree reported. "I used the mosquito and went underground when the workers lowered it. There is a large, open room with bathrooms. Some bands sent their equipment ahead, and it's stored there. So, each time the stage raises, the members will be on it ready to perform. When finished, it lowers for the next band to take the stage in the same manner. There was a door that I couldn't get under that I believe leads into the tunneling system. I won't know how many guards will be down there until the bands arrive this evening."

"Were you able to locate Carlos' office?" Sydney asked.

"Yes, it's located where the middle windows are on the third floor," Rodger showed them. "There is no computer on his desk. We checked all the windows in the building, not finding one computer. I ran a scan with CC's iPad using JAKE Technology. It didn't locate any computers on the property."

"With all this high-technology, that's hard to believe," Sydney changed keyboards. "I'm pulling up the satellite to scan the property better."

"RJ and I are worrying about Light Crimson's safety," Brock declared. "There are civilians involved, and this will not end as a sit-in at Asbury Park. When do you need us there?"

"Carlos will text Paris with the schedule," Ramsey stated. "Light Crimson is the grand finale. Jay and Jack's cover will be stagehands to help protect the members. We have a surprise for Carlos before the British flag falls, revealing Light Crimson. Alonzo's team, along with Stephen and Will, are to help with getting the band members back to the safety of the van."

"I do know that there will be fireworks behind the palace after the concert," Hiltree stated. "I saw the firemen setting it up."

"Hiltree and I created the perfect distraction for the band to leave if something goes wrong," Rodger declared. "Let's say it will end with more of a bang than Carlos anticipated."

"There is a side gate that is in the middle of the barn for Bernadette to take the horses to safety," Hiltree added. "The C-135 has an area we can cord off to transport them. I have sedatives to keep them relaxed and groggy."

"Hiltree, you will be on the grounds too," Ramsey requested. "You have firsthand knowledge of the area. Also, I'm sending you Cmdre. McIntire's cell phone in case we need to use them."

"Yes, ma'am," Hiltree agreed. "I do know him."

"Ramsey, Carlos just texted me," Paris interrupted. "He wants me to arrive at the front gate with the paintings at 2000 (8:00 PM UTC). I am to get the paintings situated. The unveiling of the palace will begin at 2100 (9:00 PM UTC). Then, the concert will begin at 22:00 (10:00 PM UTC)."

"Okay, teams, we're ready to begin," Ramsey stated. "Will, Stephen, take the motorcycles and find a place out of sight close enough to the palace to get the drones in the air."

"Ramsey," CC pulled up the Aerial. "We found the perfect place for them to work the drones. Carlos is planning a gated community near the palace. A tall, empty tower is the only thing built so far."

"That is perfect," Stephen agreed checking the Aerial, "it's close enough with no one around to see or hear us talking."

"As soon as they are in place, Paris' team will leave in the bulletproof van," Ramsey ordered. "CC, what does the security inside the palace look like?"

"There are guards in every room and hallway," CC showed them. "There is a forcefield around some of the doors, like the president's office that we could not enter."

"Hiltree and I couldn't locate the power source to shut it off," Rodger declared.

"Stephen, send the mosquito to enter the palace with Paris," Sydney watched the screen. "I'll try to locate the source and look for a way for Kathe's team to get inside. Their main mission is to locate the source Carlos plans to upload the video and switch it with ours."

"Hiltree, Alonzo, Pauli, your job is to eliminate the guards in the towers and on the roof," Ramsey continued. "Then, set the charges to blow the fountains and tunnels under them."

"Yorg, you are to pilot the Huey," Sydney affirmed. "As soon as Carlos steps outside the palace, two helicopters always appear to protect him. Your job is to locate and destroy them along with the pilots. I've programmed Chameleon to mask the Huey as one and project the second chopper with a hologram. When Carlos goes to the stage, you are to fly over. We won't know what to expect after the video plays; be ready for anything."

"Copy that," Yorg agreed.

"May God be with all of you," Ramsey added.

"Mikey, here's the key to the van," Hiltree stated tossing them to him. "Stephen, and Will, the keys are on the cycles."

"Great, let's pack it up to leave," Mikey suggested. "It's 1945 (7:45 PM UTC)."

"Will and I can help you carry one of the paintings to the van on our way to the cycles," Stephen offered.

"Paris, remember that you don't know who Carlos is," Ramsey cautioned. "Let him introduce himself to you."

"I've heard so much about him," Paris sighed. "I feel like I already know him."

"He's sharp and paranoid," Ramsey cautioned. "One wrong slip; he's onto you!"

Tuesday, July 7th
2000 (8:00 PM UTC)
Unexpected Guest

"Ramsey, there is a guardhouse with four guards stationed at the gate," Will reported. "I see the van arriving with Paris. I'll turn up the sound."

"State your name and reason for being here," Marco demanded.

"Mikey Goldenrod, I'm with Ms. Paris L'Ville delivering two paintings to the palace," Mikey declared.

"Just a minute," Marco scrolled down the guest list. "Yes, Ms. L'Ville's name is on the list," he reached for his phone. "Sir, Ms. Paris L'Ville is at the gate with two paintings."

"Is she alone?" Carlos asked.

"No Sir, a man and woman are accompanying her," Marco reported.

"I instructed her to come alone!" Carlos snapped hanging up.

"Ms. L'Ville, there has been a misunderstanding," Marco looked in the van. "You were instructed to come alone."

"There is no misunderstanding," Paris disagreed. "When the courier paid me, I specifically told him that I have to bring two of my staff members to help hang the paintings. I can't properly hang them alone."

"Sir, it's Marco again," he called. "Ms. L'Ville has two of her staff to help with the paintings."

"Have her leave the paintings!" Carlos demanded. "I'll hang them myself!"

Marco relayed the message.

"Absolutely not!" Paris refused. "My reputation is at stake! Paris L'Ville's paintings must have the right lighting and hang perfectly straight! My price included the setup fee. Anything less is unacceptable!"

"Sydney," Ramsey sighed. "She's Tierney talking to Márquez in Cuba on steroids!"

"Paris is doing what she advertises," Sydney smiled. "I'm sure Carlos read her website; I did."

Again, Marco stepped away from the van and relayed the message.

"Ms. L'Ville, you may enter," Marco stated. "Drive to the front doors. Gunther will scan you for weapons before escorting you inside the palace."

"Don't worry," Sydney consoled. "I'll encapsulate the scanner with Chameleon. It won't detect your weapons."

"Stephen, be careful with the mosquito," Ramsey requested. "CC warned some of the doorways have a forcefield."

"I put the mosquito on infrared when it entered the front doors with the team," Stephen explained. "The forcefield wasn't activated."

"You are to wait here," Gunther stopped them in a large, rounded entryway as a well-dressed man wearing a white, silk shirt with the first three buttons opened showing a thick, gold Crucifix walked down the curved stairway.

"Ms. Paris L'Ville, I'm Carlos Prado," he introduced. "Welcome to The Presidential Palace. The new president asked you to paint his portrait and recreate his favorite Garden in Paradise Cove."

"Recreate is the perfect way to describe the beauty," Paris shook his hand. "The courier that delivered the sealed envelopes mentioned the man in the portrait planted every flower and tree inside the cove. I was surprised when I opened the envelope after he left. I wasn't aware that Omar Barrick was into floristry?"

"Mr. Barrick has many talents," Carlos chuckled. "He learned floristry from his grandmother."

"That's a twist of the truth," Ramsey scoffed. "Johansson documented that Eduardo found Omar Barrick, AKA, Kenja Baal Akmul in an orphanage in Afghanistan."

“You should be honored that Barrick admires your work!” Carlos pointed to the empty spot in the foyer across from the front French doors. “This is where the painting of the Garden in Paradise Cove will hang.”

“Oh, Mr. Prado!” Mikey kissed his fingers and flipped them in the air while walking around the marble table. “The Paradise in Garden Cove only enhances the beauty of this gorgeous, marble foyer,” he pranced around the marble pillars to the massive teal and white marble table in the center. “This arrangement is simply magnifique!” framing the flowers with his hands in a circular fashion. “With the many entrances into this room, this painting will be the focal point from all directions for guests to feast their eyes on its beauty!”

“Who are you?” Carlos stepped back.

“How rude of me,” Paris pointed to her friends. “I forgot to introduce my assistants, Mikey Goldenrod and Bernadette Adel,” Paris introduced. “They’ve worked with me since the beginning of my career. Mikey has an excellent eye for lighting paintings. Bernadette helps me hang them with precision.”

“Nice way to stop the friction, Mikey!” Ramsey admitted. “Paris, try not to ruffle his feathers.”

“I feel that with Mikey’s creativeness, it might take a while to light each painting,” Carlos walked back to the steps. “Gunther will assist you in getting your equipment and bring you up in the elevator. We’ll start in President Barrick’s office. I have quite a bit of work to finish before our guests arrive.”

“As you wish,” Paris smiled as Gunther opened the doors.

“Mikey’s performance worked,” Sydney grinned. “He also gave us more time to find what we need.”

“Stephen, have the mosquito follow Carlos to the office,” Sydney requested. “It sounded like Carlos is uploading the video.”

“It’s over him,” Stephen said as the elevator door opened. “Oh, no!” Stephen pulled the mosquito away from the doorway. “This room is blocked with the forcefield!”

“Yes, it is,” Sydney scanned it. “It would have fried the mosquito and alerted Carlos. It uses a magnetic component that I haven’t seen,” he typed more commands. “I’m having the computer check for the best way for Chameleon to stop it.”

“Mikey, I left my sunglasses in your van while I was helping you carry the paintings,” Stephen advised. “Put them in your pocket facing forward. Sydney can activate the electronics once you’re inside the office.”

"With the pin that Kathe gave Paris, it gives us two cameras," Sydney confirmed. "Just don't go near the forcefield with them activated."

"I see them," Mikey stuck them in his pocket.

"The mother-drone has marked the locations of the guards on the grounds," Will reported.

"Perfect," Sydney smiled. "All teams, I'm uploading the locations of the guards on the grounds to your phones. Stephen, while you're waiting, check for the best way for Kathe's team to enter on that floor."

"I will," Stephen agreed.

"Stephen, once we're inside, I'll use JAKE's mosquito to help us dodge the guards," Kathe agreed. "I just need to see the layout of the rooms, the position of the elevator, and steps for a possible escape."

"Copy that," Stephen complied.

"Ramsey, we need to wait a few minutes for sundown to begin our duties," Alonzo replied. "The way the vegetation is placed around the grounds and the guardhouses, it will be difficult for us to stay out of sight."

"Skip, Mack, help them when they're ready," Ramsey requested.

"Copy that," Skip answered. "We're pulling up the cameras."

"It's time for me to takeoff," Yorg reported remotely using an app on his phone to activate a small Tub to back up the Huey. "I've located two small airstrips that Carlos' pilots could use to hide his helicopters."

"Turn on the camera system in the Huey," Ramsey cautioned. "There's a drone inside if you need it."

"You've got it, Boss Lady," Yorg chuckled.

"Paris' team is entering the presidential office," Ramsey noted turning up the sound.

"The forcefield only affects electrical impulses," Sydney noted. "Paris, I'm activating the artist pin now," he said as Paris looked around the office. "Mikey, I activated the glasses as well."

"I see you found where the painting will hang," Carlos joined them from behind a partition on the far-right of the room.

"Of course," Paris sighed staring behind his desk at the blank wall between two large windows. "Knowing now that Barrick has an artistic talent that he hid from his activist political career, his ego commands the focal point of the room for his portrait."

"Is Paris crazy?" Ramsey questioned.

"You're exactly right," Carlos chuckled. "My fath. . . I mean . . . I know Omar Barrick well. But don't underestimate his genius and foresight into the future for the good of all people. To me, that demands utmost respect!"

"Paris," Bernadette interrupted carrying the ladder behind the desk. "We need to get started with the measurements," she climbed up and reached in her carpenter's belt for her tape measure. "We still have to hang the other painting before his guests arrive."

"Thank you, Bernadette," Ramsey sighed. "Paris, please don't ruffle his feathers! Since you missed the memo, it means don't upset Carlos or me!"

"Mikey, will there be any problems with the lighting in this spot?" Paris questioned moving from side-to-side in front of the desk. "I feel these tall, wide windows on each side will destroy the effect."

"Paris, you're pushing my buttons!" Ramsey warned.

"It's not the perfect choice," Mikey declared joining her. "According to the lux meter, the afternoon glare will be a challenge. However, there is a covered electrical outlet behind the desk on the ceiling. Mr. Prado, may I access it? I need to add a lighting bar to hold four lights," he clasped his hands together under the side of his chin and grinned.

"I don't know how you noticed it!" Carlos exclaimed. "I specifically designed it to blend unnoticed into the ceiling."

"I have a good eye for details," Mikey threw his hands up in the air. "I am a photographer, a lighting expert, and anything my Paris needs me to be."

"Mikey, don't you start with me!" Ramsey warned.

"I'm ready for the frame," Bernadette stated climbing down the ladder. "I'll have it up in five minutes," she reached for the nails and cordless electric screwdriver. "Mikey, can you hand it to me?"

"While you do that, I need to check on something in the other room," Carlos signaled Gunther and walked behind the partition.

"What we are looking for is behind that partition!" Sydney exclaimed typing more commands, pressing enter. "Chameleon has located the source of the forcefield! It's in the basement!"

"Kathe, can your team get to the basement and shut it off?" Sydney asked.

"We just made it to the second floor around the guards," Kathe answered. "It will take us a while to get back down. There are guards everywhere."

"We can do it," Alonzo offered. "Skip, Mack, get us to the nearest fountain."

"Copy that," Mack answered. "It's the perfect time to move around. The fountains aren't lit yet, even though it's almost sunset. I'm showing you've got a clear shot to the fountain in front of you; the guards are looking the other way!"

They watched as Alonzo and Pauli made their way around foliage and trees to the fountain.

"Sydney, the lock is electronic," Alonzo whispered ducking down behind the waterfall.

"There is no forcefield," Sydney typed commands. "Chameleon is reading the lock. It's open."

"Thanks," Alonzo whispered as Pauli opened the door surprising a groundskeeper.

"There's no place to hide the body," Pauli whispered.

"I'm getting the mosquito up," Alonzo showed him. "We'll find a place while we're in here. There is a guard halfway down the corridor by the elevator. This is strange. Look at the sizable, square indent in the wall between the elevator and us that you can hide inside. I'll distract the guard long enough for you to get inside it."

"Wait a minute," Ramsey noted. "With the size and shape of the indent, could it be a holding tank for prisoners?" Ramsey stated watching Alonzo buzz the mosquito around the guard's head.

"Yes, I located sensors on the walls for a forcefield to activate across it," Sydney advised.

"Pauli, move now," Ramsey requested watching Pauli hurry down the corridor. "Pauli, the guard didn't see you. Take him out when you're ready."

Pauli stepped out of the room, hurling his knife into the guard's side.

"I'll put him inside this room for now," Pauli said as Alonzo joined him.

"You're clear to go," Alonzo watched flying the mosquito ahead. "I found what's marked the Security Operation Center."

"That glass window is a two-way mirror," Sydney scanned. "There are six people inside monitoring the computers."

"Three people are watching different areas of the G-Summit in Japan," Ramsey declared zooming in on them. "Hiltree, warn AG Kolouski that Carlos has men monitoring the G-Summit."

"Copy that," Hiltree agreed reaching for his phone.

"Chameleon has located the main source for the forcefield," Sydney smiled. "Interesting, Chameleon found that one of the forcefields is so condensed that people cannot walk through it."

"So, we were right about the holding tank for prisoners!" Ramsey gasped. "Impressive. Can you shut them off?"

"Chameleon has taken control of the forcefields," Sydney grinned pressing enter. "The workers are oblivious to the fact that they no longer control them," he typed more commands. "Now, I'm in control of their entire security system!"

"We can't tip our hand too quickly," Ramsey cautioned. "We haven't secured the perimeter or downloaded the video."

"Ramsey, I programmed Chameleon to give me advance notice of the guards trying to change the forcefields around," Sydney laughed. "Chameleon will humor them by altering their reality. It's also checking for security alerts."

"We're heading back outside," Alonzo stated sending the mosquito ahead of them.

"Wait," Sydney smiled. "I just located an incinerator near the fountain you entered. Dump the bodies in there."

"Consider it done," Pauli replied stopping at the holding tank.

"Ramsey, we're inside a room on the second floor," Kathe whispered signaling Sam to check the hallway.

"Stephen, have your mosquito on standby to get inside that office," Ramsey requested.

"It's on its way," Stephen agreed.

"Paris, I'm done here," Bernadette stated closing the ladder. "Gunther, I need to get started in the foyer."

"Just a minute," Gunther opened the door. "I have a man outside the door to take you. Tallo, take this woman to the foyer, and stay with her."

"Yes, Capitán," Tallo answered.

"Paris, hand me the lighting bar?" Mikey asked reaching for it. "I just need to put two screws and plug it into the outlet," he said putting one side up and then the other. "Gunter, I need you to lower the shades so I can focus the lights."

Gunter walked to the partition, "Mr. Prado, they need the window shades closed for a few minutes."

"I can do it from here," Carlos said lowering them.

"Paris, can you turn off the lights?" Mikey requested.

"Sydney," Mikey whispered twisting his body for the sunglasses to show the partition. "Something Carlos is doing is illuminating the partition."

"It's a monitor or computer screen," Sydney confirmed typing commands. "Stephen's mosquito is on the way to join you as soon as it can get inside."

"The far-right light needs to twist to the left a tad," Paris instructed. "That's good. Yes, the middle two are angled correctly. Now, the far-left light needs to twist a tad to the right," she watched. "That's it! Mikey, you're the best. I'll turn on the lights."

"Bernadette marked where the lights go above and under it," Mikey shared. "I'll be done in a few minutes," placing the top light and climbing down the ladder. "One more," he screwed it into the wall.

"I've got the lights," Paris hurried to turn them off. "The light on the bottom is spot-on; the one on top needs a twist downward," she watched. "Now, check with the luxmeter."

"The luxmeter agrees with your keen eyesight," Mikey winked. "Why do we even bother with this thing?"

"Because I'm not as perfect as a computer," Paris chuckled placing the luxmeter on the desk, winking back at Mikey. "Just in case," she mouthed.

"Mr. Prado, you may open the shades," Gunter said. "We're finished and going to the foyer."

"Finally, no more interruptions!" Carlos opened the shades. "I can't believe it's already dark," he turned back to the keyboard. "Glad they came here first," he turned on a few lights and continued working.

"Mack, is the coast clear for us to leave the fountain?" Alonzo asked.

"The sun in Dubai goes down very quickly," Mack advised. "The fountain lights are on now," he checked for more cameras. "Alonzo, stand down! Sydney, Ramsey, I spotted more security cameras facing the guardhouses. We need, pardon the expression, replacements for the guards."

"This might be what we need to get Carlos away from the partition for Kathe's team to get inside," Ramsey smiled. "How many replacements?"

"There are four at each post," Mack checked.

"Hiltree, how quick can McIntire's men get here?" Ramsey asked.

"The Navy Seals are outside the back gate," Hiltree responded. "With this many guards, I wanted them close and ready. Their earbuds are ready to join our network temporarily."

"Great decision," Ramsey appreciated.

"I've located their earbuds and connected them," Sydney pressed enter.

"Capt. Bob Radcliff is in charge on the ground," Hiltree introduced.

"Capt. Radcliff, I can jam the entire electrical system long enough for your men to climb over the back fence," Sydney explained. "I can't keep them off long."

"Copy that," Capt. Radcliff stated. "It should take thirty-seconds to climb up and take over the guardhouses. We are in place and ready."

"Mack, is the coast clear?" Sydney asked.

"Stop!" Skip warned zooming in on the generator. "The generator has spotlights with sensors that will activate the second the electricity goes off."

"Glad you saw that!" Sydney confirmed. "I'm shutting the entire electrical grid down, including the generators for thirty-five seconds. That's all the time you can have."

"Kathe, is your team ready to enter the office?" Ramsey asked.

"We're almost in position," Kathe replied signaling her team to hurry.

"Ready on three; one, two, three," Sydney pressed enter.

"Carlos, the entire electrical system, along with the generators, just went offline for no reason!" Cho alerted from the Security Operations Center. "We can't bring it back up! It's like our keyboards don't exist!"

"Reboot the system from the back of the monitor!" Carlos snapped.

"We tried!" Cho exclaimed. "It won't reset!"

"Pull the emergency electrical switch and it will reboot!" Carlos screamed.

"We don't have control!" Cho shouted. "It's like someone else is controlling it!"

"No one can control my system!" Carlos snapped. "I'm on my way!"

"Yes, leave the office," Sydney grinned.

"It worked!" Ramsey congratulated watching Carlos' storm out of the room. "Kathe, how quickly can you be there?"

"We're waiting for an opening to get past two guards talking in the hallway," Kathe replied. "Do you want me to take them out?"

"Negative," Ramsey warned. "One shock for Carlos is enough right now."

"I can do it," Paris whispered signaling Mikey to watch Gunter.

"Stop!" Gunter yelled as Mikey cut in front of him with the large painting tripping him.

"I'm sorry," Mikey apologized. "She forgot the lux meter. She'll be right back."

"Stephen, stay with Paris," Ramsey ordered watching Paris closing the elevator door before Gunter could stop her.

"Good job, Paris," Sydney declared typing commands. "I'll slow down the elevator when it returns for Gunther to give you some time."

"I'm inside the office," Paris whispered hurrying behind the partition. "Carlos is downloading the video to a satellite named ESPGOTU1000!"

"I see that," Sydney stated watching Stephen's camera.

"Kathe, I need you in that office!" Ramsey exclaimed. "Take the guards out, and stuff them in another room!"

"Copy that," Kathe signaled CC and Sam.

"The electricity, generator, and back security cameras are back online in five, four, three, two, one," Sydney warned pressing enter.

"We accomplished what we wanted," Ramsey declared. "Stephen got a mosquito behind the partition," she looked at the tunnel monitor. "Paris, get out of there! Carlos left the Operations Center. He's getting into the elevator. Stephen, you'll have to leave the drone above the screen and use another one."

"But I can't leave now," Paris sighed. "The video has 1% left to finish the download. Should I push stop or escape?"

"Negative!" Sydney declared. "Get out of there! I can see you with your lapel pin until Stephen gets another mosquito inside."

"Okay," Paris agreed racing to the desk for the lux meter and to the door.

"What are you doing in here?" Carlos demanded surprising Paris.

"I accidentally left the lux meter on the desk," Paris held it up. "We need it to finish in the foyer."

"You were behind the partition, weren't you?" Carlos grabbed her arm.

"No, I was only at the president's desk!" Paris twisted away from his hold. "I was nowhere near the partition! My friends and I are leaving! And you'll hear from my lawyer for grabbing me!"

"Carmine!" Carlos grabbed Paris by the arm, dragging her to the doorway. "Put Ms. L'Ville and her friends in the holding tank in the tunnel! I'll be down later to deal with them."

"Yes, Capitán," Carmine pushed Paris with his rifle to the elevator as it opened. "Gunther, why did you let her get away from you?"

"Ms. L'Ville hurried off before I could stop her," Gunther said. "The elevator isn't working right. It was the slowest it's ever been."

"Carlos said to put them in the holding tank," Carmine said. "Let's go!"

"Mikey, Bernadette, be ready," Ramsey warned. "Sydney, activate the sunglasses again."

"Oh, we heard," Bernadette whispered leaning her ladder against the wall as the elevator opened.

"Come with us!" Gunther demanded holding his rifle on Bernadette and Mikey.

"Paris, position yourself by the controls, and locate the stop button," Ramsey requested watching the door close. "When I say so, hang onto the rail beside you, and hit that button. The elevator will come to a sudden halt."

Mikey slowly moved his hand to the rail and winked at Bernadette as the elevator started down.

"Now!" Ramsey ordered watching the elevator abruptly stop, jolting the guards forward. Mikey grabbed Gunter's rifle, slamming him into the wall, choking him with it. At the same time, Bernadette quickly grabbed Carmine's gun, shoving his nose into his skull with its butt.

"What do we do with them?" Mikey asked.

"When the elevator opens, drag the bodies down the right side of the corridor," Sydney explained checking with the Security Operations Center. "I'll show you where to stash them. Chameleon alerted me that at 2100 (9:00 PM UTC), the president's new military troops will arrive and surround the palace after the video plays worldwide. General Rukar will arrive in a few minutes for Carlos to brief him."

"That name sounds so familiar," Ramsey wondered.

"Gen. Ababa Rukar killed the most American Soldiers in Afghanistan as well as civilians!" Hiltree snapped. "He used the women and children as human shields!"

Tuesday, July 7th
2100 (9:00 PM UTC)
Presidential Palace in Dubai
The Grand Finale

"Alonzo, have you cleared the guard towers?" Ramsey asked checking the monitors.

"We just finished the last one," Alonzo reported. "Each tower has Navy Seals ready to strike. When we heard we're getting company, more Seals arrived behind the back gate and hoisted up extra equipment."

"Paris' team is waiting to come out of the tunnel to join you," Ramsey declared.

"Understood," Alonzo acknowledged.

"Mack, Skip, are we clear to the same fountain?" Alonzo asked.

"Yes," Mack checked. "I don't see anyone other than our people."

"Me either," Skip confirmed.

"Alonzo, I heard them," Mikey opened the door. "We're coming outside."

"Bernadette, Mikey, position yourselves in key spots in the trees to stop an invasion. I believe that's what they have in mind."

"Sweet," Mikey agreed. "We picked up extra sniper rifles from the guards we whacked."

"Ramsey, the van carrying Light Crimson is at the gate," Hiltree reported. "It's time to get them into place."

"Jay do not tell the guards who the band is," Ramsey cautioned. "Say, it's a surprise band for Mr. Prado from the president."

"Copy that," Jay whispered turning around. "People stay quiet. We're next in line to the guardhouse."

"Mack, Skip, do we have someone near the entrance to the guardhouse if there's a problem?" Hiltree asked.

"Give me a moment to check," Mack checked the cameras.

"I see that Capt. Radcliff is the closest to you," Skip pointed out from his camera's view.

"Hiltree, I have men inside and outside the gate, ready to assist them," Capt. Radcliff reported.

"Thanks," Jay appreciated. "We might need some assistance getting inside with a surprise band. They are checking ID's and invitations."

"Radcliff, you are to standdown unless they don't buy Jay's story," Ramsey cautioned watching the van stop at the gate. "From this moment forward, timing is everything to take Carlos and an army down."

"Copy that," Capt. Radcliff confirmed. "A guard is approaching the van."

"This is a private event," Marco stated after walking around the van. "Your tag number is not on the approval list. You are to turn around immediately and leave."

"I was instructed to escort the surprise band for the grand finale," Jay stated looking Marco in the eyes.

"I'll have to check," Marco stated stepping back and reaching for his phone. "The tag should have been registered with us."

"This is a surprise gift from the new president to Mr. Prado," Jay cautioned handing Marco a piece of paper. "As you can see, the new Presidential Seal is on the bottom."

"I'm under strict orders not to let anyone inside without the right credentials," Marco insisted stepping back.

"It's your neck, not mine," Jay declared. "You've seen Prado's violent temper! Give me back the paper, and we'll leave. Then, you explain what happened to the grand finale act before the fireworks! I was told the president would call Carlos to go outside to watch. Where can I turn around?"

"Wait a minute!" Marco peered inside the van. "Do you know where to take them?"

"Yes, of course," Jay stated flashing a paper. "It's on the invitation."

"Let them pass," Marco ordered as the gate rose.

"Good job," Ramsey complimented. "Capt. Radcliff, make your way toward the van, and stand by to assist them with the guards under the stage."

"We're on our way," Capt. Radcliff agreed.

"Yorg, you heard about a new militant, military arriving?" Ramsey quizzed.

"Yes, ma'am," Yorg admitted. "I'm loading extra supplies in the Huey from Carlos's helicopters. One of the pilots told me that they were to shoot into the crowd watching the show. I'm well prepared to greet them."

"How did you get him to talk?" Ramsey asked.

"You and Kathe aren't the only ones that can be persuasive, Boss Lady," Yorg grinned.

"Are you getting cocky with me?" Ramsey snapped. "What is it with everyone tonight?"

"No, Boss Lady," Yorg laughed. "I know better than to ruffle your feathers."

"Kathe, are you in place?" Ramsey asked.

"Copy that," Kathe replied. "We're in the next room, watching Stephen's camera for Carlos to leave again. JAKE alerted me that Carlos has been in constant communication with his satellite."

"Yes, Carlos is sending information to multiple satellites, one at a time," Sydney answered watching the front gate. "I'm waiting to get inside the computer for JAKE to locate which ones. Chameleon is scanning the files for the last sequence of events. Carlos has multiple programs running to hide the information from the military satellites he's using."

"Mr. Prado," Marco called breaking his concentration. "General Rukar has arrived."

"Have the general meet me in the foyer of the palace," Carlos stated rechecking the satellite. "Have all the bands arrived?"

"Yes, I believe the last one went through a few minutes ago," Marco replied. "They are under the stage waiting to perform. The special guests are arriving with a steady stream of cars following them into the driveway. Your idea to entice the locals worked."

"Good," Carlos put on his white suit coat and checked the satellite's screen one more time. "Good, I guess that was a glitch earlier. Everything is going as scheduled," Carlos beamed leaving the office. "Escort the few special guests inside the palace for the unveiling as soon as they arrive," he ordered taking the elevator to the second floor and switching to the curved staircase to greet them.

"Yes, Sir," Marco agreed.

"We need to know who the special guests are," Ramsey declared.

"They have to be five of the nearby Emirates that weren't on the final list to attend the G-Summit," Hiltree declared. "AG Kolouski sent me a text to watch out for them. They were supposed to attend in coalition with President Trumore outlining a peace plan."

"Tell Kolouski that we'll watch for them," Ramsey requested turning up the audio.

"Gen. Rukar," Carlos reached to shake his hand. "What a pleasure for you to be the first guest inside my father's Presidential Palace."

"It is everything I expected of a man with your extraordinary talents," Gen. Rukar admired looking around. "That painting commanded my attention the moment I walked inside," he walked over to it. "It's an original Paris L'Ville! I've heard in several circles that she's the next Monet!"

"That's why my father insisted Ms. L'Ville paint his portrait and the Garden in Paradise Cove," Carlos bragged.

"Stephen, stay with them," Ramsey ordered.

"Yes, ma'am," Stephen complied.

"This way please, we need to go over tonight's final sequence of events one more time," Carlos led Rukar into the living room. "Did King Ashwie agree to our offer?"

"As you thought, Ashwie will not go along with the plan," Gen. Rukar answered.

"He is an old-fashioned, stubborn man!" Carlos snapped. "I was surprised that lately he's leaning toward democracy. He seems to have taken a fancy to the new American President's policy on business. Don't worry; his replacement is in place at the G-Summit."

"Sydney, JAKE discovered that Carlos is uploading the video around the world via five satellites," Kathe reported.

"Sydney, each satellite is password protected," Rodger stated scanning the files.

"We need those codes now to upload our video," Kathe warned.

"Kathe, keep JAKE beside it," Sydney requested watching the screen. "JAKE can help us locate them," he quickly typed commands. "I've enhanced JAKE to assist Rodger uploading our video faster."

"CC, Sam, did you find Johansson's final instructions?" Ramsey asked.

"We're still searching," CC answered. "There is a lot of notes to go through on his CYA file. Here's one about Gen. Ababa Rukar. He has placed his armies around the world to force 'One World, One Vision' on countries. Those who resist, die."

"I hate to do this!" Ramsey snapped. "Sydney put me through to AG Kolouski."

"His phone is ringing," Sydney said pressing enter. "He might not answer an unauthorized number."

"Can you extend the ringing time?" Ramsey asked.

"Okay," Sydney typed commands. "Let me try this," pressing enter.

"Ramsey?" AG Kolouski questioned walking away from the president's desk and the people with him.

"Yes," Ramsey said. "I see you just landed at Osaka, Japan."

"Yes, we did," AG Kolouski admitted. "We're staying aboard Air Force One until it's time for the president's speech. I've gone over your intelligence with President Trumore and Secretary of State, Matthew Lane."

"We found Carlos is monitoring the G-Summit from Dubai," Ramsey informed him. "Carlos is taking over five satellites from different countries to run his video worldwide. We need to know the name of the countries to stop him."

"An advisor just quickly stepped out of the communication room, handing the president a paper," AG Kolouski shared. "The president is asking for me. Stay quiet for a minute," he put the phone in his pocket. "Sir, you were asking for me?"

"Yes, this might have something to do with what we talked about earlier," President Trumore declared handing him the note.

"I believe it does," AG Kolouski glanced at it, and then hurried away reaching for his phone.

"Ramsey, China, and Russia sent out a memo that some of their satellites are missing!" AG Kolouski confirmed.

"That's two out of five," Ramsey thanked hanging up the phone.

"CC, Sam, search for the names China and Russia!" Sydney ordered.

"Got it!" CC shouted. "The password to get into the Chinese satellite is ESPGOTUCHINA1!"

"ESPGOTURUSSIA2," Sam located.

"I'm erasing Carlos's video now," Rodger typed commands. "I'm uploading our video to them. JAKE is speeding up the process."

"Wait a minute!" Stephen warned. "Carlos wants to show Rukar how his satellite is using other countries to relay the video. They are getting in the elevator."

"Kathe, be prepared to leave," Ramsey warned. "Alonzo, we need a diversion to pull Carlos outside!"

"I've got a perfect one!" Pauli laughed throwing lit firecrackers under a car coming through the gate.

"Perfect, the car ran into the gate," Will zoomed in on it with his drone. "The guards are racing to the car. Marco is on the phone."

"Carlos and Rukar got off on the second floor and are running downstairs," Stephen said following them with the drone.

"Marco, what happened?" Carlos watched from under the front porch roof.

"Sir, something popped several times under the car, scaring the driver," Marco alerted. "The people inside are shaken up."

"Move the car to the side!" Carlos snapped. "Then, see what popped under the car! I'm waiting!"

"Kathe, Rodger, continue," Ramsey requested.

"Mr. Prado, someone threw firecrackers," Marco discovered watching his men push the car to the side.

"I warned you not to have this concert!" Gen. Rukar warned.

"I did it to show the youth in the area who's in charge now!" Carlos glared at him. "They've been cowered down to old foolish ways for too long! They will join our resistance! And you better remember who is in charge, and how you talk to me!"

"Yes, Sir, as you wish," Gen. Rukar backed down.

"ESPGOTUAUSTRALIA3," CC confirmed.

"Thanks, CC," Rodger declared typing more commands.

"We need two more," Kathe stated. "JAKE is locking onto another one. ESPGOTUBRAZIL4."

"ESPGOTUGREENLAND5!" Sam found. "That should be the last one."

"No!" Sydney grinned. "JAKE alerted me that ESPGOTU1000 is scanning Alby's Satellite. That's why Carlos's program was so slow. He can't get through our security," Sydney quickly typed commands. "Chameleon is only letting Carlos think that he broke the code. Let's see how Carlos likes what I'm going to do," he pressed enter.

"Sydney, Ramsey, all our videos are uploaded and ready to activate," Rodger confirmed.

"Chameleon will activate them when Carlos hits his app," Sydney grinned. "Kathe, have JAKE fry the keyboard and get out of there. Carlos and Rukar are coming back inside."

"It's done!" Kathe exclaimed signaling her team to leave.

"Sydney, the fans are filling up the grounds in front of the stage," Alonzo cautioned. "It's going to get noisy outside."

"I'll filter out the noise for you," Sydney typed. "I tightened up our network. You're good."

"Copy that," Alonzo smiled. "The stage is rising with the first band."

"We're keeping Light Crimson in the van until the last minute," Hiltree reported. "Jay sent our mosquito inside the tunnel. As you can see, there are quite a few guards down there."

"I counted over twenty guards," Jack reported. "We'll have to clear them before we take Light Crimson inside."

"Jack's correct," Jay agreed. "One of the guards might recognize them and call Carlos. That would tip him off that we're here."

"I kept Capt. Radcliff and two Navy Seals near you, if you need them," Ramsey declared.

"Thanks," Hiltree confirmed. "Radcliff, make your way to the first van parked in the driveway. We must assess the situation to formulate a plan of attack. There are several bands down there intermingled with the guards."

"We're on our way to you," Capt. Radcliff declared signaling his men.

"Carlos and Rukar have entered the office," Stephen alerted. "They are behind the partition."

"I've got this," Sydney typed commands. "Chameleon is showing their satellite entering Alby's Satellite. Listen!"

"I did it!" Carlos sat down. "I breached Alby Airlines' Satellite! Now, when I start the video Alby Airlines will take the blame for all the chaos as well as Linda Ramsey, Dr. Sydney, and their teams like my father wanted. It's the perfect frame. It's just like when my father framed Antonio Falcini Sr. for killing those two CIA Agents years ago!"

"Then, my military will waltz in when the chaos begins and take over!" Gen. Rukar laughed. "We will go down in history as greater than Hitler's Nazi Germany!"

"Chameleon pulled it off!" Ramsey exclaimed. "They bought it!"

"Sydney," Will cautioned. "Marco just signaled four limos to pass straight through the guardhouse without stopping to the palace."

"People, this isn't over," Ramsey cautioned. "We won a battle, not the war, yet."

"Carlos is on the phone with Marco," Stephen declared. "They are leaving the office."

"Stay with them," Ramsey approved watching the driveway. "It's the Emirates that didn't attend the G-Summit tonight," Ramsey identified watching them get out of the limos. "We must get them to safety! Kathe, have your team protect the Emirates."

"We're on our way!" Kathe agreed flying the mosquito ahead of them. "Sam, get us near the foyer."

"Tanks and Hummers are pulling up to the palace gates," Will showed. "There is also a military presence in the skies."

"Carlos thinks he finished uploading his video and is home free," Sydney grinned. "Yorg, be ready to get this party started."

"I'm locked and loaded," Yorg agreed. "I'm hovering over Stephen and Will in the tower."

Tuesday, July 7th
2200 (10:00 PM UTC)
Presidential Palace in Dubai
Meeting with Five of the Emirates

"Your Royal Highness'," Carlos greeted bowing to each of the Emirates as they entered with their bodyguards. "Please, make a circle around the table with your guards standing behind you," he waited for them to get into place. "Welcome to the new Presidential Palace. I'm Carlos Santa Prado, the new Chief of Staff. I'm sure you have many questions."

"He's using his full surname again," Ramey noted.

"We are curious to know who our new neighbors are!" Prince Talib demanded. "This Palace was built rather quickly without notifying the United Emirates Nations!"

"I checked the filed deed to this parcel of land," Prince Shaaran declared. "The deed to this parcel of land has been missing for years! We always blamed Israel!"

"It is odd that it suddenly appeared after all the strife between our countries and Israel for decades?" Prince Jahara questioned. "This land was part of my family's domain! No prince was exiled to return in this region!"

"He is not a prince," Carlos chuckled. "As soon as the president is ready, he wants to introduce himself to each of you. I'm sure all your questions will be answered the moment you see him."

"When will we meet this new president?" Prince Talib demanded.

"He has a special presentation prepared to introduce himself to you at the same time as to the world," Carlos smiled pointing to the hors d'oeuvres, and drinks on the marble table. "Please enjoy his hospitality while you wait. We will watch his announcement together from the living room on a big-screen television," he waved his hand toward the painting. "This painting recreates one of his favorite past times. He loves floristry and designs this garden in Cuba as well as the gardens around his palace."

"How long has this president been in exile in Cuba?" Prince Jahara demanded.

"Not as long as you may think," Carlos alluded pointing back to the painting. "Note his love of exotic flowers as well as inhabitants. He creates a special environment for them to cohabitate in a non-indigenous region."

"We're not interested in his hobbies or environmental experiments!" Talib snapped. "We demand to know who he is, and why the sudden appearance?"

"Again, the president will give you the answers," Carlos checked his watch. "I'm glad you agreed to come to the unveiling. Especially after you suddenly declined to attend the G-Summit."

"How do you know that we declined the invitation?" Talib asked.

"I have eyes and ears everywhere," Carlos grinned.

"Then, the rumors were true," Prince Hahirah stated.

"It all depends on what kind of rumors you heard?" Carlos questioned.

"We're here to draw that conclusion before we announce it," Prince Shaaran declared as the general entered from the living room. "Gen. Rukar! We heard you died in Afghanistan!"

"Are you watching this?" Kathe whispered. "His soldiers are surrounding the bodyguards with rifles drawn."

"What can I say?" Gen. Rukar picked up an hors d'oeuvre. "Here I am with an old friend. Now I'm in charge of his new worldwide military," he signaled his soldiers to kill the bodyguards.

"You won't get away with this!" Prince Jahara exclaimed grabbing his bodyguard and laying him on the floor.

"But I already have!" Gen. Rukar laughed. "Take them to the tunnel and stay with them. I'll be down to execute them when I'm finished talking with Carlos."

"Kathe, that can't happen!" Ramsey ordered. "That will cause instability in the region!"

"We're on our way," Kathe answered.

"Sydney, I need that secure line again," Ramsey stated.

"You're on," Sydney pressed enter.

"AG Kolouski," Ramsey called. "We've located the Emirates. They've been taken into custody for execution. A team is on the way to save them."

"Rumors are speculating the executions happened an hour ago," AG Kolouski warned. "They aren't responding to messages, and neither are their guards. I need them at the G-Summit to prove to the world that they are alive."

"They'll be there!" Ramsey promised hanging up the phone. "Kathe, after we save them, Sam and Hiltree are to take them to the Dubai Airport. The Mustang Citation can get them to Osaka, Japan before President Trumore's speech. Capt. Mill will have the engines ready for takeoff as soon as they arrive."

"Copy that," Kathe agreed sending the mosquito ahead of them to the emergency stairs. "Sam, I'm showing no one is in the stairwell. That's the best approach."

"Let's go," Sam led the way down to the basement and peered out the small window in the door. "They're just getting out of the elevator."

"CC, flash your Alby Airlines' Security ID to the Emirates without them seeing where it's from," Ramsey requested.

"Carlos is instructing Gen. Rukar of the sequence of events this evening," Sydney explained turning up the sound. "Listen to them."

"As soon as the last song plays tonight," Carlos began, "my people will activate the rings at the G-Summit from here. That's when the satellites will take over all television, radio stations, and phone systems worldwide, including the monitors at the G-Summit. It's the only thing that will play on audio or video for two weeks while your men take over each country. The astronauts will land at 1100 (11:00 AM EST) tomorrow, putting fear at the Cape. Benjamin's temperature will escalate to 104 degrees, and Astronaut Jane Wells' fever is 103 degrees showing it is highly contagious. The doctors will quarantine them as soon as they land. Pasha will sneak back into the Sego Lilly Hospital tonight at 1000 (10:00 AM EST) to watch the chaos on television with my parents. As soon as the chaos begins, Pasha will administer the vaccine to them. Within an hour, their fevers and other symptoms will be gone. Then as Dr. Pasha Kamenkovich will go on television with my parents and announce a cure for the virus. Dr. Kamenkovich will say he's going to Florida to administer the vaccine to Benjamin and Wells, but instead will fly my parents to Dubai as the first casualties die in the United States from the virus."

"Thus, creating chaos with a virus the United States brought back from outer space," Gen. Rukar grinned.

"Correct," Carlos laughed. "The world's attention will be on the death of the astronauts instead of a former president and his wife in quarantine. The video that will play implicates Alby Airlines' executives confirming they are working with Pres. Trumore. My father will declare what happened and blame them. He'll take over as the first president of the 'One World, One Vision.' Then, he will lay out his plan to save the world."

"My Special Forces are in a position in the capitals of each country waiting for your orders," Gen. Rukar confided.

"We need to move swiftly," Ramsey concurred. "Sydney, is Dr. Ylia en route to Canaveral?"

"She'll be landing in a few hours," Sydney admitted.

"Kathe, have JAKE stop the rings from activating from the palace," Sydney requested. "I blocked the ones on the list Mikey got from Dano. Now, I know I don't have all of them."

"Copy that," Kathe agreed flying the mosquito outside the stairwell. "They put the Emirates in that holding room you discovered earlier."

"I see it," Sydney agreed. "To the left of the elevator on the right side is the Security Operations Center. Six people were working earlier. Don't worry; it's soundproof. They can't hear what's going on outside the room."

"Kathe, use the mosquito to take down two of the guards watching the Emirates," Ramsey suggested. "When the others turn to see what happened, that's when the Emirates need to see you take them down."

"Can bullets penetrate the forcefield?" Kathe asked.

"Negative," Sydney advised. "And the Security Operations Center is bulletproof as well."

"Ramsey, the mosquito is on the way," Kathe flew the mosquito to the last one in the line and landed it on his neck. "One down," Kathe declared finding her next target. "Is that enough?"

"Yes," Ramsey agreed. "They're trying to figure out what happened to their friends."

"We're ready to attack," Sam signaled slowly opening the door.

"Go for it!" Ramsey approved. "Their backs are away from you; go now!"

"Put your hands up!" CC shouted squaring her Glock off at them.

"You heard the lady," Sam held his gun on them.

"Don't move!" Rodger demanded walking toward the other side.

"Kathe, the one on the far-left is slowly slipping backward," Sydney cautioned. "Don't let him run down the corridor. He can get outside from there."

"Yes, Sir," Kathe moved around Rodger as the guard made a run for it.

"Stop!" Kathe ordered watching him continue to run. "Stop!" she warned and then shot him with JAKE's laser.

"Ramsey, what do we do with these two survivors?" Rodger asked.

“Have them trade places with the Emirates for now,” Ramsey grinned. “Then, go with Kathe while CC and Sam take them outside to Hiltree. Pauli arranged transportation to the Citation. Jordan is ready for takeoff.”

“Kathe, I sent JAKE the codes to shut the forcefield down,” Sydney pressed enter. “The sensor is at the top-right corner.”

Kathe held JAKE toward the censor. “JAKE, turn off the forcefield.”

“Kathe, the forcefield is off,” JAKE alerted.

“Prince Shaaran,” CC flashed her badge. “Please, it’s safe to come out. I’m Security Agent, CC Sims. AG Kolouski sent us to rescue you before we stopped Carlos Santo Prado from taking over his planned worldwide coup.”

“On behalf of all of us,” Prince Shaaran spoke. “We thank you for rescuing us.”

“We must go at once to the G-Summit,” Prince Jahara urged.

“Yes, rumors are already speculating that your execution already took place an hour ago,” CC confided. “AG Kolouski was just notified of your rescue and has arranged transportation for you. We’ve learned that Rukar’s men have taken over the airport. More of Rukar’s military is waiting to take over this complex after the video plays that Carlos prepared to disrupt the G-Summit and world. Then, they plan on taking over your countries by replacing you with look-a-like imposters. Please, come with us. Special Forces Marine, Sam Biggs, and Navy RADM Jeremy Hiltree will accompany you to Japan.”

“Rodger, go with Kathe to stop the rings,” Ramsey requested. “There are six workers inside. She may need help.”

“Copy that,” Rodger agreed hurrying with Kathe to the Security Operations Center.

“Sydney, I need that secure line again,” Ramsey requested picking up the phone.

“AG Kolouski, we have the five packages and will deliver them to you,” Ramsey stated. “Their replacements are somewhere in Osaka. They need to be removed before these arrive.”

“Understood,” AG Kolouski sighed. “Our ground intelligence has reported that some dignitaries wearing different looking rings are acting nervous.”

“I’ll see what I can find out,” Ramsey declaring hanging up the phone.

“Kathe, hold JAKE up to the window,” Sydney requested typing commands. “I’m using JAKE to help Chameleon scan for the list of rings.”

“And, possible different looking rings,” Ramsey shared. “Some dignitaries are now wearing them.”

“Kathe, duck!” Rodger whispered as Kathe dropped to the floor. Rodger moved away from the door. “The two-way mirror switched to a window. One of the workers turned his head looking this way and got up from his station.”

“Chameleon has the camera system and controls the panic button on the main desk,” Sydney warned. “He might have seen JAKE. He’s opening the door with his gun drawn. He’s moving very slowly, poking his gun out first. He’s very apprehensive about facing your way,” Sydney watched Kathe slowly standing up as the door widened. “One of them pushed the panic button! They’re all reaching for their weapons.”

“Kathe, we don’t need a confrontation!” Ramsey cautioned. “Use the mosquito!”

Kathe signaled Rodger of her intentions and then sent the mosquito around the door behind his neck.

“What happened?” one worker screamed pushing the panic button again. “It’s not working!”

“They’re trying to lock the door electronically,” Sydney typed commands. “Chameleon blocked it.”

“Get inside and take control!” Ramsey requested.

Kathe moved the mosquito behind the woman that screamed, landing it on her. She fell to the floor.

“What happened to Riley?” one shouted bending over her. “She’s dead!”

“They’re panicking,” Ramsey relayed. “They’re holding their hands up. Go inside and take them to the holding room.”

“Put your hands up!” Rodger ordered opening the door wide.

“Come with us!” Kathe demanded squaring off at them. “You two men,” she pointed her Ruger at them. “Bring Riley; she’s not dead. Rodger, grab the guy; he’s not dead either.”

“Nice job,” Ramsey commended watching Kathe open the forcefield and then resetting it.

“Kathe, put JAKE on the console in the center,” Sydney requested. “Rodger, I’m opening the files for you.”

“Got it,” Rodger sat down skimming through them. “Here’s more to add to your list, and another list is marked targeted with no replacement.”

"The rings they are wearing look different than the ones we've encountered so far," Ramsey noted. "That's the ones Kolouski's men discovered."

"I see that," Sydney typed commands and pressed enter. "I stopped each ring. There were twenty dignitaries I missed that were slated to be terminated, if they didn't do what they were told."

"They must have woken up wearing rings and were threatened," Ramsey assumed. "Since they didn't have replacements, they were motivated by fear."

"Chameleon is replacing those workers in the Security Operation Center now for the cameras," Sydney typed more command and pressed enter. "What do you think?"

"Holograms!" Ramsey exclaimed. "Sydney, we need to talk after this is over! They look so real."

"Kathe, Rodger, plans have changed," Ramsey cautioned. "Find a way to get to the room under the stage. Capt. Radcliff can't figure out a way to take out the guards without harming the band members. The third to the last band is lowering to switch places."

"It's time to get Light Crimson in place," Kathe approved hurrying down the corridor. "Jack, bring them inside the tunnel. We're almost there."

"Copy that," Jack answered. "We will bring Light Crimson down the elevator now."

"Ramsey, the Emirates, Hiltree, and Sam have arrived at the Citation," Alonzo reported. "They are ready to leave."

"Understood," Ramsey called Wanda. "Have Keith make a flight plan for the Citation to Osaka, Japan. Then, Sydney will help them takeoff."

"Yes, ma'am," Wanda agreed.

"Is everyone in place to catch our mole?" Ramsey asked.

"Agent Terrance Sims and a few of his men picked up L'Simonette with a mosquito-drone as soon as he pulled into the parking garage this morning," Wanda grinned. "They have followed and recorded L'Simonette in the Control Tower, demanding to know the whereabouts of the Citation. Currently, he has Air Traffic Controller Brundage searching for the Citation around the Sea of Oman. Brundage keeps showing L'Simonette on a camera view at Heathrow that the Citation is parked at Gate E12. He's proving it on the radar as well."

“Good,” Ramsey smiled. “Now’s the perfect time to move it. Where are the FBI Agents?”

“The agents are in your office with the blinds closed waiting for L’Simonette to arrive any minute,” Wanda cautioned. “They watched him storm out of the tower, mumbling that Keith is manipulating the facts.”

“Is Agent Terrance Sims with them?” Ramsey asked.

“Yes, ma’am,” Wanda relayed watching the elevator outside her office.

“Thanks,” Ramsey switched calls. “Terrance, Sydney is ready to run a little interference for you. He’s hacking into L’Simonette’s phone and sending the audio to your drone.”

“Copy that,” Terrance approved. “We’ve already observed L’Simonette in the Control Tower. And caught him sneaking into an empty cubical to use a computer to check for himself. When he saw what Brundage showed him was true, he stormed out of there.”

“L’Simonette just got off the elevator,” Wanda whispered. “He’s loitering in the hallway on a phone call.”

“I’m ready for him,” Sydney pressed enter. “Chameleon is sending L’Simonette’s phone’s audio to the mosquito over his head.”

“It’s loud and clear!” Terrance laughed. “We’ve got him!”

“Glad to be of service,” Sydney smiled. “Keith, I see you’ve got the Citation’s flight plan ready for me.”

“Copy that,” Keith stated. “My computer is ready for you to log into it.”

“I’m in,” Sydney split the screen showing Alby’s Control Tower and Dubai’s Tower. “I’ve found a perfect spot for the Citation to takeoff,” he typed the new flight number into Dubai’s lineup. “The tower will have a visual, but they’re off the radar. Capt. Mills, are you ready for takeoff?”

“Copy that,” Jordan replied.

“Okay,” Sydney grinned, “you’re number one for takeoff. Have a safe flight.”

“We’re on our way to the runway,” Jordan turned to Sam. “Get ready to wave to the people in the tower.”

“Let’s do this,” Sam chuckled as the Citation slowed turning onto the runway. Jordan instantly throttled up the engines.

“Have a nice evening!” Sam waved to the men in the tower as they passed over it.

“We’re up,” Jordan smiled. “Thanks, Sydney, for the assist.”

"Thank you, Sydney," Terrance laughed peeking out the blinds into Wanda's office. "L'Simonette received a phone call from the Dubai Tower. Someone changed the order of departures, and they witnessed a jet taking off that was not on the radar. He's upset and heading for Keith's office."

"You're welcome," Sydney grinned. "Throw the book at him!"

"Yes, Sir!" Terrance agreed watching the mosquito following him. "Let's go!" he signaled his men.

"Keith!" L'Simonette snapped entering the office, slamming the door shut and locking it. "Where's Ramsey's Mustang Citation? And don't give me this garbage that it's at Heathrow!"

"Actually, it just left Heathrow and is heading towards Scotland on its way home," Keith declared turning his computer screen towards L'Simonette.

"You're fired!" L'Simonette screamed. "Dubai Tower had a visual of the Citation taking off from there! Somehow their computers changed the order of departures for it to be first in the lineup! And it didn't show up on the radar!"

"Impossible," Keith insisted. "I showed you on the radar where the Citation is currently. Someone's knocking on my door," he stood up.

"Sit down!" L'Simonette screamed. "Don't move! I've got all of you this time!"

"Wayne, open the door," Terrance listened outside.

"It's locked," Wayne stated. "Should I use force?"

"Yes, use force," Terrance requested as Wayne kicked the door open.

"Ramon L'Simonette, you're under arrest for espionage and treason," Terrance held up the warrant. "I'm FBI Agent Terrance Sims. You have the right to remain silent. Anything and everything you say can and will be held against you in a court of law. You have the right to an attorney . . ." he finished as Wayne handcuffed him.

"Agent Sims," Wanda stood in the doorway holding up a large bag, "I brought just the thing for L'Simonette to wear out of the airport. He seems to have a problem accepting reality. When he insisted that Dr. Sydney's bookshelf was an elevator, we moved it, and jumped on the floor proving it was solid. Keith and I reported his behavior to HR and requested a psychiatric evaluation. We can't have one of Alby's VPs off his rocker," she grinned like a Cheshire cat.

"You did no such thing!" L'Simonette insisted. "You don't have the authority to do that!"

"Yes, we did," Wanda held up a paper. "First, we reported his behavior to Ramsey as protocol requires. Then, I faxed the request to Ramsey. She signed it and sent it back. Where do you think I got this straight jacket?" she pulled it out of the bag. "Our observation was corroborated by Controller Brundage. They've been observing you ever since."

"L'Simonette also has a major obsession with the Mustang Citation taking off without appearing on radar," Keith smiled turning his laptop around. "See," he showed the screen. "The radar is showing the Citation is over Scotland on its way to Greenland."

"Dr. Sydney did this!" L'Simonette screamed. "I have proof there is an elevator inside his bookshelf!"

"Wayne, get Mr. Crazy out of here!" Terrance order

Tuesday, July 7th
2240 (10:40 PM UTC)
Presidential Palace in Dubai
The Grand Finale

"I've got my mosquito inside the dressing room," Kathe reported assessing the situation. "Jay, bring your mosquito. There are too many innocent people inside to begin with guns. We need to thin out the guards first."

"Copy that," Jay agreed. "We're almost to you."

"Ramsey," Stephen alerted. "Carlos and Rukar are watching the guests at the concert on the television in the living room. They are also double-checking the grounds for places where Rukar's soldiers should enter."

"Stephen, we've got to help Kathe now," Ramsey glanced at his cameras. "Access the situation and advise us when we need to help you. Alonzo's team has mostly secured the inside grounds."

"Copy that," Stephen agreed.

"Jack, keep an eye on the corridor in case a guard tries to get away," Ramsey cautioned. "We don't want anyone to escape and warn Carlos. He's doing a final check of the outside property with Rukar."

"Understood," Jack replied.

“Capt. Radcliff, keep Light Crimson out of the way for a few minutes,” Kathe requested. “We’re going to thin out some of the guards. This might get a little tricky. Jack will need some help.”

“I’m on my way,” Capt. Radcliff agreed signaling two of his team to come with him. “Jamison, stay with Light Crimson until I tell you to bring them inside. Jack, I’m coming to help you.”

“Copy that,” Jack answered.

“I’ve got something that might help,” Rodger reached into his backpack. “I saw the ventilation system’s room,” he whispered to Kathe.

“Good idea,” Kathe smiled. “I’ll tell you when.”

“Okay,” Rodger hurried down the corridor.

“Kathe, with that many civilians inside, this situation is going to be difficult to turn around without civilians getting hurt,” Capt. Radcliff cautioned.

“With guns blazing, yes,” Kathe agreed. “With drones, no! Jay, you take out the guards on the right side while I work the left side. Jack, Capt. Radcliff, keep an eye on the corridor. It looks like some of the band members are scattered around the room talking. They could leave with the guards during the commotion.”

“Will do,” Jack agreed. “We’ll keep them separated.”

“Kathe, we should see the same scenario that happened in the Operations Center,” Ramsey speculated. “Hopefully, all Capt. Radcliff and his men have to do is help Jack round up the rest of the guards and put them in the holding room with the other captives.”

“I can open the forcefield from here when they’re ready,” Sydney informed them. “I’m using Chameleon to mask the security cameras under the stage, so Carlos won’t know what’s happening.”

“Kathe, begin when you’re ready,” Ramsey approved.

“Jay let’s do this,” Kathe signaled.

“We’re putting them to sleep, right?” Jay asked.

“Of course,” Kathe answered.

“That’s enough to scare the people to disperse,” Jay agreed watching the mosquitoes enter the room.

“What the hell?” One guard screamed leaning over his friend. “He’s dead!”

“This one too!” Another guard screamed from across the room.

“Capt. Radcliff, Jack, they will rush the door any minute,” Ramsey cautioned. “They’re panicking.”

“Rodger, do it now,” Kathe grinned. “Let’s flush them out.”

"It's done," Rodger admitted adding liquid smoke to the ventilation system.

"Is that smoke or gas coming out of the air conditioning vents?" A guard alerted.

"Carlos is gassing us through the ventilation system!" Another one panicked nearby.

"I'm having a hard time breathing!" A female guard screamed rushing toward the door to the hallway.

"Follow me!" The guard closest to the door opened the door for her as the rest of the guards stormed behind them, along with some band members.

"Weed the band members away from the guards," Ramsey ordered. "We can't lock them up with the guards."

"Put your hands up!" Capt. Radcliff ordered holding his rifle on them.

"You two," Jack signaled out the band members. "Step against the wall behind me. You three as well," he pointed to them.

"Put your guns down on the floor!" Capt. Radcliff ordered signaling some of his Seals to surround them.

"He said to put your guns down!" Seal Blumenthal grabbed the rifle out of a guard's hand.

"I saw that!" Seal Swanskin shouted knocking a guard to his knees, taking a knife out of the guard's pants pocket.

"Capt. Radcliff, we need to move those guards quickly," Ramsey requested.

"Yes, ma'am," Capt. Radcliff answered signaling Blumenthal to led them.

"Kathe, the stage is lowering with the last band," Sydney noted. "Light Crimson can't enter while the other bands are inside. Get those musicians to calm down and take them outside."

"That may be easier said than done," Kathe replied. "The people are pretty shaken up."

"Threaten them!" Ramsey ordered watching Kathe enter with Jay and Jack, flashing her credentials.

"People, calm down," Kathe requested. "We're sorry about the confusion. Your host got word of a possible breach within the ranks of his guards. We were sent to escort you outside to safety."

"Who are you?" Jump Fire's lead singer, Cameron Driggs demanded. "Did you kill those guards?"

"Yeah," Walton Smith, his drummer agreed. "Where are you taking the rest of our guards?"

"That's none of your concern," Kathe smiled. "The outside guards are reliable. You'll be safe watching the last act."

"We're not going anywhere until we get some answers!" Driggs demanded getting into her face.

"Your host doesn't owe you an apology concerning an internal security problem!" Kathe knocked him to the floor. "I'm not asking you to leave," she pointed her gun at him. "I'm telling you," Kathe pointed to Capt. Radcliff entering the room with his men. "These are your new bodyguards. They'll escort you outside to safety."

"You heard the lady!" Capt. Radcliff commanded. "Let's go!"

"Ramsey, Chameleon found in Johansson's CYA File, a file marked with a backward letter C," Sydney stated. "When I opened it, there was a report on Carlos. It seems that since middle school, Carlos has loved music. In the tenth grade, he started a rock band and was the lead singer. Carlos favored American Rock and Roll. He auditioned Rita Garcia-Sanchez as a backup singer and dancer. They harmonized so perfectly that he hired her on the spot. Rita favored Latin music and dances over American. She began teaching Carlos's dance moves to add to the show. Carlos's favorite was the Brazilian Tango. They slowly added some Latin songs and dances to the lineup. She influenced him to transform the band solely to Latin music within six months. They couldn't get a record deal. Carlos talked his father into opening Santo Prado Record Label Company. They sold not only music albums, but also videos of them dancing. But Eduardo didn't like the influence Rita had over Carlos. He devised a way to separate them. The day Carlos graduated high school, Eduardo pulled his money from Santo Prado Record Label Company, closing it down. He forced Carlos to go to Columbia Engineering School at a college in Atlanta. They dated a few months long-distance before Eduardo secretly gave Rita a scholarship at a University in Monte Claros to pursue a professional dancing career. Johansson noted when Carlos found out about it; he never forgave his father for coming between them. Then, his parents adopted Shabz and Kenja. Worried about losing his father's wealth, Carlos started winning awards for his designs and devoted his life to his father's cause."

"If you can make Chameleon do what I think you can, I have an idea," Ramsey smiled. "Kathe, Jay, Jack, stay on stage with Light Crimson. Once we manipulate Carlos to go outside to see his surprise, we don't know what he'll do. Rodger, the stagehands running the audio and light equipment are nervous wrecks. I volunteered you to help Brock. That's a strategic place for you to improvise if we need it."

"Yes, it is," Rodger agreed.

"Why am I on stage?" Kathe asked as Carrie Anne walked up to her.

"Because you and Yorg took several courses in Latin Dance while you were in Anguilla," Ramsey declared. "Have Carrie Anne find you a costume to wear. Capt. Radcliff, after you take the other bands outside, find Alonzo. He knows some of the places Rukar's men will enter that need reinforcement."

"Copy that," Capt. Radcliff agreed signaling Swanskin to open the last door to a fountain leading outside. "We're taking them outside now."

"Good," Ramsey watched. "Take them around to the audience, and then take your places."

"Yes, ma'am," Capt. Radcliff agreed watching the last of the performers file passed him outside.

"Kathe, put that ring back on Joe's finger," Ramsey requested as Kathe finished changing clothes. "We'll use it to signify that Eduardo sent them."

"Joe," Kathe hurried to him.

"Are you going to be on stage with us?" Joe asked. "You're dressed in a long, sexy, slinky dress!"

"Yes, in case something goes wrong, and I need to dance with Carlos," Kathe said reaching in her backpack. "I need you to wear this ring again for Carlos to see."

"It won't kill me?" Joe asked.

"No, Sydney disabled it," Kathe said. "Are the guys comfortable with Latin Music?"

"Luckily, we learned one for a friend's birthday party a few years ago," Joe smiled. "I never thought we'd use it again."

"Ramsey," Stephen cautioned. "Carlos is now checking inside the Security Operations Center. Rukar is telling him that something isn't right inside."

"Sydney, it's time for Carlos to go outside," Ramsey declared. "Brock, get the band topside."

"Yes, ma'am," Brock signaled RJ and Payton.

"Ramsey, Carlos just agreed with Gen. Rukar that they need to check out the Security Operations Center," Stephen warned. "They're heading toward the elevator."

"This phone call should stop him," Sydney pressed enter.

"Carlos," the computer called as Carlos stepped into the elevator.

"Father, you weren't supposed to break the silence until after the fireworks tonight," Carlos insisted holding the elevator door open.

"This couldn't wait," the computer imitated. "You know how spontaneous I am. Your mother and I planned a special surprise band for the grand finale. It's our way of thanking you for believing in our family dream all these years. We hope you enjoy it. Goodbye."

"My father and mother sent a surprise band for the grand finale," Carlos told Gen. Rukar. "They want me to go outside and watch."

"Doesn't that seem a little strange to you?" Gen. Rukar alerted. "Your father gave you explicit orders to follow. He wasn't supposed to contact you yet. We need to check out the Security Operations Center. I tell you; something is wrong!"

"Sydney, turn up the audio to the microphones outside," Ramsey requested. "Gen. Rukar isn't buying this. Rodger, do something! Make an introduction!"

"What?" Rodger asked grabbing a microphone.

"Carlos is hesitating," Stephen noted. "Rukar is insisting Carlos goes downstairs."

"Ladiesssss, and Gentlemennnn!" Rodger improvised. "Tonight, we have for you the hottestettt bandddddd on today's chartssss as a gift to our gracious hosttttt. It is my great privilege to introduce to you, and Mr. Carlos Santo Pradooooo! Let's put our hands together while the stage is rising, and show this band that Dubai knows how to partyyyyyy!"

"Rodger, not too shabby," Ramsey grinned as the fans began to chant, "Carlos, Carlos, Carlos."

"What is going on out there?" Carlos ran back into the living room to check the cameras by the stage. "The fans are chanting my name! My father has always been eccentric doing things on the spur of the moment. You stay here and keep an eye on the monitor," he called his pilots.

"I will only after I check the Security Operations Center," Gen. Rukar protested. "This doesn't feel right!"

"Yorg, you're up next," Sydney intercepted Carlos's text. "Carlos is leaving the palace."

"I'm coming to the palace now," Yorg grinned enabling Chameleon's hologram on his helicopter and a second one. He hovered over Carlos until he got in the bulletproof, private viewing box.

"You mimicked them perfectly," Sydney complemented watching from Stephen's camera. "Carlos glanced in the sky and then signaled you to leave when he got inside the box."

"I watched the video footage when Kathe and Hiltree noticed the helicopters in Miami on the way here," Yorg admitted.

"Brock, RJ, bring up Light Crimson!" Ramsey requested.

"Payton, it's time!" RJ alerted.

"You're the Number #1 band on the charts!" Payton exclaimed walking them inside a flag-shaped curtain. "Joe, take control of this audience, and let's rock this place down!"

"Bringing the house lights down now," Brock signaled Rodger. "Up you go!" he shouted listening to the fans continually chanting, "Carlos, Carlos, Carlos."

"Carlos is waving at people in the crowd!" Ramsey noted. "Look in his eyes! He is reliving watching his fans cheer him performing on stage! Joe, it's all up to you now!"

"Surprise, Carlos Santo Pradooooo!" Joe announced as the platform raised showing multi-colored laser beams hitting the curtain forming a small British Flag. "Dubai, Light Crimson is here!" Joe shouted as their first hit song's tempo sped up as the platform stopped. The flag filled the curtain, exploding into the words Light Crimson, and then burst into stars projecting throughout the audience. The screaming fans jumped to their feet as Collen struck the first chord on his electric guitar. The flag dropped to the floor; the stage brightened as Joe hit the first note. Fans continued to scream watching the stage come alive with Joe leaping from the top tier of the stage, down to the bottom, singing the first hit song.

"It's Light Crimson!" Carlos reached for his cell phone.

"Carlos is calling his father," Sydney grinned typing a command on the computer.

"Carlos," the computer impersonated Eduardo's voice. "I hear you're at the concert!"

"Yes, Father!" Carlos exclaimed. "How did you arrange Light Crimson to be here? I thought we couldn't locate them!"

"Check Joe's hand for the ring that Bencivenni put on his finger," the computer stated. "Spinello discovered Jenkins kidnapped Joe and got him back. Pasha is here giving us the vaccine."

"Joe is wearing the ring on the hand holding the microphone!" Carlos exclaimed. "I don't know how you do things like this!"

"I'll never tell," the computer hung up.

“It worked,” Ramsey grinned. “Carlos bought it!”

“Welllll, Dubaiiii!” Joe began exciting the crowd. “Dubaiiiii, it’s great to be here tonight!” He raised his arms in the air as screaming fans jumped to their feet. Joe blocked the bright spotlight with his hands to see out into the crowd. “Where’s our host? There is Carlos Santo Prado, in his private viewing box! Mr. Santo Prado, what do you think of your surpriseeeee?”

The crowd clapped chanting, “surprise, surprise, surprise,” and then settled down.

“Well, Dubaiiiii,” Joe jumped to the second level and looked over his shoulder. “Well, Dubaiiiiiiiiiiii!” He faced the crowd wiping his forehead. “Dubaiiiiii!” he bent over slightly, walking backward, waving his fingers for them to watch him. “Dubaiiiiiiii, do you know how to make some noise to thank our host!” Joe raised his hands in the air, enticing the audience to scream louder. “Tell me, Dubaiiiiii,” he jumped up to the third level as the crowd roared. “Do you want to rock this place or what?” Joe jumped up in the air and came down on the second level.

“Dubaiiii, I bet Collen Jones,” Joe pointed to Collen as he did a quick guitar solo. “And Rick Travis, our bass guitarist,” he pointed to Travis as he strummed up and down the chords while the fans cheered.

“I told them that you’d remember our new version of Pieces of Loveeee,” Joe raised one hand in the air and held his other hand with the mic over his heart as the crowd roared with excitement. “Well, guys, I guess I won that bet!” He licked his finger and drew an imaginary line down. “That’s one for me!” he bragged, and then Troy played a drum roll.

“That’s the thunder from Troy Thompson on the drums!” Joe waved toward Troy as he played up and down all twelve drums, ending with both High-Hat Symbols, and then grabbing them to silence.

“Do you remember my newest backup singer, Ms. Carrieeeeee Anneeeee Mobleyyyyyyy?” Joe introduced as the spotlight switched to Carrie Anne.

The crowds cheered as cell phones flickered.

“Thank you, Dubaiiii, for the great welcoming!” Carrie Anne waved as Steve played several chords.

“Steve Day, our rhythm guitarist agrees with you,” Joe introduced as Steve played a few more rifts.

“Well, Dubaiiiiiii, how about a medley of our older songs?” Joe jumped down to the second level. “I can’t hear you?” Joe jumped in the air doing splits, touching his toes as the crowd soared. “That’s much better!”

Joe said catching his breath. "Boy! Travis," Joe put his arm around Travis's shoulders. "I was worried for a moment that the fans fell asleep!"

Travis agreed by playing a scorching solo while RJ brought out a bottle of water and towel for Joe.

"We changed around some of the songs in our medley," Joe shared after Travis finished. "I hope you like them," Joe signaled Collen, and the medley began. The crowd sat down, singing along with every song.

"Carlos seems nervous," Stephen showed them. "He keeps checking his watch."

"That's fine unless he starts to leave," Ramsey stated.

"Rukar's soldiers are tightening their ranks around the property," Will showed them. "Stephen, duck down now!"

"What's wrong?" Stephen asked moving away from the window in the tower.

"A squadron of military helicopters is landing behind us on the empty field," Will warned.

"I see them," Yorg answered checking his radar. "I have to stay around Carlos; then I'll visit them."

"That's right, Yorg," Ramsey agreed. "You must hover around Carlos as long as he's outside. Capt. Radcliff, are your men ready to hold the soldiers outside?"

"Almost," Capt. Radcliff confirmed. "Alonzo, Pauli, Mikey, and some Seals are thinning out some of the soldiers and planting charges on their tanks and Hummers. My soldiers in the towers are ready to stop anyone trying to come over the gates. One question for you; why would Carlos have all these civilians for a concert, only to harm them?"

"To strike more fear into the surrounding UAE Nations," Ramsey assumed. "The plan is that as the concert ends, the video will play, and then the military will advance, killing some and taking hostages."

"He's using the youth to strike fear in this entire region," Capt. Radcliff confirmed.

"That's correct," Ramsey agreed. "Anarchists always begin by spreading fear among the people in an area."

"Well, Dubaiiiiiiiiiii!" Joe raised his hands. "I'm impressed that you knew all the words to our old songs!" The crowd screamed. "Well, Dubai, let's see if you know the lyrics to the new version of Piecesssss offff Loveeeeee!"

The crowd jumped to their feet, chanting, "Kathe, Kathe, Kathe."

"Ah, you remembered her name!" Joe licked his finger and drew another imaginary line. He looked toward Collen, "That's two for me tonight!" Collen replied with a rift of chords as the stage lights dimmed, and a single spotlight surrounded Joe as he began to sing.

The crowd settled down, hanging on every word Joe sang with the most profound emotions in his heart, pleading for forgiveness. He tearfully spoke of a tender new love turning to turmoil and heartbreak. Then, the spotlight faded on Joe, slowly lighting Carrie Anne.

Carrie Anne won the fans over immediately, singing the chorus about one heart they shaped together, ripped apart into two lonely souls.

"Rodger, split the spotlight on them until they finish the duet," Brock requested as Joe, and Carrie Anne faced each other singing.

"Now, as soon as Carrie Anne finishes, dim the spotlight on her, and brighten Joe," Brock requested watching Rodger perform the perfect sequence of lights. "You've got this. I don't think I need to help you."

"I have a way with computers," Rodger chuckled dimming the lights on Carrie Anne as they reached toward each other until she was gone.

"No!" Joe screamed falling to his knees.

The screaming crowd jumped to their feet, flickering cell phones as Joe stayed on the floor.

"Get up, Joe!" Ramsey demanded checking the look on Carlos's face. "Carlos wants to leave!"

"Well, Dubaiiiiiiiiiii!" Joe sprang to his feet as the crowd sat down. "I see that's one of your favorite songs!"

The crowd stood back up, screaming, and cheering.

"Ramsey, Carlos answered his phone and is getting up to leave," Stephen warned.

"Carlos just signaled me," Yorg declared flying toward Carlos. "He's waiting at the doorway to leave."

"Kathe, are you ready to change identities?" Sydney asked enabling Chameleon around her.

"It's not working!" Ramsey snapped. "She's still Kathe. Carlos must stay! Alonzo and the others aren't back inside the grounds yet!"

"Joe, you heard Ramsey, announce the song!" Kathe demanded. "Sydney, can JAKE help?"

"Yes, it can!" Sydney exclaimed pressing enter. "I can project Chameleon through JAKE!"

"That's it!" Ramsey shouted. "Joe, announce the song!"

"Now, JAKE can get close enough to Carlos to find and replace the video app on his phone!" Sydney exclaimed.

"Well, Mr. Santo Prado!" Joe called out as Carlos glanced back at stage. "We have another surprise for you tonight! A little birdie told us that your favorite dance is the Brazilian Tango! We were asked specifically to play one of your favorite instrumentals for the dance! Your parents sent your favorite dancer, Rita Garcia-Sanchez, just for this one song, and dance with you on this special night! Then, they said, 'you're on your own with her,' if you know what I mean!" Joe tilted his head toward her, raising his eyebrows.

Rodger slowly raised the spotlight on Kathe, showing her wearing a low cut, sequenced, navy blue, long, sexy dress with a slit up to her right thigh.

"Rita!" Carlos gasped raising his phone. "Pilots, I'm going on stage."

"Yes, Sir," Yorg answered.

"Now, split the spotlight from the third tier to the first," Brock requested. "You're going to have to stay on them dancing."

"Got it," Rodger agreed as Jay handed Steve a Spanish Guitar. Carrie Anne and the backup singers reached for their maracas on the floor in front of them.

Joe signaled Steve to begin the lead into the song. "Well, Carlos Santo Prado, are you coming to dance with Rita; or not?" Joe asked reaching one hand toward her.

The crowd began chanting, "Carlos, Carlos, Carlos."

"Pilots, watch me walk to the stage, then keep an eye on me from a distance," Carlos ordered the pilots.

"Yes, Sir," Yorg answered as Carlos left his box and walked up the steps on stage.

The crowd cheered as Carlos took off his white coat, spun it around his shoulder with one hand. The other hand reached toward Rita as the spotlight split, revealing Rita and Carlos miming tug-of-war with a rope to each other. Steve played faster. Carlos dropped his jacket, miming tugging her with both hands to him. The quicker the music played, and the maracas shook, the two tugged at each other. Until Kathe mimed throwing her rope down, flipping forward to the second level, then again down to the first level next to Carlos. He took Rita by the hands as they circled each other provocatively several times, switching directions every other time. Each time Kathe moved her right leg out and around his left leg, showing her shapely legs. Troy and Travis picked up the Latin tempo as Rita strutted away from Carlos. He followed, putting his arms under her shoulders, twirling her around, and then lowering her to the floor as he danced back to center stage.

"That's a pretty steamy song Joe chose for the dance?" Ramsey snapped watching Kathe get a running start to Carlos. He lifted her over his head, throwing her in the air, flipping her over, then he twirled her over his head. As the tempo slowed, Rita spiraled closely around Carlos's body until she sat on the floor.

"Carlos is running a second phone hidden inside this one!" Sydney exclaimed typing commands, pressing enter, typing more commands, pressing enter.

The crowd stood cheering as they watched Carlos stepping over Rita, bending down, and pulling her through his legs. She leaned back against him as he ran his hands slowly down her shoulders to her hips. Rita danced away from him, taunting him to come after her. He followed her, turning her around, lifting her over his head. Then, he lowered Rita as she slid provocatively down his body to the floor again. He picked her up, holding her close as she again wrapped her right leg around his left leg. Then, he dipped her toward the floor. As the song ended, Carlos pulled her up, dipping her in the other direction with one arm holding her up, and holding the other arm over his head.

"That move got Kathe close enough for me to use Chameleon to encapsulate his phone!" Sydney pulled up the hidden phone. "There's the app we needed! That dance did it!"

"Right under his nose!" Stephen declared. "Carlos is clueless. He didn't miss a dance move, and man, he enjoyed every second of it! Look at his face," he zoomed in on Carlos.

The crowd shouted, "more, more, more!"

The music began again as Rita strutted away from Carlos, and then provocatively slowly slid her right leg out, taunting him to join her. He danced his way to her, quickly turning her around, holding his right hand under her neck, dipping her head toward the floor.

The crowd gasped, watching her strength as her body bent in an arc.

Not a sound was heard from the audience as Carlos lifted her head up. He picked Rita up by her waist, twirling her around his body as she held her body straight while twirling around him. He flipped her up over his head, twirling her several more times, and then she slid down his body to the floor. As the song ended, he pulled her quickly up to him in an embrace. She pushed away, turning to mime tug-of-war again at Carlos.

With each tug, she backed up. He mimed strongly pulling her back. Still with each tug, she stepped back. They tugged back-and-forth until they mimed dropping the rope. They both flipped toward each other. Carlos landed on one knee as Rita landed sitting on his leg. She crossed her legs, showing her thigh, and then crossed her hands on her knee as he held his right arm in the air.

The crowd jumped to their feet, screaming with excitement chanting, "Carlos, Rita, Carlos, Rita!"

"I linked the phone with his satellite to play our video when he hits the app!" Sydney slapped his hands together.

Rodger turned up the stage lights as Rita and Carlos took a bow.

"Just like old times, mi Amoré," Carlos whispered holding her hand in the air as they took another bow. "Your perfume is so arousing to me. Tonight, we'll recapture our love," he whispered taking another bow.

"Joe, break it up before he tries to kiss her!" Ramsey ordered.

"Well, Dubaiiiiii, what do you think of Carlos and Rita?" Joe asked holding his hands toward them. "Ms. Rita Garcia-Sanchezzzz!" Joe introduced as Rita took a solo bow. "Mr. Carlos Santo Pradooooo," Joe announced as Carlos bowed. "Wellll, Mr. Santo Prado and Dubai, thanks for having us!" Joe exclaimed as the band members took their bows.

"Come with me," Carlos pulled Kathe off stage reaching for his phone. "Pilots, I'm leaving the stage," he said as his phone rang.

"Sydney, block the call," Ramsey ordered. "Stephen, stay with them. We must get Kathe away from Carlos! He's trying to take Kathe with him inside the palace!"

"Rodger, we need the crowd to block Carlos from the palace!" Ramsey declared.

"I have an idea," Rodger stated flipping the outside lights off and, on several times, causing the fans to panic.

"That worked!" Ramsey exclaimed. "Rodger, keep it up."

"Carlos's keeps trying to call someone," Stephen warned. "The fans are fleeing around them to get to their vehicles."

"Kathe, perfect time to get away from Carlos through the crowds," Ramsey ordered watching Kathe pull away from Carlos as his phone rang again.

"Rukar is trying to reach him," Sydney stated. "I blocked it again," he said watching Carlos trying to get through the crowds.

"Jay, Jack, get to Kathe and take her away from there!" Ramsey requested checking another camera. "Rukar found the people we locked in the room! That's what he's trying to tell Carlos!"

Chapter 10

Wednesday, July 8th
0000 (12:00 AM UTC)
The Final Stand

"Brock, RJ, take the band back to their van!" Ramsey ordered as the stage lowered. "Exit from the nearest fountain. Alonzo, Pauli, and Capt. Radcliff have cleared the way for you outside."

"Copy that," Brock answered. "Alonzo, we're coming out now," he said as RJ opened the door.

"This way," Alonzo led them to the driveway.

"I see you had a little problem," RJ looked around.

"Nothing we couldn't handle," Pauli shook his head. "What a shame greed has over one's life."

"Carlos is still trapped in the crowd," Stephen zoomed in on him. "He's hitting the app for the rings!"

"Chameleon stopped it!" Sydney grinned. "Carlos thinks that the rings are activated."

"Ramsey, one of the helicopter pilots in the field, received a phone call," Will warned. "Rukar gave the order for his pilots to attack."

"Yorg, you'll have to take them out before they get off the ground, and the pilots before they warn Carlos," Ramsey ordered.

"Yes, Boss Lady," Yorg turned around hurrying to the helicopters in the field. "Ramsey, the pilots are warming up the rotors."

"Take them out!" Ramsey commanded.

Yorg pointed his helmet in their direction, firing his laser across each of the rotor masts, severing them, and then hitting the gas tanks, exploding them. "It's done. All pilots are down," Yorg turned the Huey around as the sounds of explosions, followed by flames, and smoke filled the air. "I'm on my way back to the palace."

"Carlos turned to see what happened, still trying to make his way through the crowd," Stephen reported. "He's trying to make another call," Stephen moved the mosquito closer. "He can't get through to the person."

"That's because he's trying to call Rukar, and I'm blocking it," Sydney grinned.

"Rodger, announce for people to stay in their cars!" Ramsey ordered. "It's not safe for them to leave! Tell them the truth!"

"People, this palace is under attack from the militant General Ababa Rukar," Rodger warned. "There's no need to panic. Our forces are inside the gate to protect you. Walk orderly to your cars and stay inside them."

"Mikey, Bernadette, some soldiers are climbing up the middle of the fence," Pauli warned.

"I've got them in my sights," Mikey pivoted to the right, taking them out one at a time.

"I've got this side," Bernadette concurred firing at them.

"Carlos still can't move," Stephen reported. "He's answering his phone," he moved the mosquito closer again.

"Carlos, I'm using another phone to get to you," Gen. Rukar snapped. "I checked the Security Operations Center. It took me a while to get inside; the keypad was disabled. The people inside were holograms! Someone locked my guards and the engineers in the holding tank! Start the video! I signaled my soldiers to advance during the video! They're on the way!"

"I'm trying to start it!" Carlos shouted forcing his way toward the front porch. "No one is advancing! We're under attack! I repeat; we're under attack!"

"Oops," Sydney pressed enter. "Since you're having an evening of surprises, it's time for you to watch our video."

"We did it!" Ramsey cheered watching Carlos turn around and glare at the big screen on the side of the stage, showing Eduardo and Carlos walking away from the airplane crash on Sugar Mountain. Pietro Bencivenni and Angus Muldanero picking them up in a helicopter . . . The Newspaper Headlines announcing to the world their deaths. Catarina and Eduardo with their adopted sons, Shabz Rukhma of Pakistan, and Kenya Baal Akmul of Afghanistan. It switched, showing Gen. Thompson vetting Shabz as Connor Johansson to work in the Pentagon and helping Kenya get into politics as Omar Barrick.

"Carlos is furious!" Stephen showed a close-up of his face as he stared at the video showing each accomplice with his or her role under the names. It showed Carswell getting out of the single-person drone, meeting with Eduardo wearing a mesh-mask in the cove. Then, it switched to the Sego Lilly Airport, showing the jet carrying the Barricks and Carswell blowing up.

"What?" Carlos screamed. "Rukar, shut the video down! Someone switched it with the truth about us!"

"Carlos is on the move!" Stephen followed Carlos as he knocked people over, pushing his way up the steps. "How did they get pictures of

Carswell, and the Barricks getting into that jet?" He screamed into the phone, hurrying inside the palace.

"Paris, hit your app for the paintings!" Ramsey requested as Stephen's mosquito followed Carlos into the foyer.

"What video did you upload?" Gen. Rukar shouted when he met Carlos in the foyer. "You're incriminating us worldwide!"

"That's not what I uploaded!" Carlos stopped glaring at the painting. "What?" he pointed. "The painting is a hologram of the cove continually blowing up!" They ran to the elevator and hurried into Carlos's father's office. "This portrait too!" Carlos screamed watching it show blood coming out of Eduardo's eyes, ears, mouth, and noise at the same time he morphed into a skeleton. "She did this!"

"Who?" Gen. Rukar asked following Carlos behind the partition.

"Paris L'Ville!" Carlos screamed trying to stop the video. "I caught her in here earlier," he sat down at the computer. "She broke the keyboard!"

"Shut down the satellite!" Gen. Rukar demanded.

"I can't!" Carlos screamed trying several ways. "Someone has taken over our satellite! Where's the airstrike?"

"Blown up!" Gen. Rukar pointed out the window at the end of the room. "The question is, where are your parents?" Gen. Rukar demanded turning around. "You assured me they couldn't be arrested! Look!" he pointed to the video on the computer screen showing them in handcuffs being taken into custody. The mug shots of Eduardo and Catarina morphed into Omar and Ellie Barrick. "That's why your father chose them as replacements!"

"According to the U.S. Constitution, a former president can't be charged with a crime," Carlos gasped. "The Feds couldn't have found out. The surgeries were perfect!"

"Capt. Amnion and Capt. Ali aren't answering!" Gen. Rukar proclaimed.

"The plan was perfect until we hired Paris L'Ville," Carlos gasped. "What's this?" Carlos asked as a green Chameleon appeared on the screen, crawling out of a hole. It stood on its back legs, shaking his finger, saying, "Carlos Santo Prado, you've been a very bad boy with your parents and adopted brothers. Your game is over; compliments of a hacker better than you, your father, and Johansson!" The Chameleon turned around and shook its tail back-and-forth at him before crawling back into its hole as the screen went blank.

“Where’s the ground firepower?” Carlos fumed following Rukar to the window on the side of the president’s desk.

“My commanders aren’t answering me!” Gen. Rukar shouted watching explosions rip outside the grounds. “My tanks are exploding!”

“Ramsey, I’m back online with you,” AG Kolouski rejoined the conversation. “The Emirates warned their countries and the surrounding nations. Each is sending troops to help you crush Gen. Rukar’s soldiers. I told them the old Huey is on their side.”

“Thank you,” Ramsey appreciated. “Yorg, did you hear? Turn off your hologram and fly strictly as the Huey.”

“Chameleon is disabled,” Yorg reported. “One jet just veered away from me.”

“Ramsey,” Will alerted panning the area with infrared. “The Emirates’ ground troops are arriving now. They are surrounding Gen. Rukar’s soldiers. It’s funny. Their tanks and equipment have either exploded or wouldn’t work.”

“It’s funny how a few missing wires can make a difference,” Alonzo laughed looking at the parts on the ground.

“People, job well done!” Ramsey congratulated. “It was all our joint covert participation that paid off!”

“It’s poetic justice watching the Arab Nations round-up Rukar’s soldiers,” Will stated.

“Poetic justice is receiving phone calls from around the world that Rukar’s soldiers were stopped,” AG Kolouski reported. “Our phone lines haven’t stopped ringing. I have to tell you that watching the holograms on the paintings that Paris converted was an eye-opener for Carlos,” he chuckled. “Paris, you did an excellent job!”

“Paris, are you online?” Ramsey checked. “Paris?”

“Paris is online,” Sydney alerted locating her GPS. “She’s not answering. Her phone is inside the elevator, passing the second floor!”

“We’ve got Paris,” Kathe whispered. “I spotted her entering behind Carlos,” Kathe signaled Jay to take out a guard coming down the steps from the second floor.

“Jack,” Kathe pointed to a guard slipping into a room near the elevator.

“Paris is after Carlos!” Sydney sighed. “I told her not to do it! It won’t bring her parents back!”

“I’ve got Paris coming out of the elevator on the third floor,” Stephen moved the mosquito to show.

"It's been Paris' mission, since she was five," Ramsey watched the camera. "I wondered if Paris would face him alone."

"Paris has to face her demon if she ever wants peace in her life," Kathe whispered hurrying up the steps.

"Paris is carefully peering inside the office," Stephen warned. "Her hands are violently shaking. She can't shoot like that!"

"She's doesn't have the edge!" Sydney snapped. "She's no match for Carlos and Rukar!"

"Sydney," Bernadette interrupted. "I'm in the tree across from the office windows. Gen. Rukar is looking out one of the windows."

"Take the shot!" Sydney ordered.

"Copy that," Bernadette squeezed the trigger. "Direct hit," she said slinging her rifle over her shoulder, shimming down the tree.

"Gen. Rukar!" Carlos screamed running to him and turning him over. "Who are these people?" He crawled away from the window.

"Carlos," Paris entered holding her Walther P38 at him. "Now, it's just you and me, the children of two very different families. One set of parents tried to stop the other from destroying the world. I've had nightmares of your fathers when he watched the murder of my parents since I was five-years-old. You weren't there that day! Were you safe with your mother? I was with my mother as she covered me while bullets struck her body above me! At first, I thought it was Antonio Falcini, Sr. for ordering the murder, but then Ramsey found the mask your father used in Wiltz!"

"We're on our way to help Paris!" Alonzo shouted watching Paris' bravery.

"What?" Carlos slowly stood up.

"Yes, the mask your father wore in Wiltz that day with Pietro Bencivenni and Tomme Boy Dano," Paris declared.

"I don't know what you are talking about?" Carlos demanded trying to reach his pistol.

"Don't move!" Paris warned. "Keep your hands where I can see them. I'm not that five-year-old, scared, little girl anymore."

"You're crazy!" Carlos denied. "I just hired you to paint two paintings!"

"Really?" Paris laughed. "What happened to the man that ordered me, and my friends taken to the holding tank? Oh, by the way, the guards never made it out of the elevator alive. My friends are contract killers for the LaBasco Family, compliments of Alonzo DiMeglio."

"You're insane!" Carlos slowly inched closer to the desk.

"Am I?" Paris asked. "We heard you bragging to Rukar this evening about your father witnessing the murder of Daniel, and Cynthia Sydney in Wiltz, Luxembourg. I rented the flat under a different name a week after Dano left. I found the disc my parents hid in the flat. You know, the flat Spinello rented for Tomme Boy Dano to move into to find the evidence the police couldn't find. The disc which proved that Bencivenni replaced people with look-a-likes and placed a ring on their finger to control them."

"You couldn't have found it!" Carlos insisted. "Dano was a trained assassin."

"Dano didn't watch my parents hide them as I did!" Paris confessed. "I'm Paris Olivia Sydney. I use Aunt Deanna's maiden name L'Ville professionally, to honor her for raising me as her daughter."

"You destroyed my family's dream!" Carlos shouted lunging behind the desk.

"Yes!" Paris screamed shooting at Carlos, and then diving behind the couch.

"Carlos is edging around the desk on the right side," Stephen warned. "Jack, there is another doorway into the office from the room on the right. It opens across from Paris."

"I found it," Jack slowly turned the doorknob as Carlos shot at the door.

"Jack, are you, alright?" Ramsey asked.

"I took one in the leg," Jack turned sliding down against the wall.

"Paris, answer us!" Sydney begged. "We work as a team!"

"I'm sorry," Paris cried. "I knew you would stop me. I have to do this!"

"I'm in the doorway across from her," Bernadette stated raising her rifle. "Do you want me to take the shot?"

"Yes, and no!" Sydney sighed studying the situation.

"We're all in position," Pauli admitted. "If Paris can, she needs to do this herself."

"Don't worry; his gun will never fire a shot," Mikey insisted stabilizing his rifle.

"I've got Carlos in my sights, too," Pauli shared.

"I've got an idea," Kathe declared by the office door in the hallway. "Jay, take over my position. I'm going in from behind the partition," she stated heading to the room on the other side of the office. She crawled out of the window onto the ledge, edging her way to the next window.

"Be careful," Ramsey gasped watching Kathe open the window.

"Stephen, I'm entering from the window at the end of the partition," Kathe whispered slowly walking toward the desk. "I need to see both of them."

"You've got it," Stephen flew the drone up to the ceiling over them. "How's that?"

"Perfect," Kathe whispered picking up the mouse to the computer's keyboard as she walked past it. "Paris, stay very still," Kathe peered around the partition. "Carlos is edging toward the chair facing the couch. I'm going to give you a little edge," Kathe whispered throwing the mouse at Carlos.

Carlos turned toward Kathe as she shot him in his left side and leg. "L'Ville, this is your fault!" Carlos screamed falling to the floor and rolling in pain. He started firing randomly in her direction.

"Paris, stay down on the floor, and take the shot!" Sydney ordered watching Paris follow orders, steadying her Walter, shooting Carlos in the left arm.

"You did this!" Carlos screamed trying to pull himself up to the chair with his right arm and leg. "There's no way you could have known about the rings!"

"JAKE, enable Chameleon again," Kathe stated as it answered, and she appeared as Rita again. "Well, actually, she had a lot of help!" She admitted stepping out from behind the partition.

"Rita!" Carlos gasped. "You're in on this?"

"Actually, I'm not Rita," Kathe chuckled. "JAKE, disable Chameleon."

"Kathe, it's disabled," JAKE stated as she transformed.

"I hear your father has been looking for my husband and me for years," Kathe grinned holding her Ruger on him. "I'm Kathe Tierney. Chameleon works beyond what your father dreamt. Like you are sensing the smell of Rita's perfume on me. I'm not wearing any. Oh, and the pilots with your helicopters. It was Yorg flying only his Huey. Chameleon Technology is an undetectable Holographic Technology with Virtual Intelligence that easily morphs to mask its presence while altering reality. That's what brought your father's idealism down, not Paris L'Ville."

"We all had a hand in helping Paris find the murderers of her parents," Mikey admitted as everyone stepped out of different places, pointing their weapons at Carlos.

"You're that obnoxious person lighting the paintings?" Carlos stammered.

"No, I'm a hitman for the LaBasco Family," Mikey grinned.

"You know," Alonzo DiMeglio laughed. "Carlos, this goes to show you that you can't use this many entrances, even though some are hidden into a room. The foyer is designed the same way. It has too many ways for people to get to you, as well as you to escape," he walked over to Paris.

"Alonzo DiMeglio!" Carlos struggled raising his pistol toward him.

"Alonzo!" Mikey and Pauli shot the gun out of Carlos's hand.

"No!" Carlos screamed falling to the floor, screaming in pain.

"Thanks," Alonzo smiled helping Paris up. "Carlos is disabled," he shrugged his shoulder, raising his hands. "Paris, this is your call. He's down and can't move. Stephen can turn off the camera, and we can walk out. They'll be no witnesses for you to kill your demon. Or you can leave with us knowing that Carlos will sweat bullets waiting for what is to come next."

"He's just a pathetic man that couldn't live his own life the way he wanted," Paris sighed watching Carlos's roll on the floor. "Without all his bodyguards, he's no different than me."

"That's right," Kathe agreed. "Every one of us has had to face our demons."

"Knowing when to walk away is what makes you a great security agent for Alby Airlines, if you want the job?" Ramsey offered. "I can speak for what Jenkins did to me. Retribution isn't always the answer. I walked away with a clear conscience, and he got what he deserved at the hands of somebody else. I'm glad I didn't have to do it."

"Thanks for the advice and job offer," Paris cried hugging Alonzo. "I'm happy being an artist. But, if you ever need my help, I have the perfect alibi to help you."

"Let's go," Alonzo took Paris out into the hallway. "Let's take the elevator."

"Jay, help Jack to the helicopter," Sydney requested.

"It's just a flesh wound," Jack replied getting up. "I'll be fine."

"Use the laser over the wound to help it heal faster," Sydney requested.

"Bernadette, Mikey, get the horses to the airport," Ramsey ordered.

Ramsey signaled Sydney to mute the console. "Yorg, when Paris is away from the scene, and Bernadette secures the horses, you know what to do."

"You've got it, Boss Lady," Yorg hovered away from the palace.

Chapter 11

Breaking News
Tuesday, July 14th
1400 (2:00 PM EST)
The White House

Breaking News: "This is Robert Morwitz with FNN News reporting from the Rose Garden this morning," he pointed to a closed door behind him. "We are waiting for President Trumore, along with several UAE Heads of State, and Israel's Prime Minister to announce a Multi-National Peace Treaty. President Trumore is approaching the podium to speak first," the cameraman turned to the president.

"Ladies and Gentlemen of the world," President Trumore began. "This past G-Summit will go down as one of the best in history. While attending the Summit, we received an intelligence report stating that former President Omar Barrick, his wife Ellie, and his Secretary of State, Charles Carswell, were killed leaving Sego Lilly Airport outside of the DC area yesterday. This information led investigators to uncover a known terrorist, Gen. Ababa Rukar plotting to strike several nations in the Middle East and the United States before going global. It is not yet clear as to how the former administration was involved. Our nations," President Trumore pointed to the leaders behind him, "immediately formed a Multi-National Task Force to bring Rukar's evil plot to a screeching halt. Together we joined with other countries to hit his military from all global angles. We are happy to announce that we destroyed his army, and his headquarters. As a result, today in the Rose Garden we are signing a Peace Treaty between these nations present and the United States."

"As you can see," Morwitz recapped what the president said, showing them signing a treaty for each nation. "This is just the beginning for bringing peace to the Middle Eastern Nations."

"We will hear from each of the leaders," Morwitz said after they finished signing. "Let's listen to this auspicious moment in history," the camera switched to the podium.

"There you have it," Morwitz declared after they finished. "We heard all leaders say that this is just the beginning for peace in the Middle East extending globally," he said as President Trumore turned with the leaders and walked inside the White House.

"Also, the world-renown artist, Paris L'Ville, was in attendance at the White House after the Rose Garden Celebration," the camera switched inside the Oval Office. "Ms. L'Ville presented the First Family with a family portrait," Morwitz announced as the screen showed President Trumore and the First Lady accepting it.

"In other news," Morwitz added as the camera switched to London. "Light Crimson has returned home to practice for their concert this weekend in London, before hitting the road again to promote their new album. AG John Kolouski stated that none of the accusations that lead singer, Joe Sherrod was a spy were true. The new backup singer, Carrie Anne Mobley, has signed permanently with the band. Rumors are circulating that Mobley and bass guitarist Rick Travis, are engaged," he said as the camera switched to Florida.

"World Entrepreneur and Documenter Stephen Brown of Gabby Mobile Productions will release his latest film this Friday," Morwitz reported as the DVD cover appeared on the screen. "Its title, 'Hummingbirds: Sweet-Innocent VS. Violent-Warriors.' I interviewed Mr. Brown last night at his studio," the camera switched to Brown's studio in Holly Hill, Florida. "Mr. Brown, I was told that you had captured footage of hummingbirds fighting, which was once thought only to be winsomely used in poems and songs."

"Yes," Brown answered. "In this documentary, you will see firsthand how these tiniest of birds have a penchant for violence using their astounding beaks. I have proven they are truly warriors."

"I heard rumors that you also filmed the smallest Hummingbird in the World; is there truth to the rumor?" Morwitz asked.

"Truth," Brown admitted. "Not only did we film the Legendary Hummingbird Topaz but caught it mating."

"What a tremendous record find?" Morwitz exclaimed. "Where did you find the Topaz?"

"In the Sierra Maestra in Cuba of all places," Brown shared. "It was believed to be non-native to that country. Our find was cut short due to the political unrest in the area. Once the area is stable again, we will return. But, for now, this find was so promising we had to finalize the documentary. We were able to include photos of rare Hummingbird Moths. Just remember, once we get back into Cuba, there is more to come."

"Lastly, in other world news," Morwitz continued as the screen split from Florida to Cuba. "In Cuba, the people are rebelling against Presidente Castrello. Intelligence reported that the rouge Gen. Yetsun, hunted by the

Russian government, was located and destroyed on the top of the mountain in the Sierra Maestra. It is reported that several of Castrello's advisors were involved. We will keep you informed as we get the information on this intense situation. This is Robert Morwitz with FNN News returning you to your scheduled programs already in progress."

Tuesday, July 14th
1530 (3:30 PM EST)
Newark, Liberty Airport

"Alonzo, is everything in the underworld returning to normal?" Ramsey asked as they sat around the conference table in the HUB.

"Yes," Alonzo stated. "The families that had leaders switched have corrected the situation. It was the first time all the families came together to stamp out evil. Mr. LaBasco is working on an agreement between the leaders to ensure this doesn't happen again."

"That's great news," Ramsey agreed as her phone rang. "AG Kolouski, what a surprise?" She pressed the speaker on the console. "You're on speaker with all teams presents."

"That's fine," AG Kolouski approved. "President Trumore wanted me to personally thank you again for bringing this world crisis to our attention and helping us stop it. He also wanted me to tell you that he'd love for your teams to join his administration. Your technology is impressive and would benefit our country. There are some high-ranking jobs coming available in the next few days."

"What technology is he referring to?" Ramsey asked. "We are merely security for Alby Airlines."

"I told the president that you would say just that!" AG Kolouski chuckled. "Your covert teams have the ability to gather information that our agencies couldn't, or should I say, wouldn't. Our phones haven't stopped ringing with gratitude from leaders around the world. Let's just say goodbye for now," he cleared the line.

"It's time to get back to work for Alby Airlines," Ramsey admitted. "Keith, you may give us your report at this time."

"Several chief pursers have noticed a number of single men and women traveling with children that seem lethargic," Keith reported. "I called around to some of the other airlines and got the same report."

"After what we just experienced in Cuba, we need to look into this immediately," Ramsey declared. "Human traffickers won't stop with the border wall. Those kinds always find another way to do business."

"I'll have my people check around Europe to see if anyone notices the same problem," Alonzo added. "Human trafficking should have been eradicated years ago."

"This is something we must look into," Ramsey appreciated. "We can't let them use the airlines to do their bidding."

"I'm surprised AG Kolouski gave up that easily after watching what JAKE and Chameleon could do?" Kathe questioned.

"He didn't," Sydney surprised them. "In the wee hours this morning, I received a call from President Trumore. Intelligence picked up murmurs that Barrick told certain members of Congress about Chameleon."

"Mr. LaBasco and I were afraid that what Mario Jr. started would morph into something else," Alonzo admitted. "The problem with who controls Chameleon is just beginning, and not just with some of your Congress, but other countries now know about it. We've noticed many times that some of your Congress seem to have major benefactors in China, Iran, and Russia. Mr. LaBasco pledges our continual help."

"I knew we could count on you," Ramsey smiled.

"Again, the mishandling of Chameleon plagues us as well," Alonzo stood up. "How do you think we noticed who some of your Congress were seen with for the last few years? Let us know what you find this week, and we'll be back to confer notes. Remember, you are family now. And family never says goodbye. Pauli, Mikey, Bernadette, we need to get back to Corté d Azuré. I've been away from Mr. LaBasco too long. His voice the last couple of times we spoke wasn't as strong as when I left," he turned around. "Oh, and Paris made the right decision. I'm proud of her. Kathe, Yorg, take care of those beautiful children," he said as Pauli opened the door.

"I wish we were on our way to take them for a fun vacation," Kathe shook her head. "Unfortunately, we need to address our problem with Joe."

"I don't think Joe will do anything stupid again," Alonzo winked. "He knows our strengths, and resources."

"I wish it was that easy," Kathe admitted.

"You heard Alonzo," Ramsey declared. "You have one week to solve your can of worms. I need you two back at work to help CC, Sam, and Rodger check out Keith's report."

"We'll be here," Yorg declared. "Alonzo's right. Politicians seem to turn a blind-eye to human trafficking, and it's clear that some have been bought off by special interest groups."

"After what we discovered about the former administration, I agree that some high-officials are involved." Ramsey agreed. "Otherwise, Congress would have already stopped this at our borders years ago. President Trumore and some of his administration seem to be the only ones concerned about it."

"That proves that getting their hands on Chameleon would benefit not only human traffickers, but drug cartels as well to easily move their commodities around the world," Kathe confirmed.

"I was just thinking the same thing," Sydney admitted. "See you a week."

"So, I should have my father extend my leave to stay with Sam, and Rodger to begin researching this problem?" CC asked.

"Actually, your father assigned you to stay with Sam and Rodger already," Ramsey handed CC and Rodger an envelope. "I believe this gives you permission. He's vetting Rodger to work in the FBI. He is also relocating Rodger's family to New York to be with Rodger."

"I appreciate everything you've all done to help me," Rodger said.

"Don't just thank us," Ramsey grinned, "Terrance Sims and AG Kolouski watched you work with our teams. They arranged this for you."

"You're a great asset to our team," Sydney agreed.

"Okay, people, Wanda has your next week assignments," Ramsey concluded. "You are dismissed."

www.ingramcontent.com/pod-product-compliance
Lightning Source LLC
Chambersburg PA
CBHW080943020726
47505CB00009B/2131

9780999336342